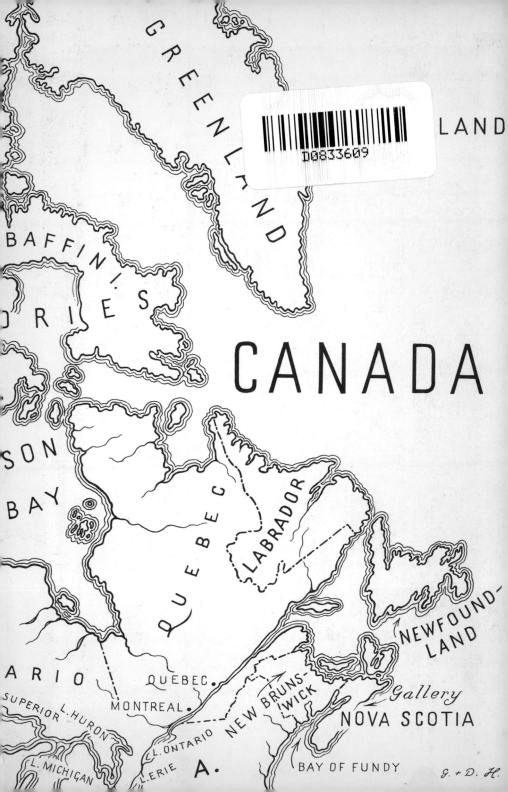

WHERE THE HIGH WINDS BLOW

BY DAVID WALKER

WHERE THE

HIGH WINDS BLOW

HOUGHTON MIFFLIN COMPANY BOSTON

THE RIVERSIDE PRESS CAMBRIDGE

TO JOHN ELPHINSTONE

AUTHOR'S NOTE

There are no real people in this book.

I have taken a few liberties with historical and geographical fact. For example: Simon Skafe was some four years ahead of his time in drilling for oil in the Arctic Islands.

I would like to thank those who made possible my northern journeys in 1950 and 1956, and to thank many people who befriended me on my way. I am also grateful to the experts who have checked this novel for technical accuracy, and have helped me to make it as true a fiction as I can.

BOOK ONE

CHAPTER ONE

THE WATER was slack at the inner bank. He rounded a spit, touched bottom once, and here was the next sweep of the river. It swings and it rolls, he thought in the boat on the river—fast at the cut bank, slow at the inside of the bend, for a thousand miles or thereabouts, I guess.

It is murky green; then the Liard joins to split the Mackenzie, brown water on the left, green water on the right, to blend a long way down the river; then at Norman the Bear comes in, clear blue or green below Bear Rock, pretty for a mile until the pellucid Bear is swallowed in Mackenzie, and down it goes, the ever-rolling stream, five miles wide or half a mile or two, and at the delta it is *habitant* pea soup. This was his Canada, immense about him.

He made for the other bank. The wind was chilly out on the river. He gave full throttle, and he had power; yet he lost ground as he edged across. But the current eased, and then the trees stood still again, and then he climbed past them, spiky spruce, ball-topped spruce, the muskeg forest.

" 'Frankie and Johnnie were lovers . . .' " he sang. He was happy on his way, singing for the thought of South and Out and Home, not for company, the river being that to him. " 'Roll me over easy, roll me over slow . . .' "

"Roll me over," he said, after singing. "That's just what you'd do if I gave you the chance." He respected the river, and did not fear it, and did not love it.

It was 10 P.M. on the twelfth of June. He was Simon Kepple Skafe, aged twenty-six. The mosquitoes were bad again near land. Duck flew low down the river. He saw what they meant about the bosom of a river, because this river was so great that you could see the swell of the curve of the earth. There were birds and flies, but not a mammal—neither moose nor mouse nor man in sight along the river all day long.

He was hungry. The river curved ahead, and the bank overhung where current gouged it. He would have to cross again unless he found a place.

But then he found a place. Things quite often met him on his way. It was an opening in the bank, an inlet, and the water from it made a small riffle into the lip of the Mackenzie. That meant a flow, and that meant a brook, and that meant fresh supper possibly.

He put over the tiller and headed in. He sounded with his pole, five foot or better. The engine was loud in here. He nosed upchannel a hundred yards until he came to the fall of the brook. He throttled back, set bow to bank, and jumped ashore. A spruce tree made a mooring.

The mosquitoes hummed in thousands or millions. They bit and did not much bother him. Needle-jabbing bulldogs, the size of small bumblebees, bothered him or anyone. He swatted half a dozen, put three on a hook, and threw the weighted line below white water.

Bluefish were taking. He caught twelve in ten minutes, cleaned and washed them, went back into the cabin, lit the stove, melted fat in the pan, rolled fish in flour, and drooled at the mouth as he fried his supper.

He ate four good arctic grayling, and bannock, and was drowsy with a laden stomach. He drank a mug of black tea and smoked his pipe. Mosquitoes darkened the screen and clamored. They suck blood to live, he thought, or to breed and die. Well then, how in this godforsaken semi-bloodless wilderness do they eat?

It was a mystery, and he was not an entomologist. He was a Bachelor of Arts from Queen's. He had worked his way down on the company boat two summers ago and met up with Jim Willis in Aklavik. They went as deckhands out of Tuk-Tuk on the Arctic Ocean. They trapped and hunted in the Barren Lands that winter. Jim taught him to trap and to hunt. First summer and first winter gone. The second summer they prospected to the Yukon border, and panned a little gold. Then they separated. Jim Willis came up by river boat to trap west of Lightning River; but then he married a trader's daughter, so the story came down at Easter. How much time did the bridegroom spend on his trapline this past winter? Simon Skafe bought the old mission boat and nursed it up to Norman and worked on it until freeze-up. Then he trapped in the Franklin country, and did well with mink and cross fox, and once he nearly starved for meat.

The furs were here in the boat. The tang of them was strong again, fried fish smell gone out through the screen. The embers settled in the stove. This was his third summer, two years nearly to a day since he had started down the muddy Slave from Smith.

He was through for this time. He was going Out. Jim would not go Out, because Jim couldn't handle liquor, unless his new wife had changed him, which was impossible. But Simon Kepple Skafe—called Husky before he ever saw a Husky dog or an Eskimo—he could handle liquor. I can handle anything, he thought.

Including a woman now, he thought. Most of this time he had forgotten women, being busy and not bushed enough for northern ladies. But now this last week in the boat, now that he had begun his journey, women were bothering him, not the girls he remembered—nice, possessive, pretty, bitchy—but Woman, piece of pleasure.

There was still a stretch of the Mackenzie, then Great Slave Lake when the weather was fair and the ice was out, and then up the Slave to Smith, and sell the boat or leave it for sale, and portage at the rapids which someday somebody would tame for power.

So portage to Fitzgerald, and then the Slave again to Athabaska—all the northland in that name—and up the Athabaska to take a train at Waterways for Edmonton and really Out. Three weeks should do it, thought Simon Skafe. But three weeks is a long haul to a piece of pleasure.

Push on? he thought. Or sleep? He had been traveling for thirty hours. Fifteen more should take him to Providence. He hoped they had gas. If they had no gas left, or not enough, he would have to wait for the first river boat, and that might mean a week's delay. And what is a week in the great North Country? A week is a week or the mood you're in.

He lit the oil lamp to inspect his samples. They were rock fragments, all from one small area in the country where he had trapped last winter. Some were black-gray with an inky luster; others were orange-yellow without luster. Some showed the pinkish bloom of cobalt; some the greenish bloom of nickel; some held silver, and pyrite crystals, and traces of copper. Only the first two might be worth mining north of Great Bear Lake. The heavy black samples were uraninite, or pitchblende; the heavy brown samples were pitchblende weathered or altered into gummite. Both were sources of radium. Skafe had only a practical smattering of geology, but he had been to Port Radium on Great Bear Lake, and had seen the deposits there. These were as rich, but how extensive? He had staked claims.

Jim Willis would be pleased. Fifty-fifty on furs or findings had been the agreement when they parted. Fifty-fifty on everything, and meet in mid-June at the head of the Mackenzie, Skafe to sell the catch of furs outside.

But since then Jim Willis had married a wife. Jim will turn up all right, he thought. He might even have found that gold he dreams about. Nuggets of gold and bottles of rum put a similar gleam in old Jim's eye. He is about the most generous guy I know, and straight as a die, and he can't wait beyond a quick return. That's the trouble about this pitchblende. Jim knows what extracting radium involves—money to prove deposits, then capital, moving equipment to the backside of beyond—it involves at the best big risks and long delays, and big risks and long delays are not for Jim, who will want to sell out to the first man to show him a few hundred-dollar bills, and that means a half-interest gone to some goddam crook.

What I would do, and I'm not sure why, a hunch—what I would do is sit on this thing, keep the claims worked, Jim could do that—and bide my time, and watch how they do at Radium. That makes sense in a depression, but it means the kind of patience Jim Willis does not possess. I'll have to talk to him.

He put the ores in the deerskin bag and tied it. You know, he thought, a poke of gold dust is so much cash right there in your hand. Even the thought of it gives Jim a fever. But that isn't my kind of money, I don't give a damn for gold in the hand to blow on rum. What I want money for is to make things with to do things with. That makes constructive sense.

He had all the time in the world to think, and thought, but was surprised at his philosophizing now about the creative use of money, ideas complete, it seemed, on a subject he did not recall considering since college days, and then as a dull abstraction. Well, I'm on a new road, he thought. I'm starting Out.

He sprayed insecticide and left the cabin to stand at the bow. There was a red sunset to the north. He could not see the silent river from here below the noisy brook. He went ashore and squelched through muskeg on the frozen earth to have a look at the river before he slept.

The river was gray and silent at dusk. Duck and geese still flew down the great cold river. A sharp breeze kept the flies away. He watched nighthawks twist and slip and dive about the sky. There were mammals now too, apart from himself. He heard a beaver's double smack of tail.

I'm going outside, he thought to the river. I'm going the other way from you. You won't miss me, but it's possible, after all, that I will miss you. This is the real world here.

He piddled into the Mackenzie. He went back to the boat to sleep.

CHAPTER TWO

THE INDIAN'S CAP hid one eye. He wore a grease-blackened shirt and store pants, not an immaculate Indian. "Jimwillis?" he said. "Sure. Seenim'n hour back." He pointed between islands. A run of lake ice was coming down. Flat white slabs jostled, clinking nicely.

The Indian looked over to the left again. He sang a song or dirge to himself. He watched a smaller channel, a few strong stakes spaced across it. They quivered in the tug of current. The Indian took his hand from the gunwale of Skafe's boat. He paddled fast, still singing. The stakes seemed to quiver equally, but he had chosen one; he hooked an arm around it to check the canoe, hauled in hand over hand, clubbed the fish at water level, and boarded it, a neat quick trick.

He baited the hook and threw it back and floated down, grinning widely and briefly, cadaverous. It was a big lake trout, perhaps thirty pounds.

"Plenty fish here?" asked Skafe. All the fish in the world, he knew.

The Indian's dogs howled behind him on the bank. They were scrofulous, emaciated to starvation point and not quite starved. They staggered, howling. The Indian cursed them to silence. "Plenty fish," he answered.

Skafe cut him a wad of plug. The Indian chewed, content and glad enough of company, but not loquacious. In a while he squirted a long brown spit. He watched his trembling stakes, and then watched nothing, bored.

The run of ice was nearly over. "I guess I'll be going," said Skafe. "So long."

"S'long," said the Indian. "Nice boat."

Skafe went on to find Jim Willis. He bucked some ice, but it was harmless stuff, thin tailings of the run. Two more hot days, he thought, and a west wind to hold it away from this end of the lake, and I could start across.

There were many islands, green beside the cloudy green of water. He knew that Jim's cabin was over to the farther shore, but the Indian said that Jim was tending nets among these islands. Think of a temperature of eighty plus, he thought, sweating in the sun away from the wind between the islands—and Great Slave Lake just breaking. He thought about the violent North, frozen for eight or nine or ten months of the year, bursting with growth for two or three or four.

He saw Jim Willis. Jim stood on a shingle beach, waving with both hands. Skafe headed to run the bow ashore.

"Sonuvagun," said Jim, "the one and only Husky!"

"It's good to see you, Jim," he said. And it was.

Jim wiped his hand on the seat of his pants, and they shook. "Tell you the truth, I never thought you'd make it in that tub. But here you are, the middle of June just like you said. Got a new motor, did you?"

"Not new," he said. "I made a trade. It has the power; heavy on gas is the biggest trouble."

"Husky Skafe is the biggest trouble." Jim laughed. "Jeeze, it's great to see you," he said. "You look kind of younger without the beard. Say, tell me . . . !" His thoughts and his tongue raced one another. ". . . How did you make out, trapping?"

"Not too bad," he said, and told him his catch. "How about you, Jim?"

"Just fair," said Jim. "That country's darn near trapped out." The flow of talk dried up for a minute.

Jim Willis was tall, with the stoop of a tall man who humps a pack. There was no better trapper in the North, when Jim would trap. He was five years older than Skafe. Now he talked again, playing with pebbles with his feet. The talk poured out of him, lone man finding a human audience. Skafe was no great talker, but he knew the feeling. But Jim's married, he thought. He has a wife to work it off on.

". . . So he said: I can allow you seven hundred and twenty-two, fifty for the lot. Christ, a whole winter's catch! Not the lot, I says, just the fox, I'll sell. For the lot, the bastard says again, take it or leave it. Well, I was needin' gill nets and staples and other gear, so I had to take it— there's no independent trader there. That's three hundred and sixty-one and two bits I'm owing you, Husky." Jim looked at Skafe.

I might have doubled that outside, thought Skafe. And half is mine. But he smiled. "It's a cleft stick, Jim," he said. "What else could you do?" Yet he thought, from Jim's face, that there might have been more to it than Jim needing staples at Eastertime. He and Jim had lived a whole year together without disagreement, plenty of time to know Jim.

"One more net, and I'm through." Jim got into his canoe and paddled to a net across this sheltered channel. "Not too good a place," he called, "but that goddamned ice . . ." Skafe walked along the shingle to watch.

Jim took four fish from the gill net, two drowned and two alive. He killed them, frowning.

Fish made a pile in the canoe—whitefish, connies, jackfish, suckers, bluefish, trout. "No cause to starve," said Jim. "There's enough in this place to feed five million, not five thousand." He laughed at his joke. "Well, let's go."

"Is it far to the camp?"

"A couple of miles." Jim paddled a stroke, then held water. "Husky," he said. "I guess you heard?"

"Heard what?" asked Skafe, smiling at Jim whose face wore his moods, eye restless always.

"That I got myself married in the fall?"

"Sure," said Simon Skafe. "No secrets, not even marriage, in the North. Congratulations, Jim!" He had been waiting for Jim to mention it. When white men married into the country, they did not do much mentioning. The wife kept house, kept cabin, made dark-haired babies.

"Anna's her name," said Jim. "She's a great girl, Husky, and clever too, you got a lot in common. We'll be glad of company. It's kind of lonesome for a woman here." He rattled that information off about his wife, coiled the rope, and started the kicker. Jim was as deft as an Indian in a canoe. He idled the motor again, and shouted: "How much do you draw?"

"Two foot," called Skafe.

"Keep right behind me, then."

He followed the canoe. Jim ran upstream, swung right, and wound slowly through a maze of islands. Then he turned down the river and down the wind. There was some ice on the river again. The air was hot. It feels wrong to be running downstream, Skafe thought, and then he had a foolish fancy, having climbed so far—of himself being drawn on down by Jim, to keep Jim and wife company on the river. He was not keeping Jim and wife company one minute longer than he had to, good as it was to see Jim again. Skafe was on his way. Besides, he thought, a man with a wife is not the man.

He saw smoke beyond a bluff. Jim swung wide of the point and headed in. He beached his canoe below the high bank and beside a scow. He waved his hand to say: *Run hard ashore*, which Skafe did. They climbed a slant-path of silt, powdery dust, soft underfoot. Jim's tethered dogs gave tongue for fish.

"Anna!" he called. The cabin was rough, but with two small glass windows and a screen at the door, a fair good cabin. "Anna!" Things lay around, traps, firewood, nets and junk, none too tidy. "Maybe she's asleep," said Jim, with a glance at Skafe, and he walked to the cabin.

"What is it?" Jim's wife stood in the door.

"Husky Skafe just got in," said Jim.

"Why not . . . ?" she began to say. She nodded to Skafe, unsmiling. Mrs. Willis had been asleep, to judge by the tousle of black hair, a pillow mark down one cheek. "I was sleeping," she said, and went in again.

"I'll give the dogs a bite." Jim went down the bank for fish to feed his dogs, which were lean and healthy.

Skafe looked across the river. He wondered how Jim Willis had found himself this wife. Jim was the type who would end up with a breed or Indian. But this was a white girl with a sulky face.

"Hullo," she said, and he turned to shake hands. "Did you have a good trip up?"

"Slow," he said. He smiled at her for politeness; then looked across the river. "Jim seems in good shape."

"Yes," she said. "Did you start from Norman?"

"Soon after breakup," he said. "Pretty here, isn't it?" Pretty was not what he meant. The river was no more pretty than Jim's wife.

"It's strong and beautiful," she said. "The North starts here, I always think."

Which was what he always thought, looking back on it from the North, and seeing it today again. But no one else had said that to him. "Have you been In long?" he asked her. It was not a voice that had always been In.

"Two years this time." She waved at the flies with a handkerchief, green silk, an exception from or contrast to her clothes, which were a man's: bush shirt, blue jeans, moccasins. She was nearly as tall as Skafe, but he was not a tall man. "And you?"

"Two years altogether," he said. "Jim and I met up in Aklavik the summer before last."

"Oh, yes," she said. "I know all about that meeting."

A commonplace remark, yet edged, he thought. "Now I'm for the city lights," he said. "They look pretty bright at the moment, too."

No comment.

"Do you like cities?" he asked.

"Not particularly," said Anna Willis.

Here came Jim from his dogs. "Big stuff," he said about ice that was passing on the stream. Some floes were ten feet across, and high in the water, clear green ice. Not a hope in hell of bucking that, thought Skafe.

Jim put a fond hand across to his wife's farther shoulder. "What's for supper, honey? Husky can eat the best part of a steer."

"Fishy hand," she said, and twitched that shoulder. Jim dropped his fishy hand.

My God, thought Skafe. What has Jim picked himself? But Jim's wife turned to him. "There's fish and moose and moose and fish and so on," she said smiling at him, hair black as an Indian's, eyes brown, mouth wide, cheekbones puffy with mosquito bites, Jim's wife come alive. "Which menu would you fancy, Mr. Skafe?"

"He answers to Husky," said Jim. "Husky's his name, and husky he is."

"So you keep . . ." she said and stopped. "Well?" she said, unsmiling again.

"Whatever's easy," he said. "Is moosemeat easy?"

"A pushover," Jim said. "Right there in the electric fridge." He nodded at a small log icehouse. "I'll get you a husky-sized steak, the very best."

"You built this cabin, didn't you, Jim?" he asked, walking with Jim, and behind Jim's wife. She had wide shoulders for a woman.

"Five years back," said Jim. "I trapped two seasons out of here."

"How did you do?" he asked. Jim's wife had a small waist, shirt gathered in tight in belted jeans.

"Beaver and marten were good in them days," said Jim.

"Do you think you might trap here again next winter?" She had long legs, molding the cheap cloth at calf and thigh.

"Well, I might," said Jim. "But I don't see no sign of beaver close to. What can you expect with the goddam Indians cleaning the lodges right out, no breeding stock?" Her body moved full and free in the sheath of her pants. She went into the cabin. He and Jim went after moosemeat.

After that, he helped Jim clean the rest of the fish, and put them to dry in the sun. After that, he shaved and washed and was ready for the dinner party. Then he smoked his pipe and sat watching the river. He never tired of that. Wherever I go, he thought, I'll always see old man, cold man Mackenzie River. He liked moose steak, but was not too keen on the dinner party, so he watched the river until Jim hailed him, and then he went up.

The wind had dropped and the flies were bad. Cloud massed to the south, indigo in the sun. "Looks like a bad one," said Jim. A robin sang at the edge of the clearing, its breast bright orange in the tree against the storm.

Jim's wife wore a dress now, red flowers on white, and an apron at the stove. "Smell that!" said Jim.

The smell of moose steak was good. Anna Willis asked Skafe how he wanted his, and then she put the meat on tin plates, and a Yorkshire pudding she had made, and peas, and she served the men.

"There!" she said, patting Jim on the back.

He looked up at her. "You're the best little cook in the whole darned North Country," said Jim, proud and loving, patted on the back.

"Little cook, little woman," she said, and took off her apron and sat between them. Jim looked puzzled.

Why does she pick on him? thought Skafe. "Fair-sized cook and man-sized steak," he said. "It's wonderful, the steak." He said that without double meaning, but to say something. Jim laughed loudly, and Anna Willis quietly, both pleased with him for joking, it seemed.

He ate his tender meat. He heard thunder far off. He sat on her right and looked at the cabin, which was moderately tidy. It had log furniture, well made—a table, a finished chair for him, a half-finished chair for her, a crate for Jim.

Skafe had seen one single bunk behind him. There was a double-decker at the other end, the top bunk in use, the woman's things on the lower. Married eight months, he thought, and she sleeps in a top bunk at the opposite corner. What kind of a setup is this?

He looked at the girl. She put down her knife and fork, took a bit of bread to mop up gravy, no fancy manners, although he knew from her speech and from other things that she had not grown up in log cabins in the wilderness, sopping gravy. "Won't you have some more?" she asked him.

"I couldn't," he said. "Decks awash already." They laughed again, an easy household to get a laugh.

"Jim?" she said. "Just a sliver from near the bone?"

"I guess I will," he said. "No seconds! What's got into you, Husky boy? You used to carry an appetite."

"Too much sitting around in boats," he said.

"You look well on it. You look like the girls won't do too much sitting around Outside." Jim chuckled, and Skafe smiled, and the girl, her face impassive, went to cut Jim a sliver of meat from near the bone.

"Are you still set on staying Out?"

"For a year or two, anyway," he said. "I'll be back, though." He thought of telling Jim now about his ore findings, but decided to wait until after supper. He must talk to him tonight, because a storm could finish the breakup fast. The thunder was louder, the lightning bright in the cabin.

"I love thunderstorms," said Anna Willis. "Wind is the thing I hate." She looked at Skafe, animated now, a girl of twenty-two or three, the brood and the sulk quite gone, the face strong-cut in a flash of lightning. He looked away.

"I'll light the lamp," said Jim.

"No," she said. "We can see."

Dutiful Jim sat down again.

"Apple pie?"

"You're a wonder," Jim said. "How did you dream up apple pie?"

"I rooted around in dried apples," she said, smiling. "Are you from the East?" she asked Simon Skafe.

"From New Brunswick," he said, "but raised in Ontario. Dad was a railroader, in Upper Canada most of his time. He's retired now, runs the farm at home." And keen that I should take over the farm, he thought. Which I won't do. I wonder how they are? He had not heard since the last boat of the previous summer.

"Were your people Loyalists?"

He nodded, surprised a little. "Yes," he said. "We came up after the war—in 1783, I think my father says. I'm not good on history myself."

"Seventeen and eighty-three," said Jim. "That's old stuff all right. Where your folks come up from, Husky?"

"Massachusetts, Jim," he said, and, to avoid history, asked Anna Willis about her family.

"Scotch on both sides," she said. "I'm only a first generation Canadian, or should I say second, I forget." End of communication.

"Anna's dad came fresh from Bonnie Scotland to the Mackenzie River. The Company hooks them young."

She thinned her lips, looking down. It was almost dark, but lightning flickered on the faces in the cabin.

"You've been Out a lot, though?"

"All my schooling," she said. "And two years at College—UBC. My aunt lives in Vancouver."

"You're educated people," said Jim Willis. "Fifth grade was my education."

"Book learning isn't everything, Jim," she said kindly. "Look at all you know about animals and birds and things."

"Sure," said Jim. "But could I write it down worth a damn to tell other people?"

Jim might have been a naturalist. But hell, thought Skafe. Jim doesn't have the brains. Well, perhaps the brains. Jim doesn't finish. Jim makes one good chair and half the second. He . . .

"Oh, look!" She went to the window. The flash had plotted its zigzag on Skafe's near eye. He stood beside her as that peal began to rip, to run, to tear, to thunder, but the rain and the wind had not come. Cloud squatted over the river and islands, a waste of water, a silhouette of land. He heard her sigh as the rain began; then he heard the wind on its way, by lake and island and river to here. He heard Jim close the door.

The great flash hissed to explosion, and Anna Willis leaned against him, her leg, her thigh, her hip, her arm, her shoulder, unknown woman against him; and then her body moved away from him, and she turned to ask Jim to light the lamp.

Jim and Skafe sat with tea while she washed the dishes. Jim's eye roved, unsettled as always. He watched his wife. It was clear that Jim loved his wife. Then he drummed his fingers on the table, and made finger patterns. Then he looked at the roof in the roar of rain. Then he looked at Skafe. Jim was an affectionate man. I only once saw him quiet in himself, thought Skafe. "Say again, Jim," he said.

"Got your plans all made for Outside?"

"First I'll have myself a bit of a time," he said. "And then I'll look around a while to see what's what. Can I help dry?" he asked Jim's wife. "That was some feast you gave us."

"No, thanks," she said. "I can manage. You and Jim have yourselves a nice time together."

"What kind of a job then, Husky?"

"I don't know," he said. "The way I see it is to see the trends—see something that's coming, and get into it." He had been seeing surprising whole ideas all the way up the river.

"I bet you'll make a million," said admiring Jim.

"A million?" he said. "In a depression?"

"Might take a year or two," said Jim. "I tell you what, Husky, you send me a three hundred Winchester, telescope sight, the works, when you make your million. Is that a deal?"

Skafe laughed. Anna Willis was watching him. "It's a deal," he said. He never did send Jim Willis a rifle.

"Talking of rifles," he said. In fact, it was not of rifles but of the only time he had seen Jim at ease with the world and himself that he was talking; and it occurred to him that Mrs. Willis might benefit from some praising of her husband. "Talking of rifles, do you remember that grizzly on the Penitence?"

"Still makes me sweat," said Jim. He smiled. His eyes swung in his wife's direction.

She came to sit with them again. "Tell me," she said to Skafe.

"A short story," he said. "We were panning the stream—or Jim was. The Penitence is not much more than a brook up there, in a gully of rock. Well, I left Jim, and I went on a ways to see what it looked like further up. What should I meet round a corner but the father and mother of all grizzlies . . ."

"Say, Husky, that reminds me. What would you do if you met a bear around a corner in the Rocky Mountains?"

"I did," he said, "in the Mackenzie Mountains, extension of the same. What would I do? Do what I did—get out of there."

"What, with a bear behind?" Big joke.

"Oh, Jim," she said. "Go on," she said, watching him.

"My jackknife was all I had. Jesus!" he said, remembering that, and saw Anna Willis frown at the word, and he thought: What does she think this is, a parlor in Vancouver?

"The bear stood up, and swung his right paw and roared, or it might have squealed, I don't remember. All I remember is climbing the rocks, the bear after me, and into a tree and shouting for Jim. The bear took a hold of that tree—six inches anyway at the butt—and I heard the roots cracking, and then I heard Jim arrive. I couldn't see Jim for the bear, and Jim couldn't shoot the bear for me. 'Hey, you!' Jim called from below. 'Hey, you big bastard critter.' Jim scored on the grizzly with a rock.

"A thing to remember about bears," said Skafe to Anna Willis, staring at him, the tip of her tongue wetting her lips, "is not to get below them, which was well known to Jim. The bear went down at Jim, and he fired his shot, and the grizzly and Jim went into the Penitence together, the bear expiring."

"You pulled me out," said Jim. And now, reliving his grizzly bear, Jim Willis looked easy, as he had looked in camp that night. There had been no fret at all in him that night.

Anna Willis breathed faster, white dress with red flowers on it, party dress on a voluptuous woman. She looked at Jim, and she looked at Skafe, and she smiled at them or about them, or for Skafe, he did not know. The rain had stopped. She stood again, and put on her apron. "I think I'll bake first thing," she said.

"Sing for us, Husky."

Sing for your supper, Husky Skafe. He did not feel much like it.

"Oh, yes!" she said, eager about him singing. She mixed flour and the rest of it in a bowl.

"What, then?" he asked.

"Any old song," she said. "I mean any old-time song."

"How's about 'Frankie and Johnnie'? That's one of Husky's best."

"Okay," he said. He sang "Frankie and Johnnie," one of his best, or one of Jim's favorites, a song he had sung alone on the river the other night, when South and Home and Out were in his mind, and girls for pleasure.

She hummed it with him, contralto hum to the baritone. He came to the end of Frankie and Johnnie.

"Jeeze, Anna, I never heard you even hum before."

She had hummed in unison, then harmony. "Your turn," he said.

"What about the 'Man on the Flying Trapeze'?" she said. "Together, then!"

" '. . . He purloined my lover away. Oh, that daring young man,' " she said, arms straight as she kneaded dough. She laughed, flushed and happy. They sang well together.

"Jeeze," said Jim. "It takes old Husky. I told ya Husky was the life and soul, and Anna singin' like Nellie Melba. You'd make a fortune on the boards, you two, double billing, Husky and Anna." Jim laughed to himself, dear old Jim, goodhearted bear-behind-you Jim, making up for lost laughing time, thought Skafe. "Yeah, a fortune," said Jim, and was quiet. A fortune, a pile, a million in yellow gold.

I'll speak to him now in a minute, Skafe thought. Anna Willis turned the dough onto a board and plumped it, up from each side, away and towards her. She slapped it and kneaded again. He watched her bare arms, the run of muscle from finger to shoulder. The thunderstorm had died.

"More singin'," said Jim.

"I'm sung out," said the life of the party.

"What's your real name?" she asked.

"Simon," he said.

"Hee, hee, hee!" Jim cackled. "That's rich, oh Jeeze, I never heard it."

Her fingers stopped working, deep in the dough. Her head turned to Jim. "What's so funny?" she said irritably.

"Aw nothin', honey. Just Simon don't seem to suit a husky guy like Husky."

"Jim," he interrupted this embarrassment. "I made some findings."

Jim sat up straight. "Gold?" Eyes bright, voice soft as a lullaby dream.

"No," he said. "Pitchblende, and rich."

Jim slumped. "Not worth a damn," he said. "Only gold's worth a damn in this country. Now if it was gold we could celebrate. Celebrate. Say!" he muttered, with a lust or another sweet dream. "You wouldn't have a drop with you, Husky boy?"

There was a bottle of rum in the boat.

"Little drops of rummy," said Anna Willis, "gold dust in the hand." She poked a finger into the dough, and poked again. "Now, let's see

. . . Gold dust in the hand. Make a mighty ocean, Never-never land."
She smiled.

"I missed that one, Anna. Say again!"

She repeated it. "Your theme song," she said. "The Rum and Gold song."

Jim said nothing, whipped dog, not resentful.

Whip hand, whipped dog, what she needs . . . "How smart you are, Mrs. Willis," said Skafe. He stood. "Goodnight," he said. "And thanks a lot."

Her face colored. Her nostrils arched. She did not look at him. "Goodnight," she said.

He went out with Jim. It was cool, and a breeze from the west. The flies were not up yet after the storm. He could not tell Jim that what his bitchy young wife seemed most to need was a beating.

"It's my own darned fault she gets sore at me," Jim said. "I went on the jag at Easter, good and drunk four days. This goddam booze—if it stays away from me, I can stay away from it is the best I can do. That's the real reason I sold my catch." Jim sighed with relief, the whole truth out.

"I know," said Skafe, and he punched Jim's skinny ribs.

Jim laughed. "You're a great guy, Husky. You do me good, and I tell you somethin', you done Anna good. Well, climb the bank for trout for breakfast."

"Thanks, Jim," he said. "But I guess I'll sleep as late as I can. If this wind holds, I might start around the south shore of the lake tomorrow night."

"That soon? I was hopin' you'd make a real visit with us, say a week. What's the hurry, Husky?"

"I'm on my way," he said. "I guess you know the feeling, Jim."

"Sure," said Jim. "Itchy pants to travel. Sure I know it. Well, goodnight then, boy."

It would be twilight for an hour or two. He went down the path, now ankle-deep in mud or gumbo. He boarded the boat, closed his curtains, and lay in the bunk. Ice thumped and scraped against the hull, small pieces back-watered from the stream. The ice stopped, and he listened for the ice. *Oh, that daring young man,* she had said to herself.

From here, at the beginning of the river, he tried to see the journey of the river—the run to the mountains at Camsell Bend—the Bear at Bear Rock—the chop of Sault rapids, two miles wide—the moon-canyon of the Ramparts—a last dwarf spruce at Kittigazuit.

But the journey of the river did not help him into sleep. Ice nudged at the boat again, here at the head of the Mackenzie, at the beginning.

CHAPTER THREE

THE WIND itself was an accompaniment to sleep. But then a rope began to slat against the boat, breaking the rhythm of sleep and wind. He lay awhile, teased by the rope on the starboard side, so he knew that the wind blew from the west, the wind he had wanted.

He rolled up the burlap curtain, a thing of more use than decorative value, and he stepped out to fresh air, and to see that Jim's scow was there, but not the canoe. Jim had left a message on the gas drum for him: *Brekfast at cabin*, a piece of paper weighted by a stone. He crumpled the paper tightly round the stone, and threw the package overboard, but the paper unwrapped and floated. There was no ice on the river this morning.

The cabin was out of sight from here, below the bank. He stripped, lowered himself from the stern, and went under, head and all, but he did not tarry in the Mackenzie River. It was against his private rules to squeak or gasp. He toweled away the shivers, and was warm again and full of glowing purity.

Half past eleven was late for breakfast, the offer of which he had declined last night, the prospect of which now pleased him. "Hullo," he said, pausing at the door.

"Come in," she said, and he went in as she slid from top bunk to floor, leaving her book face-down.

They exchanged good mornings. "I hope you slept well," she said politely, walking past him to the stove.

"Thanks," he said. In fact, he had not slept well. "Jim left a message asking me to breakfast. He weighted it with a stone, which reminded me of that old game—Paper wraps stone, stone blunts scissors, scissors cut paper. What does it mean?"

"I hadn't thought," she said. "Is it a circle? Or perhaps a Chinese way of saying that the biter gets bit; or that nothing means anything, anyway?"

"I guess so," said Skafe. He was watching the pleasure of thought in her face.

"You stare at me," she said. She smiled, wide mouthed, full lipped, dark eyed, turning his piece of trout in the pan.

"I was watching you think," he said.

"Think! I vegetate, skimming the top off books."

"What are you reading now?"

"*The Brothers Karamazov*," said Anna Willis. "Would you like fresh bread, or shall I make toast?"

He ate her good bread, and fried lake trout, which was fair, not the best of fish. She sat down with him. Jim can't quite spell breakfast, he thought; and she reads Dostoevsky. "Is Jim going round his nets?"

"Yes," she said. "He hopes you won't leave before this afternoon." She looked at her right hand, flat on the table, the fingers spread, a strong hand, and graceful. "Must you leave so soon?" she asked, turning her hand to look at the nails.

Leave to go where I'm going, he thought. While the going is good, he thought also now. "Yes," he said. "I guess I'll go."

"*Yes, I will—No, I won't—I guess I'll go.*" She was mimicking him, he supposed. She looked at him across the table. "Are you ever in doubt about anything?"

"Very often," he said. "If my mind is not made up, then I'm in doubt, which happens every day."

Anna Willis laughed. "But your mind gets made up, doesn't it?"

"You seem to be telling me," he said, perhaps piqued. People did not make a joke of him particularly often.

Her face was closed to him again. "That rhyme last night," she said. "—The Rum and the Gold. It was unkind, I know. I'm sorry about it."

Sorry to whom? "You can't change Jim," he said.

"No," she said. "Not Jim, nor you, nor me, nor anyone."

"How old are you?"

"I'm twenty-three," she said.

"H'mm," he said. "The younger school of determinists."

Twenty-three years old, Jim's wife, the moody beauty, her troubles gone, whatever they might be. "Irony," she smiled to him. "A rather unusual friend to meet on the Mackenzie River."

"Talking of the river," he said, "or of the lake, I think I'll run up and have a look at the ice. I might see Jim on the way. Would you like to come?"

"I would love to come," she said.

She sat beside him in the stern, not touching him. The air was clear after the storm last night, forest fires damped down, or new fires not yet burning up. "Are you all right?" he said, meaning comfortable, warm, contented in his boat.

"I'm fine, thank you, Simon."

Only his parents called him Simon, odd-sounding name, a big joke to Jim. He did not tell Anna Willis how he felt alone in the boat on the river with her.

"Why did you come North—for adventure, or to make a fortune, or just to come?"

"I had a job," he said. "Office equipment in Toronto, steady prospects, and all the rest. But after a year of it I thought: To hell with steady prospects in office equipment. I'm off on my own to live awhile."

He headed across the channel which Jim had brought him through yesterday. He supposed it was roughly the reason he had come North, to get some real life into his guts.

"It's lovely," she said. "It's so lovely on the river. *Off on your own to live awhile.* Now, after living, will it be office equipment?"

"No," he said. "It won't."

"You're so complete inside yourself," she said. "On your own will always be the way for you."

"Think so?" he said, annoyed in a sense, and pleased. I'll drop her off with Jim, he thought without conviction. Where he wanted her was here with him, not touching him, untouched and touchable. "You said you had two years at college. Then you came North?"

"Yes," she said. "My mother was sick. She died that next winter at Lightning River; and I stayed on."

"Does your father work for the Company?"

"Not now," she said. "He trades for himself." Subject closed, it seemed.

"So then you met Jim."

"That's right," she said on the boat between the islands. The flies were bad in here. She flicked her silk handkerchief occasionally.

"Did you know Jim long—before you were married, I mean?"

"Three days," she said. "One drunk, and two sober."

"Look," he said. "Why speak about Jim that way?"

"I know, I know. Poor Jim married to a bitch, you're right. Husky Skafe is always right. But can't you please just leave me alone."

"I wondered if I could help," he said. But had he provoked that outburst for her benefit? Her hand gripped the edge of the seat between them. He put his hand over hers, and she turned her hand up to meet his hand; then she took her hand away.

"He has a net just here," she said. But Jim was nowhere to be seen. "Let's go on," she said.

Skafe went on to the head of the Mackenzie River, at the west end of Great Slave Lake, where the river dips at the start of its run. They tied the boat in a sheltered place below fast water, and Simon Skafe and Anna Willis went along the beach. The shingle was noisy. A pair of arctic terns flew overhead, light winged, scythe winged, harshly protesting the disturbance. Near the nest they dived aggressively. "Easy now," said Skafe. He waved them off.

He sat with her on stones in the sun and the wind. He looked through his binoculars. "The south shore is clear," he said. "Some candle ice. I can make it along to Hay River." He turned the glasses east to the white rim of ice. It was thick, but the pack was breaking. The strong wind held it off the river.

Then he gave Jim's wife the glasses. He sat with his arms round his knees, and his chin on his knees, as a boy will sit, watching, thinking, feeling. A bald eagle fished along Big Island, finding nothing. It swung this way to the territory of the arctic terns, which rose to harry it. The eagle yielded, flapping with ungainly bulk, then soared again to kill for itself or thieve or scavenge, noble bird.

"It's strong and beautiful," he said. "The North starts here, I always think."

"I said that yesterday."

"I know," he said. "I quoted you."

"Simon Skafe," she said, alone with him. "You quoted me."

He saw the run of the river again, the frozen river again, hunger and hardship, a day on the Penitence with Jim, soft snow in the bush, hard snow on the sea, the North and his journey from the North to yesterday, here to a beginning with violence and growth, yet peace of a kind. He lay back, finding a stone convenient to his head. He closed his eyes.

"I thought you slept well last night."

"No," he said.

"Sleep, then," said Anna Willis, and she hummed a tune.

"What is it?"

"A lullaby. I don't remember."

He listened to her humming in the sound of the river. The terns were crying now again. "Dammit," he said. But he was happy, and he went to sleep.

A wind touched his face, and something else touched it lightly. He heard mosquitoes. She was fanning him with her handkerchief, a corner in each hand. "How long was I asleep?"

"I don't know," she said. "An hour or something."

"Dragonflies hunt bulldogs, and bulldogs hunt mosquitoes, and mosquitoes hunt the men and so on," he considered, "up and down the river." He was sleepy, and the wind had fallen.

"That's all it is," she said, "on the river and anywhere, wrap the stone, blunt the scissors and cut the paper, but you won't remember. Now go to sleep again."

"You're good to me," he said.

The second time he woke, she was not fanning him. The wind blew strongly in the trees. She sat beside him, watching him. "My child," she said, and kissed him on each cheek.

Husky Skafe had been no woman's child since what? Well, since perhaps the age of ten. Now, on the hard stones he was Anna's child, but truth only comes to go, be lost, be flouted. He looked at her face, and then he looked at her body in the shirt, a thin shirt of poplin or such stuff and, doing that, he snatched her child away.

He took his hands from behind his head, and held them out, and she leaned to meet his lover's hands. She kissed him on the lips. They kissed as lovers now already.

It's nothing, he had thought. I need a woman is all it is—Now listen, he had thought. She is trouble, this one, Jim's discontented cross, Jim's property—But listen, he had thought. How can you explain the shock and sympathy?

He held her from him. "We must go back," he said.

"Oh, please," she said. "Not yet." She laid her head in the hollow of his shoulder; and then she moved away. They watched the river, cold and green between the islands. The wind was strong. Here on this island, birds were nesting, a pair of myrtle warblers in the spruce above them, a fever and a flutter. Black and gold drooped wings about the brown and gold; how exquisite, how hot, how brief the mating of the myrtle warblers by the great cold river.

She stood. "Take me back now if you like," she said. "You can't take this away."

Nor could he take away the harm that he had done to Jim. Small harm? No great harm done. Least said soonest mended, and the rest. But did anything exist for her that could be mended? Jim baffled, outwitted, sat upon—yet Jim evidently loved his wife. "Can't you tell me a bit?" he said as they walked together on the shingle beach, the terns protesting.

"What is there to tell?"

He looked at her and saw that she was crying and waited now for her to speak.

"Three days," she said, "and I married him, and then there was all winter in the trapline cabin, Jim away half the time. Being alone, I don't mind that. It was the goodness, getting on my nerves, always starting things and bright ideas, always so kind and giving in to me, not forcing me, *Aw, honey!* But it was all right until we went back to Lightning for Easter."

She took off her moccasins, waded in and climbed aboard. The weight being in the stern, the bow came free. He pushed off with his pole. They started down the river.

"He was just tight that first time when we met last fall, just high like any man, and he sobered up . . . But at Easter he went on a jag, out cold on the doorstep at twelve below, and I got him in, and he threw up his rotgut hooch all over the floor, like an animal, worse than an animal, throwing up and drinking more while I cleaned it up . . . Did you ever see Jim on the booze?"

"Yes," he said. "In Aklavik. It doesn't happen often. It's just a thing about old Jim. He gets it, and he gets over it until it grows on him again." Much was explained, but all was not explained. "Did you want to marry him?"

She had stopped crying. "No," she said. "I thought he was nice, and so he is. I didn't know he was a dipsomaniac."

"But marriage! Why?"

Anna Willis took a breath. "The last boat had gone," she said flatly and quietly. "There was no way out from then to now. I escaped with Jim."

"Escaped?"

"Yes," she said. "Escaped from my father." She stared at him. "I had to, Simon," she said. "I had to."

He had heard of such things as not uncommon. He knew of such odious things, if not about them. "Does Jim know that?"

"No," she said. "Jim doesn't know, and never will. That would be the crowning insult."

The river took them on.

"Simon!"

He was thinking of one day gone by in the big hard killing country. "Yes?" he said.

"Do you like me?"

He looked at her face, which was beautiful to him, a face both arrogant and humble, shadowed with nightmares at twenty-three. *Do you like me?* How unexpected and diffident. He laughed. "It seems I like you," he said.

"Do you like me enough to take me with you?"

"Yes," he said. "But I won't take you with me. I can't do that to Jim."

"*You can't do that to Jim.* If you want anything enough, you do it or you take it. That's the kind of man you are."

"Maybe I take what I want," he said. "But I care about what I want to take."

"I don't," she said.

"Anna," he said. "It can't be done." He closed away the fancy in his mind of her with him. He knew, from the island, how it would be with her with him.

"Dear Simon," she said. "I know you're right." It occurred to him that it would not occur to her to say what she might have said: *Don't you see I can't stand it another minute? Help me!* She did not plead her own troubles to him.

CHAPTER FOUR

JIM HAD killed three willow grouse with his .22, all shot in the head. He took life for food or sale, but not with a hunter's pleasure—wolf and wolverine being exceptions in Jim's killing book.

The birds were tough, of good flavor, a farewell feast. "Just right," said Jim to Anna. "Trust you to do a swell job cookin' birds or anything."

"Thanks, Jim," she said.

"You look great," he said. "The sun and the wind done you good up there with Husky. You should get out to the fresh air more."

"Yes, Jim," she said. She pulled the second leg off her bird and ate it in her fingers. Jim and Skafe had finished. She glanced at Skafe as she bit into the thicker end: then she looked down and turned the leg, considering attack. She wore the same clothes—thin shirt and jeans, but a scarlet handkerchief at the neck, her hair brushed to an ebony gloss.

Scarlet and black, he thought, a contrast woman. She was only a girl, but he thought of her as a woman, which was also true, and painfully so. Now he turned to look through the window at the river. The wind had dropped, and smoke haze had settled in from forest fires that no men ever fought and few men ever saw. Bush pilots saw them, fires all across and around the compass clock, smoldering, undying, rampant, fanned to ferocity by the heat-wind bellows.

"I like a woman who can eat," said Jim across the table. "Eh, Husky?"

Certainly he liked the honest pleasure with which she ate her willow grouse. He gave an affirmatory form of grunt because Jim wanted male agreement from him.

"Are only men supposed to be carnivorous?"

"Jeeze, honey, I said I *like* a woman who . . ."

"Oh, never mind," she said, taking tin plates from before the men. She poured hot water, and then some cold, into the basin and set that on the table. "Do you want to rinse your fingers before I start?"

They rinsed their fingers. Then she took the basin over beside the stove and started washing up. It was hot in the cabin, hot from cooking, and hot dynamite awaiting a spark to blow the roof off. Jim remained unaware of dynamite. He patted his stomach about roast bird and such trimmings as the North could offer, full of belly, wandering of eye.

Skafe had left his ore samples on an inverted tea chest by the door. As he stood now to fetch them, Anna's head jerked round to him. *Leaving?* might be the question.

"Here, Jim," he said, turning out the bag, "the ores I was telling you about."

Jim took the first black sample, hefted it and turned it. "Pitchblende?"

"Yes," said Skafe.

"Heavy stuff. I never seen it." Jim inspected the other pieces perfunctorily, but his interest quickened at the last, and he took it to the window. "Fool's gold, goddam pyrite." He sat down again.

Anna had finished the dishes. She looked over Jim's shoulder a moment, shrugged, went down the cabin and climbed onto her bunk. She opened her book, *The Brothers Karamazov* in a cheap edition, and lay with her ankles crossed.

Skafe had to get this straightened out with Jim, and then he had to go. Damned stupid, he thought, to keep the partnership alive after we separated, to be in partnership with Jim at all. "What, Jim?"

"You're worse than me. You're chasing moonbeams, Husky."

"Sorry," he said. "I was thinking."

"I said: How far from the shore of Bear Lake is this Turtle Mountain?"

"Say fifty miles from Smith Arm," he said. Turtle was his own name for the unmapped hill. He had named it for a jut of rock from the ridge above the cliff. From one point to the west it resembled exactly the snake's head of the turtle.

"You're a smart boy, Husky, but you're way off this time. Hell, take Labine and them fellas, right on the lake, a better thing than this, and what do they have to do—middle of July at breakup, ship the stuff across Bear Lake and down the Bear with a portage in the middle, and up the Mackenzie and the rest of it, two-three thousand miles in a two-month season to get it Outside before they even start refining. It's a pipedream, Husky."

"Jim," he said. "Do you know what radium is worth?" She was lying reading on her bunk, but she had not turned a page.

"Plenty, I know," said Jim.

"Seventy thousand dollars a gram, say two million an ounce."

Jim was not impressed. "When you got it," he said. "But how much of that stuff do you need to get it?"

"Two or three hundred tons to an ounce. But Jim," he said, "I traced the vein and staked it. I don't know how much there is. All I know is it's worth keeping the claims alive until we can get deposits proved one way or the other."

"If you say the stuff is there, then I'll bet my shirt it's there," said Jim. "But the stuff there ain't worth nothing, and we won't get no ounce for two million bucks. See what I mean, Husky?" Jim was being practical, which he could be, with only his cardinal weakness about quick money. "Take gold now! Remember that one morning on the Penitence we panned out seventy dollars—right in our hands. There's money for you!"

"Yes," said Skafe patiently. "*One* morning, Jim. I know this thing is a gamble, and maybe I'm wrong, but we've got to sit on it a year or two until things pick up again."

"Sell out," said Jim. "Let some other fellas take the rap. Why, if we sell out now, we might clear two-three thousand bucks, dollars in the pocket, not down the drain."

"Nobody's speculating at the moment, Jim. There's a hell of a depression on."

"You needn't tell Granny that," said Jim, amiable as ever. "But there's always some fella ready for a plunge . . ."

"It's staked in both our names," he said carefully. "If you sold out your share, Jim, that would leave me with fifty per cent with God knows who."

"I see what you mean." Jim now had a bright idea. He appealed to his wife on the upper bunk. "Husky's got a hunch," he said, "and when Husky rides a hunch you might as well argue with a Catholic mule. What do you say, honey? You be referee."

She laid her book on herself and turned her head. "If he wants to stay in," she said, "and you want to get out, why not let him buy your share?"

Jim thumped his knee. "Smart, ain't she?" he said proudly. "I never thought of that one. What do you say, Husky?"

Her head lay sideways on the pillow. She was watching him, Anna Willis in her bunk, and he was doing business just before departure. "Look, Jim," he said. "Are you sure you want to sell?"

"Sure," said Jim. "Sure as the ice is breaking up there on the lake."

"Okay," he said. "You set the price, then." Intangibles were not worth much to Jim.

"He's a great guy to do business with," said Jim Willis to his wife. "How many fellas would make findings on their own, and come to a sleepin' partner, and say: *Here you are, half shares! Don't want the half? Well, set your price.* There's Husky for you."

"Come on! For Christ's sake can't we get this settled?"

"Say, what's up? I never heard you mad at me before."

"Sorry, Jim," he said. "I must travel, though."

"Okay, then. Well, let's see. I'm owing you three hundred and sixty-odd, and then there's a share of your catch the other way, okay?" Jim looked guilty, mindful that he had been hooked into selling the whole of his catch for too small a sum because the trader knew he must have liquor money.

"Prices are way down, Jim. It might net fifteen hundred, might do better. I'll have to settle that with you later—half shares anyway."

"Thanks a lot. Now, let's see—a few hundred in the clear would suit me fine. Is that too high? Hell, I don't want to rook you, Husky." Jim was the world's worst trader; fell over backwards not to rook anyone, least of all his friend and junior hero, Skafe.

"I'm still carrying some cash from last year. Suppose I write off the three hundred and sixty, and I pay you five hundred down. How does that sound?"

"Sounds wonderful—the best part of a thousand bucks! That's too much, Husky!"

"Jim," he said. "If my hunch turned out to be right, it might be far too little." She was propped on her elbow, watching them, a woman in a man's thin shirt, minding her woman's business; but she frowned.

"This pitchblende-radium pipedream—it won't come to nothing, that's for sure. No offense meant, Husky. Is it a deal, then?"

"It's a deal," he said.

Jim stood up to shake his hand in a jovially formal sort of way, and they sat again, Jim Willis with his back to Anna. "I'll give you a paper, Husky. My name's on the stakes, so I'll give you a paper."

"No need," he said. He counted the bills from his wallet. They were twenties.

Twenty-five twenties made a tight small wad for Jim, who put them in his pocket without counting them. "We got a pen and paper, Anna?"

"Yes," she said, slipping off her bunk, light as a circus girl from a piebald horse. She brought a fountain pen and a sheet of paper.

"I'm no hand at clerkin'. You write it, Husky."

He thought, and then wrote:

> Head of Mackenzie. June 15th, 1932
>
> In return for the sum of five hundred dollars ($500), receipt of which I duly acknowledge, and in settlement of my debt to S. K. Skafe of three hundred and sixty-one dollars and twenty-five cents ($361.25), total value received: eight hundred and sixty-one twenty-five, I hereby sell, assign and abandon all rights to S. K. Skafe of my half-share in mineral claims staked in the names of J. Willis and S. K. Skafe at Turtle Mountain, so called, north of Great Bear Lake, District of Mackenzie, Northwest Territories.

"There, Jim," he said. "How will that do? I'll give you an I O U for half my furs."

"I don't want no I O U," said Jim. "This other's different. It's legal stuff, and you got to be protected. Nobody needs an I O U from Husky Skafe."

Nobody needs an I O U from Husky Skafe. How well that sounded. But he made Jim take his I O U at the dissolution of their partnership, and he put Jim's paper, as Jim called it, into his wallet. It should have been witnessed, but nobody present was a valid witness to Jim's signature.

"Just one thing we should have," Jim said, "is a drink on it." He looked at Skafe with hope eternal, and then at his wife for fear of a crack.

"Oh, yes!" she said. "I'd love to have a drink."

Skafe hesitated, but not long. "I have a bottle of rum," he said. "I brought it for you, Jim." What harm could one bottle do to the Willis family?

Jim went down with him. The air outside was heavy with smoke, the smell of it, the haze of it, ugly cloak for the remorseless river. He gave Jim the bottle of rum.

"Hudson's Bay Company," Jim said. "Finest Demerara. One hundred and fifty-one proof." He chuckled, cherishing liquid gold in both his hands. "I may not love the Company just like my mother, but I sure do love the Company's rum."

Three tin mugs and a pitcher of cloudy Mackenzie water were on the table. "No glasses, I'm afraid," she said, quite apologetic, like a housewife in suburbia. She smiled. They all were happier at the thought of rum, and the thought of rum made a new man out of Jim. He opened the bottle, put back the cork, and set it on the table. He looked at Skafe. Jim's eyes were gleaming, but the courtesies must be observed.

"Your bottle," said Skafe. "It's up to you, Jim."

Jim poured dark rum into mugs, meticulously fair, a decent tot of double strength or fire in each. "You still drown yours with cold water, Husky?"

"Yes," he said. "Lots of it, Jim."

"That's a hell of a way to treat good rum. You, honey?"

"I'll take mine straight," she said.

"You shouldn't," Jim protested. "It'll burn you up. I wouldn't want to have you all burned up."

She bit her lip and looked less happy at the thought of rum. "Half and half, hot toddy, warms the cockles," said Jim. He went to the stove for his half and half. He starts with half and half, thought Skafe, not without compassion. Skafe and Anna stared at one another, and he felt the stir that was not compassion.

"Safe journey, Husky!"

"Here's tae us," she said in the voice of her forefathers. "Wha's like us? Damn few. They're a' deid, may the Lord be thankit!"

Jim cackled. "That's a good one. You're a card. Never know what Anna's coming up with."

"Good hunting!" said Skafe. How right Jim is, he thought. But it was time for a triangular clinking of mugs.

Anna took half of hers at a single swallow without visible signs of burning up, quite a feat for a girl, for anyone.

Jim sipped at the mug, held in both hands. He sniffed rummy steam, and sipped again, and sipped. "Anna," he said admiringly. "First time I seen you take a drink." Perhaps Jim loved her even more because she shared a love of rum with him.

"I take drink," she said, "and drink takes me. Paper wraps stone, as Mr. Skafe would say."

Jim's brow knitted at these riddles, then he said: "Jeeze, Anna, you still giving Husky Mister?"

"Just one of my clever little jokes," she said, and drained her mug and chased rum down with water to the manner born.

Where did she learn to drink like that? The campus jane? None of my business, thought Simon Skafe. My business is to get out of here. He needed help to do it, and he finished his rum. Jim's mug was empty too. Round one. The kettle sang for Jim's half and half.

"I'll coast, thanks, Jim," she said.

"A small one, Jim," he said.

"I wouldn't say no myself," Jim said. He went for water, and they looked at one another.

"Have you been to New York?" she asked, which startled him.

"Yes," he said. He saw the tall city on the island. "Have you?"

"No," she said.

Jim sat down again. He was easy at this stage, as he had once been on the Penitence, without rum. No goblins, no lullaby dreams for a short while at this stage. "What about New York?"

"Oh," she said, "I was thinking of Outside, where he's going." Not Simon, nor Husky, nor even Mr. Skafe, but He.

"Honey," said Jim. "It's lonesome for you." He put his hand on her hand on the table. The skin of her forearm moved, but her hand stayed where it was, under Jim's for a row of seconds until he needed his hand to raise the mug. "We'll save up for a trip," he said, and then Jim laughed at himself. "Hell," he said. "I never saved a penny in my life. But when our ship comes home, we'll take a trip to visit with Husky boy with all his millions. How does that sound, honey?"

"It sounds like pitchblende-radium to me," she said.

They all laughed, Jim the loudest; and when he stopped laughing, the gleam was in his eye. "Husky," he said. "You heard of the Nahanni country?"

"Yes," he said. Who in the North had not heard of the fabulous South Nahanni country? In fact, he had heard of it again and again from Jim, but Jim forgot that always, so near to him was the Nahanni legend, so dear to him the Nahanni dream. "The falls and the canyon," said Simon Skafe perversely. "Hell's Kitchen and the Devil's Gate. It must be a great river to run."

"It's not the river I'm speakin' of," said Jim. "It's what come out of it." He paused.

"Tell us, Jim," she said.

Jim told his Nahanni story—of a man who prospected there alone one year, and came out with nothing—so he said, until he paid for rum with gold at Nelson, and then rum paid back with his golden secret, so they knifed him. "They got fifty thousand dollars of a poke," said Jim, "but dead men tell no tales." Jim's second drink was low.

"It's still waiting there," he said. "It's waiting for some lucky guy." Drink finished. "Honey," he said. "What say we try our luck in August, when the flies are over? Leave the dogs at Simpson, borrow a second kicker—there's a hell of a current in that river—and take the scow, and take ourselves camping up the South Nahanni. There's hot springs, so they say. It's like the tropics, even palm trees growing in some secret valleys, though I can't quite swallow that one. The gold, though, it's gospel. Anna, would you like to make the trip?"

"Oh, sure," she said, in his idiom. "Sure I'd like to take a trip to see the hot springs and the palm trees in the secret arctic valleys."

She said it lightly. She was less hard on Jim tonight. She's fond of him in a way, thought Skafe, and he was jealous. I paid Jim too much for his share, he thought; but then he remembered things that Jim had done for him. He thought of Jim and Anna camping by the South Nahanni. "No more, thanks," he said. "I'm traveling tonight." He watched Jim pour triple number three.

"Put it off," said Jim. "What's one night on the road to doomsday?" He chuckled at his wisdom. "You persuade him, honey."

"I can't," she said. "He has an appointment with destiny or doomsday. He's got a date." Her face, somber and abstracted, came fully and suddenly to life. "'Got a date with an angel,'" sang Anna Willis. "'Got to meet her at seven. Got a date with an angel. I'm on my way to heaven.' You can't stop a man with a date," she said, looking out of the window. It was half past eleven, and the dusk was falling. "Can we have the lamp, Jim?" Jim brought the lamp.

Now I'll go, thought Skafe. He put his hands on the table.

"Oh listen! A wolf!

"Were you ever out in the Great Alone,
When the moon was awful clear,
And the icy mountains hemmed you in
With a silence you most could hear
With only the howl of a timber wolf
And you camped there in the cold,
A half dead thing in a stark dead world,
Clean mad for the muck called gold.

"I'm quite a girl," said Anna Willis. "Jenny Lind now married to Robert Service up the South Nahanni."

Skafe laughed, and so did Jim. She was certainly quite a girl. "I wish we had Husky with us all the time," said Jim, sweet melancholy, drifting to his cups. "Husky's real good for you and me." His hand stalked hers, but she moved her mug.

Jim's dogs were howling, drowning the wolf, if a wolf had howled. "Shut up!" bellowed Jim. But the eight dogs howled at their murderous cousin, Wolf.

Jim made to rise. "I'll go, Jim," she said. "I can quieten them." She moved quickly, taking the longer way behind Skafe's chair, and her fingers tugged at his shirt.

"True," said Jim, eyes on the bottle. "She can calm them down far better'n me." He nodded his head towards the door. "You watch!"

Skafe went out, obedient to the Willises. The flies attacked him, cloud army, pestering chorus, terrible tonight. Black flies can kill a man, he thought. They used to poison him when first he came, not now. He brushed at the fur of flies on the back of his hand, bloody carnage, cohorts inexhaustible. What a hell of a country it is, he thought, crazy people and frenzied dogs.

She was soothing them by name: "Snowball . . . Liar . . . Beaver . . . Moose . . ." One by one the dogs eased down. "Quiet now, Rover," she said to the big wheel dog of Jim's tandem hitch.

Skafe knew most of Jim's dogs. He stood with her, patting Rover, the best of the lot, a friendly beast, a demon to work, a fiend to fight. The wolf did not howl in the north again. The other dogs lay down, and their chains were quiet.

Skafe looked back. Jim moved in there, and then he sat at the table again in his cabin, man's pinprick in the wilderness, messy clearing in the wilderness. How much cleaner a boat on the river.

"Simon," she said, taking her hand from Rover's head, and moving away from Skafe. She looked at the river. "I want to ask you something."

"Yes?" he said.

"You hardly speak to me."

"A lot on my mind," he said. "What, Anna?"

"Do I seem sort of horrible to you now because of what I told you?" She swung to stare at him in the faded light. "I do. I can see it in your face. I have to be sure, that's all."

She had to be sure. Where was the absolute in thought, in feeling, about such a thing? *Do you like me?* she had asked him, the child, the girl, the woman's declaration. *Do I seem sort of horrible?*

He put his hands on her arms below her shoulders. "Foolish Anna," he said. "Of course not."

"Promise?" she said.

"Promise," he said. Did he tell her a lie? He kissed her on one mosquito-fuzzy cheek and then the other. She was his child that time outside the cabin above the river. How rarely may woman be a child to man.

"You're leaving?"

"Yes," he said. "I'll say goodbye to Jim."

"One last drink," she said. "Flies," she said. "Flies, flies, flies."

"Shertainly work magic on them dogs," said Jim inside.

The level in the bottle was the same against the lamp, better than halfway up. The rum in the bottle was not the same. It swirled now, oily alcohol and water blending. Jim had done a neat job of dilution. Poor Jim. Poor goddam dipsomaniac.

"A last one for the road?" said Skafe.

"S'all yours, Husky boy." Jim might have taken one quarter of the bottle down his throat in one deep fiery furtive blissful snatch. What Jim had taken was taking hold.

"Anna?" he asked.

"Please, Simon."

He poured their drinks while old Jim giggled. "'Simple Simon met a pieman,' oh for Chrissake." But he looked at his wife, and then at Skafe. "Say!" he said distinctly. "What is all this?"

"A party, it seems," she said, and drank.

Jim's thought, suspicion, whatever it might have been, escaped him. "Some party, whale of a party, s'cuse me, water palm trees." Jim set a mirthful course for the door of his cabin, exit Jim.

"Palm trees," Anna said. "Secret valleys up the South Nahanni."

Skafe sought her underneath the table. She held his leg between her legs. They did not speak in the time until Jim came back, and they did not move when Jim came back. Jim made it halfway to the table. "Oh, for Chrissake!" lying on the floor.

Skafe picked Jim up, a fair load for a husky man, and put him on his bunk. It was no good propping Jim up to keep the alcohol from his head. The alcohol was there already. He covered Jim with one blanket. "Thanks, Husky. You're the boy."

The bottle? Should he take it? But that would be too hard on Jim. He lifted the inverted tea chest and put the watered rum inside. Jim would have to sober up to find it; but Jim would find it as sure as the ice was breaking up there on the lake.

Anna went to tuck her husband in. "Husky, m'pal?"

"No," she said. "It's Anna." Her face was kindly, looking down at him.

"Here, honey!" Jim reached for her, but she pulled away. "Same li'l iceberg," said Jim, offended. He sighed and slept.

Skafe looked out of the window at the dawn. The smoky colors of the dawn were good. Mosquitoes drummed on the screen like a medium drizzle.

"I'm ready," she said. She carried a dunnage bag. She left the cabin. Skafe turned at the door. "Sorry, Jim," he said.

Jim was asleep, unable to accept his friend and late partner's apology.

BOOK TWO

CHAPTER ONE

SKAFE had spent Monday in London, Tuesday in New York, Thursday in Edmonton, Friday in the East again, a hard week. Behind him Mrs. Murton typed at high velocity, her clatter muted by the engines. Below him New Brunswick edged along.

Mrs. Murton and New Brunswick, he thought, this treasure, this scarce-frequented haunt. He let down his chair and closed his eyes to close the week away, close the door on that compartment, sleep for fifteen minutes.

He woke after fifteen minutes. Mrs. Murton's fingers flew to meet her deadline, an hour or less away. She stopped typing as he stood. "All right?" he said.

"Oh, yes. You had a nice little snooze, Mr. Skafe."

Mrs. Murton attributed nice little snoozes to him in planes, in trains, in cars in their life together, not that he took her with him very often. Queer, isn't it, he thought on his way to the cockpit, that North American women, so dominant, should make the best secretaries in the world, devoted slaves, work half the night, trim and eager in the morning, iron your trousers in a pinch, the Bisodol, the razor blades. *I picked up some avocados on my way. Mrs. Skafe does love avocados.* Even my marriage is her job, he thought.

He sat in the co-pilot's seat. "How is it going, Yarrow?"

"Twelve-sixteen, sir, I make the ETA. Wind northwest, fifteen to twenty—how does that sound for a landing in the bay?" He looked round at Skafe. It was Yarrow's first flight down here.

"When is high water?"

"Two o'clock Atlantic Standard, sir."

"The wind and the tide will make a chop," said Skafe. "Nothing much in sheltered water."

"Do you want to take her, sir?"

Skafe shook his head. "I came up for the view." In fact, he had come up to watch Mac's probationary pilot fly. Yarrow had done a tour over Europe in Bomber Command; he had instructed; he was twenty-five, married, careful—*just the type*, said Mac, the chief pilot. But, as Mac was the first to see, it was a personal relationship. You lived with a secretary. You went on living with a pilot.

Skafe looked ahead. The coast lay beyond a range of hills. He looked ahead, and sensed Yarrow's flying, which seemed good. There was some turbulence, not enough to bother Mrs. Murton.

"You're married, aren't you?"

"Yes, sir. Just a year."

"A family yet?"

Yarrow smiled. "One due," he said. A muscle moved in his jaw. He trimmed the plane again. Perhaps Mrs. Murton was moving in the cabin. The heading wandered slowly east, and he brought it back. "Mac's a great pilot," he said. "He was your first instructor, was he, sir?"

"Yes," said Skafe. "In a Tiger Moth in '37." Mac had instructed at the flying club. He might have gone on teaching all the war. Instead, he became a wing commander, Fighters, through the Battle of Britain and North Africa. Skafe himself had not been to the war. By 1939, he was right-hand man and heir apparent to old Ben Cloverley of Summit. In June 1940, Ben Cloverley had his stroke. Soon after that, Summit Construction was building airfields across the country. Skafe had tried to join the Air Force, but they would not let him. It still irked him that he had not fought.

They bumped above the hills. "We'll give you and Mrs. Murton a quick lunch," he said. "You'll get home in good time."

"Thank you, sir," said Yarrow. "Mac wants me in Edmonton, so I'm flying out by TCA this evening—which suits me well, actually, because Mary my wife is there."

The pangs of young fatherhood, Skafe remembered, the pangs of any separation. Anna grumbled that she hardly ever saw him nowadays. She had never complained about his absence in the war, but the war was over a year ago. As Yarrow let down to the sea and home, Skafe thought of seeing Anna, Sally, John, Father, a week at home, the farm and the place to keep him occupied. But Anna first.

"The draft of the speech is done," said Mrs. Murton at his elbow. "The letters are ready, Mr. Skafe."

"I'll be back to show you the local ropes," he said to Yarrow, who smiled acknowledgment, but did not look round. The opinion he formed of Yarrow was a good one, with only a reservation that he might ride the job too tensely. Mac was always with his plane. He watched and waited, the easy boss; but Mac had ten or twelve thousand hours, and was not in the least nervous of his pupil and employer. I notice that nowadays, thought Skafe. They tend to be scared of me. Well, why not, I'm forty.

He signed the letters. "You won't want me to stay over, will you, Mr. Skafe?"

He knew that Mrs. Murton cherished a hope of a little work and a lovely weekend at the seaside. He might have indulged her hope, but Mrs. Murton exasperated Anna. *That prissy paragon,* she called her. "No," he said. "I'll call the office on Monday. Oh, and by the way . . ." He rummaged in his attaché case. "I got you this in London."

It was a small Georgian silver box. "Oh, Mr. Skafe," she said. "It's sweet. You're far too kind to me."

"Not at all," he said. "You're kind to me." She was kind, supremely efficient, brilliant on the telephone, and could anticipate. Mrs. Murton had a husband too.

They were circling now; his ears had ceased to pop. "Remember your seat belt," he said in an avuncular way, and went forward.

They crossed the town of Gallery, over the wharf and the fishing boats and a few yachts of the summer season, now sardine weirs at the drop from the shore, and now the bay. It was a rippled sea, with broken water where wind and tide were in opposition. Not a twenty-mile wind, he thought. They circled the farm at a few hundred feet. The Jerseys were out. How pretty they looked against green pasture. They were not only pretty, but good. Beamish hoped to show at the Royal this year. He saw the old house below the highway, gray-shingled, his father waving on the lawn; the new house near the shore and Anna and the children. Here I come, thought Skafe, with an immediacy of delight. He pointed out the landing ramp to Yarrow. "I think we can run her up," he said, meaning that it looked calm enough in the cove to drop the wheels and climb the amphibian to land.

They flew on out while Yarrow did his landing checks—overhead, beside him, fingers to the panel. He gave himself twice the room that Mac would have taken. The biting muscle pulsated in his jaw. Now he turned into wind for the approach, full flap, holding off, holding, still holding, and then the light rip of water on the hull. Yarrow made a first-rate landing. "Good," said Skafe.

He undid his belt and went back to the cabin. "Take a note for Mac, Mrs. Murton, would you? 'Dear Mac, We had a good flight down. Yarrow seems the type. Let's take him on. As ever.' I'll sign a blank sheet and you can type it later." He signed *Husky* where indicated by Mrs. Murton. He knew that not the slightest hint would be dropped by Mrs. Murton to Yarrow on the homeward flight. It was an important decision for Yarrow; pilots were two a penny since the war.

He heard the wheels whine down. He stood again with Yarrow as they swam to the ramp, which was a new refinement. They found footing and rolled uphill like a noisy car. What more dramatic and complete home-coming—You appeared in the sky—*That's Husky Skafe!* You touched down on the water; you stepped out on the beach, family waiting. Skafe's world was good to him.

He set the steps for Mrs. Murton, and then went down himself. He kissed Anna with warm discretion in the public eye. He had not seen her for three weeks. "Boo," she said in his ear, half heard, well understood. He kissed his daughter Sally, and shook hands with John and Beamish. "That's quite a little rig," said Beamish, approval of amphibians that climbed ashore, admission that the concrete ramp might not be such a crazy waste of money after all.

"Oh, Mrs. Skafe," said Mrs. Murton. "It's just perfection here."

"It is a nice day, isn't it," said Mrs. Skafe.

Skafe introduced Yarrow to Anna and the others. The social formalities were not a bother to him, as they were to Anna.

"Please, can we see inside?" asked Sally, leader of the band.

"Okay," said Yarrow. "Up you hop."

"Will you have lunch with us, Mr. Yarrow?"

Yarrow hesitated at the cabin door. "Why, thanks, Mrs. Skafe," he said, lean and diffident, "if a quick bite wouldn't be a nuisance?"

"Not the least bit of a nuisance," she said, smiling at him. "Mrs. Murton?"

"The tiniest snack, perhaps, if you're sure I won't be a bother, Mrs. Skafe?"

"It's all ready," Anna said. "You must see the garden too."

Skafe took one bag, and Beamish the other. The women walked ahead together, trim Mrs. Murton, all contained and girdled, dark coat and skirt, white blouse—Anna Skafe, plain cotton dress, lightly girdled if at all. I wonder if many men want their wives as much as I do after three weeks' separation, Skafe considered. But he was not the sort of man who discussed such things with other men. Besides, other men had damned dull wives. "I see you're halfway through haying," he said. "What's the crop like?"

"Fair," said Beamish. "We were starved for rain in June."

"How is Father?"

"He's thinner with his age. Your dad looks good, though." Tom Beamish had owned the neighboring farm until Skafe bought him out in 1943. Since then he had managed both. He was twelve years younger than Skafe's father, and a friend of his; twenty years older than Simon Skafe, who now employed him.

"You're here a week, Mrs. Skafe was saying."

"Yes," he said. "And I hope to get down again over Labor Day."

"Doesn't sound like much vacation, not after six years without none."

"No," he said. His wife, his father, his farm manager were in cahoots about his leisure hours or days. Leisure was fine for those who could afford it. "There's a lot on, Tom," he said. "And the switch from war to peace—that takes watching."

"Oh, sure," said Beamish. "You got to nurse that goose. Well, it's good to have you around the place. Will we take a walk this afternoon?"

"Fine," he said. "I'll pick you up." *Nurse that goose,* he thought. Tom has a way of saying things.

The lawns sloped down from the house to the shore, so the house was open to the south, to the sun and the wet south wind, sheltered by woods to east and west and north. It had started life plainly in 1939—box-shaped, white-painted clapboards, shingle roof, three bedrooms upstairs, and so on—a modest summer house or cottage for a family of four. The new wing had been finished this past winter. It was Anna's idea to set it neither square to the main house, nor as a continuation of the house, but at an eccentric angle between the two. How right she was. "I like it, Anna," he said. "It's the making of the place."

"I'm glad," she said.

"Oh, it's darling," said Mrs. Murton.

Anna winced. She named a shrub and two roses for Mrs. Murton. She was not unkind to Mrs. Murton. She endured her when necessary, and sighed with relief at parting. The sort of people Anna was prone to slaughter nowadays were rich ladies and complacent tycoons.

"No, thanks," said Beamish about a drink. "I'll see you later then, Mr. Skafe."

God, he thought. Now Tom is calling me Mister too. I must speak to him. "Where do these go?" he asked about the bags.

"We're in the new room," Anna said. "Would you like to wash, Mrs. Murton, or have a glass of sherry now?"

"May I just tidy first? I know my way, so please don't bother. Mr. Skafe must be longing to see the addition to your lovely home." Mrs. Murton skipped upstairs.

He poured out Mrs. Murton's glass of sherry. "Lead on," he said to his wife. "Let us visit the new construction."

She smiled and led the way and closed the bedroom door behind them. "It's nice, don't you think?" she said.

"Come here," he said, and she came. They kissed with the same passion that was always new, and took off their clothes to join on the bed, quickly and strongly in celebration.

It's been the saving of us, thought Simon Skafe, at peace.

"What a man," she said. "You want me, have to have me, take me, perhaps the best thing for a woman. Now I've really got you back."

He had begun to think of Mrs. Murton sipping sherry all alone with a secretary's thoughts. The telephone rang beside the bed.

"That instrument," she said, reaching for it.

"Oh, hullo, Gladys . . . Yes, that was him. He's really here, inspecting the property at the moment; otherwise I'm sure he would love to say hullo . . . This evening? I'll have to ask Simon. I don't know our plans yet. Can I call you after lunch?" Anna hung up. "Gladys Broughton," she said, "six o'clock for drinks. So keen to see both of us. It's the first time she's spoken to me this summer."

Skafe dressed, and used Anna's comb. She watched him indolently from the bed. "That's a nice suit," she said. "Did you get it in London?"

"Yes," he said. Last month the High Commissioner had very kindly introduced him to Traill in Savile Row, and he had picked up his first two suits this visit. Which reminded him. He took her the jade necklace in the Cartier box.

"Simon!" she said. "It must have cost a fortune."

It had cost him five hundred pounds, about two thousand dollars, not a fortune. He was not superstitious, but he had a sort of superstition that when things were tight, then go a splurge. It was dark jade, flat pieces minutely carved. Anna was not an easy wife to buy things for, being full of pride and prejudice. She disliked pearls and diamonds, what she called *plushy mink-coat stuff*. She would wear small emeralds, but jade was a sure-fire bet.

"Lovely," she said. "Put it on me, darling."

He put the necklace on her, thinking that he had done the women well. "How do I look?"

"Like a Chinese tart, I guess," he said. He kissed her while she laughed. "Now I feel alive again."

He knew that she meant alive because of the physical him, and not because of expensive presents; and her pleasure in him carried seeds of trouble. If only it could always be like this.

"Run along now, and tell Mrs. Murton I'm unpacking for you. I won't be a minute."

He checked his appearance in the looking glass and ran along. *Run along now, Mr. Skafe,* he could hardly imagine Mrs. Murton saying. "Sorry," he said in the living room. "I was having a look around. My wife is unpacking for me. She won't be a minute."

"I just got down myself," said Mrs. Murton, sipping sherry. "Oh, it's so peaceful here, after the city and the plane, and blissfully cool. Mrs. Skafe looks wonderful, so brown and vital and tawny-looking."

"Anna does look well," he said. Yes, it was peaceful here today. "How is your husband, Mrs. Murton?" Her husband had diabetes, and worked part time as clerk in a clothing store.

". . . He had to increase his insulin to eighty units, but he can't seem to keep in balance, Mr. Skafe, sucking oranges one day, and his blood sugar way up again the next. It's hard for him, but he never grumbles."

Nor do you, thought Skafe. "If there's ever anything I can do . . ." he said.

"I know, Mr. Skafe. You don't need to tell me that."

The door opened, and Mrs. Murton turned. He saw the brief, feminine glance before she smiled. *So brown and vital and tawny-looking,* Mrs. Murton had said. Tawny was a Murtonish word, and it was true. But now Anna neither sought nor waited. She looked at him, and strolled over to pour herself a gin and tonic.

CHAPTER TWO

THE PLANE swung onto course and went. He listened to the engines for a time until they also went. He sat with his wife on a driftwood log, pitching pebbles to strike the water's very edge, thinking of things that he would do this week: The farm; have talks with Father; spend some time with John; have some fun with Sally; play golf, not much; work in the woods; do a few calls each morning; hope to fix the loan with Bob Carter; read a book or two for a change; last and most important, keep things good with Anna.

The wet collar of sand grew wider. There goes the tide, he thought, regardless of me and my idle plans. She leaned against him. The chil-

dren were walking along the beach, nothings of childhood in the sun.
"It's only half a life without you," Anna said.

"And without you," he said. Or, in a man's terms, he might have said
that it was incomplete. "The kids look well. Have their reports come yet?"

"Two weeks ago. I meant to send them on."

She meant to do that sort of thing. "What was John's like?"

"Good, except for the usual idiocies about him lacking initiative and
drive."

"Hardly idiocies," he said. "It couldn't be truer of him."

"I know," she said. "But that's John, and nobody will change him, and
I wouldn't want them to."

Why would she not admit that initiative and drive were desirable qualities in a boy? But let it go. "How did he do in his work?"

"Well in languages and things; badly in mathematics." She glanced at
Skafe, perversely glad, he sometimes thought, that his boy was not turning out to be what he wanted.

"And Sally?"

"Oh marvelous, top in everything. But I don't know what use her
brains are going to be to her."

"There are plenty of careers nowadays for girls."

"She's going to be too attractive, Simon, to last long in a career. The
boys are after her already. John says that Charlie Winter tried to kiss her
on the picnic yesterday."

Charlie Winter, a precocious little beast. Skafe looked along at Sally.
Yet not even he could quite blame the Winter boy.

"What happened?"

"She socked him on the jaw, a beauty, John reports."

Skafe laughed. He felt enormously happy at the thought of his daughter socking the Winter boy on the jaw. John and Sally looked round and
laughed; and Anna laughed. "I do love to hear you laugh like that," she
said.

He watched his children walk this way, the colt-limbed young of
Canada. A week of it, he thought, and I shall have had enough. But just
now it was what things were ultimately all about—Father, mother, son
and daughter, family unit on the beach.

"Daddy, why that huge belly-laugh?" She had her Skafe grandmother's dark blue eyes, and her hair was summer-bleached, but it would be
dark some day.

"None of your business," he said. "And ladies do not mention bellies."
So like Anna, he thought, but with a merry devil in her face, mocking
me even now at twelve.

"Dad," said the quiet one. "I dug some clams this morning. Would you like to come flounder fishing before the tide is too far out?" How diffident the invitation: Not *Let's go: Would you like to*.

"I would," he said, "but I promised Mr. Beamish to go round the farm. Why don't you come along?"

"Okay then, Dad."

"First let's have a skipping competition," said Simon Skafe. "Rustle up some flat stones, you characters."

"It is extraordinary about you," she said, alone again, "how all the characters young and old simply jump to do anything you suggest, including me."

"Do they?" he said. He supposed they did. "Have you any suggestions for suggestions?"

"Not at three in the afternoon," she said beside him on the log.

"What have you been doing with yourself?"

"Driving the children to tennis and picnics and so on. Rusticating apart from that. I garden all day and I read at night. A dull grass widow."

"Why not go out sometimes?"

"I don't want to go partifying alone," she said. "And partifiers don't often want me alone. It's very simple. Besides, just being here is what I like."

It was how long? It was a hundred and sixty-odd years since the Skafes had settled this land; and to him it was a place to visit for a week or two. But to her it was the one place that she loved.

"Phipps has been drinking again," she said. "He went to sleep in his lunch hour in the toolshed yesterday. I had to wake him at two. It's that nagging woman, I think, poor man. A bottle of Canadian sherry a day keeps the worst of the wife away."

Skafe wasted no sympathy on boozers, henpecked or otherwise. "I warned him last year. Should we fire him?"

"He's a nice man and a good worker, and he lets me tell him things. Sober him up would be much better."

"I'll speak to him," said Skafe.

"You make everything seem easy."

They all said that, or they felt it with him. He could manage the lot of them, except only this one. I'll have to break the news about the Carters soon, he thought.

Now time to skip stones, at which the women were no good. He showed John how to improve his throw, flat to the water, and the boy did ten, or even more, skip and skip to a flurry of small splashes. "Well done," he said. "You beat me," and John flushed.

"Mrs. Skafe! Telephone!" The voice of Toddy from the house.

"That'll be Gladys Broughton. I forgot about her. Darling, run and say I'll call right back."

John went, and Sally with him. "They get on amazingly well together. It strikes me more every time."

"He spoils her, like you and everyone else."

"It's rather hard not to spoil that child," said Simon Skafe. "But I do wish John would call the tune."

"He won't," she said, and turned for the house. "It's time you resigned yourself to that. Shall we go to the Broughtons'? We might as well."

"Why not?" he said. He feared that her propitious mood was gone, but better say it now: "By the way, Anna, I was talking to Bob Carter yesterday by phone. He said they would keep Sunday night supper until I could check with you."

"Supper *here*, you mean? Oh, not that pompous man."

"He's a good chap, Bob," said Skafe mildly. "But apart from that, he happens to be President of the Union Bank, and I need some money from him."

"Much?"

"Three million," said Skafe, surprised that she should take an interest.

"Darling, you aren't going broke?" Anna turned to look at him with what might be called a wild surmise, or even hope.

"No," he said. "We're expanding." There was no need to tell her that things would be awkward if he could not talk Bob Carter or someone into it by Wednesday.

"But our first Sunday evening with the children—I thought we might take our supper . . . Can't you talk your everlasting business in the daytime?"

"That isn't the way with old Bob Carter. I tell you what, Anna—Why not skip the Broughtons and stay home this evening?"

"No. They're all longing to see you. Besides, what about me? I wouldn't mind going out for a change."

"Well, okay," he said. She would mind or she wouldn't, he never knew. "I'm sorry to spring tomorrow on you. It's just one of those things."

"Just one of those business things that haunt our lives. Can't you ever stop it, darling, not even for a week?"

"Supper tomorrow," he said, "and finish, except for a few long distance calls."

"It was all right in the war. I could understand it then. But this is peace, and we simply don't have any life at all, or I don't anyway."

He might have said that a man in his position had to keep a finger on affairs; or that, unlike some husbands, he kept his business headaches to himself; or that his boring activities provided adequately for her and the children; or that she was plain jealous; or that if she so much wanted him to have a peaceful rest, she was hardly going the right way about it. But it was no use saying those things to Anna. So he said nothing, and looked at the swimming pond. It was pretty clean this year, a natural pool, dammed across the brook by the house.

"There, darling," she said, and kissed him. "Forgive me for being bitchy."

He forgave his penitent wife, as any peaceable man would do. He watched her cross the lawn, no less attractive to him at thirty-seven than she had been at twenty-three, but less well understood.

John appeared, and they took a path through the woods to find Beamish. "How did you get on at school this term?" he asked over his shoulder.

"Fine, Dad."

"What about sports?"

"I was second in the quarter mile."

"Good for you. Did you make the junior team in baseball?"

"No, I didn't, Dad."

There was a dutiful inertness about the boy and his own affairs which Skafe could never penetrate. You asked him and you got a truthful answer, finish.

"What about work? Mum said you did well except in math."

"Yes, Dad. Algebra was my worst."

"Do you find it hard?"

"I can't sort of see it."

"That's funny," he said. "Mathematics weren't much bother to me. I guess one day it'll just arrive."

"I guess so, Dad."

"Well," he said, "if you still find math difficult next year, we might get someone to tutor you in the summer holidays, say an engineering student from McGill, fellow you could have some fun with too. How does that sound?"

Silence a while in the cedar wood. "Mr. Beamish did say I could work on the farm next summer, if you'd let me."

"We'll have to see," said Skafe, and changed the subject. "I wonder if we should thin this again." It was second-growth cedar, the worst of which had been culled already, but still too thick for even growth.

"Mr. Beamish says if we thin any more, the whole wood's liable to blow because the roots are all on top, and they'll be loosened."

He does take an interest in the place, thought Skafe. And I guess he even has some ideas, if I could worm them out of him. "Tom Beamish may be right at that," he said. Or Tom might be wrong, for nobody here ever thinned a wood for a timber crop. They clear-felled the forest to destruction.

"Look, Dad, a kinglet! The ruby-crowned, yes, I'm sure it is." A minute bird with a very high *tseep*, working the evergreens. His birds and his natural world. He was keen on that.

Tom Beamish was having baler trouble. But he left the hay baler to his two hired men. "Those darned machines," he said. "Half the time they're on the blink, so you've wasted twice the time they save you."

Skafe thought that more thorough winter maintenance might mean less breakdowns in the summer, but he did not presume to say so on his first day here to Tom, who, if not a mechanic, was a sound farmer; and, if suspicious of newfangled theory, was at least prepared to give it a try.

Having grown up in railroad towns in Ontario, Skafe had no practical knowledge of farming. He therefore admired suitably and questioned humbly, sure of the quality of his man.

They saw milking cows, heifers, green oats, bull calves, and now Cobber, the old Jersey bull in his pen behind the cowbarn. "He don't mean no harm," said Tom. "Breathes hell-fire is all he does." He scratched the bull between its bulging eyes. "Old Cobber's become a kind of pet with me, but he's through, I guess. Well, what do you say, Mr. Skafe?"

Mr. Skafe again. "I'm afraid it's time to beef him, Tom," he said, that being what Tom had wanted said by him.

The fences were tight, although they did not yet look the way fences should look, and would look some day. "The place is in good shape," he said, and he thought that, come Labor Day, he would give old Tom a bonus, well deserved. But he did not mention it now. "Any other headaches, Tom?"

"Here's the worst one—the drinking pond. It always dries up in a dry spell—means we have to hand-pump to the trough up there, a waste of time and sweat."

He looked at the crack-seamed bottom, damp in places. He was interested. "Any other springs around?"

"There's one in that gully. But the banks are too steep. The cattle couldn't make it in and out."

Skafe climbed down to inspect the spring, a boggy patch of green. "Does this one ever dry up?"

"It runs strong always."

"How much?"

"I don't know—a gallon a minute anyways, mebbe two."

Skafe came out again to stand on the rise between spring and pond. Tom and John were watching him. He compared the levels. Yes, there was a fall. He had a good eye for grade. "How far down is the ledge?"

"It's deep here. Eight or ten foot, I wouldn't be sure."

"That's simple enough, then. All we do is hire a shovel and ditch it through and lay galvanized pipe—two-inch would do—from this spring to the pond."

"But hell, Mr. Skafe, just look at the cost—digging a ditch right through a hill."

"It's only a rise," he said. "Ten foot would do it. Besides, that's what hills are for, to dig through." Not bad, he thought. "An old barrel for the spring, six hours of the shovel at six an hour, a hundred foot of pipe —it would still be worth it, even if we hit rock and had to blast."

"Sixty years I've lived here or next door, seeing that pond dry up, and I never thought of it; and you settle the thing in two minutes flat."

"It's the sort of thing I had to think about in construction, Tom. If you asked me to doctor a sick cow, where would I be?"

"Well mebbe," said Tom. "But you'd darned soon find out."

Yes, he thought. I would. First of all, these people will not think a problem through. And secondly, they will not ask. And yet he was one of these people himself.

"Go and see if you can find Granka, John," he said. "I'll be along in a minute."

John walked off towards the old house, built or accumulated in the practical way of the early farms, shingled house joined to woodshed, and woodshed to barn.

"That's a fine boy you have there," said Beamish.

"Yes," he said. "John's a really nice kid." A really nice negative kid, he thought.

"He's keen to work on the farm. I said: Sure, next summer, if you'd let him."

"We'll have to see," said Skafe. "He's a bit backward in some of his studies."

"Backward? John's as smart as a whip in his quiet way." Tom Beamish hesitated, and then said: "Well, I don't know nothing about studies. I'll be getting back to that hay crop, Mr. Skafe."

"Mr. Beamish," he said. "Since when have I been Mr. Skafe to you?" They laughed and parted.

The wind had backed. It blew strongly now across the bay, and the hills were hazy. The wind brought a whiff, a nostril-touch of smoke from forest fires in a dry spell of weather. That smell always took him back to old days in the North, to the Mackenzie country. His home was in these tame lands of the South; but the North was the real Canada to him.

CHAPTER THREE

THE OLD HOUSE stood a quarter of a mile above the shore. There had been a time when all the land below was in cultivation. But first came the turnip disease—or borax deficiency, as was later known—which stopped that trade with Boston. Then later, after the death of Skafe's grandfather, and before his father's retirement from the Canadian Pacific, the place had been unoccupied. Now the forest was growing back on the lower land. Which is all that it ever should have been, thought Simon Skafe.

"You look fine," said old John Skafe.

"So do you, Dad." But he thought that his father had aged more than one year in this last year, and had lost some weight. With a countryman's tan, he looked well enough. "How's everything?"

"Mustn't grumble," John Skafe said. "I haven't starved to death, not yet." At which young John, drinking ginger ale from the bottle, spluttered. It was the *Grand Weather* in the middle of a sleet storm common irony of these parts. "Won't you come into the house?" he said with a certain formality.

"Granka, can I go and look at the boat?"

"Help yourself. There's nothing new except the windlass. I finished that at last."

"I would like to see it too." So they visited the workshop to inspect the model of a full-rigged clipper ship. He must have been ten years at his work of art. Or work of perfection, thought Simon Skafe; and works of perfection need never be finished.

"How much longer will it take you, Granka?"

"A year, John, maybe two. That depends upon what troubles I run up against. Depends on eyesight too." Skafe's father and his son were grave together. Indeed, they shared a quality of *gravitas*.

"Gosh, I don't see how you make these tiny things to run the ropes through."

"Patience," said John Skafe. "Which, at my age, is another word for passing time. Let's go through, then, Simon. I'll be seeing you, old-timer," he said to John. They went from the workshop by the kitchen to the living room. He called it parlor.

"We must have a nip to celebrate."

They drank a toast in Demerara rum, too pungent for the prodigal's taste.

"It's good to have you back. For a week this time, did Anna say?"

"Yes," he said. "Until next Sunday night."

"Tell me the news, Simon. You've been going places since I saw you last."

He skipped the implication of success. "I've had to get around a lot this year. Converting to peacetime is quite a business."

"I would imagine. Is Summit Construction the biggest in the country now?"

"About third, I guess," he said. But when we acquire Staniland . . . he thought.

"And that uranium place of yours up North?"

"Turtle Mountain," he said. "Things are getting under way. We had to go deeper than we thought to strike a worthwhile ore body. But we should be in production by the fall."

"How will you ship the ore out? Or will you refine it there?"

"We'll fly the concentrate," he said. "As they plan to do from Port Radium on Bear Lake. But ours will be exclusively an air operation, about nine hundred miles to Edmonton."

"Will it pay?"

"That's the intention."

John Skafe smiled. "Big stuff," he said. "Another world from the one I ever knew. All I did was run a section of a railroad."

"And ran it well for the biggest railroad. What's the difference?"

"One difference is that I never started anything, and never took a risk. I guess you must have got that from your mother's Irish. Are things going well in general?"

"Yes," he said. "We're doing all right."

"I like the way you say 'we,' when the punch comes from S. K. Skafe."

"No," he said. "It comes from every man jack of us, and Jill the stenographer too." True of the work, he thought. But of course there is no such thing as a corporate punch. "How do you find Anna and the kids?" he asked, to get the subject away from himself. Praise pleased him, but he did not want it.

"Fine," said his father. "I don't know how I'll ever get along without them in the fall." He looked at Skafe with some diffidence. "I think Anna misses you a lot."

"There is so much on at present that it's hard to take vacations. Better next year, I hope." She could run up to Montreal for a day or two, he thought, if she would leave her beloved seaside. "How are things with you, Father?"

"I want for nothing. I have my books, and I have my garden, and I have my ship, and a darned good house with every gadget. For a lone old codger I'm in clover." He had lost his wife in 1940. Skafe's mother had been an Irishwoman from the Ottawa valley, daughter of immigrants. She had ruled the Skafe roost. He remembered her as an affectionate hazard, and not at all as a comfortable Mum.

He looked at her photograph now, and his beside it; then he looked at his father's books. They were mostly philosophical tomes, ranging from Aristotle to Whitehead. Simon Skafe had wondered what he really knew about it. There was nobody here to talk philosophy with him, except of the grass-roots variety. But occasional scholars came to call, and stayed to argue.

So his books, his garden and his ship. It sounded like the blueprint for a widower in late years, too good to be quite true. The fact about John Skafe, however, was that he was entirely true. He had not ventured, but had gained a peace within himself. Perhaps peace and caution went together. ". . . What, Father?"

"I said I would have come down to meet you in that flying boat of yours, but the climb up home seems to catch my breath these days."

"Oh," he said casually. "Not feeling in such good shape?"

"I feel fine. Slight hardening of the arteries, Doc says, quite normal at my age."

I must call the doctor, he thought. We could send him south next winter, if he would go, which of course he won't, any more than he will be driven up the hill. "By the way, Father, I see the shingles are pretty well rotted out. Shouldn't we get the house done over?"

"No, thanks. These are still tight. They'll do my time. Besides, unweathered shingles look as naked as a baby coon." Offer categorically declined. He smiled at Skafe and said: "You set about spoiling me, you and Anna."

"You're not the easiest man to spoil." Nor was it the easiest thing to be prince bountiful to your father. He had his pension which covered living expenses, and he had small savings undisclosed. When John Skafe had made the place over, keeping a life rent of the old house for himself, Simon had insisted on paying upkeep and taxes. But house improvements were always a battle. Part pride, perhaps; part conservatism; part plain undemandingness.

They sat now, discussing the farm, and then running short of conversation. The theory of politics might interest John Skafe. Practical politics did not interest him at all. And as for world affairs, he thought the world was going mad, or gone. No philosopher, no gardener, no modeler of ships, no lover of vintage locomotives—I'm not the boy to chew the rag with Dad, thought Simon Skafe. But he revered his father, a man so far from him, a man with whom he always felt constraint.

A car came from the highway. It was Anna in a cloud of dust.

"We must surface the roads sometime."

"It wouldn't be worth it for the money," said his father. Caution, ever caution. "Well, my girl, how are you?" He stood, the familiar words and the courtly ways.

"Fine, Father," she said, and kissed him. No domestic thing gave Skafe more pleasure than the love between Anna and his father. Yet he wished that a mite of that tranquillity could be reserved by her for him.

"What's new in town?"

"Oh, nothing," she said. "I just dashed in to buy some things for our Sunday supper. It has to be good. It has to be worth a few million dollars."

"Won't you join us tomorrow evening, Father?"

"Thanks," he said, "not even for a million-dollar supper." But he raised his eyebrows at the riddle.

"It's only that Simon wants a little loan from Mr. Carter. Hence the supper party."

"A few-million-dollar loan?" John Skafe looked puzzled—a joke, perhaps—then shocked when Simon nodded. "But I thought you were doing well."

"We are," he said. "It's time to expand." We are either doing very well, he thought, or we are doing very badly. What possessed me to tell Anna that? She wants her pound of flesh.

"This big business is a mystery to me." He glanced at Simon Skafe, drew in breath, then closed his lips against the next remark he had thought of making.

"You won't forget my cutting, Father, will you? Of the forsythia."

"Let's get it right now," he said. They went out and round while Simon Skafe observed that the house had dropped two inches on its sills, or the kitchen steps had risen. "*Forsythia suspensa,*" said John Skafe. "Mind you keep the sharp sand moist, and in shade for a week or two until the roots have a chance to take."

"Yes, Father, I'll be careful." Probably knowing more about it than he knew himself. "Be good until tomorrow."

Skafe held the door of the car for her, shut it with a deliberation which was rather less than he felt at the moment, went round, got in himself and drove away. "Why did you say that?"

"What? Oh, about your loan, you mean? Why not?"

"Because first it was a private remark of mine to you, and secondly you must know that Father thinks to be in debt is to be hell-bent for bankruptcy, and thirdly why make an issue of this damned little supper party? You are my wife, you know."

"And everything I do is wrong, and everything you say is stuffy."

He could prevent a bicker being a quarrel if he said no more. By God, he thought. She does contrive to needle me into being pompous. *Me*, pompous! "Smoke in the air," he said. "It always reminds me of the North. Do you remember?"

"How could I forget?" She came nearer on the seat to hold his knee. "It seems like a million years ago. Ages, I mean, not millions, that offending word."

He smiled. How lightly she could woo him from disgruntlement.

"I wonder what ever happened to Jim Willis." It was a long time since they had mentioned Jim; and now that she did, she called him Jim Willis, as if she had never been Anna Willis.

"The last I heard of Jim was just before the war—he was trading in the Barren Lands, east of Coppermine, I think." Skafe parked the car. They heard the children's voices at the swimming pool. Poor old Jim, he thought, without much guilt after fourteen years. I sent him better than his half of my sale of furs. Turtle Mountain? Well, he got the ready cash he wanted. I took Anna, who would have left him anyway. But still . . .

They were diving, the love-child and the other one. Love-child because John had been born before the divorce went through. It took time finding Jim by lawyer's letter, but he raised no difficulties. Love-child in a second sense John had always remained to Anna.

"Watch, Daddy!" She ran to dive with hardly a splash, and sleeked wet hair back in the water. "How was that?"

"Not too bad," he said.

"Come in. It's lovely and warm."

"No time now. Let's swim before breakfast tomorrow morning."

They went towards the house. "Sally will soon be growing up."

"She has already, Simon. Technically speaking."

"Oh, Lord," he said. "What a shattering thought." He went to change and she went to the greenhouse with her cutting.

It turned out not to be, in the grand vernacular, a cocktail party, but a few people in for drinks, about twenty at the Broughtons' summer cottage or large mansion, in the hall of which an outsize Stars and Stripes was draped, exotic tapestry.

"Hullo, Anna! And Husky himself! So you really got him here."

"Yes," she said. "Or he brought himself." Anna was not at her best with the effusive Gladys, but she liked Harper Broughton. "A rye and water, Harper, please," she said.

"You, Husky?"

"The same if I may," he said. "But don't you bother. I'll get Anna's and my own."

He made to do so, rather wanting a drink, and taking time to get through the people he knew, which were most of them. It was agreeable.

"Who would that chap be?" he heard behind him as he entered Harper Broughton's bar.

"That's Husky Skafe, one of our . . ."

But Skafe did not dally to hear what Bob Carter would say about him. He got their drinks from the houseman behind the bar with the fancy bottles, like stone Van der Hum, and giant Martells and jeroboams.

It was early in the party, when snatches could still be heard along a room—"I finished four—five—four—then what do I have to do but take myself a seven at the eighteenth, darnit, ninety-two" . . . "Four dollars a day, they're all asking now, and lunch included. It's robbery, but what can you do?" . . . "He's a famous portrait painter, so distinguished-looking, don't you think? No dear, Dorrien—DORRIEN" . . . "Think of her having to go back to the city heat for a gall-bladder operation, and Mary's seventy, you know. She's a plucky girl, all right."

"Here, Anna."

"Thank you, darling." He had made it stronger than his own. She drank almost nothing when alone at home, but needed easement among people.

Blue blazers and white flannels, summer dresses, tidy stomachs, nice rubicund faces at the cocktail hour. It was safe relaxing fun with age and income group, all mostly over fifty, affluent. The room was pink. Two pictures were of highland cattle.

Anna's drink fell fast. She talked easily with Harper Broughton, who was an able corporation lawyer from New York, unassuming man. He took her out to see the roses.

"Husky, come and meet Grace Parkyn. She's the blond one. Poor thing, she lost her husband from a coronary. It's her first year down here. She's staying at the hotel."

"Parkyn, the Air Vice-marshal?"

"I think he was a service man of yours."

"I've heard a lot about you," said Grace Parkyn, shaking hands.

"I met your husband in the war. I'm sorry."

She smiled. "Thank you," she said, a decorative woman, and composed, not saying more than *thank you*. "That was your plane this morning, wasn't it?"

"Yes," he said. "The first time I've managed to get down this year."

"Do you always come?"

"When I can," he said. "My wife brings the children for the summers. I was born here, actually, on the farm; but my father's job took us to Ontario. So I'm an absentee or intermittent local."

"Rather more than a local now, I gather," said Grace Parkyn. She was exceptionally pretty, hair natural, he thought, real pearls, a diamond pin, a black dress rimmed with white, cut square in Tudor fashion at her neck. Mrs. Parkyn seemed friendly, quiet, not at all coquettish, but feminine with him. Her accent was slightly flat Ontario.

"Do you know many people here?"

"A few," she said. "They seem so nice."

"They are," he said. "Mostly older than my vintage; much older, of course, than yours." He put her at about thirty-one.

"I'm used to that. My husband was a good deal older."

He wondered if she had children; could not guess and did not ask. "Here's Anna," he said. "Have you met my wife?"

"No, but I would love to."

He introduced them, dark and fair. His wife was by far the stronger beauty, the less exquisite. "It's so lovely in the garden," Anna said. "I do wish they wouldn't coop us up in here."

"Yes," said Mrs. Parkyn. "But easier for drinks and canapés, I suppose. Gin and tonic, may I, just a tiny one?"

He went for replenishments. Bob Carter was still talking to the Englishman. They faced him now. "Hullo, Husky. This is Mr. Dorrien—Mr. Skafe."

"How do you do?"

"How do you do, Mr. Dorrien." He found a table for the glasses and shook hands. Dorrien was thin and tall, a stain on his lapel, long fairish hair and an intellectual or well-bred English head, wrinkles, unusual light brown eyes, a drinking face that fell away at the mouth, about Skafe's own age. His handshake was good, but he was not a type that Skafe encountered often, and the English were hard to place, the self-confident phony or the genuine article. This fellow had an amused, ironical air.

"I'll just deal with these drinks," Skafe said, after the quick scrutiny and the formalities. "Be right back." He found the women chatting amiably, smiling most cordially at him, but he went right back to talk to this Dorrien and, not quite incidentally, to Bob Carter, who looked what he was, a shrewd man of business, a top-class banker who had his own sizing-up system too.

The party was warming to a liquorish babble. "You're here painting, I understand," he said.

"Yes. I'm doing Hermione Merchant at the moment. They're putting me up, which is very kind. My next commission is Mrs. Broughton."

"Have you been over long?"

"A month, and I love this country." He smiled, perhaps about forestalling the Canadian question, but continued: "Among other things it is most refreshing not to have to grease some ghastly butcher's palm to buy a black-market chop. Also to find people who get on with it and aren't sorry for themselves."

"We've had nothing to be sorry for ourselves about," said Simon Skafe. And Hermione Merchant is buying your chops, he thought, a little irritated. Expatriates from such a country could do better than criticize it. Also, he was reminded of his own safe war, or safe enough except for one torpedoing. "I was in London this week," he said. "It will take them years to rebuild." It certainly would, with their Labour Government's hamstrung class-ridden attitude to that and every problem. "Were you there in the bombing?"

"No," said Dorrien. "North Africa and Italy." He was drinking a dark Scotch and soda. His eyes were evasive, quartering the room. He was an observer or appraiser too, probably for business. "I was a war artist," he said, "so called."

"Portraits?"

"Yes," he said. "I did them as well."

"I suppose you never ran up against a Canadian fighter pilot—MacNamara—he ended a wing commander."

"Mac MacNamara!" Dorrien had a remarkably mobile face, no longer bored and la-di-da, but happy. "I painted Mac."

"How did you sign it?"

He frowned, and the wrinkles flattened. "Various ways in those days, if at all. I liked that one—Yes, D.D., I think."

"I bought the original," said Skafe. "We have it in the house here. Mac is our chief pilot now."

"That was a marvelous chap," said Dorrien. "I happened to see him climb out of his Spitfire after a sortie. Hot from it. Didn't he have oil on his face?"

"Yes, from the eye to the chin, cutting across his scar. You must come and see it."

"Oh, yes." No great keenness to see his painting. "You build things, don't you?"

Skafe nodded. He did more than build, but that, more or less, was what he did.

"Husky is as Husky does," Bob Carter said, and laughed. Laughter blended in the hubbub; only staccato speech got through. "There's my wife waving at me. See you tomorrow evening, Husky."

"Yes, Bob," he said. "That'll be great. Goodnight."

Dorrien's eyes wandered and centered back on Skafe. "Interesting," he said. "Almost all these people are arrangers as opposed to builders." But his interest seemed to be a spark to flash and dart and vanish, here and there and off again. "By God, that's a paintable face!" he said.

Anna and Mrs. Parkyn had moved from an alcove to center stage, still talking. Anna turned this way, perhaps to catch Skafe's eye for home. Grace Parkyn also turned, as the other of a pair will follow.

"Which one?" said Skafe, seeing Dorrien's general direction. Two paintable faces, he thought. The only women in the room worth painting, or sleeping with, he thought dispassionately, liking women, but Anna was enough for him.

"The dark one, of course," said Dorrien. "Grace Parkyn, that's a nice commission, easy. But the dark woman—My God, what old John could do with her."

He was pleased at the compliment. He wondered what Dorrien thought of his own face. Well, a builder, he had implied. "Augustus John?"

"Yes."

"Come and meet her." As they went, he had an idea for livening up tomorrow's supper party. But you know, he thought, you never can tell with these artist fellows on the make. I wouldn't put it past him that he knew damn well whose wife the paintable dark woman was. "Anna," he said. "This is David Dorrien. He did that picture of ours of Mac."

He talked with the restful Mrs. Parkyn while observing Anna with the artist, who immediately said: "I like that jade necklace."

It had been a random shot by builder Skafe who had an eye for color too, cool green, warm skin, her summer bloom, "Simon gave it me today," she said.

"Oh, Mr. Dorrien, I would so much like to have your opinion of our two Highland pictures. They're Morrisons, you know. My father was a Rankin right from Scotland. Those wild cattle, aren't they darling? And the misty moors and the heather too, I'm so proud of them."

Skafe took the chance. "What about asking Dorrien and Mrs. P. tomorrow?" Might work or not.

"Yes," she said. "Do let's." She was watching Gladys Broughton and Dorrien before the nearer painting, which he inspected gravely, at some length.

"Very fine," he said. "An outstanding example of the Scottish Neo-Romantic school. You might well be proud of them."

He turned, face expressionless, eyes soulful if a little glassy, from Skafe to Anna, who now gave invitations.

Mr. Dorrien would like to do that, and Mrs. Parkyn would adore to, how kind of them to ask her. Could she pick David up? So the Skafes said au revoir, and thanks to those concerned, and made for home.

"I enjoyed that," Anna said. The tide was out. There was a rim of fog beyond Gallery Bay. "What a relief to hear the gulls calling and ourselves thinking after all that stuffy racket, but it was fun."

"You should go out more," he said.

"I never want to without you. I need support."

"I know," he said. Crowds and strangers did not bother him at all.

"Grace Parkyn is an acquisition. I thought she was very nice, almost too, but no, I don't mean that; and so attractive except for the voice."

"Yes," he said. "What did you think of the artist chap?"

"I don't know. He was marvelously deadpan about Gladys's masterpieces."

"They're not so bad, are they?"

"Darling, you couldn't! They're absolutely awful, like the 'Stag at Bay.' I wonder how good David Dorrien really is. I heard wonderful at likeness, but not very strong."

"His painting of Mac is strong enough. It hits you."

"Yes," she said. "Just a sketch, of course."

They were on the highway, above the sea. "What sort of women does Augustus John paint, do you know?"

"Lush dark ones mostly, I guess," she said. "Primitive types. But why?"

Skafe turned onto the drive. He stopped halfway down, in the seclusion of trees. "Come here," he said. He kissed his wife, and they went on home.

CHAPTER FOUR

IT TOOK HIM a while to get his bearings in this room with blinds half down. Anna was sleeping here, away from him; outside was fog, away from him; light puffs of breathing through her lips, the sea birds crying in the fog. He was used to a louder accompaniment, to city noises; or to camp generators, diesel racket all night long. But it was good to be wakeful early in the quiet, watching her bare brown back, a long arm on the quilt, that passion and this innocence, abandoned to her moment; and he again slid down to sleep.

He was awakened by a scratching and a drum of fingernails on the door. "Daddy!"

"Yes?" He had his bearings this second time.

"It's eight. Time for our swim."

"Too foggy," he said. "Go back to bed."

"The sun's almost through. Come on!"

"Okay," he said. "I'll be out in a minute."

"Blast that child," she muttered, turning over to him.

"I promised," he said. He might have suggested that Anna swim too, but he wanted Sally to himself.

She turned away with a discontented fling of body and bedclothes, and he put on his swimming trunks. Gained a pound or two, he thought, displeased—his sandals, bathrobe, towel, and downstairs to meet Sally and her appraising glance. What went on in their heads, particularly this quick lovely head? She kissed him. "Lazybones," she said.

"If you still swim before breakfast in the fog at forty, you'll be doing well."

"I'll be an old woman then," she said. "That's different from being you. Besides, the fog has almost gone, I told you, look!"

They went down the steps and across the lawn as the sun came through and went again. "I do love my bare toes in the dew," she said, and ran, his marvelous child.

The frogs were croaking round the pond, an explosive PINK or croak of yellow frogs. She dropped her towel, did not wait for him, but ran the board to dive in her yellow bathing suit as the yellow frogs took fright.

They bathed in the sea when the tide was high and the weather warm, and then back here to wash off salt. But the tide was out this morning. Mercifully, he thought, dipping a foot to test the water, which was chilly enough for him. There had been a time when Simon Skafe began his day with total immersion in the Mackenzie or the Bear.

"Come on, Daddy. It's warm as anything. I'll race you to the sluice and back."

He was no match for his marvelous child, who also liked to win. He panted, not in too good racing shape, while Sally crawled and floated, rode the rubber horse, dived, and then sat beside him at the shallow end. "You and the frogs," he said, seeing one take surreptitious station at the water's edge, "same yellow creatures."

"Watch me be one." The sun was high at half past eight, fog burned off or gone to sea. It shone on her through the clear brown water of the pond. She surfaced over there as modestly as a frog, hopped frogwise, turned to crouch, a frog in long-limbed mime, now croaking, veritable PONK, and then the frogs' alarm-sprung splash, spreadeagled.

Anything she does, he thought, is to perfection, showing off to me. But he felt melancholy that his child grew up, her body changing to a woman's purpose, he supposed, the object, after all, but he would lose her.

He dried himself. It was warm already, on the way to heat. "Shall I bring you a cup of coffee, Daddy, here?"

"Good girl," he said, and kept his cigarette for coffee time, and sat in the sun, considering love while the frogs began to croak behind him. Simon Skafe had most things straight and simple and resolved in principle and practice. But he thought that love, for one man anyway, was neither straight nor simple nor resolvable in the possessive terms of women. He wanted Anna and he had her, and he liked her company, and missed it. When she was unreasonable, he avoided quarrels in so far as he was able, but disliked her. He suspected male hypocrisy about married love, the best settled state of which, he thought—denied to him —was affectionate contentment spiced and punctuated with sensuality. But his feeling for Sally involved dismay at what sex would bring her as sure as frogs croaked, spawned and tadpoled in a pond. So this was the real love, demanding nothing, stormless. And yet what I fear is losing her, he thought, to some damned man.

"You look very grim," she said. "Are you plotting big business scoops?"

Which reminded him about Bob Carter. But he had thought that one right through, no need to fret. He lived with what he had with him. "Thanks," he said for the coffee.

"It must be such fun," she said, "I mean specially something new and far away like Turtle Mountain, things to beat and starting things and making things by your own self, sort of, is it, Daddy?"

"Yes, Sally," he said. "It is." She knows, he thought. She sees it. Anna either cannot or she simply will not. Now he wanted to be up and doing, but he sat on with his daughter who drank milk, put down the glass and wiped her mouth with the back of her hand.

"I would like to go there sometime," Sally said. "I would like to fly over the lakes and over the forests and on for ever to Turtle Mountain in the midnight sun. Do you have trees there, Daddy?"

"Small ones," he said, "but big enough for pit props, which is lucky. The tree line is just north of us."

"And gooey muskeg?"

"Muskeg galore, but we have an all-weather landing strip."

"And is it true?" she asked gravely, bundled head to knees in the bath towel, "is it true that mosquitoes eat men alive up there?"

"They can drive men crazy," he said. "If you're in a hut with a galvanized roof, the mosquitoes sound like rain above you, that's how thick they are."

"And is it true, Daddy, that over all the pit props, muskeg, mosquitoes and crazy men in the midnight sun at Turtle Mountain is a big white chief called Husky Skafe?"

"True," he said, and tipped the little devil from her basket chair. Nobody else set stealthy traps for him, and did he love it.

Seated again, she was quiet. "What's on your mind now, Miss Skafe?"

"The North," she said. "I can feel it, so huge and empty but I can't quite see it."

"It's big," he said. "It's big hard country."

"Could you take me North some day?"

"Some day, perhaps," he said. "Why do you want to go?"

But his child did not know or did not say why she wanted to go to the hard North some day, and Toddy was calling them to breakfast.

"Good morning, Toddy," he said. He liked old Toddy, and Toddy pampered him.

"Morning, Mr. Skafe." She had been in Canada for years, but was still as Scotch as the day she sailed from Greenock. Nanny, summer cook and general factotum—it was thanks to Toddy that the Skafe household ticked. "Look at that tangled tousle, Sally. It's a bathing cap you should be wearing."

"I hate those horrid rubber things. Why should I?"

Toddy sniffed. "You would if it was me. Away up now, and get yourself dressed in your Sunday blue, and I'll comb your hair out."

"I hate that silly fluffy dress."

"Less hating," he said, "and more doing what you're told."

She looked mutinous, but went. It might be, as Anna said, that he spoiled her. But he stood no nonsense, which was more than could be said for Anna, playing hot and cold.

"She's getting to be a handful, Mr. Skafe. It's your firm discipline she needs, I'm thinking. Sally's more trouble to me in one day than John would be all year, except the one thing lately is getting the poor lamb woken. I've been three times to him already."

"I'll stir him up," he said. "What's for breakfast, Toddy? I could eat a steer if you would cook it."

"It's not a cattle beast you're getting. It's eggs and bacon and the chicken livers."

"You're a marvel," he said. "Thank God for Toddy is my motto."

"Blether," said Toddy, greatly pleased.

He knocked on John's door, no answer, still no answer, so he went in. A school pennant on the wall, two Audubon prints, comics strewn about, the framed picture of him and Anna taken years ago, slight frowstiness of boy asleep, *For Whom the Bell Tolls* face down on the bedside table, quite unsuitable, he thought. "Stir your stumps," he said.

John stirred and shot bolt upright, knuckles to eyes. He was swinging his legs as he looked bleary and startled at his father.

"Sleep on," said Simon Skafe. "It's Sunday. If you're not slept out, sleep on. I used to be the same at your age."

"Gee, thanks, Dad." He collapsed again.

What do I do to the boy? he thought, to make him jump out of his skin that way. I don't beat him, do I? I don't bully him. Skafe was troubled at a potent failure in his dealings with his son.

"Let me get you some more soup," he said to Mrs. Carter on his right. Her name was Muriel, but she was a formidable sixty more or less.

"Please," she said. "This lobster bisque is quite delicious."

"Anna's doing," he said. "For you, Grace?"

"Thank you so much, Husky, but I simply daren't."

He wondered why she simply dare not with that figure, set opposite the plenitude of Mrs. Carter. Dorrien was talking at the other end about old days in princely India. How they got around, those fellows. And then, butterfly that he seemed to be, he switched from Jaipur polo slap to politics. "We should have given them self-government before the war," he said, "but now we'll skedaddle with noble protestations, leaving the Muslims to be slaughtered and the Princes in a Congress poke."

Mrs. Carter polished off her soup. Grace Parkyn was asking Sally about school at Brora where she had been herself. "Do you like it, Sally?"

"Oh, it's just super," Sally said with demure enthusiasm.

"And Miss Cummings is still there, I hear. Still making speeches?"

"She makes the loveliest speeches all the time. At the end of term she said that Canada's golden age is here, and all us girls must dedicate ourselves to being women of the golden age of Canada."

"Golden age, my foot," said Mrs. Carter.

"That's what she told us though, Mrs. Carter," Sally said across the table, guileless, blue eyes violet in the evening light. "But some of us just thought it would be easier to dedicate ourselves to Canada's golden age if Miss Cummings would dedicate some golden syrup to our suet pudding."

He wished that people, himself included, did not find her deadpan drollery quite so amusing. He caught Anna's eye, who said: "John and Sally, you can take away the plates." It was her idea not to banish the children from every adult occasion, a Canadian custom that irritated her.

"A brilliant child, I understand," Mrs. Carter said less loudly than her usual bark.

"She has brains," he said.

"And character, which is more important. Pity she's not a boy."

"But surely, Mrs. Carter," said Grace Parkyn, "there is a place for women of brains and character nowadays."

"Ah, pooh!" This was interrupted by the next course, help yourself to ham and cold fried chicken, avocado mousse and various salad. The cooking was largely Toddy's but the touch came from Anna who had spent the day in a turmoil about the supper party she had not wanted and was now enjoying.

Skafe sampled the Chablis and took it round. He was learning a bit about wine. "Best salad dressing I ever tasted," Dorrien said.

"I put sherry in it," Anna said, and turned to take on old Bob Carter whose relaxations were golf and bridge, not hers, but she was doing her best.

He filled his glass and sat again. It certainly was an excellent supper, and Mrs. Carter was tucking in, and Grace was toying. What now? "To revert to the question of women with brains and character," he said. "I'm on Grace's side against you."

"That wasn't what I meant. I meant that Canadian men are so conventional—no spark and bite and *nuance* about them, not up to us women is what I meant, hence a pity."

"Sorry, Mrs. Carter," he said equably. "I apologize for my sex."

"I'll except you," she said. "You have a bite and a spark all right. Agreed, Grace?"

"I hardly know him yet," she said, "but certainly high voltage, yes." She smiled at him, a womanly woman, or really girl. So he was flattered by them both, the lily and the battleaxe. Young Sally, third of his supper ladies, was looking Grace Parkyn up and down.

"I think a toast is in order," said Bob Carter down the table. Anna's face was expressionless. *Oh God*, another speech, she would be thinking. But Bob did not make a speech. "To our dear young friends, the Skafes," he said. "And may they all prosper."

Which could mean that Bob Carter had decided to come clean. Or it could mean just the opposite. Anna might say that businessmen were simpletons. And Mrs. Carter might say that Canadian men lacked *nuance*, including him by implication or omission. And they might be right about social life. But they did not know the Bob Carters on the job.

"Thank you, Bob," he said. "Good luck, everyone." He took round the wine again. Dorrien had done himself well on martinis, and now his wineglass was empty.

"Mr. Dorrien," said John, much more forthcoming than usual, Skafe had been thinking. "Did you ever see tigers in India?"

"Only one, when I was ADC to some governor. They put me in the fork of a tree at the side of the beat at a tiger shoot, as a sort of stop, you know, to prevent the poor animal breaking away from its proper doom at the muzzles of the potentates who were miles up trees in perfect safety.

"I was a few feet from the ground, utterly exposed, more or less defenseless except for being armed to the teeth with a double-barreled rifle, a trembling aspen leaf while the pandemonium drew near, and screams of Tiger—*Sher* is the word—while screams of Tiger made me fear the worst, hoping, by God, hoping for the best, yet knowing I would be a certain draw for any tiger. Sure enough, the terrible beast, a thousand tom-tabbies rolled into one, broke bounding at me from tall grasses, up to my tree with a heart-stopping woof . . ." Dorrien paused to drink wine.

"Oh, gosh! What happened?"

"The tiger passed, roaring its hate of me. I suppose a good man would have fired, thus risking a change of tiger mind, turn around and charge again, I mean. But I am not a good man, John."

Dorrien's tiger story was a success with all present, particularly young John, who laughed himself into a spluttering fit.

"A soupçon, Mrs. Carter?"

"My dear boy, quite impossible. Tell me, why always Mrs.? Don't you know my name is Muriel?"

"I do," he said. "It must be respect, I guess. Not lack of affection, anyway."

"I have long suspected that my figure is the culprit. Like Mr. Dorrien's tiger, it may bother men."

As well it might, the burgeoning bosom and the solid girth, encased in plum velvet. In appearance Muriel Carter was a *grande dame cana-dienne,* or a *grandedame* anything, immensely dignified and benign. In character she was both generous and merciless.

"It might be the splendor of the castle walls," he said, "or it might be the loaded guns inside. Or a bit of both, perhaps, Mrs. Carter."

"There!" she said to Grace. "The man has *nuance* too."

He was clearly in Muriel Carter's good books, which was to the good. He looked at Grace and Sally, the light blue eyes, the dark, both watching him—and past them to the garden and the sea. There had been smoke in the air again today. It was still hazy, but the wind had backed due south, he noticed by galley smoke from a boat in the bay, and the breeze was cool through open windows. "A change of weather coming," he said. "We can do with rain. Shall I close a window, anyone?" But nobody wanted a window closed.

"How do you know that the weather will change?"

"Because the wind has backed from west to south."

"Do you always watch the weather?" asked Grace Parkyn. She wore a gray dress with a mauve sash at the waist, semi-mourning, he supposed. She must have money.

"Usually," he said. "It's a habit you get into if you fly."

"Oh yes," she said. "Charles was the same. Are you a pilot?"

"Yes," he said. "I keep it up."

"Heavens," she said. "Is there anything you can't do?"

He looked down at Anna and smiled at her; she smiled in a moment.

"Mac says that if Daddy went broke, he could get a job as an airline pilot any day."

"Mac MacNamara?" said Dorrien across to Sally.

"Yes," she said. "And Mac's a super-duper pilot." No doubt about the genuineness of that enthusiasm.

"Mac's super-duper every way," John said innocently to his sister, and reduced her to confusion. Tonight the boy had some confidence and even sparkle, which pleased Skafe. He's shy, that's all, he thought. He'll find himself. And then Skafe thought that Sally's remark about broke

Daddy, the airline pilot, had a touch of irony in present company and circumstance.

It went on through the second bottle of Chablis, Oka cheese and strawberries and cream, adequate food and wine and people, a mixture of ages and character, a civilized continuity. The white sardine boat moved out of sight, and dusk was moving here. He lit four candles on the table: One for the Gramercy River job, he thought, and one for Killick terminal, and one for Turtle Mountain, and one for good luck with Staniland, the four of his candles a private folly. He was very much here and pleased with his wife and liking his party, but a man slips off in mind.

Now Sally and Bob Carter—Now Anna and Dorrien animated—Now Mrs. Carter drawing out John.

"You're quiet," Grace Parkyn said. "I suppose you think about business a lot."

"Good Heavens, no," he said, both honest and a liar. That he felt business away off there and with him might be strictly true. "I guess I'm just not a talkative type." The gray is too pale for you, he thought. With fair hair and a fair skin's tan, it isn't right.

She was smaller-boned than Anna. The swell to her breasts was delectable. Her face had the quality that sorrow gives to people who have had life on a platter and learn grief or hardship, but he did not know that there was much vitality, or bite, as Mrs. Carter called it. He was not a great man for women, but he liked a few, and here was one, and why not let her have that small encouragement, so he glanced from one soft pretty shoulder over to the other, and at her mouth unhurriedly, and met her eyes, told her effectively. She touched her lip with upper teeth and looked away from him to the last sun warmth beyond Gallery Bay.

You wicked fellow, he jollied himself, and then his attention was caught by a loudness of Dorrien who had quizzed and bantered and stated through supper and the best part of a bottle of Chablis, and now spoke passionately: ". . . It was certainly the most fateful and possibly the worst crime in world history."

"Not worse than Hitler and the Jews," said Anna. "Surely, David."

"Worse in its ultimate effect. Hitler incinerated the Jews out of an unmentionable pagan philosophy of the Nordic Übermensch. But we incinerated a few hundred thousand human beings without warning of any kind while singing Onward Christian Soldiers. It's just as simple as that, which is very simple." He looked about for contradiction.

"But, Mr. Dorrien," said Bob Carter moderately enough, although his color darkened, "bombs were dropped on London and Berlin, and dropped to kill. I see no difference between one large bomb and a thousand smaller bombs. Furthermore, all Western leaders have agreed that Hiroshima shortened the Pacific war by at least a year and saved many thousands of our boys' lives."

"Nonsense, our boys' lives! Don't you know that they had sued for peace before Hiroshima? Which is not the point."

"To put out peace feelers is not to sue for peace, young man." Bob Carter was not of aggressive character, nor accustomed to *Nonsense* being fired at him.

Bang from such delightful harmony to contention, to the children's faces still, withdrawn. Damned half-baked intellectual, probably a Red, thought Skafe, trying to catch Anna's eye, which he did, and she rose instantly to the occasion to dispel it. "Oh dear," she said, "everything and everyone's in such a muddle about things, me most of all. Shall we go and have coffee, Mrs. Carter?"

Bless her, he thought. Bless you, Anna, wife. But Bob Carter's anger fell more slowly than it rose, if he knew Bob Carter.

CHAPTER FIVE

"MR. DORRIEN would like to see the garden, John. Take him now before it gets too dark."

Both children went. How easily Anna managed things this evening, engineering his talk with Carter. She is amazing, he thought. She can do any damned thing if she happens to want to. He watched the lanky Dorrien go with John and Sally across to the pond. Damn the lanky Dorrien, he thought.

He and Bob Carter took their coffee and brandy to the study. It was a small room by the front door, facing inland. It had nothing much of him in it, except Mac's portrait sketch, which was him, and a photograph of the Bidsley Dam, which was him. Otherwise, leather armchairs, a desk, a wall of bookshelves with Anna's novels.

"Have a cigar, Bob. They're a mild Havana."

Bob Carter rimmed the end meticulously with his pocket knife; then cut it through. He lit his match, nearly steady of hand at sixty-three, pate mottled pink and brown. He considered the lighted end, rolled the cigar between thumb and second finger, put it to flame again, blew out the match, a minor ritual of a life completely ordered. The pulse in his throat was beating fast.

Skafe sipped coffee, lit a cigar, tasted brandy and waited.

"That Dorrien fellow," Carter said. "His manners leave much to be desired."

"Yes, Bob. He's had a good deal to drink."

"Enough drink to show his colors. To say that Hiroshima was the worst crime in world history sounds like nothing more or less than Communist twaddle."

"He might only be a half-baked intellectual, Bob," Skafe offered with respect. "You know what wild ideas these people have, up in the clouds, no contact with life." Husky Skafe, the counselor of moderation. "Which is no excuse for being rude. I thought you handled him well."

"He can paint, they say. He should, for a thousand dollars a time, bed and board thrown in."

"A *thousand*?"

"That's what Merchant and Broughton are paying. My people want a new portrait of me for the board room, and I had toyed with the idea of employing Dorrien, but he has now settled that item for me. I do not intend to pay a thousand dollars to be insulted, patronized, and painted by any bibulous Englishman."

"That's his sketch of our chief pilot, MacNamara, you may remember we were mentioning last evening. I like it very much." He wanted money from Bob Carter, but he did not want Bob Carter to think that he would come kowtowing for it.

"Fine face," said Carter from his chair. "Too slapdash for my taste, not what I call painting." He considered his plump fingers, which could not conceivably be callused by anything but golf clubs. It was easy to forget that he had fought and been twice wounded in the First World War. Now in a minute he would come to the point. "Husky," he said, with a wave of a hand at Mac on the wall, "there is no more important gift in business life than to be a picker of men, a gift you have in bountiful measure."

He says it as if it had never been said before, thought Skafe; but he smiled at Carter, respecting what lay behind the ponderous pomposity, wary of what might be coming.

"Now, in the matter of a possible loan, why do you want to extend your construction interests?"

"It is time for us to diversify," Skafe said. "The wartime government contracts are now virtually over . . . Also I very much want to increase our scope to a cross-country basis—the West has tremendous potentiality, only just being tapped . . . Another reason," he said, "is that Chris Staniland wants to sell—it's a first-rate company; the equipment is modern; the top men are good. But the business is on the downgrade."

"Why does he want to sell? I understand that there was a son in that business."

"There was," Skafe said. "But he had no flair for it. Construction is usually a one-generation job. Chris Staniland is getting on—sixty-seven." (And you are sixty-three, he thought.) "He wants to get out and still have time to enjoy his money."

"Do I understand that you gave him a verbal undertaking?"

"I undertook to pay him three million if I could raise the funds by next Wednesday."

"It seems to us," Bob Carter said, inspecting his cigar, "that three million is an overly high price for this business, good as it may have been. The earnings were down four per cent in this last year. It seems a big sum for a construction company, which, after all, does not consist of fixed assets, but in quickly depreciating equipment, in men, and in the good will that those men build up and hold. The sum is large, and I am not sure that I like what our doctor friends would call the prognosis."

"The prognosis may be poor under present management," Skafe said carefully. So Bob had not wasted the day on Friday. He had put his people right to work. A good sign, if their findings had been favorable, which it seemed they were not. "I have to say, Bob," he said, "that my opinion in this is a fairly expert one. I rose in Construction. I am confident that we can make a success of Staniland, provided we get it soon. I am prepared to take the risk."

"You are asking *us* to take the risk," Carter said. He frowned, sipping brandy. "With due respect, my dear boy," he said, "I must question your experience in financial matters. Did Staniland, for instance, agree to sell you assets or to sell you shares?"

"We didn't discuss it," said Skafe, a little nettled at the tone.

"There is a difference, you know. In the one case Staniland would sell shares and reap a capital gain. In the other case he would sell assets, flushing the cash out to himself as a shareholder, thus incurring tax. Every deal of such a kind poses a balance of convenience between how the seller can best derive a tax advantage, and how the buyer can best absorb it. Such technicalities, Husky, might seem of academic importance to you. They are by no means so, and it is my belief that if you aspire to larger things, which evidently you do—that if you were to move carefully to bigger spheres, you could not do so without competent daily financial advice. In other words, you would have to employ a top-class accountant."

"That is an excellent suggestion, Bob," he said. "I shall remember it." In fact, he had thought of it already, but by all means let Bob Carter take the credit. With his subjunctives and conditionals, the old devil was playing cat and mouse with him, had him guessing. "I beg your pardon," he said.

"I was asking if you have tried the open market."

"I have," he said. If the banker could play it fancy, he could play it straight. "No investment firm would touch it, without taking a substantial share of the equity. That was the answer I got. And I don't want it. I don't want to be bothered by minority shareholders."

"Let the public be damned, you mean," said Bob Carter.

"Let's say that I want to run my affairs my way," he said. In so far as he was running this particular affair of his, he was running it badly, but he did not like being patronized.

"If you ever become big," Carter said, "which is a possibility." He considered his cigar, a firm inch of Havana ash. "You will not be able to damn the public, for in all major essence the public is the master, yours and mine. Now as to this," he said, and he looked at Skafe, "we chartered banks do not lend money for capital expansion only. We are prepared, however, to extend a line of credit to a company or companies that is or are already substantial customers . . ." He paused.

The Union Bank had the Summit account. The Laurentian Bank had the Turtle Mountain account, and they had turned him down flat about Staniland last week. My God, he's going to do it, Skafe knew at last. "I was thinking of asking you," he said with gravity, "whether you would like to have the Turtle Mountain account."

"We think that would be a suitable arrangement," Carter said. "And you shall have your three million dollars." He smiled at him. "But the best collateral, Husky," he said, "is a man himself, and you are that man. You must believe me when I tell you that there is no other man of your age in Canada for whom I would do this. But hasten slowly, my good young friend."

"Thank you, Bob," he said. Now we can swing it, he thought. Now he could have danced a jig, or have driven a hundred miles an hour. Now he really saw the road that he would build and gravel, but he said: "What about a game of golf this week?"

They made a date for Wednesday, and went through the hall and down two steps to the living room, Bob Carter's hand on his shoulder, big league manager's benefaction.

John and Sally had gone to bed. Dorrien stood at the fireplace, and the women sat. It was dark outside, a few table lamps in here, bleached furniture, a comfortable room at nightcap time. Carter went to sit with Grace Parkyn on the sofa, watched by Dorrien.

"I must fetch the drinks," Skafe said. "But first would you like to see your painting of Mac?" You can see it now, he thought. And that gets us rid of you.

Dorrien came quietly, almost in police terms: quietly, to the opulent haze of the study. "Have a cigar. I should have offered you one earlier."

"No, thank you. I only smoke these things." He lit a cigarette, an Export, quizzing the room to come to the painting which he stared at intently for a few seconds. "That one stays quite well," and he turned away to the photograph of Bidsley Dam. A queer duck, this chap. "Did you build that?" he said.

"Yes, it's one of ours, finished last year—on the Bidsley River in northern Ontario." He glanced at the bland pale sweep of concrete, end result of an older story.

"That curve is good. Do you like going back to look at them, when they're finished, I mean?"

Skafe had not thought of it, but he rarely went back to see old jobs unless new business took him. "I guess not," he said. "They're over and done, and other things on the way."

"It's the same with me," said Dorrien. "When I've finished a thing and the glow is off, I've had it really. Look here, Skafe," he said. "I'm sorry if I was rude, as your wife implied, to that chap Carter. But for one thing, I have a bee in my bonnet about atom bombs; and for another, if people talk about *our boys*, it makes me think of Momma, and I can't bear Yankee Momma. Still, I'm sorry, particularly if I queered the pitch in any way."

"What pitch?"

"I don't know—only that Carter let drop at the highland cattle woman's party last evening with veiled bombast that there was some possibility of his being of service to you in the near future, businesswise. And when you were closeted just now . . ."

"Yes," said Skafe. There was no accounting for the hints that people would drop to perfect strangers. He never did himself, but he was not a financier, weaving webs. "Bob Carter may be reactionary in some ways, but certainly not in business ways. He is very able, and a good Canadian."

"What is a good Canadian?" asked Dorrien with that hint of mockery.

He looked at him. "You must not expect us either to talk or to behave like Englishmen," he said.

"I don't want to, but some Canadians seem to want me to expect just that. You tend, I would think, to be Husky Skafe and to hell with it."

It was a nice back-handed compliment from the artist, sober again if too forthcoming. But it was not quite true. He did adjust himself to people. "By the way," he said, "and between ourselves, I think there might be a portrait to be done of Carter for his board room, if you're interested. But not a hope unless you make it up with him; and old Bob is not exactly a light forgiver."

"A board-room job in a dark blue suit. Dull dames and presidents, my bread and butter. But thank you for the tip. I must try to ingratiate myself again, one of the ghastliest things about being a hack portrait painter. I often long for the freedom of the war, paint what you wanted with a spice in it and an end to it. You know what I mean?"

"I think so," he said. "I didn't go to the war myself." It was his rule not to hedge and not to explain.

"I've been meaning to ask you: might I paint your wife, if she is agreeable, or try to?"

So that was the reason for apology, affability, compliments tonight and last night. "What is your price?"

It cracked him back on his heels, as was intended. But Dorrien looked annoyed. "You misunderstand me," he said. "I never solicit commissions. I asked you if I might paint your wife. The portrait would be mine, at no cost to you. In fact, if it did not seem a little insulting, I would be glad to pay . . ."

"Oh, I see," said Skafe. "I misunderstood." But it occurred to him that making it up with Bob Carter, whom he clearly disliked, was not so different from soliciting commissions. Yes, it was different. "Anna's the person to ask," he said. "Not me."

"It might be exhibited, you know," said Dorrien, waving a vague hand, or a hand vaguely, for his hands were bony and hard. "As a matter of fact," he continued, "I'm painting damned badly at the moment, no interest and no punch, although kindly don't bruit those tidings abroad. I thought a really strong subject might help me possibly."

"Why not see what Anna says? I've often wanted to have her painted, but she will never agree to it. She has no vanity or conceit."

"I noticed that," said David Dorrien.

They went for the drinks, but only Dorrien had whisky, and the small party came to decorous conclusion. The Carters were driven away in their Rolls-Royce. Grace Parkyn took Dorrien in her Buick.

It was a quarter to eleven, and the children slept. He came downstairs again. "I'm here," she called from the veranda.

"I thought we deserved a final drink," he said, "especially you."

"Did I do all right?"

"You were superb," he said.

"It's easy with you—and with basic people like Muriel Carter, and different ones like David Dorrien—original people, I mean. But talking of the opposite, was it okay with Mr. Carter about your money?"

"All's well," he said, and then, because she had helped him and because he would like to feel that she was interested, and because again now he was seeing the way that things would go and would grow for him, he explained the deal in simple terms.

"Oh yes," she said. "The fireflies are wonderful tonight."

Frogs were croaking at the pond; a marker light flashed in the bay; the fireflies glowed twice, or three or even four times in each cycle, sailing slowly above the garden. He wondered why the variation, and said: "Sex, I suppose," rocking with her in the hammock seat.

"There are more unlikely answers," she said, with all time ahead of them, no urgency of time, keep time away from now. I was wrong this morning about love, he thought. I feel it with her.

"John really enjoyed himself this evening. It was good to see."

"He hit it off with David Dorrien."

"But he is usually so shy."

"Just sympathy, Simon. Like you to me when I get you to myself."

"I'm not an artistic type," he said, and was reminded. "But Dorrien surprised me by linking his job and mine, at least by implication."

"Making things," she said. "Yes, I suppose that easily could be so."

"He wants to paint you, free and for nothing."

"Paint me? Why on earth?"

"He has lost his punch, he says, and needs a strong subject. I told him to ask you."

"Oh no," she said. "He would make a mess of my awful face. I won't."

"You must know you have a beautiful face. Why say it's awful?"

"Because I see through bitchy me in the mirror. Even if Grace Parkyn gazes soulfully at you at supper, I notch it up against Grace Parkyn because she's the sort of placid woman you ought to have married."

"Do you think so?" he said and, watching the fireflies flashing two or three or four, he matched the rhythm with his hand, silk sliding silkily on skin, soon not enough, and then his hand on the skin of her leg.

"God," she said. "What you do to me." The night was cool, and the drink was warm, and here came time.

"Damn," he said. "Thrice damn!"

"I'll go." The seat swung and settled from her going. The telephone rang a second time in the quiet house.

"It's for you," she called. "Long distance."

At eleven-forty on Sunday night? "Probably some drunk," he said, passing her in the living room. He was occasionally subjected to conversations with people down from the bush, lovingly abusive to their old pal Husky, or sometimes plain abusive in the middle of the night. But that was in Montreal. Surely not here on Sunday. "Hullo," he said.

"Is this Mr. S. K. Skafe?"

"Speaking," he said.

"Husky? Wilson Pitt."

"Hullo, Willie," he said to his executive vice-president. It must be trouble. A plane crash? What? He shook his head to sharpen his head from an evening's mild drinking, from other beginnings on the veranda. "What is it?"

He saw his man as he listened, that rock of reliability and scrambled speech, Wilson Pitt, who explained the trouble in a minute of inimitably lucid double talk. The trouble was at Turtle Mountain, reported on the evening Radio Sked, just relayed from Edmonton: they had been running in and out of permafrost in the mine—pockets of it—but no water to speak about until today on afternoon shift when they had started drilling again and hit water under great pressure, immediately a fall; one man with a broken shoulder. They had cleared the mine, which was now flooded fifty foot up the shaft, still rising against the pumps.

"Mike Pilbrom was on the air for himself," said Pitt, "wanting pumps, compressors, grouting gear, which we're flying by earliest crack. But what I don't fancy is the hired help have got their pants scared off, he hinted on the sked, and that could be serious, way off in the backside of beyond at Turtle. Which is why I'm with you in the Sunday watches. Better for me get up there, Husky."

"Hang on a minute," he said. One of them must go. But Gramercy? Killick? The Stocker building and the others? All the detail that only Pitt had at his finger tips. "No, Willie," he said. "We can't spare you. I'll go myself. Where's the amphibian?"

"Here at Dorval with nobody to fly it. Mac was yacking for a pilot, likewise one overpregnant wife in Edmonton, so we sent Yarrow out by TCA last night. I'll find a pilot or I'll charter. He'll be there at five, Atlantic Standard. Bad weather coming, they say, not until later in the morning down your way. It's too bad about the vacation, Husky. But

Turtle on the skids right now would be calamity Jane. I thought you'd be for going yourself."

"Thanks, Wilson," he said. "Goodnight." He hung up, then thought that he might have told him that all was now clear for Staniland, but major financing meant nothing to Wilson Pitt, a superlative practical man with limitations.

How to tell Anna? She would understand. She always rose to emergencies. She would grumble and understand. He sat again with her on the hammock seat. His eyes grew accustomed to the dark, and the fireflies glowed more brightly. "Who was that?" she said idly, leaning to him. "One of your boys on a bender in town? ''S tha' you, Husky boy, Bill Plashter here, shovel operator, should goddam well hope you remember me, just wanna tell ya, mean old sonuvabitch, I love ya.'" She had Sally's trick with mimicry, or Sally had hers. "They do seem to have a soft spot for you."

"It wasn't a drunk," he said. "It was Willie Pitt. They've run into trouble at Turtle Mountain."

"Bad trouble?"

"Bad enough," he said, and explained briefly. "The worst thing may be that the men are scared."

"I don't wonder," she said. "Deep in the earth. I couldn't stand it."

"I must go there," he said, making it as normal, casual, unhurried as he could.

Her head turned quickly. "At the end of the week, you mean?"

"No," he said. The hands of his watch were exactly together. "In five hours' time. I'm sorry, darling. The thing is vital, and I must go." He reached for her hand, but she moved it away.

"But you can't," she said quietly. "Oh Simon, you can't."

"I must," he said again. "If we don't get into production by the end of summer—a bare two months from now—the whole enterprise will be a write-off. We simply cannot carry Turtle unproductive through another winter."

"And what difference will your presence make?"

"In an emergency like this it may make a lot of difference."

"So once again you ditch us."

Oh God, he thought. She's off. "Darling," he said reasonably. "I didn't ask that this should happen. All year I've been looking forward to this week at Gallery with you, and now a crisis has blown up. It's just damnably bad luck."

"The kind of damnably bad luck you love, any chance to grasp the nettle danger, oh you love it. Ditched again—this time for bigger and better atom bombs. That's all Turtle Mountain will ever contribute to the world—profits to you and atom bombs."

"Anna," he said. "I staked Turtle Mountain in the radium days before nuclear fission had been heard of. Before I had even heard of you," he added with a bid for jocularity. She might still calm down.

"Yes," she said, "and don't I know it, and you ditched your partner in the process."

"I paid Jim Willis a more than generous price for what I found myself. If you say that, Anna, you insult me."

"A lot you care whether I insult you. All I am to you is something to get into bed with when you deign to honor me, and something to enable you to escape your responsibilities with the children, and something to organize supper parties with all the bogus snobbish trimmings so that you can pull a million-dollar business deal on the second night of your so-called holiday."

"Quiet. The children are just overhead."

"I won't be quiet."

"Come inside then," he said and went in himself, bait that she would follow. He shut the door to the hall. Damned bitch, he thought, and he heard her bang the veranda door. She faced him across the room, lines pinched deep at the sides of her nose. "What do you want me to do," he said, "throw the capital and the people I'm responsible for right down the drain for the sake of a week's vacation?"

"If it would make you human, yes. Yes, yes, yes."

"Is it a crime to want to do things well?"

"It is an obsession," she said slowly. "And we are only chattels for your pleasure and your use between the things that matter."

"That's a lie," he said, "a wicked lie." Stop it, he told himself, but he had to yield to her ugliness of provocation.

"All right," she said. "Thirty-six hours of what? Of satisfying yourself with me. Of scaring John with pep talks and demands. Of spoiling your precocious little pet. Of working on your papers. Of wrecking my Sunday for the party the dictator ordered. Yes, I really tried for you. You, you, you. It's always you. Anything you ever do is done for the sake of Simon Skafe. You use us, you use Bob Carter, you use everyone. You never do a single thing in life without an eye to the main chance, which first last and all the time is S. K. Skafe."

"Thank you very much," he said. He watched her eyes, which were the sign, staring so widely that the pink rim of the eyelids showed, and she did not blink, the frantic inhumanity of her tantrum. She walked towards him slowly, hands clenched, arms held stiffly away from her sides.

He moved out of the way, around the sofa, and still he tried. "Anna," he said. "I have to go. You know I have to go. Toddy can cope here. Come with me to Turtle Mountain."

"Toddy can cope. Toddy can cope far better without me is what you mean. How typical of you to offer to take the Hausfrau along to Turtle Mountain just because she hates the North. But I do hate the North. I hate the mucking North and everything about it, including this."

It was a nice black ashtray fashioned out of high grade pitchblende right from Turtle Mountain, a lethal missile, but it missed him so widely that he did not even duck. The ashtray dented plaster harmlessly, and Anna slammed the door behind her.

He sat down to get his temper in control. He had never quite lost it with her yet. But some day he would. Some day the ashtray would hit or the nails would rake. It was horrible. It was a dirty filth of jealousy and hatred. And now he had better go and pack and try for two hours' sleep in the dressing room.

More doors slammed. He went upstairs. John was asleep; his handsome son lay deep in sleep. But Sally next door was wide awake, and crying, and afraid. "What's the matter, pooch?" child weeping in the moonlight in her bedroom.

"I woke up. It was the shouting, and she came just now and said: What did I mean by being awake, and all I did was show off all through supper, and she shook me hard."

"Never mind," he said, hearing himself from a distance. "I have to start for Turtle Mountain early in the morning. That's what your mother is upset about. Go to sleep now, darling."

"Daddy, couldn't you take me with you? Couldn't I go to Turtle Mountain?"

"Some day," he said, kissing a wet cheek, and then raising his head to break the cling of her arms. "Sleep now, Sally. Everything's all right."

But nothing was all right. He could endure even having lumps of rock thrown at his head. But to take her mad anger out on Sally. He turned for their bedroom door, which he knew would be locked . . .

"Mr. Skafe!" Old Toddy along the passage, dumpy shadow and sibilant whisper.

"Yes, Toddy?" Dear God, he thought, even Toddy's in on this.

"Is it all right?"

"Everything's all right," he said for the second time. "I have to leave, Toddy. The plane is coming at five o'clock."

"I'll get you your breakfast—egg, toast and coffee?"

"No," he said. "I'll manage myself, thank you very much. Goodnight, Toddy." But he knew, of course, that she would be up whatever he said.

He had made a *Thank God for Toddy* joke to her at last breakfast time.

He went past their bedroom door and the bathroom door to his dressing room. But his *Thank God for Toddy* now was not a joke as he thought of the brink upon which he had teetered. He packed his things and set the alarm clock for four-fifteen, and watched the fireflies down in the garden, and lay on the cot in the silent house.

The children, unwashed, unbrushed, in fisherman's sweaters and blue jeans, came to see him off, to row him out in the dinghy which was easier for a strange pilot than the ramp. The morning was still, so calm that you could see the flounders on the bottom. I never did get fishing with the boy, he thought. I never did call the doctor about Father. I never did speak to Phipps, the gardener. John rowed. Sally sat in the bow. He looked back to the house, but there was nobody at upstairs windows. The engines of the Summit amphibian stopped. John was getting quite good in a boat. "Hi," said the pilot, a competent-looking type, to the children, and took Skafe's bags.

He said quick goodbyes, thinking unhappily what a stout and happy scene it made, the children rowing Father in the early morning to board his plane.

He decided not to fly her himself, being short of sleep, so he took the co-pilot's seat, and looked out to see that John and Sally were ashore again, and both engines ticked over now, and Anna came running in her dressing gown.

The bedroom door had still been locked, but here she came running to stand with the children, to put her arm around Sally's shoulders. It was quite touching. It was her way of saying Sorry to him, he thought. But he also thought of Sorry until next time, the next time that he hoped each time would not occur, but it did.

He slid the window open to wave. The children waved back, and she raised her hand and dropped it again to Sally's shoulder. "Okay?" said the pilot.

"Okay," he said.

CHAPTER SIX

THE CAGE stopped. Pilbrom and Syme followed him out. "Everything's fine," he said to the waiting shift. The air was clean up here, and he took it in deep to rid himself of explosive fumes. Sleep and wind and sun and sleep were the things he wanted. Change, get out of these things and sleep. He unplugged his lamp, hung up his helmet, stripped for a shower and dressed again; and now the three of them met the sun and the wind.

"Be seeing you, Peter," he said to young Syme, whose bunkhouse lay along the lower catwalks. He and Mike Pilbrom climbed steps to the manager's hut. It was not quiet in the wind and the sun, but a great racket of activity at Turtle Mountain.

"What time does the plane leave, Mike?"

"Due in at midnight, out around one. Where's the next place you'll be shooting trouble?"

"I must get to the Coast," he said. "Not for trouble, though. We're taking over Staniland."

"That's a big outfit," Pilbrom said, a thump of rubber-shod feet on wooden steps this side of the sawmill, crushing mill, bulldozers, generators, turbine hum. "Well," he said, "I hope you're going to get yourself some sleep at last."

"Yes," he said. "That's just what I'm going to do."

"Do you know how many hours you've been below?"

He did not know and did not listen to how many, seeing the thing as a crazy jag of floods, pumps, shoring, grouting, drilling, blasting and men's pale faces and pandemonium, and he the busybody and kibitzer, and now he was very tired. "I wasted a lot of time," he said.

"Maybe," said Pilbrom. "If it's wasting time to be there to take what's coming." He was a spare man, fiftyish. They entered his office.

"Have you any management changes in mind?" Skafe asked, sleep crowding him, but he must not make this a last-minute question.

"Fire Reston after that performance."

"Can you use him above ground, if he wants to stay on?"

"I could put him into Stores, at less money."

"Give him the chance, then. So what about Assistant Manager?"

"Hire a new man, I guess."

"You wouldn't consider Peter Syme?"

"He's only a kid, and no practical experience, off at the war."

"His war was one kind of practical experience. He can get the other quick enough if he's ready to learn from the old hands."

"That's just it," said Pilbrom. "Some of them been mining thirty years, and he tells them, rubs them wrong. He's a first-rate boy, I will say."

And you are a first-rate man, thought Skafe, but an old hand too. "Why not try him out?"

"I could at that," said Pilbrom. "What about salary? He's drawing three hundred."

"Four-fifty on probation. How does that sound?"

"Okay," Pilbrom looked dubious. It might be that he saw a challenger. "Will I tell him, then?"

"Tell him that I have agreed to your recommendation, yours."

Pilbrom nodded.

"And you can tell Mike Pilbrom from me that he's doing a great job here."

Pilbrom grinned sourly. "Hell's bells," he said. "You go and have that sleep."

"You might send Syme along at ten o'clock to give me a shake. I want to have word with him." He yawned, five hours' sleep ahead of him, if he was not too tired to sleep. "Much load on the plane tonight?"

"The Boss is the load, unless Reston decides to go out, which he won't."

"When do you reckon to start ore shipments?"

"Next week with luck," said Pilbrom, turning to his table.

Why not sooner, dammit? But he must not ride him now. "Thanks, Mike," he said, and went two doors along to sleep. It was warm outside, about the same as a summer afternoon at Gallery, two or three thousand miles away. He used his light sleeping bag for a blanket. He looked at the colored pin-up on the wall, frisky black lace skirting billows of breasts and hips, no room in the waist for the lady's digestive apparatus, a cheery stork-legged truncated bit of tumble to titillate men in barren places, but not him, thank you very much. She heaved for him in a mischievous sexless way, he was so tired, and now immediately asleep.

The river flowed on for S. K. Skafe. It was his chattel, his obsession for his pleasure and his use, to go swimming down in the river deep, down below the river bottom in the moonlight where the fireflies played. The moon went out or in behind the clouds, and here came brighter fireflies, lamps flashing dashing splashing in the water. So on again. So on, the ashtray flying pitchblende. Everything for on and on, and here at last it came, two rings for haul away, for ride the cage to trouble-shooting at the Coast.

"It's ten o'clock, sir. Mike said you wanted a shake."

He felt as if he had drunk a whole bottle of whisky, which he had not done for years, if ever. He sloshed water into the enameled basin and put his face in and left it wet while he laced his boots. "I feel like hell," he said, but he felt much better.

"Those *Esquire* girls," he said about the pin-up. "They worry me. I don't somehow see them making both ends meet."

Peter Syme laughed heartily but not extravagantly at the Boss's joke. "Sit down," he said. "I want to talk to you."

Syme sat. He was sandy-headed, freckled, plain, composed.

"Mike Pilbrom asked if he could try you out as his assistant. I agreed."

"Thank you, sir. He told me."

"Thank yourself and him, not me. Now listen, Peter: I agreed to this because I've seen the stuff you have inside you, but you also have a lot of things to learn."

"Yes, sir."

"One of them is to be less absolute. Things are not right or wrong, army fashion. Things can be done a dozen ways without a drill book in the mining business or in any business."

"Yes, sir."

"The second thing follows from the first: You must employ some cunning and some patience, ask the older men's advice and take it."

"But, Mr. Skafe—their mining practices are from the ark."

"I know," he said. "But they have a hell of a lot of practical nous and knowledge that you lack. Also, if you can show a man that you respect him and his judgment—and the way to that is by the smaller things—he will respect you when you stand on principle."

"Yes, sir." The *yes, sirs* were a little mulish. He was needled, just as Skafe had planned.

"What I am getting at," he said coldly, "is that you will now be tried in a job which will give us a chance to judge whether you are any damned good at all in management—" He liked him. He admired him. He let him have it, watching him.

"Yes sir," said Syme. His mouth worked, and he burst out laughing. "Sorry," he said, "but I've heard how you dish the hell and the promotion out together."

"I must go and feed myself." He was not hungry, eight hours from a sandwich in the mine, but he could eat. He went with Syme along the catwalk. He was fairly sure that this young man was the man for Turtle Mountain later on. He said goodnight to him.

Gus Velensky produced eggs and bacon. Gus was a ten-year man with Summit, now a Turtle pioneer. He had wife trouble, which he discussed in detail with a relish that Skafe expected about other people's wife troubles. She was whoring it up, and the son had just graduated from high school. All that took time. "I'll see what I can do," he said, alone with the little man in the dining hut, "on one condition, Gus: that you tell nobody, least of all your boy."

He went quickly to escape thanks from the mawkish Gus—a fair cook so long as he kept off the vanilla essence. "Best goddam man in Canada," said Gus when he had gone.

The best goddam man in Canada went back the way he had come, on a catwalk along the lower slopes of Turtle Mountain, past the radio shack and the dispensary. There were disadvantages in a stilted camp against the hillside, with a scaffolding complex of stairs and walkways. But it meant no mud, and shelter from the north, and less snow-drifting. It meant access to the mine at different levels.

Few men moved about at eleven o'clock. The generators made the usual racket. If only they had water power, which they did not have; or coal near at hand, which they did not have . . . Oil from Norman Wells by the Mackenzie, the Bear, the Lake with portages and transshipments was an expensive headache. There were a thousand expensive headaches to this thing, the smallest of his operations, the newest and the first conceived. A phonograph was playing some old song about my love, my baby in some hut, but he did not know the name of the song.

He stopped to look at the windswept very spot where he had first found gummite, weathered pitchblende. Then he picked up his binoculars at Mike Pilbrom's hut and climbed away from the camp and up the shoulder of Turtle Mountain. The bill or the beak of the turtle did not show from here, or it showed as an overhang of rock. You could see the Turtle only from the west, as he had first seen it in February 1932.

There was a wild rose in a sheltered place beside the path. He picked a pallid bloom and put it in a buttonhole of his windbreaker, thinking that his wife, however much she might hate the North, would like the arctic rose. He had wife trouble, and no softy boss to tell it to.

He had climbed above the pockets of soil and vegetation, now nothing but lichens on bare rock. Yet even some of them had red pinpoints on the gray; flowers, he supposed, not knowing the first thing about it.

He sat on the top of the Turtle's head, back from the overhang because he was not fond of heights or of depths, which had made this week a strain for him.

The wind had gone to the north, and it was cold. He turned his back to wind and put up the glasses. On a clear day in the summer you could see the lake from here, a strip of blue fifty miles away. There was white in the strip tonight, for Great Bear Lake had not yet altogether broken up.

Then he dropped his glasses back this way to the lesser roll of hills and water, by the winding slash of the winter road through scrubby forest and over those lakes and back to Turtle Lake and the mining camp below him. I made that, he thought on his hilltop. But he also remembered: . . . *All Turtle Mountain will ever contribute to the world—profits to you and atom bombs.*

It was the first time that he had nursed a grudge against Anna. She neither understood nor wanted to understand that profits were not the point, and atom bombs were beside the point.

He had been a bit crazy this week, spending days and nights of sun in a hole in the ground, not profits, not atom bombs, perhaps even in some degree to spite her if the nettle danger should be too quick for him. That second fall, like the thunder doom of God, then the water rushing, the lights gone out, the miners' lamps demented fireflies, panic in his guts, not room for everyone in the cage. *Get in,* he said, beating down his panic. *Send it back for us.* He and Syme had waited while the water rose to their knees, to their waists, and then it stopped.

Yes, I was crazy, he thought. He turned now to face the north. The sun was riding its shallow curve, coming on for midnight. There was a single living thing in sight, a raven. You need not be a bird watcher to know the raven of the Arctic, black-bearded vagabond. The stunted birches also might be called alive, growing four feet in as many centuries; and the spruces in the draws and valleys had slow life. But the north wind kept the life of flies from him.

The plateau below him to the north was bare of all but the lowest ground-hugging life, and yet was quite green and pretty now. It was very pretty to him because it provided a solid base for airstrips. He looked north beyond this plateau to the true barren lands. He had trapped there once, between the last trees of the boreal forest and the Arctic Ocean.

The South was behind him, the North before him, and it called him on, bleak godforsaken wilderness. "Ours," he said aloud, "if we can take it." Each man may claim a vision or a dream, and this was his for Canada, for him, through him. Some day he would tell men of his vision, but not with empty talk.

A pair of birds alighted near him, hunting this or that where damn-all grew. He put the glasses on them. They would be the size of sparrows, one drab brown bird and one with black and white about the head and collar. He studied them carefully in order to report them to the family ornithologist. He could memorize a balance sheet at one reading, but the patterned blacks and whites and russets of a bird eluded him. He laughed about himself, the pie-eyed visionary cataloguing birds to please his son.

Then he thought that this was just the place for John one summer, when he was seventeen or so, to toughen the boy, and he could have his birds as well.

He thought up and back to the head of the Mackenzie where the North began for him. She hates the North, he thought, and what a dull-witted clod I was and am, forgetting that she nursed a dying mother here, and that she escaped an incestuous father here by marrying a decent dipsomaniac. But she also did find me.

He saw a pickup and a larger truck climb the easy slope to Turtle Mountain airstrip. They stopped by the hut and the gasoline tanks, probably man's last construction jobs on a line between here and the Pole and over to Siberia where the Russians were really doing something about their North.

It was five to twelve. Now, against the buffet of the arctic wind, he heard the plane, a rumor of the plane flying in from Yellowknife, southeast. He turned to search for a pinpoint in the sky, or a shadow down against the land and water. But there was no searching to be done, for the plane reflected the sun to him, a solitaire, a single jewel of the wilderness.

He watched it growing all the way, gleaming all the way until the saffron faded to a generality of pink, until his jewel was a prosaic C-47 or Dakota with its wheels down now, passing just below him, turtle emblem on the nose, TURTLE MOUNTAIN green along the fuselage.

There was pleasure too for him in watching the crabwise slipping off of height to straighten and touch at the limit of the gravel strip. That landing was authentic Mac.

Skafe left his mountain, which did not merit such grandiose description. He left his hilltop for this time again and walked and ran down to the camp. Mosquitoes were bad in the lee. He thought of the beauty of the flashing plane, a meaning of some kind, a heliograph for him. And then he mocked himself about his secret notions.

He bundled clothes in the grip, rolled up his sleeping bag and stuffed that in, and Mac arrived.

"Hi," said Mac. "So you finally broke surface."

"Hi, Mac," he said. "Yes, finally." He supposed that if he spent a lifetime as a miner, he might overcome his aversion to the black deep beast. But he would not thus spend a lifetime; nor would he forget that second fall.

"You look washed up. Have you had a sleep?"

"Five hours," he said. "I can manage more if you'll give me a quiet ride."

"There isn't a bump from here to Outside tonight," said Mac. He was a short man, five foot seven or eight. He wore a khaki shirt, a silk handkerchief knotted like a tie inside the open neck, a greasy old suede jacket, drill pants tucked into the top of his boots which were laced half-up and were dusty, but lately cleaned. His eyes were a palish mustardy shade, his nose was beaked, the scar jagged from his left cheekbone to his jaw. He looked like a killer, and might be that, but he was a gentle man, the only man Skafe knew who was wholly devoid of pretension. *No bullshit*, he often said, but not to assert that he had none.

"No bullshit," he said now, true to form, his eye caught by the pin-up. "How's that for a grove of melons."

"Who's co-pilot, Mac?"

"Yarrow."

"How is he doing?"

"Okay," said Mac without enthusiasm. "The poor sod's worried stupid about his wife—she's overdue. But I had to bring him. Talking of bringing . . ." He undid his breastpocket and gave Skafe a letter.

Anna's writing reminded him of things, and he was quite afraid to read the letter. "I'll go for some coffee," said Mac, and went.

He read his wife's letter through, and was glad that he had done so. Then, with attendant plague of flies, he went along for coffee with Mac. To believe in men, a man requires one elder hero.

CHAPTER SEVEN

Mac finished his coffee, and then he took out the pewter box to roll himself a cigarette. He used to roll them with the same deliberation from the same flat case or box when he came to the house at Outremont. That was in the old days, if eight years ago could properly be called the old days. Since then Mac had fought a war. Since then Skafe had risen in the world, changing his habits and his friends. Mac had done much and had not changed at all. Well, perhaps he had a cachet of accomplishment, ex-Wing Commander, Fighters, with his D.S.O. and his D.F.C.'s. But that was a cachet others stamped on him. In himself he had not changed from the laconic, gentle and explosive Mac who taught Skafe to fly. He rolled this cigarette and lit it.

"What's the word of the family?" he asked.

The family were fine, and the weather abominable, Anna said. "They all sent you their love."

"Thanks," said Mac. He smiled to himself, a family friend as well. "Too bad you had to cut your time down there."

"Yes," he said. He had lost the week, but he thought he had found something here. "I'll get down again over Labor Day. Why not switch yourself east, and spend the weekend with us?"

"I might do that," said Mac. "We'll have to see how this thing goes." With the two planes in the east, and the four planes based on Edmonton, Mac had a sizable air operation to control. And there would be Staniland at Vancouver.

Skafe discussed that with him now in general, not only the aircraft side of things. Mac's pragmatic commonsense, disinterestedness, and discretion made him an excellent person to try ideas out on, a sounding board, a lethal pricker of bubbles. He had no ambition for himself beyond running what he called his two-bit airline with efficiency, which he did; and being well paid for it, which he was.

Mac looked at his watch, and did not move. He spent much of his life in waiting, waiting to fly or waiting to get there. But he did not seem to wait, sitting complete wherever he was. It did not do to hurry him. Mac was perhaps too uncompromising a law unto himself, but you could not have everything. "Let's go," he announced, and they went out. "I guess Yarrow is still at the radio shack. His wife has been in the hospital since late last night, and he's trying to get word from Edmonton. You go on down."

Skafe obeyed instructions, taking the long flight of steps to the yard where the pickup was standing, a note in the cab from Pilbrom that he had gone out by truck. Skafe waited again. He was always waiting on somebody's pleasure. Nonsense, he thought. How much do they have to wait on mine? But they had company in waiting. He waited alone to leave this place, and there was not a single soul around to say *Well done, We'll miss you,* or *Come again.* He was the goddam boss, alone at the low hour of the night, and sorry for himself, which did not often happen. You get no thanks, he thought, unless they want something out of you.

But here came Mac and Yarrow. Mac got into the cab with him, and Yarrow outside. "Did they raise Edmonton?" Skafe asked, driving off.

"Yes," said Mac quietly. "They just got through now. The hospital was trying to contact him, but the infant has not arrived. So he's sweating worse than ever."

Skafe remembered chain trouble, driving Anna through a blizzard.

That was when she had John. He sympathized with Yarrow. "Mike Pilbrom says we're flying empty. With a tail wind, we can make it direct?" He left a question in the remark, that being Mac's department.

"No," said Mac. "I'm taking on gas at Yellowknife."

Skafe drove fast. He had not wanted to leave Turtle Mountain, but now he wanted to get the hell out of here. The road was bad, and he kept his foot down. He felt Mac's pale eye on him, but he did not look round at Mac.

"Why the road race?"

"Why not?" He changed gear for the hill.

"You're needing sleep. You can have a nice bunk-down in the bunk."

"I don't want a nice bunk-down in the bunk," he said, sensing Mac's scrutiny again. "Thank you very much."

"You're entirely welcome," said Mac provokingly. "Well, my God, take a look at that, town band and all!"

What Mac described inaccurately as the town band and all was a cluster of men, fifty or sixty. Skafe stopped and got out, and the damned dust swirled and settled, and he wondered what this was about, a collection of silent men, off-shift. More trouble, he supposed.

"It's high time you did something about the road surface, Mike," he said. "What's all this?"

"The boys came to see you off," said Pilbrom, "and to launch the ship."

"What ship?" But he looked at them, and he knew all the faces, mostly men he had seen down the mine these past five days, a fair lot of thugs of types and races, exiles for some good reason—for a quick stake or from the booze or from the police or from the women, and one or two because they liked it. They were not a prepossessing crew at Canada's most northerly embryo mine. They stood rather still, looking from him to the door of the plane and back.

Thus prodded, he went to see and saw inside a mound of small burlap sacks, netted and lashed to the floor.

"First ore shipment," said Pilbrom behind him. "Two tons. It was their idea to send it with the boss, so I fooled you about next week."

He was not here for fun and games to be fooled about next week. Then he thought that a few minutes back he had waited alone in the truck, knowing that nobody gave a damn about the boss except what they could get out of the boss.

He looked at the first shipment, and then he turned, ashamed and touched, unable to produce those few well-chosen words at which he was so adept. "Thank you, boys," he said. "Well, thanks. Now we're on our way." He smiled at them, and they grinned back. It was a sheepish send-off.

"Damned nice of them," he said inside to Pilbrom, "to care about us getting shipments started."

"They don't give a darn about us getting shipments started. That's not why they're missing out on beauty sleep. All the best, then, Mr. Skafe."

He looked at his bags of ore, an inefficient method, but a start. One day they would be shipping powdered concentrate. He took a seat forward, facing crosswise, and did up his belt. He was sleepy again.

Now Mac came in and passed him. "You're a good boy, boss," he said. "We're pleased with you." That sardonic grin of Mac's, seeing through his disgruntlement in the truck.

Yarrow climbed in, pulled up the steps, and closed the door. "Hullo, sir," he said politely, absently, in purblind fashion. He should hide it better, thought Skafe, a little irritated.

The engines took at once, and now they were taxiing out with the first sizable shipment of uranium ore from Turtle Mountain. What we need, thought Skafe, is a ten-ton payload, a cruising speed of three-twenty, a range of twelve hundred plus. But that would be years away.

Mac gunned the starboard engine to swing at the end of the strip, and then he ran each engine up in turn, and now both together, and they sounded good, the ship thundering, trembling, heaving against her brakes. Mac was meticulous, as always. Now they idled. Now the moment was coming.

But it did not come. Instead there came a violent "Christ!" from Mac. Yarrow shot down to the door.

Skafe guessed what it was before he reappeared, the gust lock in his hand, a clothespin device that locked the elevator surface against wind-slamming damage when on the ground, co-pilot's job to place it and remove it. No wonder Mac's blasphemy had sounded through the metallic putter of the engines. Skafe gave a spine-chilling moment's thought to what could conceivably have happened to two pilots, one president, one C-47 and one first shipment. It was more the might-have-beens than present emergencies that gave him flying qualms.

But then they were blasting north, faster, faster, lighter and lighter, a final trundle and a parting, and the wheels came up. The plane swung east. He looked back to see their dust cloud in the sun, a few buildings in the shadow under Turtle Mountain. Goodbye to that again.

He knew that he had earned the tribute of his men, and he knew that such a tribute was as rare as was a boss who stayed down mines in time of trouble. If he had shared their risks because of a certain bug in him, the bug was not a wish for popularity. Let them like him or dislike him. Well, that was not quite true. He liked to be liked upon the terms he set. Peter Syme would make the grade and like him; or he would fail to make the grade and would cherish a lifelong resentment against one Skafe. But young Mr. Syme knew where he stood.

The air was smooth tonight, as Mac had said. He looked at the waste of rock and water, toy spiky spruces in sheltered places. The harsh land was softened at early morning, or subdued. There were people who loved the North, not as an escaping ground or a refuge from temptation that they could not resist outside—simply as home, the world they liked best. But they were few, and few of them were native-born Canadians.

For himself, he did not think that he either loved, hated, liked, disliked, or feared the North. He might sometimes feel an apprehensive twinge about a forced landing at this season when the lakes had broken up. But that was Skafe the back-seat driver. If he flew himself, he had no such fear. For him the North was the wilderness to match himself against, to make one pinprick in it, always more North waiting to be taken.

In a minute he would avail himself of Mac's bunk. He took out Anna's letter again. "Thursday morning," and no date, and this was another Monday coming up.

Simon Darling,
    I telephoned Wilson Pitt last night but he said there was no news of developments at T.M. except that you had reached there safely. So this is just to tell you that you are always in my thoughts and more than ever after that exhibition and not even being in time to say goodbye. I said I hated the North but I love it too because of you. It has to be both extremes. That's the wretched kind of woman I am. Please forgive me darling. Best love from the three of us to you, and to dear Mac of course. Take care of yourself and come back *soon*. I can't keep saying that all my life.

                                                                                ANNA

P.S. Stinking weather, rain since Monday.

He had not taken particularly good care of himself in these last days. Nor had he taken particularly good care of her in these last years. He knew it, and he could not help it. *Come back soon. I can't keep saying that all my life.*

But get the Staniland deal fixed up, and Turtle and the rest. Get things rolling smoothly on ahead and back to meet him on his way, and he would improve, perhaps take her skiing in Switzerland next winter, no, the next but one; or to Barbados. Oh, yeah! he accused himself. But it was not fair to accuse himself. He needed time, and he needed one other thing, or one other man when business was big enough to afford that luxury. He needed, as Bob Carter had suggested, a really smart financial man to complement Wilson Pitt.

He went forward. Yarrow was flying. Mac stared out of his window at Great Bear Lake, immense and clean and deep, a hundred miles of lake to cross, blue as a tropical sea, but there was still ice here and there to contrast the blue. Mac looked in at the instruments, frowned at a creeping altimeter; then round at Skafe. Dear Mac was not in a sunny mood. He ignored the boss and looked at the lake.

Simon Skafe lay down on the bunk between the cockpit and the cabin. This time he slept without stress or strain. He slept through refueling at Yellowknife; aware of that silence, of flying again, of the country below him while he slept, Slave Lake and the Slave, the mouth of the Peace, the Athabaska, on to the south. He awoke, refurbished and ravenous as the sliver of inhabited Canada arrived, the farms of Alberta; and soon they landed at Edmonton.

Mac and Yarrow came back together, the latter as wreathed in smiles as he had been distraught a few hours ago a long way north. Once again Skafe guessed correctly. "Came through on the radio," said Mac. "Wife had a girl and they're doing fine."

"Congratulations," he said, undoing his belt. "I'm very glad." He picked up his bag and handed it out. He and Mac went into the Turtle Mountain hangar while Yarrow dealt with flight papers.

"Well?" he said in the office.

"The poor guy was beside himself," said Mac. "I'm only a bachelor, and Christ, I can guess what it must be like. I blame myself for taking him, but what could I do, with Thompson sick?"

"You want to keep Yarrow on?"

Mac hesitated. "Yes," he said. "Yes, I think so, give him one chance. He's young. He's mad about his wife. He's a sound pilot ordinarily. Yes, Husky."

"It isn't a question of being a sound pilot ordinarily, but of being a sound pilot always. In other words a question of character. A man can either master his anxieties on the job, or he can't. If he runs a lathe, it doesn't much matter. If he runs an airplane, it does. You saw that in Yarrow's flying, didn't you?"

Mac nodded. "All to hell," he said.

"He forgot the gust lock. He will never commit that particular one again. The next time it will be something else, or he will risk a landing that he shouldn't make. He can be treated generously, but he should go."

"One chance," said Mac. "Everybody deserves one chance unless he panics, or that order of a shambles. This chap's good, and I like him. I could give him hell and give him a chance."

"We've been working together now for a year. Have I ever interfered with you, or even advised you unless you consulted me?"

"No," said Mac. "You haven't."

"You asked my advice about Yarrow before you took him on, and I advised you wrongly. I want to put that straight."

"It's a special kind of case," said Mac, less than happy, with no sign of yielding.

"I know," said Skafe. "A wife, a baby, all the things that make a special case for all the sentimentalists. But there is a very special principle involved." He knew that he was right, but he knew that if he forced Mac's hand, Mac might throw his own job up. Try the other way. "All right, Mac," he said. "I won't interfere. Do what you think is best, and let's forget about it."

"You're a hard sod," said Mac. "But you're right as usual. Yes, he's got to go." He let out a large sad sigh, incongruous in so hardbitten a man.

"Do you want me to tell him?"

"You hired me to run this outfit. Since when do I need to hire you to do my dirty work?"

"I'm sorry, Mac," he said. He knew about the close family of pilots. He was by way of being one himself, and yet apart. "I was only trying to help."

"I know," said Mac. He looked at Skafe with that wintry warmth of affection which might or might not be unique in him. "I'll let Yarrow see his wife, and I'll tell him later. We shall have to keep him on until I find . . . Oh, goddammit," he said, yawning. He had flown about eleven hours.

"Are you going to sleep all day, or do you want some lunch later on?"

"I want some sleep, and then I want some lunch." They arranged to meet. Skafe had a day's work to do in Edmonton, and then the Coast. He had been right this time, and Mac had been wrong, which Mac admitted. But right or wrong, Mac was still a good instructor for a hard sod and former pupil who had risen in the world.

CHAPTER EIGHT

"The Lynx is the job," said Mac. "You say it's slow, but it can put two men and their gear and a month's supplies down on any piddling lake in a four hundred mile radius. If you want to start prospecting out of Turtle, buy a Lynx."

"Not yet," he said. "I was just thinking around ahead. That's quite a hydroelectric potential," he said about the river he was following.

"You're always at it—you live, breathe and eat potential kilowatts etcetera."

"You live, breathe and eat Lynx jobs and potential turbo-props." They had been bickering loudly in the amphibian since Mont Joli, and Gallery was half an hour away.

"True," Mac said. "But I'm not omnivorous. I'm even through with flying for the moment. I'm on my holidays, and you're the chauffeur."

"If we run into trouble, you'll be the chauffeur quick enough."

"No," said Mac. "Skafe pays the wages and Skafe does the work. Skafe puts us in the drink, and who pays but Skafe."

The river turned here, and they left it, flying south at four thousand feet for home, or for his summer home, his family. "Mac!" he said. He switched tanks again, to balance them.

"Well?" Mac wore his flying clothes, the half-laced boots and the old suede jacket; but with his clean blue shirt and a silk handkerchief knotted at his neck, he had a workaday panache. *I do adore Mac in his flying clothes,* Anna said. One leg over the arm of the co-pilot's seat, Mac took his ease. "What's on your mind?"

"Would you say that I have an eye only to the main chance, which first, last and all the time is S. K. Skafe?"

He could forget most of the things she threw at him, including ashtrays, but that one rankled. It so happened that Mac was the only man of whom he could bring himself to ask that distasteful order of question; and it so happened that the flying mood made this a time.

Mac glanced at him, speculative, and looked out. "People tick a lot of ways," he said. "I'm a cynical old bum, so I think that just about all of them tick up to self-interest in spite of the pious bullshit that goes on, or because of it. The point about you is that you know what you want and make no pretense about it and you damn well get it. A difference from most of puking humanity is that you might bankrupt yourself for the sake of principle or a pal. You don't behave like a rich fat aldermanic sod, not yet."

Not yet. He asked a question and he got an inimitably forthright answer. Mac's doctrine of self-interest applied to him, but did it apply to the propounder? "Do you ever get bored with flying?" he asked, apropos of nothing much but things in general.

"Cuts both ways," said Mac. "The less I do the less I like it. That time I cracked up in 1940 . . ." He touched the scar, his mark from the Battle of Britain. And what did he see of that long hot summer? "I was pissed windy when I started flying again. Well, that was being crash-happy, I guess. But the more I do the more I like it. Still, you can have too much. Flying is like a woman, you can have too much. It's a hell of a country, isn't it," he said or shouted, but the noise level was not high. Both motors ran sweetly from here on out. "It's a hell of a country down East here or up North there. A few more people, a lot more trees, a less vile winter, no other difference."

Skafe throttled back and trimmed her to drop off height for Gallery. "This country has only just begun. In fifty years we may control the climate. What are the limits to Canada then? We could support a hundred, two hundred million people."

"You can have them, chum. You can bring them in or breed them up. You can have two hundred million stupid air-conditioned muckers for your ninetieth birthday. I couldn't care less, because I'll be dead." Mac swung out of his seat and left the cockpit. This disparagement of humanity might be one change that war had worked in Mac. Or like many of the best ones, he might have come back to be disillusioned. Skafe did not see that it was possible to believe in anything unless you believed in men. Yet he himself could the better believe in men because he believed in Mac. Life's none too mucking simple, he thought in Mac's language, and flew on down to the sea, wishing that Mac would come forward again.

He circled the farm. It was a sunny day, almost too sharp and blue a day of late summer. They were harvesting oats for winter feed. He flew over the tractor and combine at a few hundred feet, but they did not hear him. He circled again to race the shadow of the plane across them. Tom Beamish looked up and waved. The oats were brown and the after-grass was green. Mac slid into the other seat in that economical way of his.

The job on the cattle pond had been done, a scar of fresh-turned earth across from spring to pond, and there was water in the pond, Skafe saw with pleasure at his elementary ingenuity. He flew on out to make a landing on the bay, which was riffled from the west, just nicely riffled to mark the water. He made a sound job of it.

"You'll do," said Mac, himself again, Olympian on his holidays; but he condescended to pump down the wheels, and raised his thumb, and Skafe ran up the ramp, and then the ear-falling silence of another journey done.

"The whole connection waits," Mac said, making room for him to pass.

"Go on," he said. "You're the main attraction."

"Dear Mac," said Anna, kissing him on one cheek, then the other. "It's so lovely to see you again."

"Good girl," he said to Anna.

Sally said nothing; but first shook hands, and then threw her arms around Mac's neck.

"Good girl," he said again, the short man, shy at meeting, seeming surprised that people should be glad to see him.

"Hullo, boy," he said to John. "How d'you do, sir," to old John Skafe. "I brought your prodigal, or he brought me."

"Simon! Aren't you coming out of that thing?"

"Yes," he said. "I'm letting you finish with the hero." He stepped down, and said: "Good gel," twice in Mac's clipped tones. It was a cheerful return.

"How's everything, Father?"

"Fine. Tom should be through with the oats tomorrow. Did you have a good flight down?"

"Perfect," he said. "Fine weather all the way."

"It looks a touch too fine to me," said old John Skafe. "What's the word of that storm down off Bermuda?"

"Moving slowly northeast," he said. "They think it will blow itself out at sea."

"The tail end is the worst we get up here. But those hurricanes have long fingers in weather. I would expect some rain, and we need it badly. The wells are dry all over the country."

"How is yours?" he asked. The weather, the water, the basic concerns and pleasurable headaches of the countryman.

"Low," said John Skafe, "but holding out. It's never run dry on us in a hundred and sixty years."

Which doesn't mean it won't some day, he thought. His father had declined to have a deep well drilled at the old house, although he had suffered Skafe to install a shallow-well electric pump. *That's luxury*, he said, content with a meager ration when he might have had all the water in the world, or in New Brunswick, at fifty feet. *If you have everything dished up on a platter,* he also said, the obstinate old man, *what is there to stay alive for?*

"How are things at that northern place of yours?"

"Going well now," he said. "I was in to Turtle Mountain again last week."

Anna walked ahead with Mac and Sally. With another six weeks of tan, she was in even better looks. They were all in brown good looks, but he thought that Father had lost a little more weight. He walked with his father and his son and a skim of desire for his wife.

"The wild pear is turning," Anna said. It was a tall shrub or a modest tree at the edge of the wood, and some of the leaves were red. "Goodbye to another summer," she said.

"They tend to run by," said Mac, "but your garden gets better."

"Do you think so? It's such a battle here, with things being winter-killed."

"Husky says that in fifty years we'll be able to control the climate."

"What an appalling thought."

And why so appalling to Anna and Mac, who grumbled about the climate?

"I don't see that," said Sally. "I would like every day to be fine like today. Wouldn't you, Mac?"

"I would like every day to be the first fine day of my holidays," he said. "Let's leave it that way, honeybunch."

"Yes, I see what you mean, Mac," Sally said.

The lawns were still quite green, a few burnt patches on shallow soil. "Your roses are wonderful, Anna."

"They're just coming into second bloom," she said, again with melancholy for back to Town on Tuesday, he supposed.

"What have you been up to lately, John?" he asked, admiring husband, dutiful father.

"Nothing much, Dad."

"Getting some tennis?"

"A little, Dad." It sounded like very little. The boy did not enjoy games, and Anna thought that they did not matter. "The black-bellied plover are back on the shore," he reported, "and the flounders are terrific. We caught thirty yesterday."

"What do you do with them?"

"I fillet them, and Sally sells them. We get fifteen cents a pound."

"Good for you," he said. He liked that very much. He imagined that

Sally could sell flounders to a fisherman, beer to a Baptist, climate control to Mac, or anything she cared to sell. They went into the house.

"You'll stay for tea, Father, won't you?"

"I'd like to," John Skafe said. "I see so little of this fellow. But you have parties to go to?"

"Heavens no," she said. "Not a thing arranged, except numerous invitations for tomorrow night. What kind of a weekend do you want, Mac—entertainment?"

"I want strong drink, feminine company, flounder fishing, in that or any order." Mac was in good form, clearly on his holidays. "I like this place," he said. "It soothes my itchy foot. Now let me get changed and let me get started."

"If you change, you won't be Mac in your flying clothes," said Sally to be quickly covered with confusion.

"I know," he said. "That's the point."

"Children, show Mac to his room."

They went upstairs. "You didn't put him in the big guest room?"

"No," she said. "David Dorrien wanted that one for the light."

"What's the painting like?"

"I don't know," she said. "He won't let me or anyone look until he finishes it, which might be tomorrow morning."

"Why don't we have a peek?"

"We can't," she said. "He demanded the key. I must say it's quite tantalizing to sit for hours every day for weeks and not know what goes on behind the canvas, even if it's only me."

"Only you're a knockout this summer," he said. "Eh, Father?"

"Yes," he said. "Yes, Anna looks great." John Skafe smiled at her and gazed out of the window with some thought in his aquiline face. "They don't come better," he said.

Skafe took his bag up to the dressing room. He hoped she would follow him. She always did. He waited for her, but Anna did not follow him today. He saw John's shore birds flying, and he heard them call. The plover called with strident melody. He went down for a cup of tea.

Skafe was not a riser with the lark, although he liked to waken early. It was the best time of the day to think of plans and pipedreams, to ride his country of ideas, undisturbed. He could be really wild, controlling climates or the Gulf Stream. He could go on ten years, fifteen perhaps, with nuclear power. He could come right down to earth, or to his bed wherever that might be, to let the facts and figures flick. It was a game for him to ride his country of ideas.

Now, at half past seven, he came down to earth and to their bed at
the old Skafe place at Gallery, or the new house on the old Skafe place.
He was not the first man who had gone out from the Maritimes. They
all went out, and the big ones all came back to reminisce to hushed
sycophants about those halcyon barefoot days at the old frame house,
of days when one fine teacher saw the fiber of one boy. Then, with a
large quid of flattery for a large quo of largesse, they got the hell out of
the place again. Well, I won't do that, he thought. I was different, anyway. I was raised in Upper Canada, and I only came home for a few
summers as a boy. He heard the plover on the shore, and remembered
how he and Lee Becker used to shoot them with a twenty-two, and
damned good eating. He must remind Lee of that when Lee came after
breakfast about the heating system. But young John would be horrified
to know that Dad used to shoot migrating plover.

Anna was still asleep. She lay the other way, brown as anything, brown
as an Indian half covered by one sheet. She was rich and round and
firm, marvelous woman animal asleep. Sex had been quiet, but now he
wanted her again. He traced the knobs of her spine to tickle the hollow
of her neck until she came from sleep. "Oh, hullo," she said. "It's you."

"Me," he said, and went to her warmth in the cool morning after a
night of sweat and love and sleep.

Wait now, wait a little, wait this second or this minute, see the brown
blank eyes, wet lips, the slave to punish with delight.

And then to drive to find this world, this teeming only world of storm,
this giant world of ours that ends in meeting.

"Never so good," she said. "Never love as good as that." She often
spoke in superlatives about it, and she meant it just as much each time.

"Thank you," he said. He thanked her for his pleasure with her wonderful strong body.

Now all was gone again. He lay with her, beside her, seeing the lines
of childbirth, the only flaws and changes in her body, but he thought,
love done and love apart, that there were changes in her mind about him.

"What's the time?"

"It's after eight," he said. He drew the curtains. It would be a day like
yesterday, when only gardeners, soon to be exiled from their gardens,
could even think of autumn. The tide was high, and the plover made
sedate small parties on the rocks. Peaceful, not a storm across the world,
until the immediate peace was broken, heightened, by a banging door, by
Sally running for the beach. The plover flew, and Sally swam. The temperature of that water might be fifty.

"I see that Sally has been prevailed upon to wear a bathing cap." He liked her best without, the careless disregard, straight from her mother.

"It's for Mac's benefit. Didn't you see the hairdo yesterday?"

"I thought she looked tidier," he said. Why should he notice hairdos?

"Run the bath for me, darling. David comes at nine."

He ran the bath for Anna while he shaved. Then he dressed and listened to his radio, too late for news, he got the weather, which would be fine but clouding over later, rain probably tomorrow, Sunday. The hurricane was stationary off Bermuda.

"I hope it stays away from here," she said in the bath. "Horrible winds, I hate them."

"It will," he said. "They always blow out to sea." They did not come here with force, but they did not quite always blow out at sea. He liked great winds himself. He liked all wind except the fiendish arctic gales, and even those he used to like to shelter from and hear them.

"Lee Becker comes at ten about the heating." Anna was keen to winterize the house, which he would do.

"Oh, yes," she said. "Are you in for lunch?"

"Of course," he said. He went downstairs. The casual attitude about his movements and his doings was what seemed new this time. It made life much more easy, and again it had him guessing.

He exchanged good mornings with old Toddy, who was always Toddy and worshiped Mr. Skafe. Then he went to have his breakfast. "You're up early, Mac," he said, "for a man on his holidays."

"It's these characters," said Mac. "They rousted me out."

"We have to catch the first three hours of ebb, Dad. That's much the best. Can you come too?"

"Not a hope this morning," he said. "There's too much on."

"Dear Daddy is a busy bee," Mac said. " 'Tain't one kind of honey, sure as hell's another."

Skafe often thought, and sometimes said, that the best vacation was a different kind of work or activity. I'm not only a pilot, dammit, he thought, smiling amiably while even John laughed with funny man Mac at him. Mac could tease Dad and get away with it. Mac was absolutely super.

Then Anna arrived. "Good God!" he said. "What's that in aid of?"

"In aid of my portrait," she said, helped herself to two fried eggs and bacon, and started on her breakfast with healthy relish in an evening dress of a deep red-crimson color off the shoulders halfway off the breasts, and his jade necklace, not another piece of jewelry, a queen, a gypsy, a courtesan. "Do you approve?"

"Yes," he said. "Yes, I guess so. Yes, I do."

"I'm glad," she said, and clearly was, smiling at him along the table. It was a new pride in Anna who decried her looks. He found it quite surprising.

He had a word with Tom Beamish, who was racing to finish the oats today; and then he walked back down the drive. He was pleased with the way the farm was coming—at a loss, of course. It might not be a loss so long, at that. Tom had turned down an offer of nine hundred for a bull calf lately. Mixed farming was no good here. High value pedigreed stock was the only sound proposition. In the long term what he needed was a college-trained man and not so many years from now Tom Beamish would have to be pensioned off. Meantime, Tom had earned his bonus of five hundred. Farmer Skafe, he thought.

He stopped in the cedar wood to consider that again. He agreed with the forestry people that it should be cut selectively. Tom said with prophetic relish that even if no more thinning out was done, the whole thing would blow in the next big wind. Lumberman Skafe, he thought.

He went round the left side of the house, away from where Anna was being painted. He found Phipps, the gardener, to whom he had failed to talk the last time. He weeded with him for some minutes in a perennial border. He knew a hundred decent Phippses, and it was a waste of time to give them pep talks about drinking. The best you could do—apart from firing them—was to be a sympathetic chap yourself, and then some straight tough talk about drinking on the job. He administered that, and listened to Phipps on the subject of his wife, and on the subject of Anna whom he admired devoutly. Then Gardener Skafe left Phipps the gardener.

He heard the fishermen, but he did not go to watch. He heard the man's voice and the two young voices, but they spoke one careless language from the water. Even Sally preferred Mac's company to his. Then the truck came down the drive, and he went to meet Lee Becker who was fifteen minutes late.

"Hullo, Lee," he said. "It's good to see you."

"Hullo," said Lee. "How's everything?"

"Fine," he said. "I got down yesterday."

"I know," said Lee. "It's all around town when that plane buzzes in."

It was a pleasant thought that it should be all around town. "Well, come on," he said. "Let's see about this heating business."

He knew what he wanted, or he put a practical application upon Anna's wants, which were hot air heating with humidity. She was always grumbling about the dryness of the Montreal house in winter. He led Lee

Becker down cellar and all over the place except to Mr. Dorrien's studio. "Well," he said. "What's a rough estimate?" In this neck of the woods tradesmen were not tied to contract prices.

"I don't know," said Lee. "Have to check with the Householder people. I'll write next week."

"You know how much duct," Skafe said. He had worked it out for him. "And you know the size of oil-fired heating unit. Why not call them now?"

Which Becker did, long distance, and got the manager on Saturday morning, and after one loud laugh with the manager, he returned. "You'll be giving me ulcers," he said. It seemed unlikely. He was plump, leisurely and middle-aged at forty-one. "It looks like around eighteen hundred," he said, "all in. Could be more."

"Including carpentry work?"

"No, I hadn't figured that in."

"Fine then," said Skafe. "Let's go ahead." He knew that he could have had the job done complete by one of his sub-contractors for fifteen hundred, or for nothing if Simon Skafe had been that kind of fellow. If he employed an outsider, nobody here would mention it, and nobody here would forgive him. Anyway, he wanted a local job. "What about a bottle of beer?"

"I could," said Becker. "I got myself a thirst." Which meant: *You got me a thirst, you local boy go-getter*. But it did not necessarily mean envy, admiration, or intolerance of the local boy.

Skafe had a bottle to be a pal, quite against eleven o'clock inclination. They sat in the study. "I was thinking this morning of shooting the plover, Lee. Do you remember? Fifteen or sixteen, we must have been."

"Yes, I remember. Good days, those were. You moved on a bit, Husky."

"I moved away," he said. He might have moved back, not away, if he had followed his father's wishes after the North. Father had wanted him to start an electrical business. There but for the Grace of God go I, he thought about Lee Becker. But no, it would have been the town, the county and the province, on from there.

"I had a mind to move out once," said Becker. "Had a chance of a job in Boston. But you get married, kids, the camp for weekends and the hunting. A team of horses wouldn't drag me now."

Out of your rut, he thought. "I know," he said. "I envy you, Lee, in many ways." He did, but by no means in the ultimate ways. He might even have been caught in the way that Lee had been caught a few years later for a shotgun marriage. Joyce was Mrs. Becker's name, and a damned nice willing first lay Joyce McKinney used to be on the moss in August when the flies were over, and a damned good wife now, he would bet. He wanted to send Joyce his love, but he thought that might be tactless, so expressed. "How's the family?" he asked.

"Pushing up," said Lee. "Joyce is expecting number six."

"Is she?" he said. "Please remember me to her."

"You bet," Lee Becker said. "Well, I must be going."

He wrote out a check for five hundred advance on the heating job, and tried to pin Lee down to a completion date without success until: "If Mrs. Skafe wants to come down in November, we'll have to see what we can do. Thanks again," he said at the door. "If you were just here long enough, we'd like you to visit with us at the camp some time."

"Thanks a lot, Lee," he said, and he was grateful. "May I take you up on that?"

" 'Bye then, Mr., goodbye then, Husky." He rattled off in his truck, leaving that diffident invitation to expire.

Skafe got the car out and drove to town for the morning paper. Funny, he thought. Every one of them feels strange with me, and not one of them feels strange with Anna.

CHAPTER NINE

THE SUMMER PEOPLE gossiped on the corner; the tourists hunted souvenirs; the tradesmen were agreeable; the sardine fishermen remained aloof.

Gallery had not changed since he remembered it, a charming place of characters and seasons, a place much sentimentalized by those who came—sweet village and dear annoying villagers. They had the weekly paper mailed to them in winter to keep up with local news. They gave largely, were sometimes thanked, and most of these fond strangers would be buried here.

It was his home town, at least in the ancestral sense, although he had spent less time here than any of the summer colony. They knew nothing of the feuds, the loves, the hypocrites, the harlots. Some, very sensibly, did not want to. Some, like Gladys Broughton, made a cozy little heaven of the place. *If only the world could be like Gallery* sort of thing. Anna called that *the Gallery drool*.

Skafe saw the town through his father's eyes, through his wife's eyes, through his own, with plain affection. If its multiple character—the smart season's rush, the winter sleeping off the fat of summer, the fishermen outside it all—made Gallery a pastiche of a town, rather than the kind of purposed competitive town he understood, he did see through the unreality to a real character and quality of breed which the Gallery droolers wholly missed. That the inhabitants irritated him by their dilatoriness and total lack of ambition was beside the point. Yet not quite beside the point, for a renegade in him admired that too.

He bought his daily paper, running the welcome gantlet in the drugstore, at the hardware corner, by the car. Each year he knew fewer of the people who knew him.

He drove home again, round by the shore and over the hill. He parked the car in the shade above the house and walked on down. Rain was forecast for tomorrow. The weather makes the wind, he thought, facing south into the lightest touch of wind. Or the wind leads to the weather. The chicken and the egg, he thought, and what about the muckin' rooster? The best of presidents must have unpresidential thoughts.

And then he thought, a few things done this morning, but nothing much to do despite his breakfast protestations—he thought that the habit idleness had its points which he could appreciate as well as anyone. Give me time, he thought, and I'll be spending half my winters down in Nassau. Not Nassau, somewhere less exotic. Anna would hate that place— or more particularly she would hate the cafe society and the Jim Crow atmosphere. His wife might be a puzzle to him, but he knew a bit about her.

He wondered, as he reached the porch, whether Dorrien had finished painting her. But the answer came through open windows, high and fretful from along the house: "How can I ever get this bloody thing if you freeze up on me? You have no more expression than a limpid cow."

Anna laughed, not loudly, but her indolent chuckle. She would laugh like that if the children amused her, or sometimes in the hospitality of bed.

"What's the joke?"

"That you should be so testy with the limpid cow."

"Naturally I'm testy—yesterday one face, this morning quite another, and now a vacuum. Here—and just here . . . The thing's as good as done, and worse than useless if I don't get . . ."

"Don't get what, David?"

"I don't know. It's the eyes, of course."

"Would it help if you changed the rules and let me have a look?"

"No. That's been half the trouble—ask for help to sell myself to please.

You can see this when and if I'm satisfied or not at all. I want you to sit tomorrow morning."

"Aren't you being the least bit dictatorial?" came Anna's voice. How calm it was, how cool, as to chide a child. Skafe listened at the porch, not his concern, but no private conversation, loud and clear.

"Am I, Anna? I had it so nearly—just half a touch from right." Something, the palette or whatever, clattered. "Tomorrow, then."

"Sorry, I'm going to church tomorrow."

"Oh, damn your church. Sunday and Monday are my last two chances."

"Sorry," she said. "Besides, after the dance tonight you won't be in any shape for painting."

"How well you have me indexed."

"Don't be silly, David." She laughed again. "Do you want a drink?"

"I do, but I shall take two off Bob Carter; then, bland with gin, I shall finish his bland visage after lunch."

"I'll change," she said, "and run you in."

Skafe moved from the porch and round the house. Dorrien seemed petulant, and Anna indulgently amused by him. If I was petulant with her, he thought, look what I would get. Not motherly chuckles, nor *Don't be silly, Simon*. Emotionally involved with me, I suppose is it.

He heard the fishermen and went to meet them. The score was fifty-one, a record, thanks to Mac, who had opened clams and baited hooks to keep the experts on the job, providing entertainment by his screams whenever a horned and mottled sculpin, nightmare creature, came aboard. "Once will do," he said. "I'll stick to trout in future." Mac did not adapt himself, yet had that faculty of being their age with them.

"They say the storm is heading slowly for the Banks of Newfoundland."

Mac looked for weather. The day was pale with change to come, and it was sultry. "We'd better move the plane," he said. "I'll fly it over after lunch." The amphibian was tethered on the concrete apron, well above high water, but a fair-weather parking place.

"Let me do it, Mac."

"No," he said. "Got to break into my holidays. Got to play fair with the boss. Besides, I want to see those assassins at Flume Hill."

"Could you take me with you, Mac?" Sally looked up at him, hair awry, salt streaked, spindly ankled in her blue jeans.

"Whatever your father says."

Flume Hill, the airport, was thirty miles away. She would be as safe with Mac as driving in a car, or safer. Now she transferred her well-known eyes of Irish blue to Father, appealing, fetching, ruthless wanter of her wants. "All right, then," he said. "John, do you want to go along?"

He watched John hunt a reason or excuse. John did not like flying any more than Anna, but he was ashamed of not liking it. He found his excuse in two pails of slithering, nerve-tremored fish. "All these to fillet, Dad."

"They could keep," Skafe said. How could the boy meet life unless he faced the trivial qualms of life?

"They get so slimy if you wait." John made small resistance, never quite stuck his toes in.

"Slimy is it," Mac said.

"Go on, you two," he said. "Get clean for lunch." He took one pail and shared the other with Mac. "You weren't too bored, I hope," he said, but his old and reticent and sometimes disgruntled friend seemed positively happy.

"Best morning I've had in years," Mac said. "I think only children make you see the sense of things, much as I loathe most brats." They crossed the lawn. "John doesn't like flying," he said abruptly. "That bothers you?"

"Not really, Mac," he said. "But you know how it is—how much you hope for a boy . . . And I see all the punch and bite in Sally."

"They come in a brown paper package," Mac said. "You can change the shape of the minced hamburger, squash it flat or duff it up. But you can't change the contents, would be my guess, and who the hell am I to know?"

"Then what about facing them up to things they don't like?"

"Yes," Mac said. "But John needs time to make his own image for himself, not a copy, but his own."

They put the dead flounders in the shade, and Mac went off to wash. Anna said it, and Mac said it. I must be patient, he thought, drinking sherry on the veranda. Mac came back to have tomato juice. "I'll keep the hard stuff for tonight," he said. "What's this great ramboodle we're on?"

"Not great. Dinner here and out to dance. David Dorrien, your artist chap, is coming."

"He was an amusing guy, from what I remember. Drank too much when he could get it. Thought the world was all to hell. Always tilting at brass hats and windmills."

"That's him," Skafe said. "There are only five of us, unless Anna rustles up another woman. The fifth is Grace Parkyn, widow of the A.V.M. Did you know him?"

"Just. Not a bad old obstructionist. She's no chicken, then?"

"Early thirties," he said, "and not entirely unattractive. Does that fit into a chicken bracket?"

"It depends on the not entirely un-," Mac said. "Could be a nice plump broiler."

The comings and the goings. Here was Anna in a cotton dress. "I took David back," she said. "He still hasn't finished my painting, and seems plunged in gloom."

"Where is he staying now?"

"At the cottage in the Carters' garden. It's nice and handy for him."

"Nice and rent-free for him too," Skafe said.

"I daresay," she said. "I don't suppose the shekels flow into his coffers. Now let me see, I think I'll have a gin and tonic. Tomato juice, Mac, why?"

"This storm seems to be edging not too far from our direction, and I don't want my plane bashed up or salted, therefore to Flume Hill."

"He's taking Sally. Do you want to drive over for them with me?"

"I can't, Simon, and I need the car. I promised Father days ago."

"Oh," he said. "What's on?"

"Hackmatack Point," she said, putting in the tonic, the lump of ice, the slice of lemon. "He likes me to help him," Anna said.

"I know," he said. Hackmatack Point was the cemetery further up the bay, where five generations of Skafes were buried. The newest headstone bore his father's name, *John Kepple Skafe 1870——*, and below that: *Alice O'Connor Skafe 1873–1942.*

No doubt it was an economy to have the job done all in one, with only a single date to add; and no doubt it showed a proper acceptance of mortality. But to Simon Skafe it spoke too much of death already in life's house. He would have liked to go with them to help tend the graves before another autumn, while they talked about flowers and shrubs and old sea captains. But he had not been invited.

"Perhaps Father would go tomorrow instead." She offered to change to come with him. They might not want him to go with them, or she might think he would not want to go with them. How obscure the convolutions and involvements of reason, trifling motive, misconception.

"No," he said. "Father never likes to change his plans. I can easily take a taxi, or send one over for Mac and Sally."

Still no suggestion that he might go with his father and his wife to his family burial place. It was a pretty place above the sea, exclusive too; lots were no longer available to the public. Anna smiled at him. She behaved with him this time as if they were a Darby and Joanish couple, not the hot-mated couple they had been a few hours ago again. She was unconcerned and friendly, and she said: "I tell you who might run you over to Flume Hill—Grace Parkyn asked me to go for a drive with her. Perhaps she's still free. Shall I telephone?"

He had met Grace Parkyn twice, and had found her very attractive, nice, not startling. He shrugged. "Much better than a cab," he said.

Anna laughed, quite pleased with him for being droll, and telephoned the Gallery Hotel. Delighted. Half past two.

"Did you have a nice morning, Mac?"

"Yes," he said. He had been sitting quiet. Mac absorbed and did not give himself away. His face had taken color from the sun to make his scar seem paler; his eyes were mustard, whites a little bloodshot, crow's-foot wrinkles pitted. "Yes," he said. "The poet and the poppet made me laugh."

"The poet . . . But John is terribly shy about his verses."

"Sally drew him out. *Tell us the little one about the plover, Jock*, she said. Which he did. How does it go?"

"Lean, Wind, lean!
For summer has been.
Cry, Plover, fly!
For the year must die."

Anna smiled to herself. "The wind does lean," she said.

What next? Yet Simon Skafe quite liked the sound of that. "I didn't know we had a poet in the family," he said.

"But, Simon dear . . ." she said. She did not call him *dear*, considering that bourgeois or plebeian. In most ways far from being a snob, she was a crashing snob in words and certain things. "But, Simon dear," she said. "You're with the family, so now you know."

He drove Grace Parkyn's car at her request. It was a gray convertible, a Buick, a smooth-rolling large machine. "Such poverty," she said about tar-papered shacks and junk piles at the roadside. "Surely something could be done?"

"About poverty in the Province, yes," he said. "But not about the hillbilly types. It's how they want to be, hence all they're good for."

"And the children?"

"If they were removed at infancy," he said, "before they had acquired the habits of their parents, yes, that might work. But then you would have a breeding pool of degenerates without even their spawn to feed, which would be worse than ever. Short of the late Mr. Hitler's methods, I see no present answer. But there are very few of them. Maritime prosperity would settle the hillbilly problem in the long run."

"And the way to prosperity?" she asked.

"Raw materials," he said. "Power. Federal aid. New industry. Most important, they could pull their own bootstraps up."

"You sound impatient with your fellow Maritimers."

"Yes," he said. "In matters of self-help and enterprise, I am."

"I'm not surprised," she said. "And yet Maritime stock gave you your own terrific spark and drive."

"You could call that ambition, I guess," he said. You could call it obsession, if you were Anna, he thought.

"And where would Canada be without ambition?" she said from along the seat. It was a muggy afternoon, but cool with the wind of passage in her open car. Her face was framed in a pale green scarf or handkerchief. It would not have suited Anna's stronger bones. "You know, Husky, what I think so interesting is that the Skafes were a first family here, and the first Skafe was a Captain in the Royal Navy, wasn't he?"

"Yes," he said. "He retired and settled in Massachusetts before the war, but how did you know?"

"Anna told me. I mean that you can't get away from breeding, can you? That's what my Charles always used to say."

"Where was the Air Vice-marshal from?" he asked.

"The Parkyns were English County," she said.

If Anna heard that one, she would wince, he thought. "How long were you married?"

"Six years," she said. "Charles took me almost from the schoolroom. We were blissfully happy, although losing the child was a sorrow to us and a bond. We were in Ottawa almost all that time. Charles was Supply. But, of course, you know that."

"Yes," he said. "I met your husband and I liked him."

"You say comforting things," she said. The highway rolled inland and back to the shore and into woods again.

It was not a dramatic coastline of cliffs and breakers. The rocks were modest, and the sea was sheltered. The coast had beauty, if not prettiness, at high water. When the great tides bared the shore, there was some nobility of ugliness about the mudflats and the seaweed. But if a thunderstorm should move across the bottom of a tide, there was a ghostly beauty, polished lightning-rippled mud, macabre.

Inland, the woods—the small hill rolling to the alder swamp, the lake, another hill, the summer trickle of a river, the green woods and the burnt woods, the hardwood and the evergreen, the slash, twenty-eight thousand square miles of wilderness, twenty-five hundred of cleared land; that was it, more or less.

"A forest and a shore," he said. "New Brunswick."

"A forest and a shore," repeated Grace, and sighed, as if with pleasure. "Let's go fast."

Thus encouraged, he put her up to seventy and once to eighty and slowed for the winding stretch before Flume Hill. "Good car," he said.

"Good driver," said Grace Parkyn. "Another one of your accomplishments."

"Thank you, madam." Praise of his character or success made him faintly uncomfortably gratified. Praise of his physical abilities or skills pleased him without qualification. Balance, timing—a car, an airplane, a horse, you rode with a light-handed rhythm. One day, when they imported them again, he was going to treat himself to a real car like a Bentley. As it was, he enjoyed her Buick, and he would not have minded driving another fifty miles in company with Grace.

He turned into the airport as the Grumman made its circuit. He watched the landing, down safe and sound. He would trust Mac with any of his possessions, including the most valuable package he now carried; and yet perhaps a reservation about that willful package. "Have you enjoyed the summer?" he asked Grace Parkyn while they waited near the hangars.

"Yes," she said. "People have been so kind, not that it's ever just the easiest thing to be a woman on one's own. But I've loved it."

"Good," he said. "You must come again."

"I've been thinking," she said. "And this is terribly confidential, Husky, of buying that brick house on Grover Street. You know the one?"

"Yes," he said. "The old Curley house. It's been empty for a year or two."

"They want twenty thousand, which seems like the earth. But I'm such a child in these things. What would you think?"

"I don't know," he said. "It depends on the condition." One good turn, he thought. Yes, why not? "I could have a look at it, if that would be any help."

"Oh, would you, Husky? Simply marvelous. Could you possibly on Monday?"

"Any time you like," he said. If he looked over the Curley house, the word would be all round town by Monday evening that he was buying the place. If he looked at it alone with her, the word would be that he was setting up the charming widow in a summer nest. Hazards of Gallery. "Who has the key?"

"Becker, the plumber man," she said.

"Fine," he said. "Lee Becker won't let on to put the price up. Perhaps best if I go alone and have a word with him."

"Of course," she said. "You're so good, Husky."

"That's not difficult," he said. They crossed the asphalt to the hangar. Flume Hill was already a decrepitude, ex-wartime station now in civil use. He had built it. There was one DC-3 in the hangar, and the Summit Construction amphibian, round which Sally prowled alone, as if she had never seen this or any plane before.

"I hope you'll know it the next time," he said. "How did you get on, pooch?"

"Mac let me fly, Daddy. He really did. He showed me how it worked —ailerons and rudder and everything—and I did it with him for a bit to get the feeling. Then he took his feet off and folded his arms and sat back in the other seat and said: *She's all yours, chum.* So we flew on straight or pretty wiggly because I was hopeless at it. But we did. And then I did turns, just gentle ones, without him helping once. Oh, hullo, Mrs. Parkyn," she said politely, in absent bliss.

"Hullo, Sally," said Grace Parkyn.

"Didn't I, Mac?" He had come from the office. "Didn't I fly it by myself?"

"Correct," he said. He was introduced to Grace. And on the way to the car, when Sally had run for the exuberance of flying, Mac said: "She has the touch, that child, the same easy nerveless hands you had from the beginning."

"Did I? You never told me."

"No," said Mac. "Tell them they're good, you puff them up. Tell them they're bad, you crack them down. Say they're doing well or doing badly, so do better."

"It sounds like a complete philosophy of life," Grace Parkyn said.

"Takes in flying," Mac said. "I wouldn't say it takes in everything." He bestowed upon her—bestowed was the word—his attention, his lurk of intention. Anna once said: *That small man is sweet and dangerous, and women know it.*

Grace Parkyn drove home, with Mac beside her, the Skafes behind. She drove fairly well, or safely. She wore two or three gold bracelets with numerous gold charms like Scorpio, St. Christopher, poodle, hunting boot on her slim tanned wrist on the steering wheel. She and Mac talked all the way. Sally's exhilaration had worn off. She leaned to her father and hissed: "Mummy hates silly tinkling bracelets, and so do I."

He was amused if apprehensive about the elemental nature of his daughter. Trust Mac, he thought, to set her straight in the kindly way, ignore her altogether now, talk another language with a real grown-up woman.

There was no demarcation line of cloud, but the blue dimmed down to plumbeous at the islands. A storm was moving out at sea.

CHAPTER TEN

THE BAND were pretty terrible, but they could strum it out and even hit the sweet slow sobs with "Smoke Gets in Your Eyes," the murky lights, the rosin shuffle of a floor that you could skate on. She hummed "Smoke Gets in Your Eyes" with a coal-black mammy's hum. They did not dance in a clinch or cheek to cheek but rather decorously, *a bed is a bed is not a foxtrot* was her *mot* with which he agreed. "Hum, hum—hum—hum, hum-hum . . ." she hummed, impeccable rhythmist, and he saw, through the kaleidoscopic swirl of faces, dresses, dinner jackets, Solly and his College Strummers, "Hullo there, Husky—How are you, Sam?"—he saw Anna in that cabin humming, it was fourteen years ago beside the old man cold man Mackenzie River. "Humdinger woman, you can hum," he grumbled now.

She laughed and said: "I wish I could keep you like this always, slightly tipsy, funny man." She wore the dress, her portrait one, of crimson brocade, or lamé would it be, who cares. It might evoke *Good Gods* at breakfast, but here in the Chalet at the apogee of Gallery season 1946 it was a flame, a flaunt, a marvel to make lesser ladies purse their lips. He wondered when and where she got it, did not know. He supposed she wore it to help the artist to his missing link. Dorrien seemed rather down tonight.

Now Solly's "Smoke Gets in Your Eyes" moaned finally, and Solly would not play again. Skafe followed her past the long table where the fashionable party sat. The Merchants were twenty-five or so (Jack Merchant of Dominion Oil), whence Bob Carter beckoned to him and he bent an ear. "If you're sitting out the next one, come on over. There's a young fellow here I'd like you to meet."

"Right, Bob," he said, and made a suave way from the table—Brewers, Lynes, Sharps, Broughtons, Williamses—"Hullo, Jack, quite a party." To which the Skafes had been invited.

So back across the floor to pink champagne, and everything was lovely.

"We'd better have another one, Marcel. And a brandy and soda; and a rye."

"R-right away, Mr. Skafe." Marcel slid the chair tenderly to meet his sit-upon, attentive maître d'hôtel, encouraged by ten dollars on arrival.

It was an egg-shaped room, with Solly and his Strummers at the broader end. The quality, lords of the manor, the cream were ranged along the eggshell walls below the band. The dance floor was a truncated yolk. The rest of the egg was occupied by hotel guests and similar common herd. It was gala night without balloons.

"Grace," he said to the lady in the sapphire blue. "Missing one, will you dance with me?"

"Love to, Husky." She was softly animated, pretty dish. Any maids and matrons round about the Chalet would be apt to feel eclipsed by Mr. Skafe's duet of women. But Mr. Skafe was sharing them with Dorrien and MacNamara. David Dorrien drank brandy and smoked cigarettes. He was melancholy sober, looking at the people, back to here. Mac MacNamara hit rye and water with a will, rolled a cigarette as skillfully as ever, licked it, lit it, a proper tuxedoed gangster on the spree. "Jeepers," he said with awe about the Merchants' party. "Look at them rocks on them poor old bitches."

That drew Dorrien from his preoccupation to cackle or neigh with laughter. He and Mac were poles apart and seemed to think each other funny.

Marcel spun a new bottle, slosh and clink about the bucket, personal service for Mr. Skafe, who drank champagne with Grace and Anna, the never-never land of pink champagne. And once again—it must have been some word that jogged the recollection—he thought of Jim Willis in the cabin, poor old Jim with his dream of gold in the Nahanni country. Queer that he should think of that world here and now when he so rarely thought of it, nor shunned it from his mind.

Solly snapped his fingers to snap the College Strummers into "Lili Marlene," a tricky time. "Come on, Gracie," said Mac. "Let's throw a leg around together." Anna and Dorrien went dancing too.

Skafe skirted the floor to Bob Carter, who sat off the end of the Merchant table with the young fellow he wanted him to meet. Bob had suggested that he employ a top-class financial man. In fact, Skafe had thought of that long ago, but by all means let it be Carter's pet idea for him. He guessed now, he had a hunch, that this casual encounter might be within a scheme of things. Bob Carter's business life was all his life except his golf, and even the golf could serve the business.

"Husky, this is Miles Sleeman."

"How d'you do, Mr. Skafe." He wore a cream-colored dinner jacket, black waistcoat with a gold watch chain and a seal, black trousers, a signet ring, a red carnation, an inverted V of silk handkerchief, brushed up hair—expensive clothes on a slim young man, a voice with overtones of English, an attentive deliberateness of manner that was striking in a fellow of under thirty, perhaps twenty-eight. Skafe had a doctor's eye for a man's age or a woman's.

"Are you down for the weekend?" he said somewhat obviously to Sleeman who sat again in a wickerwork chair with finger tips joined, the eight of them and the thumbs.

"Yes, sir. Mr. and Mrs. Carter very kindly asked me."

"I have decided to take Miles on as my personal instructor," Carter said. "He got me round that course in eighty-nine this morning—shot a seventy-five himself, and gave me fifteen strokes."

"And you pipped me on the post, sir. Mr. Carter is a hard man to beat," he said to Skafe. "What the Scots call a pawky player. Are you a golfer, Mr. Skafe?"

"I like to play at the game," he said, "when I find time for it."

"Which, with your activities in recent years, cannot have been much," said Sleeman, smiling.

"No," he said. "Not much." You're too studied, he thought.

"I wish that all my business affairs could be so satisfactorily linked with the golf links—linked with the links, not bad, eh? Apart from being my teacher, Miles is doing some tax work for me."

So his hunch had been right; and if Miles Sleeman was doing tax work for Bob Carter, he must be an able young man indeed. Skafe watched the dancing. Mac and Grace were certainly throwing a leg around. Mac did not dance in character with the meticulously careful master pilot. He danced in character with the fighter boy whooping it up on Saturday night, a gladsome romp, but he kept his balance with Grace Parkyn. Poor Anna plowed it around with Dorrien who had no sense of time whatever. He pumped her arm, stooping over her, and she was laughing. The music ended.

Sleeman stood up and away to let the dancers in behind the table. "Miles is an outstanding lad," Bob Carter said aside. "He's with Steele and Layton, marrying Busty Maxwell's girl next month. I think he's the man for you, if you can get him."

The outstanding accountant would be linked (and linked on the links) by marriage to Busty Maxwell, eminent stockbroker, best in Montreal, many people said. It sounded promising. Skafe did not intend to be railroaded by Bob Carter or by anyone. But if Bob Carter described

Sleeman as outstanding, he would be just that. "Thanks, Bob," he said. "We'll see." He stood to leave before being absorbed in the Merchant fold. "Won't you come over a moment and meet my wife?" he said. Anna was in an excellent mood.

"I should be delighted, Mr. Skafe."

Sleeman and Dorrien had already met *chez* Carter. He introduced him around: "And this is Wing Commander MacNamara."

"Wing Commander my foot," said Mac. "I'm the chauffeur."

Sleeman took that with urbane aplomb, accepted half a glass of pink champagne, and sipped at it. "Delicious," he said. He made small talk with Grace about the summer season. "It's been so gay," she said. He flicked a gold Dunhill lighter for her cigarette. "And back to town, Mrs. Skafe?"—"On Monday's train," she said. "Worse luck." She was in cracking form tonight, but even tonight she would harp about what a bore to go back to town after a whole summer's idleness or gardening. "The last time I had pink champagne," said Sleeman, "was on VJ-Day."

"Where?" said Mac. "In a foxhole on a desert island?"

"No such luck. I was in Washington with our Purchasing Mission."

"Sounds luckier than a foxhole." Mac was not offensive, but a little bellicose, his cold eyes choleric with liquor. "Where're you from?" he said.

"From London," Sleeman said. "Where are you from, Wing Commander?"

"My Daddy was from Medicine Hat, and my Mummy was from Moosejaw. You can take your pick." In fact, he came from Traill, B.C. "London, you say. Did you go to school at Eton?"

"London, Ontario," said Sleeman equably. "I went to T.C.S."

"I went to Moosejaw High, or Medicine Hat High, I can't remember which." Mac thought he was extremely funny, encouraged by Anna and Dorrien. It was so typical of Anna that if she scented business, as she always could, she would not lift a finger to be polite to someone produced by him.

So he and Grace and Sleeman talked about nothing much until the next dance began, when Sleeman excused himself. Skafe went a few steps with him. "Would you have lunch with me in town some day?" he said. "I'll telephone."

"Thank you so much," Sleeman said. He shook hands firmly, gravely. "Goodnight, S.K."

S.K. stood for Simon Kepple Skafe, just as C.D. stood for the great Clarence Decatur Howe. It was less rough and bluff than *Husky*. S.K. was a new one to him, didn't sound so bad.

"Who's that?" said Mac. "A pal of yours?"

"No," he said. "I've never met him before."

"Smooth kind of squirt," Mac said. "You know," he said, "I can take a real English Etonian SOB like this one." He indicated Dorrien by a waving hand. "I can take the goddam genuine patronizing article and like him, even love the bastard. But these imitation Bond Street Canucks with the swept-up sideburns, the suede shoes and the la-di-da—oh, Jesus!"

"Mac!" said Anna sharply. "Stop saying Jesus, please."

"Sorry," he said, and subsided in his chair. Mac was well away and going further fast. He stayed sober on and off the job, and he usually watched his language with the women, and he usually retired into a taciturn shell if he did not like people. "Thirsty," he said.

"Our dance, Grace."

It was a rumba, and she could dance. She was better than Anna, being featherlight to the hand. They danced hot Negro rhythm well enough to be the showpiece of the floor, to be Solly's favorite rhythm makers. "Dancing too," she said, and when the second encore finished, she leaned close to him for thanks and pleasure and stood away. "Lovely," she said.

"Mac's feeling no pain," he said, en route. He was not entirely best pleased with Mac.

"No," she said, "and rather pinchy-minded."

"That could be taken as a compliment."

"It does depend on the pinchy mind," she said, and smiled. "He was rude to that nice Mr. Sleeman too. I don't see why people have to be rude."

"Nor do I," said Simon Skafe. He did not think that Sleeman was nice, but he thought that Sleeman's equability and poise were remarkable if allied to the talents of which Bob Carter was so sure. " 'Dance, dance, dance little lady,' " he said now to Grace Parkyn.

"Why did you say that suddenly?"

"Because you can and do," he said, "and because I'm enjoying myself."

"Such a heavenly time," she said.

"Husky, old boy," said Mac in a bleary whisper. "How many millions in this room, just on a guess, how many?"

"I haven't a clue," he said. Nor did he; nor would he guess for a pie-eyed Mac.

"What I want to know is does it make the poor bums happy?" He tried to roll a cigarette from the pewter box, spilt tobacco. "Oh, hell," he said. "Give us a tailor-made."

"They look happy enough," Skafe said. The Merchants' table, where the main load lay, looked very happy.

"You think they're happy, Davie boy? You're an intellectual, you tell me, Dave."

"First define happiness," Dorrien said. "Two months here, how do I know? But I wouldn't say that bridge and golf and cocktail parties provide a satisfying or a stable end for wealth."

"They aren't an end for wealth," Skafe said. "They're a vacation for it. Almost everyone in this room goes back to work on Tuesday to put whatever wealth there is to constructive use.

"Doesn't that make sense?" he said, but moderately, in and out of his party mood.

"Excellent sense," said Dorrien. "I only meant that the climate and the size of Canada prevent private wealth from going into land, from living on the land. That once was the strength of Britain. Here you're still sane. Here, there is no class feeling worth speaking of, and the rich man isn't a public enemy. But here, alas, the rich man's wife spends twenty or thirty thousand to switch the summer cottage round for the sake of spending cash on something. She isn't satisfied with her whim, and so she switches it back next year. That's what Hermione Merchant is going to do."

"It's true," Anna said. "Isn't it, Simon?"

"Yes," he said. "It's a quarter truth, or even half. But do you know how much the Merchants give to charity? Or the work Hermione does in Montreal? Or how she helps people secretly?"

"I don't know," said Dorrien. "But I can guess." He was sober and reasonable, and he looked at Anna. "The generosity of people in this country is amazing."

"Half a million would help me as a deep dark secret," MacNamara said. "Asked a simple question: *Are they happy?* in the camel's eye, or you know what, was all I did, or did I? Now you make speeches. Let not your left hand know on Sunday morning, Husky boy, just tell Hermie Whatnot as a special secret." Mac was haggard, sweaty, more than middling drunk and quarrelsome. "Christ!" he said loudly enough to turn half the heads.

"Mac," said Skafe. "Pipe down!"

"Who says *Pipe down?*"

"I say it. Now you do it."

"Scared of me making an exhibition of you before the big tycoons?"

"Okay," he said, leaning across Grace's chair to Mac, his left hand out.

He was annoyed. "Either you stop it, or I'll stand you up and sock you. Then we'll really have an exhibition. Which is it to be?"

Mac smiled a beautifully loving sozzled smile. "Tough old bastard," he said. "You would."

He caught Anna's eye. She nodded. It was eleven-thirty, early yet. "Come on, Mac," he said. "Homeward bound."

Mac put his hand on Grace's knee. "Want my Gracie. Love you, Anna, but I want my happy happy Gracie. Gracie's happy, take me home."

"All right, Mac," she said. "Happy Gracie's coming too."

They slipped out by the door behind their table as Solly's drummer rolled for the cabaret, smooth exit. Mac needed only a guiding hand, and they found her car, and sat three in front.

"Sorry," Mac said. "Thought I was over it."

"Over what, Mac?"

"Bashed cranium. Seems not. Drink too much, go bang. You hate me, Gracie?"

"No," she said. "I love you when you're nice." She was good with him, must have handled drunks before, perhaps her Air Vice-marshal used to tipple. "Be nice now, Mac, I said. Don't put me through the wringer."

"I was sad," Mac said. "Got plastered." He sat quiet to the house, where he got out, kissed Grace's hand with a courtly bow, and tacked for the bathroom and the bed.

Skafe found him three aspirins, Bisodol, a couple of extra pillows. "There's a boy," he said, as to a boy. "Will you be all right?"

"Fine," Mac said. "Pay the bill tomorrow." He closed his eyes, then sat up straight. "You know," he said with elegant care, "you're the best bloody fool of the lot of them. But y'ought to see an oculist." *Oklist*, he said it, and lay back and was asleep.

Skafe sought Toddy, whose room lay between Mac and the children. She was awake, of course. "Puir lamb," she said, indulgent to the frailties of men in general, and scarred heroes in particular. "I'll listen for him."

"Does Mac often get so terribly squiffy?" Grace said in the car.

"Never," he said. "I wouldn't know why tonight. Blowing off steam, I guess. Three and a half years in Fighters, the rest of the war in Transport Command, this last year hard at it with us; never has unwound, if he needs to unwind. But you can't tell with Mac. He doesn't give about himself."

"He worships you," she said. "He gives that much about himself."

It was a warm night, hot enough for the leather seat of her Buick, top up now, to make his dinner jacket trousers sticky to his legs. He turned onto the highway, over the hill. He did not think that Mac worshiped him. Mac told him to see an oculist, whatever that might mean, if anything. Now the shore again.

"Oh, listen!" she said.

It was the bell buoy, heaving to a swell, but why a swell in the sheltered bay when the night was flat calm and no boats were passing? He stopped to listen to the lazy metronomic tolling of the bell. "It must be that storm," he said, remembering his father's phrase: that hurricanes had long fingers in weather.

"How do you mean, Husky?"

He explained that a distant storm could ring an ocean. "It's such a lonely sound," she said. She shivered in the still warm night without stars but with a glimmer of the moon through cloud; then Simon Skafe, who was not nearly old enough to know better, put a comforting arm around the widow's shoulder, and she caught her breath, much wanting to be kissed, and he indulged her wish and his.

She was not a feast of woman, but more cuddly, only word for that soft eagerness of arms and lips and all. Then she pushed him away. "You're gentle," she said, "for what Mac calls a tough old B."

It was a nice little joke, and the fog bell tolled. A car's lights were showing beyond the corner, so he started up and drove again, elapsed time a couple of minutes, and the hour was midnight. He was a virtuous husband, not given to flirtatious parkings or liaisons, although occasionally virile desperation had driven him to release. The other car went past. "If you stop just a sec again," she said, "I'll make sure I didn't put lipstick on you." He stopped while she compounded a small conspiracy with the aid of his lighter and her handkerchief, and a zephyr of that expensive perfume. "There," she said, touching his cheek with her hand. "Bad boy."

"Bad girl," he said inanely. She sat close to him until they reached the street lamps. "Widows are fair game," she said. "Almost every man I meet makes passes at me."

"Meaning me?" Meaning him would be a bit much, considering.

"Not meaning you," she said. "That's what I meant. But you're so absolutely all a man."

After which most gratifying obliquity, he drove in silence to the Chalet, or its environs, to park, and to accompany his girl friend in the sapphire blue, both casual as be damned, to more festivity.

"You were quick," Anna said. "The bar was closing, so I ordered us a final bottle."

"Good," he said. "Let's dance." He felt just great. He took a swig of the lovely prickle-tonguing stuff, and danced with her. It was "Night and

Day," another vintage tune by Solly and his College Strummers. The floor was a jostling pack of celebrants, all on high, and not one drunk. They met the rest of their party, Dorrien and Grace, the other half, as ships pass in the night, or cars pass at the Point. Dorrien smiled from him to Anna. Grace smiled from Anna to him, and so on round the rosin-rasping skating floor. "Dear Mac," she said, words tickling in his ear. "I wonder why he got so tight."

"He said he was sad; and he said that since his crash, drink sent him bang. Thought he was over that. What would old Mac be sad about? He seemed in fine form all day."

"It happens to people," she said. "Did you have any trouble getting him to bed?"

"He went like a lamb, swallowed his aspirins etcetera, lay down, sat up like a jack-in-the-box, and told me to consult an oculist." Skafe laughed. Any craziness of Mac's was quite okay by him.

"An *oculist*," she said. "Oh, did he?" They danced on round, and she said: "Let's have a drink." So they dropped the third after-dinner bottle, grand stuff to dance with on a sultry night. Anna drank even-steven with him; she had excellent capacity. He danced again with Grace, a Viennese waltz. "I'm a little bit high," she said, elated not inebriated. Her feet flew more cleverly, of their own thought, volition, intuition to match his feet, the small of her back in the frame of his hand. "I think I'd rather dance with you than anything," she informed him in strict confidence.

"Than anything?" asked the bold devil, Skafe.

"Bad man," she giggled. The party spirit was riding out.

Not all the time. "Do you entertain much in Montreal?" she asked. "Not much," he said. "Anna doesn't like it." Loosened traitor's tongue.

"Oh, doesn't she?" Grace said. "Anna's so sweet."

You don't know how sweet she can be, he thought, for he nursed a grudge about Miles Sleeman, and his thoughts were not all sweet thoughts.

It was nearly one, and Sunday morning, and positively the last dance of Gallery season Nineteen Forty-six. Solly snapped his fingers this final time, and everyone rolled out the barrel, the first one, the last one with the wife. What nonsense about grudges. A polka, a gallop, and all was done. There is no way to halt the gallop to the end of pleasure.

He faced Solly and his College Strummers for "God Save the King," at attention, knuckles touching the trouser seams. Jack Merchant, Bob Carter, most of them had served the King in an earlier war. But he had not served, and the regret lived on with him, as it always would. He was a Loyalist Skafe and, he hoped, a fighting man, but he had not fought. Also, he revered the good plain king.

He signed the bill, tipped the college-boy waiter and thanked Marcel. Ten dollars was quite enough. No, what did it matter, give him a five. "Have a good winter, Marcel."

"Goodnight, Anna dear," Grace said, "thank you a million times. Goodnight, Husky. It's been such a marvelous party. You won't forget about the house?"

"No," he said. He never failed in what he undertook to do, but why bring it up? "Goodnight, Grace."

They dropped Dorrien at the Carters' cottage. "On Monday morning, Anna, then."

"Yes, David," she said.

"Monday," he said. "Goodnight."

"Don't worry," she said. "It'll be all right. Goodnight."

"Goodnight, Simon," he said, "and thank you both for being kind to me."

They headed for the Point and home. "I'm getting to like that fellow," he said. "Much less of the inimitable arrogance."

"He's not arrogant," she said, "at least about his work. This painting seems to haunt him."

"Important subject," he said. But she did not respond to the raillery. "What was that Grace said about a house?"

"She's thinking of buying the Curley place. I said I would look at it for her."

Anna chuckled, not the indolent chuckle entirely. He would have liked to ask why, but he did not wish to be ridiculed.

"Oh, listen!" she said, same place, opposite direction, about the bell buoy tolling to the swell. "Let's stop. I do love that sound."

"We can hear it from home," he said. "Let's go to bed. Bed! Come on!" He felt a muddle of who and where and all that champagne, but he knew what he wanted.

"Always bed," she said, "and bed is nothing. Come on, then!"

Once again, as he drove her home in the growth of passion—once again tonight, he thought back to the North, to a boat in a hiss of candle ice when all was new, good, ruthless, simple. It was a making then, not a saving.

CHAPTER ELEVEN

"TROUBLE," she said in the morning. "Nothing but trouble." It was late, and he brought her breakfast up to find her still hunched in bed, staring out at the gray sea and the grayish droop of cloud that came from the sea. Her face was plain, indeed ugly, and she did not thank him for her breakfast.

He shaved, not much liking his own ugly face, pinker than usual from dissipation, pussyfooting voluptuary. His mouth was dry but he felt all right. He dressed and listened again to gale warnings, rain warnings, flood warnings for this coast. The announcer's voice had a fevered sort of gloat about trouble coming, a relish similar to that used when describing fatal highway accidents or families of eight being burned to death. Which particular horror trait made him feel ill about humanity; but the exhilaration of a storm on the way was another thing. "What, Anna? I didn't hear."

"I said: Must you persecute me with that thing?"

"Sorry," he said, and shut it off. When Anna's goblins were present— hangover goblins, storm goblins, whatever—the world was in conspiracy against her, and he was the arch conspirator. Still, he could have closed the door.

He went to see Mac, whose troubles were not the real ones of imagination but of physical pain. The blinds were down. He lay with his hands over his eyes like See-No-Evil. "Oh, dear," he muttered. He moved a hand to ward off aspirins, barbiturates, codeine. "Oh dear," beyond all oaths and blasphemy.

"Let me get the doctor, Mac." It might only be an epic hangover, which Mac deserved. But he was worried about him. What sort of lunacy would make a man with a bashed cranium get drunk? Yet Mac was flying fit. All mad, he thought. All stark raving crazy, me included. He said it again about the doctor.

Mac mumbled that the thing would wear off, what he deserved, no need of a doctor. His face contorted from the effort of speech.

Skafe had breakfast, and drove his father and his family to church. The cloud mass rolled in from the southeast, but no wind and still no rain. His mind wandered through the service. He believed in the Christian life, in the simplicity of Christ, in praying for those in peril on the sea. But he was not a thoroughgoing Christian. Anna once told him that he did not have the humility to be a Christian. True or untrue? How would he know about himself? Besides, he did not find his immortal soul particularly interesting. But he liked, he loved the Christian family at church, for his father and his children were devout, and he saw the secret haunt of *Nothing but trouble* ease in Anna's face. Old Mr. Mackenzie bumbled on about the parable of the Talents, which Simon Skafe could understand in terms of tough business but not of Christian teaching; nor, he thought, could Mr. Mackenzie.

The sermon ended and the rain began. It came in gouts and gushets, a deluge loud about the church as the organ played a preliminary verse to "God of Bethel." The wind struck at the tall elms outside. It was easy for him to feel God in the wind and the rain about the church.

"'. . . Through each perplexing path of life,'" he sang, "'Our wandering footsteps guide.'" Sally sang lightly and sweetly beside him, and Anna sang now beyond John on the other side, and the two John Skafes sang hardly at all. "Lili Marlene," he thought. Kiss the widow, embrace the wife. Oh, God of Bethel. What a muddle. But now, as the storm began and the service ended, he did know a cleanness of the spirit.

"Let's see if we can get the weather, John," he said at home. The rain slammed in buckets at the windows, and the lawn was flooded. The storm now headed to strike across Nova Scotia and into the Bay of Fundy between 7 and 9 P.M., with gusts of ninety miles an hour, but winds were expected to diminish . . . "That's strong enough," he said.

"Simon, do we have to have that thing?"

"We must get the weather, Anna," he said reasonably. Must we bury our heads like ostriches? he did not say. John switched it off.

They had roast sirloin of beef for Sunday lunch. "How nice not to carve for once," she said. The tender undercut sliced nicely, moistly, with a touch of pink. "It's perfect, Toddy," he said. "Trust you." Yorkshire pudding, horse-radish and the rest.

The wind was growing. It leaned—was that John's word?—it leaned upon the house. The rain eased for a while. "My poor roses," Anna said at the window. She went to her desk and started sorting drawers. It was always untidy; now she made a worse mingled chaos of it. She had no sense of order. Then she shuffled magazines. Then she moved a standard lamp to the corner by the dining room door and moved it back, that kind of small frigging restlessness which was not like her, but she was afraid of wind.

"Darling," he said. "Why not go and have a sleep?"

"Because I couldn't sleep."

It was Toddy's half Sunday off. He drove her to town to her friend Miss Gillespie, who was Gladys Broughton's personal maid. He saw the Buick outside the Broughtons' luncheon party, and would have liked to see the owner, no such luck. He came back, always unhurriedly on the go, to find his father in an armchair. His children played checkers in a caged fashion on the floor. He went to see Mac, who had eaten nothing, and whose head was no better but no worse. He lay with his eyes closed, oblivious of storms, of all but the pain in his head, which was so piercingly bad that Skafe could feel it out of sympathy. Mac now accepted two codeine tablets. *No*, about the doctor. *No need.*

"Father," Skafe said. "We're in for quite a blow. Won't you spend the rest of the day with us?"

"No, thanks," said that monument of obstinacy and settled habit. "I'll ride it out in my corner. I must batten the place down too."

He drove his father home. It was raining again, and harder, two or three inches already. The windshield wiper made no impression. "I'll fix that door," he said. Tom Beamish would have been around by now to see to such things, but Tom had gone to Maine for Sunday night.

The barn door opened outward. He wedged a length of two-by-four against the latch. Now the wedge was stronger than the door. A mess of small branches lay about the yard, and maple leaves were flying. He shielded his eyes against flat rain from the southeast and went into the house. His father was filling basins and buckets with water. He took some pleasure in his storm precautions, but he went about them slowly. Old men must fail in vigor.

"Father," he said. "I know how much you like being at home, but there's nothing to do here in the winter that Tom Beamish can't look after. Would you consider going south, say to Florida? Anna and I would like to find you a small house, nothing fancy."

He said that the winter was easy . . . best time of the year . . . old dogs and new tricks and so on. He said a courteous No, but he qualified it: "If you and Anna would keep me company, I might go for a spell near the end of winter."

"I'm sure Anna would," Skafe said. "You know how much she enjoys being with you. But it's not easy for me at present. I might manage a week perhaps. Why don't you go with Anna?"

"I also said you," his father said, with a rare nip of asperity. "Now for the lamps," he said, that subject closed. He poured the kerosene carefully through a filler, screwed on the caps of the old-fashioned lamps, and fiddled with the wicks. The house creaked in the wind. "Look, son . . . !" he said.

"Yes, Father?" *Look!* he said, a figure of speech. Simon Skafe looked at his father's blue eyes, the same color as his own. They were standing by the kitchen sink, and the daylight was dim, a grayish brown of storm piling in from sea. "Yes?" he said, to encourage him.

"I've been wanting to have a word with you. It's not my business, but I am your father, and I guess there are times for all of us when we might run into troubles that we could have avoided if we had seen them coming . . ."

"Yes, Father?" he said again. John Skafe needed help, being diffident and not articulate.

"You're a successful man already, bolder, abler and far more prominent than any of us have been. And, unless I'm a Dutchman, you haven't even got started yet. What's more, success comes to you fair and square, or you want no part of it. I'm proud of you, Simon. Your word is your bond, and you're doing great things for this country . . ."

Your word is your bond. It was true. Or, as a partner once had said: *Nobody needs an I O U from Husky Skafe.* It was equally true that his father did not pay large compliments without there being a catch somewhere.

The downpour eased to a heavy rain, but the wind grew on. He listened carefully to what his father had to say, which was that he neglected Anna. The children too, perhaps, but they went to good schools; they were growing up; they had all life before them. It mattered less that he was little with John than that he neglected his wife.

"But, Father . . ." he said, and explained patiently yet once more the difficulties of this critical year. For the first time he told him of his plans for a financial man.

"That should be a help," said John Skafe. "But being more at home is not just all that's wanted. What a woman like Anna or any woman needs is plain to be needed. She needs to know that she matters to you. Oh, I know that your marriage has been successful in the . . . in the . . ." he was shy about it, "in the sexual way. Anyone could see that. But sex is not everything, whatever Mr. Freud may say." His eye brightened a little about Freud, whom he thought a charlatan. "Sex goes, and then you have nothing. What I'm afraid of, son, is that your world is getting to be your own world, bigger every day, with no part for Anna in it. Then what good would fifty million dollars be?"

"I only want money to do what I want," he said.

"I know that, Simon. But you want to do a lot." His father smiled at him, less diffident now. He might be talking nonsense, but so selfless a man could not be resented.

"Father," he said. "You say that Anna needs me, but that's not a one-way street. What about me? How can I get help from Anna when all my business is anathema to her?"

"If business seemed to matter less to you, it might matter more to Anna. Have you tried taking her into your confidence, talking to her?"

"Often," he said. "She won't listen. She won't even be polite to my business people who come to the house, unless it happens to be Wilson Pitt or someone she likes. Father," he said, "is there anything indecent about a man having ambition?"

Where would Canada be without ambition? Grace Parkyn said yesterday. And who took the trouble to be agreeable to Miles Sleeman, a possible man to free him to see more of his wife and children? Did Anna? But he could not say these things to his father, who shook his head, agreeing that ambition was not indecent. "Anna is jealous, Father," he said. "Let's face it."

"Yes, my dear boy," his father said. "But what if she stops being jealous?"

She might improve for a day or two, but he did not think that it was in her nature to stop being jealous.

"You have quite a wife there, you know," said old John Skafe.

He had a wife who was intelligent, sensitive, beautiful, he ticked them off in his head. Who spent little on herself, was generous, unselfish, amusing in the mood, both passionate and sympathetic, good to the children, a saint with simple people. She had almost everything except that she had to have all of him without respecting all of him. Also beyond the fence were her intolerance and violent temper. "Anna's a great person," he said. The husband's comment, it sounded absurdly hollow.

"So are you," his father said. "Best couple I know, but I'm prejudiced. Well, son," he said, setting the lamps on the table, "I didn't want to interfere. Just thought . . . Now listen to that!" It was a first big gust. It thrummed on the house and shook the house and passed on its way.

"You're pretty exposed here, Father. Why not change your mind and come home with me?"

"The old house has stood some time, it'll stand some more, might even outlast your newfangled job." He smiled about that, not to give offense. "If the electricity fails, I have my water and my lamps and a good roof over my head. What else do I want?"

"Okay," he said. "But if the power goes off, put a lamp beside the window, and then we'll know that roof is still here. Well, I'd better be getting back. Thanks, Dad," he said, using the boyhood term. "Thanks for your advice."

"Good fellow," John Skafe said.

He put on his oilskin and his cap and went out to the tropical storm. The deluge was as warm as a tepid bath. They were born off Barbados somewhere, and spun and grew and tarried and hurried to die at last.

He held the car against wind, then was into the shelter of the cedar wood. The ditches were overflowing. No trees had fallen. It was not much of a wind, for the hurricane had not yet come, and the hurricane was on the way to dying. He was strongly quickened by the storm. It's all very well, he thought, but a woman must sink herself in her marriage, which means in her husband's career. It's all very well for Father to talk. But then he remembered that his mother had ruled the Skafe roost. Yes, but she deferred invariably and altogether to the great male mystique of the Canadian Pacific. But I must be better, he thought. I must encourage her and turn my cheek and all the rest of it.

He put the car away and found John to help him with the boat. They hauled it well above the spring-tide mark, and tied the painter to a wild apple tree. "Johnny Appleseed did his work around here," he said in the companionship of the big warm wind and the small wet job. It was one hour of flood at five o'clock. The tide now edged over glistening mud-flats. On the other side where the shore was steep, he saw beyond his aircraft ramp to the thrash of sea in a curtain of rain. Gulls turned to cry overhead, to fight the wind and to yield, tossed high inland.

They looked at the pond. The dam was holding, but the flood overrode the spillway. "See the power of water, John," he said. "If it gets much bigger, something must give."

They splashed across the lawn with a gale at their backs. "Poor Mum's poor roses," John said, or he shouted in the wind. Tight buds, whole blooms, a strew of petals—white, yellow, scarlet, crimson, pink, gradations, multicolors. "Blown petals—how does it go?" Skafe said, in his quickening to the storm.

> "There is sweet music here that softer falls
> Than petals from blown roses on the grass."

John looked at him, a wet young face. "Doesn't fall too softly, Dad," he said. They were in sympathy now in this storm.

Some garden chairs had taken flight. They put them in. "Fill the baths with water, John," he said. "And see what you can dig out in the way of candles, lamps, and flashlights." Knowing Anna, he rather doubted . . .

"Okay, Dad."

Skafe went round outside the house and found an open window in the one locked room, the makeshift studio. He had a master key to deal with that, and, after removing his outer wetness in the porch, he went to do so. The canvas stood on the easel, facing a corner. He decided to have a surreptitious peek.

"Simon!" she called from along in the study.

"Yes?" he said. He locked the door behind him.

"What are you doing? How did you get in there?"

"Darling, you know I have a master key to all the rooms. There was a window wide open. I didn't look," he added, good boy.

"You have keys to everything," she said, and took out a Katherine Mansfield to open it and slap the hard covers shut and put it back. She liked Mansfield, Willa Cather, Virginia Woolf, Edith Wharton, both the Brontës and some other women writers, but not Jane Austen particularly. Now she slapped her beloved Katherine Mansfield as if it had been an Ethel M. Dell. "How I hate this wind," she said.

He went to get her a drink, which would be apt to help. He did not know why she feared great winds so much; nor did he think that it would be because of some psychiatric link to an Atlantic storm in infancy, or any such tripe. People feared things. He feared heights and she feared winds. He was aware in a sort of a way that the storm made him a more sympathetic, understanding chap. "Here," he said. "The doctor prescribes a rye and water."

She drank half of it and put it down, and went on dusting by open and snap.

"I tried to persuade Father to go south this winter," he said. "I think he almost might, if you and I went with him."

"You?" she said. "Well, that settles that excursion."

"Perhaps not," he said, and went on to explain, doing his best to draw her out of herself and into things, about his idea for a man to handle day-to-day financial matters if he could find one, which would enable him . . .

"That bogus Sleeman creature, I suppose," she said, at another shelf, Joyce Cary this time.

What *is* the use? he thought. "He's a possibility. Brilliant, I understand. Why would you think of him?"

"Because of Bob Carter, your banking pundit and *éminence grise*. And because of your sacred business look in the middle of the party. You choose just as odd times to bring dreary people over as you do to bring dreary subjects up."

He left before his good resolutions left him. Anna wrote to the North and said: *Please forgive me;* then she worked up a contemptuous grudge. He checked the upstairs windows. If she would only ask for help about her troubles. But instead of that she took them out on him. This was a good stout house, however Father might disparage modern construction or modern anything. It shook now in the drive of wind.

When Toddy goes out, he thought, the rain comes in. He mopped up some puddles like some faithful janitor. Sally was reading in her room —*The Theory of Flight,* which she was not at all coy about. "You have a one-track mind," he said, and he gave her a kiss. "I must have another look at suffering Mac."

"He's better, Daddy. I heard him go into the bathroom and be most awfully sick at his stomach; so afterwards I went in and put some of Mummy's eau de cologne on him for the headache. He said it felt great. Shall we give him some more?"

"You're the boss," he said, which in a remarkable way was true. He had yet to see anything faze Miss Skafe. They went into Mac's room. He was still prostrate, but less waxen corpse-like. "Who's that?" he said.

"It's me, Mac. Would you like more of that stuff?"

"Lovely," he said.

She shook liberal dashes of expensive cologne onto the folded handkerchief and put it back on Mac's forehead. "Bless you," he said. He put his hand up to find her hand, squeezed it, dropped it. Mac had a narrow-boned hand for a man. Sally looked at him with nothing short of adoration. How absurd it was and how perilous it might be. Yet was not. Skafe found it a touching aspect of life or of love. The wind grows, he thought. And the wind will die.

Sally went back to flight, and he downstairs. "Thank you for being so patient with me," Anna said, which disarmed him. She did not blow hot or cold by design, but like a wild wind from all directions.

The power went off at seven o'clock. He checked with his father by telephone—"Not a leak in the place," John Skafe said. "What about you?"—"A few drips, Father," he admitted. "Don't forget that light."

Darkness, or a storm-ridden dusk, came early. This was no common gale. It howled and keened about the house. It heaved at the house. It was the biggest wind that he had known, although nothing to the winds they knew in southern places. He went upstairs to watch for his father's lamp. It shone three or four hundred yards away, disappeared and shone again. It came and went in the scud of the storm. He heard a tree come down behind the house. It must have been close to sound through the racket. I'd better eat something, he thought, because he knew that if this wind grew on until high water, which would be at ten o'clock, there might be flooding from the sea. Or a tree on the house was possible. Or this or that or a dozen things. It remained exhilarating, but had ceased to be amusing. He tried the telephone; that had gone. He ate a roast beef sandwich and sent John up to check on the lamp. "I can't even see the house in the flashes." A thunderstorm was contributing too.

"Let's have a look." They watched until a lessening of the sheet of rain showed the old gaunt house by lightning. The flash image faded in his eyes, and he saw the shape or the shadow of his father's house. "It's gone out," he and John said together. They waited through another squall. "I'd better go," he said, with a private curse about his father's self-sufficiency or pride. "Get me the best flashlight, John," he said, and made for the porch. "Anna," he called to tell her. "Anna!" up the stairwell and at the cellar door. But she did not answer.

He put on his rubber boots, oilskin, scarf, all wet, a sou'wester and tied it at his chin, and here was John, also dressed for the storm. "I'll come too, Dad," he said. His face was peaked, and his mouth uncertain.

"No, boy," Skafe said. "It's bad out there."

"Let me come, Dad."

"All right, then," he said, enormously pleased, enormously, and out they went. The storm fought them back to the vacuum of the house. "Shine it just ahead," he shouted. Shine it, point it, but he should not have brought the boy with him.

The arctic winds would freeze a man's eyelids together, or they would roar about the snowhouse, or they would slat and drum on the flimsy tent, murdering winds. But this great warm wind was a murderer too. I hate you, he thought about the wind he loved, for he did now fear the wind a little.

They climbed over cedars, trees falling everywhere, God's wrath everywhere. Now in the fury and the thunder, he remembered his mother's prayer. She was an Irishwoman, a Protestant O'Connor, and this was her prayer: "Oh God, give us strength for the storms of our journey."

They were halfway to the old Skafe house, at the top of the cedar wood; and here the south wind—it had veered to the south—here the south wind knocked them down. They sheltered, knee-deep in water in the ditch, until the murderer eased its grip, but the world was wind. "Come on!" he said. "Take the lull."

"Oh gosh it's awful . . . Awful!" John crouched in the water.

That teaches me, he thought. "Come on!" he shouted hardly, and pulled him out. He put John on his leeward side and held him in his arm and hustled him, and soon they reached the old Skafe house.

"What happened, Father?" The floor was a puddle, a strew of broken glass. The window was boarded half across, and the wind howled in; or it whistled and keened through narrow spaces. John Skafe sat in the kitchen rocker, but he did not rock. "I had a visitor," he said. The sea gull lay more or less unruffled against the other wall, a big white bird with the life smacked out.

"Only a herring gull," John said. He touched it with his boot and left it.

"The lamp blew out, of course. But I lit another through in the workshop, and I had some boards. I soon had her fixed." He coughed, and sipped hot rum. Woodsmoke puffed back through the seams of the stove. "Quite a wind," he said. "I don't know how you two fellows made it. You shouldn't have come. Sorry, boys," he said, pleased with them, pleased with his patch-up job. He looked very tired. "Help yourself, Simon," he said.

But Simon Skafe did not take rum. The wind had slackened. It grew again to whine through slits, to belabor the house. "I was afraid you might have that big maple on your head. Are you all right, Father?"

"I'm fine," his father said. There was some color now in his face, and his breathing had eased. "Just out of puff," he said. "Talking of puff, that wind is dropping. You'd better get back while there's time."

"Will it come again, Granka?" For a moment there had been no wind at all, not a sound but the sounds in here, the work of the stove, the boy's small voice.

"Yes," he said. "The other side will hit us, not so bad, though. Thanks, Simon. Thank you, John. You're a pretty tough fellow." He wanted to be rid of them, to be alone with his house. "I've been a darned old nuisance to you," he said.

It was not silence outside, but a rush of water, a far noise of wind or of thunder. A star, two stars showed overhead. It was an uncannily potent respite. "Is this the eye of the hurricane, Dad, they talk about?"

"Probably," he said. "Or one of several. That happens, I believe, when they're breaking up." He tried to give accurate information. Precision, exactitude were most important habits of mind for a boy to acquire.

They came to the edge of the cedar wood. "I was pretty well scared stiff in that ditch," John said, looking up at him in apology, confession, hope.

"You were pretty well pinned in there," he said. "You came out. I know men who would not have done so well." How pompous and pontifical that sounded, but how right. "Fear makes courage, John," he said. He and his son were far from each other, and he knew that it must be so. He saw that with perfect clarity in the lull of the storm; and he saw, too, that he would forget it again. Yet now, in this quiet middle place, they were father and son, one man together. "You did well, my dear boy," he said.

"Thanks, Dad."

They scrambled through the wreckage of uprooted cedars; Tom Beamish had been right. The wind was coming. It grew now from the west, a rumor, a rush, a roar, as quickly as that; and the stars had gone.

"What was that piece of yours, John, about the wind?" he said at the house. " 'Lean, wind . . .' Mum was saying it yesterday."

> "Lean, Wind, lean!
> For summer has been.
> Cry, Plover, fly!
> For the year must die.

"It's just a sort of silly verse," John said.

"Where on earth have you been?"

"Granka's lamp went out, and we thought the big maple might have blown down on the house, so we went up there. The wind was just terrific, Mum."

"So I would imagine," Anna said. She held a candle, no candlestick. The hot wax ran down, but she did not appear to notice it. Her eyes were black. He wondered if she had been hitting the bottle. He wondered if Lady Macbeth used to hit the bottle. He wondered random things. "That wind again, will it never stop? Why didn't you tell me?"

"I called," he said. "I called all over the place. Where were you?"

"I was packing," she said. "Pack, muddle, unpack, as usual."

"A sea gull blew through the kitchen window was what happened, Mum. Slap dead, it was."

"So you had a lovely time," she said.

"Oh, come on now, Anna!"

"*Oh, come on now, Anna!* Oh, come on now, John, let's see what a hurricane's like. Let's get on with the toughening process."

"That's not fair," John said. "I asked Dad, and he let me go."

"Of course he let you go."

"Not fair," John said again, quietly, obstinately. *Not fair,* a boy's ultimate plaint.

"Go and take off your clothes," he said, "and dry yourself. Quick now, John."

"Never mind, darling," he said. "The storm's nearly over, and everything is all right."

"Nothing is all right," she said. "Nothing, nothing, not even John."

He fetched himself a drink, his first, and one for her. The wind blew strongly from the land, but it was a lesser wind. "Here's luck," he said. He must go and change.

"Cheerio, old boy," she said. She began to laugh.

Enter MacNamara. He looked like death warmed up. Then he stared at Anna. "I'm glad somebody finds something funny," he said, not morosely but venomously.

It stopped her flat, and she looked at her glass. "Hullo, Mac," she said.

"Hullo," he said, mild again. "I'm hungry. I'm thirsty. I'm sorry." By design or by chance he had calmed that storm.

CHAPTER TWELVE

HE PUT the key of the Curley house under the Beckers' doormat, as arranged. Lee was spending Labor Day with his large family at his camp. Then Skafe went to report to the prospective purchaser. She must have been watching for him, because she came out of the hotel at once to stand beside the station wagon, farm utility as well as family summer car. They exchanged storm gossip.

"The place seems in pretty fair order," he said. It needed to be rewired. The furnace was archaic, but she might not want a furnace. The joists—all the wood seemed to be sound; and the bricks were good too . . . drains . . . chimneys . . . roof . . . "That's about it," he said, expert opinion. She wore a blue and white check tweed for the nip of this morning's air. It was well cut, and becoming to her.

"What shall I do then, Husky?"

"The financial side is okay?"

"Oh yes," she said. "The Laurentian Trust said that was quite all right within reason. Twenty thousand, they're asking, unfurnished, I think I told you. How much should I offer?"

"Miss Curley is a stenographer in Boston. If I were you, I would offer fifteen thousand—no, fifteen five sounds better—fifteen thousand five hundred for the place, lock stock and barrel, furniture, china, garden tools—everything, take it or leave it."

"But there are some darling things," she said, "like the Delft, and that highboy—I'm sure it's early colonial. Would she ever agree? And if she did, wouldn't it be rather mean to insist on having everything, just snap like that?"

"You might let her keep a few specified things, subject to your agreement, and of course family stuff. It may sound mean, Grace, but we know she wants to sell—she hasn't found a buyer in two years. Don't bargain with her is my advice. She's free to take it or free to leave it—and fifteen thousand five hundred looks appealing in hard cash. You can deal through Scrimby, the lawyer. Put a time limit on the offer, say a week. Then pay a deposit, get a sales agreement, and have the title searched. There are exchange control problems, of course, unless you pay in Canada. Scrimby can do all that. He's not too bad a fellow, if you watch him. Tell him you consulted me."

"You leave me rather breathless," she said. "Does your mind always work at this speed?"

"Business," he said, evading the point. "In some cases it pays to work fast. This is one, I think. First be tough; then if she agrees to sell be generous if you want to be, which I expect you will." He was quite sure that Grace would be generous. He looked at her lips, rather wanting to kiss her goodbye, because he would leave now in a minute. She understood his diversionary thought, and blushed. "To revert to business," said that swashbuckling adviser, Skafe, "can you remember what's in the house? Not a bad idea to know."

"Oh yes," she said, "that's a thing I'm quite good at, remembering things. It's all in my head. Thank you, Husky. How can I thank you?" Her eyes, the blue of her tweed coat and skirt, were quite suddenly and quite surprisingly wet.

"You're driving to Ottawa, you said. When do you leave?"

"On Wednesday, if I can see Mr. Scrimby tomorrow. Do you ever come to Ottawa?"

"Yes," he said, "fairly often on government business. Shall I call you? We might have lunch together."

"That would be simply lovely," she said. "I'm in Rockcliffe on Locust Avenue, I mean I'm in the book." She was flustered, he saw. "Goodbye then, Husky."

"Au revoir," he said. He decided against the kiss, this place not being entirely private, with bellboys in the offing; so he put his nearer hand, the left, out to hold her right hand for a short while, a second or two, and the bracelets jangled tunefully on her wrist.

But Grace Parkyn took a farewell initiative. "Au revoir," she said, and leaned in to kiss him on the cheek. "Such a kind Husky man," she murmured and went away.

He had almost forgotten the feeling of the feeling—that delirium, weakness, numbish surge of boy meets girl. It accompanied him, aged forty, in his respectable station wagon along the main street of Gallery where people loitered on Labor Day morning, and there was some storm damage. It rode with him round the Point where Husky Boy had dallied briefly with Gracie Girl some night or other. It was as new, almost as disembodied innocent as long languorous looks across the classroom in Junior High. In short, it was a lovely funny feeling. She was so serene, so predictable, so damned attractive. She said such admiring things, and meant them.

Come off it now, he instructed himself. He had a busy holiday ahead of him, no time to think about blondes. He would pack, and settle up round the house this morning. Then he would give the whole afternoon to Tom Beamish—there was the fall plowing to discuss; the pond to be repaired or made again; plans for showing at the Winter Fair in Toronto, a dozen things. Then he would put the family on the train. Then he and Mac would fly to Montreal. The weekend had been fun, despite stormy weather; now back to the job. He had it all mapped out in the casual flexible way he liked.

The cedar wood was a shambles. Tom and the boys had cleared the drive of fallen trees, and Tom had not said: *I told you so.* To say such a thing was very bad breeding in these parts. It would be best to do what Tom wanted—fell the whole lot and stump it out and plant in two years with spruce. Or what about Austrian pine, quick-growing to a windbreak?

There was near-silence from the studio, a mumbled word or two, which he did not hear in the wind. The power was still off, but they had fixed the telephone line. He called Wilson Pitt from upstairs, got him at home in Montreal. "I'll drop in around nine tonight," said his executive vice-president. "Give us a chance to have a thrash before the office." A *thrash* was Wilsonian for a general policy discussion. Willie played a bit of golf on doctor's orders. Otherwise he worked, a chronic case, no dancing frolics for him. Sometimes Skafe worried that Wilson—who was fifty-two—would burn himself out.

Now he packed his two weekend bags, and the one he had sent down early in the summer. He kept a few things here, of course. He took his time about it, as he did about everything. People often said how quick he was, but he did not hurry. His words and his actions trailed his mind; and trivial actions of this packing sort gave his mind a chance to roam haphazardly over the small long-term question of providing family quarters at Turtle Mountain, over the large more immediate question of carrying Turtle until full production; and so on.

He heard the plane coming. So did Sally. She ran out with her Brownie camera. She had wanted to go with Mac this morning to Flume Hill. But Skafe had put his foot down—ostensibly because Toddy was grossly overworked, and there was packing to be done. Which was a sound reason. Also slightly because enough was enough about her crush on Mac. But the real reason was that shaky Mac could jitter it out by himself in the plane. He had not said this to Mac, but Mac knew darned well he meant it. He had also read the packing riot act to John this morning. All in all, Father Skafe had thrown his weight around. Mother Skafe was not connecting. She was edgy and depressed about sitting yet again for *that wretched portrait*, as she put it.

Now, through the house—along the hall and up the stairs and into this wing—there came the sound of Anna's laughter. It was not a silvery tinkle of woman laughing. It was Anna's spontaneous merriment, uninhibited contralto. He heard it so rarely, and he loved to hear it, even if that laughter did not often sound for him.

Mac circled the house; then he flew out for his landing. There were white horses in the bay, a big enough chop of sea to make the amphibian wallow as he turned off wind to taxi in. He came fast to the shelter of the cove, squared to the ramp and climbed it, no sign of jitters. Skafe wondered if Mac had enjoyed the weekend. He had cased the joint, prowling around as a dog circles before lying down; he had been flounder fishing; he had given a flying lesson; he had got very drunk one night, and had suffered fearful repercussions, oblivious of a hurricane. Perhaps he had worked off steam.

Now he talked with Sally Skafe, posed before the amphibian for her, took a reciprocal picture of her. They were joined by John, binoculars round his neck; and the three of them strolled this way by the graveyard of Anna's rose garden. My God, he thought—it was not a thought that had occurred in full meaning to him before—there goes my only real friend, and he is on my payroll. Even Mac must defer to me when the chips are down. The thought alarmed him.

Below his window now, the children were telling Mac grisly stories: ". . . Mac, do you know the one about Johnny at lunch? He said: *But Mummy, I don't like little sister . . . Now, Johnny, you eat what's set before you.*"

Which seemed to appeal to Mac's sense of the macabre, and everyone was full of fun, and Skafe, packing finished but for odds and ends, went down for a glass of sherry.

His arrival in the hall chanced to coincide exactly with some words from along the hall: "That's the best I can do. The best I can do." And again: "Yes, the best I can do."

"May I look now, David?"

"Wait, Anna. I'll turn it." A scuff of wood on a wooden floor.

"Oh," she said.

"All finished?" he called along. He wanted to, might as well see this thing, about which there had been so much secret drama and temperament. If it was any good, he would pay a fair price, say a thousand. The market was limited, after all. If it was no good . . .

He waited. He saw the children and Mac through the living room window, a right angle more or less from them to him and along the hall. He remembered how hard it had been, as a boy, to accept that the act of seeing was only receptive. Hearing was different. You always felt that sound came from there to you. "Come and see it, Simon."

He went to suit the eye to the word. The west window was curtained. The canvas faced half north, back to him. He circumnavigated that to stand beside Anna while Dorrien put tops on tubes of paint, fiddled with paraphernalia.

He looked at the painting. Simon Skafe was a maker of things. He tried to make things well, and a thing truly made with love is art, although such a highfalutin thought would embarrass him.

"Well?" said Dorrien, clumsy-fingered at his tinkering pretense.

"It's me, David," Anna said. "How could I know?"

She turned to her husband who looked at the artist who looked at his wife. "Good," Skafe said, seeing Dorrien, and what he saw was not for him, but it came to him. "I think it's superb," he said heartily. He boomed his praise loudly enough to draw the children and their middle-aged pal.

A stage, Skafe thought obscurely in the room with the twin beds where visitors had slept and more important visitors would sleep; and the cast now stood, or moved to stand about the set.

"Golly," Mac said. "That's a knockout."

"Gosh, David," said quiet John. "It's absolutely super of Mum."

But Sally's eyes flickered from the painting to the artist to her mother, and she ran from the room.

"I'll change," Anna said, and went immediately after Sally, with whom so often she bickered. John and Mac walked out together. "You've earned a drink," Skafe said. "Come on."

Exit the actors, two by two. "What would you like—a gin and tonic?"

"Do you happen to have the ingredients for pink gin? I won't be a second. I must wash." Dorrien went into the cloakroom under the stairs.

Skafe put in one shake of Angostura, swilled the glass, poured gin and topped it up. He decided that gin and tonic was better suited than sherry to this occasion.

Dorrien drank without toasts in the upper class English way, with their extraordinary complexity of taboo and shibboleth, sometimes broken for colonials.

"You must be relieved," Skafe said, "to have it done."

"Yes," he said. "Simply marvelous. I can't describe it." It did not require description, for the slackness of beatitude was in his face. "I so nearly had it," he said, "and I almost gave up, and then a few minutes ago she laughed at some petulance of mine, and I saw a particular touch at the eyes which was what I had missed. Don't you like the contradiction in the pose of the head, so right of Anna?" Dorrien smiled with singular charm, and humility. "Don't mind me," he said. "I just think that this . . ." He hesitated. "I never know," he said. "I never can see when it's hot in me. But I'm almost sure. Yes, I'm sure. This is far and away the best thing I've done."

"I think it must be," Skafe said. "What are your plans now, David?"

"Home," he said. "I'm having an exhibition in London in October. Some of my better war things, and this. I can't tell you what a difference it makes to have done something with some guts in it again."

"I would like to buy Anna's portrait," Skafe said casually and carefully. "If I paid now, would you send it over after your exhibition?"

Dorrien was surprised, or he played reluctant. "But I told you before," he said. "This wasn't a commission, Simon."

"I know," he said. "But sometime presumably you will want to sell. Why not sell it now to me, and keep it a while, as long as you like." Surely that's generous, he thought. How much? "I'll give you five thousand dollars cash," he said.

"Cash!" Dorrien said. His nostrils arched. "I'm awfully sorry, old boy," he said. "It isn't on."

"Very well," Skafe said. "The portrait is of my wife. I want it. The thing is as simple as that . . ."

"Is it?" Dorrien interrupted. "The portrait is not the wife."

"Hear me out," he said. "If you won't sell now, then I am asking for a blanket option—the right to bid against any price offered to you by anyone. Do you agree?"

"I suppose so," Dorrien said. He frowned, resentful, not grateful as well he might have been. "I don't understand this high-pressure blanket option stuff; but yes, all right." And Anna came in.

"What will you have, Anna?"

"Oh, anything," she said. "Gin and tonic, I guess."

He dealt with that, and then he slid out by the french doors, leaving his drink, untouched so far. Drink never did mean a thing to him.

He crossed the lawn to sit on the red rocks by the shore, mudflats baring in the ebb to his left, the Summit amphibian above deep water to his right.

It was Anna warm from love. It was Anna kindled to amusement. It was the bite and the beauty of Anna. It was all that he had hoped that Anna would always be, and yet if she always was, she would not be. It was Anna loved, and more than the Anna he had loved.

There were white clouds of wind in the sky. The wind blew cold and clean, a northwest wind from the continent. They had an old saying here: *September's Monday brings the fall*, and it often did, and it had today.

The plover made sedate small parties on the rocks. They rose now, restless at the wind of autumn. "'Cry, Plover, fly!'" Skafe said aloud, alone, "'For the year must die. The year must die.'"

BOOK THREE

CHAPTER ONE

SKAFE took the key from the jeep and walked through crusted slush. He found himself a niche among some empty cable drums. He was at the west end of the camp below the hill, and the cold breeze dropped down at him over the hill. There were no sounds this afternoon at Turtle Mountain but the powerhouse racket and hum. It was early in October 1948.

He thought that he had come here unobserved. The camp looked peaceful enough—the large huts and the small, the complex of wooden catwalks linking them, not a soul about along this rocky slope. There was no soil anywhere to grow a weed or a blade of grass to mask a pile of rubble, but already snow was lining pockets.

He sat there alone to see what he could see, and to think about what he might do. Skafe had trouble. They had been smuggling liquor into the camp for some time now. It could come only by air, and it came without the knowledge of Mac's pilots. But liquor in a dry camp of booze artists could not be kept a secret. Five days ago things came to a head with a party, in the course of which a cable drum similar to those he now hid behind had been rolled down the hill to pile into a hut and do about a thousand dollars' worth of damage. Later, a man lying in his bunk had been shot through the leg by a stray .30-.30 bullet from target practice. Some harm had been done, if no harm was intended.

Pilbrom had acted promptly and rightly in firing the drunks. He had acted rightly, if less wisely, in announcing publicly that the cost of their passages to Edmonton would be charged against them—which was contractually provided for in cases of dismissal for cause.

If this had happened a year ago, the small affair would have had no repercussions. But of late months labor relations had deteriorated at Turtle Mountain. To complicate matters, or to give a fuse time to burn, the weather had closed in, and the dismissed men could not be flown to Edmonton. The day before yesterday the whole camp had come out on sympathy strike.

Skafe watched from behind his drums. It was none too warm at about twenty above. Now three men walked along the bottom of the camp in this direction. They walked with an air of purpose more deliberate than the intent of moving from warmth through cold to warmth again. One of them was a man he was interested to see. They turned into Stores.

The afternoon was dim. A flurry of snow came out of the north. He thought he heard geese flying overhead, but he could not be sure in the background noises of Turtle Mountain.

Play along with them, he had told Pilbrom when he arrived this morning. He had sat in the room next the office to listen through the wooden partition wall. The initial demands for reinstatement of the three drunks had grown to include dismissal of Peter Syme, Assistant Manager. He wondered what would be next. Wages, he expected, although they were already paid ten per cent over the running rates for hard rock miners, and board was provided at far less than cost.

Skafe had not decided what to do, but he knew the principle or tactics of the tricky game he intended to play. There was a nice balance to it. Give them—or give him, for one man was behind this strike, he was virtually certain—give him enough rope to hang, yet act and act decisively before two hundred idle men became violent.

The strike must be broken, for this was no ordinary mine. It was Turtle Mountain, a thousand miles from unions, labor pools, police and wives. It was, to some degree, a camp of misfits, not bad men, but men with this or that instability. Mob rule by labor would put Turtle on the skids. What none of them knew—not even Pilbrom, Syme, Jorgensen the geologist—was that Skafe's oldest and best-loved enterprise was already skidding for the skids.

He had had little labor trouble in his time. He paid well, demanded much, and treated men as human beings. A tough boss and a fair boss was his reputation. But now he had small labor trouble that was dynamite. There was a particular kind of man behind this strike, not a Communist, not a mere agitator. To deal with such a man, Skafe was ready to be, and had to be, anything but fair.

Not fair, he remembered John's complaint at Gallery in the storm two years ago, taking Skafe's part against his mother. Anna was at Gallery now. She had stayed on this fall to be with old John Skafe, who was failing. He felt about Anna nowadays . . . He did not know what he felt or knew about her. He did not know his wife as well as he had known her that night they left Jim Willis's cabin on the Mackenzie River.

Now he was sure that he heard geese flying overhead. It would soon be dark. He shivered, inadequately clothed in his wool-lined parka. It was ironically appropriate that the biggest construction man in Canada should be snooping behind empty cable drums a few miles north of the Arctic Circle.

Now the same men came out of Stores. They climbed the catwalk near to him. He saw that McClintock was in the lead. Skafe had not decided on his plan of action, but one thing his plan would include would be the getting of Mr. McClintock. "Keep your traps shut," the man said. "I'll do the talking." He used the word *traps*, but spoke with an educated intonation. He was said to have done two years at Glasgow University.

Skafe watched them all the way up and into Pilbrom's office. Then he walked fast to Stores. Reston sat at the trestle table, making notations in a stores sheet. Skafe kept his hands in his pockets. He waited for the man to look up. "Reston," he said then. "Are you alone in here?"

"Yes, Mr. Skafe." He had been an excellent storeman since being demoted from Assistant Manager. Behind him was a maze of bins and shelves, with alleyways between them. It was dark in the body of the hut.

"Put on your parka and come with me."

The man stared at him. Reston was quite a pleasant-looking fellow, heavy jawed, hair oiled and brushed straight back without a parting, a nose that turned slightly up, small mouth, a face of contradictions. He looked down again, put the sheet carefully back on the prongs of the looseleaf ledger. His hands were not entirely steady.

Skafe moved closer. "Hurry up," he said.

"There's a strike on, Mr. Skafe," said Reston. "No hurry, surely." He closed the ledger.

"Are you on strike?"

"No, sir," Reston said. "I'm a salaried man. You saw me catching up on my records, Mr. Skafe." Now his jaw muscles flexed, and he turned to take his parka from a hanger. Everything was tidy here—the table, the single bunk, the shelves. Two photographs of body builders in leopard skin drawers were Reston's pin-ups, and a nice colored print of Gainsborough's "Blue Boy."

"Bring the key of the magazine. Lights out. Lock up. And Reston!"

"Yes, Mr. Skafe?" Now the man was afraid.

"I am not going to say *Hurry up* again."

They walked on mud and a skim of ice and snow past the powerhouse to the jeep. The camp was deserted. "Get in," said Skafe.

The magazine was halfway to the airstrip, set into the side of the hill. "Get out," he said. "Open up." It was dark. Skafe waited until the light came on, and then he went round the blast embankment to join Mr. Reston. He closed the door behind him. Wooden boxes of Forcite were stacked by strength—fifty per cent nitroglycerin and up. "Now show me the liquor," he said. He did not much care about the liquor, but it would do for a start with Reston.

"What liquor, Mr. Skafe?" He was lying or he was surprised, too scared to show which.

"I know it's here," Skafe said. He did not know that the liquor was here. He was working on a last-possibility hunch of Peter Syme's, Reston's successor as Assistant Manager.

"But there's no liquor, Mr. Skafe. I swear it."

"All right," Skafe said. He hit him in the solar plexus. It was a fair good blow to penetrate the parka padding. Then he hit gasping Reston open handed, right to topple him, left to stand him up. He had fought men, but he had never had to jellify a man. "You crooked little mucker," he said dispassionately.

"But, Mr. Skafe, I swear . . ."

This time Skafe hit him with a glove-protected fist on the crown of his retroussé nose. Reston wept on his knees. People really do get on their knees, Skafe thought. "Either you show me the liquor or tell me how it comes into camp, or I will lock you up here to think it over. Which? You can scream all night," he said, "until I set a fuse to you and your dynamite in the morning." He had no such intention, but time was short; and the dynamite was not only here.

Reston confessed, as blood made a mess of his deerskin glove. There was no liquor now, shipments exhausted, but the liquor had come this way in Forcite boxes, McClintock's idea—McClintock made him do it.

Blackmail, Skafe supposed, but he did not ask. He suspected Reston of aberrant sexual inclinations, for which Turtle Mountain could be a happy hunting ground. "So you split with McClintock," he said. "At how much? Twenty bucks a bottle?"

Reston nodded. Good guess. Buy it at four or five. Fly it in at Company expense. Five bucks to the packer in Edmonton, five to Reston, five to McClintock. That was how such a profitable business would operate, more or less, he thought. Reston emitted a long shuddering snuffle like a child whose tears are drying up. He was a tool and a stooge, but a plotter nonetheless.

"Out of here," Skafe said. He drove to the airstrip, and on the way he extracted McClintock's plan of campaign, or as much of it as had been divulged to Reston. He parked the jeep between the C-47's, one which had been weatherbound, the other in which Mac had flown him this morning.

There was a cabin now at the airstrip, the only log construction of size at Turtle Mountain. It was a well-found job, a pet summer project of 1947 which had not cost the Company a penny, apart from materials and fittings. The men liked to come here to meet the planes. So they had built the cabin as a shelter, and a sort of reception lodge to Turtle Mountain. It was big, solid, comfortable, old-fashioned, perhaps out of place on this bleak plateau above the uranium mine, for no trapper would build a cabin in so exposed a spot. Yet for Skafe it was a link with his first days in the North, and it had been built by contented workers of a later era. So much for good labor relations, he thought angrily, following Reston. His right hand showed a desire of its own to take another poke at him; he put it deeper in his pocket. He could even admire an out-and-out blackguard like McClintock, but this sniveling conspirator . . . The inner door opened, and the storm door. "Who's that?"

"It's me, Mac," he said. "I brought the gentleman in question."

Mac looked at Reston, who was not a cheerful sight. "Take a pew by the stove," he said quite kindly. The other pilots were playing gin rummy. They glanced at Reston, and said hullo to Skafe. Roy Thompson was about thirty-five, the co-pilots younger—Mac and his quiet men.

Reston slumped into a chair by the stove at the other end. Skafe stood with Mac by the space heater. "No bullshit," MacNamara said. "You took the stuffing out of him. Did he come clean?"

"Yes," Skafe said. "Item One: they smuggled the booze in dynamite boxes. Item Two: the plan was or is to demand Reston back as Assistant Manager. Item Three: McClintock intends to give us until tomorrow. Then, if we don't climb down at least part way, he is going to start busting the place wide open." The amusing thing is, he thought, that I don't give a goddam if he does. But he did not say that, even to Mac.

"What the hell for? Is he crazy?"

"I wouldn't be sure," Skafe said. "Now listen, Mac . . ."

Mac listened. "Christ," he said, "you're wasted in the paths of virtue." He smiled and then he said: "I suppose you realize that Syme, Pilbrom and Co. don't matter a harlot's damn—you're going to be the target when the chips are down."

"I know," Skafe said. "I'll be in touch with you first thing in the morning." He went along the hut. "If you want to get out of this place alive, you had better not try to beat it back for camp. You know what Mc-Clintock would do to a squealer, don't you?"

Reston nodded, abject and hopeless. He was the weakling used and found out. He could not escape here or there or anywhere. "I'm sorry . . ." he began.

"Oh, shut up," said Skafe. "Goodnight, boys," he said to the pilots. Mac saw him out. "They will probably guess that Reston is here," Skafe said, "and they may try to get him back. I doubt if they will, though, until we have a showdown. Nobody wants to quarrel with the pilots."

"And the pilots don't want to quarrel with nobody," MacNamara said. "Still, a squirt or two would be like old times. We'll stand watches, anyway. Have you got a gun?"

"Yes," he said. In fact, the .38 automatic was in camp in his valise, where it would remain, he hoped.

"Cold as buggery," Mac said. "Why would anyone want to come to this godforsaken icebox, far less go on strike to stay here? Goodnight then, boy. You watch yourself."

Yes, why would anyone want to come here? he thought on his way to camp. The first time he had come had been in February 1932, trapping. He was caught in a storm, and he huddled it out at thirty or forty below in the shelter of the unnamed mountain for two days and nights with one frozen fox to eat. He had come again that spring to stake the claims; and had gone back west and down the Bear to Norman, and up the Mackenzie to Jim's log cabin.

The wife and the mine, he thought. My wife and my mine, the only two things I ever touched that have gone wrong for me. Turtle goes on draining profits, not only profits but the Staniland loan, while Bob Carter gripes and issues solemn warnings. And the wife? What about Anna? Well, what about her, turning the tables to leave me to stew in the Montreal house while she spends six months at Gallery, and three months last winter in Jamaica next door to her artist boy friend, quite respectable and chaperoned, ostensibly.

But Skafe shed these acidulous thoughts, for he had a battle on his hands here in the North in October when snow flurries came and went before the white winter. Wives and profits—what were they compared with this real world? He had been rough with Reston, not for sadistic spite but to find out what he had to know. And yet it was enjoyable.

He left the jeep this side of camp in a draw, a ravine out of sight of the road. Then he climbed. The sky had cleared, and there was a crescent moon. He could see the path quite well. He climbed until he was above the camp, on the shoulder of Turtle Mountain. He looked down at the lights. They made a tidy cryptic pattern in the wilderness. You might fly north or south or east or west five hundred miles and never see another light. My lights, he thought, and with bitterness. He did not think of his labor force as something to be exploited. Nor did he sentimentalize. He thought of them as his fellow men, to be paid just as much as they were good enough to earn; and to be cared for, with as little paternalism as possible. Many were, in the limited sense, his friends. But the idle men in those lighted huts were his enemies. And now, friends or enemies, the friendly lights would soon go out at Turtle Mountain. He was not the first fool to be beaten by the North.

The breeze chilled the warmth of climbing from him, and he made for camp, down to the mutter and the hum, down to a swell of cheering somewhere.

His valise lay unopened on the bunk. Against it was propped an envelope. The radio message said: FATHER HAS PNEUMONIA AGAIN HEART WEAKER HE ASKS FOR YOU STOP DOCTOR SAYS COME AT ONCE ANNA.

He had expected it, not in the immediate sense, but this summons had lain in the offing since the spring—two bouts of pneumonia, and now a third. Forester of Montreal had only confirmed the local man's opinion: that bronchial weakness and a failing heart left John Skafe little time.

Skafe sat on the bunk to think. Someone knocked. "Well?" he said.

It was Jorgensen, the geologist, trying yet again to see him. "Husky," he began, "that assay report that came in with you . . ." Dedicated to his uranium, U_{238}, an excellent geologist. To Jorgensen strikes were ore bodies.

Skafe waved him out. "Not now, Chris," he said. "How many more times do I have to tell you?"

Alone again, he thought about it, but he did not need to think about it. One life there, one old man dying. Many lives here, and danger here. Mike Pilbrom could run the mine and run it well and deal with ordinary trouble, but he could not cope with a McClintock. Syme, as Manager, might possibly have handled this. That was why McClintock gunned for Syme.

Skafe knew that he could not go until the strike was settled. His father asked for him. He shrank from seeing his father die, but he dearly wanted to see his father before he died. Yet everyone must die, and some must die alone without the granting of a wish. "Oh, goddammit," said Simon Skafe. He went out and two doors along to Pilbrom's office.

"What happened to you?" he said.

"Somebody heaved a rock." Peter Syme had a bandage round his head.

"It's nothing much. I bled a bit." He was pale and freckle-blotched, but not a tremor in his voice, Skafe noticed.

"I handed Reston over to Mac," he said. "You were right about the dynamite, Peter. It was a McClintock/Reston booze racket. Have you had your evening meal?"

"Yes," Syme said. "I was on my way back when they clobbered me."

"Okay, then. You stay here, and you move into my room for tonight."

"But, Mr. Skafe . . ."

"Do as I tell you. Now, Mike, what's the news?"

Pilbrom sat at his table. "Just like you expected: that bastard comes up with ten per cent—timework, piecework, flat ten per cent raise. He said they knew you were here, and he wanted to see you, not waste time on me, he as good as said. You told me: Play them along again. Well, I tried, but McClintock staring at me, talking away so darned cold-blooded condescendingly. Well, finally I blew my top, I'm sorry."

"And how did he take that?"

"Smiled," said Pilbrom. "Stood up. Said: *Would you tell Mr. Skafe that I expect to meet him at nine tomorrow?* and left. Hell, you might think McClintock paid the wage bill. Is he crazy?"

"I wouldn't be sure," Skafe said for the second time. "You'd better read this." He handed over the RCMP report.

Before this trouble broke, Pilbrom had written that things personnel-wise did not seem too good at Turtle—a rash of complaints about food, showers, laundry and so on; sullenness; drink coming in, but he could not find out how. Syme thought, wrote Pilbrom (disassociating himself), that the man behind it was one McClintock, a bulldozer operator who had been in a few months. Pilbrom did not see it—McClintock seemed a decent quiet man, gave no trouble . . .

Skafe had happened to be in Alberta at the time. He called the Superintendent of K Division, whom he knew. This was the dossier on McClintock: he had emigrated from Scotland as a youth in the depression, and after minor misdemeanors in Canada, he had crossed the border to get three years for robbery with violence in Seattle. When he had served that sentence, he came back or was returned to Canada, where he enlisted, went to Italy, was wounded and won the Military Medal, an excellent war record until, being not yet fit for action, he was posted as sergeant to a base camp staff. There, McClintock found real scope for his talents. He was caught in the end, tried and sentenced for organizing whore shops, a black market in army rations, a protection racket within the camp and far beyond the camp. He had not been tried for the murder of an officer who had been sent to investigate. That officer had vanished one night in Bari.

You had better get him out of there quick, said Superintendent Tilley yesterday. *We can't,* Skafe said. *He has a six-month contract specifically for Turtle Mountain, and we have nothing on him, yet anyway. Have you?* The RCMP had nothing new on McClintock. The superintendent was anxious to arrange with the Arctic Division to send a detachment immediately. But Skafe did not like the idea of police at a place where the only policemen had been welcome and friendly guests on routine patrol. Also, it was both too early and too late for the police. *Give me two days,* he said. *This may be a storm in a teacup . . . All right,* said Tilley. *But I warn you. One of our best men in the Force served in Italy, and he knows all about the McClintock case. He says that McClintock is the only plain wicked man he ever came across. But he says too that McClintock has an Achilles heel. He has a power bug—starts quietly, and it takes possession. That was how they got him at that other camp. I wish you'd let us . . . If you don't hear from me in two days,* Skafe said, *you can start organizing posses.*

That was why he was here, and why he must stay here although his father might be dying; and why he had told Pilbrom to play along with McClintock; and why he had dealt brutally with Reston. He thought now of the sway that men may have over other men. He watched Pilbrom read the dossier through and pass it to Syme.

"Jesus," Pilbrom said. The room was hot, always too hot, but not hot enough to make a man sweat in dry steam heat. He blinked from the sting of sweat in his eyes, and mopped his head. "If they seize the camp," he said, "what the hell can fifteen or twenty of us do against two hundred? That bastard snake will stop at nothing."

"Quite," said Skafe.

"Why don't we turn off the heat and freeze the buggers out?"

"Because we would freeze every waterpipe in the process. Because the buggers would burn the place up for warmth." Skafe laughed, and drew a wan smile from Pilbrom. "Also," he said, "because if there's any burning to be done, it won't be done by them there buggers." Syme laughed, and held his head. "I'll see you later, Peter. Stay inside, as I told you, and wait for me."

Syme handed back the paper. He left the office, not quite steady on his feet. The sound of muffled cheering came again. It seemed that McClintock had eloquence among his talents.

"Look, Mike," Skafe said. "You must take it easy about this thing."

"Take it easy?" said Pilbrom. "Take it easy? Hell, in thirty-four years in the mining business, nobody ever . . ."

"I know," Skafe said. "But this is a one-man show, and the one man is a cold sane madman who is trying to make us lose our heads. Keep calm, and we can deal with him." Or I can deal with him, he thought.

"What's a sane madman, anyways?"

"Hitler was one example."

Pilbrom shook his head. "I'm out of my league," he said. "Well, thank God you're here."

"I'm going to get some food."

"Let me come along. They're ugly, Mr. Skafe. They sit and watch you, and they plugged Syme already."

"It's quite okay until tomorrow," he said. "I'll go alone."

He went by the radio hut, where both operators worked and slept. "Anything new, Gerry?" he said.

Gerry Rosenheim had a fine-drawn ascetic face. He had been a heroin addict, which was unusual for a Jewish boy, and Skafe had employed him straight from prison. He stayed safe here from the dope. "Not a thing," he said. "Sorry about your message, Husky."

"What are your instructions?" he asked, nodding his head in the men's quarters direction.

"Send nothing without permission. Report what comes in."

"Watch it now," said the other man from the bunk, and from behind Virile Magazine. "They said if we talked . . ."

"Aw, can it," Rosenheim said.

"Don't worry," said Skafe. He left that place. He would not send a radiogram by kind permission of Mr. McClintock. Nor could he send one that would be of any help.

He was hungry, and he intended to show himself while feeding himself. If Pilbrom had been a wiser man, he would have laid in an emergency store of food at the other end of camp—another thing that Syme had suggested.

He hung his parka in the porch and opened the door. The dining hut was half full of men, drinking coffee, smoking, talking, a hum of feverish talk. Now absolute silence.

"Hullo, boys!" he said. He strolled along between the tables to the serving counter. "Gus!" he called.

Velensky appeared. He was scramble-eyed. Perhaps he had been at the vanilla essence; if so, not enough to drown his dismay at seeing the man who had put his boy through college. ". . . Supper's over," he mumbled.

"Now listen, Gus," said Skafe loudly. "I'm hungry. Come to think of it, I paid for the food. Come to think of it, did you ever hear of a fellow negotiating nicely on an empty stomach?" He listened to the ripple, even perhaps the hint of a titter behind him. Just right, he thought. He took roast beef, tepid vegetables from Gus Velensky, bread, butter, cheese, apple pie. "Give me a tray," he said. He got his tray and a mug of coffee. "You little squirt," he said, for Velensky alone.

He chose an empty table, and sat alone in his jacket of Harris tweed, dark gray trousers tucked into flying boots, S. K. Skafe the President, with his back to the door of the dining hut. Two men went out, but he did not look round. He tucked into his supper with hearty appetite and some noise of implements on a tin plate in the room where nobody spoke. He drank half his coffee with the meal, and then he lit a cigarette as men came in.

"Mr. Skafe!"

"Yes?" he said, looking up. The police photograph made a gaunt un-flattering caricature of a younger McClintock. He was a dark Scotsman, thick browed, long nosed, wide mouthed—a handsome face. He smiled now with composure, with deliberation. There was potency about him, the calmness offset, even accentuated by a very small tic or tremor in the middle of his right lower eyelid. He had eyes like Mac's, of a mustardy shade, if paler. From repute, and from his impact upon Syme and Pil-brom, Skafe had accorded McClintock the rating of a menace to be dealt with. He disliked some men, but did not hate anyone. Now, instantly, he hated this man. "What can I do for you?" he said, smiling in return.

"I'm McClintock." He said the surname in the Scottish way—Mc-Clint*uck*.

"Oh yes," Skafe said. "You're the chairman of the Turtle Mountain Strike Committee." He put down his cup, stood and held out his hand. "I'm glad to meet you," he said cordially, eye to eye. Pilbrom said that McClintock was the best catskinner he had ever seen, with a fantastically accurate eye for grade. He shook hands, hearing the stir in the dining hall. He sat again. "Won't you sit down?" he said hospitably, but Mc-Clintock stood.

"Where is Reston, Mr. Skafe?"

"Reston," he said. "Reston, the storeman, ex-Assistant Manager? I will tell you where I saw Reston. It was down the mine in the month of July, 1946, before your time. We were trying to cope with water troubles by grouting—You are not a miner, I understand, Mr. McClintock, but a very fine catskinner, I hear." He watched him. The expression did change a touch. "So I had better explain that grouting involves the forcing in of a liquid cement under pressure. Anyway, we were grouting to the left of the face; and whether that caused it, I do not know, but there was another fall, a sudden fall on the *right*, and some thousands of gallons of water arrived at some hundreds of pounds to the square inch.

"That was when I saw Reston, hightailing it for the cage and safety. One or two of the boys must still be here . . ." Skafe looked over the still sheeps' faces. Most of the originals had left. "Jimmy Little!" he said. "You saw Reston panic, Jimmy."

Jimmy Little shifted on his bench, and looked down at his coffee. "That's about all I know about Reston, Mr. McClintock. I guess it's about all any of us need to know, and Jimmy Little could have told you."

"Where *is* Reston, I asked, Mr. Skafe?" He smiled as before. The eyes did not blink. The tic ticked on.

"I couldn't care less where Reston is," said Husky Skafe, "except to hope that his gutless guts are rotting somewhere. Goodnight, then," he said, yawning. "I look forward to our talk together tomorrow morning, but first a sound night's sleep is indicated. Goodnight, everyone."

He turned and walked to the door with a sensitive back, but no one moved. He had come alone and, thanks to McClintock's arrival and to some fast thinking, he had set his own personality upon the formidable personality of McClintock. Every man in the dining hut felt that; every one of the sheep now asked a question uneasily of himself. Skafe took it for granted that he would lead, and men would follow. He did not understand why nearly all men sought safety in following; but that suited him well. It did not suit him to be challenged by a megalomaniac, a cold sane madman who could lead the sheep. And McClintock must be mad. What could he hope to gain from bossing a small mine in the back of beyond? What do I gain myself? Skafe thought. Yes, what do I gain?

The catwalk thumped back hollow to his flying boots. It was colder, around five or ten above, he judged by the tingle of his nostril hairs. He had a fairly accurate built-in thermometer.

The crescent moon was setting. He saw his father down there Outside across Canada. In the eye of his mind he saw his father's aquiline, untroubled face. He thought of his dear father, who would respect what his son was trying to do, but would not approve of the way he set about doing it.

CHAPTER TWO

HE WAS AWAKE as the door handle turned. "Who's that?"

"It's Mike. Can you come to the office?"

Skafe extracted himself from the sleeping bag, pulled on his boots, put on his jacket. He debated about the pistol—take it, leave it? He left it. Syme slept now in the other bunk, but restlessly. Skafe felt his brow above the bandage. He was feverish, not very hot. "It's fabulous," said Peter Syme, and turned from the right side to the left, which was his injured side. He grunted and turned back.

It was still night, but a bulb outside gave some light in here, enough to show the sleeping man, to show the same supercurvilinear pin-up girl still on the wall. Skafe was getting quite fond of her.

"What is it, Mike?" he said along in the office.

"This." It was a typed memo sheet.

> From Labor
> To Management.
> We want Reston at Number Four by 8 A.M.
> McCLINTOCK
> Chairman, Strike Committee

"Short, to the point, and to be expected," he said. "*McClintock* without initials amuses me. Lord God McClintock."

"Nothing about that bastard amuses me," Pilbrom said. "What's he trying to do, for God's sake—with the meeting set for nine?"

"Tap in the wedge," Skafe said. "Keep tapping. The principle is sound. Now I must talk to Mac."

"The airfield phone's been on the blink since one A.M.," said Pilbrom. "They cut the line, I guess. But Jacky went out with the second walkie-talkie."

Skafe took notice of the clerk. "Did you have any trouble?"

"I got chased coming back," said Jacky Watters. He was in a Northern Adventure category, aged nineteen or so, a callow type and pleased with himself.

"Good man," Skafe said.

There was no mistaking MacNamara's radio tones, metallic as a buzz saw. "Good morning to you," he crackled. "Over."

"How soon can Able Nan Fox be ready to fly?"

"The heaters are on, and she's all gassed up—just warming time."

"Okay," he said. "Start the engines, then."

"Wilco. Out."

"Mike," he said, "Syme is running a fever and has a slight concussion, so I'm going to fly him Out, and Reston too. You, Watters, go along the inside way to the dispensary for a stretcher, pick up Chris Jorgensen or somebody your size, and come right back."

"Ay ay, sir," the boy actually said; he dashed.

"Watters!"

"Sir?"

"Calm down. Now Mike," he said, "I want you to put off the outside lights for two or three minutes to let us get clear of camp. Okay?" There was a master switch in the manager's office.

"Okay. But they're after Syme. It's a risk, Mr. Skafe."

"I know it's a risk." He was annoyed with cautious, bewildered old Mike Pilbrom. Also, Skafe blamed himself for not moving Syme to the airstrip last night, which he had proposed, but Syme had been unwilling. His violent headache and the fever had not begun until the middle of the night.

"I can walk," Syme said now in the room.

"It is better that he should not move himself," said Doc Vandelac. He had been an M.D. at Three Rivers until he got in trouble.

The lights went out. Skafe led the way. It was an old path and he knew it well. He knew the old game paths better than the catwalks. He heard excited shouting in the darkened camp, behind, above, on there. His senses recorded profane humanity, warmer weather, night thinning in the east, a whiff of diesel exhaust, trouble ahead, but where? On this path. "Stop," he whispered, and knelt to roll a boulder downhill to the left.

It accelerated well, being fairly round, to fetch up with a godawful crash against some building. The diversion worked. Skafe led his party through. He left the path to find the jeep, which might not be there, or might have been tampered with.

But the strikers had not found the jeep. It started. "Husky, are you flying Out?" asked Jorgensen the implacable. "I have been at the correlating of this thing of mine all night, and I must see you, Husky, do you understand? I must."

"I am not flying Out," he said. "Get safely back to camp and stop correlating that thing of yours for the rest of the night for pity's sake."

He drove off laughing, exhilarated. But a thought of his father came to reproach him.

"It's fabulous," said Peter Syme, delirious perhaps. Young Syme had done a first-rate job as Assistant Manager, and he had learned to manage men without a drill book. The reason the troublemakers were after Syme was that Syme was on to them and a match for them.

There were four rocks across the road. He went into low of low ratio, four wheels biting, bulldozed one with his fender, drove on and uphill to the plateau, contemptuous of that half-baked apology for a roadblock.

"Mac," he said, "help Syme into the plane. Then fetch Reston. Roy, you might radio ahead for an ambulance to take Syme to the hospital. Only slight concussion, Vandelac thinks, but he needs attention. When you arrive at Edmonton, get onto the RCMP and keep Reston alone with you until they come to take his statement. Whatever happens, keep the press out of this. And tell the police from me . . ."

Roy Thompson gunned the engines of ANF on the way down the strip. There was no wind now, or if any wind, it was a cross puff from the west. He took off north and swung wide of the camp. They would not hear the plane there.

"Why so dramatic?" said MacNamara.

"Because McClintock has demanded Reston by eight; and when he doesn't get him, he will probably come after Syme."

"You know," Mac said. "I'm real sorry for that sod McClintock."

Skafe was pleased at Mac's compliment, but he said: "I'm afraid of him, not sorry for him. The men are really brewing up for trouble now, and all we've done so far is evade the issue, which in itself tips the balance to McClintock. Meet him and beat him is what I've got to do."

"You will," said Mac, "if you don't get bumped off in the process. But I don't see why you didn't bring in the cops to arrest him; or you could have hijacked the bugger in the office."

"No," Skafe said. "If we're going to break this thing, they must see him bested in public."

"Well, you're the boy," Mac said.

"How was it here last night?"

"No trouble to speak of. Midnight, a truck arrived and took a swing around the aircraft, so we gave it a red Very light between the eyes. Exit truck. Later there were cries of 'Friend' in the barren lands—that fuzzy-cheeked youth with the walkie-talkie. I thought he had better stay the night, but he said his duty lay at headquarters. Mountie Romance," said Mac. "There's nothing like it in the North Countree. Come and have some breakfast, and I'll tell you the gen from Reston. He poured himself out to me last night."

Afterwards, Mac drove him along the runway to Turtle Mountain. It was full daylight. The sky was clear, temperature about freezing, a breeze growing from the west. "That's a good wind coming up," Skafe said.

"Are you in earnest?"

"Of course," he said. "If I'm driven to it."

"I didn't need to ask," said Mac, driving slowly on. "Sounds crazy to me, but I can just see you do it."

Queer what a tortoise the intrepid MacNamara was in surface vehicles. All queer, all crazy, and the sun was rising. A timber wolf ranged over on the left. It trotted, dark against the smattering of snow along a ridge a quarter of a mile beyond this plateau. It was a big male wolf, and it stopped to sit like a double-sized police dog, watching them, inquisitive. Then it cut the sky, loose-limbed, unhurried hunter, gone.

Wolves were not often seen at Turtle Mountain. They were more often heard as they hunted moose or caribou by night. "And only the howl of a timber wolf," some memory jogged at Skafe, but he could not pinpoint that memory, and this great wolf had not howled.

"Did it ever occur to you," said Mac, "that everywhere we go, we muck up the mucking wilderness?"

"We clear it," he said. "We develop it. Isn't that what a wilderness is for?"

"Oh, Christ."

"It grows back quick enough," Skafe said, seeing, vaguely seeing the life of the wilderness in the death of man and the works of man. "My father has pneumonia again," he said. "Sounds bad. A signal came in last night."

"And you're stuck here," Mac said. "Is Anna with him?"

"Yes," he said. Now he remembered about the howl of a wolf, another quote from Jim Willis's cabin. "If and when I can settle this thing," he said, "I want to fly right through."

"I'd better raise Eldorado, then," Mac said, "for a met on Churchill." He stopped the jeep. "You're the boy," he said again, constrained. "Take care. I'll be round there waiting."

Skafe crossed the shoulder of Turtle Mountain, taking the rocky trail that he had taken last night and so many times before. The camp above the frozen lake was almost pleasing in the morning sun—brown rock, pale pit props at the mill, silver oil tanks, a scud of furnace smoke. Careless, he thought, about poor oil combustion. He went down to his snow-sprinkled camp above the pit, the unfruitful deep. Out there on the lake, Jorgensen's drilling rig was frozen in, more wild-goose chasing . . .

A bullet cracked and smacked quite loudly against rock thirty feet or so away from him. The chips made a small rattle as they fell. He decided that it was too wide a shot to be anything but a deliberate miss, or intimidator; but it did rather clear things up for him. There were knots of men outside the huts, and drifting around the camp. They all stood still at the rifle shot. Then they moved quickly to disappear, a unanimous vanishing act. Skafe walked on down.

Just after eight, Number Six hut started burning. It was the farthest to the east, downwind today. Number Six was empty, apart from sundry perishable gear, including the sailing dinghies in winter storage. From July to September they had a lot of fun with those dinghies on the lake. "Safe way to burn your boats," said Pilbrom, more cheerful now that Skafe had moved from the background to take control of management, in so far as management had control of anything.

"Type this," Skafe said. He started giving it to Watters word by word, for the manager's clerk could not take shorthand. Nor could he type under stress, it appeared. "Let me do it," Skafe said patiently. "Dear Mr. McClintock," he typed:

It is most unfortunate about the fire. I trust that your efforts to extinguish it will be successful. I do not know Reston's whereabouts. I much look forward to our meeting at nine o'clock.

It is my earnest hope that a way may be found to meet the grievances of labor, and I assure you that I approach these talks in a conciliatory spirit, anxious to accommodate every legitimate demand. You will join me, I know, in wishing for a speedy and amicable solution to our mutual problems.

Since a venue has not yet been arranged, and since I believe in open discussion, in according to every wage earner his inalienable right to be party to negotiation, and since the morning is so mild, I propose that you and I meet alone at Piccadilly Circus. I have instructed my manager to provide a microphone and amplifying system so that the proceedings may be heard by all assembled.

Most sincerely yours,
S. K. SKAFE,
President
Turtle Mountain Co.
Summit Construction Co.
Staniland Engineering Co.
Etc.

"It's so darned conciliatory," Pilbrom said. "Won't he smell a rat?"

"There is no apparent rat," Skafe said. "They hold the cards and well they know it. But," he said, smiling at Pilbrom, "if that lake trout doesn't swallow this public lure, I never went fishing. Jacky, take the speaker outside."

Skafe looked at the fire. Number Six burned merrily to destruction. Already, at eight thirty-five, the flames were past a zenith. "This is S. K. Skafe, your president," he said urgently into the microphone. "I have a letter for Mr. McClintock. I have a most important letter for Mr. Mc-Clintock of the Strike Committee."

He switched off. "How do we get it there?" he said.

"I'll take the letter, sir," said Jacky Watters.

"All right," he said. "Hold it in your hand. Go straight to Number Four, deliver it, come right back." They were in the mood to burn to reveal their mood before the showdown, but not to molest a harmless youth before the showdown, so Skafe thought.

And he was wrong. At five minutes to nine, Jacky Watters was expelled from Four Hut. He struck the railing of the catwalk, hung over it, and then he climbed the steps to stumble past the dining hall, the radio shack, along here on the upper level. Jacky Watters moaned, doubled up. "What did they do to you, son?" said Pilbrom, at a stage of asking questions about the obvious.

McClintock had told his henchmen to give Watters a wee slap in the balls to teach him better where he belonged. That had been administered, just that, no more. The pain was wearing off.

"Very well," said Simon Skafe. He had not needed other men's advice. His counselors of moderation had been his own within him to gain his ends. He came now to the real man Skafe, as he had always been, not well known to him, for the heat of war's hunt had never shown himself to him, no less born to kill than was the wolf. He did not reason this marvelous, unreasoning discovery, but went to meet McClintock, carrying the microphone on its tripod leg, and the amplifying box. They used it for singsongs and for Bingo, and for this and that diversion such as sailing regattas on Turtle Lake. Husky Skafe had not yet started with the burning of his boats.

He counted the steps from Camp Office level down to Piccadilly Circus, so named by veterans of World War Two, with a northern man's yen for a good old whore in good old Piccadilly. A wedge of geese came over, flying crabwise a little, as a plane flies crabwise to hold course in a crossing wind. The geese called, southward bound, a mingled brazen honking in the wind. In a day or two or several, he thought, not knowing the flight plans, cruising speeds, refueling stops and ETA's of geese—soon anyway, they would reach the warm days, the skim of ice, the flaming of the forest.

He counted to twenty-one steps in one compartment of his mind as in another he thought of the fall, of days with his father in Ontario; of days with Anna, John and Sally in the back, annual Sunday drive on about this date to see the maples. Skafe drove, as did an army of fathers on the same excursion. He admired the pretty colors, but to Anna they were more than red and gold. *Alpha, Omega and Alpha,* she once said. *Lose and find, begin again to die again.*

She meant a cycle, he supposed. Now he saw one ending, another ending, and a third. He saw no cycle.

Forty-three, he counted, and was at Piccadilly Circus. There were no autumn colors here for nature lovers to swoon about, although a few stunted birches hid among the hollows. It was that time of year at Turtle when yellow leaves or none or few did hang. And Simon Skafe, by some considered soulless, was better read than some might think. He had a few hackneyed tags to lend distinction to his speeches.

He set up the microphone to suit his height and that of his opposite number who had not yet come, but the men were gathering, so McClintock probably would come. Skafe stood alone at Piccadilly Circus, from which radiated or to which converged stairs or stepways to and from the radio shack, the dining hall, the men's living quarters to the east, and on around clockwise down by the garages, the shops, the power-house, the lower entrance to the mine, and up again by the crushing plant and to the office block whence he had come, and to the topmost level and the cage house. The ore cars were disgorged up there, and all the process worked downhill, an economical and efficient use of Newton's Law; or it would have been economical and efficient if the ore had been twice rich in tenfold quantity.

Skafe puffed to test his microphone. The volume was too high. His puff made an ugly whistling roar as of some wild beast. He turned it down a bit, and heard an answering ugly sound from the men who gathered above him, on his level, below him, all away from him, all watching him. They made a muttering growl of hostility. It was a new kind of corporate sound to him, human, grossly inhuman, human beast. Anna often said that men, meaning females too, and females more so, were only animals, and largely worse than other animals, which offended him; but he did rather see her point just now. What was it that made decent individuals into hackled packs? They were curiously still. They watched him; then there was a shift, a centering of heads to the catwalk that came down to Piccadilly Circus from the dining hut.

CHAPTER THREE

McCLINTOCK wore a dark green windbreaker, trousers of khaki battle-dress, calf-long hunting boots. He came down the steps alone, unhurried and loose-limbed. He looked like a man who could run, jump, punch, or throw a steer or anything. To Simon Skafe he looked like a man worth killing. It was a nice uncomplicated feeling to wait forty-two and a half years to have.

Skafe waited, smiling off and on, shifting feet nervously. McClintock sauntered down. He did not smile this morning. Just how is it done? Skafe thought. Just how does this bastard work them into explosive putty? He waited until the man was close, until he could see the fluttering tic below the eye, and then he said: "Good morning, Mr. McClintock," polite and manly, with an upward unsteadiness of inflection to *McClintock*.

McClintock nodded. He turned on the platform, a sizable place. There was a swell of sound from up, across, below. He raised his hand, and the cheer subsided.

Skafe coughed. "I should like to open proceedings," he said, "by saying how much I welcome this opportunity to reach a settlement by frank, free, open discussion . . ." He heard his voice drone out the platitudes while he watched smoke meet the wind to be flung away east before the wind, and he saw a last blackened rafter of Number Six topple slowly, a spurt of flame, then no more flame. " . . . It has been my avowed and unchanging policy throughout my business career . . ." *I* and *my*, he spoke now for himself, the anxious president. Skafe said always *we* and *our*, and meant it, although the *I* was prodding spirit of the *we*.

He addressed the strikers and their chosen leader, who stood with him at Piccadilly Circus, Turtle Mountain, Northwest Territories. McClintock's arms were folded, his face expressionless. This platform on its stilts straddled a gully. Down in that gully, if you chanced to look, and if there was no covering of snow, you could see the silver outcrops in the rock, pure silver. Let it lie with cobalt, nickel, copper traces, waste riches of this wilderness.

He supposed that Chris Jorgensen had some new findings to report, more false alarms of plenty—perhaps in the lake bed. But there was nothing of importance there; it had been drilled before Jorgensen's time. The trouble about specialists was their biased optimism, one-track minds, or one-rock minds, not bad that. What did the Jorgensens know about anything but their pet babies?

". . . And now, gentlemen," he boomed, "before I ask your committee chairman to state his terms, let me assure you once again, my friends . . ."

"Horseshit!" It was screamed by one man, taken up by many. They cupped their hands to scream "Horseshit!" at Husky Skafe who for a moment almost lost the part he played, but he rallied to be rattled, put the finger tips of one hand to his brow, glanced wildly round and up at Pilbrom and the small management group outside the office building. Pilbrom was red with rage. It was nous, not guts that Pilbrom lacked. Skafe bowed to McClintock and yielded the microphone.

"Reston," said McClintock, facing him. His voice was pitched clear and low to be magnified without resonance. "We want Reston." He turned to his followers. "Reston," he said, rolling the R. "Reston!" they shouted.

Skafe put up his hand. "Yes," he said to McClintock. "Yes, yes, Reston. But please state everything, all your demands now together so that I may take immediate action." He spoke in a hurried fluster. "Mr. Mc-Clintock, surely my record in personnel relations, surely what I have said to you already this morning must carry conviction that I am willing, indeed eager, to meet every legitimate demand. Labor and management are, in my unshakable philosophy, a partnership. Say only what you want."

Thus Skafe humbled himself, thinking that here was a man he might have used if anyone could use such a man, if there had not always been the streak in the man—because this man was as much of a leader as he was himself. Skafe did not think that McClintock could resist the invitation to demand it all together, everything growing to all the power.

"First, we want Reston," McClintock said. The right sleeve of his windbreaker was unbuttoned. He had no gun in camp, according to Reston, but he carried a knife under that right forearm. When McClintock was thinking, or was minded to persuade, Reston told Mac, he would draw his narrow-bladed knife and strop it on his palm and clean his fingernails, the right hand and the left . . . "If we don't get Reston right away, we're coming for Syme . . ." He stared at Skafe.

"Please go on." His voice reached only McClintock, his opposite number. When the man spoke, the sheep were silent. When the man stopped, the parrots screamed. Skafe remembered a time, last summer again at Gallery, when Dorrien propounded a pet theme, mounted a hobbyhorse about the decadence of the West, failure of political democracy . . . *We might be better with Communism*, he said, *that's about all we're fit for*. Anna agreed, as she always did with David Dorrien. And to Skafe's surprise, his father agreed about the decadence, although not the Communism. Only Simon Skafe himself had argued against a general absurdity. Now alone, listening to the Scotsman make demands which were without any justification whatsoever, voice rising, whipping sane men into a violent horde, now Skafe had a doubt about the wisdom of the common man, sacred freedom, all the rest.

Second point, the original drunks, or sparkers of the strike—Norris, Greeley, and Lebel—were to be reinstated forthwith. Third point, wages. He had a pleasant Scottish-Canadian speaking voice in lulls between passion. Remarkable, Skafe thought. Hitler spoke with that quiet ebb and that frenzied flow. The passion rose now as he reached a climax. The wage increase had gone up to fifteen per cent, payable retroactively from October the First. "Fifteen per cent!" he shouted. "Not a penny less."

McClintock stopped to a perfect silence of his listeners, an imperfect silence of powerhouse, furnaces, wind. "That's my last word," he said, smiling. "You give way, Mr. Husky Skafe, or take the consequences." He looked at his watch, and linked his hands before his battledress trousers, right hand over left.

Skafe moved to the microphone. He waited through the ovation for McClintock and the abuse for Skafe. A flock of snowbirds swept down from the hill to alight among the rocks between him and his uncaptive audience. The snowbirds—snow buntings to purists such as John—were tame, demure, industrious, hunting for food, he supposed. They would do as an opener.

"The first year I came to Turtle Mountain," he said, calm and leisurely, unbombastic, himself, "I remember the snowbirds kept me company. They were moving north with the spring, just as now they are moving south with the fall. That was April 1932 when I was staking claims. It was not the first time I came to Turtle Mountain. The first time was in February of that year, extending my trapline. Do you know where I set my last trap? In this gully right below Mr. McClintock's feet and mine."

It was not strictly true, because the place was farther up the gully, but it was true enough and good local color. "A storm blew up," he said. "You know the way these arctic storms can come out of nowhere. And I was caught. I took what open shelter I could find against the mountain-side. I had no food until a cross fox obliged in this trap on the second day, not bad eating, better than skunk . . ."

"Tough guy!" came from his audience. The flock of snowbirds flew away.

"Oh no," he said, "I don't think a tough guy, even then. But I had things fairly tough."

"Stop the blether," said McClintock.

"Blether perhaps," he said, "but I did have things tough in those early days. Also," he said, smiling at the hostile men, "I found this place, and I waited twelve or thirteen years to make this place. Can you wonder that Turtle Mountain, although small among my enterprises, is in some ways more important to me than all my other enterprises put together?"

McClintock stepped up to interpolate: "More reason to give labor a square deal at last." Which brought a tempest of cheers and catcalling. "Get on with it," McClintock said. "You haven't all day for cackle."

Skafe had enticed the man here to stand alone with him; he had wooed the man into committing himself and his fellow strikers to a list of demands that were dictatorship set upon extravagance. In short, Skafe had given the megalomaniac leader his head. How right McClintock was that Skafe did not have all day for cackle. He had a few minutes only, while McClintock continued to share Piccadilly Circus with him.

He faced the hillside crowd, but he kept McClintock in his eye. "Before I come to the question of concessions," he said, "I may as well tell you that Reston is no longer here. Perhaps you did not hear the plane. Peter Syme has also left with a head injury, inflicted last evening by a person or persons unknown with intent to cause grievous bodily harm, or worse. So much for a squealer named Reston, and so much for a straight-shooter named Syme." He looked at McClintock, who looked at him, right hand over left before his body, tic fluttering below his eye. McClintock did not move.

"In the last five days," Skafe said, "we have had illicit booze and drunkenness in this camp. We have had willful property damage. We have had two cases of assault. We have had attempted murder by rifle shot." Untrue, he thought. But who could be quite sure except the marksman? "We have had arson. Do you know, for instance," he said, "that every man who watched Number Six hut burn—let alone the men who set it on fire—that every man who let it burn—and that means every man jack of you—has committed arson? And do you know what sentence the law provides in cases of arson?"

He himself did not know, but it did not matter. The crowd stood still and quiet in the background noises of Turtle Mountain; and then the men nearest here—they were McClintock's cronies and bully boys—began to shout at him.

Skafe—the piker, the mucking crook, the jerk, four-flusher, plutocrat, rich bleeder, SOB—perforce let them shout at him while he smiled at McClintock, and McClintock, surprisingly, at him. The yellowish eyes were blank. Skafe looked past McClintock and down to the lake where the west wind was breaking up the ice along the shore and against the drilling rig. He thought that McClintock would not move while the men were demonstrating their support for him and their hate for Skafe. He looked back to the crowd, ranging northeast, east, southeast from along the hill. He observed that a good many men were not shouting now.

He waited patiently for the demonstrators to run out of breath, which they did. "Cut!" Skafe said into the microphone.

The heating furnaces stopped their roar. The two big diesels stopped their clatter. The generators stopped their hum. Of a sudden, after these years again, there was no sound at Turtle Mountain but the touch and the rush of the good west wind.

"Listen!" he said. "Listen, the wind!" He stole the words from a book about flying that he had loved, and would sometimes still read, by Anne Lindbergh. He smiled at McClintock, expecting McClintock now to move. He knew very well from his boxing days that eyes signaled movement. But the draw of a knife was a single light flash of movement, not a cumbersome one-two of feint and punch. He saw curiosity, inquisitiveness in the wolfish face.

"It sounded like this when I first came," he said. "It sounds like this today a mile from camp. There is no man-made sound, except occasionally the voice of an Indian, within a hundred miles of Turtle Mountain, damned few within a thousand. The caribou are scarce nowadays, still a long way to the north and east of us at this season. There are a few wolves about—I saw a big male timber wolf this morning just before you fired at me." He glanced at McClintock, no movement on the way. The man looked a little puzzled. "There might be a willow grouse or two," Skafe said. "You people might know about that because some of you do make short excursions from camp to shoot them. But apart from the wolves, the foxes, the small birds and mammals, there is nothing, as I learned long ago. The lakes are not passable yet, nor is the muskeg. No one except a man experienced in the North—and that means none of you—only one man out of two hundred and fifty-odd men here would have a chance of surviving in this godforsaken bog of wilderness. That man happens to be myself."

He paused. He had their whole attention in the unwonted silence in the good west wind. "But here you are," he said, "living in this comfortable camp, with heat and light and fresh food flown from Outside. The waterpipes run in steam-heated jackets, or they did until a few minutes ago. The wooden catwalks link the wooden huts. It is a compact mining camp in which you can live more comfortably at fifty below than many people live Out there in Canada.

"I found this place," he said again. "It is the only thing I ever found and made myself. I love it, as I told you. But if you imagine that sentiment would persuade me to be held to ransom by the best paid and best cared-for miners in all Canada, you are far mistaken."

Here it comes, he thought, as McClintock stirred. But it did not come. The right side of McClintock's upper lip was rising towards the flutter of his lower eyelid. Skafe watched him. "There is no water pressure for hoses now," he said, "and none in the sprinkler system. With this wind, fire would take Turtle Mountain Camp from hut to hut, and along by the catwalks in a very short time, not a chance in a thousand of stopping it. I have men waiting to light the fires. Either you . . ."

Now McClintock moved. His left hand thrust upward from his right. It held the narrow knife that Reston had described. Skafe swung the microphone across to parry that. He took one step left and round the tripod leg. He kicked McClintock in the crotch. It was a dirty sort of trick against a dirty knife. He had been measuring this action all this time. The action worked much better than he had expected, or perhaps than he deserved.

"It hurts," he said, "as young Jacky Watters has good cause to know." Then he hit the agonized McClintock. He felt a knuckle or knuckles crack against McClintock's jaw, and a minor jab of pain. McClintock slid backwards through the Piccadilly Circus railing to topple down among silver, cobalt, nickel, copper. He fell heavily and slid on down the gully.

That was McClintock, but that was not all. Skafe turned. The possible bullet did not come. McClintock's lieutenants, four of them, came along the catwalk from Number Four. He went to meet them. His fists were not of much use against spanners, although his fists were still quite useful. You forget that your father taught you many things. One thing that John Skafe, a gentle man, had started him on at the age of nine was boxing.

"Stop!" he said. Fortunately, they stopped. "Now shake some sense into your heads," he said, "and get the hell back where you came from." Skafe returned to his microphone, still in commission. McClintock stirred below, but he was not in commission. "Some of you must know," Skafe said, "that McClintock organized the booze racket in this camp. You may not know that his personal cut was five dollars a bottle. There are a good many other things you may not know about the chairman of your Strike Committee. I know, because I took the trouble to find out from the RCMP. Now listen to this!" He read the dossier, or most of it, to his silent audience in the wind. ". . . That down there," he said, "was described by a distinguished policeman as the only plain wicked man he had ever come across. We all have a bit of the wicked in us, and a bit of the decent too. It is known as the human mixture. That man," and Skafe pointed down the gully. What an act, he thought. "That man is the great rarity who lacks the mixture. Why? I will tell you why: because he is a megalomaniac, a power bug, as well as being a crook.

"If you want to stay out on a wholly unjustified strike because a crazy criminal robbed you of your senses, you are very welcome to do so."

He stopped. He watched them. He thought that he had it won, but he could not be sure that he had it won. "I am not bluffing," he said. "And I am just as much entitled to my craziness as you are." They stirred. Every man shifted.

"Unless you agree to go right back to work on precisely the same terms of employment as before, I am going to burn this camp down. Take your choice."

Fascist, she would say. Or she would say that such a draconian threat made a ludicrous hypocrisy of his professions about the freedoms of the workingman and so on. *But Simon,* his father would say. *You can't turn men out in the arctic wastes to starve. You can't do it, son,* John Skafe would say, if he could find words at all; or would have said if he could have found words.

Nor would Skafe let the greenhorns and weekend hunters wander to be lost in half-frozen muskeg. He would let them camp in a disused mine and would fly them out in a day or two. But his wife and his father would be as wrong as he was right. There were none of the balances of society here. Either management managed at Turtle Mountain, or better no Turtle Mountain. Better no Turtle Mountain in any case, he thought. He loved this unprofitable place, but who does not want to burn failure's boat?

He felt the warmth of the sun and the nip of the wind. He heard a raven croak. McClintock was cursing him from the gully, and a trickle of snow water ran down the gully. "Hands up for going back to work," Skafe said.

"Thank you," he said, discomfited by his victory. He did not want to dominate men so completely. She might call that hypocrisy too. "There are one or two things," he said. "The first is that no serious damage or injury has been done, so no charges will be laid except against McClintock. The second is that if you have complaints of any kind about conditions at Turtle Mountain, I hope you will make them. Set up a workers' committee. It's time we had one." But how much more time for workers' committees? he wondered. "The third thing is a request from Mike Pilbrom. He said this morning that if you agreed to go unconditionally back to work, would I agree to his reinstating Norris, Greeley, and Lebel. They got drunk. People have got drunk before and have beaten places up. If you keep the booze out of here, I agree."

There was a murmur of approval up and across and down, but it was guarded. Now they were thinking for themselves. He wondered whether, in breaking what he had had to break, he had broken also a tie that had always existed between him and his men. It became less personal as the thousands of employees grew, but the spirit of it still existed. Were his true colors broken out? Was he becoming a typical highhanded . . . ?

"I'm sorry about all this," he said, to close the book well for him and for them; for him, he supposed. "I would like to tell you that there are no hard feelings on my part, and I hope there are none on yours."

Nothing was said. They looked at him. They admired him; he could sense that. He also sensed a fact of life that he might have concealed from himself, or had not admitted to himself—Labor stood across a no man's land from management. You could have good relations, but always across a no man's land. It was strange how long one could take to agree to a simple truth.

"Mac!" he said more loudly into his public address system.

The jeep stopped below the gully. MacNamara and two stretcher bearers disembarked. The plan had not included stretcher bearers, but only the arrest of McClintock by MacNamara, chief pilot linked to management, yet apart, a legend in his way, far more of a legend at Turtle Mountain than Husky Skafe had been. They climbed.

Skafe watched the man he had hated and defeated. He did not hate him now. He was more inclined to feel—it was absurd—he was more inclined to feel: There but for the Grace of God go I.

McClintock, who had broken a leg, from the angle of it, did not look down at Mac. He strained round, with an elbow for a prop, to stare up here. "Next time," he said distinctly. He made no resistance and said no more.

"We'll fly as soon as you're ready, Mac." Skafe's hand had begun to ache. He looked at it. He was none too happy about himself. He climbed the catwalk to the office. The small crowd was dispersing. The powerhouse and the furnaces came to life to make an illusion or a dream of recent events. It was Turtle Mountain up to date again, busy between that first wilderness and the wilderness that would return.

They were waiting for him, men always waiting for him. In time? Or not in time? Or Father rallied? He was not psychic. He did not have second sight, nor hear far voices in the wind.

He brushed past them, including Norris, Greeley, and Lebel, who seemed intent upon speaking to him. "Okay, boys," he said. "Don't thank me, thank Mike Pilbrom." Loyalty to his manager, what a lot of crap, he thought. He made for the office, but his eye was caught by Rosenheim coming from the radio shack. His eye was always being caught by something; and his eye, although not gifted with second sight, could read a drift of things from a face.

He opened the radiogram from Anna. It said: YOUR FATHER MUCH WEAKER DO PLEASE COME.

Gerry Rosenheim looked at Skafe with what almost might be some love and some compassion, and went away.

Skafe talked a minute with Pilbrom in the office, then went to roll up his sleeping bag. "Oh, hullo," he said. "You'd better ride Out with me, Chris."

"But I must show you these latest cores." Jorgensen meant the test cores from drilling. He had been plumbing the depths at large expense in pursuit of his belief that somewhere at Turtle there was a great vein of pitchblende. Jorgensen had raised many hopes that turned out to be flashes in the uranium pan. You had to use specialists, and most of the best ones were fanatics—the geologists, the engineers, the work-study men and God knows what—no sense of balance or proportion, no wood for trees. "I tell you, Husky . . ."

"For Christ's sake tell me, then," he said.

"What you mean for Chrissake? Have I not yust tried to tell you twenty times since yesterday?" He was Norwegian born, a placid fanatic, now irate.

"I've been busy," Skafe said. "I have actually been engaged in more important things, and they are settled, and I am flying Out. Now will you shut up, or will you tell me about your epic discovery?"

"I will hand you my resignation," said Chris Jorgensen.

"Okay," he said, putting the bag on his shoulder and taking the valise in his good hand. "I'm sorry, Chris," he said. "Come on, then."

Jorgensen feared that the catwalks had ears. He followed and would not speak until they were alone in a pickup truck. "There," he said, pointing at the lake. "You see my rig. The vein runs right across, two thousand feet long and open at both ends, and two feet thick and the lowest intersection three hundred feet. My cores are in average about point five per cent. Do you know what that means? It means ten pounds of U_3O_8 per ton. Now do you see the methods in my madnesses?" He drove away from the camp.

"Who knows about this?" Skafe said.

"My drillers have no knowledge and no Geiger counters. Only Peter Syme, I told. For the mining possibility, I consulted him. Not another soul. I did not tell Pilbrom yet, because he has been too busy, like you too busy. Also," and Jorgensen cleared his throat, "old Mike does not have the grasp of the big ideas."

"But the lake is deep," Skafe said. "It's a hell of an extraction problem . . ."

"Difficult, Syme says. But it can be done at a price. I tell you, Husky, this is fabulous. There is no other thing in Canada . . ."

"You're absolutely sure of the extent?" he said.

"I am certain, positive, unless there should be a geological miracle the other way, which there is not. Must you doubt me always?"

"No," he said. "I apologize, Chris. You see . . ." But why should he ask Chris Jorgensen to see the things that made only a fable of this fabulous discovery? He forced himself to think. "We'll be refueling at Dorval," he said. "Ask Mike to get Wilson Pitt and Sleeman to meet me there. Wherever Willie is, tell him to get there somehow. You're a great fellow, Chris," he said, "and I am grateful."

"*Me* a great fellow from a man like you? Did I not also watch you at that Piccadilly Circus?"

Skafe flew over Turtle Mountain and Turtle Lake. He looked back at the camp, where hoses now played on the smoldering ashes of Number Six hut. He had done what he had come to do. He had been lucky, at a price. He flew away again.

CHAPTER FOUR

TACTFULLY enjoined to be short and unpoetical, Mr. Mackenzie spoke of John Skafe as a gardener, an artist with his hands, a philosopher, a man of no rancor who was loved by men. It was true and good, if conventional; but John Skafe had in most ways been a conventional man.

Old Bumblehead, his father used to call Mackenzie, affectionate also in that criticism. Skafe's right hand was painful. It nagged on at him, here in this holy peace. There was a kind of holy peace. It nagged on at him about a world where men kicked other men in the balls. Sally's head turned a little to him and away.

Mr. Mackenzie could not resist a word about the God-fearing Skafes of Gallery, staunch pillars of the kirk. Simon Skafe did not want to be indirectly thanked for restoring the cemetery in town, for a thousand here and five hundred there, deductible. Nor, of course, were his benefactions mentioned. But they lurked annoyingly, embarrassingly, pleasantly about the crowded church at his father's funeral.

"I conclude these words with a few verses from Luke, Chapter Two. 'Lord, now lettest thou thy servant depart in peace, according to thy word: For mine eyes have seen thy salvation, which thou hast prepared before the face of all people; a light to lighten the Gentiles, and the glory of thy people Israel.' "

There was a prayer and a closing hymn. The congregation sang but, by some Presbyterian rite, the family of the dead one did not stand or sing. They sat in holy gloom while the people sang of the Lord their Shepherd.

The pallbearers wheeled the coffin on a chrome steel carriage with roller bearings to the door of the church, and then Tom Beamish and the others carried it down the steps and to the Cadillac hearse. *All men of all walks and denominations take one ride in Cadillacs,* John Skafe had once remarked to Simon at a funeral; but perhaps that dry quip was not original with him.

Skafe held the car door for Anna. Someone had moved the new station wagon to its appropriate place in line. There were minutes to wait while the flowers were stowed in the cavern of the Cadillac, and then Tom Beamish came to ride with the Skafes to Hackmatack Point. "Warm for the time of year," he said, looking short, scrubbed and squeezed in his navy blue suit.

"It's too early, isn't it," she said. "Indian summer comes later, I think."

"Yes," Skafe said. He drove out of Gallery at the pace he was set. He steered with one hand to keep the other out of view. He tended to be a careless driver at low speeds.

"Big funeral," Tom Beamish said. "Biggest turnout ever, I would say."

"Yes, big," he said. That was one thing he could be sure about: that the people of this small, kindly, acrimonious place had loved his father.

The last of the Skafes, they would feel, if not directly say, for fame and fortune make a stranger of a next-door neighbor.

The autumn coloring was at its best, but not particularly good this year, never particularly good on this shore of Gallery Bay, where the woods were predominantly evergreen.

"So perfect," Anna said, meaning a perfect day to be buried, he supposed. Her simplest remarks had an extra implication. I wish I could have a real good cry, he thought, but that was denied to him. He was too close again. He dropped back, which would mean a chain reaction all the way down the funeral line, the party line. When he arrived, he had tried to explain his lateness, but she cut him off: *I knew there must be some reason,* she said. So that had been denied to him.

"Grand weather at last," Tom Beamish said. "I wish your dad could have seen the day he was buried." Thus Tom completed it for Anna. They are all religious, thought Simon Skafe. They all believe in the life to come. Why then do they wish that your dad could have seen the day he was buried on? Does Simon Peter keep them incommunicado in some prison block on some Ellis Island?

"I think I like the color of the ashes best," John said. He had a man's voice now, without a ring or a bite to it. "Brown as old brown shoes," he said.

"I like the maples," Sally said. "Red as cardinals' scarlet breeches. You're an awful old opposite-liker, Jock." The dear child made a joke, and then the dear child began to cry. "Idiot," she said, rather like her mother.

The constable had taken station, and opposing traffic lined up beyond while John Skafe in a great rich Cadillac turned down a puddled dirt road to Hackmatack Point. "Just look at them oats," Tom Beamish said. The oats had been laid in a flattened tangle, unharvested. "Never knew such rain," he said.

Simon Skafe wanted to lend his daughter a handkerchief, or to say something in the way of comfort, but he was none too secure himself, and so he drove austerely down to Hackmatack Point where the Skafes were buried. It was a grand day after such rain as Tom Beamish had never known. A figure of speech, but not quite, for every day is some kind of record in some particular country way, thought Skafe—late, cold, wet, windy or the opposites, the combinations. To him, weather was a past or present fact, a future gamble. To them it was a part or a portent of God or something. But today he was thankful for the weather.

He stopped the car, leaving room on Tom's side, and Tom climbed out with visible if not audible creaks. "Arthuritis," he said cheerfully, and went to carry his fair share with Lee Becker and the other able-bodied. The honorary pallbearers were either too old or were not hardened to heavy work.

Simon and Anna walked together. "Oh, that dreadful imitation grass," she muttered, meaning the mortician's rug of lushest viridian fiber that hid the earth surrounding the grave, and put nature's greens into eclipse.

She was tired out at the time of his arrival. She told him that his father had died peacefully. *Did he say anything?* he asked, meaning or hoping that Father had left a message for him. *About five he said: Simon is busy, I suppose. Then he went to sleep, and he died at eight.* She was standing at the living room window. She had lost quite a lot of weight, he noticed. He liked her better with curves than angles. He knew that she did not mean to be cold-blooded, because he knew that one person she loved was his father. *It's up to you,* she then said, meaning his business, not hers. *But could you ask Mr. Mackenzie not to quote all those ghastly poems?*

If he had done all things to please her, he would also have mystified the undertaker by requesting no dreadful imitation grass. But he had forgotten that one. *Simon is busy, I suppose.*

"Barbarians," she said now quietly. "What's wrong with the common brown earth?"

He did see her point, but then what about pallbearers' shoes in muddy weather? What about so many more important things than the niceties of artistic feeling or good taste?

He wanted to say to her: *Anna darling.* He could not say it here and now to break the deadness of his father's death between them. He stood, looking stern and commanding, he supposed, as people said he looked; looking handsome, as people also said.

The larches at Hackmatack Point were old trees, crooked within the single-shafted habit of their growth. They were shedding some needles, small and brown and idle in the falling to lie on dark cloth, to hide in natural grass, to speckle the mortician's variety. The tide was about high. The colors across the bay were very fine above the water, and quivering in the water, double blessing.

A shot sounded now inland, the hard crack of a rifle, not a shotgun's bland explosion. It echoed across and about more freely than another rifle shot that he had heard much nearer to him three days ago. It was a single shot, perhaps at a deer in an apple orchard. Every settler family had their orchard. Almost all were now overgrown, lost in the forest; but deer love apples.

"Earth to earth," said the Reverend Mr. Mackenzie. "Ashes to ashes . . ." And at that moment Sally made a small splutter, probably about the ashes, ash trees, brown as old brown shoes. Her sorrow and her sense of humor played a game on one another. It was really quite peculiar, like a Chinese maiden laughing at her Granpa's funeral.

So the thing was done, and they moved away from the grave and the headstone that bore the name of John Kepple Skafe, but not yet his second date, to receive the kindness of Gallery people. Skafe shook hands a good many times, each one a little more painful than the last. But he grinned and bore it, or he bore it with stiff valor, trying to catch hands short by the fingers. It was damnable. He had been too busy, he supposed, to have a doctor look at it. They shook hands with the unfeeling Husky Skafe—or Mr. Skafe to most of them, or no name used—and moved on to have a word with Anna.

Then the good people went away. A few—the old C.P.R. men, the second cousins from Fredericton, Tom Beamish, the Beckers father and son, ten or twelve others and Mr. Mackenzie, old Bumblehead—were to come to the house for cakes and coffee or something stronger.

But now the Skafes were alone, gravediggers smoking cigarettes in the offing, lowering tapes bundled up, the undertaker suitably rewarded, the plain oak casket six feet or whatever it was down in the earth. Anna went over to a dry stone wall that bounded the cemetery, and John went with her, and they picked some flowers. They came back, carrying goldenrod and wild blue asters, withering at this season. Skafe stood with Sally in her biscuity-colored school uniform, most unbecoming, while Anna in a dark gray flannel coat and skirt—the nearest concession she would make to mourning—while Anna and John added wild autumn flowers.

Skafe wished that he could find some vulgar, sentimental common man to let his hair down with—some Gerry Rosenheim, Jimmy Little, Gus Velensky—but they were all his employees, so they would not do, even if available. Some feckless stranger like Gabriel the Indian tending his nets on the Mackenzie, he might do. Or the fat kiosk woman on St. James Street, she might do. So either a stranger, or some rare person he knew quite well who was not on the payroll, nor in the family, who knew that there was more to him than Husky Skafe the tough tycoon. Someone, in other words, who did not feel jealous in giving comfort. It once was so different, he thought, and left his father's grave.

"We should be going, Anna, I suppose."

"Yes, Simon."

The family Skafe, of which he was now *de jure* head, drove home to entertain with cakes and coffee or something stronger. For once he gulped at a drink. It was a cheerful if not hilarious small party, the old people glad of company and another day. He thanked Mr. Mackenzie for speaking well, and so did Anna. The children were much admired as waiters, handsome, attentive, smiling, then sometimes remembering solemn stranger death. The guests did not outstay their welcome. "All the best," said Lee Becker, his boyhood friend. "I guess you're feeling it pretty bad."

"Thanks, Lee," he said. It was wonderful that someone should realize that; and he loved Lee Becker. "I'm going to be here a few days," he said. "I hope I'll see you." He had sent Wilson Pitt to Turtle Mountain. He had put Miles Sleeman's brains to work. He did not know that it could be done, even if Chris Jorgensen was right altogether one hundred per cent. "What, Lee?"

"I said: Why not us spend a night at the camp, and have a day's hunting? The deer are plentiful this year."

"That would be great," he said. "I'll call you." But Lee's handshake reminded him forcibly of his trigger hand. The doctor would want to have it X-rayed, he supposed.

"Don't wait, Mrs. Cooligan," Anna said. "I know you have supper to cook at home. Sally and I will wash these up."

The women occupied, the men walked up to the old Skafe house. "A Myrtle," John said, and explained: "The myrtle warblers always stay late." Simon Skafe did not see the myrtle warbler. He was thinking of Omega and Alpha, the year ending to begin. He was five foot eleven, and John now five foot ten and a half. Simon Skafe was much smaller than that and much less than fifteen the last time he had been at Gallery in October.

"Did Granka ever finish the boat?"

"Yes," he said. "Two weeks ago, your mother says." They went into the house and to the workshop. The boat, or the clipper ship, was covered with a cloth. Unveiled, it was perfection, no other word—running blocks of ivory the size of matchheads, boxwood panels of the cabin, masts of birdseye maple, all to scale, every moving part an exquisitely useless working model. John Skafe's black clipper ship with golden trim was in full sail. She had been named. Her port of registration was Gallery.

"I never thought somehow that Granka ever wanted quite to finish it."

"I know," he said. "But he finished it. My father was that kind of a man. He always got there in the end on time."

They went along into the house to do some tidying, like putting some empty rum bottles and some empty medicine bottles and some empty ketchup bottles into a carton. "This is a good trick," Skafe said. "Look, John!" He showed him how you crisscross the four flaps of an opened carton lid, but John did not grasp that good trick easily. The kitchen and the parlor were not quite so tidy as before because Anna was not a very tidy person. "You might just put the books in shape," he said, and went upstairs to his father's bedroom. It looked out above the half-grown forest to the sea. His father's body had not been on view. *The ghouls will want that, I suppose*, she also said before she went to sleep. That she should get on so well with simple or common or garden people while having such a horror of their customs about death and mourning and the like was another remarkable thing about a remarkable woman. He shared her views about such things, or most of them, but he never could help feeling like a clodhopper schoolboy, afraid of what those views might be. He would not tell her, for instance, that he had spent two vigil hours here with his father while the sound of the rain on the maple tree came through the open window. The big maple was lovely today after the nip of last night's frost.

"Well, John," he said downstairs. "This makes you the second man of the family. I mean it puts us both up a generation."

"Yes, Dad," John said. "I hadn't thought of it like that." He was friendly, interested, dutiful, yet wary.

Skafe had had no chance for a talk with the boy, and would have none on the way to the train this evening, with Sally's nimble vitality leading the talk. "How's school this term?"

"Fine, Dad. I'm in the second under-sixteen at football."

"Oh, good," he said. *Second*, he thought. "And your math—did the tutoring this summer help?"

"I think so, Dad." He sat forward in his grandfather's chair. John had long unmuscular hands, and bitten nails.

"Well, John," he said, "I know how fond you were of Granka, but he lived to a good old age, and death comes to all of us." Listen to me, he thought. He moved, tempted to abandon this conversation, and saw relief in John's face. But Simon Skafe rarely gave up what he had begun. He pushed ahead with it: "So in a way," he said, "your grandfather's death marks a start for you as a man. Everyone grows up, and to judge by the size of you, you will soon be leaving me behind."

John smiled, pleased at that. "Yes, Dad?" he said, quite encouragingly.

"So all men come to responsibility," said Simon Skafe, "but not all to equal responsibilities. In other parts of the world men may inherit great landed estates. In Canada large inheritances tend to be in the form of money or business interests, which are more perishable down the generations.

"Now if I go broke, you will have nothing." They shared a laugh about that possibility. "It might happen," Skafe said. "But it won't, I hope. So in the ordinary course of events you may expect to be better blessed with worldly possessions than all but a small fraction of your fellow men. This is an advantage, but it is also a great responsibility for which you must train yourself, train yourself."

"Yes, Dad."

"It's early yet at fifteen and a half," he said. "But have you had any idea about a career?"

"Not exactly, Dad."

Dogged Skafe went on. "There is External Affairs," he said. "Our small diplomatic service is one of the finest in the world. The foreign service is in some ways, perhaps, a frustrating life, but you would . . ."

He continued by the Law (a fine training for any career), Medicine, Accountancy (at which possibility even that inert young diplomatist, John Skafe, winced), Engineering, Geology, Higher Education. ". . . And, of course, there is business," he said, "as honorable a career as any. In a growing economy such as Canada's, business has tremendous potentiality. Our own interests are expanding all the time, and in the not far distant future may . . ." He wished that he could detect a glimmer of enthusiasm in that well-bred young face. "I don't want to rush you a bit," he said, contriving to talk less like an annual report. It was extraordinary how he blundered into heavy weather with John. "I just want you to start thinking."

And John now seemed to be taking interest. "You say Engineering is necessary in the construction business, Dad. But you're not an engineer."

"No," he said. "I picked it up." It might be more accurate to say that he dug engineering out, theory and practice, with a power-driven shovel. His knowledge was wider in a general sense than that of most of his engineers, as they well knew. "You know, John," he said, "construction and mining are not the dull soulless sort of work that people imagine. There's a fascination to it, as to any productive business, in the finding and the making, in the financing too. A kind of artistic creation, you might almost say." It was David Dorrien who had suggested that to him. "Like a poem or a painting, almost, not that I would know." He was doing better, reaching him at last.

"Yes, Dad, I guess there is. I hadn't thought of it that way."

John gave his head a shake. He looked straight at Skafe, and said quite strongly: "I think I will take Engineering, Dad."

"It's your own life, John, and I don't want to influence you, although of course I want to help you." And what did that mean? "You're sure there's nothing else, no other really worthwhile career you have in mind?"

John left his chair and went to the window, where his arms swung out from his sides a few inches and back. It was a habit of his grandfather's, unobtrusive, uncannily reminiscent here and now. "No, Dad," he said.

"It's a great secret for a man," Skafe said, "to have something in life to work for, to take risks for, to make his own way towards."

They went out. "What will you do with the old house, Dad?"

Why *you*, why not *we*, a part of the family place which would be his some day? Why were all things put into Simon Skafe's own personal lap? "We'll have to see," he said. "The roof is none too good." But somehow he did not fancy the thought of putting new shingles on the old gray house before this winter.

Sally came to meet them. The school uniform might be designed for that purpose, but did not succeed in hiding the astonishing promise of her figure. It made him think of rich golden cream pouring slowly from a skimpy vase into a long curved vase, some lovely thing not yet quite filled.

At fourteen, she was petulant, a woman and a child, intensely aware of and contemptuous of boys, already admired by all males young and old, already accepting that without conceit, as the most gifted and beautiful women do. Her I.Q. was something astronomical. Her gift for mathematics was the most brilliant in the headmistress's experience. In short, Miss Sally Skafe had almost everything that others had not got. She was a marvelous warmhearted ruthless virgin queen, and could be very bitchy.

"Mummy wants you, Jock," she said. They might have been twins, they were so completely *en rapport*, and yet two children could not be less alike. No longer children, he thought, but it seemed the more remarkable that the stress of puberty should not have altered that relationship. They still preferred one another's company to anyone else's company. They still took up at meeting as if they had never parted. Now she looked at John and, *click*, something slipped across as well as *Mummy wants you, Jock*.

"Let's go by the pond, shall we, Daddy?" she said.

He would go by the pond or anywhere Sally chose to take him. The dam had held out through these rains, as any Skafe-constructed dam would hold. He could often be wrong about trees and strikes and people, not often about dams. "Your mother," he said. "How does she seem now, pooch?"

"She washed the dishes, crying," Sally said. Her own upper lip began to waver, and it steadied. "That's better, though, isn't it?"

"Yes," he said.

"Mummy loved Granka so much. Would that be somehow because of something about our other grandfather?"

"I don't know," he said. Anna's father, Torquil Frazer, had been drowned in the Liard River at Fort Liard in the Northwest Territories. He knew that, and the date, no more than that; nor did Anna. "Why, Sally?"

"She never has talked about him ever. She talks sometimes about our Scotch relations, but about him she just won't, not even if you ask. So John and I thought that perhaps Granka was like a father of her own, only more so."

"It might be true," he said. He knew it was true, but he could not tell an old unholy story to his own young daughter. "They didn't get on," he said carefully. "Some people don't."

"We get on," she said. She asserted it, protested it, defended it.

"We're lucky," he said. They sat on the rocks above the sea. The sun would soon go down, but it was warm, about seventy or so. He put his arm across Sally's shoulders. His hand hurt him, and she leaned against him, and he took his hand away. It is not given to many men to weep out sorrow. "We're lucky," he said again; and so he felt with Sally. He began to play his idle game of pitching pebbles to strike the very lip of the tide. He was not much good at that, left-handed.

"How did you do it, Daddy?"

"What?" he said.

"Hurt your hand. I noticed you not steering with it in the car; then I saw it now. Polishy swollen, the knuckles don't show."

"Oh, nothing," he said. "I just knocked it a bit."

"Can't you ever tell any of us anything?"

"Oh, Sally," he said, poor fellow. Then he told her without prettifyings or withholdings. He, who never told any of them anything, told Sally the story. She sat, her hands round her knees and her chin on her knees, watching the ebb of the tide. "That's all," he said. "I don't know what else I could have done, but I'm sorry about it."

"Why sorry?" she said, looking round at him, her eyes dark blue, the whites of her eyes amazingly white.

"Various reasons," he said to his daughter confessor and admirer. "I didn't get here in time to see Father is one thing. Bludgeoning labor is another. They've always trusted me, I think," he said.

"Everyone trusts you," she said. "They're afraid of you too. Except me, I'm not afraid of you."

He laughed. She could do with him what no one else could do. Now time to take her in to have some food before he drove them to the station. It was convenient that they could take the same train from here.

"So you think this new ore strike is really terrific?"

"Yes," he said. "And only six people know about it. You're the sixth, so absolutely mum's the word, okay?"

"Okay," she said. "In that case I should think much the most important thing to do now is find an efficient freight plane. The C-47's are years out of date. There's the Flying Freighter; and they say turbo-props are the next coming thing."

It might be elementary, but she had put her finger straight upon the crux of the problem. "Yes," he said. "I'm sending Mac on the rounds next week."

"How is Mac?" she asked.

"He's fine. He sent you his love."

"Oh, did he?" she said. "Dear Mac." She was different in so many ways from her mother—in self-confidence, in that practical whip of mind, in happiness the common state and not the passing mood. But sometimes the same woman spoke, at fourteen years old or thirty-nine. *Dear Mac,* they would say, in a tone reserved for Mac alone.

Simon Skafe had scrambled eggs with John and Sally in the kitchen. "I'll have a sandwich later," Anna said. She drank rye and water. She drank more nowadays, and showed no effects.

"Goodbye then, darling," she said to John. "Goodbye, my darling," she said to Sally. The Skafes were not a demonstrative family, but both children hugged their mother with what seemed to be a passionate compassion.

He had hoped that she would want to drive the thirty miles up there, then back with him, a chance to settle together again in a leisurely drive at night. But she did not offer to come, and he did not suggest it, seeing how worn she looked. "Go to bed early, darling," he said.

"Oh, no," she said. "I'm not a bit tired."

He was in good driving form. He always drove well, but tonight he settled to a rhythm through the dusk. John was a dreamer, and Sally was unusually quiet, and Simon Skafe had his thoughts. They spoke hardly at all until an average buck stepped from the evergreen forest to the road, looked at the lights, crossed into the other wall of the forest.

"I wish I could have seen the Indians' woods before we spoiled everything," John said. "The deer and the cougar, the passenger pigeons and the Indians, and not a white man in the old great forest."

"Not you, then, either," Sally said. "No Skafes at all, Jock."

"Would that matter?" John Skafe said.

What engineer would say such a thing? Skafe thought, but he did not speak.

He put John and Sally into their single bedrooms on the train. Anna thought lower berths were quite good enough, but he did not see the point of that. He tipped the kindly porter. He drove back to Gallery, down through the walls of the white man's forest.

CHAPTER FIVE

HE DROVE in and stopped the engine. The car made hot clicks and cracks. He rolled down the garage door and stood a moment, hearing the small sounds in there, the larger stillness of the night. The air was patchily warm and cool as he walked by damp woods to the house. He caught a familiar whiff of some dying plant, a rank and fecund scent of the fall. He opened the door between the carriage lamps, or the lamps from some old Skafe gig.

"Home," he said, to announce identity. "I'm going to get myself a drink," he said. "For you, Anna?"

"I have one, thank you," she said from the living room.

She sat in the chair beyond the fire. He put on two birch logs. The bark flamed up, and he closed the chain curtains against sparks. The room had the live warmth of a fire. She was reading a new book named *Cry, the Beloved Country*. He had read it himself, not that he read many novels. It was Anna's kind of book, he would bet. "Good, isn't it?" he said, sitting down on the sofa.

"Yes," she said. "The biblical style is mannered, but right for this." He expected her to dive again into her book, but she closed it and dropped it onto the carpet, lover of books but not a respecter of them.

"We saw a buck on the way," he said. "Otherwise no excitements. The children were a great help, weren't they?"

"Yes," she said. "So kind, both of them." She drank a little rye and water, and set down her glass. The firelight was on the right side of her face, and the lamplight too, flickering and steady. She looked pale even in the lenient light, her face half shadowed. "Simon," she said. "I want you to divorce me."

The bark had burned up and the wood had now caught. He liked an open wood fire. He supposed that nobody, not a single eccentric in the whole wide world didn't like a fire on an autumn night. No, nobody didn't; everyone did. *Simon, I want you to . . .*

"Will you?"

"Will I what?"

"Will you divorce me, Simon?"

It had been too much for her, he thought. People could go on so long, still longer, longer yet until eventually . . . He stopped watching flames and smiled at Anna. "Darling," he said. "You must be exhausted. Let me put a hot water bottle . . ."

"Oh, please," she said.

Then he saw that she was calm. Her dark eyes did not stare roundly and widely at him as they did when Anna was in a stew. Her eyes were deep and she watched him with concern, as on the few occasions in their married life when he had been sick. "But, Anna . . ." he said. His hand was aching. He put it up inside his left lapel to let the blood drain down from it. Humor her, he thought. "Why?" he asked.

"I've told you why," she said; "because a divorce is what I want."

"But *why?*" He sipped at his drink and put it down. She sipped at her drink and put it down. They drank the same rye in roughly the same proportions with two lumps of ice. Darby and Joan sipping whisky together beside the open fire—it was ridiculous. This must be the *crise* or the breakdown he had often feared would happen and wondered how he would handle when it happened. But it was happening peacefully. "There must be a reason, I mean," he said. "Or reasons."

"A reason and reasons," she said. "That's it exactly." She smiled at him in a friendly way and looked at the fire in their comfortable living room at night. "I know you think I've gone crazy," she addressed the fire. "Screw loose. Unhinged. But actually, I have come to my senses at last."

But actually, the English said. And actually she had so tuneful an ear for speech that she could not be long with people without reflecting their words and intonations. After sixteen years, he knew her well in many ways. He also knew now that the unbelievable was happening. "You'd better explain," he said.

"The reason and the reasons," Anna said. "The reason is David, as you might have known if you had been able to comprehend that any man could rival you. But a reason does not come suddenly and simply out of the blue, or like uranium ore out of Turtle Mountain, or like a contract to the lowest bidder. Reasons are not so simple, Simon, as you find them."

He let her take her time on the day or the night of his father's funeral.
She's wrong, he thought. The most convincing reasons do come simply
and suddenly out of the blue.

"Before we were married," she said, "and when we first were married,
and when the children were very young, I did have a part of you. We
were so furiously in love that the differences between us didn't matter.
Differences alone don't matter, anyway. And we had our children. Your
work possessed you even then, but you gave me and the children some
of the rest of you, and so your work belonged to me too. And then the
war came, and I lost you to the war. I knew I had to lose you, and I
knew how much you wanted to fight in the war, and couldn't. So all
through those five or six years when we would meet and make love, meet
and make love and part again, I never complained."

"No," he said. "You never complained." Why the hell should you? he
thought.

"I thought all that time: *When the war is over, I will get him back.*
The war ended, and that made no difference. Or it made a great difference because I saw that it hadn't really been the war at all that kept you
from me. It was your ambition."

"That's not true," he said.

"Perhaps not true for you at the time. But what happened afterwards?
You were getting big by then. You had to convert to peace. You soon
decided that to stay big, you had to get bigger. If things don't get bigger
and better, they get smaller and worse. That's true for everyone and
everything, I suppose. It is even true for marriage."

"How right you are," he said.

"I know I have failed you in many ways, like being intolerant of your
business people—friends, you call them. But none of them are real
friends. Don't forget that I have had to lose the few good friends you
left behind. Only Mac now—he's the only one. And dear Mac stays your
friend because he is your hero; also because he fulfils a useful function."

Skafe, slow to anger, was becoming angry. Is anger my new habit? he
thought.

"I don't mean to be unkind," she said. "And I don't mean really that
you make use of Mac. Things don't seem so simple to me as they do to
you. I know a wife has to be a sort of appendage, or even a mounting
block to stand upon and climb up by. Husbands do it and children do it.
But she also has to be in a way the anchor—what you would call the firm
base of the family. She has to be a partial reason for life itself.

"When business haunts the few waking hours she spends in her husband's company; when every dinner party has a dollar sign lurking some-

where; when even the children in the holidays are dragged in as charming family evidence of the great man's quality—can you wonder if the wife thinks that the whole thing is a sham? Can you wonder that the convenience gets bitchy and bloody-minded and anti-social? Perhaps she still has bed or love or whatever you like to call it to make her feel occasionally that she is wanted. But by that time she has learned enough about men, or about one man, to know that however lovely a comfort bed can be for her, all it is for him is ease the manly beast and back to sleep."

Anna looked at him. She said these monstrous things quietly and dispassionately. "So there I was," she said, "a means to an end, or two ends at most." She smiled, perhaps about their joint libidos. "You were always kind, always considerate, always patient when I saw you; but I had no share of you for my sake ever, only for your sake. I asked you long ago . . ." She looked at the fire.

"You asked me what?" he said.

"It was on Great Slave Lake the first day we were together. I asked you then for a share of you—I meant a share of you for my sake as well as yours."

He remembered that day when the candle ice hissed and tinkled on the boat. There might be truth in what she said so quietly. "Anna," he said, "if I have failed . . ."

She raised her hand to stop him, and he stopped. "Too late," she said. "Those were some of the reasons that helped to make one reason. I know it seems incomprehensible to you, because you are so sure of yourself— not arrogant, I don't quite mean; and not conceited, not yet anyway— just supremely self-confident about everything, including me."

"You're wrong," he said. "These last few years I've never known where the hell I stood with you."

"Simon," she said, "I sound as if I'm blaming you. But really I blame myself. I did my best sometimes. More often I either did nothing or I did my worst with those competent morons, your business friends. I know I'm a jealous and possessive woman, but I simply couldn't bear to see you gradually corrupted."

"Corrupted?"

"Yes," she said. "Corrupted from a sense of proportion and liberal ideas into being a superefficient materialist tycoon. I couldn't bear it, so I stopped trying and became an even worse handicap or halter of a squaw around your neck. The truth is," she said, "that I'm just the wrong kind of wife for you. You need a gentle serene little-woman kind of wife."

Anna looked at him again, but she did not go on to say what he knew she was thinking.

"I cared terribly," she said, "and then gradually from two years ago I cared less until I discovered that I didn't really care because I had found someone I did matter to, and he mattered to me, and I could help him, and we spoke—we spoke the same language. David isn't strong like you, nor efficient, nor reliable, nor calm, nor considerate in small ways. But he happens to be a human being and a very gifted one who can laugh and worry about the world, and not see the millennium in a balance sheet."

"The world you mention," said Simon Skafe, "is full of parlor pinks who despise balance sheets, yet are only too ready to profit from them."

"It's no good," she said. "You can't provoke me."

"Also," he said, "I don't think your numerous reasons that add up to or subtract down to David Dorrien sound particularly convincing."

"Not to you," she said. "But they convince me altogether. Which might be said to be what matters."

"I don't see it," he said. "I don't see how you can suddenly do this without any previous warning whatever except for an outburst or two during a tantrum or two. It doesn't make sense."

"That's your trouble," she said. "Only the logical makes sense to you. Always logical, always in control, always Husky Skafe, that man of steel."

"Shut up!"

She shut up, perhaps knowing that she might be in danger from that man of steel. He finished his drink. "For you?" he said, and went to get replenishments. It was a breather too. He had said almost nothing up to now. His wits were no match for hers, when her wits were calm. It's a funny thing, he thought, but I never saw Anna so sure of herself, so—what was the word she used about the suitable wife?—so serene.

"Sorry I shouted," he said, and she smiled a little to acknowledge that. He put her drink on the small table while she sat still, looking at the fire. He put his left hand lightly down to cup the round of her shoulder bone. It fitted as always, just as always, soft and strong in the palm of his hand.

"Don't!" she said sharply.

He went back to the sofa. "All right," he said. "Now tell me what you want me to do."

"Adultery is the only ground for divorce in Quebec," she said dispassionately. "So we shall have to produce the evidence."

"You seem to take a lot for granted," he said. "I haven't agreed to a divorce."

"I think you will agree," she said. "Because when you face up to things, you are going to see that a divorce is what you really want yourself. And what you want you always get."

"But John and Sally—don't you give a damn about leaving your children?"

"Sally doesn't need me now," she said. "She never did need me much. And John is growing up. He's much better without me than with me in the dead misery of an unhappy family."

"You didn't speak to the children about it?" Surely not that enormity, but he did not know; he never knew with Anna.

"No," she said. "But they both have perception."

"You chose a peculiar time and occasion for this," he said. He was being quite moderate. The conversation had now settled to a nightmare moderation.

"I know," she said. She looked across at the table by the door where his father's photograph stood. "Father did need me," she said.

John Skafe had needed her. Simon Skafe did not, in her estimation. It was that same strain of ruthlessness in Anna which had enabled her to encourage a decent dipsomaniac of a first husband into drunkenness and then skip with another man without regret or a pang of conscience so far as Skafe had ever known. The veneer of the outer spots might have changed, but not the leopardess. In many ways, he was seeing now, it would be a relief to be free of the leopardess.

"About money," he said. "You would have the trust income, of course." He had set up a trust, a quarter of a million, from which the income went to Anna in her lifetime. At her death, the trust would fold, and the capital sum be divided between John and Sally. He had done it for various reasons of taxation, and to let Anna have more independence than the direct favor of an allowance, and because she did not have a clue about money.

"I don't want anything," she said. "David is making lots." Rather crudely stated.

"A trust can't be broken," he said. "The income is yours for your lifetime." He might have said that he had been simple-minded enough to think that she would remain a deserving recipient for her lifetime. *Husky Skafe divorced that wife of his, did you hear?* he thought now.

Anna shrugged her shoulders, the magnificent shoulders of Dorrien's portrait. The absurd thing was that he had grown quite to like David Dorrien, who could argue passionately in earnest, or preposterously for the sake of argument about any subject under the sun except such subjects as those competent morons, Skafe's business friends, could argue about.

"And then there's this house," he said, drawn on inexorably, work it all out. The new house and ten acres were in Anna's name, again for taxation, and again for an extra reason—that she loved the place. "The best thing would be if you would sell it to me." What was it worth by now? Perhaps fifty. "I suggest I pay you a hundred thousand," he said.

"Oh, please!" she said. When he touched her shoulder, when he spoke of the house, she showed emotion. "It isn't mine. I never paid a cent for it. And can't you understand I don't want money?"

"Yes," he said. He did know that. "And can't you understand that I'm not going to let you run away penniless with an improvident artist?"

"You were always so generous," she said. "I'm sorry, Simon."

"Are you really sure about this?"

"Yes," she said. "It's the best thing for both of us, and for the children now that Father's gone." Her face bore concern for him, he thought. It was peculiar. "I think Father saw that too," she said.

"Did he speak of it?"

Anna nodded. He opened the fire screen to bring the warmth of the dying fire. She stopped crying, and did not tell him what his father had said, and he did not ask her. If she said so, it must be true. That was Anna.

"Are you in love with Dorrien?"

"Love," she said.

"Where is he now?"

"In New York for his exhibition."

"Is your portrait there?"

"Yes," she said. "He always shows it."

"I am well aware of that." When he had offered to buy it from Dorrien in 1946, first year, Dorrien had said: *The portrait is not the wife.* Since then the wife had also become the artist's property . . . "I didn't hear you."

"I said that the Museum of Modern Art tried to buy it last week, but David wouldn't sell."

"That's interesting," he said. He wondered if she knew that he had a blanket option to bid against any price that Dorrien was offered for that painting. But probably she knew, because Dorrien had come to depend upon her in many ways. They had seemed innocent ways, such as asking her opinion about his work in progress; or asking advice about his prices now that he enjoyed some fame and a vogue.

Anna as an art adviser made some sense. Anna as financial counselor was quite laughable. David Dorrien the painter, well born, cultivated and amusing, had come to depend upon Mrs. Simon Skafe. So had old John Skafe depended on her. Oh, stop it, Skafe told himself, for the sad thing was that he knew his wife to be a woman whom men might love in many ways.

"Have you been living with him?" he asked.

"Not noticeably," she said. What a damned cold-blooded comment that was, or sounded.

"Your plans, then?"

"There's nothing more for me to do at Gallery." She looked once round the room, quickly once and back to the fire. "Leave as soon as possible," she said. "Tomorrow morning, if I can get a seat on a plane." She must be anxious to get the hell out of here, he thought, if she's willing to fly. "Then pick up a few things at the house in Montreal. Then go. Should I see the children, Simon?"

She depended on him for advice and help, for bookings and tickets and everything; for the money she genuinely did not want. But who would buy Mr. and Mrs. Dorrien's tickets? "Yes," he said. "I think perhaps you should see the children. This is your baby, after all." *Baby* was apposite, or could have been. Another child might have done the trick. But she had been most carefully and thoroughly determined not to have another child. "Yes," he said. "Take them each out to lunch, and explain the situation, and say goodbye. I could get Mrs. Murton to arrange with the schools, if you would like me to."

"No, thank you," she said. "I shall spare the efficient Mrs. Murton." But she looked round at him, and now with supplication. "Do you mean that I have to say goodbye to them for always?"

"Oh, I wouldn't say that," he said. "By the way, you might tell Dorrien that I want to see him in Montreal next week."

"Is that a summons?"

"No," he said. "It might be called a *sine qua non.*"

"You won't . . . You won't hurt David?"

"Why would I bother?" said Simon Skafe. "I don't depend upon you or him or anyone, do I? No reason for me to take it out on Mr. Dorrien."

"I know I'm not fair to you," she said.

The telephone rang, and Anna started in her chair. There was a fluid grace about her tensed to move—the long legs unlinked to meet before her at ankle and calf and knee, the long hands gripping, the bosom still. "That'll be Mac," he said. But on the way he thought that it might be Dorrien for her.

It was Mac, who had been shuttling key personnel to the dockyard job in Halifax. His two-bit airline was becoming a major ancillary enterprise, and, like other things, it was only beginning. Skafe spoke briefly to him from the telephone below the stairs.

"Lucky chance," he said. "Mac will pick you up at Flume Hill at ten o'clock. I'll run you over. That takes care of excess baggage problems."

"I have only one trunk of clothes," she said, "and the two small cases."

"But, Anna . . ."

"I don't want anything."

"Not even books?"

"No," she said. "No, thank you, Simon." She looked up at him—he was standing before the fire, which was low again—and her eyes were wide pupiled, almost black. "It's the best thing," she said. "I know it is. Don't hate me too much always."

"I won't," he said. But he might be bitter against her. "You could call it a love affair," he said.

"Yes, a love affair. Do you remember John's little verse: 'Cry, Plover, fly! For the year must die'?"

Skafe did not believe that the year in question was really dead. But better cut short than allowed to linger. "Father's ship," he said. "You must take the *Anna*."

"No," she said. "I couldn't bear to take it. Besides, what would I do with it?"

Yes, what? he thought. And what will you do with yourself in studio apartments in New York City, and rented villas in Jamaica? "Am *I* to have the *Anna*, then?" He could not help turning that screw.

"Tom Beamish might like to have it," she said, "to keep for John, perhaps."

"I'll ask him," he said.

"I wish you'd be horrible," she said.

He took both her hands and pulled her from the chair and dropped her hands and gripped her shoulders in the soft cashmere sweater and held her to him to feel her against him and she to feel him against her because he knew that she was the woman to his man no less than ever.

But she tore at his hands. "No, damn you!"

It was an excruciatingly painful twist of his bad right hand. He squeaked like an injured urchin as Anna pushed past him and ran from the room.

He tidied papers and magazines, emptied ashtrays, rinsed glasses, drew back curtains, opened a window a crack, poked the last of the fire and closed the screen, picked up her book, locked the front door, switched off the lights and so to bed, his chores completed, his wife's small strewings tidied. He had always quite enjoyed doing that. She provided the carefree touch, and he the order, a good balance in a house if both principals agreed to live with their differences.

"Your book," he said at the bedroom door. "I'll just put it down."

"Oh, thank you, Simon," she said. "Goodnight."

He prepared himself for his second sleep at Gallery. Two sleeps, he thought. It is two sleeps from here to yonder, as the Eskimos say. His first sleep had been for a few hours in the dressing room, back from his father's house to tiptoe up and use the other bathroom, not disturb Anna in her first good night's rest for a week or more. Now he did all that again, a considerate man, as she had said.

I can get her now, he thought in the narrow bed. It's probably locked, but all I have to do is insert my master key, and hey presto, she is mine again, as she knows so well and fears so much.

But the question was: Did he want Anna back for more lasting reasons than to ease the manly beast, as she had so crudely described it? *Too late*, she said, and he thought that she was right, not altogether only for the reasons she thought, but because she had said too many things calmly and carefully to him tonight. Things said in heat or by fools can be forgotten, but not things coolly said with intelligence.

The tide was high again. The small waves lapped the shore. She said *lapped* was a cliché word, but that there was no better word for the sound of the wavelets at Gallery. Such natural sounds meant little to him; they meant a mystical much to her. And she was deliberately throwing it away—the sea and the house and the children she loved; the man she still wanted physically. For what was she throwing it all away? Well, for what?

He saw now how much easier it would be: Do what he wanted; ask whom he wanted; not have to endure the acidulous post-mortem on some perfectly decent, if limited chap; not have to sit along the table from heavy silence, or from: *Not really, Mr. Jones, You see, actually, I think more and more, that ore is such an awful bore.* She said that once.

His hand throbbed but no longer ached. He had taken a 222. He never took drugs, but this was a small exception. He heard an owl hoot in the woods. Hoo-hoo-hoo, three times, five times, and then once. He wondered whether she had heard the owl, the deep lament.

He went into sleep and into dreams. The dreams grew on about rifle shots, about a coffin that sank in a bright green sea or a dull green river, old man, cold man Mackenzie River; and rose again, and the lid popped up and his father stepped out to look around in his diffident way. It must all be a false alarm, Skafe thought, asleep. Dad's alive and kicking.

Nobody dreams about dead people. *Simon is busy, I suppose,* said old
John Skafe.

He went on dreaming on and on. *I'm McClintuck,* Lord God Mc-
Clintock brutally kicked. *And where would Canada be without ambition?*
Oh, shut up, Grace. Grace, what do you want? What is it, Anna?

He woke as the sprawlings of his dream died from him. What a disgust
and a slimy pit and an easing too. He went back to sleep.

The morning was dull, and the colors just one day past their best, she
thought. They were like old buddies together in the car. It was remarkable. She noticed his hand at last and made him promise to see the
doctor. He did not resent it that she had failed to notice his hand before,
because he knew that she had had much grief and many troubles in her
mind.

"Tell me about it," she said. And so he told the story a second time.
He even included the dirty words where dirty words were true. He omitted
only to mention the new discoveries, not because he did not trust her,
but because she was cluelessly capable of letting such things slip out. No
criticism from her, no sniffs or scowls about draconian behavior—frank
praise, indeed. "Husky boy," she said to the President. "You're a crackerjack. You're lethal."

They laughed extravagantly. It was a stout way to say goodbye. It
made sense of everything. The trouble was that, turning into Flume Hill
airport, his own moribund creation, he thought that he had never loved
her so wholeheartedly, nor been so well understood by her.

Mac was waiting. He had made good time with a following wind,
which always put Mac in a slightly good mood. The plane was gassed
up already. Skafe went with him to get flight clearance.

"Mac," he said. "I'd better tell you, I guess. Anna's leaving me. She
wants a divorce."

Mac stopped on the asphalt. "But Jesus Christ," he said, without
blasphemy. "You looked happy together just now for once."

"I know," Skafe said. "I know." He left MacNamara.

"Goodbye, Anna," he said.

"Goodbye, Simon," she said. They kissed one another in the cabin.
He left the plane. "I'll be seeing you, Mac," he said.

But his old friend had nothing to say to him.

CHAPTER SIX

He usually walked downtown to reach the office by nine, but he was late this morning, having come in on the Maritimes train. He picked up a cab at the corner of Sherbrooke and Guy. "Where to, Mr. Skafe?" said the driver, strange to him.

Boulanger was the name on the operator's license. Boulanger or baker.

He talked French with M. Boulanger, the taxi driver. Skafe was not bilingual, even in the sense loosely used by English Canadians about people with a modest knowledge of French; but he could get along, and was improving.

He took the elevator for twenty-one. "Good morning, Mrs. Murton," he said up there. It was good to be back up there. She followed him in to speak about his father, which she did sincerely and nicely, and he thanked her. He would have inquired after Mr. Murton, with diabetes, but she looked at his cast, and looked a second time, seeming startled by it. "Your poor hand," she said.

"It's nothing," he said, "except that the cast makes writing awkward. I broke the bone behind my middle finger."

"That's one of the metacarpals," Mrs. Murton said. "I remember from my nursing days."

No doubt she had been as competent and selfless a nurse as she now was a secretary. He could not quite see and yet did see himself having a bed bath with or from Mrs. Murton. She was so perfect—*such a prissy paragon,* Anna said, Anna used to say—that he strayed into improbable thoughts about her.

She went through the letters, nothing of much importance since the batch she had sent to Gallery.

There was a hospital meeting at three o'clock—he had agreed to head the new drive for funds. It looked like being a reasonable day; and now Pitt and Sleeman awaited him in the board room.

"The press keep calling, Mr. Skafe. They're on to some story about the Turtle Mountain strike, I mean the trouble there. I said we didn't know whether you would be in today."

"Which papers?"

She mentioned five—Toronto, Ottawa, Montreal. "And I don't know, Mr. Skafe. I didn't really think until I noticed your hand, but perhaps you should see this." Mrs. Murton held out a local tabloid by the name of *Glare*, folded to page three. Among her innumerable services, she kept a hawk's eye on the newspapers for references, however oblique, to him and his activities.

Skafe read the single sentence: "Did the typhonic tycoon spill Turtle Soup on his good right hand, or was it Mock Turtle nearer home?" A clever, double or triple-edged little squib, and only two words annoyed him. But the mocking of Turtle had always annoyed him. He wondered who, just who could have known enough? But then he thought that it might be partly a bow at a venture, for Anna's views on business were hardly a secret, and their longish periods of separation no secret either. "Yes," he said, old poker-face, and returned the paper to Mrs. Murton.

"I'll tell you in a minute about the press," he said. "Oh, and one other thing: If Mr. Dorrien calls, you might let me know. Thank you, Mrs. Murton."

She went, leaving him alone at his desk or table. It was a good mahogany reproduction, no files or papers on it, nothing but two telephones, the office speaker system, a pigskin writing set, an enlargement of Anna and the children on the beach at Gallery. What does one do about ex-wives' pictures? he wondered vaguely, the innocent. Then he walked across his good Persian carpet—heraldic tigers, peacocks, trees.

He said good morning to Pitt and Sleeman. Willie Pitt glanced shiftily at Skafe's black tie. "Sorry about your Dad," he said, shy in such matters. "My sympathy, S.K.," Sleeman said. "However much we may expect them, these things come always as a shock."

And you come out with a precise formula for everything, he thought. "Thank you," he said to each of them, glad to be done with condolences. "The press are on to the Turtle trouble," he said. "It was bound to happen, I suppose. The question is: See them or not see them? I haven't quite decided, but it must be soon, if at all. What do you think, Willie?"

"They could make heck for us. Slant the thing wrong—I wouldn't put it past them. If we sit mum, the duck will be dead in a day or two." Wilson Pitt was extremely good with reporters as people, innately suspicious of them as tools.

"That may be true for the solid press," Skafe said, "who wouldn't slant it wrong anyway. But if the left wing made a big story of the thing, then the others would have to take it up, and questions in the House would be the next thing. I think better to break it to the reputable papers, thus spiking the gutter guns." What a dyed-in-the-wool reactionary I sound, or am becoming, he thought. "Not that I give a damn, anyway," he said. Nor did he, in the personal sense. He had trodden warily, threatened when he had to threaten, done what he had to do. But this would be a bad time for doubts to be raised as to his moderation or stability. "What do you think, Miles?"

"Handled skillfully," Sleeman said, "as you would handle it, S.K., I think we should benefit from a press conference, not only for the sound and primary reasons you mention, but also futurewise. First, the public knows little as yet of Turtle Mountain, and the place should be put in the public mind. Second, your own name should be kept before the public, not overdramatically, I mean, but as a name about which a legend might be growing—strong, moderate, dynamic. You don't want that, I know, but we need it."

Skafe could not say honestly to himself that he did not want that. Who but a saint could dislike the idea of becoming a strong, moderate, dynamic legend?

"Third," said Miles, "it would be a good opportunity to make some reference to the extraction difficulties we have experienced in this past year—indicate disappointment, but guarded optimism for the future. Or, in other words, by what you do *not* say, paint a faintly dubious picture." One, two, three, he ticked the points off on his fingers.

"The news of the ore strike is bound to bust," said Pitt. "You get too smart with all this double-guff, and then where are you?" He paced up and down, or he ambled, bearlike.

"Not too smart, I agree," said Skafe. Which was why he would prefer old Willie to young Miles any day with any reporter. "You're quite right, Willie. The news will break sooner or later."

"Why not sooner, then? It strengthens our fist." Pitt frowned, bear in a dump of intangible cans.

"Not with the people who matter to us now," said Sleeman. "They want facts, not stories. But public confidence is quite another matter. If we should wish to make a large psychological impact on the public, then later is the time—no fizzling squibs, but an explosive story. But I am going too fast." He smiled. He had a brain, all right, and not only for finance.

"Better see them, I think," Skafe said. He summoned Mrs. Murton, and instructed her to ask the *Gazette, Star, Journal, Citizen, Globe and Mail, La Presse,* for twelve noon; and nobody else who wanted to come unless she consulted him. "Better rustle up some Scotch," he said. "And Willie—you might come along to hold my hand. You'll get a free drink, too."

"You mean also, or two?" said Willie Pitt.

"Let's sit at the window. How's Amy?" he asked.

"Ugly as ever," Willie said. He was fifty-five. He and his fat childless wife loved one another, not to distraction as some people love, but to contentment.

"And Cynthia?" Mrs. Miles Sleeman, Busty Maxwell the stockbroker's daughter, was pregnant again. She had produced her first as painlessly as going to the bathroom, by peace of mind and calisthenics. She was on the right charities, like the Junior League. She wore a felt hat in the station wagon. She was a healthy athletic aseptic Young Executive's wife. And Cynthia was a damned nice girl. *Flourishing,* said Miles. "What about Miles Junior?"

"He's walking, S.K. He did three steps last night to me across his playpen. Tottering, you know, but he really did."

The suave Sleeman glowed with honest pride, plain unaffected love and pride. It was quite thought-provoking. How simple the simpletons who named men either cold or warm, sonsofbitches, angels. *Things don't seem so simple to me,* said Anna, *as they seem to you.* Of course they did not, and of course they did.

Skafe sat facing the window. His cast made a hard tap on the round table. He noticed that neither Pitt nor Sleeman inquired about Anna. It was a dull Octoberish morning in the city, and the sounds were loud. "Let's start at the beginning," he said. "What did you make of things at Turtle, Willie?"

"All true one hundred per cent," said Pitt. "The stuff is there, not a doubt in a pig's whistle. Mike Pilbrom said an impossible extraction problem, and I wasn't too sure myself, but Syme convinced me. You can do it, for a great fat slab."

"How is Peter Syme?"

"Still has headaches, but the medicos gave him a clean bill. He's a top boy, that one."

"Yes," Skafe said. "And Pilbrom?"

"It's going to be too big for Mike. He's out of his league, as he says himself. But he has a chip about Syme. Plain jealous. That happens."

"Yes," Skafe said. "It happens."

"We'd better put Syme in charge of the new development, responsible to me direct. Leave Pilbrom with the present operation and camp management. He won't like it, can't be helped. That's the way to bake the pie. Okay, Husky?"

"Yes," Skafe said. He sat between them, Wilson on his right, Miles on his left, and not by chance. On the one hand fifty thousand a year's worth of solid drive and nous, on the other hand thirty-five thousand a year of intangibles, not quite a proven investment. "Yes," he said. "Okay for the baking, Willie. But first find the fuel to fire the oven. You've given Miles all your figures, have you?"

"Yes," said Pitt. "You want to hear them now?"

"Later, I think," he said. "Well, Miles?"

"From the geological information, and from what Wilson tells me of the engineering costs involved, I would estimate, S.K.—and it cannot be so much an estimate as a guess—I would estimate that the Turtle Mountain property is worth this morning ten million, more or less, on the market."

"To sell, you mean?"

"Yes," Sleeman said. "I think I should say that first, because it would be a long time, and many million would have been expended before any such profit could again be realized. Also, and in view of the fact that the equity of Turtle Mountain is held entirely by you, S.K., such a sale, even after loan repayments, would mean a large personal gain to you."

"No," Skafe said. "I haven't waited all these years in order to sell out." But he was pleased that Sleeman, whose big chance lay in new financing, should not have ignored the possibility of cashing in. Sleeman knew, of course, that he would not cash in. "We're going to do it if we can swing it. Go on, Miles."

"From Wilson's calculations, the development of the new findings, extensions to camp and airport facilities, provision of up-to-date aircraft, Edmonton terminal, and so on—to develop the potential of the property as a going concern will cost some forty-five million."

"Forty-five," Skafe said. "Whoopee!"

Willie Pitt laughed largely. Everything was large about him except his height—big boned, heavy muscled, jowled. Willie ate too much, drank too much, worked too much, and did not exercise enough. He was a great chap, Willie.

"Now, there are various ways, or combinations of ways, by which forty-five million could perhaps be raised—from the public, from mining groups, from the banks . . ." Sleeman was warming up, deceptively ponderous, a slow-spoken young man of thirty-two. "But before any financing can be done, there is a prerequisite: firm contracts must be negotiated and concluded with Ottawa. Without an assured government market for ore, we can make no beginnings."

"I am aware of that, Miles," Skafe said. It was only Sleeman's way, but the child-guide approach did not endear him. "I'm going to Ottawa tomorrow."

"Just what I hoped, S.K. Now, I have done quite a bit of thinking on this. But before I develop my line of thought, I had better restate the assumptions on which I have worked since our brief meeting at the airport last week. First . . ." Once more he began to tick off those fingers. "First, I understand that you want to retain control if at all possible; and that, in any case, you will not allow control to pass into American hands?"

"Right," Skafe said. Canada by Canada for Canada could not be true in the overall sense. Already a majority of all invested capital was American. But for Simon Skafe it was going to be true if he could make it true.

"Second, that you feel it advisable to interest one of the big mining groups—just possibly the Van Ingen group of New York—in the venture, so that we can benefit from their technical experience and resources of specialist personnel."

"Right," Skafe said. "You agree, Willie?"

"You bet. Take the extraction problem alone . . . Yes, the Van Ingen people might be just the ticket," Wilson said, with respect, albeit unwilling, for Sleeman's suggestion. "They were behind that Colombia job."

"Third, you want to give the Canadian public an interest in this."

"I want to *sell* them an interest," Skafe said. "Philanthropy is not the object." Which made Willie chuckle. "Also," he said, "I think that if the Canadian public are in, it will give Turtle Mountain a national stamp, as well as diluting the interest of any mining group. But control is what I must have."

"You are asking a lot, S.K., perhaps the impossible. It would be something new in the Canadian financial picture if forty-five million could be brought into a company, and control still be retained in one man's hands."

"I know that," Skafe said. Pitt stared through the window and down at the harbor at things he understood. Sleeman took a gold pencil from his pocket, turned up the lead, and began to write figures, dashes, squares and lines, a sentence or two across and down the blank sheet of foolscap. He jotted, frowning.

Skafe waited—Husky, the maker; S.K., who was no financial fool— Simon Skafe, driver, coach, and referee. "I suppose you're going to say it can't be done," he said, aware from the preliminary pessimisms that Sleeman thought it might be done, that some rabbit idea would emerge alive and kicking from the conjurer's tall hat. For a young man, he had a remarkable sense of timing, if an undue and transparent self-satisfaction. There was always a naïveté about self-satisfied people, however intelligent. Skafe waited patiently. Miles benefited from occasional deflation. But first let him produce the rabbit.

Sleeman put down his pencil, joined his finger tips, another of those mannerisms, and then began to talk. "I have the germ of an idea," he said, "which in skeleton is this: the present capital of Turtle Mountain is one hundred thousand shares of no par value issued and held entirely by you, S.K. On the basis of the new fabulous strike, and with government contracts assured, I estimate that the properties are worth some ten million on the open market. I propose that we split the stock a hundred to one, thus arriving at ten million shares, each worth approximately one dollar. In addition, and for reasons I will explain later, we increase the authorized capital by two and a half million shares, thus making a total of twelve and a half million shares, of which ten million will be issued and outstanding in S.K.'s name.

"Now for the raising of funds. One thing is perfectly clear: no large and reputable mining group such as Van Ingen would touch so speculative a venture as this unless they acquired sizable share holdings—twenty, thirty, forty per cent—in other words, if not actual control, then at least a powerful interest and the opportunity for capital tax-free appreciation . . ."

Miles Sleeman's rather pedantic, pedagogic air of condescension left him now. He talked swiftly. Wilson Pitt came back from the harbor to stare at the sheet of paper across the table. ". . . Thus, the mining group provides twenty-five million dollars, secured by first-mortgage bonds on all the properties and plant, and receives the unissued two and a half million shares. You, S.K., sell two and a half million of your own shares to the public on this or a similar slogan: *Buy a share of your Canadian North.*

"This would leave you with something like a fifty-nine per cent interest, S.K., but the mining group might insist, as I have said, on a higher share participation, which could be provided by a small reduction in your holdings, or in the size of the public issue. Thus, we have twenty-five million, and still need twenty, which might be obtained from the Union Bank or other chartered banks, or otherwise—first-mortgage bonds ranking equal with the bonds held by the mining group, but used only *after* the group's money is exhausted, and to be repaid *first*; in fact, a simple 'last in first out' deal. I am almost sure that the banks would insist on that. Do I make myself quite clear?"

"Just as clear as *habitant* pea soup," said Wilson Pitt.

"I'll go through it again in simple terms." And while Sleeman explained to the baffled Willie, Skafe half listened, rounding out his own understanding. The plan was daring and farfetched, too farfetched, but with panache, and it might just work. It was Sleemanesque of him not to say, but to leave S.K. to work it out for himself, that this plan, on the best terms envisaged, would put two and a half million dollars into Skafe's own pocket. If that much, then that much less a hundred thousand to each of them.

At this stage, as Miles was careful to say, it was no more than a skeleton on which to build the blood and muscles, sinews, flesh and skin—not an attractive simile, but typical of Sleeman, whose world of ciphers had real life for him. He might see ultimately to a main chance of his own, but that did not stop him being entirely loyal to the main chance of his employer, one Simon Skafe. Come to think of it, thought Skafe, who does not see ultimately to his own main chance? But then, as in all generality of truth, he saw the exception, Willie Pitt, who sat now, trying to take in what was quite beyond him, resentful, suspicious and admiring.

Each man with limitations, each man to be used; and now the more useful man was not the better man. If we can swing this thing, thought Simon Skafe, I shall have to put Miles on near-equal salary terms with Willie. Simple enough. And this is particularly simple, because either I pay Sleeman what he is worth, or Sleeman will supply a demand elsewhere.

The explanation to Pitt was a waste of Skafe's time, but he did not interrupt. He stood at the window, watching a white and gold C.P.R. ship draw into harbor. It was a coming and a going. We come and we go, he thought—bigger and better, smaller and worse, for better or worse, to love and to cherish, to go away. His personal troubles were more real to him here today at this very moment than the financing of his future. He turned to see old Ben Cloverley's portrait on the wall, and to be reminded of his past. It was old Ben who had given him his start in Summit Construction. But again philanthropy had not been involved, for Ben was aging and needed a man; so he found a man and made use of him. But Ben Cloverley's limitations were the same as Willie Pitt's whom Skafe had outdistanced in Summit Construction.

Mrs. Murton's single knock, and in she came, and to him with a slip of paper upon which was typed: "Mr. Dorrien is on the line. Will you speak from your office now? Or shall we call him later? NOTE: All arranged with the press for noon."

"I'll come to the office," he said, thinking that she who knew all things knew that he would not take this call in the board room. Nor did she say Dorrien's name before the others. She typed the message on a piece of paper. How did she know, and what did it matter?

"Hullo," he said.

"Oh, hullo. Is that you, Simon?"

"Yes," he said. "I suggest we meet this evening, if that would be convenient for you."

"Yes, of course. That's why I came. Say where and when. I mean, you tell me." Dorrien sounded peremptory in his acquiescence, which meant that he was nervous, a new condition for Mr. Dorrien.

"Now, let's see," Skafe said, although he had thought this through before. "A club or a bar would hardly do in the circumstances. Nor would the office. You'd better come to Arbour Avenue at six o'clock. You know the number?"

"I'll be there, then, at six, old b . . . Goodbye."

Old boy Skafe made another call, and went back to the board room. David Dorrien knew the number well, 462 Arbour Avenue, under *Skafe, S. K.*, and *Residence* in the telephone book. It had been slightly a home from home for David Dorrien when he had been painting in Montreal, and Mrs. Skafe had been in residence. That was the early spring of 1947, over again from England. She had helped him find a studio. It is not possible for even a simple-minded fellow to see his wife enjoy the company of another personable man without small thoughts or questions occurring to him. But it had been entirely innocent and platonic then on her side, Skafe was sure. Indeed, Dorrien's presence in town for those three months seemed to make Anna a more amenable wife, not rude to anyone, and most affectionate with S.K.S. himself.

"So there we are," said Sleeman. "It is only the bones of an idea, as I have said. Do I get through to you, Wilson?"

Wilson nodded, glum.

Sleeman was like them all, he needed praise. He deserved praise now, and got it in three words: "Well done, Miles."

Thus encouraged, because Skafe did not throw bouquets all over the place, Miles Sleeman said: "I happen to be lunching with Mr. Carter at the Mount Royal Club. Should I pave the way by mentioning our project in the strictest confidence?"

"No, you should not," Skafe said. "When the time comes, I will deal with Bob Carter." He considered Sleeman, wondering if he could be relied upon not to indulge his ego by dropping a breath of a hint to old Bob Carter, who as sure as hell would try to shove his eminently wise and cautious oar in. "Content yourself with doing what I tell you. What I want you to do is see Small and Shield about draft propositions for a public issue, and get them to rough out some ideas for a contract with a mining group. I have just telephoned Arthur Shields, and they expect you."

"Right, S.K. And underwriters? Would you want me to approach one of the leading firms on a purely tentative and confidential basis about the public issue?"

"You can do that too. But make our position clear before you talk with anyone—the chicken is not hatched, and the egg must not be known about. In this office, any secretarial work is to be done by Mrs. Murton only at present."

"Very well, S.K. Actually, my own girl is perfectly . . ."

"I have no doubt she is reliable," Skafe said. "But I said Mrs. Murton."

Miles Sleeman stood. He wore a glenurquhart check suit, dark gray with a dark red line, a pair of suede shoes, his gold watch chain. He took the single sheet of foolscap, folded it and tore it, tore it again, and dropped the small pieces into an ashtray for Mrs. Murton's personal attention. And now for the first time strongly, Skafe felt the thrill of what he would do, of the men he would drive, of the thing they would make together. "Okay, Miles," he said. "You deal with your brain-child now. Willie and I will get down to the brass tacks of the matter."

" 'Tain't brass tacks Husky means," said Willie Pitt. "What he means is you need a good strong prick to make a brain-child." He guffawed, and Skafe laughed too. There was something to be said for having two right-hand men, or a right-hand man and a left-hand man who were poles apart. There was a lot to be said for it if both knew who was boss; and both did. Interesting, he thought—a touch of divide and rule, when the essence of all we do is teamwork. He watched Sleeman wince at Willie's coarseness, no affectation about that. "Too many metaphors around here this morning," he said. "But to use a last one, nobody ever yet solved that problem of the chicken and the egg. All I do know is that we're grateful to you, Miles."

"That's right," said Willie Pitt heavily.

"Thank you, S.K." Sleeman turned to go and turned back. "I don't bear the risks," he said. "Nor will it be my reputation that will attract very large loans in return for small equity. Nor my reputation that will cause an oversubscription of our public issue. I tell you, though, that both these things will happen."

With which poised prophecy, and with a humble if not entirely ingenuous admission of his own place in the scheme of things, Miles Sleeman left the board room.

"You picked a clever cook with him," said Willie. "Not that I trust the guy."

"You're wrong," Skafe said.

"So I'm wrong, and you think I carry a chip, and I do. But I don't mean not trust him with the kitty. I mean not trust him to stand bare-arsed in a snowstorm with you."

Skafe laughed. "I hope I don't have to see your bare arse through a snowstorm." Next to Mac, he was fonder of Willie than of any man. Willie was much more able than Mac, and much more limited than Mac, that caustic idealist and cynic. Willie was a trusty rather than a friend. Why did Anna's remarks about friends keep bothering him? Willie, good as he was in dealing with all manner of people and complications, had the engineer's suspicion of lawyers as connivers, of financiers as shady jugglers, of any winding way to an end. If we get very big, Skafe thought, Willie won't be up to it. Then what? Or more to the point: then who? "Okay, Willie," he said. "I'm listening. Shoot."

Willie shot until twelve noon. He was forceful, sound, a brilliant practical man, talking that scrambled language so peculiarly his own. Then they went together to meet the press.

CHAPTER SEVEN

SHE BROUGHT the drinks into the study, and went to draw the curtains. "No, leave them, Agnes," he said. So he sat in the dim room with a dim casement window open a bit, and a dim drizzle in the garden below Mount Royal. Four-Six-Two Arbour Avenue was a robber-baronial mausoleum of a house, engulfed by trees. Here some rich men had rested their heads, and one still did, but he would sell it. He was slightly rich, depending on the league you're in. It was six o'clock. He had chosen the study because it was impersonal, no visible mark of the mistress. He rang the bell. She came, dutiful to the rich man's whim. "Oh, Agnes," he said. "I think the Big Room, after all. Sorry to be a nuisance."

"You're not a nuisance, sir," she said, loving him dearly. Almost all the ladies loved him because he was a just-lovely man to work for—austere and indulgent and sometimes quite joky and never cross. They were like so many pet lady poodles to him. He thought that almost any minute now he would make history at 462 by screaming.

Instead of screaming, he took a snap decision and dialed Wilson Pitt in Westmount. "Hullo," said Willie's fruity voice, and Skafe hung up. What a thing to do to Willie. He had nearly done a more alarming thing to Willie by saying: *Willie, I've changed my mind. I have decided to sell out Turtle. You might tell Sleeman, will you? Now over to you, Willie. I shall be away for months.* But he did not quite bring himself to say it. Chop and change, such vacillation from Husky Skafe, strong moderate dynamic legend in the making. There was a tune when he was a boy: " 'My cutie's due at two to two,' " he sang loudly, walking through his dim old pile. ". . . He's coming through on a big choo-choo. He's been away for months . . ."

He would say: *Nothing doing* to David D., and he would get on a big choo-choo or an airplane and descend upon New York City, the Algonquin, Forty-fourth or so, near Fifth where the bohemian Mrs. Simon Skafe was staying. First he would beat her and then he would rape her and then he would growl: *Get dressed woman,* and then he would take her out drinking and dancing at this one and that one and El Morocco, and back to a friendly discipline. Then the south of France or a slow boat to Capetown. But he had not yet brought himself to tell old Willie that he was through with Turtle. He entered the Big Room to see Agnes a-hover by the other door, smiling because Mr. Skafe sang so cutely about the cutie and the big choo-choo. "Agnes," he bit. "Why the hell can't you close the curtains?"

The silly thing put her hand to her droopy chest, utterly poleaxed, stricken, and she panted to obey his brutal question. Then Agnes scampered out.

But how could he give up Turtle now? He had found it alone, and then he had bought out his sleeping partner who, incidentally, had earned no right to the claims. I wonder what's become of old Jim Willis, he thought. Must find out. He would not find out. Jim was written off and forgotten. Now it was Husky's turn. But how could he leave Turtle, after long waiting, development, disappointment, trouble—leave it now at the real beginning? Besides, what in God's name would he do with himself on a slow boat to Capetown?

His thoughts were disturbed by a cough from Toddy, arms akimbo at the door. "Yes, Toddy," he said. "What is it?"

"That's what I'm asking myself," she said. Toddy was no timorous parlormaid; she was a tough treasure. "Here's Agnes in hysterics. *Leave the curtains, draw the curtains.* How's a body to ken yer fancy?"

"I didn't mean to bawl Agnes out," he said. "Most unreasonable of me. Say I'm sorry."

Toddy sniffed. He wondered why it was that Scottish spinsters sniffed.

"Agnes's in no fit condition to answer the door. And I'm not to answer the door for yon man."

Which, in Toddy's language, meant not that she was forbidden, but that she would not. Toddy was outraged by Anna's behavior, not least by her recent behavior in this house. "*Go to a movie, Toddy. Or have a lovely jaunt to Eaton's. Or drive round the Mountain in a calèche. But leave me alone and take your key.* And what do I find when I gets back but the whole house lit up like Princes Street, and her away, and the place a shambles."

He had endured the tale on arrival this morning. Toddy sniffed again. "For Christ's sake stop sniffing, Toddy," he said. "I'll answer the door myself."

"Poor soul," said Toddy, and went away. She was a true ally, but he had it against her for taking his side, and now for *poor souling* him.

It was twenty past six, and still no Dorrien. He went through to the dining room which had, notably, two Canalettos and the Hepplewhite chairs; and then back here to the long high room, which she did not call Drawing or Morning or Living, but Big. Four-Six-Two was a dim pile in all external ways, but this was a good room after curtain time. Gallery was the house that Anna loved, and this was the house that she disliked (yet she would not let him cut down trees for light and air); and this was the room with Anna's mark. She could not abide formal period ensembles, nor what she called curlicue stuff. She liked plain things and mixed them up, except the modern in furniture. The Chippendale secretary was plain, with the desk top closed, concealing residual chaos. The Adam gilt mirror above the fire was plain. He had hoped to substitute a portrait for that some day. The Corot was a muted small painting of riverain trees, in the lambent mood of the "Bridge at Mantes," but a much lesser thing, of course.

Almost everything here had been found by Anna. But, as it happened, the thing she loved best, even more than the Corot, had been found by him in Brussels. It stood alone on a pedestal table. It was a *sang de boeuf* Chinese vase of some dynasty he had forgotten, seventeenth century, a bargain, he was assured, at the equivalent of six thousand dollars; not that she ever knew the price. The things he fancied invariably turned out to be the most expensive in the shop. She looked at the red vase when it arrived, and at him, and said, in better days not long ago: *Darling, you extraordinary man, such exquisite natural taste.*

A compliment, she meant, as she implied a bewildering contradiction. Some of those cave paintings in France and Spain showed exquisite natural taste.

But Anna had left her Chinese vase. She had taken some jewelry, things she liked less, such as pearls and diamonds, *the mink coat stuff*. But what she liked best, she had left behind. It was a contradiction, if not particularly bewildering.

He heard the front-door bell, and went to answer it, or to open the door with his good left hand, and put his poor right hand on the edge of the door. One doesn't shake hands, old boy, particularly with plaster of paris. "Good evening," he said.

"I'm afraid I'm most awfully late," said dripping Dorrien, like Anna always most awfully late. "I had to walk. Not a taxi in the whole town."

"They *are* bad at this hour of night," Skafe said, "particularly when it's raining. Put your coat down anywhere." He had not had a drink himself, and smelled Dorrien's whisky. "What will you have?" he asked at the tray.

"Whisky—Scotch and soda, if I may." Dorrien did not actually go round the room, because he knew this room well. But casing rooms was a trick of his. He took the Big Room in again. "I think it's quite lovely," he said; and then thinned his lips, as at a gaffe, which it was.

"When did you get in?" asked Simon Skafe, handing over whisky. He helped himself to rye. Perhaps she would switch to Scotch and soda.

"This morning on the New York train," said David Dorrien, a drink or two under his belt, but sober. He smiled vaguely at Skafe, like a gangling, affectionate, guilty schoolboy. "God, that color!" he said about the *sang de boeuf*. The curtains were ultramarine or some such strong blue, to mark her single red treasure in the room.

"Do sit down," said Skafe. What I ought to do, he thought, is break the mucking vase on the mucker's head. But he did not want to.

Dorrien sat and lit a cigarette, a Lucky. Then he crossed his legs the wide way, ankle on knee. Then he uncrossed them and put his lanky legs out straight. He wore an old brown tweed suit and old brown suede shoes and a yellowish silk shirt with the collar frayed and a dark green tie. He looked pretty clean this evening. He must have been fair when young, but now his hair was chestnutish brown, overlong at the back of his narrow head, a man of some distinction, no denying it. For the first time in a sporadic acquaintanceship, Skafe saw him ill at ease. "How's Mac?" Dorrien said, fingering the brush of curls above his neck.

"Fine," Skafe said. "He's over in England, looking for new aircraft. I spoke to him today."

"Mac's a marvelous chap," said Dorrien, on the safe ground of mahvelous Mac.

"He flew into Berlin yesterday with the Air Lift, to see loading techniques. He seemed much impressed."

"Thousands of tons a day—I suppose it is impressive. If leading nowhere, at least not backwards." Dorrien's drink was halfway down.

"I should have thought it leads clearly somewhere—to stop the Russians."

"Reaction," said Dorrien. "They do something—we try to meet it. The fact is that they have blocked the roads to Berlin, and the roads stay blocked. Who wins?"

"We win," Skafe said, "if we make them back down in the end, which we will." Behind these remarks lay Dorrien's old argument or hobbyhorse —the decline of the Free World. No belief, he said; and against a strong and burning belief what initiative could indulgence and no belief display? And so on.

Dorrien did not pursue Berlin as argument, but said, perhaps grasping for postponement of the topic in the offing: "I suppose the Air Lift is of interest to you because of that uranium mine in the North."

"Yes," Skafe said. It was of some interest. Any large air transport operation would be of some interest.

"How are things up there?" Dorrien's eyes flitted by the plaster cast. So she must have told him.

"Not too bad," Skafe said.

"There must be a great fascination in opening up the back of beyond."

"Yes," he said. "I suppose there is." But where now was the fascination of *profits for him and atom bombs*, her view of Turtle Mountain's contribution to the world? I will let him finish that drink, he thought, and then I will say in a fairly friendly way, or not offensively: *I have decided against divorcing my wife, so it would be best for all concerned, and particularly for David Dorrien, if you would pack up your paints and bugger off.* ". . . I wasn't listening," he said politely.

"I was only lamenting, Simon, that there seem to be so few Canadians like you who *want* to risk and find."

"Are there so few?"

"I think so," Dorrien said. He faltered, drew breath, and plunged on: "No spirit of adventure except in war, which is extraordinary when you think how this country was peopled—at the expense of the poor benighted Indian, it's true, but that added spice to the adventure. Perhaps it's because the place is so damned frighteningly big, or perhaps it's some kind of a revulsion from the frontier days, I simply do not know. But you can't travel across Canada without noticing how little love or feeling Canadians have for the land itself. And as for wildlife, not one in a hundred knows a warbler from a sparrow, a spruce from a pine, or a weasel from a mink, except at the fur-coat stage. Here they are with the greatest country on earth, and they only feel comfortable in a huddle in a city."

"Doesn't most of humanity only feel comfortable in a city?" said Simon Skafe. He had heard all this before, and it annoyed him, but he could not deny it altogether, nor did he give a damn about warblers.

"In ghastly crowds, you mean? Yes, I fear so. Look at Butlin's camps in England. But this is the big free land of hope, and do they want it or cherish it? Either they plunder it, or it scares them. In which case, the only risks they want to take are by proxy with an investment dollar."

"Which seems to settle Canada," Skafe said.

"I don't mean it like that," said Dorrien. "I love this country and Canadians. I don't think any of you could ever quite realize what it means for us jaded specimens and misanthropes to meet the warmheartedness of people here. But I just wish I thought that Canadians were matching the future that comes tumbling into their laps."

He did not like it. He disliked these half-baked generalizations very much, although he supposed that Dorrien's nervousness of him had caused another Dorrien steed to take the bit between its teeth. But the risking and finding, how true it was. How many young Canadians would up sticks and go for the sake of going, would do what he himself had done? Simon Skafe had told her on the Mackenzie River. He had said: *But after a year of it, I thought: To hell with steady prospects in office equipment. I'm off on my own to live a while.* He had always despised security, and he provided it for all who served him.

It solved the whole thing for him. Which was the more important: A woman who would never go his way? Or the way that he himself would go? It was a simple matter in the end.

"I sent for you," he said. *I sent for you,* as from husband Two to future husband Three was arrogant and right. "I sent for you," he said again, "because Anna asked me to divorce her. Well?"

Dorrien made a hissing sound, like an engine, a big choo-choo, easing itself in the station. Then he sat up straight. "On those terms . . ." he began loudly, and stopped. "Look, Simon . . ." he began less loudly, and stopped. Now he did not bungle from lack of self-assurance. Dorrien was himself again, but curbing his notably hot tongue.

"Won't you have a drink?"

"May I?" He went for whisky, a moderate one from the brief gurgle; and when he had sat down again, he said slowly and directly to Simon Skafe: "I'm not going to make a maudlin speech, but I have to say that I like and respect you very much, and I apologize."

It was honorably said, not said to disarm. Skafe had grown to like David Dorrien, if not to respect him. Now he did, momentarily, respect him. "Right, David," he said. "I suppose I had better ask if you're perfectly sure about all this?"

Dorrien nodded, and looked at his glass, a paler one than usual. "I'm sure, if Anna is sure, and she seems to be sure." How well articulated all the s's and the shushes.

"Yes," Skafe said. Whether Anna was sure or not, he was sure now himself, and hardened.

"I'm not much of a chap," said Dorrien, "but I'll do my best to take care of her. It may seem odd at my age," he said, "but Anna is the only woman I ever met . . ."

It was not finished because that extraordinary Englishmen's code or reserve or hypocrisy made them boggle over a four-letter word. They could drool *I love her* about the spaniel but not about the woman. Whatever love might be. But Skafe had known on Labor Day two years ago last month that Dorrien was helplessly bemused, besotted, in love with Anna. She did not appeal to all men, as her daughter might. She was eclectic, picking, drawing the few in many ways. And Dorrien's way was more of the intellect than the body. He did not look the sort of man who would tumble her into indolent peace. She had deluded herself to the notion that bed did not matter. But she would find that bed mattered more to her than anything else in life, including tastes shared and a share of a man. One day she will come back for it, he thought. This lanky loop won't give her what I gave her.

His body stirred, as it often stirred at sensual thought of Anna. What a wonderful loving hating woman; but he had decided. "I set up a trust," he said, "from which Anna will have a life interest of the income."

"You're damned generous," Dorrien said. "But she doesn't want to take it." Being an inveterate sponger, he did not say that he did not want her to take it, but he said nobly: "I'm earning quite a lot nowadays."

"You must persuade her to take it," said Skafe. "I prefer that she should have means of her own." It did not sink in. The skin was thick over money. "Produce the evidence," he said. "And I'll take steps about divorce at once."

Dorrien's hand wandered right jacket pocketward, as if he had private detectives' statements or whatever with him to give over to the cuckold, but his hand had second thoughts and wandered back to pick up his glass. In most ways he was a most intuitive fellow, and quite guileless, as such people often are. "I'll see to that," he said, embarrassed. "Oh, and Simon, there's one other thing—about the children. Anna wondered if she could see them. I mean have them to stay every now and then."

"Certainly," he said. "Would a month a year be adequate? And she could meet them any time passing through, of course. All right?"

"Fine, thank you," Dorrien said. He smiled, perhaps thinking of Skafe's children, to whom he was devoted.

"Does Anna want that incorporated in the Bill?"

"No. She said that you would be better than your word."

"That's nice," he said, and saw from a flicker of Dorrien's expressive face that Dorrien saw through cold-blooded matter-of-factness to some human pain. "Anything else?" he said.

Dorrien shook his head.

"I have one thing," Skafe said. "You may remember my first refusal on Anna's portrait?"

Dorrien's face clouded instantly to an ominous thought. "Oh, yes?" he said. *Oh, no! Not that again,* his face said. "Yes indeed, I remember."

"And you may remember saying, when I offered to buy the portrait of my wife, that the portrait was not the wife."

"Yes, I do," said Dorrien. "Haunted by that ghastly remark. I'm sorry."

"You needn't be," Skafe said. "But things have changed. Then you had the portrait; I had the wife. Now you have the wife; I have the portrait."

"But Simon, I don't want to sell the thing. Only lately the Museum of Modern Art tried to buy it off me, not that I could have sold without consulting you. But I need it, you see. Anna's portrait is still far and away the best thing I've done. I always make it the chef d'oeuvre of my exhibitions; and actually my reputation, such as it is . . ." He talked on, hurried, diffident, brown eyes pleading, a little bleary and full of thought, as when his betraying brown eyes went round the walls and to the mantelpiece to replace the Adam mirror, disbelieving, not crediting . . . "They offered me twelve thousand," he said. "But of course I said nothing doing."

"I want it," said Skafe. "I want it shipped to me care of the office within a week, customs clearance arranged—you would know about reimport—you can send it C. P. Express collect."

"But I tell you, I don't want to sell the painting."

"You are not selling," Skafe said, "any more than I am selling. Let us call this a barter deal, no cash transaction involved. Do you agree to the swap?"

Dorrien got up and walked away in the long high room, which was large enough for it to be quite a stroll to the Chinese vase, the *sang de boeuf*. "But what would you do with it?" he said to the Chinese vase.

"That's my affair," Skafe said, "or my investment. I have faith enough in you as an artist to think that the value will accrue. A straight business proposition, no sentiment involved."

"It might be called a pound of flesh," said Dorrien to the Chinese vase.

"You could call it that," he said. You could call it a pound of flesh for either of them. *You could call it a love affair,* he said to her on the last night down at Gallery. *Yes, a love affair,* she said.

Dorrien turned to walk back. "Simon," he said. "May I say something to you?"

"Say away," he said. He had some affection for David Dorrien, even the glimmerings of respect for him, but he looked down on him. One dog's tail is higher than the other's. But the boss dog wins the female. But men and women are not dogs and bitches, he thought. Not entirely.

"Do you know the word Daemon—D, a, e?"

"Yes," he said. "I suppose so."

"An essential force, a daemon of the spirit, I mean, and it is very rare, and both you and Anna have it. If I had had it, I might have been a great artist. But two daemons don't rest easily together. I'm under no illusions, Simon. I know who is Anna's man, but she might live more peacefully with me."

"Yes, David," he said. "I see what you mean."

It took the man who took his wife to explain the thing, just as it had taken the man who was taking his wife to bring Skafe finally to decide to let her go.

He went over to the desk and opened the lid and took out the Cartier box. She had left her favorite things in various places in the house, and the jade necklace happened to be here beside the other thing she loved. But he would keep the other thing. "Anna forgot this," he said. "You might take it to her."

Dorrien opened the box and shut it again on the green necklace of his portrait. He looked upset.

"Let me call you a taxi," Skafe said.

"I like walking in the rain," said Dorrien, putting on his coat, holding his green hat in his right hand. "Goodbye then, Simon," he said, and went. "Good luck."

"Good luck," said Simon Skafe. He watched him down the steps, and down the steep driveway—a menace in winter—and onto Arbour Avenue. The lights of the cars swung up, swung down along Côte des Neiges. The cars swished wetly on Côte des Neiges. He watched the lanky loop go under a street lamp down in the night. He closed the door of 462.

Skafe drove in the Lincoln and was not troubled by cops. "Ottawa, here I come," he sang at ninety miles an hour. He was quite a speed bug, was the President. He rumbled decorously in, and registered, and walked up Wellington Street, past the Parliament buildings—which were the dignity of Canada for him—and on down to the sprawl of temporary huts in good walking time for his appointment; then lunch together at the Rideau Club; then later an unexpected and gratifying summons.

The Minister did not waste much time on him, and he did not ask expected questions about fabulous discoveries of ore. He knew all that already. He spent three minutes of the five or six administering a thunderously lethal rebuke. It was a corker, but then the Minister was a corker. His great power was that he wielded great power without confusing himself and God. ". . . How old are you?"

"I'm forty-two, sir," said Simon Skafe. He was so bewildered, befuddled, browbeaten by the onslaught that he almost said: *Sir, I'm forty-three next birthday on March the fifth.*

"Old enough not to indulge in fisticuffs with the hired help," said the Minister. The grim glimmerings of a smile appeared. "In other words, Simon," he said, "you're getting to be a big boy now. I will say that you handled that press interview with some finesse." He put one stubby finger on the *Ottawa Journal*. "Do you have political ambitions?"

"No, sir. Not for the present, anyway."

"Which is your party?" He knew quite well.

"I am personally a Conservative," Skafe said. "But fair's fair as a hedging job on both."

The Minister laughed and stood. "I'm due in the House," he said, "to answer some foolish questions." They said he was a better man than a politician, which meant a better man in Skafe's experience, which meant *No bullshit* in Mac's expression. "Hasten slowly," he said to Simon Skafe. "Let me know if you're in trouble. But life is largely trouble," he said.

Skafe was much heartened by the dressing-down and the trust in him, and by *Life is largely trouble*.

It was nippy without a coat at the open place on the way to the Château where the north wind whips from the river, up the staircase of locks of the old canal, to pinch pale men, tired girls and hags and children waiting for the bus; and the north wind blows on by the arch of the Dead.

He had a bath, and leaned on his elbow on the bed, drinking a strong cup of tea—a habit from Anna, whom he wished well, now that all was settled—and he read with some gloat and satisfaction six versions of Turtle Mountain trouble in six newspapers. Then he dressed in his new dark pinstripe suit from Traill, and brushed his hair for about five minutes to a glossy sheen like any uncropped college boy. Then he examined the small ruby and emerald brooch in the small Birks box. Then he exchanged hearty greetings in the elevator with a man from Saskatoon. Then he sweetened the doorman with a dollar.

"You might drop me off at the corner of Howick and Mariposa," he said to the taxi driver, Mr. Evan Jones lately out from Cardiff, but you couldn't be too careful until you saw your lawyer.

"Goodnight," he said. He walked along from there and up a shadowy Rockcliffe street where a woman exercised a Boxer dog, but he did not know the woman, hence not the Boxer. His tie was tidy, buttons done up, sleek hair unruffled. His heart went pit-pat. Hearts do go pit-pat in Rockcliffe, where all seems decorum and Mayors are Reeves.

He slipped in and up, quick nonchalance and devilish discretion, and rang the bell, which was answered by the owner smartly, and in he popped and he shut the door.

"Oh, Husky, is it really you?"

"Me," he said. "Is it really you?"

He was feeling quite shy, but she settled that in the nicest way by putting her soft bare arms around his neck and her softness against him and her soft lips up to his. Grace was helplessly in love with him, and he was very fond of her. She was a gentleness, a comfort, and she said: "Now tell me every single thing about yourself."

BOOK FOUR

Now THE RUNWAY was coming up to meet him, coming nicely, he thought, air speed a hundred and twenty-five. The Crusader was new and fast and heavy. He was satisfied with his approach until, in his right eye, he saw Roy Thompson's hands stab forward to the control column, overriding him, to drop the nose. "Air speed," said Thompson, removing his hands when he felt Skafe there again. Yes, it had dropped ten miles an hour; and why had he not reacted instantly?

The landing was good enough. The Crusader drew up in a blast of reversible props. Roy was right, thought Skafe, annoyed with himself, and hence with Roy. The fact is, he thought, that the Crusader is too much airplane for a weekend flyer of forty-nine. Either I must fly twice as much, or I must give up flying this order of aircraft.

He turned off the runway and taxied to the Flume Hill hangar where a knot of people waited, and one of them was Sally. The propellers milled on and stopped. "Thanks, Roy," he said, undoing his belt. "I was slow on that."

Roy Thompson, who was Mac's senior pilot in Skafair, smiled, but briefly. "It would have been heavy is all," he said.

Skafe went aft to the cabin, where Miles and Cynthia Sleeman gathered light belongings, and the co-pilot was putting out steps. "Hullo, Dicky," he heard Sally say to him; and here she came to embrace her father.

"Happy birthday," he said, kissing her. And then he watched her shake hands with the Sleemans and Roy Thompson. "But no Mac?" she said.

"The Dewline supply is giving us a lot of headaches," he said. "Mac couldn't make it. He sent you all sorts of messages."

"Oh," she said. "I *am* so sorry." She did not hide her disappointment, and did not dwell on it. "The press await you, Father dear," she said.

He followed the Sleemans and Sally out to the brisk air and the warm sun of his native province, and to photographers.

They took two pictures of Skafes and Sleemans, Miles cutting a dash in his panama hat. "Now you, sir, Mr. Skafe, with Sally beside the plane. That's fine, just fine, let's have a laugh."

They laughed together for the local papers, who said: "That's terrific," and her old man basked in his daughter's glory.

"Can you give us a quote about being back in New Brunswick, sir?"

"I have nothing new to say," he said, "except that it is always new to be home again in this wonderful air with the people I came from." He took a deep breath of the wonderful air, and wonderful it was. "Yes, great to be home, and never better than on my girl's twenty-first birthday."

"Just one last shot of a birthday kiss, eh, Mr. Skafe?"

"No," he said. "New Brunswickers don't kiss in public."

The press laughed. Miles Sleeman smiled approval. He kept a personal eye on public relations. *You cannot escape it, S.K., he said. By which I do not mean that you must live in a glare of publicity. But it happens that you have a personality which is news. You also have a remarkable flair for dealing with reporters. It is often a bore for you, I know, but you never seek—you are sought. Thus we, businesswise, need not seek publicity, but are sought for it through you; which is a heavensent P.R. situation.*

What an inveterate pontificator, and what good sense he made. So Skafe was long inured to the flash bulb and a few words easy off the cuff.

"I won't be a minute, Miles," he said, and stayed to discuss flying plans with Roy Thompson while Sally talked to Dicky Farmer the young co-pilot, another slave. She wore her charcoal shorts, almost to the knee, and the cotton blouse with bistro scenes that her father had found in Paris this spring. It was a miracle to see his lovely child. She took his arm as they walked to the car. "Mac promised to come," she said. "I did so want dear Mac to be at my party."

"He sent you his love. If things roll better in the North, he hopes to join us fishing next week."

"I don't think I will go fishing next week."

"Oh, come on!" he said. "Why not?"

"Jock and I thought we might take a toot to Cape Breton in the Jag."

He had tentative plans for John which might include work and exclude salmon fishing and toots to Cape Breton in Jaguars. But he did not mention them to Sally. "I see you so little," he said. "Don't you know how much I was counting on the fishing trip?"

"You're madly sweet when you feel neglected," she said, "like Tiger shedding a lonely tear."

He was not a temperamental man, in vales of despond or on mountains of joy. But strong warm happiness came to him from her. "Let's see now," he said at the car. "Cynthia, would you like to sit in front with me?"

"I would adore to, Mr. Skafe."

He held the door for Cynthia and shut it. There was pleasure in hearing and feeling the soft firm click. He walked round his new bottle-green Bentley and sat in her and adjusted the seat and sniffed her goodness and he loved her. They said that riches brought unhappiness, but Skafe was a rich man contented with his blessings and possessions. He started up and drove away to a rush of air by the open windows. Cynthia and Miles were suitably admiring, and Sally teased him about his Bentley passion. "I like good things," he said, "like the American Crusader or the British Bentley. I like machines that are made as near to perfection as they can be made, not machines made to wear out by the million. Don't quote me in Detroit."

"Planned obsolescence makes an interesting study," said Miles Sleeman. "On the one hand is the ethical question you hint at, S.K. On the other hand, the advantages of sustained employment, of a continually renewed consumer demand."

"It seems rather a bogus principle on which to base prosperity," said Sally. "Don't you think so, Miles?"

"Not necessarily," Sleeman said, and he was off.

Skafe listened to the discussion between him and Sally, methodical brains and spontaneous brains. He heard her set a trap, lead the expert on, catch him out, to the evident pleasure of Miles Sleeman. She might have taken mathematics, economics, any of half a dozen honors courses. But she had done her finishing year in Paris, and then had waltzed through to an Arts degree at Vassar. It was a frittering of talent, a disappointment in a way to him.

Now all she seemed to do was gallivant from lesser love to love, the old flame dead, the new one lit. She appealed physically to all men. Intellectually, she was all things to all manner of men—a simple date to a chunk of football player, a sparring partner to a scholar. He could even hear it happening mildly now to Miles; and he fancied, from Cynthia's silence beside him, that she could hear it happening.

God knows, he thought, I don't want to lose her yet. But it worried him that what had been a human acceptance of attention now showed signs of becoming her necessity—to scalp every handsome head, innocent scalper, no harm intended. Sometime I must speak to her, he thought. But he did not know how to speak to her, nor what to say. *Sally my darling, you must stop being so attractive.* And Grace could not speak to her. Friendly as they were together, Grace could not get to first base with Sally. I suppose she'll run off with some goddam crook of a gigolo, he thought, who will beat her or something.

It was a shattering thought which made his right foot go down and the Bentley fly to hit a bump. "These damned roads," he said to Cynthia; and then he indulged himself in a grumble about provincial spending—millions on far too elaborate schools; money squandered on fancy liquor stores to encourage the secret drinking which was all that a temperance-haunted government dared allow. They wanted tourists, provided execrable highways, and forbade the civilized consumption of alcohol. Timorous bungling and hypocrisy annoyed him. I must watch it, he thought. I'm becoming intolerant. He drove through the fair, if untidy countryside of his own people, the two behind still arguing vivaciously about planned obsolescence. He and Cynthia did not have much to say. She was an attractive young matron, daughter of the eminent stockbroker Busty Maxwell; a good mother, a devoted wife to Miles, whom she had greatly improved.

Skafe swung from the coast. A better stretch of highway allowed him speed. The last miles were a romp, if that was a word for the solid command of the Bentley in the wind. He turned down the asphalt drive.

"It's such a lovely place beside the sea," said Cynthia. She said agreeable things, if not the most unexpected things.

"Yes," he said. The place looked especially good this morning of July, with the top fields mowed, and neat bales strewn on the face of the fields. To the left were cattle pastures and the main farm buildings; ahead the fields dropped to woods to the sea; on the right was the old Skafe house; and half a mile over, Tom Beamish's place. Every fence was tight, every ditch uncluttered—it was a practical farm in being.

The road swung by the old gray house. It, alone, looked decrepit, if not tumbledown. A few thousand—eight or ten—would make it habitable. But apart from odd patching to keep the rain out, he had not touched the place since his father's death. Each year he meant to, and each year he let it go. He would do something soon, when the children married.

"You were born there, S.K.?"

"Yes, Miles," he said, knowing the question to be rhetorical. He slowed down. "We left for Ontario when I was six." He had a few smallboy memories, like the lilac brushing against his wall, like thinking the rooster was fighting the hens, like the rope swing down into the hay, like the garter snake he killed at five, to Father's displeased admiration.

"It has a plain weathered dignity," Sleeman said. "I wonder, S.K., would you agree to our using a photograph of the house, perhaps in color, or better—stark black and white, for the cover illustration of *Summit?*" He meant of the monthly magazine they put out for the whole diversified organization. It was an excellent publication of its kind, thanks to Sleeman's interest.

"That would be marvelous," Cynthia said. "Your birthplace."

"Oh, I don't know," he said. "Who on earth wants to see a ramshackle old house?"

"Make him agree," said Sally Skafe. "He's a barefoot boy at heart."

Which remark put Sleeman into a ludicrous and unprecedented fit of the giggles. Skafe did not see that so-funny joke; but here was Tom Beamish in the red farm jeep.

"Are you free for a drive around, Tom?" he said.

"You bet," said Tom Beamish. "I was waiting for you, Mr. Skafe."

"Okay then. Follow us down. I won't be a minute."

He blew a toot to warn Grace that he was arriving. She did love to wait for him on the doorstep; and there she was, cool, slim, serene, his welcoming wife. "Oh, Husky dear," she said. "You're really back."

He was really back at the Gallery house; although, because of its beginnings, there was an unreality on first arrival, a sort of double-take to meet and pass, and soon largely forget. He kissed Grace on the lips. "Where's John?" he said.

"He went out with his glasses," she said, and turned to welcome the Sleemans. Miles was an intimate colleague of his, if not a friend; and Grace was fond of Cynthia. Pickering, the chauffeur, came for baggage.

"I know you're longing to be off with Tom," said Grace. She did not put ideas into his head, or push him off to do things. She made it easy for him to do the things he liked to do—and Skafe's first pleasure at Gallery was to look round the farm. He joined Beamish in the jeep. "Well, Tom," he said. "How's things?"

"The silage was bad—no fetch of clover—but the hay's a fair crop. We're doing a few jobs around the place—the orchard fence is pretty near done."

"And yourself—how's your hip?"

"Some mornings the arthuritis has me locked up solid. But I can't grumble, at seventy."

"You should take things easier, Tom." He had retired Beamish some years back. Or, because Tom did not want to be pensioned off, he had given him the sinecure job of supervising farm maintenance—buildings, fences, ditches and so on, but not machines. It kept Tom happy, and freed Harry Hicks from some routine work. Hicks was a graduate of agricultural college, a top man with a bachelor's degree. They got along well enough, with reservations—notably an old man's prejudice against the newfangled scientific, and Tom's resentment, not overt, that it was easy now for Harry, getting all the money he needed to buy the best breeding stock to build the best Jersey herd in eastern Canada. Skafe did not much want to make money on the farm, but because of cattle sales the place now showed a profit.

They swung up through the wood where cedars had been badly blown in a hurricane one year. Now his Austrian pine—an experiment—were doing well. Every single enterprise of mine, he thought, from Turtle Mountain down now even to Gallery Farms—every single one is doing well.

His riches were great at forty-nine. His benefactions were large, and many of them made in secret, known only to the recipient. At his last quarterly checkup, Forester said that he was fighting fit, with the heart of a man of thirty-five. His home life was contented, his wife a ministering angel—no other word for her—voted one of the best-dressed women in Canada. His beautiful daughter was a worry and a comfort. Only John was a disappointment to him; but the boy would settle down.

Life is good to me, thought Simon Skafe, in the jeep jolting up to his father's house. They had not paved that short stretch of road. He went down cellar to inspect the sills, which had to be replaced, said Tom, or else . . .

He agreed to that. New sills would not spoil what Miles called the *plain weathered dignity* of the place. I did run barefoot here, he thought, as every farm boy runs barefoot in the summer grass, no joke about it.

"No, Tom," he said, outside again. "The shingles are still holding out. Patch them, if you have to. Time for a renovating job when John gets married." Tom's small shrewd eyes in his broad creased face expressed surprise or interest at that.

"Not that there's anything in the wind," Skafe said, "but a grandfather's day must come." There was all too little in the wind. John still showed no interest in the other sex. It was another slightly disturbing thing about the boy, not that Skafe approved of early marriage. First a man should become a man, as he had done.

They drove on round the farm. It was his first time down since May. "Tom," he said, "I never saw the place in such good shape, and all the beginnings laid by you."

"The beginnings was laid a hundred and fifty years or more back," Tom Beamish said, but he was pleased.

"Yes," Skafe said, "but you made the place in its present form." Tom Beamish had also contributed, or sold, his own sixty acres to round out the present farm. "We have a lot to be grateful to you for, Tom."

"That's a two-way street, though, Mr. Skafe. Look at me at my age, just enough job to make out I'm busy, and two hundred a month, and a house and the electric." It was not easy for him directly to say thank you.

Harry Hicks was baling over to the east beyond the main farm buildings. He drove the windrows, oblivious of everything and everyone but himself and his tools in this present job. He was hatless and naked to a pair of blue jeans, dust and hayseed on his sweating body. He came from Ontario, and was not well liked for various reasons—for the unsound reason of his embarrassing zest for work; for the more sound reason that, when the long day's work was over, he had abundant energy to spend with the young ladies of the district; and for another sound reason —that he was given to boasting in a place where no one was loud-mouthed and no one boasted. There were pros and cons to Harry Hicks, but he paid dividends.

About themselves, they were a secret society; about a foreigner from Upper Canada or elsewhere, they were very willing to spill the beans, which Tom Beamish now did again, by that terse and devious implication which was the way of Skafe's own people. This was a matter of two girls, not one.

"Thanks for the information, Tom," he said, with a sarcasm well understood.

He got out and crossed the crisp short grass to Harry Hicks, who had turned at the end of that row and had waved a hand, getting on with the job. Now he stopped the tractor and idled the engine, and the baler motor pounded on. "Hullo, Harry," Skafe said. "How does it go?"

Hicks leaned down to shake hands, the big delighted bucko. "Fine, Mr. Skafe," he said. "It's great to see you. I've really got things rolling this year."

"Good," he said. "I'll be up at milking time." He waved and left him to it. Nowadays machinery maintenance was properly done, and farm breakdowns reduced by half. Which had not been Tom Beamish's fault entirely—he was an excellent old-time farmer, not a mechanic.

Skafe decided on two things: First, he would advise Harry Hicks to hurry up and find himself a wife. Second, he would take Harry Hicks down a peg or two. He enjoyed giving a good man hell when he deserved it. In Skafe's own uncosseted world, good men did not need to be treated with kid gloves.

"Harry's a good man," said old Tom Beamish, using the words that Skafe had been thinking, as likely by that bucolic insight or awareness of theirs as by coincidence. "I didn't mean nothing against him except . . ."

Except what you meant, thought Skafe. "I know, Tom," he said. "You did right to mention it. I won't let on."

After that, he admired a new culvert of Tom's, or commissioned by Tom, and a new high orchard fence to dissuade the deer from plundering his apples. He was very well served and he was grateful. At one time or another they all, from Miles Sleeman down, considered him hard and demanding; but they trusted him. In fact, the initiative lay the other way. It was a cardinal basis of his philosophy that he chose men he could trust, and trusted them wholly. If he made a mistake, he remedied it in short order; but the mistakes were few.

They went to the bull pen to inspect Gallery Grandee, yearling champion at the Winter Fair last year, thickening out to be a splendid beast. "There's another one that does a good job with the heifers," said old Tom Beamish, a farmer's crack.

Skafe smiled perfunctorily, not his order of a jest. "I think I'll walk down, Tom," he said.

"You look a mite tuckered out this time," said Beamish, eying him. "Just take things easy. Can't walk at a gallop all your life."

Walk at a gallop was new to him, and not quite meaningless. Gallop at a walk might be more apposite in his case.

He never hurried on his way, and he did not hurry now by the side of the brook, with the pleasing prospect of chilled Dubonnet and a slice of lemon awaiting him down at the house.

They were untouched cedar woods, with a few open places, green-circled glades of fern and moss. He had wanted to tidy these woods long ago, but Anna objected, saying that he would ruin the path beside the brook. And the path beside the brook remained important to her during the years that she remained with him, because the first time he had brought her down to meet his parents at Gallery—after John was born, and just after they were married—they had caught two trout on worms in the brook, and then, hot and happy, they had taken their clothes off to splash one another in the only deep pool in the brook—so the actual place could not be forgotten—and then they desired one another again, and they made love cool and wet on the hot happy day among the ferns in company with mosquitoes. *There, darling,* she said, a fern in a blue sky in her eyes. *We belong to this place now.* To Anna, people were linked to places, not places to people. Thus, love to a glade in a cedar wood. It was a difference in them, one of many. But he remembered that act of love in a river of acts of love forgotten. *We began Sally here,* she used to say in later years, while the years were still good.

It was a possible one of several places, but to Anna it was Sally's place. He felt tired now. Perhaps he was a mite tuckered out, as old Tom said. So he sat down in a glade below that of memory to smoke a cigarette, and to think of the vexing, perplexing love of his youth. He sometimes wished that they had parted with cruelty or dishonor. But it had not been so. He missed her still, and did not want her back.

He put out the cigarette with care, and was about to leave his shady place among the ferns, with a boulder against which to rest his back, and not a mosquito in this dry summer, when he heard voices. They came from the far bank of the brook, not that the bank was far, as the brook was ten feet wide and could be crossed dry-shod on steppingstones at many places. There was that tone or that intimacy in the voices which makes a man not want to be a spoilsport. So, from being a slightly tuckered-out tycoon taking his ease, Simon Skafe became an innocent eavesdropper, pinned to his sequestered spot.

The voices stopped, and the boy and girl came into sight. She wore one of those abbreviated playsuit things of a canary hue. He wore a pink Brooks-Brotherish shirt and dark gray flannels. They went hand in hand, the tall boy, and the girl whose black hair reached his chin. She lifted his hand in hers, bringing his hand up and across to hold it to her bosom, between her breasts. That spoke her thoughts or her feelings frankly, and the boy turned to the black-haired girl to look down at her in his arms. "Those silly things," she said. "They hurt."

He swung the binoculars from his chest around over his back. "Oh, Molly," he said, and he kissed the girl. Skafe could not but watch the scene unless he closed his eyes, which he could not do.

He stared popeyed with a thudding heart and a drain of blood and a rush of blood until John Skafe and Molly Phipps, the gardener's daughter, moved on, and stopped to kiss again, and went, timeless entwinement in the woods.

CHAPTER TWO

As HE SAT there, the forest stillness was disturbed again by a largely swooping bird. It arrived to batten itself against a tree, to compose its wings to black, to tense a red-anviled head, to hammer the trunk like a demented pendulum upside down. It was a pileated woodpecker, a comparatively *rara avis* known to hunters as the Cock of the Woods, known even to S. K. Skafe. To John Skafe, with the seven-by-fifty featherweight Zeiss binoculars (a coming of age present from his mother), the woodpecker would have been an ornithological excitement. But John was otherwise excited. Skafe closed his eyes against the Charles Addamish creature. The hammering stopped, and the bird was gone.

Sex, he thought, heading square away from the brook and lovers, breaking through face-lashing cedar twigs. They were crazed with it. Here was John with that voluptuous floozy. There was Sally, murmuring by moonlight with the current one—the *Time* correspondent aged thirty-eight, the wet baronet in the Irish Guards, the amorous physicist, the string of playboys, even a hockey player, God Almighty. Had he not sat and tossed and sweated about that girl? And now John.

He emerged onto the drive, composing himself. Oh, come on, he thought, old prig. Didn't you roam these woods with Joyce McKinney at sixteen, precocious little beast? Yes, he thought. Yes, I did. But sixteen isn't twenty-two, when a young man should know enough to stick to his own kind of people. But then he had to admit to himself that Molly Phipps was just the type of roly-poly piece that might appeal to anyone, even to respectable older men.

He made himself walk slowly down, and he thought more temperately about John, about how the boy had limped on with his engineering at McGill, getting poorer and poorer marks, until last winter, the middle of his fourth year, when he failed Structural Design and Strength of Materials. He was twenty-one then, with a generous allowance. Without any warning whatever, he took off for Ireland to stay with his mother, Mrs. David Dorrien, at the place in West Meath that Dorrien had inherited from some aged aunt. They spent a third of the year there now, with lots of bottles; a third of the year in rented studios in London or

New York; a third of the year in Jamaica, so Skafe understood the pattern more or less to be.

A letter soon came from Anna: "My dear Simon," she wrote, going on to say that John seemed distraught and unhappy, and worried at letting his father down, but she thought that he simply could not face the University just now. "He wants to stay here quietly for a while," she wrote. "Please don't think that I have tried to influence him. Love. Anna."

Certainly she might have tried to influence him. But if she said she had not done that, then she had not done it. Love from Anna.

"P.S.," she wrote, a great one for the punch-line afterthought. "From what he says, I think he would like to go back soon—in a few months— if not to McGill to finish engineering, then to the North where you have always wanted him to go."

Skafe made no fuss. After a talk with the Dean of the Faculty, he wrote a kindly letter to John, enclosing a draft for two hundred pounds, and told him to take his time, perhaps travel a bit. "And love to you all from us." It was very civilized. John replied gratefully.

But a difficult boy. When they were young, Skafe had given them no more than any father of middle means. But he decided that, as they grew up, they must accustom themselves to the circumstances in which they would later live. For example, on John's coming of age last year, he had given him a present that would thrill the heart of any sport-loving young man—a two-seated Jaguar, a very fast car, dangerous in reckless hands, but John was perfectly sober and reliable about such things. Well, if you please, he had never used the Jaguar, unless to be driven by Sally in it. In fact—and how absurd—his father and his sister had all the Jaguar fun together. Perhaps I just wanted a Jaguar, thought Skafe, with mordant bite about himself.

John had no time for girls, but now suddenly he was having a passionate affair with the gardener's daughter. I should have got rid of that shiftless Phipps long ago, Skafe thought. John had no time for Jaguars, but now suddenly he might go roaring it up with Molly Phipps around New Brunswick and into Maine and stop an hour or two at a motel. But no—if that was all that might be involved, no great harm done. But he knew John better. There would be no Jaguars where John was going.

He entered the house. "Grace!" he called. "Where are you, Grace?"

"Coming, dear," she answered from the kitchen regions, and she came, wearing a white housecoat over her dress.

"Are you busy?" he asked, knowing that she was, but knowing also that when he needed her, he was her top-priority business.

"Of course not, dear," she said. "I was just helping the servants about tonight, and that can wait. Shall I bring you your Dubonnet?"

"You're good to me," he said, and he gave her a kiss because she was so good to him. "I'll be upstairs."

He sat on the chaise longue in her bedroom, and, sex-haunted this morning, he thought of an epigram, aphorism or *bon mot* by Dorothy Parker or someone like that about exchanging the hurly-burly of the chaise longue for the deep wedded bliss of the double bed, or something like that.

He smiled wanly, pleased that his sense of humor had not entirely left him. Then he heard her light step, and she came in with the silver tray. Not only did Grace see that the bottle was ice-chilled, but the glasses too, so that his lower lip touched frost as he took his first sip of Dubonnet with a slice of lemon. "Delicious," he said. Grace smiled, and then she drank. His Dubonnet after twelve was a small ritual of hers. But he hardly ever drank his Dubonnet in her bedroom. "This is a lovely idea," she said, "just alone together. Husky dear," she said. "You look a little tired. Have you been doing too much?"

"No," he said. "I'm perfectly all right." First Tom Beamish, and now Grace. He was not used to being told that he looked a mite tuckered out, a little tired, and it made him feel a mite, a little petulant, which was unreasonable. He looked at his long lean face in the long mirror across the room; yes, haggard a bit. "Listen, Grace!" he said, and he told her whom he had seen with whom, doing what and where.

"Oh, no!" she said. "Oh, no!" Grace looked her best in pastel shades, soft colors like this coral or peach or whatever a woman would call it. Trim in her housecoat, and now so feminine, and she was much upset by what he told her. "But John," she said. "How *could* he with that common Molly Phipps? I just don't understand it."

"I do," Skafe said. "She's an attractive little dish. He has no experience. Unless I'm much mistaken, and I'm not, Miss Molly Phipps has him hooked and panting for her."

"Husky, do you think they . . . ?"

Skafe shrugged. "All but, if not, from what I saw. What's her reputation?"

Grace was no scandalmonger, in fact the soul of discretion, but she accepted confidences from the local help. "Mrs. Cooligan says she isn't a *bad* girl in the way that people mean. But she leads the boys on without . . . oh, you know."

There was a rude word for that kind of girl. If he had been less worried and upset, he might have said it to make Grace give one of her

small shocked *oh, you bad man* giggles, which were a nice thing about
her, sometimes irritating.

"If it was anyone but John," he said, "I wouldn't worry. The young
are the young, even if nowadays they seem to be obsessed by sex in a
way we never were. I mean, even Sally . . ."

Grace nodded. "Yes, dear," she said. "I sometimes worry too. But
Sally is so sensible and level-headed underneath it all. I'm not sure about
John. If he fell in love, it might be desperately," Grace smiled at him.
"Just as desperately as I fell in love with you," she said.

She had lost the only child of her first marriage. *I could never give you
children, Husky dear*, she had said on the night in Rockcliffe when he
went with circumspection to her house. *I don't care*, he said. Which was
not quite true, because he would have liked to have more children, two
or three, and one of them would have been the son a man needed to
follow him. *I don't care either*, she said, dear gentle Grace. *All I ever
want is you*. So it had been, and so it had remained. Love could be many
things, including provocation. But contentment was a part of love. The
word Love bothered him, and he avoided it in thought and speech.

Skafe held her hand a moment across the table between his couch and
her armchair. Her pliant hand in his bony hand was as womanly as everything about her; a deception too, for it was a skillful hand at any woman's task. "John is so quixotic," he said, "such a woolly idealist." He
spoke disparagingly, perhaps, in that; but he did not mean to disparage
the boy, but he knew him well enough to know that a picayune affair
might become a life or death affair to John. *Oh, Molly*, he said, gazing
down at her. "I can see it standing out a mile," Skafe said. "I'll bet that
wench has him all summed up. Virtuous my foot. A bun in the oven is
what she'll arrange; and then she will know that come hell or high water, John Skafe will marry her."

"But Husky, he *couldn't*. Your son marry a gardener's daughter? I
mean Phipps is a nice sort of man himself, but they're a shack family
really. And as for that Mrs. Phipps—there's bad blood there. Think of
a Skafe marrying such a common little creature. It's unthinkable."

He knew someone else who might have agreed that such a thing should
be prevented, but she would have mocked him, saying: *It's not unfunny
that the Skafes and the Phippses came on the same boat from Massachusetts in 1783. Who was then the gentleman?*

But the first Simon Skafe had been a captain in the Royal Navy, retired to settle at Dedham, Mass; the first Phipps had been a sergeant
in the Loyal American Regiment. So there was a difference way back
there when the grants were made; just as there was a difference way

on here, when one grant had prospered and the other had long been lost, forgotten.

"What will you do?" she said, sipping Dubonnet, putting down her glass with a fairy tinkle from her bracelet with all the golden charms. She was so sweet and kind that he had made it a rule, and he almost always kept his rule—not to let her know the little unimportant things about her that annoyed him mildly.

"One thing I have decided," he said, "is that Master John is leaving for Turtle Mountain on Monday morning."

Grace looked distressed. "But, Husky dear, he's only been home two weeks."

"I know," he said. "I'm sorry about that, and I wish I could have seen more of him, but it can't be helped."

"But John can sometimes be so obstinate. He might just refuse, and then it would be awful for you."

"He said he would go to Turtle Mountain. So he will go. He's like his grandfather about an undertaking."

"He's like his father about an undertaking," she said. "*Nobody needs an I O U from Husky Skafe.*"

Maclean's had done a piece on him—like one of those New Yorker profiles, but with illustrations. The *nobody needs an I O U* had been one theme of it, parallel with the dynamic theme. They had been saying that about him for a long time now; he could not quite remember how it started.

"Tell me," he said, being not too comfortable under too much praise. "Is it true that Harry Hicks was after the Phipps girl at one time?"

"Yes, and Mrs. Cooligan thinks she was in love with him. But apparently—well dear, you know his reputation about the only thing he wants from girls—apparently they had a quarrel. All I know is that last year when Molly was working for me in the kitchen, Harry Hicks used to bring the special thick cream down himself, and she always fled."

"The nuptial flight involves a chase . . ." he began thoughtfully.

"Oh no!" she said in a minute, shocked. "You couldn't *arrange* a thing like that. It wouldn't be right."

"Not arrange," he said. "Promote. Harry's a decent fellow despite some faults. All he needs is to settle down. I was thinking that earlier this morning. And girls don't hide from men they don't give a damn about. I see a suitable young couple—for both of whom I feel responsible—I shall be very glad to help them make a start."

"But Husky, doesn't it seem just a bit—just a bit cold-blooded?"

"Perhaps," he said. "But I don't feel cold-blooded about my son. Besides," he said, "don't you know that most marriages in the world are arranged without the couple ever having met, or at least not having expressed a choice? Yet they live happily."

"Yes, dear," said Grace. She frowned, no doubt because of a slight to her romantic view of love; but the frown lifted at another thought. "Of course," she said, "that class aren't really quite the same as us."

Once more the past came up to mock him, to mock her division of mankind, to mock him for letting the remark go by. He took Grace's hand again. "Now let's hear about the dance," he said.

It was all in train, as he knew it would be. The marquee was on the lawn, beyond the new swimming pool, which paralleled the jink of the house, good landscaping, good design. They had sited the filtered heated pool just about where the rosebeds used to be. He looked down at the water, which was as crystal a blue as the Great Bear River, at the striped marquee, at floodlights placed about the lawn. How pretty the Gallery house and surrounding woods would look tonight.

He sat on the couch again, and she told him who was coming. Everyone was coming—A Governor, a Federal Minister, a Premier, an Ambassador, the Church, the Summer Colony, including Lord and Lady Haydon and their son, Piers Whitfield, over staying with the Merchants. Grace dropped the names. "There's only one thing still to settle, and that is Sally's toast. I know you wouldn't want long speeches, dear. But a very old and distinguished friend should propose her health. Would you think Bob Carter or Foster Bovill?"

"One of those two," he said. "But old Bob on his hind legs about youth and beauty—he would lay it on with a trowel for half an hour or worse."

"He might be hurt if he wasn't asked."

"I don't think so," he said. Or if so, it did not matter. He had Bob Carter as Chairman of the Board of Summit Enterprises, the holding company. Old Bob's ego was well looked after. "Foster Bovill is the man," he said, "if he will do it. Shall I call him now?"

Bovill was a New Englander who had come to Gallery for many summers, an American with whom Skafe had no business ties, but whose courtly grace and spirit he admired. "Thank you, Simon," said Foster Bovill on the telephone. "I shall be honored to propose your dear child's health. Five minutes or so would do, I suppose?"

So that was settled by Simon Skafe, his only nonfinancial contribution to the arrangements for Sally's dance. Which reminded him that he still had not given her the diamond watch. He would get her alone for a minute.

Meanwhile, he had his wife alone with him. "Come on," he said. "There's room for two," and he took Grace in his arms, about a hundred and fifteen supple pounds. There might have been some hurly-burly on the chaise longue, but she escaped from him with giggles. "You're so naughty," she said. "You muss me up like a big bad boy."

He could have had his will of her with a bad boy's insistence, but he felt rather tired, or not sufficiently naughty to apply persuasion. To Grace, love did slightly tend to have its proper place and time, as scheduled in *Woman's Day* or the *Ladies' Home Journal*.

It seemed vaguely immoral now to think of it, but he remembered how he and Anna used to meet after absence. Nor did it matter one tinker's damn to her if she had just come straight from having a hairdo. "I'll be seein' ya," he said, to divert the mental subject and to make Grace giggle, "right here right after that li'l old dance is over."

She laughed suitably and kissed him and filled his glass. "I must go down," she said. "Stay here and rest a while, dear, until luncheon. It's been so worrying for you."

"I'd like to get John alone this afternoon," he said. "Say between two and four—I have to be back for milking. We might go out together in the boat, if the Sleemans can be otherwise entertained. Could you arrange it, Grace?"

"I think so," she said. Although not a clever woman in any intellectual sense, Grace was an extremely skillful social contriver, without ever seeming to contrive. "But must you talk to John before the dance?"

"This is Friday," he said. "If he is going to leave on Monday, I think it's much fairer to the boy to see him now. Less draconian, I mean, to give him warning. By the way," he said. "Don't drop a hint of any trouble."

"Of course not, dear," she said, and went to the door, and turned. "You won't be too hard on him, Husky?"

"No," he said. "I don't think I am ever hard on him."

"I know that, dear. But it's just that you're such a strong and terrific person . . ." Grace blew him a kiss, and went away. Neither of the children had ever quite accepted her, but both were fond of her (Sally impatiently), and both used her (John in particular) as a kind of ambassadress to Father.

Grace was a Christian person, so conventional, predictable and good that sometimes a husband might feel the secret irks of boredom—try never to indulge those irks, be thankful for one in a million in this woman-straddled continent.

They went out at two in the *Fair Alice*, a fifty-foot twin diesel boat, sleeping six. She cruised at fourteen knots, and had everything, including radar. Skafe sent the *Fair Alice* to Antigua in the winter, and he and Grace usually spent a month cruising down the islands to Barbados and Grenada; or cruising up to the Virgins and Puerto Rico. A quiet day or two at sea, another social round ashore—he liked both aspects; and, fortunately, Grace did not suffer from seasickness.

"I have to be back by four," he said to the skipper, Elmer Kirby, at the float at the wharf below the house. "So let's just potter around the islands."

"Ay ay, sir," said Kirby, an ex-chief petty officer, RCN. Of Skafe's private male employees—and they were now quite numerous—this might be the best. He was a small, crabbed, monosyllabic man who kept the *Fair Alice* like an admiral's barge. He disliked humanity, except a few individuals, one of whom was Simon Skafe, it seemed. In three winters, he had taught Skafe much about the sea.

Now father and son sat in the stern, the blue ensign of the Yacht Club fripping out behind them. The sun was warm, and there was a brisk small chop. The wind held nor'west, which meant no fog to chill the dance tonight.

John scanned the sea for birds, while Skafe enjoyed being at sea again; a sheltered sea, but it was salt. He had spent one short summer long ago working as a deckhand out of Tuktoyaktuk on the Arctic Ocean. Apart from that, he had come later than most men to learn the sea; and he wondered if it was the old Skafe blood still in his veins, or was that sort of notion so much romantic gobbledegook? Or was it that he always liked to pit himself—not against this kind of choppy millpond, but against a risk, a gale, an arctic winter, or an untamed river?

The old sailor blood certainly doesn't course in John's veins, Skafe thought. John is bored by boats, except as observation platforms. He seems to be bored by most things. He likes books, birds, his mysterious natural world, putting pen to paper, and now the gardener's daughter.

Skafe wondered how he was going to broach the matter—not of the gardener's daughter, if he could help it; oh God, he thought, I hope he hasn't got her in trouble already—but of leaving for Turtle Mountain on Monday morning. It was ridiculous, but he was nervous of his son. What with Turtle, Summit, Staniland, Precambrian Pulp and Paper, Lindores Cement, Skafair, Skafe Exploration, he employed around twelve thousand men, and he could deal—not that he did—with any single one of them without a qualm. But his own son made him sweat. Plenty of time, he thought.

"I liked your story, John," he said quite loudly, the wind, the wash, the engine and exhaust, the ensign fripping.

John started, and turned his blue eyes from his mother's expensive glasses. "What, Dad?" he said.

"I said I liked that story of yours in *New Encounter*."

John let the binoculars hang against his chest, his face alive with pleasure, clouding to be wary of paternal pats, or of some qualification of that praise. "Did you really?" he said.

"Yes," Skafe said. He had read John's story in the little magazine most carefully three times; he had also got the opinion of one of Montreal's literary pundits, who tried to be clever rather unsuccessfully. Aptly, in view of this morning's developments but quite by chance, Skafe thought, the story concerned a young man's anguished choice between girl and duty, not an original theme. But the treatment was unusual, in that the choice or dilemma before the young man became fully known to the reader only at the end.

"I like those stories of mood," Skafe said, "in the *New Yorker* style." He thought carefully, not wishing to presume to blunder in where angels fear. "And I don't mind them being unresolved, because life, after all, is largely unresolved. I think, though, that the best of such stories have a thread of plot, a small carrot to draw the reader donkey on."

"That's interesting," John said. "One needs to be reminded about plot." He looked round at Simon Skafe with warm surprise. *Click*, they were in tune together. "What else did you think about it, Dad? I mean, what did you think was wrong?" The eyes in that introspective face pleaded: *Nothing wrong*; but still he asked; he even asked his surprisingly unphilistine father.

"My only criticism," Skafe said, "might be that none of the three characters seemed quite whole, quite of a piece, if you know what I mean. Not that I have a clue about these things," he added humbly, and largely sincerely. "But I felt they were too unpredictable."

"But that's just what I'm after, don't you see? In real life, people *are* unpredictable. In real life people aren't absolute." He gave his father a speculative glance, which that not-unintelligent man took to mean a possible exception in the case of S. K. Skafe. "But almost all fiction seems to me to oversimplify character. What I am trying to do—and there's nothing really new about it, look at Shakespeare—what I am trying for is the Jekyll/Hyde, the generous/mean, the cruel/kind, the contradictions—I want to make real people as real people really are. It's terribly difficult, I know. And I know I need experience. But do you see what I'm getting at, Dad?"

"Yes," he said. "I do." And at last he saw a light burning in his son, and he resented it while respecting it. "That's a pretty tough jungle, the fiction business, isn't it?" he said.

"Yes, Father," John said. "But if you're good enough, you get there in the end. Not that I want to get there much in the sense of making fortunes and being famous. I just want to do what I want to do, and have people want to read it."

They were rounding an island now, in the cooler air of Fundy itself. You don't need to make a fortune, thought Skafe. And you even question or feel ashamed of that ambition which has as its fruit some pleasure in fame. "How much did they pay you?" he asked.

"Ten guineas, Dad. About thirty dollars. I must say it's a terrific feeling when somebody finally decides that your work is worth buying."

"Yes," he said. "I can well see that. Ten guineas, a little less than thirty dollars."

The talk lapsed, and John became glued to his glasses again, remarking porpoises, remarking a bicker of gulls over there at a school of herring. "Oh look, Dad," he said, unslinging the binoculars, which he, this young stranger, lover, friend, had turned round to his back, the less to hurt Miss Molly Phipps's bosom when he kissed her.

Skafe adjusted the glasses to observe four terns, a sedate party on a small driftwood log, like four small sailors dressing ship. They were rather cute, bobbing alone there on the sea; and they flew away.

"There's a wonderful lazy rhythm to the flight of terns," John said.

"Yes," he said. He remembered a pair of lazy-flying, angry terns harrying an eagle at the head of the Mackenzie River. He saw those others now in memory because he had been alone a first time then with John's mother. "Terns go sailing," he said absently, and somewhat to his own surprise.

"The world is beautiful," John Skafe said, perhaps feeling some communion with a newly sympathetic father in the beautiful world this afternoon.

"Yes," he agreed again. "We're lucky God put the world here for us."

"Or put us here for the world is the way I like to think of it," John said. "If you see the difference, Dad."

He saw the difference, and saw in it the blurred mystical pantheism of the David Dorrien, Anna Dorrien, John Skafe league. He gave the glasses back to John, and sat in silence, and Elmer Kirby turned her head to wind for home.

"How did you find your mother, John?" he said. It was the first time he had spoken to the boy since John's return from some months in Ireland and in Europe, and he felt it proper that he should ask.

"Mum is fine," John said, and paused. "She hasn't changed a bit except that she's becoming a little gray," he said, and paused, and his father thought that it was seven quiet years since he had seen John's mother. "She's crazy about her garden at Inniscarra," John was saying. "It's quite lovely."

"And David Dorrien?" Skafe asked.

"Oh, David's fine," John said too loudly. There was embarrassment. He might be feeling: *Poor old Dad has to ask his duty questions.* Also, John was fond of David Dorrien, who was rumored now to get tipsy every night.

Skafe thought that Anna and David were at the back of all this half-baked writing business. He felt some bitterness against them. "Did you write your story there?" he asked, mild and friendly, about John's ten-guinea one-and-only published work of fiction.

"Yes, Father." It was sometimes Dad and sometimes Father. "It's a big old house, and they gave me a room. I wrote hard all the time. That's to say when I could think of things to write."

"And since you came home?"

"No, Dad. I'm slightly stuck between things. I find ideas are the very devil."

Ideas are the very devil. Authentic Dorrien, he could hear him say it. John had his mother's infectious ear for speech. And no doubt he found that writing ideas were the very devil with Miss Molly Phipps to philander with. "I was reading a piece the other day," Skafe said, "by some old fiction-writing hand. He said that half the battle of ideas lay in having lived—in having experience of life and people and events."

John looked quickly round, as if suspicious, and Skafe smiled at him. What an appealing face, he thought, a diffident Sir Galahad. Who could blame the Phipps girl if she really fell in love with him? "True, Father," John said, "depending on the genre, of course. But whatever you write, you must know for yourself, that's true."

He could see the house now across Gallery Bay, the large house beside the shore below the small house on the hill, his birthplace. Home was five miles away, or twenty minutes. I can do only what I think is right for him, Skafe thought. And I cannot postpone it any longer. Now, this moment.

"John," he said, "I'm very glad that you have had these six months in Europe—a chance to think things out for yourself. And I do quite understand about McGill, much as I regret that you could not make it through to a degree. Your dean tells me that you tried honorably and hard, but he feels that your real bent is not in engineering. As to what you are going to do in life is not for me to say. It is for you to decide yourself. If it is to be writing, then writing it will be."

He stopped and looked at John, and he saw some trust in John for him. Why did that damned little girl have to make this a shotgun marriage, trial marriage with the North?

"The only thing I ask," he said, "is that you should do what you wrote from Europe and said that you would do—go North for a year. You know that I have always hoped that you would follow me in business. You have all the brains and commonsense required, engineering degree or not."

But do you have the flair, the punch, the pertinacity for business or for writing or for life, that is the question? thought Simon Skafe.

"Lots of people take time to make their minds up," he said. "I was twenty-four, two years older than you are now, when I threw up a safe job in office equipment and went North to find out what I wanted to do. I found it in the end, and so will you. Business, writing, whatever it may be—time is going to tell you."

"Time has told me, Father," John said. "I know it's a disappointment to you, and I'm very sorry for letting you down about the engineering, but I have made my mind up. I am going to write."

"You agreed a few minutes ago," Skafe said, "that to write about life, a man must have lived. Indeed, a man must have lived a little to know what life means at all for him. I have never told you this, but the North is Canada for me. The North is my life for me."

"I knew that, Dad," John said.

"All I ask, then," he said, moved, penitent, remorseless, "is that you leave for Turtle Mountain on Monday morning."

"On Monday?"

"Yes," he said. "It's very short notice, I'm afraid, but unavoidable, because old Wilson Pitt—who has been running our production side since we began—Willie decided only yesterday to make his summer visit. He's a grand fellow, Willie, as you know, and I want you to go with him. He will tell you the Turtle story in his own wild language—and it is quite a story, John. And he will start you off on the right leg with Peter Syme, who still runs that operation for us, but will move on to bigger things when Willie Pitt steps aside next year. I would like you to spend the first six months learning every phase, from the ore extraction to our final process—uranium concentrate."

"Port Hope next stop on the way to Strontium 90," John Skafe muttered.

Skafe ignored that interjection, or he felt it resentfully in his guts, but did not speak to it. "In late December," he pushed on, "when the sea ice is strong enough, we shall be running tractor trains across from the arctic coast to the Nunangiyak Islands where our exploration company will begin to drill for oil next year—we have very strong indications there. If that would interest you, I would like you to go along. The North may be empty, John, but you will find life there, as I did."

"I am not you, Father," John said. "And oddly enough, I don't want to be. But I will go along. I said I would."

They came to land and, as was proper, the son of the owner stepped first from the boat. The owner himself went ashore. "Thank you, Captain," he said, paying the sailor's compliment to Elmer Kirby.

He walked alone up the wharf as John strode away alone ahead. He was tired again, home on the dot of four to watch the milking.

CHAPTER THREE

SOLLY and his College Strummers were on hire from the hotel. This year he had a better lot of strummers than the usual. Suitably primed, they played favorites ranging from middle-aged *South Pacific* by *Annie, Get Your Gun* and *Oklahoma!* back to the jazzy ark, like *Coal Black Mammy*.

It was a buffet dinner-dance, food in the big marquee, dancing in the house, a hundred people, and the moon was full. *I want everyone to have unstuffy fun,* was Sally's watchword for the party. But she and Grace had planned with all the care required to reap a harvest of unstuffy fun.

Skafe moved about urbanely, pleased with everything. Lobster Newburg was the only hot food, perfection; likewise cold meat, things in aspic, salads galore; likewise jumbo strawberries grown by Phipps, the head gardener. It was a groaning board. Heidsieck '47 slaked his thirst.

Foster Bovill spoke to Sally's health with a patrician absence of superlative. "Jock will say thank you for me," Sally said. Which John had done in a few sentences. He had a way with words, if not a strong way of delivering them. But the old man and the young man shared that dignity which the New World tries so feverishly to shed.

Skafe danced some duty dances, as with Muriel Carter—Bob Carter's lethal battleaxe of a wife; as with Hermione Merchant—who had wit and kindness. It happened that most of his duty partners were the kind of older ladies who amused him. He also danced with Lady Haydon, but he did not like her. Her husband seemed a decent long-nosed chap, who might have been a peer of the realm or a hissing groom, but nothing much between, and was the former.

He also danced with Grace, by no means in the line of duty. "Gracie," he said, his hand at the curve of the waist on her shantung sheath from Hartnell; her diamonds and her pearls, her pale brown skin. "Y'know, Gracie," he said, as they danced extremely well together to *One Enchanted Evening*: "You're a smasher of a footloose dancing woman."

"So're you," she said, "except not quite a woman, I would guess." Grace was good value on a party. He remembered the first night they had danced together. He remembered it because Mac got very drunk, and after they had taken Mac to bed, the bold devil Skafe had kissed Grace Parkyn, and had danced again with her, and she had confided to him that she would rather dance with him than almost anything. "I love you in your dinner jacket," she informed him now. She did not say such things to flatter, but because she meant them warmly. "I don't see John," she said. "I wonder."

"Yes," he said. They wondered with one mind about a woodland tryst, the girl who waited, and the boy who stole away from lobsters and champagne, from her father's jumbo strawberries, from toasts and high society to meet her in a glade below the moon. It was a poignant thought to anyone no longer young. The thought accused him, but unjustly.

"Poor John," Grace said. She sighed in his arms, and the dance was over. People moved from the house to the flagstone terrace to replenish there, or at the marquee beyond the pool. "Where is that Maître D?" she said, one of her wincifying usages. "We need champagne."

But Marcel and a minion now appeared with more dewy magnums. The Skafe kitchens had provided food; the liquor commission had produced wine by special order. Marcel and his waiters came from the hotel to mastermind the service. Solly masterminded music. Grace now slipped inside to mastermind the whole affair, so Simon Skafe made cordial rounds. "It's a marvelous party, Mr. Skafe" . . . "Husky, as usual, you've done us proud" . . . "I'm glad you're enjoying yourselves," said the lordly host. Or he said: "It's all the women's doing. Don't thank me" . . . "This dance is absolutely super, sir" . . . "Have a good time," he said to the young people, who clearly were having a wonderful time, although some couples danced all night with one another. How dull that seemed to him, a cautious generation.

A remark of Dorrien's—made in the course of that improbable, final interview—had stuck with him: *I was only lamenting, Simon, that there seem to be so few Canadians like you who want to risk and find.* He thought that a prescient remark—it grew more true. It suited him very well, that as a large employer he could command the best young brains the country had—lawyers, engineers, geologists, and so on. But the personal side of him regretted it. A boy should risk and find, as he had done. This going steady seemed to him to be another escape to security. He supposed that the perils of the times might have something to do with the whole affair—our masteries had grown too great to face alone, thus go steady to early marriage, safe employment.

He had such thoughts as he passed among these younger people, who were gay but always careful, in his observation. The young were dear to him, and they liked him too. "It's the best dance ever, Mr. Skafe."

Yes, he thought. The dance is a wow, and where is John? What about this risk and find? he thought. Would John not be doing just that in writing? But he must know life. For example, a little experience at Turtle Mountain might persuade young John that *Port Hope next stop on the way to Strontium* 90 was a . . . Well, what was it?—A sort of half-baked cynical despair about a great adventure in energy, perhaps the greatest adventure in human history—not warlike in its true potentiality.

This time Solly played a Viennese waltz, and this was his dance with the *raison d'être*. Sally stuck to no partner, although she favored one or two, much cutting in. It looked to her father—if he read the signs aright —that the Haydons' son, Piers Whitfield, would be the next swain on the list.

"Ours, I think, Miss Skafe," he said at the french doors to the house. The night was still young, and warm alike outside and in. Sally's dress was the blue of that deep delphinium when grown near the sea. She wore no jewelry except his diamond watch. There was a bloom to her skin, like Anna's bloom in summer. Sally was fairer, though. It was slightly a miracle, if you considered the appalling plainness of mankind, that the Canadian family Skafe should be so well-favored. He could close his eyes when he danced with her—which, of course, he did not do— and he would be dancing with Anna again, with the firm plenitude of Anna, the perfect rhythm and the not quite perfect lightness. It was a complicated business being father to the daughter of a mother lost and not forgotten.

The old-fashioned waltz was a lively dance for them together, and no one presumed to cut in on him. "I don't see John," he said, going clockwise.

"Jock has probably vamoosed," she said, as he reversed her at the verge of his being dizzy.

"Gone *away*, you mean?" he said. It was a possibility that bothered him—of a Jaguar flying in the night, and a gardener's daughter cuddling to elopement, but he thought not, he was sure not.

"No," she said, "but I wouldn't blame him." Sally looked quite radiant, and looking radiant, the cynosure of all the passing, circling pairs of eyes, she said distinctly and quietly to her father's ear: "I don't know what possessed you to be so calculating—yes, and ruthless—to poor Jock."

"*What?*" he said. "How do you mean?"

"I mean he says you tricked him. You took him out in the boat, and you softened him up, being so encouraging and sympathetic about his story, about writing in general," said Sally, looking radiant. "John says the timing was a work of art. He says the marching orders came out smoothly as you neared the wharf." She smiled at her father with a hostile devil in her dark blue eyes.

"But I didn't trick him, Sally. I meant every word I said. Besides, he promised he would go North this year."

"Yes," she said, "and the very first time you see John again, you send him North at three days' notice. Daddy darling," Sally said, and no one could guess from that smiling face what she was telling him, "I don't know how someone so sweet and kind as you could be so hard and blind and stupid as you are with John. He wants to write. Why bully him into the arctic wastes because of some dream that is yours, not his?"

She did not know that he had another reason, and he would not tell it to her. His children had no secrets from one another; and therefore it was a certainty that Sally knew of the Molly Phipps affair. *Never explain*, his mother used to say. Not a bad precept, that. "I think you're unfair to me," he said. "It happens that Willie Pitt starts North on Tuesday— he only decided yesterday. All I have done is to ask John to be loyal to his word."

"Not to his word. To you," she said, still smiling. "But you expect too many loyalties to come to a focal point on S. K. Skafe."

It was an impertinence. "Now look here, Sally," he said. "When I want your criticism, I shall ask for it."

She looked at him, no longer smiling. "I know you don't want criticism, but you've got it."

She did not have Anna's unbridled temper, but she had a temper in control. She laid her young cheek against his cheek. "Darling," she said. "I'm sorry if I've been unkind."

It was remarkable, but she, aged twenty-one today, could be unkind to the olympian Husky Skafe. For the first time now she had rebuked him, as no other man or woman would. He took it from her, wishing an old wish he had never truly wished—for who would want such change?— that this strong and vital girl had been his son.

The dance was over, and they went outside. "Oh, thank you, Miles," she said. "I'd love to after this." Grace had contrived a game of golf— Sally and the Sleemans—for the early afternoon. Even Miles, that impeccable benedict, showed signs of Sallyitis as he asked her now to dance, a boyish touch of it, a slightly coy infection.

"Let's sit down over there," she said, "and not be bothered." They found two chairs in shadow on the lawn, in a place made darker by contrasting lights. "I do wish Mac had come," she said. "He is always such fun. Mac is a sort of catalyst for us."

"Yes," he said. It was a good description of old Mac. He was more testy now, and no less intolerant of pretension—still incapable of seeing beyond the façade of Sleeman, for example, to the quality of Sleeman. But in general Mac was a catalyst, an unchanging, undemanding helper. "Sally," Skafe said. "It's no good my speaking to John, but please tell him that I didn't mean to do him dirt."

"All right, Daddy," she said. "I will." Sally had said that she was sorry for being unkind, but she had not retracted a word that she had said; and he knew that she still had it in for him, if not for motive, then for method. "There's Jock now," she said.

John had come to stand by the swimming pool, alone, not far from people, but away from them. His face was pale, his fair hair none too tidy, his black bow tie askew. He looked distrait, perhaps a little tight, well bred as always. Bob Carter and Foster Bovill were standing near, and Skafe thought that Bob Carter spoke to John, but he did not reply. He stared down into the swimming pool, blue water and white tiles. It was illuminated. John stood alone; the party and the pool were alien to him.

The next dance had begun, and people were moving to the house again. But one young man came against the tide. "John!" called Charlie Winter loudly. "Have you seen Mr. Skafe? He's wanted on the phone, long distance. It's important."

John looked at Charlie Winter. He laughed. "No, Charlie," he said, "I haven't seen him; and in case it interests you, I couldn't care less where the crummy bastard is."

Twenty or thirty people heard it and accelerated to the dancing. Bob Carter, a good family friend, a stickler of the old school, took a pace forward. "Young man . . ." he began angrily.

"No, Bob," said Foster Bovill, "not that way." He went over to John, who stared again morosely at the pool. "Hullo there, John," he said. "I haven't had a chance to hear about your European trip. If you're not dancing this one, shall we stroll?"

John started and swayed and pulled himself together. "Yes, Mr. Bovill," he said. "Of course." The two tall men walked off together, past the marquee and down the lawn in moonlight to the shore. They were oddly alike in an austerity of distinction.

Oh God, Skafe thought. What have I done? He might have done the right thing wrongly, but he had done what he had done. And then he stood, remembering the telephone for him. More trouble, he supposed.

Sally caught his hand and went with him. "You must never let John know you heard that. Promise, Daddy!"

"All right," he said. He went in and upstairs to take the call. *Life is trouble,* someone once said to him. But it was not. For seven years he had moved along, not without problems—indeed, they were unending; not without things that failed—indeed, the failure headaches spiced success. He had moved on, and if the road had been rough in places, to fill and grade and surface, he had built a good road as he went along. Until today . . . Oh, to hell with roads, he thought. To hell with inadequate analogies. Simply face the fact that the not-so-omniscient Husky Skafe had made a mess of things; that one of life's climacterics was making trouble for the not-so-omnipotent Husky Skafe. *Crummy bastard,* he thought. By God, John's right. But I was right too, and I will not change.

He spoke on the telephone. It was a somewhat important person from Ottawa. Skafe, who had contacts in many places, had heard by the grapevine of this possibility, so was readied to say with respect and gratitude how much he regretted that pressure of existing business—and new plans which he could not mention by telephone but would be only too glad to explain in person—made it quite impossible for him to accept the South American ambassadorship, honored as he was, and vitally important as he knew the post now to be in view of Canadian trade etcetera, and so on by a few courteous nothings to a cordial goodbye. Quite a compliment, he thought, considering that I'm inclined to the other side of the political fence. But then, their industrial development down there . . .

Grace would have liked it, he thought, returning to festivity; and she would have made a first-rate ambassador's wife. He might have liked it too himself in some ways, but it was not a sufficiently important post to justify considering even for one moment the shelving of plans for the drawing of steel within his orbit. Gaining control of Algonquin Steel would require finesse, yet was as simple in essence as it was honorable in practice, but it would hardly do for His Excellency Simon Skafe, one of Her Majesty's Ambassadors of Canada.

Later on, he thought, and it was a private ambition he divulged to no one, hardly to himself—later on might come a day, Conservatives back in power, the High Commissionership in London . . .

He felt encouraged. That invitation lessened the load of his personal troubles. He told Grace about it the next time they danced together; and she was thrilled at the honor, if disappointed at his decision. "You know best, dear," she said cheerfully.

The older guests began to fade away before "God Save the Queen" at one o'clock. Youth, and some mutton dressed as lamb, instead of swimming in the best private pool in all New Brunswick, elected to depart in droves for one of New Brunswick's lovely lakes nearby. So Simon Skafe was in bed by two.

He was still awake at three. I was a fool, he thought, to have those after-party eggs and bacon on top of everything—lobster, Virginia ham, avocado mousse (made by Toddy after Anna's recipe), strawberries and Jersey cream. Too much is more than enough, he thought, turning over to his left side. That did not help the heartburn.

He tried to slow his mind to let sleep gather on him. But the day kept racing, from a smooth flight to a muffed approach, Flume Hill and home to Gallery, the farm so prosperous, the minor problems, the woodland idyll—yes, it was that, he thought remorsefully. And then Sally's day, the happiest of days went wrong, went right, became a kaleidoscope of daughter dishing out the hell, crummy bastard, happy people, Solly and his College Strummers '55, Heidsieck '47. And so to bed and indigestion.

Grace slept in the other bed beside him. She was a soft light sleeper as she was a soft light woman in a million, spoiling him. Sometimes he wished that she would bite his head off, scream at him or something; but she never did, and just as well.

He felt blown up. He tried to get out of bed as quietly as a bloated mouse to go for Bisodol, but Grace woke up. She did not mumble and grumble like a sleepy tigress like another woman, but stirred instantly from sleep to wakefulness, and sat up straight. The moon wore down beyond the south and gave some light in here upon her slightness and her charming breasts, not hidden and not flouting nylon nightgown. She always put it on again. "What is it, dear?" she said.

"Indigestion," said Husky Skafe. "Some Bisodol."

"You have such healthy appetite," she said. Or was it plural? She went back to sleep.

Safely returned, and feeling cold, he lay to hear the wild loon laugh at him. *What have you got?* it laughed at him. *Millions. Ha ha, millions!* You shut up, he willed the moonlit loon on Gallery Bay. Sure enough, the loon obeyed him.

The Bisodol seemed to help a little. The balloon stopped inflating against his chest. A car came down the drive and stopped, the Buick wagon from the sound of it. That would be the Sleemans, who had gone off swimming too, led by Sally and Piers Whitfield in the Jaguar.

They came into the house, and to their room, which had been a rumpus room until this year. Grace liked making changes. By poor design in the heating system this room shared a cold air return with that room below. The register was behind his bed. The voices floated up by pipeline. She should have found it out, he thought testily. Once again the wretched Skafe could not but be party to a private scene. It was embarrassing, a muted altercation. You never knew with people, did you? Even Miles and Cynthia—woman spits and man resents, and *Quiet, can't you? Don't you know that they're asleep?* Hissing, horrible, the cruel waves of it. He felt damned cold in his hands and feet, but not in his swollen middle.

He shut his ears, but that made such a roaring in his head that he unplugged to hear the raucous whispers, seething jealousy and hate from nice kind Cynthia. Just because Miles had lost his senses over that intelligent man-crazy female, was she, his wife, expected to go swimming naked with a lot of juveniles in a lake?

But now silence, such relief from that, but not from the thought of that—of naked swimming parties—*in the nude, dear,* Grace would say. This sex, thought Skafe, father of the man-crazy female. It's simply terrible, a scourge, a pest, a horrible constriction and expansion. But we did that when we were young, he thought. And it was no scourge in the summer moon. It was quite lovely and innocent, bare bodies shining, and the water's touch.

The thing was blowing up inside him and—a funny thing—he felt so awful, but he saw the beauty that was life—cruel, lovely, hateful, precious. Not much of a chap for so-called beauty, but he saw it now. He heard it truly in a sob, a laugh, "My darling" from below. And that was peace, a blessing called catharsis. For the first time he felt some real friendship toward Miles, the human being in his silk stuffed shirt.

But then a clamp closed on his chest. He managed one loud belch and Grace turned over. She would not object to that rudeness if it meant relief.

It meant no relief. It was not a pain exactly, but like broken ribs strapped up too tight. His heart was racing in the ice.

But he remembered. He knew suddenly from an article that he had read in something, *Reader's Digest, Coronet* or something. Symptoms. Dear God, he thought, and called to her.

"What is it, Husky?"

"Sick," he said. "Please help me."

Her lamp went on, and she was round beside him. "Darling," she said, "your brow is cold and clammy."

"My heart," he said. *Please, God,* he prayed, the frightened boy, God near to him.

The operator must have been dozing, but she answered in a while. Dr. Pugsley might have been asleep, a hand stretched out, a bald head shaken. "Yes?" his voice came on at once.

"It's Mrs. Skafe. My husband's sick—his heart, I think. Please come." Grace put the spurs to Dr. Pugsley, but she was calm. She circled the beds from telephone to him again. He tried to sit up to ease that tourniquet across his chest, but he could not make it.

"You mustn't move," she said. "Now close your eyes. Relax, dear, if you can."

First, a warm damp sponge to wipe his face. Next, a hot water bottle to his feet. His heart went on a fluttering rampage while he thought of many things, of all past projects, struggles and achievements, all for this. So what were they? But nothing. Where was he? But nowhere, dying in a room. He prayed.

The house had been sleeping, but it woke. A house had life too, of its own, and sleep and creaking pain and death, slow death, like the old house where he was born but it survived him. This house perked up to wakefulness, doors, footsteps, whispers. "Done for," he said.

"Lie still, dear." She seemed almost cross that time.

Now he heard two cars, the second one the Jaguar. He knew individuals in machinery, their own life too. That would be Sally home from the moonlight swim, chancing to follow an M.D. license down the drive. The house was buzzing now. The vultures gather, thought Simon Skafe. It was an unfair, unreasonable thought to be regretted.

The doctor felt him, listened to him, questioned him about his feelings—real pain or extreme constriction?—then about his latest checkup.

Who was the doctor? Forester? Then about his food, which Grace remembered perfectly. "H'mm," the doctor said.

Now Simon Skafe was speechless, just about to burst. He did. He exploded with a colossal belch, a mammoth eructation. It was very rude, but it did not kill him. The tourniquet around his chest was marvelously loosened, and he lived.

"What's that?" he said about the injection.

"To make you sleep," said Dr. Pugsley.

"But *what?*" he said.

"Morphine, one-quarter grain, if you want to know," said Dr. Pugsley, not well pleased. How grudgingly they parted with their Hippocratic secrets, even to the rich. The poor got nowhere, asking.

"How bad is my heart attack?" he asked. Or how bad was it? he might have said, because a lull was here. He felt very tired and very cold, but marvelously eased. They come again, he thought he remembered from that article, so it would have been tempting providence to ask about his heart attack as been and gone. They called the bad ones *massive,* did they not? "Is it massive?" he asked. He wanted facts, and he could face them.

"It looks to me more like a massive case of indigestion," Dr. Pugsley said. "Too much to eat and too much excitement, and you have paid for it. Go to sleep now, Mr. Skafe." Dr. Pugsley was not sympathy itself. He would have made a poor ambassador to some South American republic. "Stop worrying," he said, hard-bitten, lantern-jawed, bald-tonsured devil. "You're going to be all right. Now sleep."

"Damned lot of nonsense," he said when the man had gone. "Of course it was a heart attack."

"You don't know better than the doctor, dear," said Grace. "You must be calm and go to sleep."

"Bah," he said about their conspiracy to spare him the truth. "Who had it, him or me?"

She tutted at him. Then she kissed him.

"Thank you, Grace," he said, her grateful child, and he was sleepy, not so cold.

"John and Sally—would you like to see them for a second?"

"Yes," he said. He opened his eyes to see his tall son in a dressing gown, and his daughter still in her short evening dress of that vivid deep delphinium blue.

"Good boy, Dad," John said.

"Dear darling," Sally said.

He shut his eyes because of tears, the silly fellow, love around him, love undeserved, and love was true, and where was Anna?

"High time you were all in bed," he said, and he went to sleep to dream. I hardly ever dream, he thought, but he was dreaming. He was in the boat again, in Winter North Atlantic. It was bloody cold, the salt spray freezing, Simon Skafe taking charge, of course. *Let's sing,* he said, that being the hackneyed, sensible thing for shipwrecked mariners to do to keep their spirits up. One chap had died, and many were in shock. They had taken a spread of three torpedoes, bow, amidships, stern —not quite exactly funny. *Frankie and Johnnie,* he sang. *Sing up, damn you!* It was an old favorite song of his from northern days on the great cold river, old man, cold man Mackenzie River. *Frankie and Johnnie were lovers Oh Lordy, how they did love* . . . He bullied them and got them singing, and he tried to keep his hands warm in his pockets when not chipping ice, holding her small St. Christopher on his key ring in his pocket. A destroyer picked them up at noon. That was one good thing I did, he thought, asleep, and down he went into deep water, Winter North Atlantic.

"Can Toddy bring your breakfast up? She wants to, dear."

"Why not?" he said. It was nearly twelve, what a time for breakfast. It would be breakfast in bed from now on, he supposed, the best he had to hope for. He felt dopey, washed out, hungry.

"That's not much of a breakfast, Toddy." She was getting pretty old and fat. She'll bury me, he thought.

"It's all you're to get," she said. "Juice, toast, marmalade and coffee— Dr. Pugsley's orders, to be easy on your stomach."

"Well anyway," he said. "Thank God for Toddy's still my motto." He often said it, a ritual saying. But now he particularly wanted her to know. "I can't imagine what we would have done without your goodness to us all these years," he said.

"Och away, Mr. Skafe," she said, and she went away, or rushed away.

He had one piece of toast, and was hungry for another, but he feared the next attack, and so denied himself. Grace came in. She looked pale and tired. "You look tired, my love," he said.

"Do I really, dear?" she said. She took away the tray and brushed crumbs from the quilt. Damned messy meals in bed, he thought, but not strongly, because it was better to be an invalid than to be sinking down and down in Winter North Atlantic. It had not been a dream. He must have nearly died asleep. "The sheerest stroke of luck," she said, "but Dr. Forester was vacationing in Nova Scotia at the Digby Pines, we traced him down, and sent the Crusader from Montreal. He should be at Flume Hill any minute now."

"I knew it was a heart attack," he said, with some peculiar sort of satisfaction, being right; and with a jab of fear.

"You knew nothing of the sort," she snapped at him. It was unkind of Grace to be like this, so different from herself. "Dr. Pugsley thinks you had an acute attack of indigestion, not a coronary. But a second opinion from a specialist just makes sense."

"Pugsley doesn't have a clue," he said. "He's only an old horse doctor from the sticks." Miles, the brains and flair; and Peter Syme, the man —the two of them can swing it somehow, Simon thought. I've been training them for that very purpose all these years. But he had not. He had been training them to take the load off him, another matter from replacing him.

"People come from all over to consult old Dr. Pugsley," Grace said, with some tartness. "Don't you know that?"

She left, and John arrived. "How do you feel now, Dad?" he said, easy and kind, the strong one with the weak one. It was a far cry from that *Fair Alice* conversation yesterday.

"Better, thank you, John," he said. "Not raring to go exactly." He was troubled with an essential thought, because when a man comes near to death, he sees through social trimmings and snobbery to things that matter. Suppose young John did love young Molly Phipps, and want to marry her. Why not? You cannot take a lost love with you either.

He thought of saying : *Don't go North, John,* for a start. But John sat in a chair and looped one leg, dark gray flannel, bare shin, yellow sock and loafer over the arm with a careless sort of elegance, and told him about riding a Vespa scooter from Turin over some pass (being John, he had forgotten the name of it) to Grenoble. It was amusing, casual, laconic. There is much of the bohemian in him, Simon thought. Sally is a practical Canadian, like me. I have my vision or my dream, of course. But Simon's dream seemed unimportant now.

He sat at John's feet in quite a new manner of speaking until various cars arrived, including Sally and Dr. Forester in the Bentley. Pickering, the chauffeur, had brought a technician and an electrocardiogram machine from the local hospital. So all the rigmarole of inspection, embarrassing questions and electrodes went on for ages. Then Dr. Forester, who looked fit and bronzed from the Digby Pines, went out with Dr. Pugsley for some professional cahoots; and Simon Skafe lay with his heart.

He feared the worst, and awaited it in trepidation until Forester returned, full of a heart specialist's hearty cheer and the best of tidings. The cardiogram was entirely normal and similar to the one last month. He concurred wholly with his colleague Dr. Pugsley's diagnosis. Unlike Dr. Pugsley, he was a man-to-man, now-this-is-the-picture, spill-all-the-clinical-minutiae-of-beans kind of medico, which made great sense to Skafe, when the news was good. "We think you should rest today," he said, "and resume a normal easy vacation life tomorrow. You must be more careful of your diet. Do not burden your stomach with heavy foods. As I told you before," he said, "fit as you may be, you have reached the age of forty-nine, and you must realize that you are not immortal."

They went downstairs to be refreshed, while the mortal Skafe lay happily in bed. But he began to reproach himself for being such a sissy. He forgot about that when Sally came to hug him before she drove Dr. Forester back to Flume Hill and the best executive aircraft in Canada, and back to the Digby Pines, another great C.P.R. hotel. "What'll he stick you up for, Daddy?" she inquired. He guessed about five hundred smackers, to confirm what that uncompromising but in a way impressive old physician Pugsley had said already for five bucks a house call.

Grace came up. "It's wonderful, dear," she said, but she did not seem wonderfully pleased with him.

"Yes," he said. "Even if they know darned well they may be wrong. A cardiogram quite often doesn't show a thing."

"Will you stop it?" she said. For the very first time she spat fire at him. "You might think you were the only person in this world who ever had been a little sick. It's not like you at all."

Nor like you, he thought. She is tired, he thought. She looks worn out. But she has seen my feet of clay. "Grace," he said. "Let's have a glass of Dubonnet, shall we?"

"Not today, dear," she said. "Tomorrow when your tummy's rested."

"I'm all right," he said. "I want my Dubonnet today, right now."

"Just a tiny one, then, dear," she said, but she went with alacrity.

He saw it. He was always seeing something that he had not known. One wanted me fallible, he thought. And one wants me only strong. "Thank you, darling," he said. He sipped his deliciously iced Dubonnet, and, being so empty and exhausted, he felt it rush to his head at once. "You must be tired out," he said. "I suppose you didn't get much sleep."

"Not after," she said. "Not a wink. I just couldn't bear it . . ." Grace cried a little.

"Sleep now," he said. "Lie down beside me and go to sleep."

She lay down on the other bed and slept. He thought about life and death and a meeting place. To be a Christian suddenly, calling on God, imploring Him—that is the worst thing, Simon thought, damned coward-ice. He was ashamed. The storm was over, and his good wife slept.

CHAPTER FOUR

THE POOL was wide down here. After a week he was in a careful habit, covering the water cast by cast from each side to center below the canoe. When he had all the line that he could manage, just more than he could comfortably manage, he reeled in. "That is the end of it," Pierre Roland said.

"Let's try one more for luck, Pierre," he said, and sat while they dropped a little. The lead caught on bottom again. The river ran quietly past them between the woods. He fished that last drop, which brought no more luck than he had expected.

"We should rest it now a piece," said Roland. "Then try the old Black Dose."

He had caught one grilse at the top of the pool, hooked it with his second cast of the evening. He had killed eight salmon and three grilse in this week, not spectacular, but satisfying. He felt rested and well again, no recurrence of his indigestion, or whatever. A week on the river was enough.

"You will be leaving tomorrow in the morning, sir?" Roland said in French. They used both languages together.

"Yes, Pierre," he said. "Tomorrow early."

"*Dommage,*" said Roland, poling ashore. "Some rain, and the big run comes," he said in English.

"*Vraiment?*" Skafe said. "I've heard that one before." They joked mildly about the big run of salmon that would always come with rain. Roland was a man of this river—he had been born beside it; he lived beside it, lumbered beside it. He drove pulp and logs down the river, hunted and trapped along the river. He knew every shift of every pool each year in the thirty miles below the dam, every change of lie in chang-ing water. He was a carefree type, a voyageur type, living, working, breeding, carousing beside his river.

Skafe wondered what it would be like to live with a river in all its moods. Would the river not become a sort of god to the man who lived with it? He had been wondering a lot of things in his idle hours and his fishing hours this week. A week was enough for him on a river.

Roland beached the canoe and settled to watch for fish. Skafe walked in his waders across the shingle bar on the inside of the bend at the Bogan Pool. They called it the Bogan because of a large backwater at the start of the sweep that made the pool.

He sat in some comfort against a stranded stump he knew. The smoke of his cigarette rose undisturbed. Mosquitoes bit him but did not much bother him. Those northern summers twenty-three and more years ago had given his blood a built-in bad taste or a lasting resistance. He heard Mac yell as he hooked a fish in Hubbard's Pool upstream. It was Mac's habit or eccentricity to emit a brazen scream of pleasure; then a banshee howl of disgust if things went wrong. "He is into that one good," said Roland down by the canoe. Even Roland, the professional, who hooked most of his sports' salmon for them, respected Mac as a virtuoso.

Skafe watched the top of the pool, which was the best of it. A salmon rolled, up and over and in, like a porpoise, clean silver fish. "Twelve, fifteen pounds," said Roland. Skafe went on watching, but the salmon did not break again. He watched in a riverain trance until the flow of the river tired his eyes, and he looked up to see the trees flow backwards. It was seven forty-five, the last hour of daylight coming. Have patience, Skafe. The best hour comes.

Cloud was building, and a breeze came from the south. It had been hot weather all the week; hence leisurely fishing: from eight until noon; from six until dark. Tomorrow Montreal. He felt a zest for his luncheon meeting—he and Miles Sleeman, Buxton and Kindersley of Algonquin Steel. When we get Algonquin, he thought. When and if, we shall be rounded out, as big as I think we want to be. I might change then, he thought. I might change and give them all a shock, Husky Skafe, the elder playboy, dilettante, patron of the arts. Might change, my foot. Might die of boredom. *You must realize that you are not immortal.* But to be as immortal as a man may be, a man must live.

The sound of an outboard came upriver. Skafe had three miles fishing, a mile below the camp, two miles above. A week's free salmon fishing was a most effective form of business entertaining. The sound grew and faded on the river road below the forest. It would be Sally, he thought, he hoped. She had driven Piers Whitfield this afternoon to catch a train. He was the heir to a peerage, just starting in the investment business in Toronto. Many English immigrants still seemed to expect a living as by right while looking down their noses at all things Canadian. But the best, the few, were very good indeed.

Piers was one of them—intelligent, flexible, of humble mind about this country. He would have made a good match for Sally, except that he was not a match for her. All this fishing week she called the tune, and Piers danced puppy-dog attendance. She led him to sit away on the veranda in the dark, to murmur the nothings of yet another fleeting flame. Skafe knew the signs well, and finally he struck. He walked her up the road from camp, and wasted no time on preliminaries. *This nice boy will go,* he said. *And you will sigh, and you will forget him in a week. But what about Piers? Will he forget you in a week? Do you want him to forget you? No, you don't. You are getting so that you want every personable male extant to pine for love of Sally Skafe.*

She did not like criticism any more than her father liked it, nor any prima donna likes it. *How right you are,* she said. *The nymphomaniac . . . You take that back,* he said. *Or by God, I'll beat you, twenty-one years old or not.* She took it back, poor child, but he had not finished with her. *Now consider Mac,* he said. *You're always longing to see him again. What happens when our oldest friend spends a week fishing with us? He and Grace and I sit every night in constraint while you and Piers whisper interminably twenty feet away. What about, for God's sake? . . . You're old,* she said. *You don't understand. Or you've forgotten, if you ever knew.*

Yes, he said. *Perhaps old people do forget.* He knew that his shining Sally awaited a thing that had not come, and might not come for her. He had thought often this week on the river of that exquisite pain which was love to find and love to lose.

The canoe came at full throttle, a snarling kind of music on the river. The tempo dropped as Sally crossed a bar; then the kicker ran loudly again in the middle of the river. It puttered out below the Bogan Pool. She stood to pole through the shallows this side of the salmon lie, past Roland. "Hi, Pierre," she said, and on up here, to hold the pole under her armpit against her breast, outlining her breast in the plain red shirt. The pole trembled a little in the stream. She wore a pair of man's drill pants. Her face was pensive. "Any luck?" she said.

"One grilse," he said. "There's a fish in the pool. We're resting him. You didn't bring Grace?"

"She said it was a quiet chance to pack. Tight lines, then, Daddy. I think I'll go on up to Mac." Sally thrust with the pole, and the metal tip clinked again on bottom. She could pole a light canoe as well as a man, more gracefully than a man. Above the pool she sat, turned, pulled deftly once, and the motor caught. The noise ebbed round the bend. Now evening was drawing in.

"She is like one of us in a boat," Pierre Roland said.

It was time to fish the Bogan Pool again, the last time for him in 1955. But there came a sound on the shingle bar behind, a scampering rattle, and a fawn ran past him on spindly legs, dappled small creature, quite alone. It fled close by Roland to splash in the shallows and then to swim. Small head, bell ears—the infant deer swam down the middle of the river, ran over sandpits and swam again, neither stopping nor looking around. Skafe watched it a long way, perhaps half a mile. "What happened to that one, Pierre?" he said.

"The mother was killed," said Roland, "by a bear or a bobcat, or people may be hungry too. It runs from fear."

"But in the open straight down a river? I never saw that before."

"It feels safety in the middle underneath the sky, not knowing eagles. Did you see—down the middle of the middle?"

"Yes," Skafe said. He was sorry about the defenseless infant of the wild alone. "Does it have a chance?"

"Not one chance," Roland said. "It needs mother's milk. It is not old enough to fully find its food. It will starve or it will be killed." He spoke without compassion. The fawn would die, and that was God.

Skafe changed from the Silver Grey to the Black Dose, a No. 6. One reason he liked this pool was that you could wade the top and better half. What a know-it-all he is, he thought. Men have faults, and gay Roland is a know-it-all. The fisher does this, the marten does that, the mother doe was killed—I, Roland, say it. Roland knew all about all that lived along his river, excepting only his river itself.

Skafe fished it down to the big-rock eddy, the best lie at this height of water. I shall get this fish, he thought. He was not a good fisherman at the beginning of a week, being impatient of results. But the rhythm, the habit hypnotized him into patience. This last evening—and he was glad to be nearly done with it again—he was a fisherman.

The salmon took quietly—a hesitation in the float of line, let it be —a swinging furrow in the current, let it be—a light jerk, certainly a fish, but let it be—a firm tug now to meet, to hold. The hook was set. The line hummed, taut; and still the salmon did not run. Then it ran.

The salmon climbs a river to spawn and to die one time, but the salmon fights for life downriver, through the fight and the flagging to death downriver. He took his last fish.

"Home, Pierre," he said. Home at success, the moment unfaded. He sat in the bow and dipped for some water and added whisky and drank his tot to happy endings. Then he swilled out the top of the silver flask, and handed the works over his shoulder to his guide, Pierre. "All yours," he said.

That gave Pierre some four ounces of whisky to warm his heart to float down to camp, by the wide reach where the fawn had swum, through the white water where Roland said: "Know what she done to me here one time? In the fall it was, and one of them hurricane winds from the south or them places was blowing up, or blowing downriver to meet us right here. With me and the kicker we was riding low in the stern, and the bow took a couple of bumps in them rapids, and Jeez-us, you know what she done to us, Mr. Skafe?"

"I'll buy it," he said, looking down the river. It was dusk, pink on white water, a sheen on smooth water.

"She took the twenty-one foot boat, turned it right back over the head of us in a big blow of wind, arse-and-tip, you say? Jeeze, that goddam propeller near took my neck off, and was it cold. You never know what the old bitch will do, bad as a woman."

The wind had picked up the boat or canoe and turned it end for end; but for Roland the river did that, not the wind. "Let that be a lesson to you," said Husky Skafe. "A woman can be right there on top before a fella knows it."

Roland rocked the canoe about humorist Skafe. They floated on down the quiet river, a hundred yards wide in shallow places. They touched bottom once, a nudge and a scrape. The river was low.

"There!" said Roland. The fawn lay close to them, dark against a white pebble beach on an island of the river. Roland held with his paddle. "It is too tired to fear us," he said. "Or it does not know this enemy." The fawn looked at them, then turned its delicate and lovely head to watch upriver.

"They might have been separated after all," said Simon Skafe. "Perhaps the mother will be along."

"No," Roland said. "It hopes for the mother who is dead."

Skafe did not question the pundit. "Come on, then," he said, and they floated down. Good luck, small friend, he thought to the fawn. He might hope that fate would bring the mother back. Yet he would shoot that mother if he needed meat—man, the hunting sentimentalist.

"This Mackenzie of which you have told me," Roland said. "How long you say?"

"About a thousand miles," he said, "from Great Slave Lake to the Arctic Ocean."

"How wide you say?"

"One mile, three miles, five. In one place there are rapids two miles wide. In one place it narrows to half a mile." He saw the moon-canyon of the Ramparts of the Mackenzie River.

The nighthawks were out, twisting, slipping, diving for insects in the sky. They rasped nasally in the gloaming here, as there in the North. "Jeez-us," Roland said. "Must be some river. So goddam big—couldn't seem like a river, not to me."

"It does, though, Pierre," he said. They were nearly at camp. He watched the lights, and he thought of the great cold Mackenzie River.

"Starts smaller, I guess?" Roland said.

"No," he said. "It starts full size from Great Slave Lake." He saw the green dip at the start of the river. *It's strong and beautiful,* Anna said. *The North starts here, I always think.* The river, the love, both started full grown.

Pierre beached the canoe by his own small river. "You done plenty things, Mr. Skafe," he said.

"A few," Skafe said. He went ashore.

Grace awaited him. "It's so lovely to have you well and strong again," she said, kissing him in the cabin, which was a comfortable rambling house.

"And to have you here waiting for me," he said. The other canoes came down under power. Sally brought Mac, and the guide brought Mac's two salmon. The first weighed twelve. Mac's last fish was a big one, twenty-three pounds.

"It doesn't sound too good," he said, coming back from the telephone. "This low may hang around until noon, they think."

"And Montreal?"

"Dorval is closed in," Mac said, "which rules out flying for tonight." They had one of the amphibians at an airstrip of sorts ten miles away. "Thank God," he said. "I ain't got no itchy foot to sleep in no city. Nor do I fancy night take-offs from a pisspot strip like that." He was cautious, even overcautious, Skafe sometimes thought. But Mac ran his airline Mac's own way, to which the safety record bore testimony. "I'm grounded," he said. "I may as well have a snifter."

His snifter was a bottle of beer. They went to join Sally and Grace on the screened veranda. The air was heavy with rain, but it did not rain yet. Skafe told them about the fawn, and Mac spoke of an otter he had seen. Grace was knitting a pair of socks for her husband. Her fingers fairly flew at the knitting, which kept her company on fishing trips—in camp, or out with him when the flies were not too bad. She was interested in things that people told her, but because of people, not deer and otters.

Mac rolled himself a cigarette from his pewter box. "Could you do one for me, please, Mac?"

He rolled a cigarette for Sally, who smoked by whim occasionally. "You'd better lick it, woman," he said.

"Oh, come on, Mac," she said. "I don't mind your spit." He gave her the almost perfectly even cigarette. "It's magic," she said.

"My parlor trick," he said. "Unto each man his parlor trick. Unto each woman her cigarette." Mac was droll in the mood, funnier than the things he said; and his mood was better tonight, the four of them, no strain of romance in the farther corner. "I was just thinking," he said. "If it wasn't to be a boat, I might settle for a river. Or would a river to live with get you down?"

"I wondered that myself," Skafe said. "I think it might."

"So a boat I've decided on," said MacNamara.

"How do you mean a boat?" asked Grace. It was a pleasure to watch that dark green sock grow under those nimble fingers.

"To live on when I retire," Mac said. "Which is as soon as the boss will let me go after my fiftieth birthday in October."

"You really mean it this time, Mac?" But he knew that Mac meant it this time. He could find a man to run Skafair, and run it as well as Mac for less than he paid to Mac. But Mac's worth to him was not in the competent job he did. It could not be measured with money, nor held by money, because Mac gave less of a damn about money than anyone he knew. "How about a raise?" he said perversely.

"No," Mac said. "No carrots to this donkey. And may I say," he said, "that nobody ever had a straighter-shooting more considerate hands-off old bulldozer of an employer—and I might say, pal—than me. I never thought it could work, but it did."

"Thanks to you," Skafe said. He was touched. Thanks to both of us, he thought.

"I can't think of you as nearly fifty," Sally said. "You've always been Mac to me since I was little. No age. Just Mac."

"Institutions, like old soldiers, fade away," said MacNamara. He went to the screen door and shaded his eyes to see into darkness down to the river. "Erebus tonight," he said. He turned to sit again, economical in movement. His face was more creased, the scar from his left cheekbone to his jaw less evident now among the wrinkles. The spirit had not altered; therefore Mac did not seem to change as other people changed with age.

"What kind of a boat?" Skafe said. He supposed that, through savings, bonuses, options, and some sound advice about investment, Mac might be worth a couple of hundred thousand now. He could buy himself an adequate boat and live on it for life. Every penny he has, Skafe thought, came to him through me, and now he is going to . . . "A cruiser?" he said.

"No," said Mac. "I've lived with damned noisy engines nearly thirty years—listened to them, sweated about them, depended on them. I'm through with engines. What I want is a good tight boat I can sail by myself to Trincomalee."

"I didn't know you were a sailor, Mac." Sally watched him, smiling. He was an enigma to all of them.

"I'm not, to speak of," he said. "I can learn."

"But Mac," said Grace. She drew some wool and paused in her knitting. "After being so busy and living so full a life all these years, won't you find that just sailing a boat isn't much of a challenge?"

"Not much but enough," he said. "The next place I'm sailing for—that can be my challenge. Stay a while and on again. I never was blessed . . ." Mac smiled, sardonic. "I never was blessed with a big ambition, which is why I'll rest easy in my good tight boat. As your old father used to say," he said to Skafe. "*The world's gone crazy*. Well, I guess I can still escape the worst of the craziness in my boat."

"Crazy or not," Skafe said. "I doubt if anyone can escape it." And I certainly would not want to, he thought.

"You could be right at that," said Mac. He looked at Skafe, his pale eyes pursed by wrinkles—oddly baleful, those eyes—but Mac was not baleful. And he did not escape from life. He took life as it came to him.

"Won't you be lonely, Mac, in your good tight boat?"

"You keep busy, alone," he said to Sally.

Grace now suggested bed because of an early start for everyone. She and Sally were driving back to Gallery tomorrow, nearly three hundred miles around the province. She was always rather withdrawn here at the river, away from her bright life of people. She said goodnight.

"Goodnight, dear Mac." Sally kissed him on the cheek.

"Goodnight, you Sally," he said.

The men took a flashlight out with them. They went down to the river. "Anna would have liked this place," said MacNamara.

"I know," Skafe said. "I often think of that."

Now the rain began. It pocked the river and hissed on the river; then eased to a drizzle. "I'm going to miss you, Mac," he said.

"Me too," Mac said. "But a time does come when a chap must go." He did not enlarge about why a chap must go, if there should be a reason or reasons beyond indeterminate reasons given. They turned to walk up in the warm night rain.

"This lunch tomorrow," Skafe said. "It's damned important. We're trying to persuade them to let us make an offer to the Algonquin shareholders. Buxton is wavering, but he is the kind of pettifogging procrastinator who has to be taken quickly or not at all. His toes stick in with second thoughts."

"We'll do our best to get you there," Mac said. "Next port of call on the way to the next. Do you know what I would like you to do?"

"Say on," Skafe said. He could guess.

"Get this Algonquin deal fixed up. You'll have to do that, because the ants are hotching in your pants about it. Then get the hell away for a year or two. Do anything, do nothing, but get away to have time to think. Sleeman can run things, with old Willie and Syme to check him."

"Why time to think?" Skafe said. A change was an idea that he had considered and discarded on the river.

"Because you've been too busy growing too big too fast. Just to be a bigger frog than all the other Canadian frogs might become the object. But there's more to you than that, chum."

He had had a hint of this from Mac before. He must be patient with him. Inside again, he said: "Isn't developing Canada and the North a good enough object?"

"I guess so," Mac said. "If you can see beyond to why and where."

"I think I can," he said. "Can't you?"

"What I can see," Mac said, "is not of the least importance. I am not Husky Skafe. The point is, my boy," he said, the elder by six months, "that I have hopes of you."

"Go on, Mac," he said.

"If we're going to survive against the Commies, we must be better than the Commies. It's just as simple as that. And I don't mean bigger bombs and Dewlines."

"We are better," he said. "But that doesn't make it any too simple to cope with thugs and despots."

"Very simple," Mac said. "Be better."

It was no good arguing with Mac's simple-minded idea that such things were simple. "And how do I come into it?" he said.

"Because you're a new kind of capitalist in a new kind of age when the workingman holds his share of the cards. It's not only the eye of the rich man's needle that is small these days."

"I couldn't agree with you more," Skafe said.

"But your needle needs watching too." Mac rolled himself a cigarette. "You're powerful now, Husky. The more power you get, the less you can see with other people's eyes, and the less you like being crossed. So nobody crosses you."

"Sally crossed me the other day," he said. "And how!" He had told noncommittal Mac about the John troubles.

Mac smiled. "But Sally is Sally," he said. "Just as Anna was Anna. Just as Grace is the perfect wife for you in everything but curbing you." He looked morose, after smiling.

"So you think I'm too big for my boots," Skafe said.

"All you need to do is rest your feet and contemplate your navel," MacNamara said. "Then you'll see what I mean. Well, I'm for bed. Goodnight, old friend."

"Goodnight, Mac," he said. He thought, before he went to sleep, that Mac had paid him compliments for being a considerate employer, but had not evinced the smallest regret about retiring at three months' notice after all that Skafe had done for him.

Montreal was clear in the morning, and good weather on its way east. The good weather had not reached here yet. They had three hundred and eighty miles to fly, a ten-mile headwind, a cruising speed of one-forty, half an hour's drive in from Dorval, ten minutes to change for his lunch at one with Buxton and Kindersley of Algonquin Steel. Nine-twenty, Atlantic Standard, would be the latest possible take-off time.

Grace and Sally drove them in the Buick wagon to the airstrip, which was a gravel slash through burnt-over forest, gray and dim in the mist and drizzle, a depressing place. Mac warmed the engines. Then he came over. It was nine o'clock. "It should be clear in an hour or less," he said. "I checked again."

"An hour isn't soon enough," Skafe said.

"It's in the lap," Mac said. He wore his suede jacket, green pants and khaki shirt, the dandified silk handerchief knotted at his neck, Mac unchanged, in the lap of the gods, but subject to his flying rules.

It's only local, Skafe thought. We'd be out of it in no time. First get rid of the women; then work on Mac. "Don't wait for us, Grace," he said. "We know it's going to clear, and you have eight hours driving ahead of you."

"No, dear," she said. "I wouldn't think of it. You might be stranded in this horrid place. Besides, Sally and I have forever to get back to Gallery."

Thus balked by unselfishness, or by her unfailing concern for him, he said: "Come on, Mac. Let's check on that weather again."

"I checked on it ten minutes back," Mac said. But he went with him.

"Look," Skafe said, on the way to the plane. "We can still make it if we go right now. The risk is virtually nonexistent."

"Nothing doing," Mac said equably, if curtly. "Half a mile and three hundred feet is not enough by the standards we adhere to. If we lose an engine on take-off in that soup, we've had it. In an emergency I would go. No emergency."

Skafe went aboard to get a Met from the American base a hundred miles away. *West winds, clearing, wait.* And he thought: This is the first time I ever asked Mac to lower his blasted standards. It's a tiny risk. He knows the importance. He refuses flatly. Skafe made a decision.

"Satisfied?" Mac said, outside. He himself seemed satisfied that the visibility was no better yet, the ceiling no better yet.

"I told you," Skafe said. "This meeting is vitally important."

"I know," Mac said. "But your blue-eyed boy Sleeman is there. He can cope."

"That's just the point," said Simon Skafe. "Miles, alone, hasn't got the right touch to deal with Buxton."

Mac looked along the runway, no more than a wide dirt road in the drizzle, running into mist. "I've broken the rules a hundred times in a pinch or on a rescue job, but never otherwise, as you well know. I'm not starting now. Sorry, Husky," he said. "We'll have to wait." He was not aggressively unyielding, as a weaker man might be. He was adamant.

"All right," Skafe said. "Grace and Sally are going by Fredericton. You can get a TCA flight from there. If you won't fly this thing, I'll fly it alone."

Mac moved casually to stand at the door of the plane. "Don't be a bloody fool," he said. He seemed amused.

"I mean it," Skafe said. "I employ you to run Skafair, but you are not here in that capacity. You are here as my guest. I'm not asking you to take any risks. I am telling you that I intend to fly my plane without you. Now get out of my way."

Mac glanced over at the station wagon where the women sat, unaware of this, for no dramatics were evident, a conversation piece beside a twin-engined amphibian. He looked along the runway, no improvement. He looked at Skafe, and he did not move.

"Very well," Skafe said, too angry to stop himself. "You can buy your boat with the money I paid you just as well now as in October. I shall see about severance pay when I reach Montreal."

"You can do you-know-what with your severance pay when I reach Montreal," MacNamara said. "In the meanwhile you can consider the ingratitude of the common herd who sponge upon the great. In other words, you can go and muck yourself." His yellowish eyes were murderous. He turned his back on Skafe and went into the plane.

Simon Skafe did some considering, as instructed, but his conclusions were the reverse of expectation, at least about Mac, if not about run-of-the-mill humanity. "Mac," he said in the cockpit. "I apologize."

And, being true friends, they flew as friends when the weather cleared. He missed his luncheon with Algonquin Steel.

CHAPTER FIVE

HE HAD various ways of walking to the office. Sometimes he would go along Pine Avenue on the mountainside; sometimes he would go by the splendor of Sherbrooke Street; sometimes he would go down Guy to St. Catherine's or to Dorchester before turning east. This morning he chose to meet the polyglot bustle of Canada 1955 on St. Catherine's Street. They were Slavic, Teutonic, Anglo-Saxon, French, everything Caucasian and more besides in the gateway city. They were not prepossessing.

The crowds made his walk a less restful daily dozen, but he felt the vitality of people on the move. It was a very different street from the St. Catherine's of prewar days. Also he liked pretty French office girls in summer dresses, and many of them liked him. It was nice enough to be recognized as the famous Husky Skafe, and he often was. But more agreeable that young ladies still approved of him in his linen suit, tanned handsome grizzled stranger on St. Catherine's Street. It does an old fellow good, he thought, striding with a young fellow's limber vim to work.

So on and down by Beaverhall Hill. It was a hot morning. He might have got Pickering to pick him up with the Bentley halfway to the office, but Pickering had gone to meet Grace at Windsor Station. Or he might have taken a taxi, but he did not take one, and arrived a little warm.

"Good morning, Mrs. Murton," he said in the coolness up there. "What's on?" He knew pretty well, but he liked her to feel that she was the mistress of the master's schedule: and she was.

Then he read letters, the most interesting of which was an invitation from the Financial and Industrial Association of Canada to a luncheon in his honor on his fiftieth birthday, March 5th, 1956. "I must say that's extremely nice of FIAC," he said.

"It's a great tribute, Mr. Skafe," she said. "I happen to know that they have done it only once before."

"Really?" he said. He had two things before Miles Sleeman came at ten: "I'll see Mr. Driscoll now," he said, following his custom of the unpleasant first. "Oh, and Mrs. Murton, you might take a note of the conversation, not on tape, though." He considered it dishonorable to record conversations unless both parties were aware and agreeable.

He dealt with Driscoll, suspended manager of Summit, Maritimes Division. The damned knave and idiot, it hardly seemed credible, but Driscoll had been taking bribes from sub-contractors, and there was proof. Normally, Willie Pitt would have handled such a matter of next-to-top echelon personnel; but Willie was still away on his cross-country inspection tour, due back today.

So Skafe did it himself and enjoyed the doing. He forgave or excused stupidity and human weakness every day. But he had never forgiven a breach of trust by a man in a position of trust, and he never would. He gave Driscoll his choice: either dismissal and forfeiture of all pension benefits, or criminal proceedings. The latter would have been bad publicity. The former accepted, he blasted Mr. Driscoll from the office, from Summit, and from all hope of future employment in big-league construction.

"Mrs. Murton!" he said into the microphone; then shut the thing off. She arrived, looking shaken about the rough beast she sometimes glimpsed or heard in her kindly Mr. Skafe.

He went to his window to look over the city to the harbor and the shipping. He had a thought about iron ore from Labrador, about ships and a Seaway soon to be, about the Great Lakes and steel. But, as always, it was a lesser vision, a means to his vision of the North, the empty land still waiting. He stood there, getting Driscoll out of himself. "Now for my pleasant task," he said.

Mrs. Murton took the box from the Chippendale corner cupboard which was the hiding place before bestowal. It was a fine mahogany case of flat silver from Birks. She put it on the refectory table near the window, tenderly loving a present, especially a wedding present. "Now ask Françoise to come in," he said. "But you stay too, Mrs. Murton."

"Françoise," he said to Mademoiselle Dupuy, assistant to his secretary, "I want you to accept this wedding gift as a small token of my appreciation and gratitude for all the good work you have done for Mrs. Murton and myself in these past three years. I wish health and great happiness to you and your future husband." He spoke with the avuncular formality that was right.

She was an excellent girl, no beauty, but nubile now on the verge of marriage. "Oh, Mr. Skafe," she said, "engraved with the R even too!" R for Roy being the young man's name. Françoise Dupuy was overcome, but she rallied to thank him with demure vivacity, so charmingly French.

"He works for Quebec Hydro, I think you said?"

"Yes, sir," she said; and Skafe caught Mrs. Murton's eye to remind him to drop a small word in the right large place about Jean Roy, electrical engineer.

Mrs. Murton stayed to say that she thought she had found a suitable French-Canadian successor to Françoise.

"I think we'd better stall on that one for the moment," he said. "I'm not sure yet, but Sally might be coming to help us, Mrs. Murton."

"Your Sally, Mr. Skafe?"

What other Sally? Mrs. Murton's lightning brains needed only a moment to mull that one over—a daughter in the office, the secrets of the office. "Oh, that would be lovely, Mr. Skafe," she said. "And Sally is so brilliant. I'm sure she would be the greatest help."

"It's by no means definite," he said. Nor was it, but Sally's own ideas had a way of becoming *faits accomplis*. He thought it fair to forewarn Mrs. Murton. "When is Mr. Pitt due in?" he asked.

"Ten-forty is the ETA at Dorval," she said. "He spent last night in Toronto."

"I shall hope to see him this afternoon." He wanted to hear about it all but most he wanted to hear about John. He hoped that John would get on with Peter Syme at Turtle.

"Thank you, Mrs. Murton," he said. "You and I—we watch them come and go." He said it sincerely, and it reached her faithful, jealous woman's heart. Now it was ten o'clock, time for Sleeman.

"I see Algonquin's up another point," Skafe said. It had risen five in a week. "I suppose the rumors are going the rounds."

"Yes, S.K., and fostered by them, I have no doubt." Buxton had not agreed to a generous offer to the Algonquin shareholders; and from what Sleeman had told him, Skafe did not think that his own presence at the luncheon meeting would have made any difference. Buxton's attitude— a traditional one among the old school fuddy-duddies—had been suspicious resentment, as if there was something piratical in wanting to buy a man's property from him. "If we sit quiet, S.K., that small bubble will soon burst on Mr. Buxton's head. Then we can start buying in. By the way," he said, "I hear that FIAC want to have a big affair for you on your fiftieth birthday."

"Yes," Skafe said. He was pleased about that, as any leader of industry would be. I bet Miles put them up to it, he thought.

"If we could so time our action, S.K.—and there are many imponderables to be faced—if we could so time it that we announced control of Algonquin just about the beginning of March . . ."

"Wouldn't that be a bit flamboyant?" said Simon Skafe. Big news a day or so before the luncheon—*Skafe has got Algonquin Steel*. It was another one of Sleeman's brainwaves.

"I think not, S.K.—dramatic, yes. Flamboyant, no. As I keep saying, the judicious use of public relations . . ."

"We'll see," Skafe said. The man was a genius of a kind, with imponderables, intangibles (favorite words of his). He failed only in assessing the imponderables of individual human beings, and that less often nowadays. They talked until eleven. It was one of those anomalies, breakthroughs in relationships, that he had grown much fonder of Miles since Gallery three weeks ago when he had learned for the first time, under trying circumstances, that the impeccable paragon could falter, be susceptible, drag his wife off to swim by moonlight in the buff, have a corking row and make it up. All overheard *in extremis* through the cold-air register.

"I'm going out now," he told Mrs. Murton when Sleeman had left. "First to the Hide-Out to think a bit, and then to the Ritz to have lunch with Mrs. Skafe. The train must be late, or she would have called, so perhaps you would remind her, a quarter to one. I shall be back at two-thirty."

Mrs. Murton would make a point of reminding Mrs. Skafe. It had long been clear that she preferred the second to the first Mrs. Skafe, not that Mrs. Murton had ever dropped a verbal hint of that to him.

He took a taxi to the Hide-Out, the penthouse apartment that he used sometimes, particularly in summer if the family were down at Gallery. He had first taken it at the time of the divorce when he could not endure the old Arbour Avenue house. The Hide-Out had started as a place of retirement in time of trouble, and had remained or become a secret, known to Mrs. Murton, to Grace, and to a few other people. His name was not on the card downstairs. The telephone number was not listed. *I have to have some pied-à-terre*, he had told Grace early on, *where I can do business in absolute privacy. There are times when the office, a club, or even the house . . . Yes, of course, dear,* she said. *I quite see that.* She never spoke about it, nor had she been there.

He pressed number fifteen button. The elevator was no express. Then he let himself in. They kept it ready for him always—asters in a shallow bowl, the air-conditioner running this morning. You get what you pay for, he thought. He paid plenty for the service he got, here in his Hide-Out and everywhere. Skafe was no penny-pincher, nor did he throw it vulgarly around.

He sat in the big armchair below the paneled wall opposite the window. He had had that paneling put in and waxed—old weathered red-pine boards from the barn at Gallery. He sat with his eyes closed and his fingers linked, and he thought from eleven-ten until eleven-fifty without movement and without interruption.

Here and alone in his penthouse hide-out—there was an inaccurate sort of parallel between him high up here and him at the head of Summit Enterprises, the holding company—he traced the web of control—Summit and Staniland, construction companies east and west—Turtle Mountain Uranium—Precambrian Pulp and Paper—Lindores Cement—Skafair—Skafe Exploration. Only the last of these did he personally own outright. The rest, total assets some fifty-five million, he controlled by personal holdings of just under eighteen million.

People found it incomprehensible, or witchcraft, but the intricate weave and weft was clear to him. Add to these eighteen million the proceeds of his sales of stock to the public at various times since 1948, and you had a man with a fortune—the larger part of it liquid—that had grown on a rising market to some fifty million dollars. He had reason for satisfaction, but not self-satisfaction. To be self-satisfied was, inevitably, to be static. Now for Algonquin. . . .

He was big, and he had the cars, the planes, the superlatively dressed and jeweled wife, the houses and the rest—the appurtenances of bigness. But he did not affect the airs of bigness. He had not changed, whatever might be thought, and he did not much care what people thought.

He left the flat at twelve for the Ritz to have a haircut, a dry shampoo, a shoeshine, but not a manicure. Husky Skafe had never had a manicure in his life.

He tipped the shoeshine man, and was thinking of a drink with Grace now at a quarter to one, and was paying the barber's bill at the counter near the door when the telephone rang. "Mr. Skafe?" said his barber. "He's right here."

"Yes?" he said. He did not much like being traced to barbershops.

It was Mrs. Murton, speaking a little more slowly than her wont, a sure portent of trouble. She did not apologize for disturbing him. She said that Mac was overdue on a flight from Turtle Mountain to Edmonton. He had radioed Yellowknife that he had lost one engine, and had excessive cylinder head temperature with the other. After that, no word.

"Where?"

"A hundred and thirty miles west of Yellowknife," she said.

That's somewhere near the Horn Mountain country, he thought. "When?"

"Three hours ago, Mr. Skafe. The last message was sent at nine thirty-seven by our time, Eastern Daylight."

On one engine he would make for Simpson or Providence, eighty, a hundred miles. "And no more word, you say?"

"No, Mr. Skafe. They say he must have . . . must have been forced down somewhere in the wild."

In the wild. "Has the Crusader arrived with Mr. Pitt?"

"Yes, Mr. Skafe. They're refueling now. Françoise has Captain Thompson waiting on the line."

"Tell him I'll be right out. And tell the house I'll pick up my bush clothes."

"We called them, Mr. Skafe. Your things are ready. I had some trouble finding you, and then I just thought about it being time for your hair again."

"Well done, Mrs. Murton," he said.

"I do hope . . ." she was saying as he hung up.

He could not see Grace at first in the lofty room that paid dim flattery to raddled faces. But then she waved from the far left corner where she sat with two other women, and she came to meet him, a dash of a hat and a summer dress, blond wife.

"Mac is three hours overdue on a flight in the North," he said, "which means a forced landing somewhere in the bush. He probably is quite all right, but I'm going to start west immediately." And why had Mrs. Murton been so sure that he would start west immediately? They must have said to her what he himself had thought: The loss of one engine, the other overheated, then silence from the wilderness—not very good. But Mac could belly-land a C-47 in a football field, provided he had power to reach that field.

"I'll come to the airport, dear," she said in the foyer, people passing, people smiling.

"No, Grace," he said. They went through the glass doors to the heat, ninety-five and humid. He sent the doorman for Pickering. "Oh, and about the dinner, please make my apologies." Lord and Lady Haydon on the eve of sailing back to England—Piers Whitfield's parents, you never knew—and eight interesting people to meet them at dinner tonight. That was why Grace had come up to town.

"Should I cancel it, Husky?"

"No, no," he said. "The best hostess in Montreal cancel a dinner party just because her husband isn't there? Besides, it may be a false alarm, and I'll be back." But he was in a hurry, a rampaging hurry for once in a way. "Dear Grace," he said, embracing her in public on the street. All the men looked at her on the street.

"Do please be careful," she said. "Please take care of yourself, Simon darling."

"I will," he said. "I'll drive," he said to Pickering. He was *Husky* to her, *Simon* in crisis, in intimacy; another reversal from Anna. He drove by the house, and on to Dorval.

Three hours out of Montreal, no word. He watched the forest and the lakes, smoke to the north. It was a striped pattern of land and water from twenty thousand feet. Mac did not do so much flying nowadays. He ran his airline. But he had taken in a Dewline load in the Eastern Arctic two days ago, and then had worked west along the embryo line to see his pilots fly in, to hear their gripes and troubles about half-built strips, and waste of time unloading, and water in the gas. The Dewline race was on. He had come south to Turtle to spend last night, and to make for Edmonton early this morning. Young Dicky Farmer was his co-pilot in the C-47, Able Nan Fox, one of the original Turtle Mountain planes.

Four hours out of Montreal, the forest and the lakes, the smoke, no word.

Five hours out of Montreal, he was looking at *Fortune* magazine, going through it backwards, but he put it down and watched the hazy land and lakes, the ribs of the Laurentian Shield. It couldn't possibly have been water in the gas, he thought, not out of Turtle, impossible. "Yes, Roy?" he said.

"Our own people spotted it," Thompson said. He was a deliberate individual, bulking over Skafe in the maroon and silver overplush cabin of the Crusader, flying at about three hundred miles an hour on automatic pilot to Fort Smith on the sixtieth parallel of latitude. "One of the Tamerlaines—Gilchrist—southbound. Here, sir!" A pencil-circled blue point on the map. For Christ's sake get on with it, Skafe thought, but he said again: "Yes, Roy?" The Tamerlaines were the new Turtle Mountain freight planes, four-engined turbo-props. "Crash-landed on a strip of beach at the edge of a lake, one wing smashed up, one chap sitting, no sign of fire."

"What chap sitting?" he said.

"Don't know, sir," Thompson said. "Gilchrist came low, but he says there was a lot of smoke around, made it hard to see, and you know how they chew up fuel at low altitude, but he says that lake is small and shallow and full of rocks. He thinks it's even money about a floatplane getting in at all, let alone out."

"Helicopter?"

Thompson shook his head. "Not a one," he said.

"Are our Minks anywhere available?"

"They're both far north with Exploration."

"What about Yellowknife or Smith? Who's the best man with a Mink? Where is he?"

"The best man would be Brian Fiske," said Thompson. "He runs a small outfit called Aurora Air out of Yellowknife. He's quite a guy, is Fiske."

"See if you can find him," said Simon Skafe. "If he's near enough, offer him double-charter, anything he wants, to meet us at Providence."

"Right, sir," Thompson said.

Skafe was alone again to wonder why—why one engine out, then nothing more reported? But Thompson had put him straight on that. *It's what*, he said in his slow gentle way, *not why that matters.*

He came aft soon again. "We located Fiske," he said. "He's shuttling firefighting parties, but he will meet us at Providence."

"Good, Roy," he said. He dozed through the sixth hour and part of the seventh until the Crusader began to drop off height. They flew over Athabaska, the first great lake on the northern way. And then, far to the west, he thought he could see the Peace River's confluence with the Rochers to make the Slave. He had some good timber rights along the lower Peace. He saw smoldering fires, and the flaming slash of fire on the rampage.

They dropped to the silt lands at Fort Smith, where the Northwest Territories begin. He looked at the rapids of the Slave. Once he had persuaded a bush pilot to fly him down those rapids, ten feet above the mad brown welter, a quarter of a million horsepower there to be tamed someday. They had flown too close to the ferocity of Pelican Rapids, aptly named, for a grotesque white pelican had risen, startled, from a rock. The pilot hauled back on everything. They missed the pelican and dropped a wing and just got it back. The pilot was somewhat shaken. Flying was his business, and you must keep alive to stay in business. God, the stupid risks I've taken, Simon thought. He took risks too readily and lightly. He had tried to persuade Mac to take a trifling risk the other day; and then, balked, had lost his temper. What a son of a bitch I can be, he thought. He never used to lose his temper.

They took on fuel at Fort Smith and flew again. He saw buffalo herds in Wood Buffalo Park, fore-burdened creatures of a fresco in a caveman's cave. As he grew older, he came more to deplore the white man's slaughter of this continent, the forests and the fauna, a spree of destruction spilling west. He disliked profligate waste. He liked sound harvesting of trees and buffaloes, but some buffalo were coming back.

They flew by the flatlands south of Great Slave Lake. Base metals here, but base metals did not ring a bell for him. "Roy," he said to the telephone by his chair, "I would like to have a look at the start of the river on our way into Providence. You might swing along south of Big Island at a thousand feet."

"Roger," Thompson said.

He had seen the head of the river often enough from a height and a distance to the east, but it happened that the last time he had been close to the dip of the river from the lake was in the month of June, 1932. He looked now at the many small islands and the one big island. "There it is," he said aloud by himself in the cabin. And there it was, the island with the shingle beach where he had slept, and when he woke, she said: *My child* to him, and kissed him on both cheeks; but seeing her and waking to desire her, he had snatched her child away.

The wind was strong. Here on this island, birds were nesting, a pair of myrtle warblers in the spruce above them, a fever and a flutter. Black and gold drooped wings about the brown and gold. How exquisite, how hot, how brief the mating of the myrtle warblers by the great cold river.

And the next morning, looking back from his boat, the *Mabel K.*, as they set across the lake, she had said: *Goodbye. I hope I never see you again,* to the green islands at the dip of the Mackenzie River. She had called the place strong and beautiful, and hoped not to see it again.

He looked for Jim's cabin. But that had been swallowed long ago. "I wonder what became of Jim Willis," he said aloud. Died of drink on a jag in Edmonton more than likely. But if Jim was alive, he ought to do something for him. But he would not find out to have to do. "O.K., Roy," he said. "Let's go on in." He looked at a river boat with its squat family of barges, strapped two and two ahead and one on each beam, starting down the river.

Some people awaited him at the Providence strip, the Hudson's Bay manager, a sergeant of the RCMP, and others.

"The managing director radioed from Winnipeg," said the company man. "Everything we have is at your disposal, Mr. Skafe."

"How very kind," he said. "Has that pilot with the Mink arrived? What's his name, Roy?"

"Brian Fiske," said Thompson.

Fiske had not arrived, and Skafe sat in somebody's pickup truck to bump into Providence. They talked about Mac, and they were sure that he would be all right. Mac MacNamara was a flying legend in the North where Husky Skafe was only a tycoon legend, more or less. Husky Skafe had nothing to say to the friendly people.

He stood on the top of the steep bank above a float, waiting for this Fiske to come; and he watched some ducks fly along the river, which was a mile wide upstream, three or four miles wide below. The black plane with golden-yellow wings came in without warning or circuits to land downriver and taxi to the float, where Skafe now held a wing tip while the pilot moored one pontoon fore and aft to the float, two half-hitches, one-two, one-two, and it was done.

"My name is Skafe," he said.

"Brian Fiske, sir." He was a man of Skafe's own height or a little taller, the middle-weight boxer's build, five foot eleven, a hundred and sixty pounds. Fiske's hair was black, and his eyes were bloodshot. Skafe caught a whiff or a tang of smoke from him as they shook hands. Then he stood, hands on hips, and said: "I'm sorry to hear old Mac has had trouble."

"Yes," Skafe said. "Do you know that lake?"

"I'm not sure," said Brian Fiske. "If it's shaped something like an L, then I think I do; and if that is the one—which sounds likely from what your pilot said—it's a bad proposition, a few feet deep and loaded with rocks. But the only thing is to go and see. This might have to be a helicopter job. No choppers around, though."

"Do you need gas before we start?"

"Yes," Fiske said. His feet planted wide, he swayed a little from one to the other. He held his right forefinger out and brought it to his nose to squint at it, and away again. "I must sleep first," he said. "I've been flying forever, and that darned smoke. My vision is all to hell. Two hours will do me." He yawned. Skafe could see the swim of fatigue in him.

"But we must . . ." Skafe began to say.

Fiske cut him off. "I know, sir," he said, "and I must see straight. We'll start at nine, Mountain Standard, if that suits you." He was not so much cocky as imperviously self-assured. He turned now and climbed the dusty bank. "Hullo, Father," he said. "Can you give me a Catholic bed for a couple of hours?"

"Come, Brian," said the oblate priest.

"We can gas her up for you, Brian," Roy Thompson said. "That would save time."

"Thanks, Roy. One drum is all I want, eighty-seven octane." Fiske and the priest, the khaki and the black, walked away together.

The Hudson's Bay trader asked Skafe in for a bite of supper, but he had eaten on the plane. Or coffee? Or a small snifter, perhaps? "Thank you very much," he said politely, "but I think I'll just hang around."

He hung around to help Roy Thompson and the Crusader co-pilot refuel the floatplane, a slow meticulous business, filtering every last drop of the drum of aviation fuel from the Wells. Skafe did his spell at the pump. "This Brian Fiske," he said to Thompson. "What's his history?"

"He flew Saber Jets with the Americans in Korea, sir; but he's a Canadian. Then he came out of the service, and bought a Mink. Since then he's grown to Aurora Air—two Lynxes, a Beaver, an old Anson—three of those on the Dewline—and now I believe he's dickering for a Venture."

"There have been a lot of those shoestring outfits," Skafe said. They always fold, he thought.

"Brian is something different," said Roy Thompson, "or that's what the boys are saying. They swear by him, and not just as a crackerjack pilot."

It was high praise from Thompson, who was not a bush flyer primarily but a methodical airline type, with many thousand hours. "That's it," he said, the fueling done, the time nearly eight P.M. by Mountain Standard, the silent audience on the bank, the silent river flowing. He looked at Skafe. "Want a walk, sir?" he said.

"Yes, come on," Skafe said.

"You'd better watch this thing, Les." They left the co-pilot and climbed past the Indians and the breeds, inanimate adults and solemn children, no time in their watching and their waiting.

"I guess there's almost no pure Indian blood left," Thompson said, walking upriver. "Is that right, sir?"

"Probably," he said. "Even a dash of negroid now, from the workers on the Canol Project in the war." He saw the shiftless people, and beyond them, as it were, to a writhe of miscegenation, and back to captive wards of well-intentioned government, victims of the fur market whim, helpless, vitiated muddle.

"You lived in the North once, didn't you, sir?"

"I came in twenty-five years ago," he said. "Stayed two years, and then I went out by boat past here. I haven't been on the River since then."

"It must have changed a lot, sir, I guess."

"Still the same river," he said. "Are there fires in that country, do you know?"

"Further west, sir, I think," Thompson said.

I wish he'd stop calling me Sir, thought Simon Skafe. They walked out past the Catholic mission where the crackerjack pilot was having a sleep, and past snarling scrofulous skeletons of dogs, tied according to law by their Indian owners to starve the summer through. "It's a hell of a country," Roy Thompson said, as others had said before him.

Skafe picked a pallid wild rose and put it in a buttonhole of his shirt, and thought better of that arctic rose, and threw it away. They walked back past the Catholic mission, handsome school and so on, and they met a priest, Father Legrain, or it sounded like that. "My name is Skafe, and this is Roy Thompson."

"Hi, Roy," said the priest. "What's your first name?" he said to Skafe, but Simon Skafe did not give. It was a plunge twenty-five years back to the hearty brassy boys-together approach of some of them. He liked it no better now. He thought of saintly Father Robin at Good Hope. They talked with this priest a while. He was quite a nice arrogant chap, and, provoked by Skafe, he soon made urbane remarks about the Protestant missions along the river who acquired converts by tobacco, bags of flour, or similar appeals to cupboard love.

It was twenty to nine, but no Fiske yet. They said goodbye to that priest and walked downriver in the smoky air. "The Anglicans are just as bad or worse," Roy Thompson said. "I run into them at Smith and Yellowknife. You might think the other outfit represented Satan. I'd like to knock all their goddam stupid Christian heads together, wouldn't you, sir?"

Skafe laughed. "Yes," he said. "I would. What Church are you, Roy, if any?"

"I'm a Unitarian, sir," Roy Thompson said, and he gave a short enthusiastic talk about Unitarianism, toward which Skafe thought he might have leanings, never having been able or possibly willing to understand that Trinity business. But his mind wandered, coming to the float, the black plane with the golden wings. "What are you, sir?" asked Roy Thompson, a decent Unitarian fellow and a clumsy help in trouble.

"I'm supposed to be a Presbyterian," said Skafe. "And I wish to Christ you'd stop calling me Sir." Then he was like a small boy, sorry about that blasphemy in time of trouble, not very sorry. Who was he to be Sir to this limited honorable master of his trade, Mac's senior pilot in Skafair, and a friend of Mac's?

Now Brian Fiske arrived at ten to nine with his priest, who was a flying priest, they said. Sky pilot, thought Skafe. What inanity will I come up with next? Fiske's eyes were clear again after two hours' sleep and perhaps some soothing lotion. He would be twenty-eight or thirty, Skafe supposed. People moved aside for him. There was a certainty about him, a gravity until he smiled at Skafe. "Let's go, sir," he said.

They taxied upriver. Some ducks were flying low along the river, and that river boat was coming down with three barges, the others left above Providence Rapids to be relayed later. The name of the Northern Transportation boat was *Radium Yellowknife*. There was some waving, as always on the Mackenzie River. "Do you know Stony Thorsteinsen?" asked Fiske.

"No, I don't," Skafe said.

"Good fellow," said Fiske, and said no more.

Fiske ran the engine up, and tested magnetoes, curving about the Mackenzie River, and was satisfied. "All set?" he said, with that brief and vital smile. They took off northwest into sun and breeze, a wallowing, a lightening, a rough pump of stick and onto the step, smack, spank, and they were flying. The Mink was the plane for the job, if the job could be done.

CHAPTER SIX

TWELVE MINUTES out, and at three thousand to clear the hills, Fiske said: "You still fly, don't you?"

Skafe acknowledged that he still flew, and the wheel was swung over to him to do the driving while young Fiske's finger edged up the map on his knee. I was flying when you were in Grade Five, Skafe estimated, but it was pleasing that this fellow knew he flew, old Skafe still flew, not very tactful. He set his mind to flying a noisy utilitarian Mink again. The smoke was not too bad, but thick enough to haze such individuality of landscape as there was below—spruce, muskeg, water, rock—drab, godforsaken. Fiske looked out of his window and on ahead and at his map and out again. He gave one or two small changes of course, and otherwise said nothing until he said: "You can come down to two thousand now." Skafe supposed that he had been asked to fly the Mink to give him something to do, not because the ex-Saber Jet pilot needed to be free to map-read. It was bumpy.

"Thanks," Fiske said at forty-seven minutes out. "I'll take her."

He turned steeply, so that the port wing cut far below the horizon, curved across the indeterminate land. Skafe saw the gradual escarpment to the west above them, the drop to marshlands a long way east, but no lake—no trees below and no water, nothing but scrub and rock.

Then it swung into view beyond the wing, a wide-angled L of gray water wrapping round the hill. "A million lakes all over the map," shouted Brian Fiske, "and old Mac had to hit this puddle in a rockpile for a deadstick landing from four thousand. Is your belt done up tight? I'm going to throw her around."

Skafe tightened his belt. Now Fiske threw the Mink around in narrow eccentric above the lake, the one arm and the other, not an L so much as a boomerang set in against the hill, one arm pointing north, the other southwest. On the southwest arm on the upper shore was Able Nan Fox on its belly, the port wing torn almost off against a rock, the nose slewed into undergrowth at the end of that small strip of beach. Skafe glimpsed it once, and a second time. Gilchrist, the Tamberlaine pilot, had seen one man sitting. How long ago? Four hours, perhaps. Now a man still sat, his back to the rock that had taken the wing. There was life in the man, but he did not look up. Mac's pilots dressed for the bush in much the same raffish way as Mac. They tended to ape him, you might say. The views were too brief, and the light was too bad to identify the man.

It went on and on. He flew the one arm, a vertical turn, and crabwise back. The lake was dotted with surface rocks, with the paleness of rocks just submerged. Now the other arm. "Crosswind either way, too, dam-mit," said Fiske. And now he did it all again at slow speed, still lower. And now, at last, he was coming in to land, a narrow rock-free channel, Skafe could see it. He nearly touched; then gunned the engine. It was interminable.

You can get in, Skafe thought. To hell with getting out again. Get in. What's your plane worth? Twenty-five thousand? I'll pay you fifty. But he stopped himself. He did not say it.

"Here goes," said Brian Fiske. He sideslipped steeply, almost vertically, whistling soughing complaint of wind, down to square at the ultimate to smack heavily, and they were in on the southwest arm. It was a fabulous job, no other word. It was so fabulous that Skafe did not quite have a word to say as they puttered gingerly to ground in shallows. "That's the nearest we can do," Fiske said. The propeller milled to a stop.

Skafe got out to wade with a mooring line ashore. The water was cold, not too bad, colder than his heated, filtered swimming pool at Gallery, New Brunswick.

The man who sat was Dicky Farmer. He had a compound fracture of his left forearm. It was a bloody mess. With his right hand he was arranging pebbles neatly to make the letters R.E.F., probably his initials. Then he mucked that pattern up, and began again to make the letters from the pebbles on the sand.

Skafe went on into the willowbrush, a thick high tangle of it, where he found that the nose of Able Nan Fox was blunted into rock. He looked through the pilot's window to see Mac strapped in his seat and Mac's head tilted sharply forward to the wheel of the control column, which Mac still held.

Now Fiske was beside him, and wind stirred the light-leaved willows, and mosquitoes came. Then, without speaking, they went down the silvery side of Able Nan Fox and through the door and up past the drums, the ubiquitous steels of the North which in this case held uranium, the concentrate, and some of that yellowish precious stuff was spilled about the place for the same whiplash reason but with a less neat result than the whiplash that had broken MacNamara's neck.

They undid Mac's belt and got him out. The stains on his suede jacket were from Dicky Farmer's blood. They laid him on the beach and covered him.

Fiske unslung a small satchel from which he took and assembled a hypodermic syringe. Then he dissolved a morphine pill in distilled water in a test tube. Then he charged the syringe, held it up to get rid of air, wiped the needle with rubbing alcohol on a bit of absorbent cotton, and he said: "Look at that!" He meant the scour marks of Able Nan Fox's belly from the far end of the beach along to here. "It was fabulous to get in at all," he said. "If there had been no rock hidden in those willows, Mac would have had it made. But old Mac didn't make it this time. Come on," he said. "Let's deal with that poor chap. What's his name?"

"Farmer," Skafe said. "Dicky Farmer. Dicky," he said, "leave those pebbles for now. We want your good arm to give you a shot."

Farmer surrendered the arm, but he did not look up. "Lost everything," he said. "Lost Katie, shirt, everything—oh, Jesus!"

Fiske gave him the injection, quite professionally. "We need something for a sling," he said to Skafe, who found a towel in an overnight bag in Able Nan Fox. They had lost one plane before this, but never a fatal accident in ten years. "Do you think a tourniquet?" asked Fiske. Now he asked for advice.

"Not unless it bleeds again," Skafe said. "We could fix one that you could tighten if need be."

"Right," said Fiske. "The light is none too good and getting worse, so I don't think I'd better wait for that morphine to work, do you?"

"No," Skafe said. "Go now! Dicky," he said. "We're going to take you to the plane. If we hurt you, shout your head off."

They carried him and they hurt him, and Farmer screamed. It was difficult, but they got him in and fixed his belt and arranged Skafe's knotted handkerchief and a screwdriver as a loose tourniquet to be tightened if need be. The morphine was working on Dicky Farmer.

"Can you get out of this place all right?"

"With one passenger nip and tuck round the corner, I guess so," said Fiske. "There's rain over there." He pointed northwest to cloud beyond the hills. "It may help the smoke, in which case I shall be back in a couple of hours. If not, I'll have to wait for light. Or if the weather gets bad . . ." He shrugged. "Will you be okay?"

"Of course I'll be okay," Skafe said. "What do you take me for?" He was petulant about it.

"I take you for a stout sort of chap," said Brian Fiske. "Now turn me round and give me a push."

Skafe did that. He pushed the Mink until he was thigh-deep in water. Then it taxied away, and he turned his back to the blasting chill, and he waded ashore to watch and wait. There was nothing much to taking off round corners. Bush pilots often did it when they lacked for space. There was more to it in this particular boomerang lake, a crosswind tonight on either arm, the elbow of the boomerang a narrow channel leading from one narrow channel to another. I wouldn't try it, he thought. I wouldn't be good enough to try it. Mac could have done it, but Mac was fabulous, as Brian Fiske said.

They are the fabled ones, he thought. They are the men of this new North. They bring us in, and they take us out. They have it made until one time they don't make it.

Skafe waited. He was not a hunch-ridden man, but he was the son of an Irish mother. He waited with foreboding that Mac would have company at a nameless lake. He heard the guttural roar, the Mink's distinctive voice, and he watched the corner which the Mink would turn. It slithered round fast, at sixty or so; then it straightened to run its narrow course past him, a pretty aurora borealis emblem on the nose, took off with some to spare, sagged left from the hill, and flew away south. He had been wrong about that foreboding.

He sat on there a while. He heard thunder behind him beyond the hills. The wind was fitful. Sometimes it chased the mosquitoes from him, sometimes not; but they were less fiendish at this season. The sky and the rocks and the water of the lake were gray. The reeds and the willows were wishywashy.

He felt small in the wilderness with Mac, and he went over to Mac and took off the cover—it was a canvas cloth or a light tarpaulin from Able Nan Fox, the kind with metal eyelets—and he looked at Mac. He went down to the shore. It was not full daylight, but by no means dusk. It was like a city, say London in November smog, not exactly cheerful, but the people go on bustling with good cheer. But there was no bustle here. There was a squelch of his boots as he went up again to look at his peaceful friend again.

He went through Mac's jacket pockets, a wallet and a pen, a pewter box with the makin's, and some small oddments like a rubber eraser, wooden toothpicks and a thirty-thirty shell. He rolled himself a clumsy cigarette, returned the box, covered Mac up, and took the wallet to do what somebody has to do.

He smoked while he went through Mac's papers—his pilot's license; his driving license; two old receipts for registered letters; twenty-three dollars in two tens, a two and a one; some telephone numbers from Vancouver to Quebec to New York City, a pilot's ports of call across a continent, not that the cities were named, but Glad Pl 4212 could mean Gladys at Plateau 4212 in Montreal. There was one item which Skafe smiled about and buried in the sand. There were these verses, typed on a faded sheet:

> Be Thou my vision, oh Lord of my heart,
> Nought be all else to me, save that Thou art,
> Thou my best thought, by day or by night
> Waking or sleeping, Thy presence my light.
>
> Riches I heed not, nor man's empty praise
> Thou mine inheritance, now and always
> Thou and Thou only, first in my heart
> High King of Heaven, my Treasure Thou art.

"It sounds like a hymn," Skafe said, but he did not know it. Nor had he known that Mac would value such a thing. But who could tell that Mac had valued it?

Lastly, there was a newspaper photograph of King George the Sixth pinning a D.S.O. on Squadron Leader MacNamara D.F.C., October 1940, just out of hospital.

It was the miscellany of a good mortal sinner.

There remained now only the back compartment of the wallet, from which Skafe took three things. The first was a small snapshot of Sally Skafe beside a plane. He remembered that occasion well. It was Labor Day morning, 1946, when David Dorrien finished a portrait, and Sally took Brownie pictures of her pash her crush her lately drunken super-duper pilot hero, Mac; and he took one of her, and this would be it, sent on to him. MacNamara declined to own cameras, for reasons known to himself.

The second snapshot was of Sally too. It had been taken last month on a New Brunswick river. The child of twelve and the girl of twenty-one— it could not be said that the one was more beautiful than the other.

"I don't know," Skafe said aloud, alone. He was *dear Mac* to her, a man apart. But Sally to him? Was she his old friend's child? Or a dis-embodiment? Or was she what a middle-aged bachelor must sail away from in a good tight boat? "I don't know," he said again by Mac-Namara's lake, and the reeds chafed in the wind, and no birds sang. He put the pictures of his Sally in his pocket.

Now he unfolded the final item from Mac's pocket book or wallet. Properly enough, it was Mac's will, written in Mac's decisive hand:

This is my last will and testament.

1. I leave all my money, investments etc. to the Pilots' Provident Fund of Skafair.
2. I leave all other goods and personal possessions to my friend Husky Skafe and his family, Sally to have my pig.
3. If I buy it in the bush, I want to be disposed of there.

It was signed, dated June of 1955, witnessed by Roy Thompson and K. C. Wilbraham.

A lesser man than Roy Thompson might have spoken of that will as they walked beside the Mackenzie River. He might have wondered about presentiments of death, and have spoken of them to a beneficiary. Even Mac had his good-luck charm, a small brass pig that he kept on his key ring, which might be in Mac's trouser pockets. But Roy had said nothing. Roy was a solid sterling chap, but not the right man to succeed Mac in Skafair.

The wind blew strongly, clean of smoke. The thunder grew from rumbles to a rip or two above the hills, but rain did not come. The storm fell back, and the wind died altogether at nearly midnight. Skafe was wet and cold. He wished that Fiske would come. The light was bad, so he hoped that Fiske would not take undue risks in coming.

A muskrat swam along. Its nose cut a V in unruffled water, lowly muskrat, decks awash. Once he had shot a hundred and sixty-seven in one night from a bobbing canoe in the Mackenzie delta. The price was less than a dollar a skin in those days, 1931. Oh, them were the days. In them old days a white man could come In to trap and hunt. But that was all stopped to preserve the game for Indians and Eskimos, and rightly so. But that had made the white man a commuter or a stranger to his North.

Now he came In to do a job—prospecting for the likes of Husky Skafe, or mining, or building a Dewline, or to be a DOT radio operator, be a real Northern man for six months or a year. Many of them spent all spare hours going to seed in bunks in comfortable huts. Few ventured beyond camp until they were flown Out with beards to the TV set. I wonder, Skafe thought. I wonder if there might be a way . . . He had the germ of a bright idea.

But the flies were intolerable, even for a real Northern man, so he found a piece of cotton waste in Able Nan Fox and soaked it with oil from the smashed-up engine, and retired to a safe distance from gasoline fumes to make himself a smudge at the shore of the lonely lake. The smoke kept the flies away a bit, but it did not keep loneliness away from him with his old friend lost to him. Now who do I have? he thought. *No bullshit*, as Mac would say: I have no friend now to love me straitly.

But I have a son, he thought. And, being lonely now, and sorry for himself, and sad also for his valiant friend, he wished that John might be with him here. He did not know John (who had called him a crummy bastard, most unlike John), but he knew that John would understand this here.

A breeze came again, and it was cold. When he was young, when strait was the gate and narrow was the way to keep alive, in days when he did find life, he had learned to live with cold, to force it down, still and strong, go down, you cold! Now he tried it again, and he was still that man, and he dozed with strength for company until he heard a mutter of a plane at two o'clock, the sun somewhere east of north.

It was the same northwest breeze again. The Mink flew over once, and then Fiske landed. Once seen, and known—that young man's self-confidence was prodigious. He ran it aground and brought the line ashore. "Sorry, I've been so long," he said. "It rained like hell at Providence." He wore his waterproof or windbreaking jacket with the Aurora badge, an impressionist fan of green northern lights from a frozen North, quite artistic.

"How is Farmer?" Skafe asked.

"They were giving him plasma before they set his arm. In shock still, but he'll be all right."

"He didn't say anything about the crash?"

Fiske shook his head, and looked at Able Nan Fox on its belly. "*Lost everything* sums it up, I guess," he said. "They'll send in some wizard to find out what. But a chopper can bring him, not me."

"You'd better read this," Skafe said.

Fiske read Mac's will through twice. "Authentic Mac," he said smiling. "Who's Sally?"

"My daughter," Skafe said. And if she saw you, he thought, she would add you to the string of scalps. But if she added Mac, he thought, she never knew it, and she never will. She will get Mac's porker from Mac, her pal. Skafe had it in for Sally, knowing that he was unfair to her. "Mac wanting to be disposed of here," he said. "Is it legal? I don't know."

"If Mac wanted it, that's good enough," Fiske said, "and I see his point and so would I."

"In the lake, then," Skafe said. It would require dynamite to dig a hole here for Mac, even if sufficient soil existed. "Is there a deep place, did you notice?"

"Up that end," said Fiske, and he nodded to the one small cliff below the hill. They considered the matter. "I'll rustle up some rope," Skafe said. "You might empty all his pockets."

He found just the thing—a length of the nylon cord that had been employed to lash Able Nan Fox's freight. Fiske had extracted Mac's key ring with brass pig attached, some change and the pewter box, in which Skafe stored the other small things, and he pocketed the box.

"Do we put the rocks inside or out?"

"One each end, outside, don't you think? We don't want to put too much strain on that cloth."

They rolled Mac in his light tarpaulin, and, threading the eyelets, they trussed him safely. Then, to each spare end of cord they tied a narrow-waisted rock. They thought two of twenty pounds should be enough to sink Mac's hundred and forty.

Skafe took his end, ninety pounds or so, but the rock made it a damned awkward load, and near the water's edge he stumbled, clumsy idiot, and they both fell down with Mac. They laughed. It was mighty funny. Skafe could hear Mac chuckle.

Then they waded out and put Mac along a pontoon where Simon also perched precariously, one hand holding Mac and one a strut.

"I shall have to keep moving," said Fiske. "Just roll him off as I swing by that cliff."

"Okay," Simon said.

Fiske coiled up his mooring line, pushed the Mink and climbed aboard. They taxied slowly up the lake and round by the cliff where Simon, who was numbed by the propeller wind, let Mac and his ballast roll plop into black water. Nobody knew how bottomless the deep end of this shallow lake was, and probably nobody ever would.

He thought of "ashes to ashes and dust to dust," but he remembered some more appropriate words from a burial prayer at sea—they buried some that time in the war—and he said: "'It hath pleased Almighty God of His great mercy to take unto Himself the soul of our dear brother here departed. We therefore commit his body to the deep.'"

He felt some unease with himself, not being sure in faith, but he said the good words with good will, which God might consider to be what mattered, he thought, looking back to see bubbles break. He climbed in beside Fiske.

They went fast down that arm, and then down the other until Fiske, who was fussy, seemed satisfied. He turned. "All set?" he said with that smile.

Skafe nodded. He feared great heights, and he feared black depths; not much else in life except the dim expunction of life by sickness, as he had recently discovered. Now he feared this take-off. The corner raced up, and he closed his eyes and held himself in a pit of fear. But they were around. The floats scamped more lightly. He opened his eyes before Fiske could catch him being a coward. They were off, swinging left from the lake where he had seen one muskrat while he waited, mosquitoes and one muskrat, not another sign of life.

"Thank God for that," said Brian Fiske.

"Thank you," Skafe said. He did not mean thank Fiske rather than thank the Almighty. He meant humble thanks to all concerned.

"I hear Mac was set to retire in October," Fiske said, or shouted at climbing revs.

"Yes," Skafe said. "He was going to buy himself a boat. He said he wanted a good tight boat he could sail by himself to Trincomalee."

"Where's that?"

"Ceylon," he said.

Then he talked about Mac and their days together, and as he talked a bit of it out, he thought of how little he knew about Mac beyond Mac in person. His parents used to run a bakery in Trail, B.C.; but both were dead. He had no relations of whom he spoke. Mac was not secretive when asked. But he did not give because he did not think that there was much worth giving. Skafe talked to a stranger, as people will do. He could not but admire Brian Fiske, who was no stranger after this; yet so olympian a young man that it was not easy to know whether sympathy lay in him, or much warmth of heart.

"I saw Mac occasionally these past three years," Fiske said. "He gave me some darned sound advice about starting this outfit."

"He would," Skafe said. "Roy tells me you're expanding fast."

"We're getting going," Fiske said. "The Dewline is a help."

"And after that?"

"After that, something," said Brian Fiske. "The way I see it, the North is only just beginning. Don't you agree, sir?"

"Yes," Skafe said. "I do. But there are a lot of risks involved." For example, those risks you took tonight, he thought, and could not say. "I mean that a run of bad luck, even a patch of slow business—and a small company, any kind of small company, is in trouble." He did not want to pontificate, or to condescend from his own not inconsiderable experience.

"In one way you're right, sir," Fiske said. "In another wrong. I know that bad luck may break you, but luck is what you make yourself, too. We're earning good money now, and I'm putting every cent back in. If things work out, I'll be getting a Venture next month."

How blandly this fellow told S. K. Skafe that he was wrong. *But luck is what you make yourself.* My God, he thought. How often do I hear a young man say that? "Look here, Brian," he said. They were losing height slowly to the river. "I have a proposal to make: It is that you sell us Aurora at book value plus a fair price for good will; and we won't argue about that. Then run Skafair for me at a starting salary of twenty-five thousand." He had made his best choices in this way, not quite on the spur of the moment but not much slower. He had seen enough of men, and of Brian Fiske tonight, to know that Fiske was his man. "Does that sound a fair offer to you?" he said.

"It sounds like a princely offer," Fiske said. "But I wouldn't be interested, thank you, sir."

"Oh," Skafe said. So instantaneous, so firm a refusal of a princely offer was something new to him; but in several ways this Fiske was something new to him. The fact of no explanation was in itself new and arrogant, considering their respective positions in the business world, and the lesser business world of flying. "Oh," he said again.

"The thing is," Fiske said, and now he did hesitate for words, coming down to the Mackenzie River, where a measure of life had begun for

Skafe. "The thing is that I started Aurora on my own, and I want to take my risks to make something for myself—control what I run, is partly what I mean."

"But you would control Skafair," Skafe said. He was nettled, and tired, and his mind too full. He had chosen this time wrongly to make himself seem cold-blooded, but life and life's business must go on without sentimental pause, as Mac himself would have said. "You would have a free hand," he said. "Carte blanche, within limits of policy."

"That is just it, Mr. Skafe. Your policy, not mine."

He did not argue the point, which he saw in a way, but the cool disdain baffled him. Did this youth not realize what opportunities . . . ?

They circled Providence—Police, Company and Signals, the mission and the humble flock, a larger settlement than most along the river, the next one a hundred and fifty miles downriver.

"A lot of people loved old Mac," Fiske said, beginning the approach. "But I guess you were his only friend."

"Was I?" he said. "I suppose I was."

"You don't lose that," Fiske said.

They landed and taxied back. There were a number of people waiting on the bank, which was not unusual. A man sleeps in the northern summer when a load of sleep climbs on his back.

"I think I should warn you that the press are here," Fiske said. "A plane load came in just as I left."

"Oh, no," he said. "Not now."

Fiske looked round at him. "I'll deal with them," he said. "You stay in the plane until I call you."

He got out at the float and closed his door. "Hullo," he said to a dozen reporters and photographers who were crowding for Husky Skafe. "You can see him when he's had some sleep," Fiske said. "Not before."

"But this is a hot story . . ."

"Not so hot for some concerned," said Brian Fiske. He was quite unmoved, quite lackadaisical and quite impressive, and he willed them. "I'll tell you all I know," he said, "which is all we know. Mr. Skafe will see you later. Come on, sir," he said.

They made way for Skafe. "Hullo, boys," he said. "Hullo, Greg. Hi there, Barney."

"Too bad about Mac."

"Yes," he said. "Too bad."

Simon climbed the muddy bank, and, before sleep at the trader's red-roofed house, he went to get a report on Mac's co-pilot for that flight. The river flowed past him, down against him, down the same silent way.

BOOK FIVE

CHAPTER ONE

". . . Only the other day, and with this most welcome task in mind, I posed a casual question to him: 'Tell me, Husky—who first said: *Nobody needs an I O U from Husky Skafe?*' . . . 'Oh, I wouldn't know, Bob,' he replied in that modest way of his. 'Some misguided character, I suppose.'

"Yes, gentlemen, some character, some thoroughly unmisguided character must have coined that phrase, which has become a watchword about Husky Skafe."

For God's sake get on with it, Skafe thought. He looked over applauding tables and up to a discreet gallery opposite him where the women sat —Grace and Sally, Muriel Carter, Cynthia Sleeman, Amy Pitt, Peter Syme's young wife, Hermione Merchant, one or two others, and Mrs. Murton lurked there too. It was like Purdah at the Maharaja's banquet.

". . . It has been my privilege," Bob Carter was saying, "to watch, and in a small way to assist at the rise of this legendary figure. Nor would I deny that there were times, a mere handful of years ago, when a certain conservative banker—I do not speak in the party political sense of that word, I need hardly say, gentlemen—" Pause for amusement, "when a certain conservative banker was anxious lest this dynamic and intrepid venturer should overreach himself. But Fortune smiled on him. One might better say that Husky Skafe forced a smile to the lips of Dame Fortune . . ."

Skafe looked up to look round the room, more than seven hundred men, most of whose faces were familiar to him, but he did not pinpoint any face at any table. He stared again at his coffee cup with that dejected deadpannery which is a must for modest men under paeans of praise.

". . . Only this very morning we read in our newspapers that a change of management had taken place in a great Canadian corporation. Mark you, my friends, these tidings were something less than a large surprise to some of us . . ." Bob Carter smiled amid loud laughter. "And what has happened to Algonquin Steel since the market opened at ten this morning? Has it fallen, as might be expected after the gains of these past months? No, gentlemen, Algonquin Steel has risen four further points. And why? We all know why—because the world knows now that Husky Skafe will lead Algonquin Steel to greater things . . ."

He makes it sound like a pretty piece of philanthropy in the common weal, thought Skafe. In fact, it had been a cold war for control. By the time Summit had acquired a twenty-five per cent interest—more voting stock than Buxton could command—the market price had been pushed from 30 to 44. Then Skafe had threatened a proxy fight; and only then had that obstinate bungler, Buxton, capitulated. But when he broke, he broke altogether—a proud man, a humiliated wreck. It had been an honorable affair, but not a pretty piece of philanthropy. Skafe sensed some reserve in the applause about Algonquin.

". . . And so, gentlemen, it is with a profound sense of pride and pleasure that now, on behalf of all members of our Financial and Industrial Association of Canada, I make this birthday presentation to a man in the very prime of his years, to a great Canadian, Simon Kepple Skafe."

It was a silver casket, about two foot by one, a giant cigar box on lion-paw legs, all crenelated curlicues. It was very fine, indeed a noble ornament, just the thing for the board-room table. It was what his first wife would have called a splendiferous enormity.

Skafe accepted it from Bob Carter. Bob, who had moved from the presidency to the chairmanship of the Union Bank, had long been a stout ally and counselor to him. Skafe put the casket down, and now he stood before the three microphones, one for amplification, two for the networks. They photographed him while he faced the room, and glanced once to the gallery to see Grace smiling.

"Mr. Chairman," he began. "Your Excellency, Mr. Minister . . ."

He thanked them for this magnificent gift, and for the honor they had done to him. He spoke of Bob Carter as a Canadian who had served his country in peace and war, a symbol of integrity and of a fine tradition; and what he said was true about Bob Carter, and he said it more tellingly without the fulsome rotundity that afflicted Bob Carter on his hind legs making speeches.

He accepted the casket, Skafe said, not as a deserving individual but as a man who had been privileged to work with a team. He turned to his henchmen at the head table, Sleeman to one side, Willie Pitt and

Peter Syme to the other, not mentioning them by name, but looking at them, and thinking of many stout men of his who were not here.

He said these right and proper things, first in English and then in French, to an audience of individuals who were as ready to admire great success as they would be ready, while making appropriate disclaimers and expressions of regret, privately to relish a mighty tumble from a great success. He had that thought about them, for they were human beings; and as he spoke he knew that many might be wondering, questioning within themselves whether this Husky Skafe really had something (except phenomenal luck) that some others had not got. But he had, and well he knew it.

Skafe had been a doer all his life, not a talker, but he could talk straight practical sense or talk around a point, his tongue running servant to his brain while his brain thought on aside. It was a gift few men possess.

". . . When I was a young man," he said, "even more in my prime than Mr. Carter says I now am . . . When I was a young man, I saw down to Canada from far away . . ."

He spoke of the country he had seen—a country three or four thousand miles in length, a country that was no more than a sliver or strip of habitation set upon a populous continent. Since those times, twenty-five years ago, Canada had burgeoned to power and prosperity, thanks in great measure to her peaceful neighbor, that most generous nation on earth, the United States.

He paused for the applause, and he bowed to the Ambassador two chairs along. But he was thinking, as others here were thinking, that a Canadian could not now travel freely in his Canadian North without first obtaining security clearance or permission from the United States. It was inevitable in the cold terms of a continental threat. It was inevitable, considering who would pay a half-billion-dollar Dewline bill. But it rankled.

Now twenty-five years later, he continued, the narrow land had prospered, but almost all her prosperity still derived from that strip of habitation. And yet, he said, the narrow land of Canada was the widest or deepest land in the world. If she were to achieve her destiny, if she were to become the great nation she so lightly called herself, she must turn to the North.

"The North is ours by right," he said, "ours to take if we can take it, or we shall lose the North by default. It is not enough to talk in a self-satisfied way about this great land of ours, nor enough to finance mineral exploration or other ventures from office chairs in Toronto and Montreal with someone else's money. For what is the truth, gentlemen? The lamentable truth is that few Canadians will even go to the North unless to earn a quick grubstake working for the likes of me.

"But we must learn for ourselves. Above all, our best young men must live in the North to learn the North. Only then will Canada be Canada of herself by herself and for herself. Indeed, in the long term she cannot otherwise survive."

He had their still attention. He must curb the visionary gleam. He spoke from a practical and material success unparalleled in recent years. They were hard-headed men of business. Success talked turkey to them, as it did to him.

". . . Last summer," he said, "Skafe Exploration established a camp in the Arctic Islands. Since January we have been moving equipment by tractor train across the sea ice, preparatory to the start of drilling operations in the coming season. My son John made the first round trip from the Arctic coast to our camp, which—whatever the results of drilling for oil—we intend to establish as a permanent base for operations in the Archipelago. Our people have chosen to name it Camp Husky, but I prefer the Eskimo name for those islands—*Nunangiyak*, the islands far from land. I hope to visit Nunangiyak next week when another of our tractor trains will be due in from the south."

They applauded him. Some of them, perhaps fifty of them, indirectly a hundred of them, he had clashed with and ridden roughshod over in his time. So he had enemies among admirers.

"I had a friend," he said, "named MacNamara. Many of you knew him personally. Most of you knew of him in his lifetime. All of you will have read of his death last August at a northern lake. Mac was not a businessman in the usual sense, although he became that too, and he ran our air operation with notable success. Mac's great renown was as a pilot, a fighter ace in the war, a northern flyer off and on for almost thirty years. But Mac had little use for fame. Indeed, he was a man without ambition for himself who saw our free world and our Canada, the weakness and the strength, with a particular disillusioned idealism of his own."

Skafe waited for the applause, and then he said: "While I sat beside that lake, I thought of my testy guide, blaspheming philosopher and friend, and I wondered how it might be possible to pay tribute to his memory in a way of which he himself would have approved—not that Mac would regard his memory as worth preserving. But he was an adventurer, a fabled pilot, an adventurer. And so I announce the MacNamara Fund . . ."

The capital sum in trust was five million dollars. The purpose was to provide grants of ten thousand dollars for a year's work and travel in the Northwest Territories or the Yukon. Subjects of study: Any or none at all. Condition: Available at first only to native-born Canadians. Condition: At least six months of the twelve to be spent away from northern centers of population.

"You could call this a bribe," Skafe said, "which is precisely what we intend it to be." Slightly a royal We, he thought. "As Mac would say," he said, "*sure as hell it's a bribe.*" He watched them stir to the punch of that. "In more polite language," he said, "we hope that a MacNamara grant will be an inducement—a larger inducement in terms of cash than any job now available to a young man or woman straight out of college. The numbers will be small, twenty or twenty-five each year. An insignificant number, you might say. But if twenty of our most able young people go out alone each year to seek the North, then that is a beginning. Let them do what they want—explore, paint pictures, study Eskimos, prospect. And in the matter of prospecting, gentlemen, I should perhaps mention that there will be no strings attached to Skafe Exploration . . ."

There was a ripple of amusement, but they were listening intently to him, even if they might think that Husky Skafe had gone off his rocker. "Thus we hope," he said, "to encourage some people to know their North. A man who has sat out an arctic blow the hard way in a tent, or has sat out enough of them to lose his first fear of them, will not forget that on his backside in an office chair.

"So what am I saying, gentlemen? I am saying that life is an adventure, or life is nothing. Canadians must adventure from the narrow land, or Canada will be nothing. Our adventure waits there for us."

He sat down, and they cheered him. He had never said it publicly before, and he thought that perhaps he had said it badly. What, indeed, was the truth of his vision about the North? Was it for Canada to find herself and to save herself from being swallowed? Or was it for Husky Skafe to match himself against? What dreamer could know the truth about his dream? And his audience—what, if anything, would remain with them when the spell of an eloquence had died?

They went on cheering him. Then he was paid compliments here at the table and across the table as his hosts said goodbye and made tracks for the office, or to catch a plane, or to see more of Montreal. Some had crossed Canada for this.

The women awaited him in the lobby. "Oh, Husky," Grace said. "You were superb."

"Well done, darling," Sally said, her face bright with pleasure for him and about him.

He talked with the others, or they said admiring things which he lapped up with grave depreciation. Mrs. Murton hovered in the offing, and he went to speak to her. "I'm so glad you could come," he said.

"Oh, Mr. Skafe, I can't tell you what it was to sit and listen to your inmost thoughts and dreams after all these years of working for you."

"Of our working together," he said, a prophet not without honor in that country which he shared with Mrs. Murton. "No one ever had a stauncher right hand." He was a little lightheaded after it all, prone to giggle about his staunch right hand and his innermost secret dreams, so he said briskly: "I'm going to the Hide-Out now to think a bit. I don't want to be disturbed unless anything of importance turns up at the office."

He went to the door with Grace, and said that he would be home by half past six. Then he collected his coon coat and astrakhan hat and walked a few blocks to the Hide-Out. It was a raw day, the streets dirty brown with slush, too mild a day for a handsome dreamer to be wearing raccoon and astrakhan. He let himself into the apartment.

Bob Carter might speak of him as in the very prime of his years, but on a man's fiftieth birthday the prime of the prime hardly lay ahead. A dry old road was looming ahead. Yet no man could have had a more encouraging start to a second half-century.

Fifty, he thought. I can't quite believe it, and he went through to the bedroom to inspect himself in a mirror against the grim light of March. The hair was gray, the lines were deeper, the underside of the chin was not so cleancut as it used to be; but there were no sagging jowls, flabby dewlaps, vein-blotchy cheeks, no ancient rheum or telltale tracery of pink about the eyes. The eyes were blue and sharp and white.

"There's life in the old dog yet," he said, encouraged by that inspection, elated still by the virtue gone out in speaking, by the tributes paid to him. Husky Skafe was slightly on high. He went back to the paneled sitting room and the dropleaf table—it was a good Tudor piece—where the latest copy of *Summit* lay. The cover illustration was a black and white photograph of a farmhouse, weathered, dignified, austere, a little tumbledown. Above was the caption: *The Birthplace of our President*. Below was this caption: *The old Skafe Home at Gallery, New Brunswick*.

He had come here, not to think a bit, as he had told Mrs. Murton, but to steady back from too much adulatory excitement. He could feel it wearing off. He thought he would have a well-earned snooze for half an hour, so he sat in the big armchair, stretched out his legs and closed his eyes and slept.

The telephone rang. "Yes?" he said. The daffodils on the table by the telephone had a pleasant scent of spring not far away.

"Oh, Mr. Skafe, I *am* so sorry . . . I know you don't want to be disturbed but I really didn't know . . ." When crises arose, Mrs. Murton battened her woman down and spoke more slowly. But now Mrs. Murton was aflutter.

"What is it, Mrs. Murton?"

"Well, you see, Mr. Skafe, your first husband, oh dear, I mean Mrs. Dorrien just called. Sally was out of our office on an errand, so I took it myself."

"Where is Mrs. Dorrien?" he asked about his first husband.

"She's in town, Mr. Skafe, at the St. Sauveur. She said would you call her please at . . ."

He wrote the number down. "Thank you, Mrs. Murton," he said. "No doubt Mrs. Dorrien has come to see Sally, so we shall keep it as a surprise for Sally."

He hung up, and stood at the window. It was snowing now. The city was muffled under snow, but the traffic thrashed and stalled and hooted down there in dismal slush. It was seven and a half years since he had parted from her. He dialed the number and asked for the room.

"Anna," he said.

"Oh, Simon," she said. "Many happy returns."

"Thank you," he said. "Thanks, Anna. When did you get in?"

"This morning," she said, "after a loathsome flight from Shannon. I'm on my way to join David in Jamaica." Her voice was much less Canadian, or more English, but the same voice to hear it and listen for the shadows of it. "Are you still there?"

"Still here," he said, "if slightly poleaxed."

She laughed. "Me too. Mrs. Murton sounded so poleaxed as to be almost human. Where are you?" Anna said. "Where's here?"

"I have a sort of hide-out flat," he said. "Will you come?"

"Yes," she said.

He warned the doorman to show her up and to let him know. Then he went to brush his hair. If he was fifty, Anna was forty-seven, both as old as the ark to the up and coming. Then he looked at his paneling from the barn at Gallery. Then he waited after waiting all these years; and he watched the cram of traffic in the city. The telephone rang again, the doorman to say that the lady was coming up. In the first years he had thought often that he would see the lady again, today, tomorrow, somewhere, somehow, at a corner, on the Mountain, in the Berkeley, on Fifth Avenue. But later his expectation seemed to fade.

He left the door open and went to the elevator and it lumbered to a stop, and he saw Anna again, not having anything to say and not knowing whether he should kiss her, what to say or do, so he said: "Hullo, Anna," and closed the elevator doors. She was taking off her coat, a camel's hair coat for a traveler from an Irish winter to a West Indian island, under that a gray coat and skirt, a dark red blouse, a jade necklace he had given her. No overshoes, needless to say. She grumbled about flecks of mud at the ankles of her nylon stockings. She had put on some weight, but her legs were the same long undulant legs. He hung the coat with his coon in the cupboard in the lobby place, and he followed her in.

"Such bedraggled dimmery," she said at the window. "I was hoping for a bright hard day with a squeak in the snow. How are you, Simon?"

"I'm all right," he said, watching her look at bedraggled dimmery far down on the street, up at the wet roofs of the city in the sleet; but here it was dry and warm, a light by the chair. He switched on another. "And you?" he said, moving to stand beside her and behind her, willing Anna to turn, which she did. They kissed one another lightly, quietly, softly on the lips. Then she went to sit, her knees together, her hands linked at her knees. "I came round this way," she said, stopping at that statement of fact. "You're grayer," she said, "but not much changed. I'm gray too, and rather fat."

"It suits you," he said. "You have big bones to carry a bit of weight."

"Like a steeplechaser," she said, and she chuckled her indolent chuckle and stopped. When he kissed her just now, he had felt that same animal strength of Anna, that same smell of Anna's skin, that same instant knowledge of Anna. So time had gone and grayness had come but nothing had changed, so how could they be easy together?

"I love your paneling," she said, "such a soft pale color; but the room is bare."

"I found some old pine boards in the barn at Gallery," he said. It had been an expensive craftsman's job. He hesitated. He went now and put the key in the small hole in the knot, turned the key and slid the two sides of the central recess apart to let Anna see herself framed in the paneling of the wall.

"Oh," she said, before the portrait of the woman in the evening dress of deep red crimson lamé or such stuff, off the shoulders, half off the breasts, a jade necklace, not another piece of jewelry, a queen, a gypsy, a courtesan. "Oh," she said. "Did I really look like that?"

"Yes," he said. It was Anna warm from love. It was Anna kindled to amusement. It was the bite and the beauty of Anna. It was all that he had hoped that Anna would always be, and yet if she always was, she would not be. It was Anna loved, and more than the Anna he had loved. "David saw you like that," he said. But who made you like that for David to see? he thought.

She looked quickly at him with some feeling for him. Then they sat on the sofa, he at one end of it, she at the other. "Did you really think of me?" she said, ever surprised that anyone should think of her.

"What the hell do you imagine?" he said. "Why did you come?" he said.

"I came round this way because I wanted to see Sally—she sounded so unhappy in her last letter—and because I wanted to get her to talk to you about John; but then I listened to you speaking on the wireless, on the radio, and then I felt I had to see you for myself just once again."

"I've been waiting all this time," he said.

She looked at her portrait, smiling. "There!" she said. "Let reality shatter recollection. Dumpy old frump."

He laughed. "Still Anna," he said. It was four o'clock. He had two hours before going home to Grace. The only other painting in the room was Dorrien's sketch of Mac, which Anna was now looking at. He had brought it from Gallery after Mac was killed. So his two paintings here were by his first wife's husband, quite peculiar.

"Dear Mac," she said. "You must miss him terribly."

"I do," he said. And he did, in his thoughts each day, no Mac to see again. But Mac was gone, and Anna was here, his splendid woman, *dumpy old frump*, she said, his woman, but he did not know her wants for him. "When I went to find Mac," he said, using Mac without scruple to lead her wants to him. "When I went to find Mac, we flew by the head of the Mackenzie into Providence. I saw the island where you and I were that first day together. Do you remember?"

"I remember," she said. "You slept, and I watched you all the time."

"And do you remember next morning, the hard ice on the river and the candle ice on the lake?"

"I remember," she said. Do you remember? I remember.

There was a headwind on the last miles of the river. Anna slept beside him, knees on the seat, head pillowed on her arm. It grew chilly, so he let the boat fend for itself and went past the racketing engine and the gas drum to the cabin for a blanket which he put over her. She did not stir. Her face was soft, asleep. Somebody wrote that sleep was death's counterfeit, or death's twin brother. Not true, he thought, watching Anna asleep, his to touch into life again. He wished that she would waken, so that he could know her better. They came to the island of yesterday. She woke now, without a word or a touch from him.

"Our island," she said, as a woman will, and she moved along the seat to meet him while the old boat strained by the side of the island.

Someone was shouting. Skafe broke from her. It was the Indian, fourth and perhaps only other human inhabitant of these upper reaches—Jim out for the count in a cabin, Indian kibitzing from their island, Skafe and Anna kissing hotly on old man, cold man Mackenzie River.

One eye hidden by his cap, the Indian had a squatly rakish look. He was pointing upriver. Skafe throttled back. "Big ice come!" the Indian shouted.

"Hi, Gabriel!" called Anna.

Skafe waved acknowledgment. He did not seek shelter, but went on to round the point to see this ice. He considered coincidence—that she should be whose wife she was; that he should meet her here in one of the less populous regions of the unpopulous Dominion; that Anna's acquaintance, Gabriel, should observe them kissing, as one might from someone else's private island observe a couple kissing on a Sunday on MacGregor Lake or Georgian Bay or the St. Lawrence at a Thousand Islands.

Then he saw the ice. Indeed, by coincidence, the ice met him as he rounded the point. The south shore of the lake was clear. This ice came before the wind and current from the main pack to the east. It came in slabs, the smaller ones flat and white at water level, the larger pieces with a freeboard of a foot, heaving and tilting in wind and current, hard green ice. The floes came sailing in battalions, advanced guards here already.

There was danger of smashing his wheel on solid ice; and he carried no spare propeller. There was danger of big floes running aground in shallow water, crushing his boat.

He stood to see farther ahead, and saw that to yield was the better hope. He edged right for deeper water, but the ice closed on him, scraping, grinding on timbers, clinking. He threw the shaft out of drive just as the wheel jarred into ice—no harm done yet.

They drifted at six or seven miles an hour past Gabriel, the Indian who had admired his boat. The name of Skafe's boat was the *Mabel K.*, but he did not much like the name, so he call it the *Boat*. Skafe, the boat, the ice, and Anna Willis went down the river, so much flotsam past a string of islands.

There were shallows ahead, broken water. He had come through them upstream with his shallow draft; but the ice would not go through. The big ice would strand, pile up, smash the boat.

"We'll have to risk the prop," she said, meaning risk using power to force a way through the vanguard of the ice. Anna spoke calmly, floating homeward down the river.

Simon Kepple Skafe was lucky, not for the first or last time. He nudged his way ahead and out with power, and led the race through shallow water. He ran on until he was well ahead of ice, and could see the wooded bluff that hid Jim's cabin; and then he turned into a sheltered channel between islands.

Sweat stung his eyes. He wiped them. "I wonder if old Jim's all right," he said, at a tangent from what he most strongly felt—relief at escaping the consequences of besotted carelessness. Skafe measured risks and took them. He did not run blindly, kissing women, ignoring warnings, into ice. He had just done that, though. He also did wonder about old Jim.

"Of course Jim's all right," she said without the slightest compromise to sympathy. *Our island,* she said sentimentally. *Of course Jim's all right,* she said.

Skafe found an ice-free way upriver. He approached their particular island again from the other flank. The Indian did not appear.

Gabriel had shown no surprise at their embrace. It would be recorded in his head, as all natural phenomena were recorded, and when Jim came to make the painful enquiries of sobriety: *See the boat? Where? Was she in it? Heading?* and so on, kissing and hugging would also be reported. To leave a kissing story with an Indian added untidy insult to Jim's injury.

They drew up the island for the second time. The run of ice had finished, and the remaining pack was far out on the lake. He thought that must have been the swansong to the river of break-up 1932; and it had nearly pipped them. He wondered what she thought about, beside him. "What are you thinking about?" he asked.

"Nothing," she said. "I'm sitting with you."

But once again they were not alone. It was the first river boat of the year, the Hudson's Bay Company *Distributor.* Square bowed and sterned, a box afloat, she pushed two barges in line ahead. Her woodsmoke kept pace in the easterly breeze, her house flag flew, her sternwheel turned slowly, lazily splashing watermill. She was like some old something from Mark Twain's river; one went north and the other went south, the two great rivers. The *Distributor* blew a short blast on her way. Even small boats rated casual notice on this river. The queen of the river whistled greeting, a second, if unknowing witness to elopement.

There might be a third witness in the shadows, a man named Mackenzie who went by canoe that way this month, a hundred and forty-three years ago.

Skafe headed roughly east by south. He would keep land in sight all the way to Hay River. This south shore of the lake was shallow, and treacherous in storms. Even the large river boats often had to shelter. There were mares' tails in the sky, but the wind had moderated. He did not think it would blow in the four or five hours he needed to cross.

They were an hour from the last island when she turned, and said: "Goodbye. I hope I never see you again," to the green islands at the dip of the Mackenzie River. She had called the place strong and beautiful, and hoped not to see it again.

"Never mind," he said. He put his arm round Anna's shoulder to give her comfort. But then desire made hypocrisy of comfort motives, and he kissed her, letting the boat look after itself on Great Slave Lake until they were into hard ice again. He pushed Anna away, and steered his boat, the *Mabel K.*

"Start-stop, start-stop—do we have to go on like this forever?"

"Not forever," he said reasonably, "but we must make sure of getting across. One near-shipwreck is enough for one day, don't you think?"

They ran on through some patches of candle ice, no obstacle, the last stage in the rotting process, slivers like candles, or like the long glasses of a candelabra. It was warmer now, and the wind had dropped. They made their own small breeze. "Are you hungry?" she said in a while. "I brought the ptarmigan eggs, hardboiled. Jim said they were fresh. I tried them too, and they sank in water. Shall I make us some tea as well?"

"I'd better gas up first," he said. He filled a can from the drum and poured it into the tank. He had to be careful about fire. There were numerous ways of being shipwrecked. "Okay now," he said when the fumes were gone. Did she hardboil Jim's eggs especially for this picnic breakfast? Did we plot Jim's selling out to me? Did we jump at the rum idea to make Jim drunk? Hell, he thought. I've never been troubled by pangs of conscience.

She brought eggs, bread and mugs of tea. "You keep the boat so tidy and clean," she said politely to the stranger. There were three eggs each, man-sized mouthfuls.

"They're very good," Skafe said. "Hardboiled eggs are the best things on a picnic." He yawned.

"You're half asleep," she said when they had finished. "Let me take the boat for an hour. I'll call you if we run into ice or anything."

Hay River was flat on the brown horizon. They might be halfway or more across. He lay on the bunk with a backlog of sleep, and now that he tried to sleep, he could not sleep. The voices and specters of fatigue swirled round him, and he listened to the engine running well, and he thought of her steering the boat across the lake to Hay River.

He gave up sleep after half an hour and went out to surprise her sitting shirtless in the sun. She grabbed for the shirt.

"Please don't," he said. "I want to see you."

She smiled at him. "It's quite a help to hear that at last," she said, and put down the shirt.

"Aren't you cold?"

"No," she said, looking down at herself. "No goose-flesh even, see?"

And no prudery. She was glad that he wanted to see her voluptuous body, and even then he thought of others who had seen her body, and had used it, and perhaps had pleased her, using it.

He sat with her, not touching her at first; but then his willful ambassadors took charge of him and her. "Simon," she said. "I haven't slept with Jim since Easter."

Why did she feel impelled, compelled, to say such things? Or was she right to answer a question he did not ask? Poor old Jim, still adoring his same li'l iceberg, hoping for his rights since Easter, dreaming of them, seething with them in a drunken stupor, possibly.

Hay River might be ten miles away, no other boats in sight, only this boat on the inland sea. "I won't be a minute," he said.

He stopped the engine. It was a fine day now, a few herringbones in the sky, no wind at all, a swell on the lake, the air warm enough and cool enough, the spring and the summer marching, and she waited for him.

"It isn't the widest of feather beds," she said. But she stopped smiling, watching him, and she put out her hand to touch him. "Man," she said. "Take me quickly."

He took her as she asked and as he wanted. Then he heard the candle ice against the boat, and he thought how incongruous the listing boat, how quiet the relief of passion spending, spent; and now the impulse to go somewhere else, go anywhere but here. But she held him, smiling up at him. "I knew it," she said. "I knew that all my horrors would be gone." Her hands caressed his back, and traced the touchings of their bodies. "Please," she said. "Please don't let me lose you." She held his head to kiss him, softly, deeply, hardly, the protagonist. "Do you like me?" she said now, as they began to love again.

"A lot," he said. "Very much. Very much indeed." They laughed together, letting love come slowly.

"It would have been nice beside the river."

"Why the river, Anna?"

"Oh, I don't know, river flowing, terns objecting, warblers mating, minds and bodies by the river."

She went along the way with him, down along the river, down between the trees, and on, no river now, no trees, blind truth, and back to Great Slave Lake again.

"The first time I saw you," Anna said. "When was that? Was it yesterday?"

"The day before," he said. He saw her untidy, with a sleep-smudged face at the cabin door. But that reminded him of Jim—not too pretty, was it, clean a man's trapline in the trapping country. He was sorry, but he did not care, he did not give a damn. He lay with Anna in his arms. She was lighthearted, ruthless, passionate or kind or angry by the mood, honest always. Skafe was a man who suited things to him, who went where he was going. He hardly knew gloom or discontent. But happiness was a discovery with her.

"You can always have all of me," she said. "I can't have all of you, I know. Just give me a share."

"What with?" he asked her. The wind was rising. Love was an episode. The time had come to be going on.

"A share with my competitors," she said. "Ambition might be one." She kissed him, and she watched him dress. "But I have to be more than an appendage. That's my kind of woman, darling."

The wind blew from the ice again. He steered for Hay River. There would be the crossing to Fort Resolution, the muddy Slave and portage to Fitzgerald, the Slave again, the Athabaska, take a train at Waterways, and south to Edmonton, and Out at last.

His great cold river was behind him. His woman slept in the cabin of his boat. Simon Skafe was on his way.

CHAPTER TWO

THEY TALKED in the afternoon. With a window open (she complained of heat), they heard the noises of the city in the afternoon. They talked and thought and lived again some old beginnings, as they could. They thought about an ending, but avoided it, for such things talked about are dim recrimination. The past lay there; the future did not call for them together. They were happy in the present on that afternoon, with excursions back and on, and some edged comment, being less than saintly people.

"How is Sally doing in the office?" Anna asked one time.

"As well as you might guess," he said. "Give her five years, and she could run the whole caboodle." He looked pleased and baffled that any such lustrous apple of a father's eye could quite exist. In that, at least, he was transparent. "Mrs. Murton is supremely good at working from experience. But Sally initiates, or she could and would if she weren't careful not to steal Mrs. Murton's thunder. It isn't easy to have so many gifts." Now Simon frowned.

"Is that prissy paragon jealous of her?"

"There were signs," he said. "But Sally caught on, and now she simply coasts with efficiency in the outer office, charming the pants off all who call. A waste of her time, but she won't take on a worthwhile job like Public Relations, which I offered her. She could do that ten times better than the present man."

"Perhaps she wouldn't want to steal *his* thunder."

"Perhaps she wouldn't know what she wants," he said. "I wish you'd talk to her, Anna. Grace and I are flummoxed." He looked round at her like an ordinary uncertain man. How incongruous that seemed, and how endearing.

"We made a tentative date for tomorrow, if she can have the day off."

"You spoke to Sally? I didn't know."

"I telephoned this morning. That was how I knew about your speech. I must say she did seem pleased to hear me."

"Not surprising," Simon said.

"She always blamed me," Anna said. And John never did, she thought. "Almost the first thing Sally said was that I should see you. *Please see him*, she said. *Please, on his birthday. I won't breathe a word.* But I said no, and then I heard you speak, and then I weakened, typical. But I thought it rather touching that she would want us to meet again, that she would even know that two such ancients might still want very much to meet again."

"Yes," he said. "I find that touching." When he showed feeling, it was reluctantly. He had not changed in that or anything, except to be more than he had been—more olympian, more formidable. I wonder if he missed me at all, she thought. Or did he shut me off, close the door on that compartment until I turned up and he wanted me? "But Grace?" he said now.

"I'm to telephone Sally this evening out of the blue," Anna said. "Conspiracy," she said. "I'm sorry about that sordidness, if not about anything else."

"It doesn't matter," he said, "as long as Grace doesn't know. You're not a conspirator," he said, kissing her. "You never conspired in all your life."

"Quite often," she said. "And once with you—we conspired against Jim Willis." There was David's kindly shadow, and far back was Willis, throwing up his rotgut hooch, and here was the man who possessed her still. "*Nobody needs an I O U from Husky Skafe,*" she said unkindly.

His hand tightened on her shoulder. "I know," he said. "I wasn't thinking when Bob Carter asked me, and then he had to trot it out today. Not too pretty, not that it matters."

But she had not finished with him. "There is one other aspect. Three people heard that remark in that log cabin," she said. "Jim Willis would not have been likely to say it again. I never repeated it to anyone any time. Someone else must have coined the watchword sometime."

"*Touché,* I suppose," he said. "You always did like to tread on my hairy heels." He sounded hurt but not combative. She could not provoke the man beyond a mild riposte, and why should she want to provoke the man when she had him for this afternoon?

"I thought your speech was marvelous," she said.

He smiled. He absorbed praise as his due.

"Perhaps that was a simplified romantic idea about either the North for Canada, or nothing in the end for Canada; but then strong ideas must be simple."

"You used to say that things were not so simple as they seemed to me."

"I say some very silly things," she said. "Occasionally one might be true."

He laughed at that circumlocution. There were many facets to Simon Skafe, who saw things simple, rounded out, but was hardly a simple man.

"I was thinking as I listened," she said, "wishing that sometimes you had told me a little about the vision you saw beyond the job."

"I used to try sometimes," he said. "But when I tried, you cracked down on me." Which might be true. But how could she have known that mattered to him if he had never bothered to answer sarcasm? God, how bitchy I was to him, she thought, and would be again, and never have been to David.

"It's nearly five," he said. "Would you like a cup of tea?"

"I would rather have a drink," she said. She had taken to Scotch, with David. "A rye and water, may I?" and she watched him go. His waist had thickened, but he was the same unhurried prowler for her drink. Would he have one himself? He might, for company, not easement. Thus well she knew him.

He brought two drinks. "Hop in again," she said.

He hopped in again. Propped against pillows, they sat up in bed together. "Like a gin scene from Hogarth," he said. "I wish the hosts of FIAC could see the speaker now."

"It's so lovely," she said, "that you still seem to like me faded and fat."

"We're growing old," he said. "Isn't that what love means, growing old?"

Damn him, it made her weep, she who never wept, that Simon who shunned the word love, and was ignorant of love, should say this truth of love to her. She wanted to say to him, sobbing like some silly sentimental woman, which she was—she wanted to say to him: *I did right, didn't I, for you and the children and us all?* But she did not say it. She stopped her mawkish sobbing and said: "Idiot."

He laughed and held her to him. If you weakened, he was wonderfully kind, like Jehovah bending to soothe the mortal. "How's David?" he asked casually, as about some mutual friend one might remember from the comfort of Jehovah's bed.

She said that David was all right; that he depended upon her entirely in his painting now; that he drank too much, and so did she, but that she had given it up in the autumn with him, and that he had been worse without it—lost, nervous and morose—and now drinking again. "David is not complete within himself, and neither am I," she said. "We're not like you." She spoke of David with a whole understanding that was love again, thus love confounded. "It's hard to believe," she said, "but I'm quite a decent wife to him. Darby and Joan—blowsy and boozy at the proper hours, no cross words spoken."

"Oh, I'm glad," he said, but something like sadness—or was it doubt? —crossed that austere countenance. He was an austere man, Simon, yet a passionate splendor of a man in bed. He was a human man about the frailties of lesser people. She had not reached his mind, and she could not reach it now. "Have a top-up," he said.

He took her glass away. David was an admirer of one Simon Skafe. *What you cannot see, my love,* he said, *is that the man is an artist in his way, in a far bigger way than I shall ever be, but in a similar way. He has a thing he wants to make, and that is all he wants to make, and nothing will stop him making it.*

Nothing will stop him bulldozing it, she said. She was the more bitter about Simon in those days because of the blessing of contentment that David had brought her, the blessing of a share, of being some help to someone who mattered. I told Simon long ago, she thought. I warned him what kind of a woman I am.

Now he brought her second drink; two would be enough to get her out of here, away from him; but he got in beside her again. "Tell me," he said. "Who buys the tickets in the Dorrien ménage?"

"I do, of course," she said. "Who buys them for a great Canadian when Mrs. Murton is away?"

"Grace does, of course," he said. What fun it was again.

"How is Grace?" she asked, for the proprieties. Ask about David and ask about Grace, feeling neither regret nor embarrassment. Ah no, but ever pursued by some words of Christ. The snow had stopped. The sky was clearing. Soon the sun would set. No other windows in the city gave upon this window.

"Grace is a marvel," he said, "a saint to me, and I think she is happy." He said it quite humbly, with gratitude, with firmness. Thus, both of them had said it firmly.

"Are you sorry about this?" she said. "About us this afternoon? It's wrong, I know, but I'm not sorry."

"Not so long as Grace doesn't know," he said, "and she won't."

I wonder, Anna thought. I would know, the other way round. But then I'm not nice, saintly, unimaginative, trusting Grace, insipid too. "What, Simon?"

"I said that I see now you were right—for us and for them, and even for the children." So he had said it, bless him. "But I can't pretend to be cured of a vexing, perplexing thing called love."

"A vexing, perplexing thing called love," she said. "You say things sometimes."

"I'm literate, you know," he said, raising an eyebrow at her, perhaps indulgently irritated at what he took to be condescension, but if she had ever condescended to him or cracked down on him, it had been defensively and jealously.

"Are you and Grace going away this spring?" she asked.

"Grace is flying to Antigua as soon as I leave for the North."

"For Camp Husky, or the Islands far from Land?"

"Yes," he said, "for Nunangiyak." When he spoke about that bleak hideous North, his eyes brightened, as they brightened about Sally, extraordinary man. "Then after that I'm joining Grace. We plan to cruise down the Windwards to Granada. I do manage to drag myself away occasionally from the office," he said blandly.

"I know," she said. "I wasn't fair to you. Besides, you got that dough now, baby."

He laughed. She loved to hear the austere enigma laugh like that, like a schoolboy, give himself complete to laughter. When he stopped laughing, she heard the city rumble, rush and hoot. "Oh, look!" she said. "The sun is coming out to set."

"I can't see it from here," he said, on the side away from the open window.

It was not cold on a mild March evening with a window open. It was just bearably not too hot for her after the cool house in the balmy winter. She had grown fond of Ireland, but this was her country, and she had left it and did not want it back. "Come and watch the sun set with me," she said, although sunsets did not mean a thing to him.

He laid his head between her shoulder and her breast. He used the same pleasant-smelling stuff on his hair. She opened the fingers of her hand to bury them in his hair, still thick, but gray. The back of his neck was seamed as a peasant's neck is seamed by wind and weather. She turned his head and kissed his neck below the hair. "I'm happy," he said, making the sorrow of her happiness a danger to self-control again. They watched the sun go down from this high place. "Gone," he said. "Now that I'm getting old," he said, "I begin to see a sunset and be grateful for it." He lay in her arms. It was so many years since he had given himself to her to be her child, and now he was her child again as the lights of Montreal came on. A clock struck six to take him from her. "Oh, dammit," he said.

"I'll run you a bath," she said, and went through the sitting room, past David's portrait of Anna Skafe, to fetch her camel's hair coat, but she decided on his coon instead, and came back drowned in that to amuse the master, and then to run the master's bath. She had lost him now, and she must go, back to the hotel to drink and have some food sent up. She did not drink so much as she had given him to think, but tonight she would soak herself alone to sleep, but first she must telephone Sally to compound conspiracy before her speech was slurred. First the children, blast the children they had made together.

"You're a more efficient mistress than a wife," he said, lowering himself into his bath.

"You mean that I haven't been with you long enough to become a bitchy millstone round your neck again," she said, sitting on the lid of the bathroom seat in Husky Skafe's coon coat.

He looked at her, the master and the man of steel: *No scenes now, woman. You behave yourself.* Then he started soaping up.

She needed a drink quite badly, but she did not like to ask for number three. "About Sally," she said. "Do you want her to marry this Piers Whitfield?"

"I want her to do what she wants to do," he said. "He's a charming boy, good prospects, able, everything. She could do much worse."

"Is she in love with him? She didn't sound so from her letter."

"She is fond of him," he said, "and attracted by him. She likes him well enough to have stopped compulsively capturing every personable male extant. I had to speak to her about that last summer."

"Don't you think that might have stopped because Sally is haunted by what you said last summer? Hence Piers Whitfield—steady, nice, a peerage coming, safe with a rich girl's money, acceptable to Father."

"I have neither plotted nor planned," he said. "If that's what you mean. Surprisingly enough, I only want my daughter to be happy." He could say these things, and no doubt they were true, but he sounded cold and hard. "*Our* daughter," he said then, a rebuke in that, or to himself that he had spoken of his daughter to her mother. He rarely forgot the corporate aspect of production. Simon had all the niceties of feeling, if he had the feelings. "It might be better for her to be the more treasured party," he said, "rather than the more treasuring. Other people have found that out."

"Yes," she said, and thought about it and let it pass. "Are they seeing a lot of one another?"

"Every weekend—here, or skiing up North, or in Toronto. By Friday afternoons she's wild to be with him. On Sunday nights she comes home, won't speak to me, is rude to Grace. Last night she burst into tears for no apparent reason. Thank God her temperament doesn't carry over to the office."

"Her temperament might be frustration. Do they sleep together?"

"How would I know?" he said, scrubbing himself with offended vigor.

How could you bear to ask? she thought. "But I don't think it is frustration," Anna said. "I think from what Sally wrote to me that she is so fond of Piers that she doesn't want to hurt him, and she drifts on with him, knowing that she will hurt him either now or later, and she knows it should be now. What you said about it being better to be the more treasured one is true for many people, Simon darling, even for us.

But not for Sally, I think. She is not only dominant like you, but willful like me. It wouldn't work."

"You know best," he said. "You always were better about these things. You talk to her." He washed off soap and lay back in the bath and closed his eyes.

"If I were you," she said, "I would wash that woman right out of your grizzled locks as well."

He took her advice. "John did well on that trip," he said. "I was proud of him."

"He said he drove a tractor. What do you call it?"

"He skinned a cat," Simon said. "Catskinner John Skafe." He smiled, eyes shut, rinsing his head, at a thought that might be improbable but was most pleasing to him. "Not a picnic at fifty below," he said.

How Simon has longed that John should be in Simon's image, she thought. And she said carefully: "John told me that he would always be grateful to you for sending him North."

"Did he say that?" The great man sat up in his bath and turned his blue eyes to her, pleased about that pat on the back. No doubt he had pats and plaudits every day of life, too many of them, and he showed some signs of too many of them, but this was a kind word at second hand from John. "I must go home," he said, getting out of the bath. He was a good man too, but good or bad, he was more dear to her than she could well endure, but she did not want him back. She wanted weak kind David.

"Leave it for me," she said, and she took his bath. What did the children matter, even John? But she must not fail in this, having failed in so much. "Don't go away," she said. How right he was that she could not conspire.

"Simon," she said, too abruptly. "John has done nearly nine months in the North. Let him come back now."

"But he hasn't asked to come back," Simon said, surprised. "Besides, John promised he would do a year."

"I know," she said. "He won't ask because he gave you his word. But he did that trip, and you're proud of him. Isn't that enough?"

"No," he said. "John is learning the whole Turtle operation. That's what he went to do."

"And is he learning it? Do your people say that he's doing well?"

Simon shook his head. "Peter Syme says not. He says John tries, but that he is slow. I know John isn't slow. A little more time, and he will learn, as other slow starters learn." He frowned. "Syme is wrong."

"So you won't let him write. You intend to trap him in business somehow." She was no better able than she had been to hide her blind impatience about Simon's blind hopes for John.

"I said: *Do the year you promised. Then do what you want.* If he intends to write when this year in the North is up, let him write by all means. I know he can write, but I doubt if he has the real ability or the punch to make a go of it."

"You might be surprised to hear," she said, "that John was much struck with your criticism of his short story." She might have been surprised herself, except that the depths of Simon Skafe were unknown to her.

"Oh, was he?" he said noncommittally. You could butter him up a little bit, not much. He had a sharp nose for cupboard love, if not so sharp a nose for flattery.

"Why not be honest and admit, to yourself if not to me, that you're determined at all costs to wear John down, to cheat him of the right to be himself, to do what he wants to do to prove himself?"

"That is a fairly sweeping statement," he said.

"But it's true. And haven't you done what you wanted all your life?"

"In some respects," he said. "So John is the reason you came this afternoon."

"No, Simon darling," she said. "Please believe me. Will you believe me?"

"I always believe you," he said. "But why do you want John to come Out now? What difference does three months make when he gave an undertaking? They're all the same nowadays. No spirit of adventure, and no sense of obligation, softies writing home to Mummy."

She did not say what John had written. He had written: *I know that Father was pleased about me making the trip. And he was right when he said that the North would give me experience, if writing was what I decided to do. What Father might be less pleased to know is that my experience of his beloved North is humanity lost in a death of winter, and humanity does not suffice. He won't like it when I write it, which I will.*

"John didn't ask me to speak to you," she said. "He made his bargain and he intends to stick to it. Meanwhile you mumble like Colonel Blimp about no spirit of adventure." As she said that, she thought how typical of her to say such a thing to Simon Skafe who never mumbled like Colonel Blimp. "Might it not be John's own spirit of adventure that makes him determined to write his novel? But how can he write it, working twelve hours a day at a uranium mine?"

"What is John's idea for a novel?" He seemed mildly interested.

"I don't know," she said, which was true more or less. "Something from his trip, I suppose. If they get an idea, they want to write it, not lose it by telling people about it—that is, if they're any good; and I know John is, or he will be."

"Do you know many writers?"

"A few," she said. "We run up against them."

He knotted the towel at his middle. "A whole new life for you," he said, "the kind of bohemian life you always wanted. Mine is still the same life that bored you so much, and is the one I wanted."

"You never bored me," she said, using the wet cloth on her face. "I couldn't take the boring life. It might just be said that I couldn't take it."

"So why should John take the North, you mean?"

"Oh, Simon," she said. "John is not me, and John is not you. John is himself. Do you deny him that?"

"What precious sentimentalizing bores you intellectuals are," he said. "I'm going to dress." He slammed the bathroom door behind him, leaving his ex-wife flattened. If only he had dealt with me like that, she thought. But no—always kind, patient, considerate, impersonal, magnificent, the very perfect belted knight to make a woman scream. And now I have condemned John to a life in business.

She dried herself; a bit of weight, it suited her big bones, he said—and she had been hunting two days a week all winter, so she was no soft trollop. She left the man's coon coat and walked a few naked steps to the bedroom, but he had gone, and the other door was closed. Her girdle was worn out, of course, but it would have to do. She dressed quickly and did her face, which might have been more awful. It had some older resemblance now, she thought, to David's painting. There were no signs of other women anywhere that she could see in Simon's Hide-Out, not a single hairpin on the floor, no sniff of perfume in a drawer, none of her business, fated to be a woman. She had to leave him now. *Goodbye, Simon. It's been lovely meeting you again. Thanks for giving me what I never could forget.*

She went into the sitting room. "Well, that's all right," he said. "I called Edmonton. There's a plane out of Turtle in three hours' time. They'll put John on it. He should be here by tomorrow afternoon."

Rat-tat-tat, the master acts, the master speaks. *"They'll put John on it.* What about John? Doesn't he have a say? The last thing in the world he would do is break his word."

"You know what John wants," he interrupted her. "You always did." He paused, and some unsaid thoughts about her defection came across from him to her. Then he smiled. "I was wrong," he said. "I've always been wrong about the boy. He must try his own adventure for himself. If he succeeds, more power to him. If he fails, let him fail alone."

"You're not going to cut him off?"

"Don't be ridiculous," he said. Simon hesitated. "Which reminds me, darling," he said, what pleasure and pain in hearing him say that word. "How is the cash situation?"

"Oh, fine," she said. "David is earning lots." In fact, he was earning less because of a bottle at his elbow, or on the sideboard noon and night, and sometimes mornings.

"You've never used the income of the Trust," said Simon. "It's yours. Why not?"

"Because I don't deserve it," Anna said. "We don't need it either," she said. They still scraped comfortably through for whisky and other necessities of life, if not for new girdles, undercover frills of life.

"You took nothing," he said, "not even that necklace." He looked at it on her neck and in her portrait. "Some pride, I suppose," he said. "More honesty. Sometimes I wish we had parted with dishonor."

"I know," she said. "I thought of pinching the Corot and the Canalettos, but I didn't have the guts to do a thorough job. I'm glad, though," she said. "We meet as friends and lovers now again."

"But that trust money," he said. God, he was a persistent mammoth terrier with a bone. "It's going to waste."

"No," she said. "The children will get it."

"The children won't need it," he said. "I know you need it. Please take it now."

"No," she said.

"You never could take," he said. "You only could give." He said some things to her that afternoon to make her wonder. "People pester me all my life for money, and ninety per cent of the thanks I get are only hopes for more. But you want nothing for yourself. Are you too proud to take it?"

"It's not that," she said.

"Father said: *They don't come better.* Do you remember?"

"I remember," she said. "And I remember the night of dear Father's funeral. If they don't come better, they don't come worse."

"Promise me something," he said. "That if you need money, you will use it."

"Darling," Anna said. She went into his arms. It was no good. "Don't let me cry again."

"Then go and fetch my plutocratic coat," he said. "You left it in the bathroom."

When she came back, he was saying: "Oh, Kippen—you might get me two taxis. I want them now."

There was a difference in the lordly air of those for whom their fellow men went scurrying. The differences accrued. She smelled the daffodils, and saw a magazine named *Summit Enterprises* on the table. "The old house!" she said, but she did not mock him with *The Birthplace of Our President*. She thought that on the whole our President had put up a fair fight against the perils of his legend. "Gallery," she said. "How I would love to go there again, not to our house, but the old house."

"You easily could," he said, "if John lives there. He has to live somewhere with his pen and ink. We might do it over for him." Now Simon Skafe had another project: *Get that boy started on his writing.*

"You'll have to see what John says," Anna said, with emphasis on *John*, tactful woman, she had had her way.

"There is one slight snag," he said, "about John living on the farm. You know I sent him North at pretty short notice?"

"Yes," she said. "I know."

"The reason was that one morning, when I had just reached home, I took that short cut from the farm to the house through the cedar woods. We caught two trout, and then had a little dip together once, if you remember?"

Anna laughed. "I remember," she said. "Go on."

"I was sitting, having a cigarette. Enter John and Molly Phipps. They passed by oblivious and very much entwined, in fact so evidently enamored that I decided I'd better pack him off before worse happened."

"Oh, really?" she said, not always so honest as Simon thought. In John's last letter he had written: *I have a sort of clue that the reason the old man whisked me here at three days' notice was that he tumbled to a warm romance I was having with Molly Phipps last summer. Perhaps Tom Beamish dropped a hint to him, I wouldn't know. Anyway, I hear that Harry Hicks's marriage to Molly has been sweetened almost blatantly with everything from checks to washing machines to a trousseau fit for any princess, so I have suspicions. I was mad keen on her, but now I'm over it. Somehow the thought of that stud-bull Harry Hicks is putting off.* "It could have been awkward," Anna said, "even if when Adam delved and Eve span, the Phippses were a first family too."

"I knew you would say that," he said. "I remember thinking of it at the time." He seemed to have been thinking quite a lot. "Now she is married to Harry Hicks, the farmer, an ideal match. But what about John, I wonder, if he lived there?"

"I wouldn't worry, Simon," she said. "Young people forget when a thing is done."

"I suppose they do," he said.

The telephone rang. "That's the taxis, sir," the doorman said.

"Good, Kippen," he said. And to her he said: "You'll telephone Sally later, will you, Anna? Give me time to get home. And we haven't met."

"No, Simon darling," she said. "We haven't met."

"Until sometime, then, my love," he said.

"Yes," she said, "until sometime somewhere."

"You go first," he said. They kissed one another lightly, quietly, softly on the lips. And so they parted.

The elevator trundled down. He went back to close the paneling on Anna's portrait, which one cabinetmaker had seen in its hiding place, and he and she had seen. Then he did some remedial chores, like folding bath towels, stripping a bed, flicking powder off a dressing table. Tidy after careless Anna. He looked at the city in the night. "We meet as friends and lovers now again," he said, and he left that place.

The taxi driver discussed the Jordan crisis. He was an English immigrant, a loquacious one. "They got a decent climate there," he said. "What they want to fight for, sir, I ask you?" He was tired of Montreal in March, as anyone might be, even people with that city in their bones.

"Who wants to fight about anything?" said Skafe, philosopher, and said no more.

Grace was at her dressing table. "You're late, dear," she said as he bent to kiss her.

"Yes," he said. "I had a sleep, and then I had a drink, and then I had a bath."

"You look rested, Husky," she said. "Much better for it. I was so proud of you today. Fifty people must have called to say it was the best speech they had heard in years, and quite inspiring."

"Oh, good," he said. "What a lovely dress that is," he said. "How many people for dinner, I've forgotten?"

"Thirty, dear. Someone's sure to propose your health, so you will have a few words ready, won't you?"

"I guess so," he said. "But I'm spoken out. What do I say?"

"Just say that you're the best husband on his fiftieth birthday that any woman ever had."

"Okay, then," he said, and he kissed her again, and he went to put on his dinner jacket.

CHAPTER THREE

SLEEMAN and Syme got up to leave. "I hope you enjoy your trip, S.K.," said Miles, "not that I envy you those arctic breezes." He said it easily, no longer at pains to dissimulate about the frozen bee in S.K.'s bonnet.

"I'll see you at Turtle, sir," said Syme, who did not waste words.

They left thus, casually—the one for the Lakes to straighten out Algonquin at the administrative level; the other for Turtle Mountain to hand over within the next month or so to his successor, and then to take on from Wilson Pitt. Miles Sleeman was just forty, and Peter Syme was thirty-eight.

"You picked two good horses there," said Willie Pitt.

"Yes," he said. "But you trained them, Willie." He remembered occasions in the past ten years when he had sat back himself and had let old Willie (to whom every working man was a fellow man) take Sleeman apart. But now Willie's active days were done. He would move up in semi-retirement to be Chairman of the Board of Summit Enterprises, taking that over from Bob Carter, who was getting out of most of his directorships. "Miles learned a lot from you, Willie," he said.

"Not a sausage from me he ever learned about finance."

"True," Skafe said, "but you taught him the facts of life."

Skafe was going north, and then he was going south. When he came back in six weeks' time, Miles Sleeman would be in full executive control, responsible only to Skafe himself. So Willie Pitt had taught the younger man the facts of life, leading to the moment of his own eclipse.

Willie taught him a lot, thought Skafe, as they left the board room. And Miles taught himself a lot. But I was the one who taught Miles balance. It was a theory of Skafe's, or a conviction, that balance was the key to real quality in men and their works. "Well done, Willie," he said.

"Well done yourself," Willie said. He shambled off, short of breath, overweight, too red in the face. One of these days the sterling man would finally go pop. The doctors had been warning him for years.

Everyone has to go pop sometime, Skafe thought. He summoned Mrs. Murton, dictated various letters to her, and said to her: "When I'm away, and now that Mr. Pitt is moving to the chairmanship, I want all policy matters channeled through Mr. Sleeman."

"Very good, Mr. Skafe," she said, wondering, he knew, because of the carte-blanche tone, whether Mr. Skafe himself intended some sort of semi-retirement. But what Mr. Skafe intended was not retirement. He intended now to follow Mac's advice, proffered one night by a salmon river. *So you think I'm too big for my boots,* he had said to Mac. *All you need,* Mac said, among other things he said, *is to rest your feet and contemplate your navel. Then you'll see what I mean.* "Henceforth," Skafe said, bowdlerizing him, "I intend to take more time to think about the larger things."

"That's so wise of you, Mr. Skafe," she said.

"How is your husband these days?" he asked. Mr. Murton's diabetes had been a shadow over this good woman's life for many years.

"Not much change, Mr. Skafe," she said, and went on to explain with an ex-nurse's relish about Units, NPH, blood sugar, whatnot—and to explain in sympathetic terms the burden that the unending injections were, and worse for him now that he had heard of a new drug from Germany which could be taken orally, but it was not yet available . . . So now Mr. Murton's hopes were raised . . .

"Would it be any help if I wrote Hans Rademacher at Essen? He could put his people on to finding out."

"Oh, that would be wonderful, Mr. Skafe—so kind."

"Not at all," he said, "the least I can do." He dictated the letter to Rademacher. "You open the answer if I'm away," he said, "and if Rademacher suggests treatment over there, consult with your husband and his doctor. Then, if they're agreeable, lay on a trip to Europe, at our expense, of course. You might like to take in England too, Mr. Murton being well enough."

"England in the summer," she said, after thanks gracefully expressed. She did that well. "It's always been my dream, Mr. Skafe, so beautiful and old—Oh, Stratford and the Abbey, all the ritual, those quaint thatched cottages, everything."

"Fine, then," he said, stemming the tide. "I hope it works out. What else do you have this morning?"

"That's all," she said, "except that Sally wondered if she could see you, Mr. Skafe, if you're not too busy."

"I'm here," he said. "Sally's there. She brings stuff in all the time."

Mrs. Murton gave a quaint thatched-cottage sort of laugh. "It's just that I think she wants to ask you something for herself, and you know how Sally never presumes in office hours. So I'll ask her to come in, Mr. Skafe, but first I want to tell you, sir," she said in gathering tones, "that Sally has been a treasure to me in the office, just a treasure, Mr. Skafe."

Mrs. Murton went out, leaving a hint with *has-been* that the treasure's office days were numbered; and after a minute Sally arrived, wearing a plain woolen dress, from Eaton's probably, no better than any of them wore, except that it clothed Sally.

She left her troubled private life at home. In six months in the office she had somehow, and incredibly, contrived to change the atmosphere, to make Skafe a sort of father image around the place. Now men and women positively beamed good mornings to Sally's Dad. It was ridiculous. It was her magic.

"Hullo, darling," he said. He might have made some light remark about only daughters asking for interviews with only fathers but she had that melancholy air which worried him so often when she allowed herself to be her private self these days. And so he said: "Can I help you, pooch?"

He sat by his table. Sally went to the window and stood, her back to him, her mother's younger figure to him. He had not spoken to Anna again, and Sally had not spoken of her talks with Anna. Piers Whitfield would be the subject coming up. The more he thought about it, the more sure he was that Piers would make the right husband for her.

"A zero day," she said. "The trees will be snapping in the woods. Daddy," she said. "There's not going to be much pressure of work in your office this next month or two, with you away, and especially now that Miles is taking over, is there?"

"No," he said. "It will be quieter."

"And you're flying straight to Turtle Mountain tomorrow?"

"Yes," he said.

"And switch planes there; then on to that Nunangiyak place?"

"Yes," he said with patience. She had seen his itinerary.

"I want to ask something for myself."

"Ask away," he said.

"Will you let me take a job at Turtle Mountain?" She kept on looking out of the window, her exquisite figure silhouetted against the window.

"*You?*" he said. "But why on earth?"

"Because I want to," she said. "You always promised you would take me North, and you never have. I'm asking you to take me and to leave me there."

"But, my dear girl," he said. "Do you realize that the temperature this morning at Turtle Mountain may be forty-five below? Do you realize that the breakup doesn't come until July? Do you realize . . . ?"

"I know all that," she interrupted him, "and I know that there are women and families at Turtle Mountain. So why not me?"

"But *why* you?" he said. It was preposterous.

"First," she said, "because, as I told you, I have always longed to go North. Second, I think the idea of a productive community of a thousand people in the wilderness is fascinating in itself—I mean the ordinariness of it, like a mining town in Ontario or Quebec, people just doing a routine job; and then the Turtle Saloon, the school, theatricals, the hi-fi group and all the rest. Jennifer Syme says there is more community spirit at Turtle Mountain than anywhere she has ever lived. And Peter told me that some of them even buy their houses from the company . . ."

Sally's dejection was gone. She seemed enthusiastic.

"Yes," he said. "We encourage them to own their homes, on a buy-back guarantee, of course. It makes for stability. What we have found at Turtle, as they have found at Port Radium, is that there are plenty of Canadians—not cranks or misanthropes—who, once they get used to it, prefer that life to life Outside. They go to the office, just as we go to this office in Montreal; but they find a spirit and a comradeship beyond working hours that doesn't exist elsewhere. It is largely a matter of management, of course. And the essence of our management principle is that we manage as little as possible, apart from the job itself . . ." He talked on a while, forgetting how this most interesting and important topic had cropped up.

"So then, may I come with you? I happen to know that they're short of girls in the manager's office." She would happen to know anything she needed to know to work to her ends.

"Sally," he said. "It is one thing for you to work here in Montreal, and you have done admirably, but . . ." He paused, in search of words.

"You have your North," she said. "Why shouldn't I have it too?"

First his son could not abide the North, and now his daughter wanted the North. What a ludicrous situation. "There must be another reason in your mind," he said.

"There is," she said. "I have to get away. If I go to Jamaica to stay with Mummy, it will be the same old thing. So I'm going somewhere right away."

"There are women and children at Turtle Mountain," he said, "but they are in a small and sheltered minority, and they are not Sally Skafes . . ."

She rounded on him. "So you still harp on about my habits. I want to go to Turtle Mountain to make a corner in pants, you mean."

"Don't be childish," he said. She was no exception to the rule that they did not forget and they did not forgive, or they could forgive until they thought of it again. "What I mean," he said, abandoning diplomacy, "is that unless you lived in total purdah, you would disrupt the place. It's not your fault, darling," he said. "It seems to be the nature of my sex."

She was not amused. "Have I disrupted this office?"

"You have been an excellent influence in this office. But this office disperses to the four winds at 5 P.M." He awaited some ultimatum from his daughter. He could see an ultimatum coming, and it came:

"Very well, Father," she said. "Either you let me prove that you are wrong, or I'll go away altogether."

"Go where?" he said.

"Oh, I think Paris first," she said. "Then Rome. All the conventional places where the best fun can be had. In other words," she said casually, "I'll go whoopee on the town."

He left his table and walked past her to the window to look at the ice on the river, at wisps of ice-fog scudding down above the open waters of the river, and to see a wolfish horde—smooth Frenchmen, debonair wops, expatriates, existentialists, pansified ballet dancers, counts of the Holy Roman Empire, skilehrers, gondoliers—all the riffraff to ferment the rich girl's honey. He saw it or them with horrible certainty against the river.

He was not dealing with a melodramatic girl of twenty-one. He was dealing with Sally Skafe, the one person who could meet him and match him in all respects, and whose troubled moods had baffled him for months. She could control herself, impose upon herself to be the treasure of the office; but a volcano had been brewing, and this was the eruption. *Either you let me go to Turtle Mountain, or you lose me altogether. Take your choice.*

"Very well, damn you," he said. "Go and see Olssen about arctic clothing, and buy exactly what he tells you, not what you think you will need. We take off at eight tomorrow." He looked at the river in the zero weather. It would soon be spring down here. He thought about the young man who had caused this theater. He was sorry for him and about him. There was a trivial appeal of snobbery, but there was quality in Piers, not only of intellect, but of a life ruled by code, by inflexible standards of behavior, not unlike Bob Carter's standards, and they were vanishing. Anna had been wrong, but he could not interfere. Give Sally time, and she might change her mind. "So Piers is off," he said abruptly.

"That's rather obvious," Sally said, now suddenly in tears.

"Piers is the one you might be sorry for," he said.

"But I am," she cried, and left him.

He summoned people to instill ginger into operations. Sally's dad stirred up Head Office, and sent morning tremors through the empire from Halifax to Vancouver. Then, some steam blown off to some good or bad purpose, he told Mrs. Murton that he would be back at half past two.

She was nervous of him when on the warpath, but she set her jaw and said: "I'm so glad about Sally, Mr. Skafe, dreadfully as I'm going to miss her. I know it's the very best thing for her that she should get right away from it all just now."

He emitted a testy grunt, wondering what would happen to affairs if he escaped from it all to Turtle Mountain or to Rome and Paris whenever life proved difficult. Then he left for luncheon. "Have you seen about that arctic clothing yet?" he asked Miss Skafe in the outer office.

"I will as soon as Mrs. Murton comes back from her lunch hour, Father," she replied with dutiful respect.

Pickering drove him to the club, where he got rid of his hat and coat and rubbers, washed his hands, and waited in the hall. Then he went into the room to watch Sherbrooke Street, along which, seven minutes late, his son came walking. He wore a parka without the hood. John had not returned with an explorer's beard. The less they did up there, the more like youthful Father Christmases they tended to descend upon the South. But John had done something, and he knew it; yet was not quite proof against strolling bareheaded through Montreal when the temperature was one below zero. *I was hoping for a bright hard day with a squeak in the snow*, his mother said the other afternoon.

John came in now. "Am I late, Father?" he said.

"Not noticeably," Skafe showed him to the cloakroom. Then he returned to write *John Skafe* and *S. K. Skafe* in the book. S.K. had grown to be the fashion. They called him S.K. to his face, and spoke of him as *Husky*, or plain *Skafe*.

He took John into the bar. "What will you have?" he said. "The rye sours are good here. Or a dry martini?"

"A rye sour sounds fine," John said.

He ordered two, it being a celebration that called for more than his habitual sherry or Dubonnet. "Some of us are not very keen on this bar idea," he said. "It seems out of keeping with the dignity of the club; but the younger fellows wanted it."

John smiled, and he said: "Are there younger fellows, Father?"

"Not by your standards." The drinks arrived, and people drifted over to say hullo. "You know my son John," he said. "Just back from the North."

John stood to shake hands gravely. He had acquired or had inherited that *gravitas* from his namesake. His hair was too long, and his collar floppy, but he looked quite respectable. He looked like a tweedy young literary type, more English than American, and not Canadian.

"So you're the lad who has been pioneering in the Arctic regions?"

"Not quite pioneering, sir."

And someone said: "Did you enjoy it?"

"In retrospect," John said. "At the time there was always that warm caboose to think of."

Skafe remembered from his own days—the blissful prospect, not of a comfortable bed, but of a bare floor in a shack.

"How do they all seem to know about that cat-train trip?"

"I happened to mention it in a speech I had to make. You needn't look so pained," he said.

And someone said: ". . . A chip off the old block, it's good to see."

"Let the chips fall where they may," John remarked when he had gone.

"You two are having a high old time," said Busty Maxwell, Cynthia's father. Indeed, it would be good to see, as it was to sense, some merry accord of father and son.

They had a table to themselves at lunch. "What about Sally?" said John at his oysters. "Are you going to let her go?"

They would be in cahoots, oh doubtless. "I saw no alternative," Skafe said. "She posed me Turtle Mountain or going on the loose. But if Miss Sally imagines that I will let her change her mind when she discovers what life in the middle of nowhere is really like, she is far mistaken."

"You know she won't change her mind," John said.

"I know she is headstrong and spoilt," he said.

"You're not fair to Sally, Father. She is very fond of Piers."

"If she is so fond of Piers—and he's a splendid fellow—why doesn't she marry him?"

"For a fairly sound reason, Father. And if Sally is spoiled, you shouldn't blame her. She didn't do the spoiling."

"You mean that I did?"

"I mean everyone did. That old chestnut about power applies to adulation too." He had always been a thoughtful boy, and now he had a measure of self-confidence.

"The same thing will happen at Turtle Mountain," said Simon Skafe. "You might as well coop up eight hundred bachelors with a youthful Ingrid Bergman."

John smiled, but he said: "I don't think so, Father. I think the boys will put her on a pedestal."

"Perhaps," he said. "And when some bohunk takes her fancy. Then what?"

"Then either she will like him well enough to marry him, or she will have nothing more to do with him. She tried with Piers, and it wouldn't work. You mustn't blame Sally either, Father, for heeding what you said to her."

"I don't," he said. "I blame our self-indulgent society that glorifies and cheapens and romanticizes sex. I think there is much to be said for the arranged marriage. It works far better."

"You think that, do you, Father?" John looked at him coolly, speculatively. Why? "So you deny love, Father," he said.

"No, John," he said. "I do not, surprisingly enough." The grilled lamb chops arrived. "As a matter of fact," he said, "Sally seemed extremely interested about Turtle Mountain, about all our northern ventures." Which is more than you ever were, or ever now will be, he thought.

"She always has been. I never remember your leaving for the North when Sally didn't say how much she wished that she could go."

"She used to ask," he said. "She hasn't asked for years until today."

"She's been having a good time growing up," the pundit said. "My sister has a strong vein of Good-time Charlie. But another reason Sally will like Turtle Mountain is that she likes people as people, any people."

Meaning that you do not, Skafe thought. "Well, John," he said. "What is your northern balance sheet?"

John hedged. He liked some things, and some things not too much. ". . . I must go back in the summer to see life in the North. The sea ice doesn't exactly live." And now John wandered in thought, but he came back to say: "I'm grateful to you for sending me, Father. I disliked some aspects quite a lot, like being cooped up with people I had nothing in common with, or just being cooped up with people. I'm not gregarious, like Sally. But it was the best thing yet, on balance."

"I was thinking this morning," Skafe said, "about the growth of Miles Sleeman, actually—I was thinking again that without balance a man, a thought, an enterprise is nothing. When you write your novel, I suppose you will have to think of balance, a foot on each side of the seesaw."

"Balance," John said, with surprise and respect. "I won't forget that."

They had Brie cheese, neither too grand a luncheon nor too plain. When a man learns at last to talk with his son, a man may be grateful. A man may even be pleased with himself about his wisdom in facing facts, whatever regrets he may have.

". . . She was saying last night," John spoke of his sister again, "that she is completely with you about Canada's character and so-called destiny lying either in the North or nowhere."

"And you?" Skafe said.

"I'm not a nationalistic type," John said. "I don't know that it matters so much if geography asserts itself. We're virtually Americans already."

"Are we?" Skafe said. He felt some warmth around his Loyalist ears.

"You're not, Father. Nobody here is." John looked round the room. "But they are not the people. And don't misunderstand me—that talk about St. James Street being a conspiracy against the honest workingman is so much crap. You only have to know a few people like Mr. Merchant and Mr. Carter to know it simply isn't true. Blacks and whites," he said, smiling at his father. "Extremes, my anti-hobbyhorse. I wonder if I can ever write the shades of gray which are the truth. But what I really mean is that it doesn't much matter Canada being swamped from down below. What matters is that if we don't look out, we shall all be swamped from up above. I thought of it often in the North."

"Swamped by war?" Skafe said.

"No, Father—swamped by peace. All the Russians have to do is make convincing peace. They believe in something. We believe in nothing. Watch what happens when peace is declared."

"But what I advocate," Skafe said, "does involve belief. On the one hand you decry nationalism; on the other hand you say that we believe in nothing; from which you conclude that we do not strive. Correct?"

"Correct, Father," John said, "except for bread and butter and bigger cars."

"You want no blacks and whites. Okay then, tell me how we strive with grays."

"You're quite an argufyer," said John Skafe, evading it.

"I haven't worked things out," Skafe said. "All I know is that men must strive or wither. Your hobbyhorse and mine," he said. "If the two could meet, we might have something."

They left the dining room. He thought about his hopes for John, and they were lost, and with the lost hopes had gone John's awe of him. Which, at least, was a credit item. But now he would write gray novels, and what adventure would there be in that? And yet there was a spark in the boy, almost a bite now in him. Perhaps he would make a road of his own to success alone. More probably he would not. And Sally? They said often that Simon Skafe was a living legend of success; but he had failed in some things some people thought to be the most important things in life—his son, his daughter and their mother. Thank God for Grace, he thought.

John was leaving by train for New York tonight; then flying with Anna to Jamaica. They would sweat it out together, hating flying to Jamaica. Skafe had a most poignant longing to be with Anna, flying anywhere;

but he put that from him. "How long will you stay with the Dorriens?"

"A month or two, I guess," John said. "Long enough to get my ideas straight."

"And after that?"

"Could I live at the old house at Gallery, do you think?"

"We can make it over for you, certainly, a good idea. There is only one thing, John," he said with care. "You're sure you wouldn't find it difficult in any way to live on the farm at Gallery?"

"No, Father," John said, looking at him. "Not in the least. You needn't worry."

Which, added to a previous remark, told Skafe that John had tumbled to the fact that he had known of the Molly Phipps affair. "That's fine, then," he said. "It should be an ideal place to write."

"Perhaps Mother could come and stay sometimes—out of season, I mean?"

"She would like that," he said. He did not think that John was aware that he had seen John's mother. Or would Sally have told him? Or did Sally know, in fact? *We haven't met*, they said at parting. "How did you find your mother, John?" he asked.

"Just the same," John said. "The best value of anyone I know."

"Yes," he said, and when he looked up, his son was watching him. "I must get back to that office," said Simon Skafe.

They stood on the steps in the zero weather. The Bentley slid up. It was a handsome car. "Can I drop you anywhere?" he said.

"I think I'll walk," John said. "Thank you for everything, Father, including lunch. It was damned good fun to talk to you." He had seemed at ease most of the time in the club, but now his old shyness attacked him as they stood alone together on the steps. "I'm sorry I've failed you," he said.

"You have not failed yourself," Skafe said. "So how can you have failed me?"

He was rewarded by John's face at that pontifical and paterish and right remark. My God, we clicked at last, he thought, and sat in the car beside the curb. He watched John stroll along Sherbrooke Street, toes turned out, arms slack at his sides, Mr. Head-in-air. There goes my boy, he thought. The rush of traffic passed, and Pickering drove off.

CHAPTER FOUR

TODDY did not come to speed the parting family. She waited in her sitting room, the door ajar. Nothing would be said if you forgot, but there would be Scottish sniffs and huffy gloom on next arrival.

"We're off then, Toddy," he called. "Are you there?"

"I'm here," she said, appearing in the door, "and you're aye off some place. John home three days and away again. And now Sally—yon's the daftest notion I ever heard. She wouldn't be going to them Arctic places if it was me."

"Nor would she if it was me," he said.

"Sally was a terror from a bairn," Toddy said, and sighed. If John and Sally were his bairns or children, bright hopes and disappointments of his life, they were all Toddy's life to her. She had set her heart on Sally's marriage to Piers Whitfield, the Honorable Piers, a Lord one day. Toddy was an honest expatriate snob, who knew a real nice gentleman when she saw one. "But I ken fine I shouldn't have said what I said, I was that vexed with her," she said now. "Mebbe you could tell her from me, Mr. Skafe."

"I will," he said. He gave the old girl a kiss. "We shall be thinking of you, Toddy. Be good while I'm away."

"You've been a grand man to me," she said.

Grace was ready in her blue mutation mink. Agnes, the parlor maid, opened the front door for them. "Goodbye, Agnes," he said. "Be careful of strange men in Florida."

She giggled, Mr. Skafe was such a card. When master and mistress went spring cruising in the Caribbean, lesser capitalists took off for Florida. Toddy stayed here to hold the fort.

"What are you smiling about?" Grace said in the car, the rug on their knees, the dignified back view of Pickering through partition glass.

"I was thinking of the one and only time I blew my top at Agnes—the night before I paid a surreptitious call on you in Ottawa. Remember?"

"How would I forget?"

Oh, God, he thought. Here we go playing the remember game. Her supple hand found his, and held it on her knee. She had slept with him all night last night, after somewhat surprising him by appearing from her bathroom in stiletto heels and this fur coat, a well-heeled call girl stepping out of shoes and mink.

The one put on his coon, the other took off his mink he gave to her for Christmas; just one of those psychic coincidences that happen to a bigamist, he supposed. "Elmer Kirby cabled," he said. "The *Fair Alice* is at English Harbour, all provisioned, if you want to take some people out before I get there."

"Oh, I don't think so, dear," she said. "I think I'll just laze at the Nelson Club until you arrive. Unless the Binghams happen to be in Antigua. Rex is such fun. I might take them to St. Kitts or somewhere for a little cruise."

"They're not due until the twentieth," he said. "I heard from Rex." Rex Bingham of General Futurities in Cleveland was quite a boy. Skafe thought that the owner would prefer to be on that cruise.

They drove through Westmount, between snowbanks six feet deep or high, a sordid growth of winter, but the sun was shining on dirty snow. "It will all be gone by the time we come back," Grace said, holding hands. "Just to think that I shall be on a beach tomorrow afternoon, and you will be in some horrid igloo in your deerskin suit."

"We usually take them off inside," he said.

"In your birthday suit, then. That sounds worse in some horrid igloo." She was quite skittish for half past seven in the morning, going to Dorval with him to see him off. Gregor, the houseman, had driven Sally out ahead with baggage.

"Toddy takes a dim view of Sally going to Turtle Mountain."

"So do I," Grace said. "I think it's absolutely mad. I think it's the craziest thing I ever heard."

"Oh, I don't know," he said. After twenty hours, or however many had elapsed since the young lady put a double-barreled pistol to his head, he had quite grown used to the idea. John seemed to think that she would be all right on a pedestal at Turtle Mountain; and John was sound about some things. She is full of faults and full of guts, that girl, he thought. The prospect of flying with Sally for her first glimpse of his North was enormously exciting. "What, Grace?" It had been some remark about Sally and her mother.

"Nothing, dear," she said. Her hand lay soft and slack in his. There was little traffic at this hour, down to Decarie, and on past Ruby Foo's, and round to strike for the airport. Pickering was a sound driver at moderate speed. If Skafe was in a hurry, or if he felt like action, chew up miles, he drove himself. Sally could drive fast too. In so many things she had his touch.

"It's only a week," he said. "I'll be thinking of you." Now he pressed the hand that was a comfort to him.

"I wish you didn't have to make these trips," she said. "I think it's time you settled down to be your age in lots of ways."

"I am," he said. "I really am. You watch."

"I watch the Skafes come and go," she said. "John gets his marching orders, and Anna comes, and John comes back, and he and Anna go, and you and Sally go, a four-ring circus for me to watch." Her hand slipped away from his. "I wonder if I should start a little two-ring circus of my own." He kept his hand on her knee. Something like something seemed to be in Grace's mind. "How was Anna?" asked gentle guileless Grace, and she looked at him.

"The children both said she was fine," he said, batting no eyelid. He took his hand from her silken knee and put his arm round his wife, and then he kissed her in a comprehensive fashion to let her know what was what.

"You're the most awful musser-up," she said, making repairs. She took a Kleenex to him too. "There," she said. "Pickering is watching us in the mirror."

"Let him," he said. He thought that Grace, so conventional, so predictable, so simple a comfort of a loving wife, had read a riot act to him in the most deviously civilized fashion imaginable. But how did she know? Or did she know?

They drove round a Skafair hangar, and to the Crusader where Sally was standing with the pilots. "Good morning, Roy," he said. "Good morning, Dicky." Young Farmer had been two months in hospital with that arm, but was as good as new again, or he was better; less bounce in him; more man in him.

"All set, Father," Sally said, in her office personality. He had told her that she could damn well work her passage as stewardess-secretary and baggage mistress. Now she said goodbye to Grace, whom she used and took for granted, of whom she was very fond; but the wall of reserve on Sally's side persisted.

"Au revoir, Grace darling," he said, "until next week."

"Goodbye, darling Husky," she said. "I'll be waiting for you every single minute."

"In your mink coat on a tropical strand?" he inquired privately, and she giggled at him, and did not want to let him go. "Bless you," he said, almost saying *I love you* in farewell, which he might possibly have said, and wished afterwards that he had said, looking out of the cabin window at her, what a pearl of a glamour wife and helpmeet to a man to whom she had recently hinted: *You watch your step or else . . .* Anna, suspicious (in the days when Anna bothered), would have taken a meat cleaver or a guided missile to him. Grace blew him a kiss as they taxied out. The President blew one rather sheepishly back.

They flew all day to the west and north, over a smoke-feathered city in the snow; a black race of river in the snow; a railroad line that cut the wilderness of forest, rock and lake; a town within the wilderness; and on. Spring had not come, but the hold of winter was not absolute.

Farther north it was absolute. "I see what Jock means about a death of winter," Sally said, "but I don't agree. Methinks our Lady sleepeth underneath her counterpane. What a cozy thought," she said, like her mother. " 'For we be also a people, said our Lady of the Snows,' with acknowledgments to Mr. Kipling on the Tariff. Or be we? Shall I brew us up some coffee?"

"Not for me," he said, "but the pilots drink gallons of the stuff."

Sally took two cups of coffee forward. She did not play at being airline stewardess, but was stewardess to the devoted manner born, if not dressed for the job. Miss Skafe gave satisfaction when she set her mind to it. He dozed again, and when he woke, she sat across the aisle from him. She did not read that day. She watched Canada slide past below them.

"A penny," he said. But perhaps she was thinking of Piers Whitfield, so he should have left her with her thoughts.

"I was thinking I would like to fly North forever," Sally said. "The world a pinprick inside space, and us a pinprick above the North. *It's big hard country*, you said once to me when I was small."

"Did I?" he said. I should have brought her long ago, he thought.

She looked out again. Then she turned in her dark plum ski pants and blue suede jacket. If Sally was getting away from it all to deny the world at a northern mine, she was flying there in sensible clothes of becoming colors. "Tell me," she said. "Where does this drilling for oil in the Arctic Islands lead to? I mean, supposing you do strike it rich, what markets can you hope to reach competitively?"

"None now," he said. "But some day we might keep an ocean passage open through to Hudson Bay, and by the Bering Strait. And some day, perhaps sooner than that, we might be able to ship by nuclear submarine tanker underneath the ice cap."

"What about harbors? Aren't the Arctic coastlines shallow? Surely that would be a problem."

"So it would," he said, for the thousandth time impressed by the way her mind drove to practical essentials. "It happens that there is sufficient depth at the Nunangiyak Islands, for example. Whether we strike oil is another matter. Whether—even if the oil exists in quantity—it can be exploited is still another matter."

"And still another lovely gamble," Sally said.

"Yes," he said. He talked about some wild ideas that might never come. Then he told her the story of Turtle Mountain, which many people had said was a wild idea. How many people said that now? But uranium was a special case, and the big findings in 1948 a monumental stroke of luck. They had to have the stuff. He took his risks and found the stuff; and now for the present, he reaped the profits. *All that Turtle Mountain will ever contribute to the world is profits for you and atom bombs,* her mother said. But Sally said now, when he had told her the story of one wild idea become reality: "I have no patience with the prophets of woe who say we're going to blow ourselves to bits. I always tell Mummy and John that the surest way to be blown up is to hide. We can't halt the world in the past, and I don't want to. I'm for the moon and beyond."

"It's a long time since we have had a chance to talk about things together," he said. In these recent years she had skimmed off the cream of her quality with beaus and pleasure. Then life had caught up with her, he thought, in the shape of a good young man, to whom she would eventually return, he hoped. But now, flying North with him today, she was Sally again. "I'm glad you came," he said.

"So am I," she said. She went to get lunch ready for the pilots while Skafe had a glass of sherry. Since he had given up flying himself—that was a mid-century resolution and surrender to Grace—he saw no reason to deny himself the minor indulgences when airborne. Sally came back laughing.

"What's the joke?" he said.

"Dicky says I'm the best not-so-little cook in the North Countree," she said. Which remark by the ebullient Dicky Farmer rang a bell somewhere for him.

The Commissariat, Mrs. Simon Skafe, had provided a bang-up lunch —*pâté de foie gras,* half a bottle of hock, *fricassée* of chicken heated by the stewardess, fresh fruit and cheese. "There's nothing like roughing it with Father," Sally said in the cabin of the Crusader flying North, the dark-flecked carpet of the forest and the rock, the smooth white carpet of the lake, not a road, not a plume of chimney smoke to tell of man.

They took on fuel at Fort Smith, where he had landed last summer with Roy Thompson on their way to find Mac and Dicky Farmer. They flew again. Sally wore Mac's charm or talisman, his small brass pig on a gold chain on her wrist. She wore it always now. *Dear Mac,* she said at the

326

time. *No good tight boat for him.* Mac's death had grieved her. It had contributed to the malaise, Skafe thought.

They crossed Great Slave Lake. "Is that a pressure ridge?" she asked about a darker line that snaked across the white as far as could be seen.

"Yes," he said. "They can be tricky on the lakes, on the sea ice too."

"To cross you mean?"

"Yes," he said. "They're awkward with dogs, and damned treacherous in a bulldozer weighing eight or ten tons. We test them for thickness, of course."

The north shore of the lake, and now a town. "So that is Yellowknife," she said, having read the guidebooks to the bleak far land. She was a puzzle to him and a delight. Most people were appalled at a first view of the bleak far land. The pinpoint settlements served to accentuate the emptiness, the nothingness, for them. But Sally stared in a fascination stronger than she might feel about the Côte d'Azur or the Caribbean.

The sky was blue, and the day intensely bright. Now the ribbed white earth had blurred. "Why?" she said. Her hair was not blond, but halfway dark with a shot of gold in it against the sun, cut short in that charmingly careless new way that girls affected.

"Wind," he said, and wind might disrupt his plans. Which thought of minor troubles was strengthened soon by the intercom buzzer. "Yes," he said into his telephone.

"Can you come up a minute, sir?"

He went forward. Both engines were running sweetly.

"Turtle looks a bit doubtful, sir. Gusts up to thirty-five already, and they expect forty. It's one of these polar highs on the move. No warning, down they come."

"Oh, damn," he said. It was not bad weather. It was fine weather with a wind strong enough to fog out the land, ground-blizzard fashion.

"We may just get in," Roy said. "But it will be nip and tuck. We have plenty of fuel. The snag is that if Turtle is no good, then the Wells and Yellowknife are sure to be socked in solid before we get there. That means either a long way south again, or into the Dewline. I checked with Fifty-Eight. They're in the clear all the way along. But then there's Sally."

"Yes," he said. Miss Skafe was an exhilarating boon companion to him. But if they could not get into Turtle or somewhere with accommodation for women . . . To turn round and fly south again would be an unmitigated nuisance when he was due at Nunangiyak tomorrow. "The thing to do is go and see what Turtle looks like."

He went aft to the cabin. Unless he was flying himself—but those days were over—he left the pilots to it.

"There is some doubt about getting into Turtle," he said.

"Where do we go then, Norman Wells?"

"It's blowing there too," he said. "We might have to turn back, or even sit down on the Dewline for the night."

"What fun," Sally said. "I would love to sit down on the Dewline." She smiled, looking out of her window, asking no more questions. If she was thoughtful, it was not about being cut off from the land by a fog of driving snow. She was wholly without the disquiet that preyed upon so many people in the air.

Great Bear Lake was an indeterminate white, a thousand feet, ten thousand feet below them. "It's impossible to judge our height at all," she said. Another thing that Sally had flirted with was flying—she had taken her license at eighteen, and let it lapse, which disappointed Mac. She had no purpose in those years.

"Great Bear Lake," she said. "It's deep, isn't it?"

"Yes," he said, "immense and clear and deep. Angus Sherwood calls it a gigantic pothole."

"Who is Angus Sherwood?"

"A man of the North," he said.

Soon they were losing height to Turtle Mountain. "There it is," he said when they began to circle on a perfect afternoon. It was only the top of the hill, jutting out of cotton wool. He had thought of the North many times on that hill. "I see the Turtle's nose at last," she said, as they swung in from the west. But that was all they saw.

"No dice," said Roy Thompson's voice, harsh on the intercom. "It's either south to Hay River or Smith, or into the Dewline."

"I'll call you in a minute, Roy," he said.

"We're North," she said. "Don't let's go South again. I couldn't bear it."

He did not like that idea himself. "They're doing a construction job in a pretty rough place," he said, "and they're not equipped to handle women. Besides . . ."

"Can't I sleep in the plane?" she said.

"I suppose you could," he said, and called the cockpit. "Better make it the Dewline, Roy. Tell them at Turtle to let us know immediately that wind shows signs of dropping. And I want the Lynx ready for me when I get back there." Or would he get the Lynx to come to Fifty-Eight? No, a waste of time.

"Roger," Thompson said. They headed northeast and climbed again.

"How far is Camp Husky from Turtle Mountain?" she asked.

"About three hundred and fifty," he said. "Three hours plus in a Lynx."

"And when is the cat train due up there?"

"Tomorrow afternoon," he said, "if the weather holds."

"This weather?"

"No," he said. "That weather. It's a flat calm beyond the coast." And he told her something of arctic weather.

"So it all depends on your getting back to Turtle first?"

"Yes," he said, "unless there is something on skis available at Fifty-Eight."

"Don't they need all their planes for shuttle work?"

"Oh, well," he said. "Skafair supplies the Dewline. We're pretty good friends."

She laughed. "*We're pretty good friends* is lovely big-business talk. You didn't tender for Dewline construction, did you?"

"No," he said. "We're up to our eyes in the North already. I wanted to get more people's eyes involved. They're doing a good job, too, both outfits."

"Do you have to get to Nunangiyak to meet the cat train?"

"I don't have to," he said, "but this trip completes a most successful supply operation. I want to be there to see them arrive."

"So you will be there," she said, and smiled.

Dicky Farmer brought a message: "Sorry about windy welcome see you later Lynx in state of readiness regards Sally from us both. Syme."

"Send: 'Thanks,'" he said. "And 'regards from Sally.'"

"Roy wants to know, sir," Dicky said. "Do we break the news to Fifty-Eight about our stewardess?"

"You'd better warn them before we land, too late for protest."

"I hear a mighty howl of protest, Mr. Skafe," said Dicky Farmer gravely, and went forward.

"Will I be a nuisance?"

"I don't think he quite meant protest," said her father.

"You needn't worry," she said, her face closed off from him. She was a prickly prima donna, sometimes childish.

"I'm not," he said, although the impact of a girl like Sally on an arctic camp where men worked twelve or fourteen hours a day and ate and slept beside their naked pin-ups and their lurid amateur art might be upsetting. He had no experience of that. When they brought the families to Turtle, the houses were ready, furnished, stocked—so, one day a bachelor establishment; and the next day children played in snowsuits. But Turtle was entirely different—in personnel, in routine production. A brief stop like this would be all right, he thought. The only way it could be avoided was by flying south again, which he did not want to do, and would not do. "The Barren Lands," he said.

"You lived there once, didn't you?"

"Yes," he said, "my first winter in the North. We trapped, mostly arctic fox; and we hunted caribou, along this country south of the coast." He saw a cold kaleidoscope of that winter.

"You and Jim Willis?"

"Yes," he said.

"That was before, I suppose?"

"Yes," he said. "Before your mother met him."

"What kind of a man was he?"

"There was no better trapper in the North, when Jim would trap." Skafe thought about Jim Willis, a man long gone, but men who share hardships never quite forget. "Jim would give you the parka off his back," he said, "but he would sell the parka off his back or yours for booze. He was a decent dipsomaniac, and a good friend on the trail away from it."

"Poor man," she said. "Mummy never talked about him, any more than she would talk about our Frazer grandfather."

"No," Skafe said. "Your mother had unhappy memories of the North. That was part of our trouble," he said, looking down at the barren lands. The wind had dropped. Fly on! he thought, as they flew on to the arctic coast, from the wasteland to the waste of ice.

"It's wicked and wonderful," she said. "Or perhaps not wicked—impartial and remote and cold, John's death of winter. It's impossible to feel from up here in this ritzy comfort. But I don't think I would hate it."

"No," he said, "because you wouldn't fear it."

"You don't fear anything," she said.

"I do," Skafe said. "I fear heights, except from an airplane. I fear depths. I fear being sick. I fear myself, and what I am capable of." He had told her some fears as they reached the white desert of the sea.

Now the sun rode low. The sun gave a warmth of color to the cold as it dawdled to meet the rim of the west. They came down to Fifty-Eight, which was to be a radar station in the chain across the North to give distant early warning of aerial attack.

There was one long low building, shaped like a train, an elongated trailer or a florist's box. In the middle of the building was a frame of girders for the radar dome, not yet in place. Beside this building was the temporary camp. And everywhere, on a still evening after sunset, rose the shafts of white, of man-made warmth at one speck in the wilderness of white. "It looks like forty below, by that smoke," Skafe said.

He and his daughter dressed. They fastened their seat belts. It was sweltering. The Crusader came in to touch on frozen gravel. The engines roared with props reversed. They taxied in and stopped. Sally smiled across at him. "The wrong place," she said. "But we came to it."

CHAPTER FIVE

THE CONSTRUCTION boss was named Henniker. He was a small man who accepted mixed company as just another thing to be coped with. "Best if you and your daughter don't mind sharing my tent," he said. "I'll move next door for tonight. There's room in a bunkhouse for the pilots. Okay, Mr. Skafe?"

Skafe knew how such men worked and survived, having been such a man in easier circumstances than these. To protest overmuch served only to confuse another quick decision made. "That's darned good of you," he said, before Sally could offer to sleep in the unheated cabin of the Crusader, which creaked already to a seep of cold.

"Let's go, then," Henniker said. "It'll soon be suppertime." He was hospitable in an absent way, deferential in an absent way. This chap is driven hard, Skafe thought.

The air was so perfectly still this evening as the sunset faded, that, standing, you felt no cold but a catch of breath. The stillness contrasted with a hubbub intensified and particularized by cold. Their bags were in the back of Henniker's four-by-four.

They climbed from the airstrip, past a bulldozer ploughing snowdrifts. The driver was an Eskimo, smoking a cigar. Then they were up at the camp, the long low stilted building to the left, tent-roofed huts to the right. "You're well along with the modules, I see," Skafe said.

"We're coming," he said. "Pretty near finished except for the radar installation—but that's their headache."

"Whose headache?" Sally said, between them.

"The boys who foot the bill," Henniker said. "We're only the hired help around this place."

"How long have you been here?" she asked.

"A year ago, February," he said. "We pitched a tent, the four of us."

"So you began it and made it," she said. "That's more than just being the hired help."

"I guess it could be," Henniker said. He stopped at the end small hut of a line, got out and left the engine running.

There were two bunks, one unoccupied, a table between the heads of the bunks, a space heater, a pail of water on top of that. Henniker rolled up his sleeping bag. He seemed calm, but it was the calmness of a man who dares not be fazed by anything, lest everything should faze him. "Can you come along a minute, Mr. Skafe?"

Outside again, he said: "Here's the toilet. All yours. I'll tell the boys it's off limits for tonight. Okay, sir?"

"Okay," Skafe said. A latrine reserved for management was one of management's few and precious prerogatives. "I'm sorry about this," he said, not particularly sorry, but grateful.

"Think nothing of it," Henniker said. "I'd better warn them we got mixed company. They're not a bad bunch of boys. She won't mind a whistle or two?"

"No," he said. "She won't mind a whistle or two." It occurred to him that Henniker had seen no more of Sally than two eyes and a nose in a parka hood. He went into the tent again. She sat on a bunk, and fingered Mac's piglet on her wrist. "Only me," he said. "Are you all right?"

"I'm fine," she said, looking less than fine for the first time in this long day of flight and change. "Slight qualms about all those men at supper," she said. "The cattle show, I mean."

There was the loud clangor of an electric bell through the loudness of mechanical sounds. Henniker arrived in a few minutes. His eyes made startled appraisal of Sally without her parka. The cattle show, Skafe thought. He saw Sally's point.

"Is that your son?" she asked about the plain boy of eight or ten on the table between the bunks.

"Yes," he said. Henniker looked from Sally in her soft blue suede jacket to the picture. There was no photograph of a wife. But she was too worldly-wise to ask directly about a wife, if no picture. "Only kid," he said.

"He's like you," she said. "He will be your spitting image when he pitches his tent to build some other Dewline." How charmingly she paid respect to this small man.

"When you're ready," Henniker said, and they dressed again for a cold hundred yards. Men moved from the splash of light at each bunkhouse door, and across snow on a starlit night, muffled latecomers converging on the dining hall.

"Do the bulldozers and everything run all the time?" she asked.

"Day and night," he said, "when they're not on the blink or in for maintenance."

"So it's never quiet here," she said. "I hadn't thought of that. I suppose Turtle Mountain is the same."

"There's always a racket," Skafe said. Once only in the productive years had he known Turtle Mountain quiet.

They shed outer clothing in the porch, a hundred parkas already hanging; a clatter of eating, a buzz of talk beyond the door. She would not know that men talked little while they ate in dining halls like this. They entered to an absolute silence within the noisy camp. "Up the other end," said Henniker. He went beside Sally, Skafe following.

He looked at the faces, but few eyes considered him. It was the least noticed entrance he had made in years, following Sally, not one whistle, to the table where she turned and smiled at the room and said: "Hullo, everyone," entirely composed.

It was roast chicken for supper. Twice chicken today, he thought, helping himself to plenty, with dressing, green peas, synthetic brown gravy and mashed potatoes—similar food to Turtle Mountain. You fed them abundantly and well, or there was trouble.

He sat on the other side of Henniker, facing down the room. At this table were the camp foreman, the timekeeper, two American electronics men. He must have eaten a thousand times at such a table, looking down the same long hut at the same heterogeneous collection of men, or these men might be younger in average. He could judge the spirit of a camp with fair accuracy at a first meal in the dining hut. But not tonight. All down the room the men had their apple pie, or stewed plums and cake; and then sat drinking coffee or tea, and smoking. Talk usually started after the meal. But there was constraint, and little talk except at this table.

Again he was reminded of a silence—at Turtle Mountain when a strike was on, a hushed dining hall at night, a hushed camp on that morning with McClintock. Now, unreasoning, he looked here for McClintock, the dark Scotsman. He looked carefully around, table by table, a dark man's head, or a gray man's head, a saturnine face among the bearded—blond, black, sandy, wispish, thick—among the unlined cleanshaven faces. But, of course, there was no McClintock here. There was a hardy annual named Simon Skafe, to whom no one paid attention.

Was it unreality, or was it a complete reality crowding at him from before? "Sorry," he said to Henniker on his right. "I didn't hear."

"I was saying it's ten days since we had mail in the camp. I keep telling them if they want the boys happy for Chrissake get the mail in regular, but I waste my breath."

"That's too bad," Skafe said, sensing that Henniker wanted to tell his headaches, troubles. To give him that chance would be the best way to pay for a night's board and lodging at Fifty-Eight on the Dewline; but Skafe did not much want to be his small brother's keeper. He wanted to get the hell out of this place, shed it, leave it, go on.

Now one of the electronics men angled about his business. It seemed that a small word about a big Canadian tycoon had not reached the modules, or they might not know in Little America up there that such an animal existed. "I'm a business man," Skafe said, that being less grand than an industrialist. He had a good solid opinion of himself, but he never put on dog.

"And she's your daughter?"

"Yes," he said. "We were flying to Turtle Mountain, but the weather closed in."

"That's the big uranium mine. Now let's see—the Van Ingen people run it; you with them?"

"No," he said. "Van Ingen do have a minority interest, but Turtle Mountain is Canadian controlled."

"You sure about that?"

"Yes, I'm sure," he said.

"You don't say," his neighbor said.

Silence again in the long hut with ice at the apex of the rafters, and Sally said to the young timekeeper, an Australian, sitting across the table from her: "I had a cobber called Cobber," she said, and paused, and added with bland innocence: "He was a jackaroo."

The men here laughed, and the men there smiled about a girl's small joke they had not heard. Supper was over, but they waited.

"I guess we'd better make the move," said Henniker.

"Thank you," she said to the room. "I do hope your mail arrives to-morrow."

Thus she spoke for a world elsewhere, and they left. "Was I right to say something?" she said in the tent again alone with him.

"You were," he said. He thought that she had behaved impeccably to be a good reminder for them. "You measured up," he said. "You always do."

The pilots came in, bringing a fog of cold at the foot of the door, but it was too hot. "What's the news, Roy?" he asked.

"It's blowing now everywhere south of the coast. They don't see any change for Turtle until late tomorrow."

"Oh, damnation," Skafe said. He wanted to get to Nunangiyak; he wanted to get the hell out of here, from all the old camps crowding him, from McClintock, cold sane madman, and some other skeletons, and yet he had not seen a single man he knew among the men. "What's the weather west and north of us?" he asked patiently. God, he had to be a patient man. "Sit down," he said.

"Set fair," Roy said. "Winds five to ten, northwest. Temperature going up to thirty below tomorrow."

"How cold is it now?" Sally asked.

"Forty-four below zero."

"You hardly feel it," she said.

"The heat loss at fifty below in still air is less . . ." And Roy Thompson, phlegmatic ox who would chew a grounded cud contentedly from now until Easter if the wind or the President decreed it, began an exposé about heat loss.

"Is there anything on skis available?" Skafe said, interrupting that monologue.

"There was talk of a Lynx due in, sir," Thompson said. "An operator overheard some radio chat along the line, but nothing definite."

"Oh," Skafe said, and none of them spoke for a minute or two while the outside sounds went on, and the pot burner pulsated quietly at full blast to heat a space about ten by eight by seven with snowblocks around the walls to break the wind, and a canvas roof, and not a stir of wind tonight, this evening, so many hours and so many miles from the house in Westmount above the Boulevard where the day had begun, and this was arctic comfort, four people sitting two by two on the edges of two bunks, what madness moved the human race. "I didn't hear you," he said to Dicky Farmer.

"The fellows in the modules wondered if you and Sally would visit with them for an hour, sir," said Dicky Farmer rapidly, put off his carefree stride by the Old Man's terse *I didn't hear you.*

"Not for me," Skafe said. "Henniker asked if he could drop in." And what my small host asks of me, he thought, *noblesse oblige* accords to him. "Do you want to go, Sally?"

"If Dicky will come along. Yes, I'd love to see the . . . what do you call them?"

"The modules," Skafe said. "Unit construction. I suppose they realize that Sally doesn't have security clearance," he said to Farmer.

"Yes, sir. The idea was more of a social visit."

"Take care of her, then," he said. "I may be up later on."

Thompson thought he would check again on the weather situation. Thus, Skafe's three traveling companions left him with some alacrity. He pulled his sleeping robe from the bag, unstrapped it, unrolled it, and lay on top of it, thinking what a damned nuisance all this was, until more knocks, like a boudoir—Henniker, with a frozen patch the size of a dime on one cheek, but he thawed it with his hand.

"Have a nip to warm you up," Skafe said, producing the bottle of overproof rum from his zipper bag. He thought that a nip might improve his own state of mind.

Henniker declined with thanks; then said: "We have to be death on liquor, but I guess the boys won't smell me tonight."

They drank rum and tepid water. It was an encouragement, and Skafe rarely needed that. He saw that Henniker drank for pleasant warmth, not for a mounting compulsive need. It could be the dirtiest trick you could play a man in the North to offer him a drink, and you never knew until he drank. But this man was all right.

What he needed was a catalyst to cleanse him of his troubles. Sally once called Mac our catalyst, Skafe thought. Now he leaned on his elbow on his bunk, and was catalyst to Henniker. It was absurd that the man would trust him, S. K. Skafe, so powerful that a few words from him: *I'm not sure Henniker at Fifty-Eight is quite up to it, been in too long perhaps, seemed to have the job on his back*, would be enough to sidetrack Mr. Henniker.

If a man annoyed him, Skafe might do just that. But this was a decent fellow, hard-driven, with big brother now to tell it to—mail, weather troubles, jealousies, delays in supply, ingratitude, resentment at Americans calling the tune, but they were good guys themselves, the debits and the credits, blacks and whites, even a few of John's famous grays.

To be a good boss meant never to let your men see you weaken, and probably Henniker rarely did. So Skafe, who did not weaken to pour it out to any big brother, gave an hour of his time and a little advice, and became Hero Skafe to another man. "I feel one helluva lot better for just talking to you," Henniker said.

He stayed apart from them; he could be forbidding with them and ruthless with them. But he had only to say to an employee or to a stranger: *How are things?* and they poured things out to him.

"That's a dandy, that girl of yours," Henniker said. "No airs about her. She makes a man see what a woman could be like, makes a guy feel better, so the boys are saying."

"Sally is a good kid," he said.

"The wife ran off with a goddam chiropractor," Henniker said. "So the boy's with his granny."

"Oh," he said. "I'm sorry." The wife ran off with a goddam artist, he thought, so the girl's with her dad, who has another wife to make a guy feel better.

"I would like to do that," he said about visiting the modules, and with the intention of collecting Sally.

They met a breeze as they walked up there, the least flow of air, but enough to strike on nose and cheeks. A single-engined plane flew over, and circled out above the airstrip lights. Beyond the airstrip was the frozen sea, and beyond that sea the continent began. "Roy Thompson heard that a Lynx might be in," Skafe said. He was much interested in anything suitable that might be in.

"It's news to me," Henniker said. "But half the time you never hear nothing. Bingo, another one arrives, top secret. The security on this thing is crazy—planes flying all day, sending ETA's all day in clear—and look at the labor force, Ukrainians, Polacks, God knows what. No wonder Moscow Molly tells us all the Dewline dope."

"But does she?" Skafe said, through hoar frost on the fur of his hood.

"I guess not," said Henniker. "I guess mebbe that's all rumors." They were at the end of the building, camp lights behind them, the North Star and the northern lights before them, but the northern lights were weak. They rippled up and faded altogether. "You get brassed off," Henniker said. "But it's worth it for the job we're doing."

"Yes," Skafe said, and was drawn to him, and would say no word to make Henniker question the worth of the job they were doing.

"Like a ship is the way I see it," he began his explanation, forgetting or not knowing that Skafe's own interests had done much to pioneer this stilted ship on land, which swallowed ice to be melted as a side process by the diesel motors—thus: heat, light, water and humidity, a closed sewage system. Yes, it was like an insulated air-conditioned ship. So, on a smaller scale, was the camp at Nunangiyak.

They entered past the ice conveyor belt—which was giving trouble—and went on by powerhouse, water tanks, radar area, washrooms, and living quarters. The doors were open along the corridor. He noticed half a dozen men in one room, but no Sally. Where had she got to? Always an anxiety to him, a damned nuisance to him here and now. He and Henniker came to the radio room at the end of the building, but no Sally.

Roy Thompson was here, leaning against a counter by the main transmitter. Three men stood in the middle of the floor. Two were listening, facing Skafe. One was talking, his back to Skafe. He did not speak in a conversational tone, nor did he rant. He raised his voice in brazen uninhibited exasperation. "I get instructions to have a Lynx at Fifty-Eight to fly a party of three east along the line tomorrow. Okay, I'm here, and now you say that you won't fly tomorrow early, and when you do fly, won't be by stages east, it will be eight hundred miles west to Alaska, God Almighty, in a Lynx—and we have a Venture aircraft and two pilots sitting on their bottoms doing nothing."

They were patient and apologetic. They had not known that a C-124 was due with equipment. They must wait for that. As for Alaska, they were sorry about the switch. Someone had slipped up in not passing that signal. And yes, they did understand about utilization, but they would ensure that Aurora . . .

"It isn't only utilization," said Brian Fiske. "It's the pilots. We try to do a decent job, but how can my boys do a decent job when they never know where the hell they are? Warm up, cancel. Who wouldn't be browned off? It's not good enough," he said. "And this damn silly security is half the trouble."

"That's what I say," said Henniker, who had joined them.

"We can't help it about security, Brian," said the taller American. He seemed a good type, conciliatory and patient. "Everyone knows Aurora is doing a darned fine job," he said.

Skafe looked at Thompson, and raised his head, and Roy came over. "Any change in weather?"

"No, sir," Thompson said.

"I see a chance, then. If you took this party west in the Crusader on subcharter to Aurora, I could take the Lynx on subcharter to Skafair. Sally is the only complication. Where is that girl?"

"She went back to your tent," Thompson said. "I sent Farmer with her, and told him to wait if you were out."

"Good," Skafe said. "She can't stay at Fifty-Eight. She can't go with me. You could take her. How would that be?"

"That might be okay," said Thompson. He was slow except in physical emergency, infallibly reliable about a million dollars or a woman. "You're set on meeting that cat train, sir?"

"Yes," Skafe said. "I am." He might have explained, if he could have explained, but he did not bother. "Come and see what they say."

Fiske held his parka on his arm. He wore a green quilted waistcoat of nylon or silk. "Hullo, Brian," said Skafe.

"I heard you were here," Fiske said. "My God, Mr. Skafe, it's good to see you."

"And you," he said. And it was. He had met many men, but few men with this young man's force. He should be building the whole damned Dewline, Skafe thought, not running a shoestring outfit under impossible flying conditions. "I have a proposal," Skafe said. He made his proposal in general terms, and said goodnight, and took Roy with him to the door. "Fix it somehow," he said. "Come and let me know what you arrange."

He went down the steps from the radio room, and looked at the thermometer. It had risen to thirty-nine below. A bulldozer was still cutting back snowdrifts in this respite from the arctic winds. The camp worked on by night. Dogs howled at the Eskimo village down at the shore. He walked on packed snow to a perishing private latrine; thence to the tent, and went in to find Sally and Dicky Farmer sitting in silence, but Farmer stood to leave.

"Roy is in the radio room," Skafe said. "You had better go and have a word with him. Goodnight, Dicky."

"Goodnight, Dicky. Thank you for looking after me."

"A pleasure," said Farmer, and said goodnight, and left.

"I'm becoming a thanks-to-the-gentlemen phonograph record," Sally said. She yawned. "Madly sleepy," she said, "But first I must seek the geography."

"I'll show you," he said. He went with her to stand guard away from that place, to be troubled by a waggery or aphorism of Somerset Maugham's about the functions of the female of the species, an offensive cleverness to him, but perhaps he was squeamish. Anyway, it had put him off Mr. Maugham for keeps.

"Gosh," she said, emerging. They went back together, and brushed their teeth and so into sleeping bags on bunks. "What's the plan?" she said. "I know something's cooking."

"Why?" he said.

"Because the glint is back in Father's eye."

"A Lynx has come in," he said. He outlined his switch idea.

"And what about me?" she said, facing him, her cheek on her hand. Anna used to face him like that.

"You can't stay here alone," he said. "I think you should go in the Crusader. If Turtle is clear by that time, they can drop you off—otherwise the Alaskan trip. That's a town. They could look after you properly there, if you had to stay over."

Sally shook her head. "Oh, dear," she said, and looked at him again. "I've come so far. Please can't I go to Nunangiyak with you?"

"It's out of the question," he said. "Four hundred miles in a single-engined plane to a place like that? Impossible."

"But the camp is a small version of these Dewline modules. You told me so."

"I told you so," he said. "And I'm saying No."

"And why should you risk yourself with any old pilot just because you have this bug to get there somehow, anyhow? They were saying tonight up there that some of the pilots are terrible. One man's nerves were so shot that he started out four times in perfect weather for Yellowknife, and turned back each time with some excuse about the gaslines freezing up, and the fifth time he taxied out and stopped and got out of the plane and ran away from it."

"I wouldn't fly with any old pilot," Skafe said. "But I would fly with Brian Fiske, the man who took me in to find Mac. Yes?" he called.

It was Roy Thompson. "That's fixed, sir," he said. "As a matter of fact, it helps everyone out. And we raised Camp Husky—perfect conditions. The cat train should be in on schedule around fourteen hundred to-morrow."

"I have been trying to persuade my father to let me go with him," Sally said. "Not that I don't like flying with you . . ."

Thompson looked at her thoughtfully, and at Skafe thoughtfully. "Brian Fiske will be ready at seven," he said. "Goodnight, then."

He went out, leaving Skafe with the impression that Thompson would prefer not to take her along to Alaska. A responsibility he did not want? Some other reason? Some other reason such as Dicky Farmer, the irrepressible, the gay of spirit, sitting glumly here with Sally. Enough was enough. Enough was too much, was the *femme fatale* of the polar regions. And it was not her fault . . . She did not want it now. It was not her fault that in her were combined an extraordinary physical appeal and an extraordinary comradely, vital appeal, the girl men hoped to meet but no man quite had met before. And if Simon Skafe were to be honest with himself, he could not deny that he felt it too.

Now Sally knelt beside the other bunk to say her prayers. Once upon a time he used to say his prayers. He wondered now as he watched her praying; he wondered if life was a slow corruption from the truth of childhood. It was a thought or a fear that had bothered him occasionally, and it bothered him now, watching Sally pray.

"Shall I put down the heat a bit? It's wide open at Seven."

"To Five, I guess," he said. Even then it would be too hot to lie in a closed arctic sleeping bag, designed for forty below, supposedly. He unzipped his down the side.

"Goodnight, darling." She kissed him on the forehead. "We came a long way together."

A long way toward the islands far from land, he knew what she meant.

Sally switched off the lamp at the head of her bunk. Electric power was commonplace in the Arctic nowadays. Such air-conditioned apartment houses as the one up there would soon be commonplace. But outside was the cold.

The stove flickered. He turned in his search for sleep and saw that Sally slept. But sleep stayed away from him. *I would like to fly North forever,* she said today. *The world a pinprick inside space, and us a pinprick above the North. It's big hard country.*

"But, Piers darling, don't you understand?" she said in the tent in the noisy camp in the wilderness.

Now Simon Skafe fell away to sleep, not to peace and a nothingness of sleep, but to dreams, to this dream, and again this dream: He sat on a sled behind the driver, idle Skafe watching the ice, the forms and the fancies of the ice until the other team came chasing up, the big white lead dog, behind it dogs two by two in double tandem, and the leader homed on him, trotting strong and steady a thousand miles a day, right up now, right here. *I'm McClintuck,* said the lead dog.

"What's the matter, Daddy?" she said, across from him.

"Sorry," he said. "I had a dream." Now sleep was kinder.

CHAPTER SIX

FAR OFF to the right was land. On the port side a dark ellipse of cloud reflected open water many miles away. Ahead, the sea ice went on to a vague meeting with the sky. Four thousand feet below, the snow was featureless. Above, the sky was blue. They were an hour and fifty-five minutes out—halfway, he supposed. All's well, he thought, comfortable and contented behind Brian Fiske and Sally.

He dozed a little, hearing *One—Two, Buckle my shoe,* the words of the rhyme saying themselves for no reason with no meaning to the periodic of the engine rhythm, or that kind of marriage. He heard Fiske try for contact ahead with Nunangiyak and back with the Dewline, but he made no contact.

Skafe was dozing nicely until things went wrong, not gradually as could happen flying, nor in catastrophic fashion as could happen, but decisively in the form of a viscid deluge of oil on the windshield. The oil pressure dropped.

Fiske throttled back and put down the nose. "What's it like your side?"

"The right corner is almost clear," Sally said.

"I'll take that seat. You get back. Look for a lead," he said to Skafe.

Visibility was good, but there was a oneness, indeterminate white, and no perspective except in the roughest ice. It was hard to make out . . .

"There, I think," Skafe said. "Yes, there!" One stretch of smoothness between a relief of broken ice.

"Right," Fiske said. He turned for it, and looked over his shoulder. "Not in the seat," he said, "on the deck, facing aft, soft gear behind her back. Quick now!"

Skafe undid his belt, and arranged Sally and sleeping gear as instructed, thinking that if they should bounce, she might be worse off unstrapped on the floor than strapped in a seat. "Okay?" he said.

"I'm fine," she said. "But I'd rather see." Her face was pale.

Skafe sat again. The windshield was now opaque except in that dwindling corner through which Fiske peered. "It's okay," he said, "but too short for comfort. Hang on."

Skafe saw the ice, snow-covered mounds, bare green triangles, crazy columns rising to his side window, and then the Lynx was down on the lead, hitting hard, not bouncing, skis trundling, slowing, almost stopping, and he braced his hands against the seat in front. "Hang on," Fiske said again. They struck at a modest speed, no more than ten miles an hour, crunch, stop. "Get everything out!" A few minutes from *One—Two, Buckle my shoe* to abandoning ship at the end of a lead on the sea ice.

Skafe threw most of the gear out to Sally, and passed some breakables to her, working fast against fire, but no fire came. "That's the lot," he said outside.

One propeller blade was bent in by ice. The port wing rested against a spear of ice, and gasoline feathered from it to melt a patch of snow on the lead. The fumes were not strong. Fiske held an extinguisher, but the oil smoke stopped. Sweat beaded into hoar frost on his forehead, and now he pulled up the hood of his parka. "No bonfires, anyway," he said.

"You did well to get us down," Skafe said. Half blinded, he had done well.

"I did badly to pile the bugger up," Fiske said. He climbed to the top of the pressure ridge against which the plane had run. Skafe and Sally joined him.

In every direction the ice rolled like a bumpy countryside—fields, boulders, crisscrossed walls under snow, but a splash of green ice here and there. "Is a lead where the ice formed last?"

"Yes," Skafe said. "Or it can be open water. What now, Brian?"

"I'd better try to raise someone before the battery gets cold. Can you pitch the tent?"

"Yes," he said. "You have a snowknife?"

"In the grub box." Fiske jumped down. He looked at the bent propeller. "That settles that one," he said, and he went into the cabin of the Lynx.

There was a faint breeze from the west. Skafe probed with the snowknife, found a good place in the lee, and pitched the tent with Sally. It was light single canvas, a two-poled tent. "Shovel some snow around the foot of the walls," he said, and went to seek a drift of uniform consistency for snowblocks. It was a long long time since he had cut a snowblock. His nerves were steadying.

"What next?" Sally leaned on the shovel. "I slightly thought we'd had it," she said.

"In another half minute we would have been blind," he said. "With another pilot we might have had it. Are you all right, pooch?"

"Yes," she said. "Keep me busy."

He lit the gas stove and told her how to melt snow for tea. Fiske was calling on the radio. Skafe went back to cutting long snowblocks, eight altogether, he was clumsy at it. Then he set up his windbreak round the head of the tent.

"You cut a nifty snowblock," Fiske said. "Where did you learn to do that, sir?"

"In my salad days," he said. "Did you get through?"

"Not a peep out of anyone. The nearest is about a hundred and forty miles, and at this time of day at sea level . . ." He shrugged.

"What's the temperature?" It was twelve below zero by the plane thermometer. The sun was now hazy, the rim of the sea ice indistinct.

"Tea ready," she called from the tent.

A tarpaulin on the snow, boxes to sit on. "It's as warm as a house," she said. They drank sweet tea at noon, ate frozen doughnuts and discussed the situation. They had not left Fifty-Eight until nine, delaying to watch a monster C-124 open its maw and disgorge many tons of equipment.

"We were due at Camp Husky around one," Fiske said. "So by two, things might begin to buzz; by four or five someone will be looking for us—probably the Crusader, if they haven't taken off before we're missed."

"Weather permitting," Skafe said.

"Do you think it's going to blow?"

"In my day it usually did from a quick rise in temperature."

Fiske smiled. "Or from any change," he said. "Or it just blows. When did you winter in the North, sir?"

"Nineteen thirty to thirty-two," he said, but he thought: In forty minutes from now we would have been circling that tractor train—the yellow cats, the drilling gear on the sleds, the smoking caboose, archaic modern caterpillar crawling at four or five miles an hour into Nunangiyak. But here, perhaps there, perhaps everywhere, it was going to blow. The tent was perfectly still. The gas stove hissed. Now he put might-have-beens away.

"It was an oil line, I suppose," she said.

Fiske nodded. "A fracture from the union. It's just had a five-hundred too." He put down his mug on the snow of the tent, laid the back of his hand against his eyes, and took it away. He looked tired, drained out. "Sorry," he said.

"You got us down safely," Sally said. "We have food and a tent and a stove, and all the snow in the North to make tea. Don't apologize."

"Things go wrong," he said. "It's somebody's fault. Therefore mine."

But he smiled, sitting on a box in his dressy green waistcoat, quilted swansdown. "What next, would you say, sir?"

"Tie down the plane," Skafe said. "How much snow is there on the lead?"

"An inch or two."

"Then we'll have to chip ice to set the toggles. Melt us lots of snow," he said to Sally.

She pumped up the stove. She was as adept with mechanical things as her brother was clumsy.

"Come on," Skafe said. Fiske seemed dull after his immediacy of action, brilliantly taken, but now only passive measures to be taken. Skafe knew the feeling, the let-down condition; he would be over it soon. In the meanwhile, take charge of him. "If it blows," he said, "it may blow all round the compass. The plane faces west. Shall we settle for west?"

"Whatever you say," Fiske said.

It took some time to chip small trenches with the hatchet, one for each wing and the tail, and set the anchor toggles, a line to each, and pack them with snow, and add water to freeze them in.

"That should hold her," Fiske said. "If they harden in time."

Now the sky and the snow were one. Now you could see to a pressure point a hundred yards away or to a sea mountain twenty miles away, whichever, whatever it might be. Now you could not distinguish flat snow from a hummock at your feet, subdued immeasurable world. "It is extraordinary," Sally said.

"A white-out," Skafe said. "*Hila kapuk*, the Eskimos call it." He was pleased with himself for remembering.

"And so quiet," she said. "Like a great din of quietness."

"Yes, it's like that," Fiske said. "What now, sir?" He was cheerful and alert again, but not bossing the expedition. He went to the plane. "One above zero," he said. "Spring is with us."

"And so is the wind," Skafe said. It came quietly, a puff from the west. Sometimes the winds came with stealth. Sometimes they came full strength out of calm. This vanguard of wind brought chill, and did not stir the snow, and passed on to the east. "No sleeping skins?" he said, meaning for the floor of the tent.

"No," Fiske said. "You can't get caribou for love nor money."

"We can use my deerskins. Separate them, Sally, all fur to the outside."

"Won't you wear your deerskins?" she said.

"Not in a tent. Put everything we need inside with us, and the rest back into the plane. Quick, now!"

It was almost three o'clock, time frittered away in the muted weather. Now the wind grew as they did the few things still to be done—deerskins, tarpaulin, food, gas, kerosene, lamps, a .30-.30 carbine in a case. Fiske came back from the plane. "Everything aboard," he said.

"Check the tent pegs," Skafe said, the boss. Well, naturally.

They watched the wind grow from the west to pick up snow, to run gravelly wisps of it, modest beginning, an idle scurry of white along white. The wind gathered to pluck at the snow and spin it to snowdevils that scuttled merrily along the lead, this way and that way to die against the walls that framed the lead. And now the wind rapped on the tent, rap-smack, rap-smack.

Inside, she said: "I thought fine weather was the forecast."

"So it was," said Brian Fiske. "But highs, lows, warm fronts, cold— the Met boys can't compete. You usually get some warning, and I guess there was today for those who heard it."

"Have you often had to do this?" she asked.

"I've had to sit down for weather a few times," he said. "I never cracked up on the ice before. We could have made it in a Mink," he said. "We could have made it in the Lynx in colder weather."

"Why?"

"Because cold snow is slow snow." He laughed. "But we didn't make it. No more spilt milk."

"You don't spill much. Who runs Aurora when you're away?"

"Tim Roncaroni is my Number Two," he said. "He's in Yellowknife at the moment. Are you hungry, sir?"

"I'm famished," Skafe said. He explored the emergency rations, a Skafair box, an Aurora box. This fellow could have managed Skafair, he thought, starting at—what was it I offered him?—starting at twenty-five thousand, on top of a whacking good purchase price. But no—he had to run his own piddling show, and run into this sort of thing, just what I warned him about, a crack-up or two—Goodbye, Aurora. "There's stew," he said, "or bully beef . . ."

They agreed upon stew and dehydrated potatoes. Skafe let the others do the work. He took his middle-aged ease as wind grew to pester the tent on the sea ice, and he watched Sally slice shavings deftly from a snowblock to fill a pot, two aluminum pots, and set them on the burners. She put her bare hand to a can of stew. "No," Fiske said. "That sat at thirty below in the plane all night. It'll burn you." He touched a finger to cold metal, and showed it to her, the tip blanched instantly white, but color came back.

"There's lots to learn about this kind of picnic," Sally said. She seemed engrossed and happy; and now, using a glove, she put the can of stew into melting snow.

"We might as well light the primus for tea," Fiske said. It made a throaty roar in the tent, which was hot.

"How are we for food and fuel?" Sally said.

"A week's rations anyway," he said, "two gallons of kerosene, plenty of gas. We're sitting pretty. Listen!" he said sharply, and pushed his head out through the flap.

The stove and the primus made small loudness in the wind. Fiske came back, his head white with snow, but he rubbed the snow from his hair and eyebrows. "What was it, Brian?" Skafe had heard nothing out there but the wind.

"A plane, I thought," he said. "Probably not. Did you hear anything?"

"All I heard was the wind," she said. "They wouldn't be searching, would they, in this?"

"A waste of time," he said, "or worse." He had black hair, as black as Anna's when she was young—wet black hair, and a wet face, red from the wind, grayish eyes, life in this young man in the pallid light of the tent. "Here, I'll do that," he said, and employed the can opener.

Now the stew was hot, the potatoes ready. "Supper's up," she said. They ate from tin plates with spoons.

"Full marks to the cook," Fiske said. He was quite pally with her in a casual way, like John with her.

"Yesterday we had *pâté de foie gras* and chicken and a potable hock for lunch in the Crusader; today the best stew in the world for supper in a tent. Life with Father. You're quiet," she said to him.

"I was thinking," he said. He had been thinking that by now the news would be out; by now Grace would be at the Nelson Club in Antigua, BWI, and someone would have told her. Dear Grace, he had been thinking. *Husky Skafe overdue in Arctic*, he had been thinking.

The wind grew by lull and by gust to higher points of strength. The direction was changing. It had begun from the west, square to the eight-foot pressure ridge, the tent in the lee, the strike of the wind at the peak of the tent. But now the wind was backing south.

They had pilot biscuits and raspberry jam. How delicious the hard-tack tasted. What well-being from Brian's strong tea. "Warm and snug," she said, "while the cold world thunders. I must look out." Sally parted the flaps. "Not so nice," she said, turning to sit again, and she shivered from cold, or at a first sight of the fiend out there. "What if the tent blows away?" she said.

"It won't," he said. "But we could build a snowhouse. I remember the first time I was caught in a blow . . ." And, telling her of his fear that first time, he eased Sally's horror of the blind white rack that she had glimpsed.

"You love it," she said. "You thrive on storms and trouble."

"No," he said. But he did in a way. "It's like being sick," he said. "You see through to the essentials. One essential is that I shouldn't have landed you in this."

"I landed myself," she said. "Plumb up to my neck. You know I did."

"Yes," he said. He laughed at his daughter whom he had cosseted and spoiled all her life, and he had worried about her and had almost lost her, and she had prevailed upon him, and here was his daughter.

"I would say she landed plumb on her two feet," said Brian Fiske. He smiled his vital smile at each of them, and then he said: "That thing on your wrist—Mac's porker, isn't it?"

"Yes," she said. She undid the chain and handed it to him. "Mac left it to me, and now I seem to be a Jonah." She spoke with some haunt of being a Jonah.

"Jonah spent three days in a whale of an arctic blow," he said. "But Jonah popped out safe and sound." Thus, quickly and lightly he turned aside her thought of being a Jonah, and he dropped Mac's pig on the gold chain back into her hand.

"Mac in a tent on the ice," she said. "I bet he would have been funny." She laid the chain on her knee, and her wrist on the chain, and she did the catch up. "I can almost feel Mac here with us," she said.

Now the wind was broadside to the tent. The south wind drove at the tent by Sally's head, and the canvas drummed, and she looked up at it, and said:

> "Lean, Wind, lean!
> For summer has been . . .

"But this wind doesn't lean," she said.

"Who wrote that?"

"My brother John, when he was a boy."

"Is he older than you?"

"A year," she said.

They were quiet in the wind, which grew to be mighty, and Fiske said: "There's cord in the plane, and pegs, I think. Extra mooring lines to the peak of the tent?"

"We might as well," Skafe said. "Do you want me to help?"

"I can manage," he said. Fiske put on his parka, which was of American type, with a better hood than the Canadian, woolen gloves and mitts. He took the hatchet.

"Don't worry, darling," Skafe said. "It's quite all right."

"Like some beast," she said. "I'll get used to it." She put on more snow to melt, but her hand was trembling. He had not seen her afraid before. "I see Mummy's point about winds," she said.

"How did you find your mother?" he said. *How did you find your mother?* he asked them, and now he asked Sally in a tent, to take her mind off the wind, but he wanted to know.

"I didn't find her," Sally said crossly. "Sorry, darling," she said. "Mummy was . . . Oh, I don't know. She was fine."

The man sang out there on the weather side. He sang: "'. . . Down a shady lane in the sugar cane, a burly bum come hikin' . . .'" He sang strongly in the strong wind, securing one line to the peak of the tent, and then another. He sang overhead: "'Where the limmonade springs, and the bluebird sings, On that big rock-candy mountain.'" He sang lustily in the wind, and hammered tent pegs into hard snow, and then the wind drowned his voice.

"He flies like Mac," she said. "Did you notice?"

"Yes," he said. When she had said: *I can almost feel Mac here with us,* Skafe had felt that same thing, a live presence of his dead friend, Mac. It was true that this boy rode a plane like Mac in the fabled company of the few; but Mac flew no more, and Brian Fiske had met bad luck. Where was he now?"

Skafe put his head out. "Brian!" he called. It was snowing as well as blowing. He could see the outline of the plane fifteen yards away, and he could see the grotesquerie of the pressure ridge near at hand, the plane and the ice and blind white snow. "Brian!" he called.

Fiske came downwind and into the tent. He took off mitts and gloves, and held his hands to his face until the ice loosened. "I don't like that toggle on the windward side," he said. "It's working loose."

"Can we set it again?" Skafe said.

"If the temperature would drop . . ." But through the wind, and through the soundbox of the ice came a loud smack and complaint of metal, smack again. "There she goes," he said. "Now everything is well and truly mucked. I beg your pardon," he said politely, and went out again.

Skafe prepared to follow him. Dress, undress, what a clumsy, maddening business. It was dusk, but he could still see a silhouette of the plane, wing up, wing down. "Stay here!" he said to Sally. He had the flashlight in his inner pocket.

He met the wind, and a whiff of gasoline in the wind. Snow plastered his face, nose, eyes and mouth, and burned cold pain between his eyes, and froze his eyelids together, and he shielded his eyes. "Not very clever," Fiske said round there. He had all his weight on the half-inch nylon which had tethered the wing to the toggle in the ice, but the toggle dangled from the rope. "You hang on," he said. "I'll chip it out."

Skafe took two turns round his mitt, and put weight on the rope, his back to wind, and shone the flashlight for Brian Fiske. It was blowing hard. It blew a gale. It blew like the fiends of Hades or some cold place. The wind danced him like a marionette suspended from the wing. But he hung on while the wind shifted again. It backed to the east. The wind was colder, still more wicked, but now the change of direction eased the wind's grip. Fiske had finished chipping ice. "Need more rope," he said, for the wing had risen. He took off his mitts and worked to free the knot. The flashlight beam was dying in the cold.

"Here's water," Sally said, adding her weight to her father's weight on the rope, and the wing came down.

"Good for you," Fiske said. He set the toggle again, packed snow, poured water, more snow, more water, but then the water pot had frozen solid. "That should hold her now, with the wind from the tail."

They were in the tent, in the blissful heaven of the tent. Any heaven must be blissful, but it was bliss, a painful bliss of thawing out. Fiske had nipped his nose and two fingers. "You have faces like Eskimos," he said to the Skafes, rubbing his hand back to life.

"I was only outside a minute," she said.

"We should have tethered her facing south," Skafe said. "My fault, Brian."

"You can't tell which way the winds will go," he said. "This is just not our lucky day, let's face it." He was more human, less arrogant than Skafe had thought that other time.

"There was a smell of gasoline," he said. "Your starboard tank must have sprung a leak."

"Yes," Fiske said. "Which puts paid to a number of things, the Florida climate being the first. But we have a primus and plenty of kerosene for cooking."

"What else does it put paid to?" Sally asked.

"I hoped to fit a new prop and patch her up and fly out of here, but now she won't hold gas." Fiske lit the hurricane lamp, and the place was more cheerful. The wind had backed half a compass to blow from the east at the flaps of the tent, which were lashed tight, but the wind fought through them. It grew colder, but did not now grow in strength.

"We should get ready for the night before the gas stove dies on us," Skafe said. "If you want to go out, Sally," he said, bluff and impersonal. How else to be about that hideous excursion? "Remember that the plane and the tent are against the pressure ridge, so stay between them and close to the ridge."

"All right," she said, and dressed and went out while he and Fiske spread the sleeping bags. "We'll put her in the middle," he said. "Is that rifle loaded in case a bear should chance along?"

"Yes," Fiske said.

They lay in the cold tent in the wind. "How long do they last?" she said.

"A day, two days, sometimes even three," he said.

"Now let's see," Sally said in the dark beside him. "How did it go? 'A man who has sat out an arctic blow the hard way in a tent, or has sat out enough of them to lose his first fear of them, will not forget that on his backside in an office chair.' End of quote. It holds for a female too, I guess."

"Who said that?" asked Brian Fiske.

"Simon Kepple Skafe," she said, "also called Husky, the arctic dreamer."

Fiske laughed loudly and heartily in the wind. "The Canadian family Skafe," he said. "You're quite an outfit."

And half of the broken outfit were here. Now the wind came in gusts, a long way growing on the ice to buffet and thunder at the tent, a long way dying, and the next gust came.

"What else lives in these parts?" Sally asked, between them. "I mean animals."

"A bear hunts a seal," he said. "A fox and a raven take the pickings. That's about all, on the sea ice."

"It doesn't feel like a sea," she said. "And people?"

"There are a few Eskimos and a mission at Hummel Point," Fiske said. "Thirty-five miles north of us, I make it. Otherwise no one."

"Thirty-five miles," she said. "It might be thirty-five hundred in the wind. Daddy, what was our grandmother's prayer? You used to say it some wild nights when we were small."

She was an Irishwoman, a Protestant O'Connor, and this was her prayer: "Oh, God, give us strength for the storms of our journey."

"Amen," Sally said.

"Amen," Brian said.

Simon put his head inside the bag, with an airhole for breath. His breath formed ice and a frigid trickle. The wind blew steadily again. It piled into the tent and heaved at the tent, but the sound of the wind was muffled. He was cold. He was contented, strangely contented, strong for this storm of his journey.

CHAPTER SEVEN

THE WIND blew in the morning. "I light, you cook," Fiske said. "How's that?"

"Okay," she said from inside her sleeping bag.

The primus made a homey, homely, homelike promise in the tent. "Over to you," Fiske said, and he went out.

Sally sat up. "It takes the edge off," she said about the stove. "Did you sleep?"

"Off and on," he said. "I dozed in limbo." The night had been wind, a snatch of sleep, and cold—it went on through blowing, sleeping, waking, freezing, on and on. Sally looked all right, wearing her sleeping bag to her middle, wearing her parka, wearing her green woolen tuque that Grace, amid a welter of packing, had found two hours or three or whatever it was to knit for her as a present for this expedition, typical of Grace. *It's the craziest thing I ever heard,* she said in the car two days ago, and had said much the same thing when she applied the finishing touch—a red tassel for Sally's green woolen hat. A *toorie* was Anna's Scottish word for tassel.

"It's a corker this morning," Fiske said. "Twenty-eight below from Greenland's icy mountains. The prospect rivals man for vileness." He looked less cheerful than his scramble of that hymn. "I don't get it," he said. "The wing seems all right, and yet both tanks are empty. I suppose the gas siphoned from the starboard tank through the crossfeed system." He sat down, white from head to foot.

"You must brush off your snow," Skafe said, "or this tent will be a frozen puddle." He was strict about it.

Corned beef hash again for breakfast; then pilot and jam, but the jam was frozen; then a brew of tea to bless the spirits of the party; then they went out to the wind to erect a wall of snowblocks. There were new drifts, which made the snow bad for cutting, but the master cutter achieved some indifferent blocks, and his assistants built the wall against the killer wind, which still blew as it had blown all night; at the flaps of the tent, and drifting in.

They thawed themselves, put off the primus, and went back to bed, or to bag, wearing everything except flying boots. They had fleece-lined overboots, adequate for Dewlines, Camp Huskies and that sort of circumstance, not adequate for this open air.

The day dreamed on in a sort of dream of talk in the tent, which the wind attacked from Greenland's icy mountains. Or probably it was a cyclonic spinner of a storm, but the wind was not to be imagined as anything but a straight wind round this narrowing world, still a long way from the Pole, thirteen hundred miles or something. If there was an east wind at the Pole, which way did the wind blow but from the south? That kind of brain-teaser triviality; and also talk about the only people who quite existed in the wind-torn world.

"Where do you come from?" she asked on her stomach, face propped on her gloves in the middle of the trio.

"From Vancouver Island," he said. "But we moved there. I was born in New Brunswick, on the Nashwaak River near Fredericton."

"And I was born at Gallery," Skafe said.

"Really?" said Fiske. "I didn't know." He was not at all abashed about not knowing the birthplace of one of New Brunswick's more notable sons, most notable bar one or two.

"Which makes our small world still smaller," Sally said. The wind changed tone. It ran on past them and away; and for a second or three or five or ten, there was no more wind than would blatter a tent. One could even imagine a world without wind. But it came again. "My land!" Sally said in the voice of a lady of a far kindly land, "isn't it just lovely to think of them fine barefoot boys goin' out from dear old New Brunswick."

Talk in the morning, listen, talk, laugh as the joke wears thin, talk, listen, go inside bag as a child into tent of darkness in his bed.

"Let's have a brew." It was noon again, twenty-four hours in residence. The primus warmed the upper reaches. If you stood in the peak among steaming socks on the wash line, you felt quite cozy, and your lower half remained quite cozy in the bag, like a sack race. The wind had put on new rhythm. Now it blew in long peaks and troughs around the world, the great wind growing to a seventh wave of wind, or so you might imagine.

"Perhaps this is the swansong," Sally said.

"I think it must veer first," said Brian Fiske. "When it unwinds with the clock, the wind will die."

"I like that," Sally said. "The wind must unwind with the clock to die."

"It was an odd thing at Fifty-Eight," Skafe said. With strong sweet tea in him he felt like talking; and he spoke of his feeling of the mad McClintock, even of McClintock lead dog in his dream.

"So that was why you shouted," Sally said. "Tell him about the Turtle Mountain strike." And he told that story. He was not ashamed of it, not much; nor proud of it, not much. But life had taken turnings at that time for him.

So put out the stove and back to bed. "I spy Canada," she said. "What do you spy down thataway?"

"From here?" Fiske said. "I spy America, I guess."

"That's what my father said in a speech," she said, "about a narrow strip of us set on America."

"I said no such thing," he said, the pedant. "This is America. That is America. But this is Canada, and that is the United States." He was a testy splitter of hairs of some small importance.

"Are you anti-American, Mr. Skafe?"

"Of course not," he said. What a juvenile question. "Some of my best friends are American. You might say I'm pro-Canadian."

They talked on, but he wandered away in thought, because from this tent on the ice in the wind, this only real place, he could look back to himself down there, not liking much of what he saw of him down there. *Some of my best friends are American.* It was true. He had more in common with some of them than with Canadians. They had more breath. They were less bürgerworthy.

But who were they, his Canadian, American, English friends? They were big league boys like him, no axe to grind with one another, safe playmate acquaintances, mutually admiring in the easy weather. Men on high plateaus talk much of friends, he thought, but few tolerate friends to love them straitly. That is our corruption. I had old Mac, he thought, and the last time I saw Mac alive, he said to me: . . . *In the meanwhile you can consider the ingratitude of the common herd who sponge upon the great. In other words, you can go and muck yourself.* I apologized, he thought. We flew as friends a last time together.

But that is not me down there, he thought. This is becoming me up here. The others were talking of French Canada, vested citadel, skeleton excuse in cupboard, civilizing vivacity. They disagreed intelligently, and he went to sleep.

When he awoke, the wind seemed quieter and the weather colder. All this time there had been the chorus of wind, many-tongued beast, but now: BOOM—BOOM, through the very pinnings of this world. "*What's that?*"

"Ice pressure," Brian said. "Like the sonic boom, it's nothing lethal."

"I forgot about the cold sea underneath," she said.

"What I was saying," he said, and he talked so quickly on, Skafe thought, to take Sally's mind from another cold beast, "is that I started in flying, and we're making a success of it with Aurora, if the luck holds better than this sort of episode; but on the whole, luck is what you make yourself . . ."

"Well," she said. "I suppose so."

"I mean you have to meet your luck head-on."

"And if you met worse luck than yesterday head-on?"

"You still would be meeting it," he said.

"I must say that's absolute and good," she said. "Go on."

"Flying is not what I'm after ultimately, but you have to use your beginnings to take you on. As I see it, Aurora can be the link for me between the established South and the new North—just a linking service, a start, if you see what I mean."

"I think so," she said, "but a link to what from what?"

"To the new things that are coming, the sort of development in the far North that so far only your father has done much about." Skafe lay submerged in his sleeping bag. He listened, and they thought he slept.

"And a link from what?" she said.

"Here's an example that came to nothing: I had an offer last month from Anglo-Petroleum, the second biggest British outfit. God knows how they heard of me, or what made them ask me, but anyway I went Out to Edmonton to meet the head chap, thinking they were on to something big in the North. But no. They want to get into Canada, start in a small way with filling stations in the east, and work across slowly and carefully, then possibly north for exploration at some future date, the usual ultra-cautious anglified approach. So I took a bit of that, and then I said: *It's no earthly good starting small in this country. If you want to get anywhere in Canada, go big. Spend millions. Splash it around, and then you might get somewhere. This picayune stuff is a waste of time.*

"Well, he was one of those do-the-Colonies-a-favor-out-of-our-vast-experience kind of Limeys, and he didn't like that much."

"It was hardly tactful of you, if you wanted the job."

"I didn't," he said. "I was giving him some sound advice for free. But he stood up and said: *I see there's no meeting of the minds. We do not want to be taught the facts of Canadian life, nor to have our policies framed for us. All we really want is some local help, if you know what I mean, old boy, to do the hackwork in the local language.* Or something equally condescending. They're all the same, these English, when you prick them."

"They're all the same, and you know everything, and I'm going out." A scuffle with boots, a scramble with flaps, and Sally went angrily out to the wind.

"I was only gassing away to keep her mind off this bloody storm."

"I know," he said. "But caution with that particular subject, Brian."

354

"Oh, I see," Fiske said.

It happens like that, Skafe thought. It's happening to me—down to essentials, down to the core, and then you see a truth or two. From this cold tent in the wind, she sees to Piers Whitfield, the man for her. "I was interested to hear you talk just now," he said. "We share some ideas about the North. You are right, too, I think, to consider Aurora as a link on your way."

"Oh, yes," said Fiske. "I wonder if both tanks are quite bone-dry. There's a length of rubber tubing in the plane. When she comes back, I think I'll see if I can't siphon a cup or two for the stove." It was a clam-up or a brush-off about business matters.

Sally crawled in. "It's snowing less," she said. "I saw blue sky once above." The tears of the cold east wind were icicles on her face, but she took off her gloves to thaw her face. What possessed me to bring her? Skafe thought.

"Where has he gone now?" she said, getting back into her bag.

"To see if he can get some gas. He's a stout lad, Brian, if opinionated." My God, he thought, if anyone is going to use that young man, it will not be the likes of Anglo-Petroleum. "But opinionatedness is youth," he said. "You're all the same."

"Are we?" she said. "Oh, listen!"

Sure enough, it was a plane, twin-engined, he thought, growing louder in the wind. They went out, and through the blizzard they saw a smudge of moving silver against the blue beyond the racing veil of snow. The sound died away to the east. Fiske called something from the black plane with the yellow wings, just visible, but they could not hear him, and they went in again.

"They can't have seen us, Father."

"No," he said. "It's like a lace curtain. You can see out from the house. But you can't see into the house from farther away."

"Some house," she said. "Will they find us?"

"Of course," he said. "When the blow stops, they'll find us right away, or in short order." Or so he hoped. It was not quite as easy as pie. "Did you think they might not?" he said to his valiant daughter.

"I didn't know," she said. "Nobody brought the subject up. And what then?"

"Then they'll take time to pick a lead, and collect us."

"And what about his plane?"

"I don't know," he said. "It depends on the damage. But we'll see that Brian doesn't lose out on the deal."

"Magic," said Brian Fiske, putting down the tank of the gas stove. "I squeezed half a pint." He brushed his snow off. They were learning that discipline. The stubble on his face was thick and black. He looked tough, and was.

Now the timeless drift of the day had stopped. Now a plane and warmth brought time back here. "Such heaven," she said, shedding clothes to her blue suede jacket, and combing her hair, but Miss Skafe did nothing silly like putting on powder. Her right cheek was chapped from a frost burn, and her lips were cracked, and she looked remarkably beautiful, cooking supper, or heating it. "The likes of us don't cut no ice," she said, "not what you'd notice except right here. But . . ."

"But what?" Fiske said. He had the primus going too. It was a splurge for warmth.

"But think of the headlines about the captain of industry lost in his beloved North."

"That will be all from you," Skafe said. He had been thinking of that hue and cry. It was his due, and it pleased him, and might serve some purpose: *Safe and sound. I told you there's nothing to it.* Still, he crossed his fingers about the *Safe and sound.*

The tent was getting messy. Tea leaves and frozen slops, cigarette butts, empty cans in the snow—one night was enough in one camping spot. The young ate largely, and Skafe ate less. He felt quite well, except that the chill was deep in him now. However skin-warm he might feel, warmth did not reach his marrow of chill. Brian and Sally washed up. "I didn't mean to be rude that time," she said.

"I didn't mean to sound off," he said. "A couple of our pilots are Englishmen, and they're red-hot. I meant the other kind."

"It takes all kinds," she said, "and all kinds of people within the one, as my brother John keeps saying."

"He sounds a good kind of guy," said Brian Fiske.

"He is," she said. "He's just gone to Jamaica to stay with our mother."

"You have a house there, then?"

"No," she said.

Skafe went out before bed. She would tell Brian Fiske, who himself seemed a good kind of guy in a lordly way, that her parents were divorced. She would be sure to do that to prevent embarrassing remarks in camp. It was a fearful shrink of cold as he piddled. Who could enjoy the Arctic wastes? Not Husky Skafe.

The wind had blown from the east for twenty-four hours, easing this afternoon, gusting by long waves, long troughs, the sea of wind.

But now the wind grew again to solidness, changing again, edging north. It was the worst wind yet, the coldest wind, the strongest wind, strong enough to take the flimsy tent in his fist and whip it away from them, and then he would have them defenseless on the ice to work his merciless will on them. He was a killer god, the wind.

Skafe thought of broaching rum, a sup, a *schluck* for each of them. But no. From the wonderful warmth to a doubled pit of cold.

"Will it never stop?" she said.

"Tomorrow and tomorrow and tomorrow, it's a corker, chum," said Brian Fiske, and then he sang about the shady lane, the sugar cane, burly bum come hikin', lookin' for his likin'. And he sang: "'. . . I want to go where there ain't no snow . . . And the wind don't blow . . . The Big Rock-Candy Mountain.'"

"You can sing," she said. "Sing again."

"That was for the never-never land of milk and honey," he said. "That one was for the birds. This one is for the storm. Do you know the choral part of Beethoven's *Ninth Symphony?*"

"Sure we know the tune," Sally said. "We're cultured folks."

So they sang a wordless ode to joy. But Simon himself remembered those words.

> Freude, schöner Götterfunken,
> Tochter aus Elysium,
> Wir betreten feuertrunken,
> Himmlische, dein Heiligtum,
> Deine Zauber binden wieder,
> Was die Mode streng geteilt,
> Alle Menschen werden Brüder,
> Wo dein sanfter Flügel weilt.

"Now to sleep," Sally said in the wind.

Being young, perhaps they slept at once. But Simon lay awake. He remembered singing with Anna once upon a time beside the green Mackenzie River where the North began for him. And now in the tent in the great north wind they had sung of the brotherhood of men, of puny men, of men. Now Simon's breath condensed to trickle and to freeze, and now his few tears of joy and sorrow added dampness, and he slept.

It was nearly three. The north wind battered at the tent, and something that was not the wind nosed at the tent. "Light!" said Brian Fiske.

Skafe brought out the flashlight that stayed alive in his sleeping bag with him, and Fiske held the .30-.30 carbine, but the visitor departed, took leave, stayed away, and only the wind nosed at the tent.

"A bear?"

"Yes," Skafe said. "That was Nanuk, the Polar Bear. They don't bother you." You're telling me, he thought. You're telling me you don't feel bothered by them. "They hunt downwind in a blow," he said.

"Seekin' milk and honey," said Brian Fiske. "Seekin' blubber for no money."

"Now I'm not afraid," she said, between them.

"Sleep again," Simon said.

They had a late breakfast of bacon and pilot biscuit soaked in bacon fat, gobs of warm fat to crave for warmth, for caviar, for oysters, a Lucullan banquet, fat, blubber, bacon fat. The wind held north. It had abated at the start of this third day, but still blew hard enough to keep the blizzard flying on the ice. The snow-filled tracks of a big male bear ran on to the south.

It was their enemy the wind that brought the sound of dogs, a yelping excitement on the wind, come racing with the wind. Then a man shouted his dogs to silence. Thus swiftly out of the north came a man with dogs. He set the grapnel anchor into snow and tipped the sled. "Dogs hunt Nanuk," he said, taking off his mitt to shake hands. He was an Eskimo named Charlie Avakana, short, square and broad with smiles.

They gave him a hearty welcome, a slug of bacon fat, a mug of tea. He pulled his deerskins over his head, and sweated in a shirt. He spoke little English, but it transpired that some radio at Hummel Point was on the blink, and that this camping party was a surprise to him, although it did not seem to surprise him much. He said that his dogs followed the trail of the polar bear. He pointed south, and spoke of open water far away, no doubt that same open water reflected as a dark ellipse of cloud two days ago when they were flying. *Two days ago?*

"Big blow," he said about the wind in which he jaunted after polar bears. "*Nowna,*" he said, not knowing when the wind would die, tonight, tomorrow, sometime. "Can travel," he said, very happy about taking them to Hummel Point, about losing his chance to kill Nanuk who had led him here. He was a very happy man when laughing, which was often, but his face in repose wore melancholy. His face was light mahogany, or russet-apple, undiluted slab-faced Eskimo.

"We can leave everything except our personal gear," Skafe said, and he asked Charlie Avakana if he could manage sleeping bags and other bags, as well as passengers.

"Sure," Charlie said. "Sled light for Nanuk." He was full of glee. "Get Nanuk other time," he said.

"I'd better stay here," Brian said.

"You can't do any good by staying," Sally said. "If you came to Hummel Point, you might fix the radio he says is on the blink. Transmitter

358

radio?" she said to Charlie Avakana. "Send messages?" She made out-sending gestures with her hand.

"Yeah," he said, raising eyebrows in the affirmative. "On blink, not much."

Brian wavered in doubt. For once in a way he seemed unsure. "Well, I guess that makes sense," he said to Sally.

Skafe put on his deerskins, which had served as insulation at the central part of a floor of snow. He turned the young caribou hidefur-inward, the outer parka fur-outward. His deerskins had been presented to him by some pretty good friends with big interests in the North. He made Sally wear his buttoned parka on top of her own, his two layers of pants. Thus, she was double or quadruple clad against the cold, swimming in his clothes. But she was a fair-sized girl, not swimming much more than her mother had swum in his coon coat one afternoon. "Are you going to be warm enough?" she said to Brian Fiske.

"All I possess is on me," he said. "And I can run."

Outside, the wind blew moderately, and outside now, two dogs fought in a fury of hate. "Rover! Moose!" Avakana shouted at them, and he quelled them brutally with a chain.

"You have to hang on," Skafe said to Sally, behind him on the sled. He had forgotten almost everything that came rushing out of long ago to be remembered. "Ho!" called Avakana. "Ho!" And the big white lead-dog swung left from the pressure ridge, swung left again, Avakana running, guiding the sled through rough ice that bordered the lead. They turned their backs to wind. The black plane with the yellow wings was gone in the snow, and the tent was gone. The snow hooked into the lee of their parka hoods, into their faces, but it was not bad.

Avakana rode square to wind. There was some music in his shouting, his cajoling, his encouragement, calling them by name: "Idivaluk—Screwball—Beaver—Kingi—Moose." The lead dog was named Liar, but he seemed a noble animal, reminiscent of the white lead dog of Simon's dream.

Hours sitting on the sled, fifty jogging paces now and then for warmth. Fiske ran often, being the least well clad. Sally ran, for she was young. Skafe ran no more than he could help, being fifty years of age last week.

They stopped once to melt snow, ice up, eat a doughnut, brew tea. Avakana smiled often, but he did not talk. The steel runners were coated with a few inches of frozen mud, and to this smooth surface ice was applied. He iced his runners with a wet cloth in his bare hand at whatever the temperature might be, perhaps thirty-five below zero Fahrenheit, sixty-seven degrees of frost. Then he ran up and down his runners, flipping the rag for a final pebbled gloss. Then he blew on his hand and laughed.

They traveled again. The wind veered now. It swung to the east as it fell, and now you could see in dim white weather—the flutings of the snow, the cornices, the anvils which were the patterns carved by the last great wind, and it had been from the north. Avakana ran against the pointers of that wind for home.

The wind and the day wore down until snowdevils ceased to spin, until not even a gravelly wisp of snow ran across the surface of the snow, until Avakana pointed to a headland, orange in the sun, and the dogs strained for home and a chunk of seal. The runners hissed. The sun shone on rough ice between here and land.

"All that time in the tent," she said, "and then the polar bear, and then the Eskimo. Now the wind unwinds, and the sun comes out. It seems like God to me."

"And to me," said Brian Fiske, who sat at the back of the sled on Avakana's frozen seal. He got off to run for warmth, or to ease the load.

They came to rough ice, not big, but twenty or thirty yards of humps and hollows, of a blue-green jumble in the sun, to swing between, sweep through, watch your feet, and Avakana ran beside his sled, leaning, guiding, nimble as a squat brown ballet dancer.

"Watch out," Skafe said as the sled began to tip. But he said it too late to Sally behind him. Perhaps she was not holding on. Perhaps she was looking back. He turned to see her tumble, do a somersault, and roll. Avakana stopped the dogs.

Brian Fiske ran up to her. She lay laughing on the snow in her numerous outsized clothes. Then he took the mitts from his hand, and held his hand to her; and she took the mitts from her hand, and put her hand in his, and stood with his help.

They walked here hand in hand. They bore Simon tidings of a joy of theirs. "Children," he said, for both were his children after the wind.

The dogs gave tongue as they galloped for home, round the headland, past a beached schooner, to a pittance of huts and buried tents, yet a church above this godforsaken place. But not godforsaken—an oasis, a Manhattan Island.

Some children ran, and some elders gathered, as is the way at the rim of the world where strangers come few and come far.

One man was tall. He wore a duffel parka. Skafe had wondered at the names of the dogs, but he had not asked Avakana. If this were to be the irrational authentic tap of fate, then let fate tap for him. Let it boom for him. Boom—boom through the very pinnings of this world, the cold sea underneath, the shore at hand.

The dogsled stopped, and people came, and Simon Skafe dismounted. "Hullo, Jim," he said.

CHAPTER EIGHT

"Well, for Chrissake!" Then, upon astonishment there swooped astonishing delight. "Husky! Hell, I says to myself a thousand times: One of these days the one and only'll show up." Jim Willis pumped his hand.

"This is Sally," said the one and only. "And Brian Fiske—Jim Willis."

Jim said he was pleased to meet them. He spoke some Eskimo with Avakana. Then he turned back to Husky Skafe, who told him that they had been flying to Nunangiyak . . .

"Makin' for Camp Husky, eh, the latest one?" Jim laughed. "And out in that blow! Come and get warm." They walked to the nearer of two huts, into Jim's warm house.

"Ida," Jim called to an open door at the end of the room. On the other side was an alcove with a radio transmitter. "The wife," he said, when Ida came. She shook hands all round, and went to make tea. "Set down," Jim said. "Take the chesterfield. Relax." He was elated, looking at his onetime partner. "'Tain't much of a place, but it's home."

"It's the nearest thing to heaven I remember," Sally said, sitting between Brian and her father.

Then Jim noticed her. He stared at Anna's daughter, and looked away, and his eyes flickered back to a substantial ghost. "Well, for Chr . . ." he mumbled, and went to the stove to Ida, his Eskimo wife, who wore sneakers and a shapeless cotton dress.

"Is this chap crazy?"

"Ssh, Brian! I'll explain."

Simon's face was burning. He burned outwardly, and chills shivered him to the core. The heat in Jim's home was the nearest thing to heaven he remembered, but he remembered nothing. "Yes, Jim?"

"You need a good sleep," Jim said. "But first we got to put the warmth back in. She can make a fish pie pretty decent. How would that be?"

"Great, Jim," he said. He watched Jim and his silent wife set about the making of the pie: or Jim fetched a frozen char, and chopped the head and tail, and let Ida go to work. Jim's children came in. "This is Noel," he said. "Nine last birthday, drives his own team of pups. He don't speak hardly any English." Noel was a round-faced child, and solemn. "And this is Junie. She's five, ain't ya, honey? Got a kiss for Uncle Husky, June?"

Skafe suffered himself to be kissed. How he loathed kisses from strange children, let alone to be Uncle Husky; and he sat again on the complaining sofa. The boy went away. The girl sat on Jim's knee. He stroked her hair.

"It's good to see you, Jim," he said heartily. "You haven't changed." Except to become a gaunt old man of fifty-five, he thought.

"I got skinnier," Jim said. "You got to look more solid like. But I don't remember you right without the beard. There's my honey," he said to June, inert in his arms.

Jim had known him two days without the beard, when Jim had been host at the head of the Mackenzie River. "We trapped together, Brian," he said. "Jim taught me all I learned, which wasn't much."

"You learned quicker'n any fella I ever saw," said Jim.

"Jim," he said. It was inspiration. "Do you remember that grizzly on the Penitence?"

Jim nodded. He looked as happy as could be about that memory.

"What happened?" Sally said.

Skafe told them the story of the bear from which he had been saved by Jim. The slow Arctic dusk was deepening. Jim lit two oil lamps. "Generator's on the blink," he said vaguely, picking the child from the chair to pet her on his lap again. "We panned some gold on the Penitence," he said. "You panned some black gold since them days, Husky." He did not speak with any kind of edge, but in due reverence.

Ida brought the fish pie. "There's nothin' like *Irkalukhik* for puttin' warmth into a fella, so tuck in."

Skafe tucked in moderately, and did not feel internal warmth. He felt vastly tired and sleepy, and well enough in a thrum of heat and chill. He wanted sleep, the floor, that sofa, anything in Jim Willis's house. But now another white man arrived, Canon Harper, the missionary, who was old, bearded and serene. He smiled as sweetly, as expansively, as fleetingly as an Eskimo, and declined fish pie. "Our first Outside visitors since freeze-up," he said. "How delightful strange faces are." But he made no inquiries about the strangers; nor did he ask for news of the world. He simply sat. Everyone simply sat after supper, including some Eskimos who had come to call, and Jim stroked his daughter's hair. If you looked at the Eskimos, they smiled. Otherwise, they simply sat. Time was not here. Time was less here than in the tent in a middle eternity of wind. The Eskimos sat in a row against the farther wall, below a daguerreotype

362

of Queen Victoria and a calendar of the Montreal Canadiens 1954 in color.

The old partnership—fifty-fifty on furs and findings—shared Jim's chesterfield or sofa, plus Jim's little daughter puss. Canon Harper had the garden chair, the folding canvas kind that lasts a few seasons on the patio of some lovely summer home. Sally and Brian sat on at the supper table, their knees touching below the table, he could see, their hands side by side on the greasy oilcloth of the table. The one with three days' black growth of beard and the one with the frost-chapped cheeks looked down at their hands that lay together. They simply looked, and Skafe simply yearned for sleep, to sleep forever with his timeless chills, but that would be rude, and he looked at Jim's library beside him in two orange crates. There were birds and beasts and arctic flowers like Roger Tory Peterson in hard covers, and there were bosoms and whips and death-splayed prostitutes like Mickey Spillane in paperbacks, the library of a catholic taste, and now the one and only Husky yielded to a timeless sea of sleep, but Brian brought him weaving back to time and life and sanity by saying: "Your generator's on the blink, you said?"

"Can't seem to get it started," Jim said. "How long is it—a week, two weeks I haven't sent a goddam Met report—sorry, Rev."

"Ah, Jim," the Canon said.

"Perhaps I could have a look?"

"Sure. Sure, thanks a lot. Mebbe tomorrow when you're rested out."

Skafe pulled himself together. "We're missing, Jim," he said. "Planes will be searching for us. We must let them know that we are safe."

"They can't be searchin' in the night, so what's the hurry?" Jim cackled, stroking Junie's hair. Everyone grinned happily against the farther wall.

"Please excuse us," said the Canon. "We forget other ways. Show the young man," he said to Jim.

"Okay, then. Go to Uncle, honey."

Honey Junie moved to Uncle on the chesterfield. She snuggled up. It was appalling.

"A most affectionate dear child," the Canon said.

Sally came over from the table. Her mouth twitched at the cozy scene; then she held a finger to her lips. "Awfully sore," she said. "I must put some cold cream on them."

"Cold cream," the Canon said. "Capital stuff for cracked lips."

"I'm going to help Brian, Daddy," she said. "Will you be all right?"

"I'll be asleep," he said. "Wake me up if there's any news. If you do get through to Turtle, send messages to Grace and John; and tell Syme I want both Lynxes here—one to take me on to Nunangiyak; the other with a propeller, a heater, whatever else Brian wants, and the best mechanic we have. Is that clear?"

"Yes, Father," she said. Her eyes were violet blue, and they were deep, profoundly happy and compassionate, and she bent to kiss him on his stubbled cheek. "Mad hatter's, isn't it?" she murmured. "Never mind."

Junie snuggled. Sally went, and Jim returned. He was a gangling man, shaped much like David Dorrien, but thinner than the Dorrien last seen by Skafe in 1948, more stooped, emaciated, loving than the Willis last seen by Skafe in 1932.

"This poor man bears a mighty burden for the land of Nod," the Canon said. "We must consider sleeping quarters. Now let me see—there are two bunks at the mission, and Jim's sofa here, which is young Noel's bed, but no doubt you could find the boy some corner, Jim."

"Sure," Jim said. "Take him in to doss with us." He nodded his head at the open door through which Sphinx Ida had lately passed.

"Any bit of floor would do me fine," Skafe said. He fought for wakefulness, head nodding again. "Yes, Jim?" he said.

"I says Junie's taken to you. Loves big he-men, Junie does."

She snuggled like a pussycat against her unwilling sofa mate. "Yes, Jim?" he said.

"I said: the girl and him—they ain't married on a honeymoon?"

"No, they ain't," Skafe said. "There you are," he said inanely to the child, and eased her off and stood. "You're very kind," he said. "Sally and I at the mission, and Brian Fiske here, if that would be all right?"

"Fine," Jim said. "Whatever you say, not but what it's not a right welcome . . ." His voice tailed off. "Come on, then, Rev," he said. "We'll show old Husky to his bunk. Stay there on your botty, June. Daddy be right back."

Now quite a bustle and quite a company of willing hands to take him to the mission bunk. Jim pounced on his zipper bag, which was the heavy one. The night was not particularly cold. They walked up to the mission. "Look at that!" Jim said, turning. "Well, can you beat it?"

It was a far light to the south, and a far sound in stillness. "What on earth?" the Canon said. "Or in the heavens, I should say?"

"They're lookin' for Husky is what," Jim said. "So I was wrong. And you know why? Because my old pal Husky is the biggest bigshot in the whole goddam North. Sorry, Rev."

"Ah, Jim," the Canon said. The light sank to be a glow at the horizon, and they went in. Two flames were burning at the altar. The Canon crossed himself. "Our church, our home," he said. "My room to the right, yours to the left. Shall I lead the way?"

Jim put down the zipper bag, moved it a few inches, took his hand away. The bottle, from which two tots had been taken at Camp Fifty-Eight, made a small slop or gurgle in the bag.

"Now, Jim," said the Canon, "we must let your friend have his well-earned beauty sleep. So off you go now, back to Junie."

Jim looked at Skafe, and at the bag, and said goodnight reluctantly with vague affection. They both went out. Skafe unrolled his sleeping bag on the upper bunk. He did not like upper bunks, but she would be late, sure to be late. *They ain't married on a honeymoon?—No, they ain't.* What next, indeed? But nothing mattered next but sleep.

"I say!" It was the Canon, knocking.

"Come in," he said.

"I was so sorry to rush him out like that, but he suspected a bottle in your bag, poor Jim. This drink, it is a fearful curse for him."

"It always was," Skafe said.

"You are old friends, then?"

"I knew Jim long ago," he said. He had a maudlin impulse to tell this clergyman about his last meeting with Jim, or his last parting from Jim; but instead he unzipped the bag, took out Jim's fearful curse and offered the Canon a drink.

"Not in Lent, thank you very much, forgive me for not joining you. But take a good noggin yourself. There is nothing like rum to warm chilled cockles." The Canon dashed for hot water, and then sat timelessly, benignly, while Skafe sipped toddy. It went into him and through him, down and up, the swim of rum, the wonder warmth. "How long has Jim been at Hummel Point?" he asked.

"Fifteen years, would it be, or thereabouts. The Company were generous to him when they moved from here—they let him have two buildings at quite nominal cost. Since then Jim has trapped and traded—no better trapper in his day, no less effectual trader." The Canon chuckled. "Poor fellow, he would starve were it not for his weather reports by radio when the radio is working. And then he guides in summer for the wildlife people. Jim does everything in fits and starts, and struggles through by virtue, purest virtue, of loving his fellow men so much that God and his fellow men love him. He is Abou Ben Adhem of Hummel Point." The Canon laughed, swaying in his chair. "Oh, everyone loves Jim."

Abou Ben Adhem soft in the head, Skafe thought. "Have you been here long?" he asked. He was half tipsy after rum, and half awake.

"I came directly from the First World War," the Canon said.

"There has been a great advance in the North since then."

"There has been a woeful retrogression in the North since then," said the Canon blandly. "Now let me show you the geography, and then at last you can be rid of me."

They went out, and came back, and the Canon said: "God grant you restful sleep."

He locked his zipper bag, stowed it under, climbed to his upper bunk, thought of escape and went to sleep.

"What time is it?" he said.

"After three. Brian fixed the generator."

"What was wrong?" He mumbled questions, coming out of sleep.

"Dirt," Brian said. "Plugs, points, carburetor, a real dog's dinner of neglect. Anyway, we got through to Turtle in the end."

"Well done," he said, now wide awake and sitting up. "And when will they be here?"

"They're all set, but the weather doesn't look too good—heavy overcast, according to the Met. It's clouding up already."

"Jim says *Hila kapuk*," Sally said. "He says *Sure as hell it's a white-out for tomorrow*." They stood beside his bunk, the one yawning, then the other, yawning and amused. "It's madly funny, isn't it?" she said. "Sort of madly funny sad."

"What?"

"Oh, Jim and the shadow wife and everything. He strokes Junie's hair all night, and says: *Jeeze, it's great to see Husky again*."

"I think I'll get some sleep now," Brian said. "We have another sked at eight. And many thanks for all your help about the plane. We could easily . . ."

"Not at all. Goodnight then, Brian."

"Goodnight, sir. Goodnight, you," he said to Sally.

"Goodnight, you," she said to him. They were completely and shamelessly enmeshed with one another, just as crazed as crazy old loving Jim, insanity at Hummel Point. She kissed Brian on the cheek, hardly a kiss at all, a touch, and he went out to the church. "It happened to me, Daddy," she said.

"I know," he said. He had known that someone must take her from him, and he had hoped that the sterling Piers would be that one, and so Piers would have been had not God or fate conspired to bring his child and this young man to meet. It was truth, and he had known truth once himself, but he had lost his truth.

"I'm going to say my prayers," she said, and left him again to say her prayers in the mission church. He prayed that she might not lose her truth. Sally came back to sleep in the bunk below him. She did not stir. He lay as quietly as he could, caught in his bunk, a *white-out sure as hell tomorrow*, a loving Jim to face tomorrow, a bigot's *woeful retrogression in the North* to face tomorrow, jealousy tomorrow, trapped.

Jim was taking stock, but as his scanty stock was jumbled all about the store, he had some difficulty, would go round counting out aloud, forget, and start again, and find another gill net, seal hook, one of a pair of mitts, an open box of .25-.35 shells, and think of something else to talk about. Skafe stood it for a while; but he was cold, and temperamentally incapable of watching scrambled work. "How about stacking things by item, Jim," he said. "That would save a lot of time."

"Okay then, you're the boss."

Just it, he was immediately the boss, and in twenty minutes they reduced a shambles to sparse order while Jim prattled on, the Company boat not due until August, they supplied him and bought his furs, the Company used him good, he wouldn't hear no word against the Company. And the Government was pretty decent. Hell, all he did was send in Weather, none too regular at that.

But now an old Eskimo woman came, and hovered in submissive apathy until Jim talked to her and gave her flour. "They're up to the eyes to me," he said. "But what can a fella do, with the husband coughing his guts out in the tent?"

And then Jim went on to speak of the beauties of Hummel Point in summer when the flowers were out and birds were nesting. "It's real pretty," he said. Perhaps the desolate place was real pretty in the summer. It was pretty to Jim at least, a lover of nature who had grown to love nature twice as much.

The caribou herds inland were almost gone—the price of white fox compared to what it used to be, twenty bucks for a real good skin against better'n fifty—the young fellas gone to the Dewline to work, shoot off their dogteams—hell, you should hear his holiness on that one. It was one helluvan outlook for a trader in a place like this, but what the hell, so we'll get by. Use people good. They use you good. Jim Willis, Abou Ben Adhem of Hummel Point, Pollyanna of the Arctic.

"Say, Husky," he said. "What d'you reckon to this goddam Dewline?"

An example of a necessary waste of money, he considered. Useless against ballistic missiles; but even then there still must be aircraft warning; and furthermore, the North should be manned, however thinly. No, it was the right decision. He gave Jim a careful little talk about the Dewline. But his opinion, and it was only a personal opinion, was that Canada should pay the bill.

"Hell, the Yanks can afford it better'n us."

"Ah, Jim," he said, like his holiness, Canon Harper, Rev.

Enter Junie, in a gaudy mother hubbard over parkas, woebegone. "Honey, what's the matter? Gotta kiss for Dad? You got sore throaty and the sniffles? Gotta kiss for Uncle Husky? No, mebbe not, if you got the sniffles. Go to Mummy. Mummy put Junie right in Daddy's great big bed."

Exit Junie. English to Junie, Eskimo to the boy. Why? Who could tell? Not Husky Skafe.

"There!" said Jim. "The place ain't been this neat in years, all thanks to Husky. Say, Husky," he said earnestly. "What's your secret of success? You tell me, Husky, mebbe I could learn."

I end what I begin, he thought. I do what I am doing. I do not love the man who stole my wife. In my end is my beginning. I am going crazy. He smiled and said: "I have no secrets, Jim."

Avakana came to announce that he would go round his seal holes. It transpired that the team was Jim's, but an arrangement with the mission too, whereby the Canon, and Avakana who was his catechist, could use Jim's dogs for travel. Everything at Hummel Point was interlooped, or communism of a sort, or something.

Now Jim took some depleted stock in double time, and as quickly lost enthusiasm, but said: "Thanks a million," with great enthusiasm, and looked out at the day, a lot warmer in the open air than in the store of Jim Willis, trader, trapper, weatherman and nature lover, Husky lover. "A white-out," he said. "Can stay this way for days, so you can make a real nice visit with us. You ain't in no hurry, Husky, now they know you're safe, eh Husky?"

He let that one go by. Surely sometime something must be said . . .

"I tell you who else has itchy pants to travel is that pilot fella. Well, mebbe not itchy pants, but on the ball for what he's on. He's quite a boy, and he reminds me . . ." Jim's reminiscence died, as always and as now. He did not seem much changed; he was only more so in most respects.

"Yes, Brian is an exceptional young man," Skafe said.

"And him and Sally are clean crazed for one another, that stands out a mile, eh Husky?"

"So it seems," he said.

"So they'll be gettin' spliced."

"I suppose they may," he said. It was another matter beyond his control.

"Love," Jim said. "It's good to see. Y'know, Husky, when I took a first right look at that kid on the chesterfield last evenin', you could of knocked me for a loop. *Jesus Christ,* I thought. *It's Anna.* She ain't so dark, and she got blue eyes, and she's more cheery like, more happy you would say, but still the spittin' image in the shape and face, and when she's laughin' too, not that Anna did too much laughin', but that was me, I guess."

"Sally is much less moody," he said, what a nightmare conversation in Jim's store. More beautiful, he thought, more gifted. Less artistic, less imaginative, too much of me in her, and she will never be the woman Anna is, or was for me. "Jim," he said. "All these years I have regretted what I did to you."

"It was me done it to myself," said Jim. "It was that jag I went on at Lightning River that first Easter, sickin' it up disgustin' on the floor, and hell, her a decent eddicated college girl raised to lunches in a parlor. Hell, you was made for one another from the first word go. But what triggered her to marry me was what I never got the reason of. Mebbe you know, Husky. Mebbe you could tell me. Was she lonely, mebbe?"

He doubted, even if he did tell Jim why Anna married him, that it would put a spoke in the wheel of Jim's sweet love for all mankind; but he would not tell him. "I guess she was lonely and she liked you, Jim," he said. "Anna always said she liked you."

"Sure she did at first," Jim said. "Why she . . ."

He interrupted the unbearable. "I ought to tell you, Jim," he said, "that Anna left me too. She ran off with an artist fellow in 1948."

It took a while, a few seconds, for that to sink into Jim's soft head. But then he smacked the counter with his mitt. He smacked his padded thigh. He smacked the duffel parka on his chest. Jim rocked and stamped and rolled around his ice-cold store in desperate hilarity, and tears ran down to freeze on the wolverine of his hood, and his panting breath filled the air with fog, and finally he croaked: "Jeeze, that's rich," he croaked, "me and Husky in the same old boat, oh Jeeze, we oughter have a drink on it." At which thought of rum, at which lullaby dream, he sobered instantly to cunning supplication: "Say, Husky . . ."

"Are you in there, sir?" It was Brian's voice.

"Here, Brian," he said. Thank God for you, he thought.

"I'm afraid the weather is pretty hopeless for today—it's snowing at Turtle, and a white-out everywhere above the coast."

"Oh, yes," he said.

"These radio messages for you." One said: THANK GOD YOU ARE BOTH SAFE PLEASE BE CAREFUL COME TO ME SOON LOVE GRACE. One said: ALL MUCH RELIEVED TO KNOW YOU AND SALLY FREE OF ICE STOP LOVE FROM MOTHER JOHN.

He read them on the counter while Jim hovered, like a small boy longing to have a peek, but he did not let Jim have his peek. "Thank you, Brian," he said, giving the sheet of paper back. "You might show these to Sally. Anything else?"

"I talked to Camp Husky. The tractor train was due to start south tomorrow, but there's trouble with one of the cats, so it will be a day or two. The head chap—Jorgensen, is that his name?"

"Yes," he said. "Chris Jorgensen, a geologist."

"He and Rosenheim, the radio operator, both said: *Be sure and give Husky my best.*" Fiske smiled. He had shaved this morning, and was bareheaded, despite the cold in Jim's store. "They seemed darned glad to know you were safe."

"Sure they'd be darned glad," Jim said. "Who wouldn't, to know old Husky was Skafe, mean safe." Jim laughed like crazy, and Skafe pleaded soulfully to Brian for relief, and got it.

"How are you for gasoline, Jim? That tank is almost dry."

"We're gettin' low," Jim said. "But hell, if we run out altogether, I won't need to send no goddam Met reports. And midnight sun is comin' —what's the need for the electric?"

"If you could just show me, then," said Fiske. He drooped an eyelid at Skafe, and this particular party broke up with an affectionate: "Be seeing you, Husky boy," from Jim.

Skafe went walking, across a wind-swept pebble beach, and down to the sea and past the dogline. Cloud was low, the world vague about him, and he stumbled once or twice, not Husky's fault in a vague white world where men who walk must blindly stub their toes. He thought of dear Grace, *please be careful come to me soon,* at the Nelson Club, Antigua. He thought of *Love from Mother.*

He walked for ten minutes across the bay to be alone, to hear nothing, to see nothing but one empty sardine can—New Brunswick sardines, to make a small world smaller—one sardine can and Simon Skafe and nothing else in the dead white dungeon of the north, the south, the east, the west, all round him nothing. The snow was hard and bore no tracks. He had to steady himself against a jab, a panicky flutter, foolish man to wander off alone without even his compass to lend erratic aid, half a mile from a pinprick named Hummel Point.

But then he cast about, and played at Eskimo, and cut across the north-south flutings of the last great wind, and found a heel mark facing west, and he had found himself again.

Love from Mother. And what would Anna say about Husband One and Husband Two in the same old boat? Would she find that amusing? Simon Skafe thought not.

He passed the dogs, curled head to tail, asleep, or they did not think him worthy of attention. He passed an Eskimo house, a bulge in the snow with a stovepipe sticking out. A man beamed at the door, and called: "Tea!" But he waved very heartily and pointed up hill and cried: "*Kwana-puk-po.*" Thanks a lot, picked that one up again, and skipped the kind invitation, because he was beginning to find that life at Hummel Point in the North for which he strove and for which he hoped so much for reasons that escaped him slightly at the moment—that life at Hummel Point was pretty well the end, *Kwana-puk-po*, thanks to you, old-timer.

He made it safely past the Willis home, and rounded a large black rock. God, what a place for anyone to call *real pretty* any time, beyond belief —and there in the open were Sally and Brian Fiske ahead of him, also mission-bound. He was very glad to see kindred spirits, to some degree his kindred, and he would have announced himself; but by honest common thought or impulse they turned now as one man, one woman, to embrace passionately, blatantly, not giving one goddam, as Jim would say, who saw them in the dim white weather, but they had not seen him.

Somehow or other it was quite a shock. He skipped behind Jim Willis's store to hide until the clinch was over, or after a decent interval cough loudly and emerge; but he met something face to face and almost worse behind the store. It was on a wooden erection like a bird table, at a safe height from dogs.

It stared at him, and he stared at it—the thoughtful eyes, the puggy nose, the whiskered dignity, like some embalmed professor at McGill, mummified *philosophe*. No, by God, not a McGill professor—the seal bore a striking resemblance to that old nincompoop Alfred Buxton, lately president of Algonquin Steel. A time to weep, and a time to laugh. He laughed.

CHAPTER NINE

THERE WERE the sentimental chats with Jim—not again about two men in one marital boat, for Jim had opened and closed that subject with a single excruciating bout of mirth. The topics were trapping and hunting reminiscence: using people good and vice versa: the traces of gold he found inland when he was guiding the wildlife fellas, a decent bunch, they used him good, and *gold is where you find it, don't forget that, Husky:* Skafe's secret of success, such golden admiration in Jim's rheumy eye, a million wasn't good enough, he was a billionaire. *Say, why'n't you pay for the Dewline, Husky, you could do it easy;* and then so penitent because an old pal did not split his sides.

Fortunately, Junie was confined to Daddy's bed. When not with June, and sometimes through the open door, and all the time at meals, and in the store taking stock—they had finished that yesterday afternoon—Jim covered a quarter of a century of arctic life. And if they were alone together, sooner or later his body would do a corkscrew shimmy, his long neck would twist, and his voice would change: *Say, Husky, what about . . . ?* Then time for the victim to take off again; or to interrupt hopes of rum with a feigned interest in the nuptial habits of some curlew. Jim was also dotty about birds.

Life with Canon Harper would have been fine for a man who shared his views. He was charming, full of fun despite his Lenten fasting, a fount of knowledge about the North, wise in all matters except the central matter of his *idée fixe.* He would even make puzzled forays of inquiry about an outside world that he had not seen for twenty years. But soon he would tire of that, and back to his Eskimos, the victims of despoilers from that outside world, of new plunderers like Simon Skafe. He did not say such personal things. He hinted delicately and urbanely.

For him, after nearly forty years with the Eskimo, Christianity of the Anglican persuasion had in a measure become the Eskimo; the Eskimo of the Anglican persuasion had become Christianity. He yearned that his flock should follow their ancient skills with Christ. Any change from this was sin against the mystique of the Eskimo in Christ.

It was fruitless to argue with the saintly man, to say to him: Canon, don't you understand that a few thousand Eskimos are no more sacrosanct than the other few thousand million human beings? They are of the world, for better or for worse, and the world is coming North, and if you try to preserve them in a state of nature in a refuge from that world, you will not preserve them, but destroy them. The result of forcing the unwilling Eskimo into a paternalistic game reserve would be that they, who have already tasted our luxuries as well as our diseases, would go the way of the Indians, to decay in a wretched middle pit. Can you not see, dear Canon, that the only hope for your Eskimos is the precise opposite—that they should be absorbed speedily into the new life of the North? So educate them.

But the Canon spoke from Faith, with which there is no argument, least of all the argument that Christian missions were the ones who started it, teaching the concept of sin in a lusty arctic Eden where nobody had heard of sin.

Yet he might have doubts. He said after church this morning: *The real tragedy for the Eskimo may be that the Arctic makes fanatics of all who love it best, excepting only the hapless Eskimo.*

Life with Sally and Brian was not awkward because of contrasting ideologies or opinions, as with the Canon; nor because woolly philanthropists make misanthropes of other men, as with Jim; but because homo sapiens at Hummel Point consisted for them only of two people. They behaved with restraint in public, and had no privacy except in the inhospitable open air, or here in this room next door to the Canon in the mission hut when Skafe went out. They were kindly and considerate to him, and he was *de trop.*

So either he was too much loved, or he was held guilty of conspiracy against God's children, or he was a spoilsport.

Now he lay on his upper bunk after forty-eight hours at Hummel Point. He was reading a book by Vilhjalmur Stefansson, which he had borrowed from the Canon. He admired incredible hardihood, but was bored by blond Eskimos and all-fat diets, so he laid *The Friendly Arctic* on his chest and listened to the wind. It made a different sound against a building. It whistled at the mission eaves and blustered boisterously, but was not like the wind immediate on a tent. How right the Canon is, he thought, about fanaticism. His physical health was good, apart from heartburn due to a fatty diet. Jim's speechless spouse had produced white whale for luncheon. His mental health left much to be desired.

A far door slammed. It might be an Eskimo to see the Canon, who was a Christian father to his people. There had been a congregation of about twenty this morning, children and adults, all devout. They stifled the coughs and sneezes which the first Outside visitors since freeze-up had brought to Hummel Point. Skafe could not but feel Christ in this static place where his own restless spirit was alien.

It might be Sally, come for something, come to pay a duty call on him to cheer him up. *You seem sort of moldy,* she said this morning. *Do you feel all right?* He felt simply fine, thanks very much.

It might be Jim. If so, he would feign the sleep of the damned.

Then he recognized Brian's rubber-heeled step, firm, unhurried, going somewhere, coming here. "Come in," he said.

"There is one radiogram," said Fiske. He handed it over. He was like some good adjutant to some Commanding Officer, the kind of adjutant who smoothes a colonel's way in peace or war. But this C.O. had nothing to command. Also Fiske had shot down six Migs in war, whereas Skafe had not been to war.

The message was: GREAT NEWS SK NOT THAT I ENVY YOU THOSE ARCTIC BREEZES AS EVER MILES.

Probably Sleeman was not feeling his oats as Number Two. Probably,

like so many annoying people, he was impelled to facetiousness by tele-
gram. "What a damned stupid message."

"Slightly what I thought in the circs," Brian said, and continued about
the weather. It was blowing everywhere . . . low-pressure trough . . .
heavy overcast tomorrow . . . Skafe got the depressing gist of it. "It's
turning out to be a bloody awful month. I raised Camp Husky too.
They've found out the trouble with that cat. Some sort of a main track
bearing will have to be flown in."

"These blasted machines," Skafe said. "You're better on a dogsled."

"How right you are, sir," said Brian Fiske. "Another thing: *Life* magazine are waiting complete with plane at Turtle to come and do a picture
story. The Arctic is in the news, and you are one item that is not a
deadly secret."

"Deadly," Skafe said. "If not a secret."

Brian smiled. He had an abundance to smile about personally, nothing
to smile about businesswise: and he did not allow romance to blind him
to business, not for one instant. We can make it up to him, thought
Skafe. "Oh, by the way," he said, "if you get a chance to talk to Turtle
without an audience, tell them to load the planes with staple food, and
some clothing too. Gus Vinblad there is an old Arctic hand. He will
know what to send. But for God's sake don't mention it to Jim. I cannot
tolerate more affection."

"He's crazy about you," said Brian Fiske, thereby linking Skafe to a
general elder queerness, craziness at Hummel Point; or so Skafe felt,
trapped in his upper bunk; next door to a Canon and a church; outside
the wind again and good old Jim; or a tin mug of tea and a tidbit of raw
caribou to taste like ice cream set upon heartburn in some Eskimo home;
and here with him the lordly adjutant, perhaps a little less sure of himself than usual, who said: "If the wind drops a bit, and flying conditions
still seem to be hopeless, I think I'll get Avakana to take me to the plane
and back tomorrow, just to check that all is well."

"Why bother?" he said. "All will be well."

"Those toggles might break out again. And don't forget, sir, that it's
close to the pressure ridge . . ."

He had not forgotten, and he saw no danger of a shift of ice. Boom—
boom, through the very pinnings of this world, his daughter came hand
in hand with Brian Fiske; Jim Willis welcomed him at Hummel Point.
"What did you say?"

"I said that Sally wanted to go along for the ride."

"You said that, did you? You have the bland effrontery to inform me
that my daughter wants to go riding with you on the sea ice. You seem
to imagine that my daughter is some sort of cuddlesome appendage to

be taken into all manner of hardship, even on a dogsled. Why? For your pleasure and your entertainment, to gratify your boundless arrogance. What Sally wants? Not at all—what you want, and what you want must trail behind you. You have many qualities, young man, but you have much to learn. Now listen to me . . ."

He did not consider whys or wherefores, justice or injustice, although within himself he heard some protest. From Fiske there was no protest. His face went white. He shook his head slowly once, to the right, to the left, to center again. Skafe sometimes pretended to lose his temper when, on necessary occasions, he lived up to a reputation as a prize bawler-out. Now he lost his temper. He gave Fiske brazen hell, and when he had finished, Brian said: "Is that all, sir?" without a trace of the afore-mentioned arrogance.

"Yes," Skafe said. Alone again, he felt much better. His heartburn had vanished. His pulse slowed down. He might be sorry soon, but the victim was a worthy one, no softy sop. In fact, having flattened Fiske, he admired Fiske more than ever. He was a young man in love. Was it such arrogance to want to have his girl with him in a car, in a train, on a dogsled? God Almighty, Skafe thought. Don't I remember myself with Anna? Now, as the wind blew about the hut, as the far door slammed again, as footsteps sounded once again, he began to feel remorse, not unmixed with trepidation: it was Sally, at her hostile best.

"It may interest you to know," she said, "that Brian flatly refused to take me with him to the plane."

"He didn't say that," Skafe said. "He said you wanted to go."

"You didn't give him time to tell you. If you have to take it out on someone, why choose poor Brian?"

"Poor Brian my foot," he said.

"Yes, poor Brian," Sally said. "Did it occur to you that this isn't the easiest situation in the world for him?"

"Well, not the easiest," he said. "Nor the hardest."

"I know it's appalling for you with Jim. But what about me? Half the time he calls me Anna. No, you're not Anna, honey, are ya? It's not our fault that you ran off with Mummy, and that Jim seems to love you madly for it."

"If he hated my guts, I wouldn't give a damn," Skafe said.

"It's poor Jim's solution. Besides, what is wrong about him admiring you?"

"What is wrong," he said, "is that I am not admirable."

"Some people seem to think so," Sally said, "including Brian. Then you go and shatter him. Is it so arrogant to have self-confidence? You ought to know."

He was cursed with a faithful memory. On the eve of departure to divorce, her mother said to him: *You are so sure of yourself—not arrogant, I don't quite mean; and not conceited, not yet anyway—just supremely self-confident about everything.* "I suppose not," he said.

"He had been steeling himself all day to talk to you; and then you just blew him out."

It was possible that the blowing out had been related to the prospect of that talk. "All right," he said. "I owe Brian an apology. Send him here." Now who sounded arrogant?

Sally turned at the door. "You won't be horrible again?" She asked him. She appealed to him. She warned him.

"Of course not," he said. "What do you take me for?"

She laughed. God, she looked happy, all the world and life discovered. "I take you for Husky Skafe," she said. "And so does he. And so should you."

It was not so easy to take himself for that well-known man, because he was not that man. He was Husky Skafe found out. He laid Stefansson aside, descended from his upper bunk, dipped his face in water, combed his distinguished gray hair, steeled himself to apology and a talk, and listened to the loathsome wind.

"Brian," he said. "I made some offensive and unjustified remarks which I did not mean. I withdraw them and apologize." The manly apologist, he mocked himself.

Fiske showed some embarrassment. He blamed himself, but he did not mean to take things for granted or be arrogant, God knows, but he seemed to be more than slightly round the bend at this particular point of time . . .

"Who isn't?" said Skafe. He got out the rum which he had been denying himself because of Jim. He poured two tots and stowed the bottle. "Sure as fate," he said. "Jim will smell it in the wind, and be along."

"He's an extraordinary chap," Fiske said, "the most affectionate old cluck I ever came across, and no fool either."

Now Skafe drank some rum, and waited. He had lost the upper hand by loss of temper and subsequent apology. He would regain a measure of the upper hand by waiting for Fiske to say whatever it was he wanted to say, and even if one was more than slightly round the bend, one could hazard a guess as to that.

One would be right. "Sir," said Brian Fiske. "May I ask Sally to marry me?"

One had been right about the subject. One had been wrong about the approach to the subject. *May I ask* was formal and old-fashioned. He felt a certainty, and it frightened him—he felt a certainty that if he said No, this young man would not ask Sally to marry him, damn him. So Simon Skafe was back on his heels again, or the war, but of course it was not a war, had been carried into his own country. "You're sure?" he said, for want of anything more sensible to say.

"Yes," Brian said. His father was a forester for Cartwright River, the lumber people on Vancouver Island. His mother was from Springfield, Mass. His grandfather owned a hardware store at a small town on the Nashwaak River in New Brunswick—so much Skafe had learned by now. It was not much to know, and undistinguished; yet there was a solid ring to it.

"And Sally?" he said.

"I told her not to speak to you until I had asked you, sir."

And what can it be but the sureness of love that makes my headstrong Sally wholly obedient to you? he thought. "But if you are sure, and Sally is sure, and she is twenty-one, why ask me?"

"Because I am in a slightly risky business. And because everything between you and Sally is . . . I can only describe it as true and good. And because I respect . . ." He let it go at that.

"When would you get married?"

"In the summer," Fiske said. "Sally wanted me to meet her mother first."

What would Sally's mother think of him? She would like him. Any woman who was a woman would like Brian Fiske. She would like the casual way he cloaked his will. She would have an intellectual bohemian's weakening of the knees if she heard him sing Big Rock-Candy Mountain and Beethoven one after the other. She would dislike his ambition, but Anna would approve.

"Brian," he said, "my marriage with Sally's mother failed. I don't think the fault was entirely mine . . ." He had never discussed the subject with John and Sally. Nor would he discuss it with them. Nor had he discussed it with anyone else, not even with Mac, because Mac had blamed him. But now he told Brian Fiske about the failure that had been his by initiative but not his altogether.

He saw it all quite well from here in a hap of circumstance at Hummel Point. He saw also what he might have seen before—that Brian Fiske, the self-assured, the one who said that *luck is what you make yourself,* the one who immediately replied: *I wouldn't be interested, thank you* to a princely offer—that Brian Fiske was another of the same, the qualities, the faults, the bite, the blinkered vision. And the wind blew on, and lurking somewhere was loving Jim. ". . . And so I do blame myself," he said. "I am telling you this because perhaps you ought to know—also because I see a similar danger for you. But there is a difference which makes the danger less, and the difference is Sally, who meets life and people and events with a gusto Anna never had. Sally does not suspect the practical mundane world. She belongs to it. You must be firm with her and cherish her."

"Thank you, sir," Brian said.

Now what? Now tell him that we made a temporary appointment from within the organization to Skafair, and that the job awaits him? Tell him the truth—that I was sure I would get him one of these days, either when he found out that luck is not quite what you make yourself, or when he had proved himself enough to himself—that I arranged for the spinning of some gossamer. Unscrupulous? Not at all. I want a good man, and I get him. But the trouble is that he has got my daughter. And now if I say: *Skafair is yours*—I never did like that word *Skafair*. It was a Sleemanism, slightly slick—if I say: *Skafair is yours*, he will pick up a wedding present and throw it in my face.

So I shall be cunning, pontificate a little, state a few generalities, work on Sally, bide my time. Now I see him disciplining himself to decline with courtesy. "You must realize," he said, "that Sally will, in the normal expectation of events, have a lot of money of her own one day."

"Yes, I know," said Fiske.

"Such a situation," he said, "makes no small demand upon the character of the husband, touching particularly his vanity and self-respect." Not a bad piece of pontificating.

"Yes," said Fiske. He looked unhappy, trapped by that rich vulgarian, future father-in-law.

But a knock on the door, Jim's tentative knock, and in he came, a gangle of smiles, and then a glazed fixation of a smile as he saw the two glasses with the rum. It was pathetic and indecent, and Skafe said: "Brian and I are having a talk. I'll be over later. How would that be, Jim?"

"Sure," Jim said. "Sure, sure." He went out. He rushed away in his sealskin boots with the fancy trim, and the door of the mission hut slammed.

"Poor sod," said Brian Fiske, not concealing a certain annoyance with the brutal Skafe.

"I shall have to ask the Canon what he thinks," Skafe said. "Now where was I? Ah yes, we were discussing self-respect. Or shall I say Pride? It is a subject to which I, as a mortal sinner, have given some thought—pride, an integrity of self-respect. Pride, vanity. Where does one end, the other begin? How easy it might be for the rich wife's husband to bitch things up for all concerned by confusing his vanity and his self-respect." He stood, and so did Fiske. "Well, Brian," he said, "that is all I have to say except to wish you happiness. Now go and fetch that girl of ours, of yours, and we will celebrate."

Fiske looked at him. "My God, you're no fool," he said, and departed chuckling.

There was a passage across to the Canon's quarters, which Skafe took. The old man's Bible was open before him. He lived to Christ's Passion less than two weeks away.

"Canon," said Skafe, who felt more like himself again, more like the prideful man who worked his will on other men, "I have two sinful matters to discuss. The first is that I much regret losing my temper with young Brian an hour or so ago. You must have heard me."

"I heard sounds of wrath," the Canon said. He pronounced it rath, as in lath. "Sometimes a rightful or a wrongful honest rage—the air is cleaner than before, and no harm done." He smiled with peace and innocence. "Very wrong of me to say so. True, alas. Is all well, my dear Mr. Skafe?"

"All is well," he said. "But all is not well with Jim. Whenever he gets me alone, he begins to ask about a drink, and I cut him off short. But he is getting desperate. What should we do?"

"Poor fellow," said the Canon. "Every year alcohol arrives—in the boat, with other visitors. We try to keep it from him. Once I poured a bottle away before his eyes; but that was a well-intentioned cruelty, and Jim in a slough of despond for months. I pray for forgiveness in this, but I believe that the best thing, the least bad thing, is to let Jim drink his fill, and then the devil sleeps in him again." The small old Canon smiled. "Would that the devil slept so peacefully in me."

Skafe thought him a most endearing bigot, and went back. He extracted the second and unopened bottle in its traveling bag from his zipper bag, and here the young people came, the comings and the goings through the wind, the children came. Also the Canon with an afterthought, dressed in his parka for the wind: "Junie is too small to matter, but Noel—I shall invite him here to spend the night with me. I have hopes for that boy, high hopes. Give me a few minutes, Mr. Skafe, to fetch Noel from the Elephant and Castle."

Simon drank to the children's health and happiness, and they drank to him, and all drank to a few in the world Outside. Then the Canon and Noel Willis came along the church, talking Eskimo. Then Skafe took his bottle and his leave. He looked at them both at the beginning of their journey, and he said, as if he had some wisdom to impart, he said humbly enough: "Be careful." He knew little, but he knew something of physical love, and he thought about it, walking through the church, out to the wind—he thought that nothing was so beautiful with love, noth-

ing so eternal in its brevity within the brevity of life, nothing so be-
smirched by prudish hypocrites. God keep her safe with him.

CHAPTER TEN

HE FOUND his way through darkness in a moderate blow to Jim Willis's
house, the Elephant and Castle of that humorous old clergyman. He
was at the doorstep when he remembered that the last time he had drunk
rum with Jim had been at a cabin by the Mackenzie River in the year of
Our Lord 1932. But it was slightly—as Brian would say—it was slightly
too late for second thoughts, so he went in—through the ice porch
which was a deep-freeze of fish, caribou, white whale, seal, potatoes,
petrified blood and guts, through the coat room which doubled as a privy,
and where he removed the parka from himself and the parka from the
rum, and he went in.

"Hi, Jim!" he said. "Shall we have a drink?"

Ida was sitting silently with Jim, but she slipped silently away to be
with Junie in the bedroom.

*Jim sipped at the mug. He sniffed rummy steam, and sipped again,
and sipped.* "Anna," *he said admiringly.* "First time I seen you take a
drink . . ."

"*Have you been to New York?*" *she asked.*

"*Yes,*" *he said. He saw the tall city on the island.* "*Have you?*"

"*No,*" *she said . . .*

"*No more, thanks,*" *he said.* "*I'm traveling tonight.*" *He watched Jim
pour triple number three.*

"*Put it off,*" *said Jim.* "*What's one night on the road to doomsday?*"
He chuckled at his wisdom. "*You persuade him, honey.*"

"*I can't,*" *she said.* "*He has an appointment with destiny or doomsday.
He's got a date.*" *Her face, somber and abstracted, came fully and sud-
denly to life.* "'*Got a date with an angel,*'" *sang Anna Willis.* "'*Got to
meet her at seven. Got a date with an angel. I'm on my way to heaven.*'
You can't stop a man with a date," *she said, looking out of the window.
It was half past eleven, and the dusk was falling . . .*

He kissed her on one mosquito-fuzzy cheek and then the other. She was his child that time outside the cabin above the river. How rarely may woman be a child to man . . .

Anna went to tuck her husband in. "Husky, m'pal?"

"No," she said. "It's Anna." Her face was kindly, looking down at him.

"Here, honey!" Jim reached for her, but she pulled away. "Same li'l iceberg," said Jim, offended. He sighed and slept.

Skafe looked out of the window at the dawn. The smoky colors of the dawn were good. Mosquitoes drummed on the screen like a medium drizzle.

"I'm ready," she said. She carried a dunnage bag. She left the cabin. Sakfe turned at the door. "Sorry, Jim," he said.

Jim was asleep, unable to accept his friend and late partner's apology.

"Hell," Jim said. "The Company use me good; the DOT use me good; the Mounties, never had no trouble with them, decent bunch, they always used me good; the Canon, bless his holy heart, he uses me good; the Huskies use me good; Ida uses me good—now see, she ain't no Anna, couldn't be, I'm not pretending." Jim was on number four, holding his liquor like a gentleman. He was a slightly screwball or screwy gentleman. "Where was I at?"

"You were at everyone using you good."

"Sure, everyone. Most everyone. Husky," he said. "You heard of the Nahanni country?"

"You bet," he said. "But you tell me more."

So Jim told more about the fabulous Nahanni country—hot springs, so they say; like the tropics, so they say; even palm trees growing in some secret valleys, can't quite swallow that one; but the gold, the Gold, the GOLD was gospel. "Say, Husky," he said, "what was that rhyme Anna spouted to us sudden, I guess she meant to be a wee bit snarky, but I had it coming to me. Rum and Gold, eh, something, was it?

> "Little drops of rummy
> Gold dust in your hand
> Makes a mighty ocean
> Never-never land."

Simon remembered it, and being annoyed with her, in love with her already.

Jim cackled. "Great," he said. "She got the brains, that kiddo. Have a top-up, Husky."

"Still got some," he said. "I'll coast, Jim, thanks." I ain't got no lullaby dream, he thought.

Jim helped himself, and brought the kettle, did not spill a drop. "I'll tell you something," he said. "You're a great guy, Husky, and you never had no vices, not rum, not women not to speak of, nothin'. Hell, I bet you don't even go pornographee."

Now he was Casper Milquetoast. "Oh, I don't know, Jim," he said. "I like to read a nice juicy bit of sex."

"Nice juicy bit of sex, that's rich—but careful, brother, Junie mustn't hear that stuff. Say, Husky, why'n't I get Junie out to sit with us? We can keep it clean." Jim stood, and started for the bedroom door.

"No, Jim," he said.

"Okay, then. You're the boss." He sat again, thoughtful with his rum, nursing the wide-bottomed mug. "That Camp Husky place of yours," he said. "That *Nunangiyak*." He pronounced it like an Eskimo. "Is it oil you're after, Husky, gospel truth?"

"Yes, Jim," he said.

"What use is oil up here? Hell, oil's a pipedream. That's good—oil's a pipeline pipedream. No offense meant, Husky."

"None taken, Jim," he said, when his ex-partner in furs and in findings at Turtle Mountain had regained solemnity. "What is your translation of *Nunangiyak*, Jim?"

Jim's sallow face was flushed. He screwed up his eyes and held his head. He had long thin dirty hands. "Something growin' from the earth, small land, far island—that's a corker, you got me there, I wouldn't know. All I know is I used to run my trapline to the Cape—I'm too goddam thin to be runnin' traplines nowadays—and then make out across after bear—shot ten, no twelve in my time up Nunangiyak way—make a landfall on that curvin' hill, and the she-bear's den up in the valley for the cubs, but I never shot a she-bear havin' cubs, or with her cubs, I'm soft, I guess. But I tell you, that's a great place, Husky, and I'll tell you somethin' else—that valley looks like gold to me, but I never got around to getting there in summer yet. One day I will. Say, Husky, mebbe your boys could put me up like I'm puttin' you this minute if I got around to boatin' thataways one summer?"

"Sure, Jim," he said. "You would be most welcome."

And so Jim would be, to exiles like Jorgensen and Rosenheim.

"But that's no dice," Jim said. "You got the mineral rights, I guess."

"You're welcome to any gold at Nunangiyak, Jim," he said. There was no gold, but nothing was impossible. *Don't forget that gold is where you find it, Husky.*

"That's mighty big of you," said Jim. He finished number five, and took a fairly modest number six. "You ought to go there," he said, "before them goddam oil rigs spoil the place."

"I plan to fly on from Hummel Point," Skafe said. He planned to fly and prayed to fly.

"Yeah, I forgot. Know that word *Hummel,* know what it means? One of them wildlife fellas—they sure do use me good, them guys—one of them, he told me a Hummel's a billy-goat or a buck without no horns. You ain't a hummel, are you, Husky?" Jim laughed wildly at the notion of a hornless Husky, wiped his tears away, and said: "Hummel, my bony arse, you sure ain't that."

Silence but for Junie's small coughing in Jim's bedroom, and the wind's small thunder on Jim's house. But the wind and the coughing were intermittent. Jim jerked his head to the radio alcove. "I heard the weather before you come," he said. "Heavy overcast. Winds five to ten southeast. That's *Hila kapuk,* sure as I'm sitting here. One helluva month it's turnin' out to be. Say!" he said. "You got itchy pants to travel, Husky, ain't you?"

"I do want to see that cat train leave." Or he could have said that he wanted to reach a journey's end.

"You won't get there by no *tigmiak-puk,* not by big flying bird, you won't, in *Hila kapuk.* So you got itchy pants, why don't you travel?"

"By dogteam, you mean? It's quite a journey, Jim."

"Quite a journey, hell. Two sleeps would do it easy, if you don't have to sit a blow. You take Charlie and the dogs. You travel. *My name's Husky. Here I come. I'll show you with your airyplanes.*" Jim's sixth drink was low. "Yeah, you show 'em," he said, yawning. "*Show 'em.* That's what you been doin' all your life. I guess mebbe that's your secret I been hunting for." He stared in bright blank loving revelation at his old trapping mate, prospecting partner.

"No secrets, Jim," he said. "What secrets has a hummel got to show 'em?"

Jim laughed again and wiped his tears. "You're a scream," he said. "You always was in your quiet way, and you ain't changed, the millions didn't change ya. I got to take a leak."

He was not quite steady, coming back, and he slumped at the table, and said: "Sad thing, sad thing is: fella I cared most about in all my life was the fella didn't use me good. And Anna—why's pretendin'—Anna didn't use me good. An' mebbe I didn't use her good, an' mebbe she didn't use you good. Mebbe it's like what you used to say about them dragonflies, they hunt the bulldogs, and the bulldogs hunt mosquiters, and mosquiters bite the goddam boss, and then where are you?"

"Yes, where are you, Jim?" he said. "I think I'll follow your example."

He was not without cunning in the steps he took out there to end the party. He gave Jim time for one deep, fiery, furtive blissful snatch; and then he went back, and what Jim had taken now upon the rest was taking hold.

"Bunk down," he said. "Bunk down to beddy-byes, okay? An' thanks a million. Thanks a million, Husky boy." Jim laughed, and then forgot what he was laughing at. He made it to the sofa. "Hell, no!" he said. "That's Fiskey's place." He was no less good of heart when good and drunk.

Ida appeared to give support with an arm around Jim's waist, to lend support with a shoulder for Jim, who turned. "Ida sure does use me good," he said. "You're a billionaire, and what you got that I ain't got, you tell me. And one thing you ain't got I got is Ida." He teetered with a dawning thought, suggestion, but it never dawned. "God bless ya, Husky, you ain't changed."

"Sleep well, Jim," he said. Unchanged, and blessed by Jim, he left Jim's house. The billionaire was inclined to think that he would take Grace any day in preference to Ida. He made a small joke of that to himself as he walked in another dying wind, first to Avakana's tent where he spent a little time; thence again en route to the mission hut. It was perhaps the kind of small joke that Grace, who used him good, would not quite understand, but that did not make her less dear to him. The dragonflies etcetera, he thought. Scissors cut paper. Paper wraps stone. Stone blunts scissors, up and down the river.

It was midnight. The Canon prayed at the altar. Noel Willis slept in an improvised bunk of pews turned inward. He knocked, and heard: "Come in," from Brian, who lay on the lower bunk, and Sally upstairs.

"I hope you don't mind," Brian said, getting out. "I looked in Jim's window, and thought I would leave you to it."

"Thank you, Brian," he said, and told them of the plan he had made at Jim's suggestion. They were pleased. They thought it was a good idea, because they thought—they had agreed this evening in their wisdom— that much more of Hummel Point would be more than he could take. "Besides, you're a tough old nut," she said, "and you'll love showing everyone on that dogsled."

Brian said goodnight, and made tracks for his sofa, so chivalrously left for him by Jim. Skafe went out. He did not want to disturb the Canon at his prayers, and so he knelt in Anglican style and offered prayers. When he had slightly run out of prayer, he sat again to find that the Canon had finished praying and stood before him. "I wondered if I might talk to you," Simon said.

"Pray do," the Canon said.

Then he told an old story quietly, while here and there the sleepers slept, a son, a daughter. Then he confessed that he was running from here to yonder where his restless spirit called him. Then he gave Sally into the old man's care.

"Have no fear," the Canon said. "They are good children. And so, my son, do penance on the trail." He blessed Simon, and he said: "May God bring wisdom to your striving." He smiled as sweetly, as expansively, as fleetingly as an Eskimo.

Love thine enemies. Strive on to Nunangiyak in the morning.

CHAPTER ELEVEN

THEY TRAVELED to the north and west. It was a monotony of white—of the creaking, hissing, bumping sled—of Avakana calling to his dogs—of the leader ranging at command to skirt another tumble of rough ice that loomed in dim white weather—of smoke a cigarette and cough and spit to see the frozen globule roll—of talk occasionally, and run occasionally for warmth, and watch the dogs scoop snow with bleeding jaws, and see them excrete in harness, dragged along—of try the pocket compass out: guess the true course to be three hundred and five degrees; then, with a variation of fifty-five degrees east, the compass course should be approximately two-five-zero; and so it was. Contrary to some opinion, the compass worked quite well in wayward fashion on the arctic sea—of watching for those cubes and chunks of ice that struck a dangling foot most painfully—of dark glasses misting up again—of the bustling, bounding square brown man who sweated as he drove his dogs, calling, cursing, chanting in his throaty voice. These were some variants, diversions in monotony, not boredom, peaceful idleness, monotony.

While he sat behind, passenger and admirer of Avakana on the cold sea ice, Simon thought vaguely, idly in the dim white weather. He thought of Grace who waited for him in Antigua. He thought of Anna in Jamaica, but she did not wait for him. From this white peace—the trundle, hiss and bump, the stout man calling, spittle-strong, the image in the ice, a rabbit's head, a lop-eared bunny fell behind—from this white peace, he saw to peaceful Grace. Love vexing and perplexing was a stranger here. And now the wind puffed up along the trail. It chased them, raced them, picked up snow to run on snow, and everywhere the snow ran on ahead to race them on the trail to Nunangiyak.

But that squall died, and he was warm again. The Canon had enjoined him to do penance on the trail. He did not see cause for much penitence about Jim. He did not see that anything that he had done had harmed Jim Willis. If Jim must live in exile, and he must, or die in alcohol, then Husky Skafe had helped him to that safety and that happiness, for Jim was happy while the devil slept. Jim wanted nothing, not even a million from the billionaire, fella he cared most about in all his life, only fella didn't use him good. Jim asked for rum, and as a tipsy afterthought, to seek gold at Nunangiyak where there was no gold that he would never get around to seeking. He did not ask for love; he gave it and he won, God damn him.

But there was penance to be done. Skafe had pitied himself at Hummel Point, two days and a half in a hap of circumstance. *Ask for this great deliverer now, And find him eyeless in Gaza at a mill with slaves.*

My thoughts were of myself, he thought. Or in a wartime phrase: I was concerned with Number One. I am gaining quick promotion in that army of the rich who change the subject to themselves. And yet I am so often praised for my interest in my fellow men. Yes, he thought, when I am free to work my will on them.

He had a few such pains of penance in the dim white weather. But he lived a daydream on the trail. The hours dawdled by as he watched the forms and fancies of the ice that every traveler has seen—the bunny rabbit and the goose, green woman sprawling welcome in the ice, the wolf cub keen as mustard at salute, the skyline of the crazy city, a Shinto gate, and on and on, they lulled him, slipping past him; and once he saw wonderful old Willie Pitt in his awful wide fedora.

"Whoa!" called Avakana. Stop for icing, tea from a thermos, bannock. The dogs lay down in their double-tandem hitch, two by two along the trace, and one odd dog, and the white lead dog, Liar, making twelve in all; but Liar's white was cream against the snow. Avakana finished icing and righted the sled. The eager dogs sat up again; the others lay. Liar faced his master, awaiting orders. They were friendly enough, if not affectionate. Skafe walked along, and cuffed them in the hearty way they understood. "Not Liar!" Avakana said.

He turned back from the handsome Liar, who was watching him. "Why not?" he said.

"Good leader," said Avakana. "Bad devil." He grinned widely. "*Audlark-ta,*" he said. "Let's travel."

They traveled again. It was not cold—twenty or thirty below; but without wind there was no yardstick. A puff of wind, and instantly the cold nudged at his back. Still air, and he was warm. *You're a tough old nut*, his darling Sally said to him last night. Yes, I'm passably tough, he thought; and Avakana is passing tough. He is the toughest old uncrackable walnut in the business, and he said in a talkative moment an hour or two or three ago that after Easter he intends to give up being a famous hunter of Nanuk, and take this year's skins which he shares with Jim— his partner in furs and findings Hummel-fashion—take the polar bear skins and sell them on the Dewline for good money; then work on the Dewline for six hundred a month, half a year's money every thirty days would be it, I guess. Thus the Canon will lose his catechist to mammon, poor old boy.

Alone on the sea ice in dim weather—but good weather for traveling, and no travel but this was travel in the proper sense—he saw the confusion of the North, as confused in change as the rough ice was confusion halted, a big cold empty place with a few indigenous inhabitants, the slaves of muddle, and a lot of transients earning dollars where they could not spend them. He saw some sensible traders; some of the best, and less than best, lone policemen in the world; some administrators not quite up to it, some not nearly up to it, but their service was new; some missionaries. The Canon and I, he thought—we disagree and speak a language, but the picayune middle-roaders speak no language.

But here alone with Avakana and his dogs there was no confusion. There was a journey of perfect simplicity and purpose from Hummel Point, one hundred and fifty miles, two sleeps to Nunangiyak.

They had found a good lead, and were running straight, no trundling bumps, only a hiss of well-iced runners. He looked back at the parallels of the trail, going to meet, but never to meet. There, Hummel and a world beyond—here, the middle point, the only point in travel. Sally said this morning that Brian refused to take her with him to his plane, if and when flying weather came again, so could she please fly on to Nunangiyak to meet him? Skafe said No; she could go direct to Turtle as had been planned from the beginning. But she pleaded; she had set her heart on it, all the rest of it—*finish the journey we began, and why should I be different?*—*Tell her, Brian*, he said. Brian looked at her, amused, enmeshed, entranced, and he had her absolutely buttoned up. *Be nice*, he said. . . . *Yes, darling*, said the slave. It was quite beautiful to see, to envy and to think about from here at the middle point of travel.

They ran for twelve hours, seventy miles, Avakana said. He was pure Eskimo, or as near to such a breed as now existed after a hundred years of hospitable fornication. He was a man of the North, still farther north than this.

They camped at dusk. Skafe set out the dogline, digging holes in the snow for toggles at each end, and packing them. Avakana pitched the tent and lit the stove. "Pitch tent, take two minutes. Build snowhouse, take one hour." He laughed heartily, and said that he used a snowhouse in a blow, or sealing. His face was happy in action, oddly melancholy in repose.

"You travel old days with Jim," he remarked, inspecting Skafe's handiwork, which seemed to be to his satisfaction. "Jim good trapper, not so good traveler," he said. "Canon great traveler." Then he went to unhitch the dogs and hustle them to the dogline. He held a length of chain when dealing with Liar, but did not hustle him. "Bad devil in morning," he said. "Tired now."

Skafe cooked the supper. They were the Canon's traveling rations—a bag of frozen beans, and a bag of stew, much better than canned food. The Canon had pressed them on Skafe, not saying that he was loving thine enemies, but saying that he would travel no more this year. Now Simon melted snow in a pot on the gas stove, and put in a chunk of beans and a chunk of stew to make their one-course dinner. He was famished.

Avakana chopped up seal to feed the dogs, and there was a hubbub until they settled to eat in their several ways, some to gobble and some to eke it out, as varied in the private liberties permitted them as human slaves. These dogs were well cared for. In times of plenty they would be fed a pound or two of seal, and rations would grow short along the trail, and then a blow, and then one night of blubber while the wind blew on, and then two days of travel without food, the last of the blubber running through them, thin black excrement, and so on to be shot, worn out at eight years old—hunger, beatings, servitude from puppydom to death. Such care as they received was to a purpose.

"You good cook," Avakana said. He loaded himself with stew and beans, and Skafe ate well enough. It occurred to him that, apart from a few unimportant physical frills and skills, like driving an airplane or perhaps a snowmobile, there was nothing in the northern world—the only real and present world—that he could do that this man could not do far better. He felt humble beside the mighty Avakana, who said thoughtfully, drinking tea, with the luxury of powdered milk and three tablespoons of sugar: "No crap two days. Do real good crap tomorrow." He grinned about one of life's important matters, to be mulled over in prospect, retrospect and detail, but mercifully his English was too limited to do the subject justice.

A dog broke loose, and Avakana stopped the ensuing fight. Skafe watched him from the tent in the half light of a hazy half-moon. One could not say that he enjoyed the beatings, but he administered them with a will, basic master of his basic slaves.

Now the dogs were quiet in the quiet night. Good weather tomorrow? Maybe, he said, with the jowliest of grins. They planned an early start. It was five hours' travel to round Cape Tulugak, and then always rough ice there to cross before a last forty miles to Nunangiyak. If the ice at the Cape was not too bad, they might make it tomorrow night—one sleep, two long days travel. But nobody had been this way this year. Skafe asked about the bears that Jim had mentioned. That was old days, Avakana said. Jim forgot that old days were not nowadays. He spoke of Jim much as the Canon spoke of him—with an everyone-loves-Jim indulgence.

Now it was time for bed, and Skafe made to go out, but Avakana said: "Piss in corner," which he did; and when he had finished, Avakana was kneeling at his prayers. Skafe wondered whether he prayed to a whiteman Christ, ten days from Eastertide; or to an Eskimo Christ; or to a pantheist Christ of men, dogs, polar bears, seals, foxes, fishes. But he was a good Christian, a lot better Christian than Simon Skafe. His only stipulation about this trip had been that he must return immediately so that he could be at Hummel Point for the last week before *Tukuvik*, the day of death. For the *Innuit*, the People, a year's sorrow and a year's joy died and were born again at Easter when the days grew long.

Avakana used the corner too. He took off his shirt and pants, and stood, squat, muscled, greasy-skinned, to put out the lamp. Then he got into his deerskin bag, said goodnight, and went at once to sleep. Superman, arctic fashion, slept peacefully.

Skafe lay awake, nearly half this last and least trying stage of his journey done. Hummel Point fell back from him down a slide of hours and miles and pictures in the ice, a daydream of small penance on the ice, faded, finished. Now Nunangiyak called to him, a passenger in safe hands, but going where he willed.

He slept. He seemed to have that dream again about sitting on a sled behind the driver, idle Skafe with nothing to do but watch the ice, the forms and the fancies of the ice until the other team came chasing up, the big white lead dog, behind it dogs two by two in double tandem, and the leader homed on him, trotting strong and steady a thousand miles a day, right up now, right here . . . He woke, and wondered if he had had that dream, but he could not quite remember.

The night was quiet. After these days and nights of great winds, middling winds and small winds in the tent or at Hummel Point, or on the trail again—and always a commotion, wind or no wind, on the trail—now it was a silent night, *a great din of quietness*, Sally had described the

silence. Not a sound from his companions, no sound but a din of quietness in the arctic night.

Avakana gave him a mug of tea in bed. That tea and that cigarette
and that stove were the best immediate things that a man could imagine.
Well, you might add to them a basic warm-skinned woman to enjoy in a
sleeping bag. That would be the crowning touch, because a man's several
appetites throve on beans and stew and long hours idle on a sled. *You
have such healthy appetite,* or *appetites,* Grace said to him. *I think it's
time you settled down to be your age in lots of ways,* she also said to
him. I could settle you down right here and now to be my age, which
is not that of Methuselah, he thought. She enjoyed soothing his healthy
appetites, but was not particularly basic.

Avakana came in again. The beans and the stew were bubbling, and
the smell was wonderful in the warm tent in the cold where a man could
not smell a thing. "Crap great," he said with honest schoolboy pride,
and might have enlarged, but it was rather too basic a subject for squeamish Skafe at 6 A.M. or at any hour, so he went outside.

The sun was up. For the first time for some days—he could not remember how many days, because all time past seemed to be a vagueness
like *Hila kapuk,* and time ahead was nothing but a journey to Nunangiyak to see Chris Jorgensen, the stout Scandinavian with a one-track
mind, a one-rock mind, whose latest obsession was petroleum; and to see
Gerry Rosenheim, the stout Jew who stayed safe from heroin in the
North—for the first time for some days he could see the sun, or a washy
brightness that marked the sun at the horizon. It looked like better
weather on the way. The aircraft might beat him to Nunangiyak yet. Not
if he knew it, the aircraft wouldn't.

The dogs were still on the chain. They were all sitting up, alert. *"Hila
nakoyok?"* he said inside. *Good weather?*

Avakana wrinkled his nose in the way that means No, but qualified it
by saying: "Maybe." He knew so much; he was so complete a man of
the arctic weather, that he professed no certainty. He ladled stew and
beans into himself, belched contentedly and said: "Too much bad
winds," presumably about the climate.

It was the first time that Skafe had traveled with an Eskimo. He had
traveled with Jim through a winter long ago, and he had traveled alone
through a second winter at the treeline. Jim had been neat and quick in
those days, a clumsy sluggard compared with Avakana, who allowed Skafe
to help him strike the tent, but the help was a hindrance, not that Avakana minded. He was merry this morning, light-handed, light-footed
gnome. The sled was loaded, wrapped and lashed. The dogs were hus-

tled from line to trace, and harnessed. Some danced and yelped in their eagerness to travel. Some sat quietly. The anchor—a double-pronged grapnel—was set in the snow, and Skafe stood on it, one useful, if lowly function. Now only Liar remained on the dogline. He was a big dog, about a hundred pounds, a menacing animal. He growled at Avakana, who took him across—but the two went on terms of some equality—to the leader's place. Once harnessed, he sat up quietly, awaiting orders. Most leaders were not the boss dog, Skafe remembered. Very often the leader was a bitch. But this dog was the leader and the strongest male.

Now Avakana peeled off his duffel parka, stood sweating, bare to the waist, put on his deerskins, saw that Skafe was aboard, laughed loudly, plucked at the anchor, took two light steps or skips and jumped, turning in mid-air to sit, and they were traveling. That first gallop was an exhilaration in the quiet morning, but the dogs soon settled to a trot across the waves, the rolling prairie of the snow.

"Liar bad dog—vicious?" Skafe said. "You beat him?"

"No beat him," Avakana said. "Good dog, hate people." He looked round at Skafe, his sweat beaded into hoar frost, a wide grin across his face. "Hates most people. Likes kids, specially Noel—Jim's boy Noel."

They ran for the Cape. It was still murky weather, the sun showing dimly, but the glare was trying. Avakana had spoken little yesterday, except to his dogs. This morning he called to them, and ran to beat the idle Screamer, and hopped on again, and talked again in rudimentary English, mostly unlinked monosyllables, from which one could get a drift of meaning. He pointed to the north, and spoke of his own country on the great island to the north where the caribou were plentiful, but one year they did not come, and the people starved. His grandfather had died. His grandmother, not wishing to live, had sat in the snow with him to die. His father had died, and his mother had died, and the children had starved one by one, until only Avakana and a young brother were still alive. They traveled with a light sled and the four remaining dogs. It was far, and many sleeps for them, traveling slowly and more slowly until they ate the last dog at Cape Tulugak, which was strange to them, but they had heard of it from the Canon, who traveled each year to that northern country when the sun returned. They were too weak to travel farther. They almost died; but the sun returned, and the Canon came to find them at the Cape. Avakana pointed to the cliff that was showing now. He laughed no more, but he had not told his story sadly. He finished it in his strong-spittled voice, and then he cried encouragement with the high thin yelp of *Tiriganyak*, the fox, and his dogs ran faster for Cape Tulugak, the Cape of Ravens.

Of all the white men and the Eskimos who traveled, none were greater travelers than the missionaries, men like Canon Harper and a few Catholic priests, ascetics, weaker in body than the Eskimo, stronger in spirit for adversity. They bowed to their God, and fought through every trial that God could set them.

"Whoa!" he said at the shore below the cliff. There were a few wisps of pale brown grass along the shore, and that meant life, incredible that grass could live in this desolation. Avakana dipped into a satchel, extracted half an arctic char, chopped from the tail and gave a piece to Skafe. "You eat," he said. "*Irkalukpik* make warm quick."

They climbed a short way to spy the North. It was not bad visibility— a mile or more across the ice field, formed in the fall of the year when gales and currents met off this headland and broke the young ice and forced it up and tore it apart and threw it about until winter settled the affair. Winter killed the heaving melee to an eccentric graveyard, white headstones and green, and all askew. But there was smoothness here and there, empty lots within the untended cemetery of the ice.

Skafe gnawed his piece of raw pink frozen fish. It made his teeth ache and it tasted like salmon, very good. Sure enough, he felt the warmth of the frozen fish rise through him.

Out to sea, and bordering this minor tumble, was one high pressure ridge; beyond that, smoother ice, and forty miles to Nunangiyak. "Bad," said Avakana about the pressure ridge. The visibility closed and opened. Sometimes the sun came nearly through, and the ice stood in vague relief. Sometimes there was a blankness again of *Hila kapuk*. "We go see," he said, and he added, solicitous of his gray-haired charge: "You no try help. You walk after. Okay?"

"Okay," said Simon Skafe. He did not aspire to a heart attack—or a coronary, as Grace would say—in a Grand National through rough ice. He had found that hard enough work when he was twenty-four years old, not fifty as now, and never quite unmindful of what that tactless old Dr. Pugsley had called his *massive case of indigestion* at Gallery last summer.

So he followed at a walk. The ice was not very difficult on the whole. It was a matter of choosing a route to squeeze between this block and that, and thirty yards clear again, and now try to the right along a small arête of ice through which there seemed to be no way, and there was no way. It was five or six feet high, beyond it smaller stuff again. Avakana put the dogs at it. He spoke to Liar by name, not loudly. The misanthropic leader, who led but did not usually pull, now heaved in his traces, and the team scrabbled up and over after him, and Avakana bounded from slab to cube to pyramid of ice, and over to ease the drop, he was prodigious. The sled seesawed at the top, bumped heavily and tipped, but they lost no mud.

Avakana went along the dogs, straightening the traces of one pair that choked together, and on past Liar, whose head he touched, to climb another pile of ice to plot his way. It was all young green ice, sharp edged, steel-hard. It was cruel stuff, of cold haphazard beauty in the sun.

Even walking, and with rests while the master sought a way, and sometimes lending guidance to the tail of the heavy sled which might weigh eight hundred or a thousand pounds, Skafe was out of breath. He panted, sweating. Avakana had taken off his deerskins and wore the duffel parka. He steamed in rivulets of sweat.

There was no other word for him—he was prodigious, lithe as an eel, surefooted as a goat, strong as a chunky ox, quick as a cat. Simon thought now, watching him, that he had seen no such virtuosity in his life, the small man heaving, leaning, dancing.

He righted the sled again. But this time it had smashed heavily to break a foot of mud from the tail of one runner. Avakana swore fluently in English. Losing mud was not disastrous. You could smooth the rough ends with a hatchet. You could patch with more mud, if you had the mud. You could patch with a paste of semolina, also used as dogfood. But such repairs involved camping, cooking, pasting, freezing, filing, icing again. If the worst came to the worst, you could knock off all your mud and run on steel, but in cold weather steel was very slow.

"Not bad," Avakana said about his loss of mud. All the dogs except Liar lay flat. That animal sat on his haunches, looking back. The sun was shining at this time, on the tilted sled and on the man, on the dark dogs on the snow, and the white lead dog against whiter snow, on the last pressure ridge ahead, where peaks of ice made a petrified jumble the height of a house, but there were lower places.

They reconnoitered, and found a way, a gully that twisted through and up between that pale green ice and over a sloping cornice to a saddle twice as high as a man, and down beyond to an end of trouble, to a rolling white desert of the sea to Nunangiyak. "Bad ice this year," Avakana said. "No see such bad ice. Make it okay." He grinned at his passenger, who was an ignoramus, not offering opinions; but Simon thought that his smaller hero might have committed himself too lightly and boldly to a narrow place where he could not turn his dogs, where the only alternative to unharnessing and unloading completely to turn the sled was to drive his dogs on to make it okay through that short steep pass.

Now they went back, and Simon saw a bird in the sky above the Cape. The black raven dived, tumbled as if for fun, croaked once and disappeared behind the bluff. A polar bear had passed the tent beside the plane in the blow one night. But the raven was the only free living thing that he had seen in the Arctic in this week, not another beast or bird or fish, and it disappeared beyond Cape Tulugak.

Liar stared at him. He growled. That so wise an animal of noble mien should cherish hate seemed quite peculiar and disconcerting.

Avakana stirred up his dogs. He lashed the lazy Screamer with his chain, and Screamer screamed. "Liar!" he called in his raucous voice, and they were running.

They swung into the defile and round and up, the small man running by his sled, and once he leapt on top of his sled at a narrow place and off again, and his voice boomed in viridescent ice, between the walls, the slabs, the overhangs, the crazy columns.

Skafe followed close. They were nearly over, the leader over, the first three pairs were over, the odd dog over, now one pair of dogs scrabbling and straining up this side, and then the wheel dogs, and then the sled, rising to the saddle of the pressure ridge, Avakana dancing by his sled, hands to it, breast to it, his feet thinking for themselves on a sawtoothed floor of ice, it was miraculous. But the sled slewed left, and the second dog forward on the left—it was Screamer—was caught by the trace round a shaft of ice. Eleven dogs heaved vainly at the silent Screamer.

The sled had been guided up that cornice on the right, had slewed, and was now perched on the overhang while eleven dogs heaved at one garroted dog. Avakana ran forward underneath to climb the ice to free the dog.

Skafe might have sensed it about to happen, or he might have seen it happening. He did not know, and he would not know.

"Watch out!" he called to his smaller hero, Avakana, the Eskimo. But he called too late, or perhaps he should not have called, because the man heard him and checked below the sled as the overhanging cornice cracked, and the tail of the sled dropped free. Skafe saw it happen—he saw the runner, of wood, steel, frozen mud and ice, smash Avakana's head against the hard green ice that framed that place. He heard the crunch. Then he saw the strangled dog and its mate, the two wheel dogs, the sled, go over the saddle of the pressure ridge.

Avakana, the square man, lightning quick, lay in that narrow cleft of ice. He wore his sealskin boots, his deerskin pants, his duffel parka. He lay on his face, and he was dead.

CHAPTER TWELVE

SOME MEN are passably tough, Skafe thought. And some are passing tough. All are mortal; and this man's head was pulped between a falling object and a static object, both frozen hard as steel, if more brittle—both harder and less brittle than the human skull.

A few drops of blood dripped from Avakana's nose onto snow that covered the floor of that place. Skafe blamed himself in some way or other—for not calling sooner, but he had called at once—for calling at all, but he could not help himself. But the milk was spilt; the blood was frozen. There were things to do; he set about doing them.

First he climbed over to find the team lying, exhausted. Liar watched him. Screamer, the strangled dog, was not quite dead. He drew out Avakana's .25-.35 Martini action carbine from its place on the front left side of the sled, inside the canvas wrapper. It was loaded. He shot the dog, unharnessed it, and dragged it away from the other dogs, who lay afraid. Then he straightened out some harness tangles.

The sled had come unguided over the crest to fall and break more mud. There were a few things he could do, but he was not competent to make a porridge of semolina, a kind of milk pudding as Anna called it (à l'écosse) that she used to feed to the children when they were small. He could not apply thick semolina to replace lost mud. There were two more broken bits—one on the middle of each runner—where the sled must have landed on arrival north of the pressure ridge. The first piece of mud had broken from the tail of a runner, not important. But these were in the middle, long gaps, four inches deep, effective brakes negating the purpose of the runners. Therefore he took the hatchet and set about knocking off all the mud from the fourteen-foot runners, down to bare steel.

All of which took time. He was not an Avakana; nor was he the greenhorn traveler and apt pupil that he had been with Jim Willis twenty-six years ago. He was damned tired and damned upset and damned sorry and damned lonely, and now he blamed Avakana for the freak accident that had killed him. Everyone knew that ice as big and chaotic as that was dangerous. But they were so brilliantly skilled, so sure, that they risked it until the one time in a million when it happened. Now, twenty-six years later, he could still see Jim's sled turn turtle on one such occasion in one such place to crash beside the greenhorn's head, miss him by an inch or six.

That was the mud all off, and he could travel. But he had frittered hours away to nearly four o'clock at the vernal equinox when the night and the day were of equal lengths here, there, anywhere, the Arctic or the Caribbean. The weather seemed to be improving, against Avakana's expectation. Simon played with the idea of traveling all night or until the small hours when the crescent moon would set. The light would be adequate; the North Star would be sitting over Nunangiyak. But his dogs were tired, and he was tired, and he was not an Eskimo. He was far from being an Eskimo, and rather far from being anywhere.

The right thing to do was to camp—pitch the tent, tie out the dogs, feed the dogs, feed himself, make an early start tomorrow morning. All the trouble lay behind. Ahead lay forty easy miles to Nunangiyak.

Now he went for Avakana. He thought of taking a couple of dogs to lend a helping hand, but his dogs—yes, they were his dogs in a manner of speaking now, if he could manage them—his dogs were strange to him. So he went alone. Avakana was frozen stiff. It was an awkward load, if not a very heavy load, about a hundred and fifty petrified pounds to stand up against a niche in the ice, and stoop to topple it over his shoulder, and then to make that exhausting climb from slab to slab—the ice was not slippery—and up the pile and to the very top of the arête. His heart was pounding. He rested a while, and then let gravity do the work. Avakana gathered speed down the northern side like a rolling pin, and that was that job done.

He looked at poor dead Charlie Avakana, as blanched and dead as man could be, a mile from Cape Tulugak where Canon Harper had once found him starving. The Canon will blame me, Simon thought. The Canon blames me for everything. I am the despoiler of the North, the plunderer for gain, waxing richer and richer at everyone's expense, including the Eskimos'. How rich I am, right here and now.

Then he righted the sled with greater effort than that to which affluent men of his age were accustomed. He unlashed the wrapper and pitched the tent. It took him about twenty minutes, as against Avakana's two, but he got it up, and shoveled snow round the walls in approved fashion to stop the drafts. The right side of his face was numb. He took off his mitt and thawed it out, got that in time.

What next? The dogline. He took great care to anchor those toggles firmly at each end, because if he lost his dogs in a murderous melee of slave kill slave, he would lose some of his more valuable assets or capital equipment.

That done, he armed himself with Avakana's baton and the length of chain attached to it, and began to move his dogs, starting with the wheel dog Rover, like his namesake long ago, a friendly beast, a demon to work, a fiend to fight. There is only one thing to do, Simon thought, and that is be tough. But Rover gave him no trouble.

The other wheel dog did. It became impatient with his fumbling to release the harness, and turned to snap at him. Simon beat the lights out of that dog. I beat you, or you beat me. Stated otherwise, the veneer or outer skin peels off when the chips are down. He beat that dog to whining subservience, and hustled it to a place on the chain.

The others were chastened by his brutality, and gave little trouble. One dog, Idivaluk, had been urinating blood, he noticed. Probably Idivaluk's guts were rotted out. All the dogs' feet were bleeding from sharp ice.

He hooked each dog by the collar to a side length of chain along the main dogline, just out of reach of one another. Now only the leader remained, and it was getting on for six, the sun slipping down along to the rim of the sea. Skafe tipped the sled for insurance, gave Liar a wide berth, and approached him from the limit of the trace. Wrong, he thought. Should be bold and brassy, treat him like the rest. "Come on, Liar," he said politely, out of reach.

The dog stared at him. It stared him out. He had never met a dog who could stare him out. "Noel, Liar," he said. "Jim's boy, Noel. Good dog, Liar." He went forward a step. The dog's lips curled. It rumbled at him, staring at him.

He had adopted a policy, and being timorous, had not stuck to it. Back to his policy. He swung the chain on the end of the baton. "Come on, you!" he said harshly, taking the step to grasp the collar.

But he did not complete the step, for Liar made at him in hate. He moved the half-empty sled until the anchor tightened; then he lunged impotently, the harness jumping up and down along the trace. Skafe was frightened, and he hit him with the chain across the back, one side and the other, and now the dog was in a frenzy. *No beat him*, said Avakana, grinning. "All right, you bugger," Skafe said. "I'll shoot you." He meant it, and he went for the carbine and brought it here and aimed it at Liar, who knew all about that rifle, having seen it kill Nanuk and lesser game many times. The dog sat still and stared him out.

He would have killed that dog who beat him, but he needed that dog, and so he thought better of showing conclusively who was master and who was slave. He gave up, not very proud of himself, and went to get their supper. He wondered whether he should chop up Screamer, but decided not to. He chopped eleven portions of seal. I don't know what I would do without you, old friend, he thought to the hatchet. He thought that this was probably the seal who had met him round the corner of Jim's store when he had taken cover from Brian and Sally in a passionate embrace; but one frozen seal looks much like another mummified *philosophe* or Alfred Buxton, late of Algonquin Steel; so he could not be sure and he could not care less.

The dogs were all crazy for their supper, excepting Liar, who sat and stared at him, and did not eat until he went away.

He set a toggle in the snow halfway along the trace so that Liar's movements would be restricted. The trace was nylon. He supposed that Liar could chew it through, or do anything he chose to suit his wicked will; but Skafe did not know.

All good officers care first for their men, and he was supposed to be the leader of this expedition and, by God, one more growl out of that brute, and he would shoot it. The last thing he must do before caring for himself was care for Avakana, who in most ways was beyond caring, but somehow or other, he did not quite know why, and there were quite a few things he did not quite know why about—the right thing to do was to roll a dead man in a shroud. Not the sled wrapper, because that was needed to wrap the load. Not the sleeping skins, because Simon needed them to sleep on; and anyway, they were not big enough. For once he hit on the right solution. If Avakana slept in his deerskin sleeping bag, then he must fit nicely into it. What better shroud for a dead smaller hero?

Avakana did not fit so nicely as all that, by reason of his bulky clothes, but Skafe managed to squeeze him in, or to pull the thing on like a deerskin sock; and was astonished to find that both ends were open, not a sock, a sort of sleeve. The whole principle was to keep the heat in, keep the cold out, for which purpose a closed double garment of caribou hide was the most efficient insulator known to man. But Avakana slept with bare toes in the cold. It was incredible. It was another kind of human animal or hero, with an improved central heating system, and the square brown man was dead. He put him beside the tent, out of sight of the dogs; and now the unheroic Skafe could care for himself at last.

While he heated his stew and beans, and brewed strong tea, he thought about Avakana, famous hunter of Nanuk, great traveler even in the company of Eskimos, so quick today, but now as dead, as stiff, almost as solid as the ice that killed him. Tomorrow he would lash him on like Sam McGee from Tennessee, and they would run for Nunangiyak.

While he ate, he thought about Avakana's wife and children back there at home in a tent in a mound of snow—the blubber-bubbling stove—the morsel of raw caribou, ice cream, latest heartburn flavor, how delicious—the fish heads, entrails everywhere—the wife, a jolly chew-jowled type

—the red-cheeked children playing around outside, stop, take off the glove, shake hands—such charming children, all God's children, and some are doomed or all are doomed.

Now he had finished, and now he would sleep. He went outside. The dogs were curled up. They were quiet, including his enemy, the Husky dog. Round one to Liar. It was not dark. It was a pale moonland below the mountain of the pressure ridge. It was cold. He piddled full force to get that over with, and got into his sleeping bag with the carbine by his side, ready to repel Nanuk, mad dogs or Englishmen or anything. But he was rather lonely all alone. But forty miles away was Nunangiyak. Two sleeps to Nunangiyak, and there was nothing else for him but Nunangiyak. Why? Why now more than ever? I end what I begin. I'll show them.

And then he had one rather nasty thought that things were going wrong for him just once too often, that this was the journey he did not end, that this was the time that they would do the showing. He dismissed that thought.

He slept with a dream of dogs in ice, the forms and the fancies of the ice, the white dog lunging at him here and now, the world a howl of dogs and wind.

And so it was, not of wind, but of howling dogs. He dressed to quell them. The dogs sat up and howled. They bayed the moon that slanted off Cape Raven, or perhaps they howled for their master, Avakana, dead master of his trusty slaves. Simon did not know. He had never slept with a dead man and a dead man's dogs before. He bellowed at the dogs, and one by one they quietened and lay down, curled nose into tail again. Even Liar quietened, lay down alone, curled nose into tail again.

The moon had passed the south, and dipped to set. It was a tranquil, waxing moon. But from the north and overhead and across the sky, the northern lights were playing. They rippled up and disappeared and came again, now green as the hard sea ice, now red, white, lemon ribbon-candy rolling, or draw the curtains, close the curtains, or send the fingers probing, riding, stabbing, draw the fingers back, the many fingers of God's hand. Simon watched in awe of God, and went into the tent, and broke a sound old rule of travelers by taking the bottle from the bag and tipping it and taking four small sips of fiery rum for strength, for sleep, and into his sleeping bag and so to sleep.

The sled was loaded, wrapped and lashed, but the time was half past nine, and his heart felt rather heavy in his chest. It had taken him ages to do the jobs because he was unskilled labor, worth a dollar something on the Dewline, ninety cents an hour in dear old New Brunswick. But he had worked carefully in his clumsy way, and there was plenty of nylon cord to lash and double lash—a mass of stuff, the tent, the grub box, bags of food, his personal belongings—and at the tail the gasoline can, shovel, front half of a seal, and on the top a dead man in his deerskin shroud. It was secure, if not shipshape, Eskimo fashion.

Now he harnessed the dogs, starting with his old pal Rover. He administered one beating to one bitch called Snowball. He laid the chain about her ribs. It was not very nice of him, but Snowball was not a Pekingese. She was a friendly bitch to her human boss, but she had just bitten half an ear off her enemy bitch named Kingi.

The anchor was set. His precautionary toggle was still in position on the driving trace. This was the dangerous time—when they were fresh and raring to go; so he hurried to dig out the dogline toggles, and shoulder the long chain, and stuff it in a bag, and now all set. He walked up one side of the excited team, straightening harness, and to the end where Liar sat, staring him out in that menacing way. His black lips curled up to show his fangs.

"You big white bastard," Skafe said. "I hate you." He meant every word of it, and the result was quite surprising. Liar's bush of tail wagged across his back, no doubt about it, he was pleased, knew a good boss when he saw one. "Good dog," the good boss said, and Liar snarled at him.

He left the big white contrary bastard, and went down the other side of the team to dig out that extra toggle. He remembered—when you are fifty, and feeling it, there is usually something to be remembered—he remembered a toy dog called Napoleon who belonged to a friend of his. It was a similar type to that hundred-pound Liar, who was strong enough and violent enough to kill two men in unarmed combat. If you wished that Napoleon would stop his tiny painful nips you said *I hate your guts, Napoleon*, which made Napoleon love you. The reverse held true.

All the dogs but Liar were dancing in their harness. Liar awaited orders from that bastard Skafe. It was a perfect day at last, a mild morning in the latter part of March. It was the kind of arctic day that he remembered. Neither the killing winds nor the dead white weather stayed in memory, but this—the sun, the peace, the blinding perfection toned down to beauty by dark glasses. But could he drive a team of dogs?

He picked up the anchor and jumped aboard "Tsee!" he called. "Tsee!" Liar swung right from the pressure ridge—what greater triumph in all his life than this? "Tsee!" Right again. A capital T, sibilant and explosive. "Ho!" he called, deep, round and wet from the bottom of his throat; and the big white leader ranged to the left, and steadied on that lead, as smooth as an ice rink, stretching on and on.

The dogs settled to a trot. He felt in the satchel bag, which was tucked into the lashing on top of the sled. It contained a bannock or two for him to nibble on the trail, and the rest of Avakana's arctic char which was so warming on the trail, and his prismatic compass to guide him on the trail.

Nunangiyak lay due north of the Cape, three hundred and sixty degrees, or zero degrees. The compass declination or variation was fifty-five degrees east, give or take a few. Thus, to travel due north, he must follow a compass course of three hundred and five. The needle swung widely, because up here, above seventy north latitude, the turning error was very great; but it settled in the end. He tried it three times, and always a bearing of three-oh-five took him straight along the middle of the lead.

Things were good at last. They could not possibly be better in this bleak magnificence of traveling alone and small to Nunangiyak. With the temperature above zero, he was making six miles an hour on steel. He knew the speed because it was just too fast for him to keep up, walking hard. But on this lead he rarely had to run to guide the sled.

He encouraged the dogs in the best imitation he could make of Avakana's coarse strong-spittled voice. He mourned Avakana. The man was dead, and Simon Kepple Skafe had fumbled and faltered and made a mess of things, and he had feared a dog; but he had stuck it out and measured up, and this was his reward: to drive his dogs to his journey's end. With God's help he was making it, and God helps those . . . he thought.

Now out of a clear blue sky in the halcyon weather, he saw the face of his dead friend, Mac. *You're the boy*, Mac said to him with that wintry warmth of affection that might have been unique in Mac. *You're the boy*, Mac used to say to him on the rare occasions when Mac was pleased with him. *You go and muck yourself*, he said to him with murder in his yellowish eyes. Oh yes, he was a killer, Mac, no doubt. Mac could be a bastard too.

And he thought: Of all the battles I have fought, and of all the victories I have won, this is my greatest. I struggled and I prevailed, and I am warm, and the runners hiss.

Now many things were settled. Now Sally had found a man, and a damned good man at that, even her father must admit. Now, thanks to his father's tolerance and good sense, John would settle to the writing of his book in shades of gray. Grace was happy, and she had warned him. But she did not need to warn him, because it had been so unbearably wonderful again to be with Anna that he could not bear again to be with Anna. That was a cloud upon the perfection of this travel.

The plane had not yet come. Any time now he expected to hear a plane grow in the east from Hummel Point, or a plane grow in the west from Turtle Mountain, or a plane pass overhead to spy him and salute him with a dip of wings. *Life* magazine, perhaps, and what a story of tragedy and triumph it would make. Miles Sleeman would be very pleased about the PR impact.

He looked back over Avakana in his shroud. Cape Tulugak fell astern; already a mirage shimmered at a double cape. He took off his wolfskin mitt and his woolen glove, and the fur of the deerskin was warm to his hand. It was a miracle of spring, no less, no more. He sang a while. He sang the Wild Goose song, Oh, he would go where the wild goose goes, but he did not know many words to that song of a dreamer of the North. And then he sang Big Rock-Candy Mountain, but it did not suit his mood. He did not want the softy tropics where the winds don't blow and there ain't no snow, because what he had here on his way to Nunangiyak—three hours gone already; another three and he would be there with Jorgensen and Rosenheim, his good men and true—what he had here was the perfection of travel on a day of arctic stillness, arctic sunlight, arctic spring soon coming, and—as anyone who had ever traveled, knew with him—it was the best thing that existed in the world—better than loving a basic woman, better than hooking a fresh-run salmon, the best, the tops at the top of the world. He sang Wild Goose again, with *dees* and *dos* and *das* for the missing words, but his trusty dogs began now to sneak uneasy looks at him over their shoulders, as if he was crazy or something, and Liar slowed down with evident displeasure, big white brute, so he stopped singing, called a few strong-spittled *hos*, and a few explosive *Tsees* to be the boss again, and Liar ranged left and right within the highway of the lead.

He saw something. Could it be Nunangiyak already—the curving hill, the long low module, the cat train waiting for him? But no, it was not a module or a string of sleds—it was a house on a snowy hilltop, a square buff-painted house ahead. Surely not Nunangiyak yet? He traveled to that house in the magic of the gleaming arctic weather until he saw that it was not a house but a wooden box on the pressure ridge that ended this lead. He had been deceived that way before, and to him the box that was a house, the pressure ridge that was a mountain range—bland fathomless illusion—was the loveliest vexing trick that the Arctic could play on a traveler alone and small and infinite.

"Whoa!" he called. The dogs were tired. They lay. There was no footing for his anchor, so he bullied them on again, to swing left to the west along the ridge, and now he found snow, and set his anchor solidly, and let them rest, and he walked along the team, cuffing heads in the hearty way that they understood. "You sonuvabitch!" he said to Liar, with growing love. "I hate you." Liar wagged his tail, and raised his lips in a snarl that was a loving smile.

He climbed the ridge to have a look. It was nothing much. He could run straight over, but he wanted to choose the easiest way, and he wanted the few feet gain in height to see a few more miles at a tangent to the curve of the cold white desert of the sea to Nunangiyak, which could not be more than twenty miles. The air was still. The sky was blue, but hazy in the north.

The box which had been a house made a small and even more delightful world of this immensity. It had no lid, and was about three feet by two by two in size. It bore the words: SKAFE EXPLORATION in bold print, and in smaller print: *Project Husky*, and a code index: CDM266SUR.

The box would have come in by sea last summer season via the Mackenzie River, Aklavik and Tuktoyaktuk, he supposed, and have been emptied and discarded, and have floated down here to be caught and ejected in the storms of freeze-up time to be locked in ice, and quite unharmed at the top of the pressure ridge. Truly, he thought, the mark of a man can carry far.

He took a compass bearing, and was sure that he could see, almost sure, or was he sure? He nibbled at a frozen bannock from the satchel, no need of that calorific fish because he was as warm as toast, so warm that for the past hour he had traveled with the outer deerskin of his hood right back on his neck, and the inner deerskin only covering his ears, above his quilted cap. There were no icicles, but only hoar frost on the wolverine trim below his mouth. He took off his dark glasses and held them in one hand, and shielded his dazzled eyes between both hands the better to spy for the truth of Nunangiyak, but he could not be sure. There was a shimmer of haze to the north.

Then, the satchel slung on one shoulder, the glasses in one gloved hand, his wolfskin mitts hanging on their string around his neck, he turned to his dogs. Avakana's shroud was a glossy brown hump on the sled against the sun. Liar watched him. All the other dogs looked the other way to the west along the pressure ridge. Their ears were cocked. He saw what they were watching. It was a black object in the infinite gleam of white. It wriggled out of its hole and flopped on the ice. The seal had come up to enjoy a first sunbath of the spring.

Skafe ran, and he could still run fast. But the dogs had taken off. Only Liar, the lead dog, faced this way, and he was tumbled head over heels and spun, and regained his footing somehow, and saw *Naterk*, the seal, and now Liar led the riot.

The dogs, the sled with Avakana's corpse, the anchor bumping uselessly, prongs up—all departed westward. The seal dived in. Liar swung from the hole and passed the hole and went on running.

Simon chased them at a steady trot. They would soon tire on steel. The anchor would right itself to engage, or the sled would tip: It was quite all right, and he was not much dismayed, and it was not Liar's fault. Liar was only human. A noble beast, he thought. By God, I'd like to tame that animal.

The dogs still galloped, not very fast, perhaps at eight or ten miles an hour. Simon steadied to a walk, and turned to get his bearings, to view that Skafe Exploration box on top of the ridge.

He saw the box, and beyond the box he saw another thing. It was a pale rim below the blue of the sky—between the sky and the flat white ice. It resembled the low-lying cottonwool of fog that lay out at sea from Gallery in the summer. He knew what that pale fuzz meant: a blow was coming.

CHAPTER THIRTEEN

SOMETIMES the winds come stealthily. Sometimes they come full strength out of calm. This was such a wind. It rolled down on Simon Kepple Skafe as fast as a Southbound Express.

No sound of wind—time to check that the pressure ridge ran unbroken east and west as far as he could see—a rumor of wind—time to see that the team were going strong, swinging southwest from the pressure ridge. Already they had ceased to be eleven dogs and a lifeless sled, and had become a black corporate caterpillar moving on the white—a rushing of wind, a curtain billowing at him from the north—time to put up both hoods, to put on his wolfskin mitts, to miss his dark glasses. Then the wind was here.

You stupid bastard, he thought to himself in the wind, not the usual thought-language of the President, but the President of this basically one-man corporation deserved abuse. But having been foolish, and cock-ahoop foolish to make things worse, he knew what he must do. On the sled were food, heat, snowknife, all his needs and all his possessions. He followed the sled.

The parallel tracks were not hard to see, although the wind whipped at the right side of his face, and iced him up, and he had to thaw himself, and the pain between his eyes was horrible. But he kept on. Sometimes the tracks were two or three inches deep in the changing immutable skin of the snow; sometimes they were the faintest indentations; but he could follow them, and now, any minute now, he would come in the loud wind upon the chaos of his dogs, dead dogs, murdering dogs and upset sled.

But he did not come upon them. He blundered into a crack in the ice and bruised his shin, and cursed about that, and saw ahead for the fifteen or twenty feet that he could see, ahead and to either side, and all he could see was bare dark ice through the wrack of snow. He went a little further to see bare dark ice, no square-cut trail of a sled that ran on steel.

This won't do, he thought. I cannot follow what I cannot see. And now that he was really down to earth in a manner of speaking and with a vengeance, he found his lost head, and retraced his steps, and was lucky enough to hit the tracks where they had ended, at the beginning of this bare dark lead. He got the compass from the satchel and took a bearing up the tracks, roughly northeast true, which meant that Liar had led his team steady southwest. Yes, that must be all right. He backtracked for a while until the tracks vanished in the new drifts of this latest wind. He had expected that, and knew what to do—walk a bearing of due north, three-oh-five magnetic, to hit the pressure ridge to find some shelter.

Now he faced the wind. It was a killer. It cut his face with knives and then it froze him up. It froze his cheeks and nose. It froze his eyelids shut. He turned his back to it, and thawed his face again, bowing his head to meet his mitts. That took some suffering time; and then he took a back-bearing, the opposite of three-oh-five, and blundered backwards from one-two-five. He leaned and struggled backwards into wind until he tripped over ice and fell and got up again and faced the wind below the pressure ridge. Now let's see, he thought. Now it stands to reason that if I go east along the ridge, I will come to that wooden box. For some reason or other, the box, which he had thought was a house in the halcyon weather, did now seem like a house or a home to him. He found it. He had been quite clever.

He sheltered below the box in a cleft or small canyon in the ice. He was protected from east and west, but not from the north whence the wind swooped over and down at him, nor from the south, whence wind and snow eddied back at him. It could be worse, but it was bad enough. He crouched in there in a fetal position, not so much because a psychiatrist had placed him back in the womb of his mother, a Protestant O'Connor from the Ottawa Valley, but much because there was no other way to shelter from this wind. But again now he had the frightening thought which had occurred to him in the tent last night: that things were going wrong for him just once too often, that this was the journey he did not end, that this time he would not show them, that the showing would be done to him. This second time there was sound reason for his thought. The wind thundered all about him in his cranny, womb or coffin on the cold sea ice.

On his head he wore a peaked and quilted cap, a double deerskin hood; on his upper parts he wore a mesh-knit undershirt (the latest arctic thing), a Vyella shirt, a windbreaker, two layers of deerskin; on his lower parts he wore jockey shorts, long mesh-knit underpants, lined windproof trousers, two layers of deerskin; on his feet and legs he wore a pair of woolen socks, two pairs of deerskin socks, a pair of thick duffel socks, a pair of sealskin boots; on his hands he wore woolen gloves and wolfskin mitts. An Eskimo might sit out a blow in these clothes for days, but he was not an Eskimo.

In his wallet he had ten fifties and some smaller bills, and other oddments. In his trouser pockets he had a penknife, a key ring and a handkerchief. In his satchel he had about a pound of *Irkalukpik*, arctic char, and two frozen bannocks. These were the possessions that clothed and accompanied Simon Skafe. I had a thought once, he thought: that all men are mortal, but that to be as immortal as a man may be, a man must live. I did not finish it. A man must live and a man must die. The thought began by being philosophical or sardonic, but then the thought became a cold naked fear, and he listened in terror to the wind, and to a lesser keening of the wind in a slit between the boards of the box above his head. It might be said also that he owned that box—although being flotsam or jetsam, questionable in law, but his by possession which was nine points here and now if the box had been of the least value to him. It was of some academic interest that Skafe Exploration was the only one of his companies that he owned outright.

The cold was seeping into him. He knew what would be the first thing to go—his feet. If your hands went, there was something you could do— put them inside your bosom, rub them—and he did that now. But your feet—could you take off your socks to rub them? Could you put them in your bosom? You could jump about and run about and waste more body heat to keep your feet alive a little longer.

"Come on!" he said sternly. "You never packed up yet." He took out the hunk of fish and gnawed at it. The blow might last half a day, a day, two days or three—what mortal man can tell about a blow? He allowed himself a small portion of the small piece that remained. He ate a chunk about the size of a matchbox, and it did bring warmth to him. It was another miracle, a thing he must have known in the days with Jim, but had long forgotten until Avakana told him at Cape Tulugak.

And where would Liar have taken Avakana? Home to Hummel Point? Impossible, and yet if Liar found another lead as smooth as the one Skafe had followed this morning, the driver of dogs, Husky Skafe can do anything . . . *Heavens*, Grace said to him quite often. *Is there anything you can't do?* Dear Grace, he thought . . . But the dogs might run a long way. Or they might be half a mile from him. But half a mile was a thousand miles while the wind blew on. You know, he thought, encouraged by his cocktail canapé of fish, I had that dream about the white leader homing on me up to get me, a thousand miles a day to get me, queer dream, starting with McClintock. But the last I saw of a white lead dog, he was leading his team, galloping lickety-split away from that bastard, Husky Skafe. Liar likes kids, especially Noel, and I wonder why? Perhaps because the little bastards aren't bastards yet.

He was warm in his body, but his feet were leaving him. He had no feeling in his right big toe. He wiggled it, or what had been it when he had feeling in it. No good. He held his knees, and with his arms to help, he stamped his feet, one-two, one-two, and kept on doing that, but no improvement.

Now this was the choice: Shelter, conserve body energy, lose your feet? Or move about, consume body energy, get back your feet? A common school of thought said: *Keep moving. If you let yourself sleep, you sleep into death.*

But that was not what Vilhjalmur Stefansson advised. He said that you should shelter, keep still, keep dry, sleep as much as possible, move a little now and then, sleep again. There might be some things—such as Blond Eskimos and All-Fat diets and a friendly North—about which one could venture to disagree with Mr. Stefansson. But about the practical rules for arctic survival under primitive conditions he made absolute sound sense. He was the oracle.

The worst of the wind did not reach Simon here in his trench below the pressure ridge, but enough reached him. Two snowblocks behind to close that door, two snowblocks above to close that roof—but what use was a pocketknife with a three-inch blade? Cut snowblocks with your hands? Impossible. Burrow into hard snow? Impossible. He had nothing to help him, give up trying—and then he had an inspiration to a slender hope, and he stood. He was badly cramped. He climbed to that Skafe Exploration box, to the full force of the wind that thundered about him and whistled through the box. It was a killer, a colder killer now, unbearable, but he heaved at the box, and a frozen board snapped.

Now he had a kind of snowknife with one jagged edge. It would penetrate the drift. He worked hard, with pauses to thaw his face and his tears of the wind; and as he worked, he thought about the missionaries, the few Canon Harpers, the few Catholic priests, the great men of God who found God here, alone with God in the arctic wastes; and for the first time he could understand it in a way, but who was God?

Then he had four snowblocks of an untidy sort. It took him hours, perhaps, to get them, but he got them, and he placed two rough blocks of snow to close the one end of his den, and two snowblocks for a roof. Now he danced about to try to drive the cold down past his heels and through to his toes. He felt pain in his heels again, but by then he was too tired to use more body heat to push the cold down further to his toes; and so he cut his losses and crawled into his cubbyhole from the open end at the south, and he crouched again in the cold womb of the wind. Sometimes now he thought of it as a murderous mother wind, or as a murderous father wind, infanticide, or as a murderous bridegroom wind to pierce the virginity of Skafe. Some virgin! he thought. It was amusing in a way to be the frightened wealthy bride to be ravished by the lustful bridegroom on the make. What an immaculate conception, fiendish blasphemy of cold.

He nibbled half a bannock as a mouse would nibble at a frozen cheese. Then he had another appetizer of the good pink fish that brought the miracle of warmth to the very middle core of him, not now to his shoulders, nor to his genitals.

He was losing. I cannot do it, Simon thought. Why try? I have traveled far. Now let me show them, not that I can go where I am going, but that I can accept defeat when it comes to me. My life has been all right, he thought. My affairs down there in the world are left in order. My trustees are: Grace, John, Sally, Willie Pitt and Sleeman—majority in the family. Oh, I suppose they will lose control because of taxes, but what does it matter, what the hell? It's a funny thing: Miles Sleeman is a brilliant fellow. He has been loyal to me. Miles is fine, but when I see Miles from an arctic blow, I do not like him quite so much. Old Willie said: *I don't mean not trust him with the kitty. I mean not trust him to stand bare-arsed in a snowstorm with you.*

Why should he stand bare-arsed in a snowstorm with me? Who but a fanatic would? Who but the sort of zealot lunatic who says: *The North for Canada, or nothing in the end for Canada?* And did the zealot speak for Canada or for himself? But be fair to him. He did not entirely speak for either. He meant that men must venture out and risk and strive, or men must wither. And who was that man? Simon Kepple Skafe, called Husky? No, that man was a flight of arrogance and fancy in the easy weather. That man does not exist. He was an illusion, just as the warmth brought by the arctic char is an illusion.

Be quiet, Simon said to his weakling self. *Go down, you cold!* In the

408

days when he was young, when strait was the gate and narrow was the
way to keep alive, in days when he did find life, he had learned to live
with cold, to force it down, still and strong, *Go down, you cold!* Now he
tried it again, but he was not that man. Yes, he was that man, but he
needed help to be that man, and he did a sentimental thing to find help
to be that man again: he took off his mitt and glove and put his cold
hand inside his deerskin clothing to search for his trouser pocket and to
find it, and to search in the pocket until he found his key ring, on which
was the gold St. Christopher that Anna had given him. He found the
small patron of men who travel, and he held him for comfort and for
strength, for the memory of love vexing and perplexing. He remembered
the prayer of his Irish mother, and this was her prayer, and he said it
in his shelter in the killer wind: "Oh God, give us strength for the storms
of our journey."

Now with that strength by God's grace from God within himself, he
pushed his way out through the feathery snow that had drifted into the
open end of his shelter, and he moved about in the twilight in the great
cold wind in the Arctic night. He hopped around on his dying feet, and
then he crept in again to doze again and to yield again.

Two sleeps to Nunangiyak. But this was his third sleep on the trail to
Nunangiyak, the small far island where the riches wait. But they would
wait in vain for him. And Grace would wait in vain for him. Dear Grace,
he thought, my comfort and my helpmeet.

But his love awaited him. They were together long ago and now again
at the head of the Mackenzie where the river dips at the start of its run,
on a green island where the North began for Simon and began for Anna
by old man, cold man Mackenzie River.

"Now go to sleep again," she said.
"You're good to me," he said.
*The second time he woke, she was not fanning him. The wind blew
strongly in the trees. She sat beside him, watching him. "My child," she
said, and kissed him on each cheek.*
*Husky Skafe had been no woman's child since what? Well, since per-
haps the age of ten. Now, on the hard stones he was Anna's child, but
truth only comes to go, be lost, be flouted. He looked at her face, and
then he looked at her body in the shirt, a thin shirt of poplin or such
stuff; and doing that, he snatched her child away.*
*He took his hands from behind his head, and held them out, and she
leaned to meet his lover's hands. She kissed him on the lips. They kissed
as lovers now already.*

He slept on a journey down the great cold river. He strove no more. He sought no more. He yielded to peace, riding down the river.

CHAPTER FOURTEEN

> Gone with the storm the waxen rind,
> And tentative and slow the knives unwind.
> All but the core is blind
> Beyond the vale of sleep.

"SIMON!"
He stirred in the depth of his sleep on the river.
"Simon!"
Don't bother me, he thought.
"Simon!"
Can't you leave me in peace? he thought.
"Simon!"
Oh, go to hell! he thought.
"Simon!"
"What is it?" he said aloud to that voice calling him, her voice calling him, his own voice calling him. Whose voice calling him? But he was awake in a great din of quietness of the wind.

He had no feet, and he had no hands. He opened his eyes to see the snow covering his feet, but the snow did not move; nothing was moving here.

I must try, he thought, but he did not want to try. He wanted to stay here in the peace with the cold in him. But being slave to himself or whoever it was, he tried. He crawled out on his hands and knees to meet this new illusion, and there was no wind.

The wind had died, and the day had come, and all the sky was ribbed with cloud from north to south. It was not *Hila kapuk*, the dim white weather, for the cloud was high, remote, beyond the touching of the mind. The sky bore the flutings of the last great wind, as this white desert bore the flutings of the last great wind.

And Simon was alone. There were no dogs, no sled with the body of his smaller hero. Simon was alone. Nothing broke the white depth of sky and sea, immutable and infinite.

But there is an end to all beginning; there is no sky that stays unchanged. He knelt on hands and knees, and strove no more in his pit of cold. He had shed his world, and he leaned over now to lie on his side to watch this last thing happen to his world.

It was a sliver of blue where the sky and the sea met in the west. It grew. He watched the blue sky climb against the white. A west wind must blow in the depth of the sky, but here there was no wind, and he could not think of that as wind, so measured and so clean the march of blue eternity against the clouds that were the parents or the children of the last great wind. The lover took the corner of the sheet and slowly drew the sheet to bare the beauty of his loved one.

Simon watched the sky peel off to blue. He saw a truth, not understanding it. He was a lover, and the sun was shining. He had seen truth to strive again. He stood. He stood on stumps, but he could stand. He turned to the north to see the box which had seemed to be a house to him before the last great wind, and has seemed to be a home to him in the travail of the last great wind; and a board from the box had been his tool to gain him shelter from the wind.

He saw beyond the broken box on the pressure ridge. He closed his eyes and opened them to see again that it was not a double image or a dream, false promise of the mirage. If his eyes saw truth, if there were such a thing as truth, then he had made his landfall.

Jim spoke of the curving hill at Nunangiyak, and so it seemed, or the striations of the bare brown rock between the fingers of the snow gave a perspective to make it so. There had been no land in the haze before the wind. He had imagined any land that he had seen. But there was land, not twenty miles away, much less.

He climbed this pressure ridge and hobbled north. He had not lost his fingers altogether, but he had lost his toes, and he supposed that he would lose some toes, so what the hell.

He shielded his eyes against the pain of light. He gnawed the last of his frozen fish. The day was very cold. It was the true fine weather of the North, and the sun put a touch of warmth upon the deerskin, and the fish put a touch of warmth into the very middle core of Simon Kepple Skafe.

He thanked God for strength in the storms of his journey. The man of the storm now asked his God for strength to be a man of peace. And so Simon came to the small far islands called Nunangiyak.